MW01135649

BEYOND the BURNING SEA

BOOK ONE OF FATE'S CRUCIBLE

By T.B. Schmid & R. Wade Hodges

Cover art by Todd Schmid

"Salt" rune based on a concept by Winston Clark

Copyright 2016 T.B. Schmid and R.Wade Hodges

Published by Lions of the Empire

Visit us at: www.lionsoftheempire.com

Print Edition License Notes
This book is licensed for your personal enjoyment only. This book may not be re-sold or given away to other people. If you would like to share this book with another person, please purchase an additional copy for each recipient. If you're reading this book and did not purchase it, or it was not purchased for your enjoyment only, then please return to your favorite retailer and purchase your own copy. Thank you for respecting our hard work.

Acknowledgements

For my family, especially my parents. To my mother, whose creativity and compassion were robbed from this world far too soon; and to my father, whose quiet strength, integrity and love have long been my keel. And my sincere gratitude to Wade for his technical prowess, constant humor and overall creative genius. If not for him, I would not have had the courage to begin. - *T.B. Schmid*

For CJ and Tess, because they are my favorite and my best. And many thanks to Tim, because together we actually made this crazy idea work. - *rwh*

Last but certainly not least, we would like to thank Joel Schmid for his tireless proofreading, valuable input and fanatical support throughout the process. - *Tim and Wade*

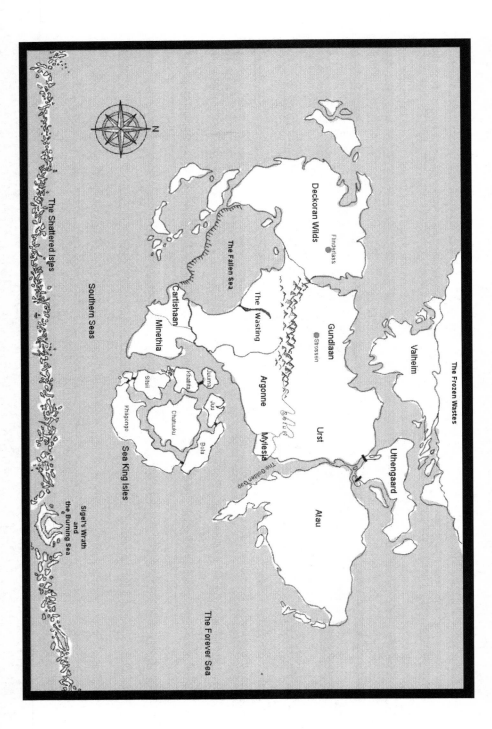

- 1 -

Ghosts in the Mist

One Year Earlier

Captain Vaelysia dug her fingers into the knotted muscles at the base of her neck as she surveyed her battered ship, wondering if she and her crew were already dead.

Her ketch slipped ghost-like through a formless, unknown world shrouded in thick fog. It was all around them like the breath of some giant beast, clinging wetly to every surface, concealing most of the chaos of splintered, tangled rigging above their heads.

Maybe the storm's killed us after all, she thought as something cold and clammy brushed its fingers along her spine. She suppressed a shiver and told herself it was anticipation, excitement, but not fear. Never fear.

She ducked under a broken batten, brushing aside a mass of hopelessly knotted stays, and winced as she felt the newly-stitched slash across her shoulder protest. She hoped it hadn't ruined her tattoo.

"Fate is the wind," the tattoo said. "You can trust it to take you home, or you can seize the helm and make it." They were the words she lived her life by... and would likely die by some day.

"But not today", she murmured to herself. She raised her voice slightly and spoke with the quiet confidence her crew expected: "Starboard echo-man, sound your range."

A lithe sailor with sun-bronzed skin leaned out over the starboard bulwark, one arm draped over the same broken batten. He cupped a hand to the side of his mouth and called out loudly, "HO!"

The rest of the landing party waited in tense silence. Their colossal ship, christened *The SKS Peregrine* not two years ago, was too large to risk in an unknown bay this tight, but she carried two smaller vessels for close-in work; two-masted, junk-rigged boats that had been modified with a rowing deck and two dozen oars. One of these boats had broken loose from its moorings and been lost in the last storm, but this one was still serviceable - barely.

Their sweeps were poised just above the horizontal, but Captain Vaelysia could only see the first four feet of gleaming stonewood before each oar disappeared into the mist. She heard the staccato patter of water dripping off the wooden blades back into the calm, flat sea, so different from what they'd sailed just a few days ago. Beneath it the low, muted rumble of a waterfall came from somewhere ahead. The echo-man's voice bounced back to them.

"I make at least fifty yards, Captain."

Her eyes slid sideways and met the fiercely green pair belonging to her first mate, which most of a Seeker vessel's crew referred to as the "Ship's Whip". Tarq smirked and shrugged. "Sixty, but who's counting?"

"Agreed. Fore echo-man, sound your range."

A stout, dark-skinned sailor named Mhorokai crouched atop the ketch's figurehead, carved and painted in the likeness of a huge falcon, with onyx gems as big as a man's fist for its glittering eyes. He'd been struck by a dead-eye during the storm and knocked unconscious and now wore a bloodstained bandage wrapped around his forehead. She knew how fortunate they were that he had survived: a survey ship without her echo-men was little more than driftwood.

Eight months out from port, the *Peregrine* had dared the Burning Sea, a feat most mariners considered suicide. Incredibly, they had survived and had even discovered a much safer return passage through a hidden channel they found after reaching the other side. Their self-congratulatory chest thumping was short lived, however: barely two days later, a vicious storm overtook them in the dark of night. They lost twenty-five good men as the tempest raged for days and blew them leagues off course into the uncharted seas beyond. They'd had two days' respite - barely enough time to tend to their wounded and release the dead - before more storms had set in.

The *Peregrine* was the first ship of its kind, a massive vessel with five towering masts. Its stated purpose was to modernize the Seeker fleet's stable of venerable survey ships - dubbed "Mappers" by most people - but its deep keel and vast cargo space made it clear that it was designed to extend the Sea Kings' reach to the farthest corners of Ruine. A true "blue-water babe", as her Master Carpenter called her, she was an impressive display of power and ingenuity.

The raging ocean, however, was not impressed.

For a week they pitched and rolled, fought and drowned, all the while driven southward, beyond the edge of the world they knew. Because of her size, the *Peregrine* was an unruly, sluggish beast and it had taken every ounce of sailing skill and experience - and as the crew believed, considerable good fortune - to manhandle her through the storms.

When at last the sea's fury had subsided in the waning hours just before dawn, Vaelysia herself had gone aloft. It had been her voice that rang out from the crow's nest with every sailor's most cherished words as the first light of Ruine's twin suns revealed a pair of rocky spires thrusting out from the horizon far to their south. They stood silent sentry less than a league out from the mist-shrouded bay her landing party was now exploring.

Vaelysia's discovery was just the latest in a series of examples why, to a man, the *Peregrine's* crew (as well as most everyone who'd ever fought, gambled or traded with her) considered their Captain to be a living, breathing good luck charm. For her part, she believed you forged your own luck, and other than the Whore, she didn't have much use for the House of Pleasures or its sibling - and now extinct - gods. The fact that they'd survived had nothing to do with luck or fate and everything to do with the skill, courage and discipline of her crew. You made your own fortune. In their minds they were lucky because of her; in hers they survived and succeeded because they were good; and they were good because she and First Mate Tarq had made them that way.

"No range, Captain," answered Mhorokai. The heavy accent of his native Sea King Isles made it sound like 'Cup-tain'. "But echo's strange. Might be the falls drownin'em."

They were in some kind of deep lagoon that was steadily narrowing; judging from the hard, flat strength of the echoes, the unseen shoreline to either side consisted of sheer cliffs.

"Port echo-man, sound -"

"HO!" The sounding call cut her off in mid-command, causing her to grind her teeth. A mapper's fourth echo-man was typically a mud-footed novice expected to learn the trade from his peers and step in only in an emergency. In the *Peregrine's* case, "novice" was being generous. Wiliamund (whom the crew's Row-master had christened "Mung", the sailor's term for the slimy black mold they were perpetually scrubbing from the ship's oft-soaked wooden surfaces) was a self-described "professional coward" whose first words to his new captain had been "I would say that you can count on me, save for the fact that I am altogether untrustworthy in practically every way." She'd immediately dispatched a courier with a request for a replacement, only to be told that Wiliamund possessed the best ears in Nyah and her request was denied. No doubt he had inherited those ears from some gods-damned nobleman with a fat purse or a favor owed.

"Ummm... two hundred? No - two-fifty... I think - sir... Lady... Captain."

She raised an eyebrow and caught the look from Tarq. She made the range at two hundred and twenty-five yards. Maybe there was hope for Mung and his noble ears after all.

"Depth, Boots?"

An old man with a peg-leg, a neatly trimmed, snow-white beard and skin like boiled leather pulled up the last of his length of rope and counted off the hash marks to the weighted bucket affixed to its end.

"Ten fathoms, Cap'n. But have a look at this." He upended the bucket, dumping a load of sand and seawater onto the deck.

A mixed murmur of excitement and trepidation rippled through the crew. A sand-bottomed bay was a good sign they'd found a decent berth to anchor and repair their battered ship, provided they could squeeze her through this gap. But it was also visceral proof that they were far from home; you'd find flows of molten lava, boiling geysers, and jagged reefs of black-rock around the Shattered Isles and Burning Sea, but not a hint of sand, and naught beyond the Isles but wind and waves for as far as anyone had ever sailed or seen. The *Peregrine* and her crew had been commissioned to explore the very edge of the known world, and they had gone over it.

"Silence!" came Tarq's growled whisper.

The Ship's Whip was an imposing figure; a head taller than almost anyone else on board, broad in the chest and shoulders, his arms and legs corded with muscle. Tarq was Khaliil - one of The Hidden Ones of the Wasting - and his entire body from the tops of his feet to his scalp was covered in intricate tattoos. They even covered his face and head, which was shaven but for a long, garnet-colored top-knot that hung to the small of his back and was braided with fat silver bands. He was fiercely loyal to Vaelysia and demanded the same from her crew, but he was also fair and quick to laugh, and the crew loved him nearly as much as they feared him. They obeyed instantly, and the ketch slipped quietly through the fog once more.

Vaelysia signaled the Row-master, holding up one finger. He nodded and raised his thick arm, meaty fist clenched. Twenty-four pairs of eyes locked on the fist and leaned forward, arms extended. The Row-master brought his fist down, smacking it into the palm of his other hand, and his oarsmen finished their stroke in perfect unison, their black stonewood sweeps coming to rest again just above the waterline, gleaming dark and wet. The stroke was sufficient to maintain their quiet momentum, keeping the craft gliding forward at a pace they could easily check and reverse if needed.

She ran a tan forearm across her forehead, wiping away the sweat. Given all they had been through, she could feel the crew's nerves beginning to fray. So she held rigidly to this slow, methodical course, repeating the same steps of checking range and depth in a cautious rhythm that was as much procedure as it was therapy: sailors, like soldiers, found solace in routine.

The low thrum of the waterfall grew steadily, but while the starboard range shrank to thirty yards, Mung's range increased rapidly before he lost the echoes entirely, indicating that the shoreline off the port side had either turned away or flattened out. At first Vaelysia swung the ship's bow a half-turn in that direction, hoping to find a beach head. The depth fell away so dramatically however that she corrected to follow the unseen cliffs to starboard again, until Boots began calling his depth between three and four fathoms. His bucket was drifting now from more than just the ship's headway; they were pulling against a slight current as they drew closer to the falls, and tiny wavelets now disturbed the flat calm of the lagoon, slapping against the vessel's flanks.

The Captain leaned out over the rail to inspect the free-board, noting that they'd settled some, but not enough to be concerned with as long as the depth didn't drop below two and a half fathoms. One of the features that made this style of launch boat so adept at its task (and a favorite of smugglers) was its shallow draught, but anything less than two and a half fathoms and they would likely snag the bottom. The *Peregrine's* keel was another story, however, and Vaelysia was heartened by the abrupt drop-off to port; if they could ease her into this bay, they could shelter, refit and restock for as long as they needed to. The prospect of her ship foundering - a very real possibility in its current condition - eclipsed the vague threat of anything that might be lurking on these unknown shores, so something like relief began to ease the knotted cords in her shoulders.

As the faintest breath of a breeze brushed her bronze skin, she realized that she could see the oar blades and more of the rigging above. The fog was thinning.

"Fore echo-man, sound your range."

"Three hundred and fifty, Captain..." Mhorokai called back hesitantly. He was one of the best echo-men she had ever worked with, so it was unsettling to hear the hint of doubt in his voice. The tension promptly returned, coiling around her neck and shoulders, worming its way into her wound. She set her teeth and did her best to ignore it.

"Is there a problem, Seeker?"

He shook his head, his braids swinging back and forth. "I'm not sure, Captain... the bounce is... strange."

"Sound again."

"Aye, Captain." He curled his hands to either side of his mouth and called out sharply.

He shook his head again and looked at her, bushy black eyebrows knitting over bright, intelligent eyes.

"The same, but there is something else I think. Closer."

"Longeye, see if you can get above this bloody fog," Vaelysia commanded and a tall, dark-haired woman with thick legs wrapped in supple sealskin boots nodded sharply and began scrambling up a ratline. She was Khaliil as well, though younger than Tarq. Her tale was still being told by the body-scribes; other than her sinewy arms, most of her upper torso was still clean, olive-toned skin. She climbed swiftly, effortlessly, disappearing into the fog.

"How close?"

Mhorokai frowned. "I cannot say. Falls make it hard, Captain, but something breaks the echo up - something big."

Vaelysia stepped to the railing overlooking the oar-deck and signaled the Row-master to back oars, instinctively flexing her knees against the inevitable lurch as the ketch slowed dramatically.

"Poles," she commanded, raising her voice just enough to penetrate through the din of the hidden falls. Mhorokai and two other sailors seized long, stout poles and moved forward to the bow.

"Firstblade," she said to a large man with long dark hair swept back in a pony tail, "claws out."

Unlike Tarq and most of the other sailors, the man wore a breastplate and single pauldron made of dark leather. He nodded and raised a gauntleted fist in the air, then opened it abruptly, spreading his fingers wide. A dozen men and women in similar armor with curved swords at their hips moved sharply to take up positions at the taffrails, the whisper of drawn steel their only audible response.

"I have something, Captain!" the lookout called down through the fog. "Some kind of tower or shoal, fifty yards ahead. It's just a shadow but whatever it is, it's tall as - by all the Wasting's sand..!"

Vaelysia craned her neck back, trying unsuccessfully to pierce the mist. She kept her voice calm and deliberate despite the ache in her shoulders. "Talk to me, lookout. What do you see?"

"It's a - it's some kind of monument, Captain. A statue, a huge stone statue of a jharrl I think - I can only see its head, but it's tall as the mainsail! Day-break's chasing the wind now, Cap and she's stiffening. Fog's lifting and you should -"

"Captain!"

Vaelysia turned towards Mhorokai and the other two pole-men. They were braced at the bow, staves thrust out in front of the ship. Mhorokai was pointing past the prow. Behind him - over him, she corrected herself - a huge dark shadow loomed in the mist.

Without headway, the ketch began to turn as the current nudged her prow aside, so that the huge shape seemed to be moving, stalking alongside the ship. Several of the crewman muttered quiet prayers or clutched any of a dozen different good-luck charms (most of which featured a few stray strands of their captain's hair) as Tarq growled at them again to hold fast.

The breeze had indeed stiffened, the heavy fog being reduced to a ghostly mist that began to tear and fade, while the monstrous shadow slowly materialized and a part of the world that had been forgotten for centuries was discovered again.

Twenty yards off the starboard rail, a massive block of dark-green stone squatted in the lagoon, its pitted, chipped top cresting the waterline by a hands-breadth. Atop it was a huge, beautifully-wrought statue of a jharrl; a ferocious beast that most closely resembled a tiger but grew nearly three times the size and had a prominent lower jaw bearing two curving tusks as long and sharp as scimitars. Equally large and deadly-looking incisors protruded from the front of its upper jaw as well. The idol was carved from some kind of smooth, black rock; marble, perhaps, but with the slightest transparency that almost gave it the look of glass.

Half again taller than the ship, the beast was standing on heavily-muscled rear legs, lunging forward. Forelegs twice as thick as a boom were extended, ending in wide paws tipped with hooked claws as long as a man, raking the empty air above their heads. Beneath the accumulation of moss, stringy vines, dirt and the detritus of centuries, the detail was exquisite - every hair and muscle ridge clearly depicted. She wondered what kind of civilization possessed the artistry and ability to work whatever material this was with such perfection and suppressed an apprehensive shudder.

The dull gray light of the fog bank was beginning to brighten, and a sudden shaft of early-morning sun found its way through to strike the monument. A collective gasp went up from the crew. The statue shimmered such that it almost seemed alive, as though the rough fur were moving as the beast breathed. It was clear now that it was straining forward, held back by a massive chain affixed to a rusted iron collar around its neck, links as thick as tree trunks leading away into the dissipating mist.

"Captain..." Tarq said quietly, his head bent back as he took in the incredible sight.

"I see, Whip." Her eyes had followed the chain as well, which lead up and away. An even larger shadow towered there, still veiled in mist, waiting.

"I think I need to use the privy, Capt-"

Vaelysia turned to Mung and silenced him with a withering look.

"Right then. Never mind." He smiled meekly.

The mist drew back further, golden and glistening in the early morning sun, but no longer thick enough to keep its forgotten secrets. Three times the height of the launch's mainmast and carved from the same translucent marble-like material as the jharrl, stood the figure of a warrior the likes of which the world had not seen in nearly four hundred years. His left fist was encased in a heavy gauntlet formed of grey-green ivory or bone, around which was wrapped the end of the massive chain leash attached to the jharrl's collar. His right arm was thrust out before him and ended in another mailed fist, this one clutching a twin-bladed sword-staff, held crosswise. The centered pommel was made of the same material as the gauntlets and other pieces of armor, she saw, though what manner of creature would yield such enormous chunks of either bone or ivory only the Sea knew. Beneath the moss, vines and salt encrustations, the pommel was covered with intricate carvings, though the long, gleaming black blades at either end were bare and smooth. She rubbed at the ache in her neck as she craned her head back to take it all in.

"Rowmaster, two points to starboard and bring us in as close as you can."

"Aye, Cap'n."

The waterfall they had heard was visible now as well. The colossus stood in a wide stance; ornate, armored boots of the same ivory material sunk ankle-deep in the lagoon, while between them cascaded a noisy torrent of water from where it fell over an escarpment behind the statue's knees. The giant sentinel guarded one end of a narrow river canyon that ran away into shadow, its broad shoulders nearly touching either side of the valley, its strange, crested helm rising higher than the cliff walls that surrounded the bay. Shafts of gilded light pierced some of the gloom at the mouth of the canyon, and from where she stood, Vaelysia could see the twisted green chaos of lush jungle growth crowding either side and spilling over the bluff in a verdant mimicry of the river.

Nearly eleven turnings of the moon had passed since they had set out to map the edge of the world they knew, and now here they were poised on the heady precipice of an entirely new one. Seekers dreamed nonstop about discovering new islands and hidden bays… but this! It was terrifying and exhilarating at the same time - and she had never felt more alive.

"Doesn't look very welcoming, does he?" Tarq inquired from beside her.

The message conveyed by the posture and composition of the warrior and the lunging jharrl was unmistakable: whomever or whatever had placed these statues here had gone to great lengths to warn others away.

"No, he doesn't."

Tarq scratched his chin nonchalantly. "So… we'll be sending an expedition into that valley then." It wasn't a question; he'd served with her a long time.

"Put a landing party together. Climbers first, including the boy."

"Halliard?"

"Yes. Reavers too."

The Whip studied his captain for a moment. "You don't honestly think that they're still alive, do you? That he's still here?"

Vaelysia stared up at the colossal statue.

"Gods I hope not."

~ * ~

From the forward to "*A Comprehensive History of Niyah After the Fall of Ehronhaal*" by Mikkel Vaun, 158th Rector of Talmoreth, Order of Veda:

The paradise of the First World was destroyed by Maughrin, the Demon Dragon, and avenged by Tarsus, last of the Old Gods. From its remains, He revived the world. From His own life's spark, He formed the Young Gods: the proud Auruim, on their shining wings, to defend His creation, and the wise Dauthir, who abandoned flight to further nurture this Second World. We, His Children, were created last, before He ascended into the heavens.

Two thousand years passed with peace and order before the Godswar, when the Young Gods turned on one another. Once again, the world would change. Ehronhaal fell from the sky, setting the very air on fire and scarring that ground which did not shatter outright.

It has been over two hundred years since the Young Gods died. Our world has suffered greatly. But we are the Children of Tarsus, and under the light of the sun He lit for us, we shall honor that legacy. Like Him, we shall rise from these ashes to reforge the world.

- 2 -

Lost at Sea

Gods, what have we done?

Triistan Halliard stared hard at his own words on the wrinkled, salt-stained page of his journal. It was mid-morning on the sixth day since the *SKS Peregrine* went down with nearly all hands, not quite a full year after having arguably made the greatest discovery in mortal history.

They were the last words he had written scant minutes before the full fury of the House of Storms had manifested itself upon the ocean. Somehow he had managed to retain the book through the chaos of the tempest, though he could not say how, or why. It would be such a simple matter to throw it overboard and claim to have lost it - provided anyone who knew that it even existed managed to survive long enough to ask. Let the Dark swallow its secrets and choke on the oath he'd given.

If he still had his stylus, he might have scratched that last sentence out. The gods were dead, gone. They had long since wiped themselves out and left men to fend for themselves.

But what we found... The irony made his chest hurt. A lie within a lie, hidden behind a secret he had sworn to conceal.

He closed the book abruptly and stared out at the vast emptiness of sea and sky that surrounded him now. Under other circumstances, it would have been a perfect day - the sea was calm, her embrace gentle and soothing, while overhead the sky was the impossibly blue arch of a childhood memory. It was the kind of day Triistan would have spent aloft once his duties were completed, lounging in a 'rig-tit', writing or reading. The jury-rigged strip of sailcloth and some spare cordage made for a cozy sling-style hammock, and his favorite place in the wide world was wrapped in the rough fabric, swaying dozens of feet above the ocean. But instead he was floating here in a battered launch, guarding a terrible secret and wondering if he would ever enjoy that feeling again.

His head ached fiercely from dehydration, his belly hurt from being empty, and his eyes burned from trying to scan the endless blue veil, but he forced himself to continue searching for a sail or the sweet, dark curve of land. Not because he held much hope of sighting either form of salvation, but because it was the practical thing to do: just because he thought they were doomed did not mean he had to accept it.

Though he could not be sure exactly where the *Peregrine* had foundered, it was common knowledge that they had been within six or seven weeks' reach of the Sea King Isles when the storm struck. Since then, he and the other survivors had been afloat in the *Peregrine's* sole remaining launch for five days and nights, and while progress was painfully slow, they had been moving in one fashion or another for all of that time. Even after the storm had subsided, the skies had remained sullen, oppressive and unwilling to allow the survivors to view the stars or Ruine's twin suns so they could fix their position. But just after dawn this morning, the veil of swollen bruises had finally drawn back, and with a bit of luck they would get a solid reckoning today. The young man told himself that they might even sight one of the small, outlying archipelagos that surrounded the Isles sometime during the next week or so.

He pushed a blonde and copper tangle of hair out of his eyes and looked across the deck at the Mattock, the crew's nickname for the burly ship's bosun, who'd had the mizzen watch and was dozing fitfully now. He had wrapped and tied his tattered shirt around his bald head as protection from the suns, but it had slipped down to cover half of his face, lending him a rare comical look. Even with all that had transpired, Triistan couldn't suppress a weak smile.

Mordon "the Mattock" Scow was loud, surly, and mercilessly demanding with his charges, but he had loved his ship. He had been meticulous about every aspect of her care; from scrubbing the mung out of every crack and crevice to the proper way to store spare cordage. No detail was left to chance on board 'his lady'. Whenever he went over the side to inspect the hull, the standing joke - told well out of earshot out of a healthy respect for arms as thick as most men's legs - was to ask what he would do if he found a hole.

Triistan never laughed at their japes, though. He knew the Mattock was a good man, an honest man, and despite the seemingly never-ending tongue-lashings - not to mention a handful of real ones given before the mast - Triistan had developed a deep respect and admiration for him. Twice now the Master Carpenter had saved his life, and he wished with all his heart that they had listened to him before fleeing Aarden.

For the first time since the *Peregrine's* capsizing, a zephyr whispered in their makeshift sails, a seductive song of hearth and home. The fickle breeze tugged at the launch's ragged shrouds - their junk-rigged, serrated edges looking like tattered wings - just enough to keep a modest headway as they continued creeping northward. Triistan saw a few of the others lift their gaunt faces as they felt the heavy tropical air stir.

At least they seemed to have moved beyond the immediate wreckage and bloated bodies. The strength of the storm had scattered crew, cargo and other debris over a vast area, but they had not seen anything save open water since the previous morning. He dropped his head and rubbed his temple with weak fingers, catching a glimpse of the foul stew collecting in the bottom of the boat. He hoped they'd moved beyond the range of any scavengers as well.

Five days becalmed in this sub-tropical heat and humidity, with only the barest rations, was leaching their will and wits, and the rowing shifts they'd organized were growing shorter and shorter. Yet every Seeker knew the old adage: "Three knots or more, bilge ye by the boards; three knots or less, the boot be the best." The Dark may be empty of light, but not of life. At sea, as on land, there were predators and scavengers with highly developed senses, and smaller ships had to be cautious with their waste. If you were making at least three knots, anything over the side would be sufficiently diluted and dispersed behind you to avoid attracting predators. Below that speed, however, and the smart sailor kept his waste in the "boot" - the bottom of his boat. It made for rather foul living quarters, but it was better than being dragged into the abyss by some nameless horror of the deep. Much to Triistan's and his fellow survivors' discomfort, they had not been making anywhere near three knots.

Of the nine survivors on board the launch, only eight of them were in any condition to man an oar. Lahnkam Voth, the ranking officer, had harangued them mercilessly for the first three days, but they were still uncomfortably close to the wreckage site.

Triistan winced and glanced at Voth where he was sprawled like some partially-crushed spider, arms and legs all askew. Calling him an officer was a stretch. A tall spear of a man with bulbous eyes, "Lanky Lahnkam" had been the *Peregrine's* Provisions Master, and as such was much more adept at counting, packing and hording than he was at leading men. His new command was derived from having the dubious distinction of being the highest ranking sailor left alive, and he approached it with the same methodical, rigid tenacity he had displayed as the ship's purser. That obstinacy had earned him the approval and gratitude of his captain, but the enmity of every mariner on board who thought they were entitled to an extra helping of rum or a new set of boots or another blanket on a cool night - which essentially amounted to nearly all of them.

At the mercy of the Sea and under the command of a bloody crate-counter, Triistan thought. *Scow should be leading us. That's the merchant-kings' navy for you, though; cargo and coin outranked capacity and common sense.* His face turned sour as he shifted his position.

Two hundred and fifty-two souls had set sail aboard the *Peregrine*, heading for home with orders to report their incredible discovery to the High Chancellor. Captain Vaelysia and the Ship's Whip had remained behind with the balance of the *Peregrine's* remaining crew: nearly three hundred pioneers who chose exile in an unknown world over the more familiar perils of the long voyage home to Niyah. At least, that was the story concocted by Captain Vaelysia, which Triistan had sworn an oath to promote. Only a handful on the return voyage had known the truth recorded in his journal, and as far as he knew, there were only two left who still carried that burden. It was a lonely feeling, but that was a small price to pay; at the moment he was glad he couldn't tell them the truth, because he still wasn't ready to face it himself.

He looked up again, scanning first to the north, where he knew the Sea King Isles should be, and just west of them, the southern edge of Niyah's mainland. He allowed himself to imagine that it was just below the curve of the ocean, about to breach, and he would be the one to call it out to the others. His gaze lingered and he brought his hand up to shield his eyes from the glaring suns, but that horizon refused to yield to his will, so he turned to the east, sweeping his gaze in a wide, slow arc from there to the south.

Two hundred and fifty-two had escaped... and now there are only nine of us left.

There had been some concerns about the structural integrity of the *Peregrine's* hull, enough to spark a heated argument between Captain Vaelysia and Scow, he recalled. The storm that had initially blown them well south of the Burning Sea and led to their discovery of the new continent had caused significant, obvious damage above the waterline, which they had set to repairing almost as soon as they had made landfall. The ship had been fitted with new fore and mizzen masts from the spare booms she carried, but they were forced to cut and haul new timber for the spars. Scow hadn't liked the look of the wood they brought back to him from the jungle - "Damn my eyes if I wouldn't rather piss boiling bilge-water than hang that soft shite on my lady!"

he'd roared - but his real concern was what they couldn't see. He had insisted that the *Peregrine* needed to be careened and gone over "from belly to batten", but the bay they had landed in did not have a suitable berth in which to do so. Not even a sandbar. A limping, one-month search east and west along the coastline had proved fruitless as well, revealing nothing but unassailable cliffs in both directions.

Eventually the Mattock was ordered to make do with what he had. They did not have the resources to build an entirely new ship, and the Captain was adamant that they had to get word of their discovery back. It had already been nearly a year since they'd originally cleared moorings at Stormgate, and while only a select few understood the full significance of what they'd found, even the dullest crew member among them knew what was at stake if enough time elapsed and another ship managed to discover the new world and report back first. Never mind the fact that it had existed here for hundreds of years before being discovered; now that they'd found it, the sense that someone else would do the same soon was overwhelming, and too many of them had already begun dreaming of the wealth and glory to come.

The Godswar and its catastrophic end had reshaped the world in every conceivable way: cultures, borders, technologies and even the land itself had been either destroyed or forever changed. Like hungry ridgebacks scenting blood, the Sea Kings sought to take full advantage of this opportunity, so they placed great value in exploration. New discoveries were richly rewarded, especially now - in the last decade, many of the mainland coastal kingdoms had nearly caught up to the Sea Kings' shipping capabilities and competition for trade was more intense than it had ever been. There was a significant movement back home by certain factions within the complex government of the Isles, pushing hard for the Sea Kings to not just solidify their power, but to extend it as well; to step into the vacuum left in the wake of the Godswar. The *Peregrine's* captain - if she survived and returned home - would no doubt receive a much-coveted Fleet Commander designation and the substantial pay raise and prestige that went with it; her officers could look forward to Captaining their own vessels, as well as fat bonuses equivalent to three years' pay; and her common sailors, besides bonuses of their own, would earn the envy of their fellow mariners, opening doors in their careers and eager thighs in every port of every town in the Isles and on the mainland, Nyah.

But Triistan knew that was only part of the story. In and of itself, the re-discovery of a lost continent would change their lives far more profoundly than promotions and a pair of firm tits in every town as it touched off a race among nations to explore, conquer and exploit limitless new land and resources. But once it was known what was on the new continent - what this new land actually *was* - it would fundamentally change the world as they knew it. That was the real reason there had been such a rush to send word home again: they needed to be warned. Darkness stalked that mysterious land, and it was only a matter of time before it came crawling after them. He struggled daily to keep his fear at bay, worrying not just if they would make it home, but whether they would make it home in time.

So, the crews had been sorted out, officers assigned, orders and contingencies provided for, food and supplies laid in, ceremonies and rituals observed, hugs, vows, lies and good intentions shared all around, and letters to loved ones hastily scribbled - or in most cases, dictated and transcribed by one of the few people who could actually write. Most of that fell upon Triistan, and had he known that none of them would ever reach home, he would have demurred, saving himself a great deal of time and the embarrassment of unwanted intimacy with his shipmates.

When they had finally set out for home, the *Peregrine* had run swift and sure, her lines thrumming with energy as she ran before the wind, almost as if the ship was eager to leave the new land far astern as well. Most of the men and women selected to crew the *Peregrine* had been only too glad to leave the strange country and its mysteries behind, many of them cheering as they passed what some were now calling "*Peregrine's* Point" while riding high on a following sea.

Such blind, happy fools then, Triistan thought.

Soon after, they had settled back into the familiar routine of watches, maintenance, navigation, cleaning, meals, and sleep that made up the pulse of a mariner's life, while they tried not to think about the daunting challenge they still faced ahead. The Shattered Isles were a belt of uninhabited islands and shoals that ran west to east for leagues uncounted. Up until the *Peregrine's* voyage, they had long been considered the southern edge of the world, and now they lay between the crew and their home port.

Legend held that the islands actually moved, slowly being dragged westward by something called the Godsfall Drift, an inexorable current believed to have been created when the gods' floating city of Ehronhaal fell. Legend notwithstanding, the myriad narrow channels and by-ways between the islands were far too small, shallow and treacherous for a deepwater sailing vessel to pass, but Seeker Command had long theorized that passage could be found through a nightmare landscape called the Burning Sea. There, a black mountain peak known as Sigel's

Wrath rose from the water, spitting fire and smoke into the sky and bleeding veins of molten lava hissing into the sea around its flanks. The water boiled and smoked, the air made men sick, and flaming boulders came rocketing out of the sky like missiles launched from the trebuchets of some ghost army defending the mountain. But the *Peregrine's* stated mission was to chart a way through, so that's what Captain Vaelysia had done.

They survived, and as they limped their way south, they discovered a hidden bay on the eastern side of the islands that ringed the Burning Sea. They put in to repair the ship and treat their wounded and sick, only to discover a wide, deep channel leading north and east from the back of the bay. As the *Peregrine* refit, First Mate Tarq sailed one of the launches up the hidden channel, returning a day later with the news that it was wide and deep enough for the *Peregrine* to traverse on their return voyage. Apparently the other end came out between a series of overlapping islands that, when viewed from the north, completely obscured the passage.

Triistan knew he was not alone in his concern that the channel would still be there upon their return, let alone that it would remain large and deep enough for them to sail through, but fortune had favored them, and the *Peregrine* passed north through the Shattered Isles with far less trouble than their southern trip had seen. Indeed, by that time most of the crew were openly stating that the Captain's luck must run with her ship, for in addition to their safe passage, they had seen very little inclement weather for most of the journey. What storms they had encountered had been mercifully tame, or small enough or far enough away to skirt.

Triistan smiled grimly. As most who spent their lives on the sea would tell you, it was only a matter of time, and the *Peregrine* and her crew had been borrowing that time heavily. Ten months and three days out from Aarden, in the small dark hours of the mizzen watch, whatever forces that now held sway over men's lives finally came to collect.

A brief gust of wind made the launch's topgallant ripple and snap above Triistan's head. He slipped his journal into the protective oilcloth pouch he had made for it, winding the leather cord sewn to one corner around the package several times to secure it. He wished he had not lost his stylus. He needed to write these events down so that he could stop replaying them in his head. He tended to become fixated on certain things, cycling through an event or idea over and over in an endless loop, examining all of the myriad factors that could be altered down to the tiniest detail. Once his musings began to appear on paper, however, the loop was broken; he could record the events as they transpired, or the idea as it had first occurred to him, as if the act of writing out his thoughts captured them, containing them in their original form as a naturalist might pin a specimen to his display board. With no such outlet, his thoughts of the preceding days continued fluttering around inside his mind, relentless.

The *Peregrine's* doom had swept in from the north and west, having marshaled its forces overnight, and as dawn broke somewhere behind its towering black mass, it swallowed them. The first blast of wind looked to the men in the fore-top like some giant silver-gray wraith scraping across the face of the ocean. It tore at her sails, breaking several of the new spars and sending two unprepared line-spiders hurtling into the ocean. They fished one out, but as they were dropping a lifeline for the second man, the *Peregrine* broached and heeled heavily. When she had straightened again, the sailor was gone.

They had managed to reef most of the undamaged sails, but one of the yards on the mainmast had snapped, fouling the braces and preventing them from taking in the mainsail completely. The ship and her crew fought gallantly for several hours, pitching and rolling across huge swells, while the wounded groans of the hull vied with the crash and roar of thunder from both sea and sky as she alternately hogged and sagged across or between huge waves.

Ultimately, the *Peregrine* had fought one too many battles with the unforgiving sea. As she crested a wave that Triistan swore was taller than her topgallants by half, a sudden blast of wind caught the partially-furled mainsail. She heeled, essentially falling sideways into the trough beyond. Another swell running counter to them took her square amidships and with a thunderous crack they could feel as much as hear, the *Peregrine's* back broke.

Triistan had been working directly across from Mordon Scow when it happened, and would never forget the expression on the Mattock's face as long as he lived: it was the look of a man who'd just received a mortal wound. Scow had just stood there, stock still, while sheets of rain and wind-blown spray hammered down at them from every conceivable angle. Triistan heard the order to abandon ship and men began running for the ketch, some fighting with each other in a panicked effort to get to the only remaining lifeboat. Yet the Mattock did nothing.

Triistan had grabbed the man's arm and shouted at him that they had to leave, but he might as well have been trying to uproot a tree. Scow shook him off and placed his two massive hands to either side of the foremast, then touched his forehead to it, almost gently, even as men pushed past them. Triistan saw Wiliamund slink by and called to him for help, but the look he received in response made it clear what the man most called "Mung" for short thought of helping anyone but himself. He never even checked his stride.

Desperate but determined not to leave the bosun behind, Triistan rounded on Scow, grabbed two fistfuls of the man's tunic and jerked him as hard as he could.

"By the Seven High Houses - *MOVE YOU STUBBORN OLD BASTARD*!!" He still wasn't sure who was more stunned by his outburst at that moment - he largely kept to himself and was so quiet half the crew still thought him a mute, and it had been many, many seasons since one of the Mattock's mates had assaulted and insulted him simultaneously - but it worked. Scow blinked and shook his head, and his square face had twisted into a snarl as he drew back his huge fist.

Triistan stepped back and raised his hands, gesturing and pointing towards the mob of men struggling to get into the launch boat. At the last moment, Scow seemed to recognize him and break out of his fugue. He shook himself and looked about, reflex and duty overpowering his emotions not a moment too soon: the ship was listing heavily to starboard and her main decks were awash, the air was filled with the agonized shrieking of wood pushed to its breaking point and beyond, and the panicked crew members risked dooming everyone to the Dark as they fought to release the launch.

"Thunder and spray, this won't do - one more wave athwart and she'll come apart right under us! Where in the Endless Dark is the Captain?" He reached out and grabbed a passing sailor by the arm.

"Stand to, lad! Where's Captain Fjord?!" Fjord had been the *Peregrine's* Second, directly subordinate to Tarq and a capable, if somewhat nervous, commander. For reasons only known to a select few, the First Mate had remained behind with Captain Vaelysia, so Fjord had been given command of the *Peregrine* for the return voyage.

The young man stammered and tried to pull away, but the Mattock's grip was iron-bound. He shook his head and pointed with his free hand.

"Overboard, sir! He and Lyhmes were -"

Scow didn't wait for him to finish. He let the man go and turned back to Triistan.

"C'mon, boy, stop standing there with your mouth a'hanging open like a bloody scupper!"

He grabbed Triistan by the collar and dragged him straight into the mob, bellowing above the storm as only the Mattock could. His roar and the presence of his huge frame knocking men and women aside soon brought them to order, and they began working together to ease the ketch overboard. Fortunately, that was the direction the ship was listing, so they did not have far to go when another wave struck them and the Mattock's prediction came true. With a horrifying cacophony of crashing and rending sounds, the *Peregrine* virtually exploded under and around her crew.

Triistan found himself falling, the sea reaching up for him with wet, eager arms. He plunged into the black water head-first, and in the terror of the moment, actually began swimming *down* until something latched around his ankle and hauled him back. He twisted in panic, lashing out with his other foot and striking the solid, broad chest of Mordon Scow.

The Master Carpenter had ignored his struggling and shot for the surface, only a few feet above his head. He seized hold of a piece of wreckage, gave a hard jerk to Triistan's leg so that he surfaced as well, then switched his grip to the back of his tunic and manhandled him partially onto the wreckage. With his head out of the water and an arm across the floating debris, Triistan choked and gasped for breath. The Dark would have to wait, at least for the two of them.

Somehow the ketch had survived and was fairly close, so they had kicked their way towards it, rising and falling with the undulating sea, apparently small enough to escape its full fury. There were already four people in the boat: Lahnkam Voth, two hulking Valheim oarsman, and an unconscious woman named Jode. She was one of Scow's apprentice ship's carpenters. As Triistan was hauled in over the taffrail and collapsed onto a bench, he saw immediately that she was in a bad way, with half a yard of splintered oar sticking out of her abdomen just above her right hip.

The next several hours had been a confused blur as they struggled to stay afloat and inside the boat while looking for survivors. Voth was useless, bulbous eyes bulging even further in terror as he refused to release his grip on the mainmast. Scow was furious, but he had been a seaman all of his life and mutiny in any form was incomprehensible to him. Instead he gave the man a contemptuous look and carried on as if the ranking officer were absent. He found some rope and had them all - even the ship's petrified purser - lash themselves securely to the jack stays. There was nothing they could do for the injured Jode as the launch bucked beneath them, though Scow held her head tightly and whispered in her ear for a few moments. When he released her abruptly and turned away, shouting orders to the other survivors, Triistan saw the girl's eyes follow him with a mixture of gratitude and determination.

Finally, the fury of the storm began to subside. It moved on in search of bigger prey, like a giant child tired of its toys, unwilling to trouble with such trifling things as survivors, of which there seemed precious few of anyway.

They pulled three more shipmates out of the water that afternoon: Dreysha, a dark-haired Mylisian beauty who made his heart race, and not because of her mean streak and the bandolier of throwing knives she was expert with; Rantham the Rogue, purported to be the luckiest man on board other than the captain, although up until they had hauled him into the ketch, grinning, Triistan had been convinced he was just very clever and very good at cheating at dice games; and Biiko, one of the Unbound from the Sea King Isle of Khiigongo, who had joined the *Peregrine's* crew just a few days before they had departed from Thunder Bay, and who's fate seemed to be inextricably entwined with his own.

He glanced down the length of the boat to where Biiko sat in front of their meager food and water supplies. That was one good command decision Lahnkam had made, anyway. The Unbound were legendary warriors, but despite their martial prowess, their spiritual beliefs required extreme humility and discipline in all things. There were many who scoffed at the idea of unassailable virtue, but so far Biiko had lived up to the legend. As Scow had put it, "I ain't gotta wet-nurse him, and he don't squawk when life pulls the tit out of his mouth." More importantly, though, he had become an invaluable friend and guardian to Triistan for some bizarre reason he was only just beginning to fathom.

Now, as provisions on board the launch began to run low, tension and mistrust began to gnaw at the worn fibers holding their odd community together. A brother of one of the most feared and respected orders in the known world, with demonstrated discipline and integrity, Biiko was the obvious choice for Quartermaster. Even given their ragged, desperate condition, to a man they all trusted him over anyone else, and no one - not even the Mattock - could hope to challenge him physically.

Triistan looked out to sea again, performing his ritual search for land, unconsciously grinding his teeth as he silently willed it to appear.

Uprising in Strossen

"No blades! You will not bare steel or you will answer to me!"

Casselle did not have a blade to draw. Assuming she survived until next week's end, she would be granted the blade and the title of Laegis Templar. As she pushed back on the mob with her shield and weighted baton, however, she did think there was a possibility she would never hold that sword.

"I'm running out of polite admonitions," growled Jaksen, immediately to Casselle's left. He was taller than her, with a strong build and a chin slightly overlarge for his face. It stuck out from underneath the helmet that was just barely too small for his head. He was from Barrowbridge, a farming community in Southeast Gundlaan, bordered by Deyshen on the east and just over the hills from the Argonne grasslands in the south. Casselle liked Jaksen well enough. He'd come from a big family with plenty of hard working brothers and sisters alike. They had that much in common.

"Why not use that terrible breath of yours?" mocked Temos Pelt, who stood immediately to Casselle's right side. Although the humble son of a trapper, Temos had excelled in the Templar academic training, much to the irritation of several other cadets who'd taunted his lack of formal schooling when he'd first arrived. He was taller than Casselle by a hand, just an inch or so shy of Jaksen, and had the natural, wiry athleticism of someone who'd spent most of his early childhood ranging the thick forests of northern Gundlaan.

"Hush, Rabbit," Raabel grumbled, playfully mocking Temos' family profession. He was on Temos' right side, the biggest of the squad, standing over Jaksen by a good foot in height. He was strong, too, and often bragged that he was helping his father collar criminals when he was but twelve years old. Despite his permanent scowl, Casselle knew Raabel's jest to be more playful than cutting, because the four of them had become strong friends during their years of training.

Perhaps it was fitting that they all perished on this, the first real challenge they faced together. Their tiny squad was set in formation in front of the gate that separated the rest of the city from the Elder Circle, which was both the name of the round building behind them and the body of men that ruled from inside it. If the building had another name, no one ever cared to use it. It wasn't the only building behind the gate, but these days it certainly was the more important of the two.

"We are servants of the Elders! Of Strossen! Of Gundlaan itself!" came the cry from the Templar Captain. He was close by, close enough for Casselle to glance over her shoulder and see the look of steely resolve in his eyes. Whatever dead god gave him that resolve was hidden behind the fingers clutched around the talisman at his throat.

"Down with the Elders! Down with the Church!" yelled an unwashed man that attempted to claw past Casselle's shield. With the weight of several others behind him, he threatened to take her down, but she widened her stance slightly and lowered her center of gravity. She also used her baton to brace her shield from behind long enough for Temos to aid pushing the man up and away from her. He was consumed by the crowd and replaced by a more respectably dressed man with a much fouler mouth. After the third insult in quick succession regarding Casselle's promiscuity, she slapped him hard across the cheek with her baton, unintentionally bloodying his nose. He screamed and pressed to get away.

"What are they on about?" Jaksen asked.

"Anarchy and disorder," Raabel growled.

"Representation at the Elder Circle," Temos clarified. "It's not..." A thrown rock interrupted his explanation, caroming off his shield with a metallic crash.

"I actually agree with you idiots!" Temos yelled into the crowd." Up until you decided to become a bloodthirsty mob!"

The mob surged. It was not in response to Temos' comment directly, but they threatened to push the squad back into the spiked iron gates where the Elder Circle building stood tall behind them. The Temple of Passages, the structure where the Young Gods had once held court with those that lived in the city, stood in front of it. At one time it had been a separate building, but since the Ehronfall it had merely become an elaborate entryway to the expanded Circle building.

"We must hold!" yelled the Templar Captain. Another glance back affirmed to Casselle that he was, indeed, behind the relative safety of the gate.

"Bloody easy for him to say," Temos quipped as he helped Raabel turn aside a man eagerly attempting to climb the gate on his own. The crowd had only grown stronger since Casselle's squad had been hastily deployed from inside the Temple. Today had been important since it was the Elder Council's monthly audience, and they had been there to perform a standard turn of watching the grounds. It gave the squad the chance to observe veteran Templar attending to their duties, but also bolstered the apparent number of Templar on site.

Not that there were a large number to bolster to begin with. Casselle knew the only reason she was here, the only reason that any of her squadmates held the shield emblazoned with the Templar's Hammer, was because the organization was desperate.

That momentary distraction cost her the sure footing she'd held up until then. Something banged against the side of her helmet and as she reflexively stepped backwards, the mob picked the best time to surge forward again, throwing her fully off balance. She fell, her ill-fitting metal cap affording her little protection as her head smacked solidly against the gate.

She did not black out. Thankfully she was made of sterner stuff. The blow, however, set the world to spinning and slapped one noise on top of another until it all was an indecipherable wave crashing down on top of her, threatening to crush her underneath. She tried to get back on her feet, but the succession of blows had addled her, making her legs unsteady. She felt the bars of the gate slam against her back as her helmet fell forward, making it hard for her to see.

She dropped her baton and fumbled for the strap that held the helmet to her head. Someone tried to grab hold of her arm. She choked down her panic and snapped a punch back in the direction she felt the arm tugging her. Her mailed fist connected with something and the hand fell away.

She rolled to her left, hoping to put herself behind Jaksen. It was a clumsy attempt and her shield got tangled in the bars of the gate. Frustrated and on the verge of panic, she tried once more to wrest the helm from her head, but her thickly mailed fingers made working the delicate buckle almost impossible.

The leather strap gave before the buckle did, and Casselle's head finally came free. She could see once more, her vision unobstructed by the helmet's visor, and the echoing cacophony of noise subsided to a loud roar.

Jaksen was in front of her, valiantly pushing away twice as many rioters as he should have been able to. Raabel had locked shields with him and was holding back more than his own fair share. Temos was shaking his head: it had been his jaw she'd connected with when he'd tried to help her to her feet.

She didn't have the time to apologize as the crowd surged forward again, pushing Temos into her, forcing Jaksen and Raabel to give ground as well, and moving them all dangerously closer to being crushed up against the iron bars.

This time Casselle realized that something other than the general frenzy of the crowd was driving them forward.

"I see a banner!" Jaksen yelled.

"It must be the Watch!" Raabel grunted.

"I can't tell! It's out of view!" Jaksen replied. Casselle watched as the space between them eroded. Despite their best efforts, Jaksen and Raabel were forced to yield some ground. No amount of strength could hope to keep off the entire weight of the mob. Unfortunately, Temos and Casselle were stuck between them and the bars of the gate.

"Hold the line!" cried the Templar Captain, sounding older and frailer than before.

"What rutting line is he talking about?" Jaksen grunted.

"Push!" Raabel screamed, obviously strained to his limit and then a bit beyond. Casselle placed her hands on his back and tried to push him forward, to prop him up as best she could. When she heard the whistles and cries of authority, she had to remind herself to breathe.

"It is the Watch!" said Raabel, sounding relieved. Casselle felt the pressure against her aching arms yield as Raabel was able to stand more solidly on his own. She watched as the crowd shifted and began to disperse, their focus no longer on getting into the Temple grounds. Constables of the Strossen Watch, with their deep blue and silver trimmed padded jack vests, were working apart the crowd with whistles, batons and the strength of their authority. It was not an orderly event, but it gave the Templars the breathing room they needed to pick themselves up and regroup. Casselle collected her helmet from the ground and checked on the status of the others.

Jaksen, Raabel and Temos (sore jaw notwithstanding) were fine. Despite the raw strength of the mob, none of them had suffered any serious damage. As they collected themselves in the immediate aftermath, they acknowledged their status to each other with a quick look and nod.

Another rookie squad that had been set outside the next gate down, however, had fared less well. As the mob was being dispersed and the gates of the Temple opened, a small group of gray robed acolytes helped them to their feet and inside. The cries of the angry townsfolk and the screams of the wounded mixed together as the Watch constables tried to sweep the courtyard in front of the Temple clear.

"Ogund be praised, we survived," said Temos, his voice uncharacteristically free from the sarcasm he put behind most of his prayers.

"We're lucky," Jaksen replied.

"No thanks to Captain Frail over there," Temos bit back, looking at the nervously fidgeting Templar Captain just behind the gates.

"Captain Brale made the best call he could," Raabel replied sharply.

"Still," Casselle said firmly, "It was a bad decision."

The others looked to her and quietly nodded in agreement.

The square in front of the gate was still in a state of chaos, but it was channeled at this point, directed by the constables and some fresh Templars from the Barracks on the other side of the city. Templar Seniors and Initiates alike worked with the Watch to restore order.

During their training, it had been drilled into Casselle's head that the Laegis were more than just heavily armored constables defending buildings and old men. History recounted that they were the army of the Young Gods themselves, sworn to stand against the Living Darkness - the dragon Maughrin and her monstrous spawn. Tales of Templars standing shoulder to shoulder against impossible odds were the kind of thing that had inspired young Casselle's hopes and dreams.

Most people still believed in them, holding the Laegis as an example of the good the High Houses had done. Of late, however, other voices had begun to speak up. Some townsfolk called them militant thugs or worse, daring to whisper such things barely out of her hearing on those days she was granted leave in the city. Dwelling on such thoughts started to make her angry, but a cry caught her attention and kept her from thinking on it further.

"Milner!"

Casselle searched the crowd for the owner of the calm, steady voice that called out to her. Temos found it first.

"Captain Taumber!" the former trapper replied happily. Raabel and Jaksen also relaxed at the sight of the grizzled Templar Captain as he emerged from behind a dispersing knot of protesters. His face was well lined and his hair was white, but his eyes were sharp and bright and he had a grace in his step that made one think his countenance had been misinformed of his actual age. He had already locked on to Casselle's squad near the gate and he made his way to them with purpose.

Captain Odegar Taumber had been one of their regular trainers on and off for their long years as initiates of the Laegis. Soon they would take the full mantle of Templar and join him as an equal, no longer simply students. He had always been stern, but vocally proud of this band of stalwart friends, watching as they bested many other, heavily advantaged groups in the training yards.

"It is good to see you all well," he said. "But I have not come to simply check up on you."

"Then why..?" Temos began.

"I was on my way across town when this riot started. I was asked to collect the Templar Librarian from the stacks at Strossen University."

"So there was more to this than just a mess at the Circle?" Jaksen asked. Odegar nodded his head quickly in affirmation.

"This discontent has been brewing for some time. It was just bad luck that it boiled over today." Odegar motioned for them to follow as he made his way to a side street. Over the tops of the buildings ahead, Casselle could see hazy smoke climbing into the sky, several plumes of it from different directions. "Come. I will need help."

The others looked briefly to Casselle, who had already fallen in behind Odegar. She considered tossing her ornamented, ill-fitting helmet to the side, wishing she'd had the comfortable sparring helm she'd grown accustomed to over her years as an initiate. Instead, she looped the chinstrap through her belt, letting it hang at her side rather than exacerbate the headache she was already dealing with.

The group moved with practiced ease, filling the small lane with the sound of rattling armor. Cats and rats vanished ahead of them, and even some particularly dodgy two-legged vermin quickly ducked out of their way, into the shadows.

"The whole city's in trouble. We were lucky enough to get reinforcements to the Temple because the Elder Council pays for the Watch. As you'll see, the rest of Strossen is in worse shape," Captain Taumber growled, motioning them to skirt a larger street. As they did, Casselle caught sight of two younger men overturning a produce cart. There was more happening, but the next alley swallowed them up before they could make sense of it.

"What in the High Houses?" Temos said.

"The Council of Elders was supposed to speak to Jonn Harrell today," Odegar replied.

"Jonn Harrell as in 'Golden Fingers' Harrell?" Temos asked.

"Yes, the self-proclaimed Merchant Prince of Strossen," the grizzled Templar Captain answered. "He has been waiting for an audience with the Elders for over a year now, to talk about his ideas."

"Bah," Raabel scoffed. "He advocates rule of the mob."

"He advocates the Council stepping aside so the citizens can govern themselves... I mean we... ourselves," Temos retorted.

"Regardless of what he advocates, he's little better than a thug himself," Jaksen interjected.

Captain Taumber hurried them across a wide street. This one was mostly empty, but the sounds of disorder were frighteningly close by. The confining width of the next alley felt almost welcome; at the very least, it was defensible.

"The Council did not have a high regard for him either," Odegar continued. "I wasn't there, but I know them, and I'm sure they were just waiting for him to slip up on some minor breach of protocol or etiquette. When he did, they moved to have him ejected. When he protested..."

"They arrested him," Raabel said, sounding strangely uncomfortable.

"You've seen that before?" Jaksen asked.

"In the past, my father had been pressed to put one or two 'troublemakers' in the cells overnight in order to quiet them," Raabel confirmed. "When I was a child I thought they deserved it."

Casselle could tell by the look on his face that perhaps the Constable's son had changed his mind since those days.

"Yes. It was all that was needed to light the fire. There were already plenty amongst his herd that were looking for a reason to pick a fight. It seems like an unjustly imprisoned leader was reason enough," Odegar explained. As they rounded a sharp corner leading into a small commons area, that was evident enough. Across the street a building burned slowly from the inside, flames licking out of the smashed windows.

Casselle felt a hot flush of anger as she watched a few young men push an older man to the ground, and would have moved to take them all on if the call of her mentor had not refocused her attention.

"The Watch will be along. We must hurry," Odegar said sharply, leading the others into another side street. Casselle, however, found herself planted firmly, still staring at the ruffians. The words from Odegar had restrained her, but she could not walk away, either. As her fist clenched tighter, she realized that she still held her baton. She stood motionless, the muscles in her shoulders and thighs begging for release, until the young man across the street happened to look up and catch sight of her. She saw the look of bloodlust blanch from his face.

He tugged at the sleeves of his friends before the beating turned ugly. All three of them ran off as the old man uprighted himself slowly, but with that situation diffused, Casselle was already gone, duty finally compelling her to follow after her comrades.

Strossen was an enormous city, by any standard, and was dominated by four main features: The Elder Circle, the University, the Cel'Dama and the Korristraad. The Circle and the University were on opposite sides of the city, near the East and West Gates, respectively. The 'Dama was at the center of town, an enormous amphitheater with a long and storied history. The hulking compound known as the Korristraad was to the North side, the hub of banking, manufacturing and business. Attempting to cross the city on foot was an undertaking on a good day, even by horseback. But on this day, in the shadows of Strossen's numerous alleys, making their way past angry rioters and frightened citizens, it was almost impossible.

Casselle continued on behind Jaksen, glancing over her shoulder as often as she spent watching his back.

"Do they expect this to make a difference? A lasting difference?" Raabel said aloud.

"They're probably not thinking that far ahead," Jaksen replied.

"This is not change," Temos said, sounding especially winded. "This is the result of frustration borne of no change. How long have the Elder Council promised that they would begin including others in the governance of Strossen... of Gundlaan?"

"Since we've been initiates," Jaksen said. "At least six years."

They pulled to a stop in the shadow of the Cel'Dama. Odegar surveyed the open streets ahead of them. Casselle looked once again at the great theatre. Used in equal measure for sports, entertainment and community gatherings, the Cel'Dama was a great coliseum, a massive edifice that easily rivaled the size of the Korristraad, which was roughly a dozen or so buildings loosely connected together. Street vendors and restaurants dominated the area around it, as well as other smaller, social venues. With the rest of the city alive with riot, it was odd to see this area so calm. Normally it was one of the busiest sections of the city.

Captain Taumber motioned for them to skirt to the South of the Cel'Dama, taking them past a pastries shop and into another long alley. These alleys were larger, more useful to the merchants who required deliveries to and from their shops. The Templars ran two abreast here, with room to spare.

"They've debated it since I was an initiate," Odegar said to them calmly, "and my Captain before me. The Council is big on debate... and little else." The group fell silent at that, the clamor of their armor masked by the sounds of civil conflict around them.

By the time the spires of the University loomed large above them, they were all exhausted, tired of the shadows and smells of Strossen's labyrinthine alleyways. There was quite a crowd here as well. Disaffected students of the University mixed in with other denizens of the city. Constables from the Watch attempted to keep the crowd turned away, but there was no heavy gate like there was at the Circle, so they fought from doorways and chokepoints provided by the campus' many entrances and exits. Thankfully, these protestors seemed to be more eager to deface symbols of authority than to actually engage in combat with armed guards.

As the squad emerged from a corner alley, they shuffled towards the building on the right side of the University's complex, the tall and well-buttressed library. Most of the rioters avoided the heavily armored group, with only a few brave or foolish enough to hurl insults or light projectiles in their direction.

A member of the Watch unbarred a door to allow them entrance to the library and ushered them all in before sliding the beam back into position. Another constable helped slide some benches back in place to brace the doors. There was a quick nod of mutual respect before anyone spoke.

"Captain Odegar Taumber."

"Constable Whitner," replied a young man with a makeshift bandage over his left temple. He appeared no worse for wear, but a few rivulets of blood had dried and matted the hair on that side of his face.

"How bad is it here?"

"Bad enough, sir," the constable replied. "We were nearby when our Sergeant sent us to secure the University. We were only two squads, so we're spread pretty thin, but I think we've got most of the buildings sealed for now."

"Have you been in touch?"

"Only with each other, sir. We've been waiting for word from our Sergeant before we do anything more than keep the buildings secured. Assuming things die down sooner rather than later, I think no real damage done." The constable paused for a moment, looking over Casselle and her squad. "It will die down soon, won't it, sir?"

"I do hope so," Captain Taumber replied. "For all our sakes." Constable Whitner did not appear reassured by that statement. Odegar continued on.

"We're looking for a Templar Librarian, Brother Maynard. Do you know if he is here? If he is well?"

"We haven't had time to do a full sweep of the building, sir. With just the two of us, we've been busy keeping the doors manned and the people here calm."

Casselle looked around, noting the nervous looks on the faces of those on the lowest level of the library. There were a few dozen of them sitting around in tight clusters, talking in hushed whispers. It was mostly an open area, with tables and chairs for reading and quiet discussion. She didn't see a lot of books around, like she would have expected.

"So you have not been upstairs to check the stacks?" Odegar pressed.

"No, sir," the constable said hesitantly.

"No worries, son," the elder Templar said with a slight smile. "You've done the right thing. We'll handle it. Anyone we find, we'll send down so you can account for them."

"Thank you, sir," the constable said with a look of relief. Odegar pulled the squad to the side, assigning them individual floors to check.

"Jaksen starts on two, with Temos and Raabel on three and four. Casselle to five and I'll head up to six." He paused for a moment and looked at Jaksen. "Screw that, I'm old. Jaksen to six and I'll take the second floor. We're here for Brother Maynard, but should you find anyone else, reassure them the building is safe and send them down here." Captain Taumber made sure his instructions had been clearly heard and then the five of them headed for the stairwells, splitting unevenly between the stairs on the opposite sides of the building.

Casselle followed Jaksen up the stairwell until she reached the fifth floor landing. The two exchanged a look and Jaksen continued onward, doing his best to hurry in his heavy armor up another flight of steps. Casselle was exhausted as well, with the excitement of direct combat finally starting to bleed out of her system. She knew that she would sleep well tonight, only to be sore tomorrow. She wondered what it was like on the campaign trail, when daily battles were a sure thing and there was no real time for rest. Would she weather that as well as the men in her squad? She didn't doubt her ability or strength, but she did secretly dwell on the doubts that most of the male Templars spoke of in unguarded whispers behind her back, looking down upon her because of her gender. Wanting to prove those comments wrong always helped push her to strive harder, but she occasionally had to fight in order to keep their insecurities from becoming her own.

The fifth floor looked more like Casselle expected. Directly outside the stairwell, she found herself between long rows of bookshelves. Something was written on the endcap of the closest shelf, and she paused to study it. Underneath a series of numbers and a couple of arrows pointing in either direction were the words "Theology & History". She listened for signs of movement, but was greeted only by the subtle creaking of aged timber settling and shifting.

In the stillness of the fifth floor stacks, she found herself trying to creep as silently as possible around the corners and through the rows, keeping her senses sharp for signs of activity. There was a dim light on the floor from high windows recessed in the wall. They allowed indirect sunlight into the room, but no direct light that she could see. She chided herself a moment later for thinking that any librarian would want candles or lamps near their precious books.

Distracted in thought, Casselle jumped when she heard the sound of wood scraping wood. A chair? It was hard to pinpoint the origin of the sound with the high roof and the long corridors of books, but she could tell it wasn't far. She moved more quickly now, trying to find an outer edge of the room in order to circumnavigate it. She broke free from the stacks on her right side (her cardinal directions somewhat confused now) and put her hand against the stone wall for just a moment to feel more oriented. Working along the wall she followed it to a corner and peered around to the left.

The sound hadn't been a chair. Down the outer lane of the stacks, Casselle saw an older man in thick robes struggling to move a ladder from one set of shelves to the next. His face was red with exertion and some of his wispy graying hair had flown away from the crown of his head, making the attempt more comical than productive. Casselle noted the cut and color of his vestment and could tell immediately that this was Brother Maynard, the missing Templar Librarian.

"Pardon..." Casselle said quietly, perhaps too quietly to be heard, given her distance from the man. While he continued to struggle, Casselle stepped from the edge and made her way towards him with steady, unhurried footsteps, attempting not to alarm him with her approach.

"Pardon..." Casselle said again, now closer and speaking louder than before. His face was lined like heavily grained wood, a gnarled old thing that had seen many years. His eyes were barely visible under the thick knot of his bushy white brows, and a pair of glass spectacles that were held in place by wire frames made them appear almost nonexistent. He adjusted his glasses slightly as he turned to look at Casselle, and made a slight clucking sound with his tongue as he quickly misjudged her by her appearance.

"Letting fat young boys into the Order now are we? Such a shame."

Casselle felt the blood rush to her cheeks. Not out of embarrassment, but anger. Why this old one's comment seemed to prickle her so much she could not tell, but she had become a master of choking back her anger and barbed replies. She answered only with a calm, if curt:

"You are in danger and must come with me. Captain Taumber requests it."

"Hm. Odegar came to save me? Must be a problem outside. Someone rile up the peasants again?" the librarian asked with equal portions of displeasure and detachment. In her head, Casselle gauged how far the closest window was and how hard she'd have to throw the old man to get him through the thick leaded glass. She was not as good with numbers as Temos was, but she felt she came to a close approximation before she silenced the thought. He stopped struggling with the ladder and stepped away from it.

"Come on, boy, help me get my books and I'll let my knees complain their way down the stairs," Maynard grumbled, leading to a table around the corner from the bookshelves. The books were piled high and deep and he casually pulled a large selection of them to pile into Casselle's arms, much to her own surprise and displeasure. After he had heaped on more than she could easily manage, he took an extra two small tomes to carry himself and headed for the stairwell.

The trip down was twice as bad as the march up had been. Not only did Casselle have to contend with the weight and unstable nature of the books stacked too high in her arms, she was forced to a maddening crawl as Librarian Maynard growled and groaned his way down each step, one tiny footstep after another, stopping to rest on each landing. It actually took so long that Jaksen caught up with them on the way down from his thorough inspection of the sixth floor.

"I stopped on five, but did not see you... Do you need help with those?" he asked. She nodded enthusiastically and Jaksen took more than a fair share of them himself, relieving Casselle's aching arms. Even after stopping for this rebalancing act, they still easily caught up with Librarian Maynard as he approached the third floor landing.

By the time they returned to the first floor, they had heard plenty about "lazy peasants" and the "burdens of those with noble blood." Casselle could tell that Jaksen had done his own calculations regarding glass windows and flying librarians. Thankfully Maynard would soon be Captain Taumber's problem and the thought of being bludgeoned in the head by an angry mob seemed preferable to the old man's blind prejudice.

"Maynard, what have you been doing with yourself?" Odegar Taumber asked as the slow moving librarian shuffled from the stairwell to the main floor. Casselle caught sight of Temos and Raabel and motioned for Jaksen to deposit the books on a nearby and conveniently clean table. He did so and the squadmates reunited, just out of earshot of the Captain.

"I see you two found him," Raabel said. "We've been back for some time. I guess he's as slow as he looks?"

"Casselle found him," Jaksen replied. "And he's both slow and rude. I'm sure he's important enough, but seems like he was in no real danger to begin with."

"I took a look out of the windows while we were searching for him," Temos said. "It doesn't look like it's calmed down much out there. I'd hate to think of trying to move him through an angry crowd. He doesn't look nimble enough to sneak by, either."

"If we weren't in this damned armor, I'd just carry him," Raabel said. Coming from someone else, it might have been considered a boast, but Raabel usually didn't say things he wasn't sure he was capable of doing. Casselle pictured the old man wailing in protest, thrown over Raabel's shoulder and being forced to bounce along like a sack of potatoes. Raabel was right about the armor, though: it was clumsy and ill-fitting. It was obvious that it had not been altered for them, and none more obvious than on Casselle. Her broad shoulders were a boon, but even bound, her breasts had proved problematic to find a properly sized chestplate from a stockpile that had been made exclusively for men. They had settled on a piece that was just slightly too large, having previously been worn by a heavyset Templar from a time before.

In thinking of it, she pondered Maynard's earlier words.

"He called me a boy," she said. "A fat young boy."

Her squadmates took a step back, shocked.

"And you did not correct him?" Raabel asked.

"Or worse?" Jaksen asked.

"To be fair," Temos said after a moment, "he is very old. It is entirely possible he has lost his will to live."

"I did want to hurt him. I do not know why it rankles me so." Casselle watched as her squadmates turned to stare at the elderly librarian, each showing their disapproval in their own way. She tried to shake the feeling, but could not. Thankfully, it looked as if duty would once again take her mind off of things. Captain Taumber moved close after leaving Maynard seated with his stack of tomes.

"I am glad Maynard is unhurt. He is a bit of an ass, but a very knowledgeable man."

"What now?" Temos asked.

"Now we help the constables fortify the buildings and keep us all safe. There is not much else we can do until the riot burns itself out or the city burns down because of it," Odegar replied.

"Do you think it will get that far?" Jaksen asked.

"I don't think so," Odegar replied and after a slight pause, "but I cannot be sure of that. Regardless, it is best to be prepared, which means I need the lot of you in fighting shape. Find a place to tend your wounds and rest. I will speak with the Constables and attempt to get a message back to the Temple about our status."

Fatigue began to settle on them and they nodded in reply. Temos found a room on the side that looked to be a supply closet of some sort or another. There were a few crates that they were able to use as chairs as well as a workbench to inspect their weapons and armor.

Casselle instantly felt more at ease with the improvised heavy plating removed. She kept on her lightly armored dressing jack, as did the others, while they inspected the plate mail for damage as well as the straps and buckles that held it all together. As usual, she finished first and found a place in the corner to sit and lean her head back while waiting for the rest of them to be done.

"Well, for complete ill-fitting pieces of mung, the armor actually held up pretty well," Jaksen said.

Casselle, however, did not hear him, nor did she hear Temos' witty reply. She had already fallen asleep.

***

Her father finished pulling the straps tight on her pack. Because she'd watched him do it a hundred times before, she knew the question she would ask next but never finish.

"Would mother...?" This is where her tongue always failed her. Her father turned and stood, strong and proud, as he had always been.

"Approve? Oh no," he said plainly, quite sure of himself. "She would have never approved." As Casselle felt her resolve slip, ever so slightly, he reached out and tenderly lifted her chin with thick, calloused fingers.

"But she would have been proud. She may not have ever said it like that, but you'd be able to see it in her eyes. She was always so proud of you, my sweet Cassie."

Casselle jolted awake from where she had fallen asleep against the wall of the room. Temos was curled up on the floor, resting his head on a makeshift pillow and snoring softly. Beyond them, Casselle could tell the lamps in the library had been lit and the yawning silence made her assume that night had finally fallen. She left her heavy, ill-fitting plate where it rested and moved from the room in her padded jack to confirm her suspicions.

The patrons of the library had tried to make themselves comfortable as best they could, clearing out a space on the far wall, furthest from the door. Casselle noticed the two constables among them as well. Jaksen and Raabel had taken their places on watch, though they both looked exhausted.

"She stirs," Jaksen said with a tired grin as she approached their position near the doors.

"Welcome," Raabel said, suppressing a yawn. "Thankfully there has been no trouble since you fell asleep, and Temos after you."

"Good timing," came the voice of Odegar Taumber, who had been positioned just out of Casselle's immediate view at another window. He motioned to Jaksen and Raabel. "You two get some sleep. Milner and I will keep watch."

Nodding in agreement, the two of them shuffled off towards the room where Temos already lay sleeping. Jaksen gave Casselle a friendly pat on the shoulder as he passed. Casselle nodded at him and watched Captain Taumber move into position just to the side of the window Raabel had been stationed at. Casselle moved to the opposite side of the door. She stared out to the right, and he the left, giving them crossing arcs of vision as well as a bit of protection instead of standing directly in front of the window.

Outside, the city was darker than usual. The lamplighters must not have come. The riot must have kept them at home, letting the shadows of the night run free. She wondered how late it was. Not that a view of the sky would have helped, but not being able to see it past the tops of the buildings outside made it feel as if the night would last forever.

"It's better, in case you were wondering," Odegar said. Casselle looked to him and lifted an eyebrow.

"The city, I mean," he added. "I don't think the trouble has stopped altogether, but I do think most of them have returned home. I feel that the worst of it has passed."

"For now," she replied, returning to her view out the window.

"Indeed," the Captain said with a sigh. "Only for now."

"Would this have happened in the days before?" Casselle asked.

"The days before..?" Odegar began to question, though he quickly guessed her meaning. "Before the Ehronfall, you mean. When the Young Gods lived among us."

Casselle nodded. More than two hundred years ago, the floating city of Ehronhaal fell from the sky, forever changing the world. Some monuments to them still stood, but the Gods themselves were gone.

"That... that is an excellent question," sighed Odegar. "I do not possess an equally excellent answer. At best I could say some have adjusted better than others. None of us, however, were prepared for it."

"Not even the Templars?"

"As you know, the Laegis Templars were drafted to act as an army against the H'kaan, the spawn of Maughrin. The Laegis fought under the command of the Gods, not only here in Strossen, but across all the lands of Niyah. You see... before the Ehronfall... before the Godswar... the High Houses acted in concert, working together as a family. Yes, each of them had different approaches, but theirs was a single goal.

"But it was not the H'kaan that decimated the Templars and slew the Gods. A fracture developed within their ranks, pitting family members against each other. When these conflicts started and the Godswar raged... well, even those of us closest to them fell victim.

"I have been told it was long and terrible, but I was too young for that. I only know what happened after it was over... when the last of them fell, never to rise again. We were all so shocked... so crushed by our grief, that I do not think, even today, some of us know how to continue on," the old Captain admitted.

"You were there?" Casselle asked, knowing that Odegar was older than he appeared. There was talk that he was Vanha, one of those who had the blood of the Gods in them.

"I was alive, yes, but not there. I was too young at the time... still a child. I remember very little about my father. My mother told me he was one of Derant's finest soldiers. I never knew him... but even then, as a child, I felt his passing." Odegar hung his head slightly. Casselle had never seen him this way before, not this vulnerable. He was quick to laugh, difficult to anger, but she had never seen him sad like this.

"Some of my oldest memories are those of my mother. I remember she would lay out an extra plate at each meal, for a husband that would never come. At first I thought she was just hopeful, later I took it for senility and it angered me. Not long after she died, I finally understood. She didn't do it because she expected him to come back. She did it because she had always done it and the act itself gave her a measure of comfort to remember him that way, carrying on with those traditions despite his absence.

"Some say we are lost without the Gods. I do not think we are lost. I feel confident we will carry on eventually. But for now we have not stopped setting a place for them. We carry on in their memory, hoping it will sustain us." Odegar said.

"But it won't," Casselle said grimly.

"It can't," he replied. "Because those of us that remember will eventually die. Just as my mother died... and her habits along with her. The best we can hope is to take their lessons and use the memory of them to make a better tomorrow."

Casselle thought of her own mother, and how distant the memories of her seemed. She empathized with Odegar's pain and the two of them sat silently, watching the night pass them by.

Blackness eventually surrendered to color and Casselle watched the sky lighten as the morning began to break. Just as they contemplated waking the others, a pair of Templar appeared outside, approaching confidently. Casselle noticed it first, but Captain Taumber caught her look of recognition and moved to unbolt the doors as soon as he saw them.

There was an exchange of names that Casselle couldn't hear clearly, but it was enough to have Odegar usher them inside.

"The danger is averted, Captain," the taller of the two informed him. "John Harrell worked with the Watch and the Council to pacify the rioters."

"Has he been freed?" Odegar asked.

"Not as of yet, but it was promised to him. The Council wishes to speak to him again before then. They are set to convene later this morning," the same Templar answered. His companion seemed content to remain quiet.

"I trust security will be better?"

"Yes, sir, though I think we all hope that it will be unnecessary," the Templar replied.

"Very good. Carry on," the Captain said. "We'll escort Librarian Maynard back." The two fresh-faced Templars saluted in return.

"If we arrive before you, we shall report your status," the Templar said before retreating through the front door and moving swiftly with his silent companion towards their next destination. Odegar watched them vanish around the corner.

"Let's wake the others and make sure the constables are aware of what's happening. We want to get these people back to their homes safely just as much as we need to safeguard Maynard." Whatever melancholy had possessed Odegar earlier had since passed... or been safely hidden away again. Casselle empathized with that, but said nothing, merely nodding in acknowledgement of her Captain's orders.

She moved to the room where the others lay and quietly nudged them from slumber. Jaksen and Raabel looked the worst for wear, since they'd had the least amount of rest, but Temos was wide-eyed and eager for news.

"The riot is over, yes? Everything's okay now?"

"Yes, the riot is over," Casselle answered calmly, staring out of the room at Captain Taumber as he spoke with the constables. He looked calm and aware and his words seemed reassuring to the guard. Casselle, however, felt less secure now than she had yesterday, in the face of the mob.

"And no, everything is not okay. Nor will it be for some time, I fear."

- 4 -

Ridgeback

Triistan is swimming in the dark water, swimming deeper, even though he doesn't want to, because something Terrible is down there in the True Dark, waiting to be discovered, unleashed. He should be swimming up, to freedom and light and air, but the journal clutched in his hands is like a great anchor and he isn't swimming anymore but sinking, being dragged down, down into the unknown terror of the deep...

Suddenly something snatches at his ankle and he is dragged upward. His panic gives way to relief as he realizes it is Scow saving him again because he was swimming the wrong way. He knows he must repeat every detail in that chain of events precisely as it had already occurred or the Terrible Thing will claim him. So he lashes out with his foot, expecting to connect with Scow's chest, but instead his foot encounters something rough yet soft and yielding, and suddenly that foot is grabbed too. He screams silently, his mouth filling with water, terrified as he is carried across the Burning Sea and beyond the Shattered Isles again. He knows that something has gone terribly wrong - some critical detail in repeating the sequence of events that he missed - and now there are strong-as-steel tentacles wrapped around both ankles, dragging him all the way back to Aarden, back to the Worm...

"Oi there, Titch have a care and stop your kickin' now!"

Dreysha's grip on his ankle was surprisingly strong as he woke to find her holding his twitching leg. His other foot was jammed up under one of the rowing thwarts. He mumbled an apology and sat up, rubbing his eyes against the late afternoon glare. He must have drifted off just after their meager lunch - a bite of salted boar, a biscuit, and two swallows of water. Tomorrow, Voth had told them, rations would have to be reduced even further.

"You can suck on that 'sorry', Titch. Next time maybe I take your foot off an' have me a little nibble -"

"That's enough," Lankham Voth interrupted her briskly.

Dreysha smirked.

"Not nearly enough if you ask me; not much meat on his b-"

"I SAID THAT'S ENOUGH!" Voth snapped and the others on the boat looked over in surprise. His nasally voice was pitched high and quavered slightly. "There will be no such discussions on board my ship, do you understand?"

Dreysha did her best to look chastised, failing miserably. She caught Triistan's eye and favored him with a sly wink.

"Aye, sir. It's your *ship*," she added and Rantham snickered. Triistan bit the inside of his cheek and looked down at his feet.

"Stow that shite, Drey, or I'll flog you myself," Scow grumbled. He had been talking with Voth about how they might possibly rig a third sail when Triistan had cried out and Dreysha yelped in surprise when he kicked her. Standing beside the reedy purser-turned-launch captain, the Mattock's wide frame seemed more solid and substantial than the boat's mainmast.

"Aye sir, meant nothin' by it," was all she said, but she gave Voth a dark look.

"You sure as the Stormfather's dick did, Seeker." Scow jerked his square chin in Triistan's direction. "Take Halliard and man that contraption of his. I think we can risk emptying the boot and you can toss your shite overboard with everybody else's."

For the first time since he'd awoken, Triistan realized that the sails were full and pulling hard, and the launch must have been making close to four knots. The motion of the boat felt good. The steady low hiss of the water sliding along their hull and the warm rake of the wind's fingers through his hair helped dispel the cold dead ones of his nightmare. It also meant they should be able to dump their filth overboard without fear of attracting any unwanted visitors.

Triistan followed Dreysha to the aft storage locker, nervously admiring the swing of her hips and the long, dark ponytail swaying above them. She still wore the sky-blue rough spun shirt, beige broadcloth pants, and faded red sash that comprised the midshipman's uniform, though her calves and feet were now wrapped in snug, supple boots of black sealskin rather than the stiff, blister-inducing deck-thumpers the Corps issued. He knew the knee-length boots had once belonged to Longeye, and swallowed a lump at the memory of Dreysha coldly stripping them from the lookout's floating corpse; a corpse he'd once called friend.

She opened the locker and held the heavy wooden lid up as he removed an odd-looking device and three lengths of hollow tubing. The tubes were actually sections cut from a tree they had found growing in dense thickets on Aarden - "criedewood" somebody had called it. The wood was somewhat flexible, very light, and remarkably strong considering it was hollow.

During those first days after making landfall, they had discovered and catalogued all kinds of new flora and fauna, but Scow had taken an immediate liking to this versatile plant. It had been he and Tarq who had come up with an ingenious method for extracting water and waste from the *Peregrine's* flooded lower decks. By cutting the criedewood into manageable lengths and whittling down one end, the pieces could be fitted together end to end and used to transport water from one place to another.

That was the simple part; they had all seen aqueducts before, so while the material was new, its use wasn't very impressive, until Tarq showed them how they could construct a pumping apparatus that forced air into the tubing and used it to push or pull the water where they wanted it to go. The handful of Khaliil on board had seen this done before as well - plumbing and pumping mechanisms had existed for decades in Ghostvale, their home - but for most of the remaining crew it bordered on sorcery and was regarded with a confused mixture of admiration and suspicion.

Triistan found it fascinating, however, and to Scow and Tarq's surprise, the normally quiet line-spider suddenly wouldn't shut up. He pestered both officers with question after question about the mechanics involved, followed soon after with multiple suggestions and sketches on how they could be improved. It hadn't taken long for Scow to lose his patience and threaten to shove one of the sections of criedewood up Triistan's arse and draw his innards out if he did not cease and desist immediately.

So the boy had retreated to his rig-tit and his silence, but his mind was not so easily cowed: thoughts filled his head until he thought it would burst, and he knew from experience that if he didn't get them down on paper they would plague him endlessly. So he had continued sketching the ideas in his journal, filling several pages with drawings, notes, arrows, scribbles, questions and half-formed thoughts that even he could make little sense of just a short time later.

It was after breakfast on the second day of the landing, as they were organizing labor parties to continue offloading supplies from the *Peregrine* to the camp they were establishing on shore, when Longeye had approached him. She had been with the crew since the *Peregrine* was commissioned - one of a dozen hand-picked Seekers Captain Vaelysia had demanded when she was given the command - and had always been kind to him. Apparently she had overheard some of his exchanges with Tarq and Scow and offered to share her knowledge with him as a native of Ghostvale. Together they created a smaller, portable version of the bulky pump that Scow had initially designed. The Mattock had watched them demonstrate the pump's quick assembly and simplified use in silence, exchanged a look with the Ship's Whip, and told them to stow it in the launch's equipment locker and get back to their original duties. Though Scow would never acknowledge it, Triistan knew he was impressed with their ingenuity, perhaps even proud of them. Assigning this task to him was as close as he would probably come to admitting it publicly.

Triistan smiled crookedly at the memory as he set the device down in the pungent, ankle-deep slop and began assembling the hollow criedewood sections. A few moments later, six days of filth was being ejected out one end of the makeshift pipe where Dreysha held it over the taffrail, while he worked the pump's plunger.

It was hard, hot work and before long sweat ran freely down his back. He stripped off his shirt, then reached back for his journal out of habit. Normally he kept it tucked inside the broad black sash that marked him as a topman, but he felt a brief flutter of panic when he realized the book wasn't there. It must have slipped out while he was sleeping.

"Be right back," he mumbled and started forward, heading for where he had been sprawled near the bow.

"Make it quick, a'fore the Mattock makes us bail it out with our sodding hands."

He ignored her, moving with an effortless, sinuous grace, slipping through the rigging and down the length of the boat like the shadow of a scudding cloud. To his relief, the journal in its protective wrap was still there, and he snatched it up and tucked it behind his back, inside his sash.

He returned the same way he'd come, sun-bronzed skin slick and shimmering in the ruddy light of the approaching long evening. He brushed past Dreysha, muttering a quick apology, and settled in next to the pump. She bit her cheek and arched an eyebrow.

"Oh don't worry about me, Titch," she said wryly. "Just admiring the view." She licked her lips and looked out at the water. "Such a lovely even' for pumping, don't you think?"

He glanced up at her and couldn't think of anything clever to say - or anything at all, actually - so he just smiled and removed his journal and placed it over next to his shirt. Her eyes followed the book.

"So what are you always scribblin' about, Titch? You a poet?"
"Sometimes."

He hated when she called him 'Titch'. The Rowmaster had coined the nickname, after the trained monkeys most ships of the Seeker Corps kept on board to catch rats; the *Peregrine* had had two as a matter of fact. Given the unnatural size of the vermin that thrived on the Sea King Isles, most cats were over-matched. The Titch Monkey, however, was extremely nimble, larger and stronger than a cat, and its dexterous tail - essentially a fifth arm - gave it a distinctive advantage. It was a highly intelligent animal and a cunning hunter, and most ships of the Corps carried one or two, with the larger galleys sometimes boasting as many as four.

Triistan was under no delusions that the Rowmaster had meant the nickname to be a compliment. Although no one could move through the tops with the speed and agility that he did, the favorable comparison fell short on the rowing deck - "the pit" as the crew called it - where you were judged by strength, girth, and volume, attributes the oarsmen found wanting in the wiry, quiet topman.

He stole another glance at Dreysha, peering out from under sweat-soaked locks of hair that had pulled loose from his sailor's braid. She stood on a coiled hawser, leaning out over the bulwark and holding her end of the wooden tubing over the side. Occasionally she twisted sideways to check that it was discharging far enough away from the launch's hull so as not to befoul it - they both knew Scow would have them slung over the side scrubbing it off if she did. The motion caused her to arch her back, while the rising breeze pressed her loose clothing tight to her body, revealing much, though not nearly enough for Triistan's taste.

"I once shipped with a rakish bastard on a run through the Golden Gap, wrote me poems and read them to me every night while the sky-fires burned above us. Thought his fancy words would tickle my thighs apart." She caught his gaze with a knowing look and he glanced away quickly, pumping harder. He could hear amusement in her voice as she continued, answering the question he could not voice himself, no matter how badly he wanted to know.

"Truth be told, I might have fucked him anyway if he'd had the courage to ask." Triistan's hand slipped off of the plunger handle and he fumbled with the device for an awkward moment before setting it upright again and resuming his task. He surprised them both by stammering out a question.

"W-Was he any god -good?"

Dreysha's gold-flecked eyes glinted mischievously. "Weren't you listening, Titch? He never *asked*..."

He felt the color rise in his cheeks and the tips of his ears grew hot. "No, no - I meant his poetry. Was his poetry any g -" He stopped and stood suddenly, looking past her.

He grabbed the mainstay and vaulted lightly up onto the bulwark, shielding his eyes from the westering suns. Dreysha, still holding the criedewood tube with one hand, grabbed the line and pulled herself up beside him.

"What? What is it? Land?"

"No," was all he said before he scrambled up the ratline to their makeshift lookout - a loop of line and a yard-long section of wood nailed crosswise near the top of the mainmast, where a man could sit with his legs draped to either side of the mast. In rougher seas, he could slip the lanyard around his waist and tie off.

As Triistan climbed, all eyes were on him, and no one saw the long, sinuous shadow glide beneath the launch's prow.

"What is it, Halliard?" Lankham Voth asked in an annoyed tone.

Triistan stood on the jury-rigged spar, holding the lanyard with one hand and shielding his eyes with the other.

"Survivors, sir! Looks like two on a decent-sized section of hull."

The others all rushed to the side to see for themselves, and the boat heeled dangerously, pitching Dreysha over the side and nearly sending Triistan plummeting ten meters to the deck. Fortunately he'd had a firm hold on the loop of line and kept his perch.

The Mattock roared his disapproval, cursing and bludgeoning them back to their stations and ordering Rantham to ready a lifeline for the survivors. Lahnkam Voth had the wherewithal to grab the helm and pulled hard on the wheel, pointing up and swinging the launch's prow to the northwest, towards the stranded men. In the commotion, they did not at first realize that Dreysha had fallen by the boards, until they heard her shouting her own Scow-worthy stream of invectives from ten yards behind the still-moving boat.

Rantham rushed aft, lifeline in hand, stumbled when the boat lurched awkwardly, then regained his footing and tossed the line out to her. Even with the abrupt change of course, she was still some fifteen yards off the port aft and Triistan was glad it was the Rogue making the throw - his luck held. A small sealed cask was attached to the end of the line, both to give it some weight for longer throws and to keep it afloat. It landed with a soft splash only three yards away from her. Relative to her position in the water, the launch was moving quickly though and the cask began dragging in a curve around her, forcing Dreysha to swim for it. Triistan flushed with relief when he saw her reach the line and begin pulling herself along its length as Rantham shortened the distance by drawing in his end from the deck.

Below him, most of the crew were hustling to obey orders, except for Scow, who was standing near the prow with a puzzled look on his face, looking around slowly, as if he were listening or waiting for something; and Jode, the injured sailor who had been pierced by a section of oar. Biiko had removed the wood from Jode's side and expertly sewn and cauterized both entry and exit injuries - apparently he was a highly skilled healer as well. Even so, the rest of the crew still assumed she would die if they did not sight land soon.

Thus far, she had stubbornly refused to oblige their pessimism, though she was feverish and only semi-conscious most of the time. Triistan could see her now where she had been lying beneath a low canopy of sail stretched out to provide her with shade not far from where The Mattock stood. She was struggling to sit up and get Scow's attention, and Triistan assumed she was trying to make sense of the sudden burst of activity aboard the boat. Whatever the reason, the fact that she was lucid enough to try was a hopeful sign.

Triistan swept his gaze out to the floating survivors, who were still beyond hailing distance but now close enough that he could see that there were actually three. Beyond them the sky was bright orange streaked with purple streamers, the second sun a ball of blood hanging just above the horizon. What at first he'd taken to be a large piece of the *Peregrine's* hull was actually a haphazard island of flotsam - bits of sailcloth, decking, broken spars, and what had to be a large barrel of drinking water called a scuttlebutt. Judging by how low it rode in the water, it looked to be about half full. Either that, or... no, he refused to consider the obvious alternative. Instead he did the calculations quickly in his mind: one full butt should contain enough drinking water to last the thirteen survivors about fifteen days. Combined with the two remaining scuttlebutts on board the launch, as well as whatever rainfall they could capture, they might have enough water to reach home now.

Food was going to be a different story.

The *Peregrine's* launch was always stocked with an emergency supply of fresh water and food: a mixture of salted pork and tough-but-protein-rich boar; wax-sealed clay jars of pickled fish; two crates of fruit (depending on the ships' remaining stores), and sacks of barely-edible hardtack. The notorious 'ship's biscuits' were supposed to be rotated out weekly, but even so, the "fresh" supply was typically the stalest, mealiest cast-offs from the cook's pantry. Finally, as per Seeker Corps regulations, every ship's launch was equipped with a "Morale Officer": a firkin of black spiced rum kept in a locked compartment to which each officer had a key. It was nothing that could withstand an earnest mate's boot in a pinch, but it was enough to keep thirsty watchmen from stealing a nip or three during the long, lonely hours of the mizzen watch.

All things considered, the launch should have been sufficiently stocked for two dozen crewmen for a month at three-quarter rations, longer if they tightened their belts. Unfortunately, when the *Peregrine* was destroyed and the launch dropped into the storm-lashed sea, the vessel had landed hard. Several of the casks and crates of food, as well as most of the fresh water supply, had broken loose and fallen overboard. Worse, according to the two Valheim oarsmen, in those first desperately confused moments while they were busy trying to free Jode from the oar, Voth had failed miserably at his final task as Provisions Master, clinging to the boat in panic while most of their stores were swallowed or smashed by the storm.

During the first few days after they were capsized, Triistan had fashioned a fishing line out of thread teased from his shirt, tied a small piece of meat to the end, and dropped it over the side of the boat. Most of the other survivors followed his example, spending the hours when they weren't sleeping or rowing attempting to fish, using a portion of their rations as bait. Unfortunately, their best efforts had only produced one barely-edible catch: a foul-tasting, boney thing called a skrell that had made two of them sick. Even so, for the first two days, the simple act of self-determination had lifted their spirits, at least until Voth ordered them to stop wasting their food as bait.

Maybe these three had managed to scavenge some food as well as water, Triistan thought hopefully, though the hope felt nearly as hollow as his belly.

The three castaways weren't able to stand on the unstable raft, but two of them were sitting up and waving their arms. The third had some kind of dark object on his shoulder that suddenly moved and began scampering from one section of the raft to another, eventually lighting on the scuttlebutt.

"I'll be drowned," Triistan muttered to himself, watching it bounce up and down and skitter back and forth. It was one of the *Peregrine's* rat-catching titch monkeys, though whether it was Snitch or Snatch he couldn't tell yet. He grinned and waved back, turning as he did to check on Dreysha's progress.

This time he saw the shadow.

It was a long, sleek thing, about as wide as he was tall but much, much longer - nearly the length of their launch, he judged. It glided from beneath the boat, a silent wraith darker than the shadow cast by their sails, but unmistakable even before its row of three spiked dorsal fins - like miniature lateen sails, each half as tall as a man - sliced the surface of the water only twenty meters astern. His heart lurched as the line of fins began curving back towards the ship.

"RIDGEBACK!" Triistan screamed.

"Where away?!" Scow shouted in response.

"Twenty yards off the starboard aft and coming about! Get her in the boat, Rantham!"

Both the Rogue and Dreysha were pulling frantically, and as the launch's sails filled, they began to pick up speed so that for a moment they were pulling away from the creature.

But only for a moment.

There was a sudden flurry of water behind the exposed ridge of dorsals and they seemed to leap forward, the jagged fins carving the surface and the bulk of something much larger below creating a long, low wave that was closing rapidly. Dreysha was only fifteen feet from them, the Ridgeback perhaps forty but gaining fast.

"Get her in the fucking boat, man!"

Triistan heard the rush of pounding feet on the deck below as Scow ordered them to retrieve the four harpoons fastened along the sides of the vessel. Triistan saw the Mattock toss one to Biiko, who snatched it out of the air, slammed its point into the bulwark beside him, and then seized hold of the lifeline in front of Rantham. Dreysha nearly flew the last ten feet to the launch, where the Unbound reached down and plucked her from the sea an instant before the pressure wave struck the side of the craft. At the top of the mainmast, Triistan jammed his arm and shoulder through the tie-off and braced for impact.

It never came, though. The ridge of fins slid silently from view, leaving only a much smaller, secondary wake to slap harmlessly against the launch's hull. The boat rocked gently.

They all stood stock still for several tense moments, listening. Triistan craned his neck to see Dreysha and found her next to Biiko, feet braced, wet clothes clinging to her skin, a harpoon clutched in her hands. She looked furious.

"Easy now, lads," Scow said quietly. "Steady. She just wanted a little whiff of Drey is all. Like as not she's gone down deep again."

"Come back for another sniff you slimy crab-buggering bitch," Dreysha growled.

"Stow that!" Voth squeaked from where he clung to the ship's wheel. Triistan could practically hear his knobby knees knocking together all the way up here.

The ship groaned and creaked its familiar song as they continued closing the gap to their raft-bound shipmates. Now all too aware of what lurked beneath the water, the crew had taken positions on both sides of the launch. Biiko, Scow, and one of the Valheim held harpoons at the ready, while Rantham was coiling up the lifeline he had used to rescue Dreysha, moving slowly to avoid making any noise.

Triistan's chest began to ache and he realized he was holding his breath. He let it out slowly and drew in a new one, all the while scanning the ocean around the ship and now, as it drew closer, the raft as well. Below him the sails luffed and snapped as Voth tacked, trying to pick up speed.

The first sun dropped below the horizon and the water turned black speckled with rose and gold where the fading light skimmed the wave tops. The long evening had begun, and there would be no tell-tale shadows now, as the second sun wasn't bright enough. Scow shared a quiet word with Rantham, who stowed the lifeline and began lighting the launch's watch lamps.

The raft and its four occupants were barely more than a silhouette, but they were close enough for Triistan to hear the titch's chattering. *Must be Snitch then*, he thought. Snatch rarely if ever made a sound, while Snitch never seemed to shut up. It made them ideal hunting partners; Snitch would move through the hold chattering and screaming, driving the rats into his silent brother's waiting embrace. For the monkey's sake, he hoped ridgebacks weren't attracted to sound.

The crew remained hushed, watching. He checked the lanyard around his arm and shoulder again and noticed that some of the others had crept back to the edge of the boat and were peering over the side, trying to see into the dark waters. He was just wondering if ridgebacks had been known to breach and snatch unwary sailors from their ships when a sudden cry startled him.

His heart threatened to burst from where it had lodged in his throat, but it was just one of the men on the raft hailing them.

They don't know, he realized. They were still some hundred yards away. The ridgeback and Dreysha had been on the far side of the launch, behind the boat and thus shielded from view, and they had no idea of the danger they might be in.

Triistan thought he knew the hailing voice, and the Mattock confirmed it.

"Bail out my bunghole, is that you, Mung?" Scow's rough baritone rumbled across the narrowing gap as they drew closer. A few of them chuckled softly. Although the sound was low and nervous, Triistan sensed the tension and fear that had transfixed them all beginning to lessen. A ship's crew needed a confident leader. Even if it wasn't the captain.

"Echoman Wiliamund, what is your status?" Voth rasped harshly.

High above, Triistan gritted his teeth and tightened his grip on the lanyard. He searched the waters around them again, but the ruddy glow of the evening sky was not enough to see by. On deck, Rantham was making his way along the launch, lighting the seal-oil watch lanterns as he went, and Triistan was acutely aware of the vast, unseen void below them.

"My status sir?" Triistan could hear the honest confusion in Mung's voice and imagined him looking incredulously at his two fellow cast-aways: *wasn't it obvious?*

Snitch was still yammering away, perhaps telling Captain Voth a few of the choice things many of them were thinking.

"You heard me, Echoman. Report!"

"Yes... I mean, Aye, sir. My- our status, sir, is that we... the three of us, sir, are cast adrift on a raft made of flotsam which - if I may say so myself, sir, was rather resourcefully done. Furthermore, we're hungry enough to contemplate eating raw monkey, and despite your less than inviting welcome, we're still very happy to see you."

There was a pause before the normally cowardly Mung added an almost-defiant, "Sir." It seemed that the threat of death had finally imbued Mung with a backbone, undoubtedly short-lived, but humorous nonetheless. There was a smattering of chuckles and a few half-whispered, wry comments.

Finally faced with something he had control over, Voth ignored them and clung to Seeker Corps Protocol like a drowning mariner to a lifeline. "Identify your- "

"Sir," interrupted Scow. "May I suggest we lower our sails and man the sweeps?" By then they were perhaps sixty yards away and liable to ram right into and through the raft at their current speed.

Voth sounded annoyed. "Yes, Mr. Scow... I should think that would be rather obvious." He called out again to Mung as Scow quietly issued orders to strike the sails and ship the oars.

"Who is 'we', Echoman?"

"Oh, sorry, sir." He cleared his throat and announced in a more recognizably obedient tone, "Auxiliary Echoman Wiliamund Azimuth the Younger, sir!"

"Able Seeker Braeghan, sir!" came the squeaky reply of an adolescent, and Triistan smiled. Braeghan was a young apprentice cooper from a coastal town in Minethia and one of the few shipmates he could truly call a friend. He was a bright but naive boy with a knack for woodworking and telling jokes that were so innocent and simplistic that even the surliest among the crew couldn't help but at least smile. It would be good to have his company again.

The third person on the raft did not immediately answer, but Triistan heard Mung say something in a questioning tone. In the awkward silence, he realized that Snitch had stopped chattering; apparently the monkey did not wish to report in to the ranking officer, either.

A long, low scraping noise issued from below as Biiko, Rantham and the two oarsmen slid the launch's sweeps into position.

"Is there a problem, Echoman? Who else is with you and why does he not report?" Voth persisted.

"My apologies, Provisions Master Voth, sir, it -"

"Captain!" Voth cut in and Triistan closed his eyes, shaking his head.

"What? Oh, yes, sir, but I don't think he can hear you. Seems to have taken a nasty blow on the head and just -"

Voth made an odd, whiny noise of frustration. "What in the Dark are you babbling about, Mung? As the highest ranking officer left, you will address me as *Captain* Voth!"

Silence. If not for the sound of the oars and Scow's quiet cadence for the rowers, Triistan fancied he could have heard Mung blinking stupidly.

"Begging your pardon, sir, but that's... well that's not exactly true, sir. Captain Fjord is right here, sir... though I cannot say if he knows he is."

A murmur of surprise rose up from the others, and now it was Lahnkam Voth's turn to blink stupidly. Triistan was tempted to whisper his own prayer of thanks, whether any gods were around to hear it or not, when the makeshift raft floated into the glow of the launch's watch lamps. He could see the three castaways: Mung and Braeghan wore the torn and filthy remnants of their uniforms, but Fjord was completely naked save for a stained bandage around his head and another around his waist. As Scow ordered his rowers to reverse sweeps and slow, Triistan realized that it wasn't a bandage around Fjord's waist, but the tattered remains of his azure and cloth-of-gold Captain's Sash. Mung's earlier responses suddenly made sense and he groaned inwardly. Soon the rest of the survivors did as well, as the *Peregrine's* acting captain sat slack-jawed, ignoring the handful of "Hail, Captain's" that broke out among the launch's crew.

"Just trading one fool for another," he murmured, but aloft as he was, there was no one to hear him save the last bloody sun and a few brave but silent stars. He heard someone curse quietly from below - no doubt sharing the same thought - and since he could no longer see anything in the failing light, Triistan climbed quickly down to the deck to lend a hand.

Suddenly, Snitch emitted a high-pitched, terrified scream. An instant later the water and the portion of the raft the monkey was on exploded upwards. Triistan caught a glimpse of something huge, black and shining. It had a broad snout and long, triangular-shaped head split by gaping pink gums filled with row upon row of jagged, gleaming teeth, and a bottomless black sphere of an eye the size of his fist. Pieces of the raft splintered, were thrown up and cascaded down around them as the front third of the thing's body crashed back down. It turned as it fell and he saw its belly flashing in the glow of the watchlamps as it thrashed its way clear of the debris, white as a drowned corpse. Somehow Snitch had leaped into the air and hurled himself towards the launch, landing only a few meters from the tip of the foremost oar where he was swimming deftly towards safety.

Shouts and screams rent the night as Mung and Braeghan begged for help. Captain Fjord remained seated where he was, oblivious and staring silently, but Mung panicked and dove into the water, making for the ship. Braeghan was nowhere to be seen, although Triistan could hear the boy's desperate pleading.

The ridgeback rolled and slid back beneath the surface, leaving half of the makeshift raft - the half with Fjord sitting quietly, insensate - still intact. The rest of it had been reduced to random flotsam in only a few seconds.

Triistan looked desperately around for Braeghan and spotted something moving along the outer edge of the wreckage. A moment later he recognized the tallow-haired head of the young cooper bobbing up and down as he swam out from behind a broken spar. He must have been thrown from the raft as well and was now heading for the starboard oars, struggling badly, alternately sobbing and choking as he inadvertently inhaled water, but his terror kept him moving. Rantham was up at the bow, tossing the lifeline out to Mung while Biiko and Scow stood next to him, harpoons held high. Closer, one of the Valheim - Pelor - was trying to lift an oar out of its lock so that he could extend it out further for the boy to grab.

Braeghan was moaning plaintively in between his sobbing coughs, "Oh gods please oh gods please please..."

"Dreysha, help me!" Triistan screamed and snatched up a second line. He half-vaulted, half-rolled over Pelor's broad back, flinging out the coil of line as he deftly landed on his feet. It was a poor throw, however, and the float at its end landed well short of his terrified friend. As he hurried to draw the rope back in, he frantically scanned the wreckage and the surrounding waters for the ridgeback, expecting to see the row of fins appear at any moment.

Snitch scampered up the oar and over Pelor's shoulder, squealing and tugging at the Valheim's hair as if trying to exhort him to save the boy. While trying to dislodge the monkey, the big sailor dropped the oar and it clattered onto the taffrail and began sliding into the water.

Dreysha was there a heartbeat later and seized the titch by the scruff of its neck, tore it loose from the oarsman's hair and hurled it aside. Somehow Pelor managed to grab the oar's handle just as it slid free of the lock, and with Dreysha balanced on the edge of the taffrail brandishing her harpoon, he leaned out as far as he could, holding the oar out.

All three of them began shouting encouragement to the boy; he was only two or three yards away from the extended oar now, and as Triistan gathered up the lifeline for another throw, he stole a glance towards the bow to see how the others were faring with Mung, who actually had hold of Rantham's rope. Scow was helping to pull him closer, while Biiko stood nearby, scanning the waters, harpoon poised.

Pelor was shouting at Braeghan. "That's it, lad! Grab the sweep now it's right there, c'mon boy, stretch..." Still sobbing and choking, Braeghan reached out to grasp the oar, but his fingers slipped off of the wet wood. He bobbed under the water and came back up sputtering and crying even louder, beseeching the gods to save him.

Triistan felt his own panic rising in response to the boy's hysterics. He watched Pelor lean out and nearly tip over the side while trying to push the ungainly sweep into Braeghan's flailing hands, and suddenly had a better idea for the lifeline. Moving quickly, he slipped it around the oarsman's waist and made the other end fast around a jack stay, allowing the man to lean out even further. This time Pelor literally poked the panicked cooper in the chest with the oar, and Dreysha's voice cut through the tumult like claws shredding flesh.

"Stop wailing like a whore, boy and save yourself! *Grab that fuckin' scull, NOW!*"

This time Braeghan lunged at the sweep and got both hands around it just above the blade. Pelor shouted encouragement and braced his knees against the bulwark as he began pulling the oar in hand over hand. Braeghan had both arms wrapped around it as if it were his mother's neck, sobbing wildly, moaning, the same words tumbling out as his mind locked onto the litany as surely as his arms had onto the blade of the sweep.

"Oh gods thank you thank you thank you oh gods mercy thank you..."

Off to his left, Triistan heard Scow berating Mung as they hauled him up the side. He could tell from the familiar sound that the Mattock was welcoming the self-proclaimed craven back to the land of the living in his own unique way. But the hint of a smile suddenly froze at the corner of Triistan's mouth as he watched Braeghan being dragged in.

For one heartbeat, the boy's body and the water immediately around him seemed to *lift*, rising up as though the sea itself were trying to rescue him. In the next beat, twelve yards of sleek, glistening cartilage, muscle and teeth exploded into the evening air.

The ridgeback's entire body breached, the pressure wave of its attack flinging Braeghan into the air just ahead of its open jaws. For one more agonizing heartbeat, Triistan thought the boy's prayers had been answered and miraculously he would be thrown free.

But the moment passed.

The beast seemed to stretch itself, the smooth black skin pulling away to expose jaws lined with multiple rows of serrated teeth, pushing forward the hands breadth more it needed to snatch him from the air. The sickening wet snapping of bones cut the boy's prayer off in mid-sentence - it happened so quickly he hadn't even had time to scream or let go of the oar - and then the ridgeback's long, tapering body was falling, rolling sideways, massive pectoral fins as long as Triistan splayed out to either side like wings.

The entire strike lasted less than three seconds, and in his shock, Pelor held onto his end of the oar, causing him to be jerked overboard. The lifeline Triistan had fastened around the oarsman's waist pulled taught so that he swung and smashed face-first into the hull, where he was crushed as the ridgeback rolled and thrashed its massive body, striking a glancing blow to the boat as it dove again. The starboard oars snapped off and the launch was slammed sideways, blood, seawater and splinters raining down on her crew.

Most were thrown from their feet and Jode screamed in agony as she was flung against a bulwark. As he fell, Triistan struck the side of his head against something and his vision blurred. A lantern knocked free of its hook to shatter on the deck, where blue flames flashed across the slick of seal oil it disgorged. As Scow and Pelor's brother tore away Jode's sail-cloth shelter and rushed to smother the flames, Voth panicked and kicked over the half-full butt of fresh water, trying to put it out himself.

Triistan struggled back to his feet and lurched to the starboard rail. Dreysha and Biiko were already there, but something warm and sticky ran into his left eye. He clawed and wiped at it, blinked and shook his head, trying to clear his vision, trying to see over the side.

Biiko was hauling on the lifeline tied around Pelor, dragging the Valheim's lifeless body back into the boat. The surface of the sea was relatively calm again, a dark wet void dotted here and there with pieces of the raft and broken oars. In the deep red glow of Ruine's long evening, it was an ocean of blood.

Off to his left, nearly bumping the launch's prow, Captain Fjord still sat on what was left of his raft, oblivious. Rantham was preparing to throw another line to him, for what little good it would do.

Of the ridgeback or the boy, there was no sign.

"Braeghan!" Triistan tried to shout, but the effort sent a searing spike of pain through his skull and his knees buckled. A strong arm slid around his waist and held him up.

"Whoa, Titch. Easy. That black bitch has had her fill of Seekers for now."

He looked down at Dreysha, his ragged emotions flaring.

"Is that some kind of sick fucking joke? He was my friend!"

She didn't seem to hear him, though, and the expression on her face made him look overboard again.

In a cruel parody of just a few moments earlier, he spotted the familiar tallow-haired head of the young cooper bobbing up and down in the water again. But when it rolled over, revealing that the ridgeback had consumed the rest, he shoved away from Dreysha and fell to his knees on the deck, vomiting.

The violence of the act brought a wave of blinding pain and dizziness cascading down upon him, the deck tilted sideways, and the world went as dark and cold as the sea beneath him.

- 5 -

Blood Moon

The ridgeback would claim two more victims before the night was through.

Triistan rose slowly to the surface. His head ached fiercely, particularly just above and in front of his left ear. When he tried to open his eyes, he saw nothing but blackness. Sounds drifted into his consciousness from somewhere nearby, muted and weirdly distorted. Initially he didn't even realize it was speech, until he began to recognize voices, and then he felt a flutter of panic because he couldn't comprehend what they were saying.

He blinked hard, misshapen purple spots blossoming across the darkness. When he forced his eyes open again, the spots remained - a drifting, random pattern like blood spatter that slid from left to right. As they gradually faded, lighter spots began to appear, cold fires flickering in the distance.

Stars.

The word came to him and with it a warm wash of relief as lucidity slowly settled the silt clouding the waters of his mind. The world rocked gently around him: he was floating on his back under a brilliant field of stars, and for some reason he couldn't quite grasp yet, that felt right.

Suddenly the stars disappeared, replaced by a large, dark shape that loomed over him. He shrank back in fear, or tried to, but the rough stonewood planks beneath him would not yield. A familiar rotting smell assailed his nostrils as the shadow moved closer, the stench driving his pain deeper into his head and turning his stomach.

A rough, angry voice with a thick northern accent rasped in his ear and he suddenly had a name to go with the horrid breath: *Sherp.*

"Should have been your busted bones danglin' from that lifeline, little Titch. It was your fucking little bunkwarmer he was tryin' to rescue anyway. Worthless mung-sucking toppers - the lot o' ya ain't worth one of us in the pit and my brother was one of the best."

Pelor. Sherp was talking about Pelor, the other Valheim oarsman. Triistan had tied Pelor off so that he could lean out further to rescue...

Oh gods, poor Braeghan.

Something solid struck the deck close to Triistan's ear and Sherp broke off, looking up sharply. Someone else had arrived. Triistan tried bringing the figure into focus, but he couldn't see past Sherp's bulk. Even the feeble effort to shift his position brought a fresh wave of pain and dizziness, so he focused on the butt end of his rescuer's harpoon instead. Sherp was standing slowly to face the newcomer, while Triistan lay flat on his back between them, feeling small and miserable.

"Just checkin' on our little Titch is all, friend. Better have a look at that hard head of his - could be a nasty wound... wouldn't want him to lose it." His forced bravado was so thin even Triistan's sluggish, bruised brain saw through it, and he realized who his benefactor must be. Biiko was the only one on board who inspired that kind of fear, particularly among the oarsmen. Sherp muttered something that sounded like "fucking worthless toppers" as he stalked away, the impact of his heavy sea boots striking the stonewood deck planking hard enough to make Triistan's teeth rattle. The boy winced and bit down hard to stifle a groan of pain.

There was a rustle of movement as Biiko squatted beside him and set his harpoon aside. Despite everything they had been through together on Aarden, the Unbound warrior was still an enigma to him. He had learned some details about the order some called the Sons of Khagan from First Mate Tarq, but very little from the man himself. Unbound on a Kattha - some kind of vision quest - apparently took a vow of silence and were only allowed to speak once each day until their Kattha was fulfilled. Those pursuing such a quest saved the opportunity for one of three things: the evening prayer, a truly urgent need to communicate verbally in order to continue their quest, or, if they should fall in battle, to curse their enemy, so that they might find them again in The Dark and have an opportunity to avenge themselves. At least, those were the stories he'd been told, but Triistan suspected there was much more to it than that.

Biiko reached out and felt his head, fingertips surprisingly warm, his movements quick with the surety of long practice. Triistan opened his eyes again.

"Thanks - I don't think he likes me very much."

Biiko ignored him and continued inspecting the wound.

"How bad is it?"

Still no response, but his dark lips twitched in what might have been a disapproving scowl, though it was hard to tell; the long scar running from his right eyebrow to his chin bisected the corner of his mouth, dragging it down and giving him a perpetual frown. He met Triistan's gaze and gently lowered the boy's head to the deck. No matter how many times Triistan saw them, he was always struck by the warrior's unusual eyes: his irises were gold-colored, but surrounded by a thin ring of vivid blue, and at the moment they looked luminescent in the flickering light of a nearby watch lamp.

His thoughts drifted back to the first time he had seen the Unbound, in Thunder Bay off the southern coast of Khiigongo. The *Peregrine* had put in to take on fresh supplies of water and food before setting out for the Shattered Isles. He'd been checking the kicker straps along one of the booms and explaining their function to Mung when he had noticed a tall stranger in dark robes staring at him from the dock. Well, it had *felt* like he was being stared at; in truth it was difficult to see the man's eyes because he had the hood of his robe pulled low, hiding his features in deep shadow. But from the angle of the stranger's head and the crawling sensation on the back of Triistan's neck, he felt sure that the man was looking right at him.

"That, my dear boy, is an Unbound, or I'm Thunor reborn," Mung had said quietly.

"How can you tell?" Triistan whispered from the side of his mouth. There had been at least thirty yards between them and the stranger at the time, but there was something about the man under the shadowed hood that had filled Triistan with foreboding.

Indeed, the figure tilted his head ever so slightly, as if he'd heard Triistan's question. Mung dropped his voice to a whisper as well.

"You mean besides that feeling like somebody just replaced your bollocks with two slabs of ice? Look again at his robe; that's a jiisahn, not some goat-herder's rags. Not to mention, who else this side of The Dark would wear that much black in this heat?"

Mung was right; what he'd at first mistook for a common hooded frock looked on closer inspection more like an ensemble of various pieces, layered and cut so that while he had been standing still, they covered his frame as a simple robe might. However, as the stranger moved towards the *Peregrine's* gangplank, Triistan had caught glimpses of dark steel beneath, as well as twin sword pommels poking from behind each shoulder like gleaming ebony bones, as if he were about to sprout demon's wings.

First Mate Tarq had been embroiled in a heated exchange with the wharf-master near the foot of the gangplank as Biiko approached. Triistan remembered being surprised to see he was nearly as tall as the Ship's Whip - an imposing figure unto himself and easily the tallest

- 59 -

onboard the *Peregrine* by half a head - and now both men towered over the much rounder and suddenly much quieter wharf-master. Triistan saw the stranger hold out some type of message which Tarq unrolled and began to read, and a moment later he was escorting Biiko onto the ship and down the stairwell leading to Captain Vaelysia's cabin. When they had emerged less than half an hour later, Tarq shot an odd look at Triistan before moving back across the gangplank, while the newcomer and Vaelysia stood together for a moment, conferring in low voices.

After a few moments, the warrior had drawn back his hood with both hands, very formally, and bowed to the Captain. He had smooth, black skin drawn tightly over bold cheeks and a broad, strong jaw line. His jet-colored eyebrows swept back from both eyes, across his temples, nearly to the point where his tightly braided dreadlocks began. Had Triistan known more of the mysterious sect, it might have occurred to him how significant it was for an Unbound to be speaking with anyone. Only later did he learn about their Kattha and Vow of Silence.

As the stranger bowed, he touched the fingertips of both hands to his forehead, then swept his arms down and out from his sides in a very elegant gesture, as if he were placing his thoughts at the Captain's feet in some form of offering. When he straightened and strode past Triistan and Mung, the boy met the dark warrior's eyes. They startled him - not just their alien color, but the intensity that burned behind them - yet somehow Triistan had managed not to look away. Even now he remembered the relief he had felt when the Unbound brushed past, releasing him from that penetrating gaze.

Mung, of course, hadn't failed to notice the exchange.

"Brave boy, but foolish if you ask me, and I know much of the latter, if little of the former."

Triistan had turned to look at him reflexively, but his mind had still been wrestling with what the Captain and this stranger had been discussing and why it felt like it had something to do with him. In truth he had not heard a word Mung had spoken, but his new friend continued on regardless - as was typical, Triistan had learned since.

"The Unbound are not to be trifled with, though being a native of the Sea King Isles I should think you would already know that."

Still trying to catch up, Triistan shook his head. "What?"

Even now he could hear Mung's exaggerated sigh. "Surely it is proof that the gods have returned that you can form coherent sentences, let alone read and write." He had then gestured dramatically with his two fingers, first at the departing warrior's broad back and then waggling them in Triistan's face. "I am *saying* that it is incredibly idiotic to try and stare someone down, particularly a mystical warrior who knows nine hundred and ninety-nine ways *to kill you.*"

"Oh... no, I wasn't staring him down. I was just surprised - did you see his eyes, Wil?"

"Haven't you been following along? No, I avoid them whenever possible. What of them?"

"He's been scrubbed."

It was odd how vivid that memory was, like he was reliving that moment right now - so much so that he flinched guiltily and looked at Biiko to see if he had heard the derogatory remark. But of course he hadn't; he was still crouched beside Triistan, examining his wound.

Biiko held his hand up, palm out. It was clear that he wanted Triistan to wait here, which was fine with him; just the act of trying to focus on the silent warrior was making him nauseous. He closed his eyes, trying to relax and rest, but his thoughts raced on unchecked.

Damn his mind! The gods knew it had its own unusual way of functioning under normal circumstances, and now in response to this latest trauma it seemed to be reorganizing itself by following old pathways, like this memory of his conversation with Mung, which now led to another, darker trail. Biiko's eyes were proof that he had gone through the highly controversial process of Reformative Memory Cleansing - "scrubbing" to most commoners - which was normally used by the Sea Kings to handle their worst criminals. Somehow they were able to destroy a person's memories, effectively erasing his or her past. Proponents believed it gave the person scrubbed a chance to redeem themselves. By removing all of the corrupting experiences of their former lives - abusive parents, traumatic events, poverty or wealth, maniacal mentors or any other of a myriad of destructive forces - you would be left with what they believed all Men began as and were by nature: a clean sheet of parchment. Unmarred, unsullied, and pure, just as Tarsus had first created them.

But as his thoughts raced along this particular track, he had the uneasy sense that there was one darker still running in parallel; the trail left by questions he had obsessed over in the past, like the shadowy path of some beast he had been hunting. He tried to remember the rest of the conversation with Mung, but he couldn't seem to move past that last thought: there was something connected to this concept of a second chance.

He remembered pressing Mung on the issue of scrubbing, asking if the Unbound were criminals. He could not imagine why anyone would do so willingly, but Mung was only too happy to correct him.

"The Unbound undergo voluntary scrubbing, though no one understands why. Something to do with their calling to 'break the chains of Fate,' or some other equally colorful metaphor." He shrugged. "Everything I've heard about them smacks of fanatical fortune-telling nonsense if you ask me."

Breaking the chains... Triistan shivered, recalling the sense of foreboding he'd felt as Mung spoke. It was somehow related to his sense now of this parallel line of thought he was missing. It was like entering an empty room with another door that was just clicking shut, as though someone had just left.

A pair of soft supple boots stepped into his field of view, interrupting his reflections, and Dreysha sank down beside him. His nausea intensified, but for a very different reason.

"You look like shit."

"Thanks," he laughed weakly and closed his eyes. "What happened?"

"How much do you remember?"

He raised a shaky hand and pinched the bridge of his nose. The sight of Braeghan's severed head was all too clear in his mind's eye. "Too much... not enough..."

He opened his eyes again and looked up at her. She was crouching, hands clasped loosely in front of her, dusky arms resting on her knees. Her left forearm bore a fresh bandage and he could see a dark stain just above her wrist. She saw the direction of his gaze and held it up for closer inspection.

"A souvenir from that big bitch. Your nursemaid gave her one better, though. Drove a yard of steel into its eye. Either ridgebacks sink like stones when they die or she's had her fill of us. Either way, she's gone." He loved the rich, throaty sound of her voice with its exotic accent, one he still hadn't been able to place. Mylesia was on the mainland on the opposite side of Niht's Haven from the Sea Kings' archipelago - not exactly 'exotic' to an Islander, but the so-called 'Knave's Haven' attracted her namesake citizens from the farthest reaches of Niyah. Dreysha could be from anywhere, and he had made a private game of trying to guess where without asking her outright.

"How long have I been out?" The sky was fully dark now, but there was no moon. Had they been in familiar waters he would have been able to guess the time from the position of the stars, but they weren't, and anyway that part of his brain still refused to cooperate.

"Not long. One bell maybe?" At two bells to a quarter-watch, he'd been unconscious for about half an hour then. With the limping, disjointed state of his thoughts, his sense of time was scrambled, so it felt like much longer.

She lowered her voice and he heard a note of exhaustion in it. "Long enough for Tall, Dark and Silent to play heroic warrior *and* healer. Though I don't think even he can save Coop."

Triistan blinked. "Coop?" The name was familiar, but he couldn't say why, or connect her last sentence to the topic of how long he had been out.

She tilted her head and looked at him curiously.

"Coop. Jode Cooper? The apprentice carpenter with the oar handle poking her insides just a few inches too high? Scow's favorite? She must have taken a beating when that giant fucking fish slammed into us. Broke something open inside is my guess."

Just then Biiko returned and knelt beside him, opposite Dreysha. He gave her a meaningful look before returning his attention to Triistan. The warrior shoved a few leaves into his mouth and began chewing, but Triistan had stopped paying attention: something soft and warm brushed his cheek. His heartbeat stumbled as he felt Dreysha's breath in his ear.

"Thank you," she whispered.

He tried to turn his head to respond but Biiko grunted quietly and placed a long-fingered hand along one side, his thumb crossing under Triistan's chin, effectively immobilizing him. With his other hand, he reached up and spat a glob of greenish paste onto his fingertips, then began applying it to the wound on Triistan's head. It smelled horrible - strong enough to burn his nostrils and make his eyes water - and he wondered how anyone could have placed such a foul substance in their mouth with such aplomb. No wonder the Unbound always looked so miserable.

Whatever it was, however, it worked. The moment the poultice touched his skin, the pain began to recede and in a few moments it had retreated to a dull throb behind his left eye. He began to breathe easier, and even the nausea receded as Biiko wrapped a clean bandage several times around his head. Then, to his surprise, he was pulled upright to a sitting position and turned so that he could rest his back against a bulkhead. Biiko squatted in front of Triistan and looked directly at him, pointing with two fingers first at the boy's eyes and then at his own, at which point he closed them and shook his head.

"Don't stare...?"

The warrior made an irritated face and repeated the gesture. But on top of the severe blow to Triistan's skull, he was also more than a little preoccupied with the warm tingle Dreysha's lips had left on his cheek. He gazed blankly at Biiko and shook his head.

The Unbound sighed in exasperation, then put his two large hands together and placed them beside his face, miming a pillow. When Triistan just stared at the network of scars etched across the dark skin of Biiko's hands, the warrior shook them for emphasis, eyes wide, brows lifted high. It finally clicked.

"Oh, sleep - don't sleep? For how long?" Just saying it seemed to make him tired and his eyelids immediately felt heavier.

Biiko pointed to the watch lamp hanging nearby, and then held up two fingers again.

"Two hours?"

Biiko shook his head. He mimed someone shielding their eyes and looking out to sea, followed by two fingers again.

"Two watches?" A typical watch rotation was four hours long. Triistan wasn't sure he was going to be able to stay awake for two more minutes, let alone the rest of the night.

"What in the Endless Dark am I going to do for eight hours?" Biiko merely arched an eyebrow, shrugged, and walked away.

Triistan looked for Dreysha, but caught sight of Sherp instead. The burly oarsman was staring openly at him, his expression full of bile. He spat on the deck in Triistan's direction and turned away, and the boy wrapped his arms around himself.

After waiting several minutes, hoping that Dreysha would come back over to speak with him, he noticed Scow seated on a locker near the bow. The Mattock was leaning forward and talking with someone, though from this angle Triistan couldn't see who it was. Not that it really mattered. He needed to stay awake, and sitting here alone in the dark with Sherp staring at him wasn't helping any. So he reached for a nearby stay and hauled himself to his feet.

The purple spots reappeared, dancing across his vision, and a wave of dizziness made his legs weak, but he held onto the line and the feeling passed after a few moments, leaving only the dull ache in the side of his head. He made his way slowly across the mid-deck towards Scow.

The watch lamps still burned, tiny flickering pools of warm light surrounded by the vast unknown that lurked beyond their touch. Triistan felt like a ghost gliding along the deck of the launch, appearing and disappearing the way apparitions did in the stories some of the sailors' told during the lonely hours of the night watches. As he drew closer, he saw that someone had constructed another low tent out of a section of spare sailcloth as a crude shelter for Jode. Nearby, Biiko sat cross-legged on the deck, mixing something with mortar and pestle, periodically raising the bowl to his nose and sniffing it. Mung was there as well and his friend gave him a haunted half-smile.

Scow looked up as he approached. Triistan paused involuntarily, struck by the haggard expression on the Mattock's normally impregnable face. As the bosun caught sight of him, however, he smiled with genuine warmth.

"Well shit in my soup and tell me it's stew, ain't you a sight to behold? Good to see you on your feet, lad." He stood and shoved the locker towards Triistan with a big, booted foot. "Now, get off'em. Just because Tongueless here tells you not to sleep don't mean you can start a parade."

Triistan glanced sharply at Biiko, then back to Scow. Had the Unbound broken his Vow of Silence?

Scow read his look and chuckled quietly. "No, lad, he's not said a word to me since he signed on with us back in Thunder Bay. But I've had my share of skull-crackers and know what advice the healers are wont to give. Now, have a seat." Under the makeshift tent, Jode shifted and groaned loudly. Scow's face fell as he knelt in front of the tent opening. He spoke in a rough, low rumble, the closest thing he could come to a whisper.

"Easy, Coop. Everything's going to be alright. Biiko's mixing one of them fine concoctions of his - have you dancin' in the foretops afore long."

Jode coughed, a wet, strangled sound like she'd inhaled a mouthful of water.

"Whaleshit..." she croaked." You always were a horrible... liar - sir. I'm broken... inside - done. It is... the will of the gods -" She bit off the last word, moaning.

Scow looked at Triistan, his eyes pleading.

What was he supposed to say? He'd never had to console a dying friend before, and even if his head hadn't felt like it was filled with bilge and seaweed, he wouldn't have had the faintest idea of any words of his that might help.

But the look on Scow's broad face reminded him of everything he owed the man. He'd practically become Triistan's surrogate father after finding him hiding aboard the *Peregrine* nearly five years ago. That moment came back to him with sudden, startling clarity as he realized he had hidden in this very launch. The Corps did not treat stowaways kindly, but fortunately for Triistan, he was already well-known to Scow and some of his crew, having spent the past month living on the docks while caught in one of what his mother used to call his obsessive "dream-fevers".

His most recent infatuation had begun when he had visited Sitsii's North Harbor for the first time to deliver a set of charts for his latest mentor, Doyen Turrell. Turrell was a Master Cartographer who had agreed to take him on as an apprentice after receiving a fervent plea from a fellow academian. The old man had told him countless times how he'd really had no choice given that he owed the scholar a tremendous favor (which Triistan had interpreted to mean a healthy amount of coin), and constantly cursed his own limitless generosity in agreeing to take on such an ungrateful, inconsiderate, rock-headed lout as Triistan. Given that this was his fifth Doyen in three years, the boy knew from experience that the truth was something closer to Doyen Turrell not knowing how to interact with someone whose appetite for knowledge was so all-consuming, and worse, whose intellect so clearly surpassed his own.

On one particular morning, faced with a series of rapid, complicated questions from Triistan that confounded him, the Doyen handed him a leather case full of charts he had copied for some ship's captain and dispatched him to run an errand that he hoped would keep Triistan out from under his feet for some time. He wondered how long the old man had waited before reporting to his parents that he'd gone missing, and whether they had even cared enough to look for him.

He still remembered that day very clearly: while fighting his way through the press of sailors, deck-hands, loiterers, fishwives, purser's men, street urchins, travelers and other errand boys crowding Captain's Way, the crowd had suddenly parted and he had found himself staring up at a massive war galley. It marked the first time he had ever viewed a large sailing vessel this close. With her canvas furled, the intricate webbing of the *Last Horizon's* rigging was on full display, and to this day Triistan could recall the intense thrill of discovery that had coursed through him as his mind seized on the pattern and purpose of every line and timber.

He delivered the charts, but more out of a sense of closure than duty, for he never went back to Doyen Turrell's service again. He spent that first day perched atop a stack of crates waiting to be loaded aboard the galley, scribbling madly in his journal as he watched the crew crawl across her massive back like ants across a tangle of vines. He had been completely lost in the moment, forgetting to eat or drink, leaving his post only when the urge to piss had become painful, and then pushing and shoving his way back to his crate-tower worrying that he might have missed something. When dusk fell and the Dock Watch and lamplighters made their rounds, he stole aboard a small fishing trawler and curled up in the relatively snug nest of her nets, too exhausted to notice the stench. He spent that first week absorbing everything he could about the *Horizon* in watchful silence, too shy to approach any of her boisterous crew, but feeling with each passing day a growing pressure from the countless questions his mind was generating.

He had some money at first, enough to purchase food when he thought to eat, but it didn't take long for a small gang of wharf rats to change that. He was tall for his age, but reed-thin and looked like an easy mark for the young toughs. Fortunately, he was quick, agile, and an excellent climber even at that age, which probably saved his life, if not his purse. From that point on, he was forced to steal and beg for food and water, but he kept his vigil nonetheless, for the hardship had only seemed to intensify his newest obsession.

The *Last Horizon* was a ship of war, so in addition to her crew, a contingent of fierce-looking Reavers maintained constant watch over her decks, as well as the wharf along her berth. Though the elite soldiers had left him alone so far, their appearance and reputation kept him from approaching the crewmembers when the pressure of his unanswered questions had reached a boiling point, so he had gone in search of a civilian vessel. He soon found himself alongside the *SKS Peregrine*, a newly-christened behemoth intended for deepwater charting. The *Peregrine* was even larger than the *Last Horizon*, but his attention was caught by the tiny figure of a man being lowered on a boson's chair to inspect something along her sleek black and yellow hull.

It had been Mordan Scow, Master Ship's Carpenter, and the man who had since saved his life twice; the same man who now looked at him with such desperate sorrow. Over his shoulder, Triistan could see Jode's face clearly, a death's mask shading her cheeks and eyes, etching the sharp cartilage lines of her nose.

He groped for something to say, some story he could tell to distract them, but his thoughts were still sluggish and confused, and the only stories he could think of swirled around his experience on Aarden - information he had been forbidden to reveal to anyone but the High Chancellor. He was suddenly aware of the awkward silence, filled only by the rustle and creak of canvas and timber, the whisper of water along the hull, and the low voices of Dreysha and the others near the stern.

Mung coughed, breaking the silence.

"Do you know the story of Tarsus... of the Young Gods and Ehronfall?"

No one answered for a few seconds, until Triistan nodded at his friend, encouraging him to continue.

"Though they are no more," Mung said with forced deliberateness, "the gods did once walk among us. Their footprints are trodden deep in the lands we know... and... perhaps... elsewhere as well."

"For most of us who do not keep to the old ways, not much is known of the Old Gods, save that Tarsus was the last of them. The others - even the memory of them - were said to have been consumed. Devoured by Maughrin, the Living Darkness and Mother of the Endless Swarm..."

"The H'kaan" Jode whispered with a shudder. Even softly spoken, the word had a harsh, guttural quality that seemed overly loud in the attentive silence. She closed her eyes and Triistan could see the whites of her knuckles where she gripped Scow's huge hand.

"I learned the story from my mother's mother," Mung continued more rapidly. "Maughrin... it is said she was a plague born in the Old World, upon which she feasted without mercy or discretion. Nothing could withstand her appetite. One by one the Old Gods fell, until she stood poised to consume the sky and stars as well."

He cleared his throat and glanced up at the night sky. The deep blue of twilight had cleansed most of the blood left by the long evening, save for a narrow stain of violet along the horizon.

"But Tarsus would not allow it."

"Pitting his immortal life against the Living Darkness, he alone battled the Swarm, until a thousand years had passed and the piles of vanquished Dark-spawn were as tall as mountains, none of them having escaped the justice of his sword."

"A thousand years?" Triistan interjected, well acquainted with the story already.

"It sounds better. Let's not quibble over a few hundred years or so," Mung replied, obviously for Jode's amusement. She was able to manage a weak smile as he continued. "Finally Maughrin took to the field to avenge her children. The battle was surely one beyond our imagining, though we do know the outcome - at least what we've been taught about it. After a fearsome struggle that almost undid them both, Tarsus brought her low, and bound the Living Darkness with cold, unbreakable chains, and cast her into the Dark of Ruine forever.

"He was victorious, but alone. He called upon the memories and dreams of the Old Gods and opened his soul to give life back to the world, restoring what Maughrin's darkling spawn had ravaged away. He used the knowledge known only to the Old Gods and reforged our world, raising a garden from its ruins.

"But Tarsus feared for his creation. He knew there would still be H'kaan in the shadows of this world, looking to corrupt all that was new and pure. And so Tarsus created the Arys, the Young Gods, to become the guardians of Ruine in his absence. From the dust and bones of what was left of this world, he shaped the Dauthir, who would abide in a new, restored Ruine. From the breath of the wind, he made the Auruim, who would live above it, thinking that distance would give them better perspective to watch over all. Together, they assumed stewardship over that which Tarsus had sacrificed himself for, each of them according to his own strengths and desires.

"Knowing that his time on Ruine was ending, Tarsus gathered himself for one final task. Some would say it was his greatest feat, though the gods might differ."

Triistan felt the weight of his secret grow heavier, but he did not interject.

"For his greatest act," Mung went on, clearly relishing being the focus of attention, "Tarsus shaped something new and beautiful, something not of the Old World. They were the huunan, naked and naive, which he then called his own Children.

"His final work completed, Tarsus ascended, soaring higher than even the Auruim dared, lighting a bright new sun for all of his creation, to stand as a shining beacon of hope for all beneath it."

"Somewhere beyond the sky, Tarsus looked down upon this and smiled."

Mung paused, smiling himself. "I remember the way she used to say that part, how she told the whole story, really. It was such a romantic fable, the perfect bed-time story. Which of course meant the proper amount of suspense and dark warnings." He shrugged. "Anyway, I'm a bit hazy on the details after that, as by then I was usually falling asleep, but I think most of us know the gist of it."

Triistan had learned that part of the story from one of his doyens almost exactly as Mung had just told it, but unlike his friend, he had also learned since then much more than he had ever wanted to know. Aarden had shown him the cold, ugly truth behind the fable, and it had nearly killed them all.

It still might, a voice whispered in his mind.

Seeking to avoid that voice, he cleared his throat and picked up the tale where Mung had left off.

"I think I can finish it," he continued. "The Arys did not waste time. Upon the ground, side by side with Man, the Dauthir constructed mighty citadels, the Dauthirian Columns, from where they would watch over their charges. Derant the Builder first raised Deranthaal, Column of the Suns, a work of such splendor and size it surpassed the tallest of the mountains of what we now call Ganar's Bones, standing so high and strong it was said that Ruine's sister suns could rest upon her spires as they made their way across the sky.

"As Derant labored in his mountain stronghold, Arcolen the Verdant raised a mighty forest of tall stonewood pines to stand vigil over the Far North. Beneath them, the bones of Valheim are comprised of the blue-white marble called 'ice rock', and it was this material that Arcolen used to shape her seat of power: Arcothaal - Column of the Moon. Though the stonewoods have since brought the walls down, the ruins still glow iridescent in the moonlight as a reminder of its namesake."

Scow grunted. "Tis true. I've seen it with my own eyes." Triistan nodded and continued.

"Lastly, Shan, the Stormfather, ever vainglorious, sought to outdo the others and erected his archipelago-fortress, Shanthaal - Storm's Eye, in the ringed southern islands we now call The Sea King Isles... our home."

"Your home, maybe, Titch," Dreysha's voice floated from the darkness behind him. "Some of us just work there."

He turned as she slid into the light and set one booted foot on the locker next to him, close enough that her knee brushed his right shoulder as she casually leaned on it.

"Go on, Lad," came Scow's quiet rumble. When Triistan looked at his mentor, the big bosun gestured towards Jode, who was lying quietly in her tent. She almost looked to be sleeping peacefully. "Seems to be helping."

Triistan shifted his position - careful not to break contact with Dreysha's leg - and continued.

"At first the Auruim dismissed these acts as boastful and self-serving. They chose instead to live together in the magnificent city of Ehronhaal, which, they built among the stars." He looked up reflexively, just as Mung had done a few moments before. The clouds that had glowered down at them for days had withdrawn and the dying light of the second sun had faded. The sky was a dream of black diamonds, vast and glittering.

"But there were some among the Auruim who were not content to watch from afar. Chief among them was Obed, the Guardian. To him fell the weighty responsibility of The Long Watch: the Auruim's self-appointed task of guarding against the return of the H'kaan. Toward that end, he constructed Senhaal, The Unsleeping Vigil, from whose high parapets he and his kin warded the rest of the world from Maughrin's darkling spawn."

He paused, considering his words carefully. He still had the uneasy sense of a riddle threading its way through his thoughts, while at the same time he was getting uncomfortably close to the secret he had sworn to protect. In a strange way, he felt as if the riddle were pushing him towards it.

"For ages, this was how the world lived. The Dauthir were both parent and sibling to Man, living amongst us, guiding us. The Auruim watched the shadows and struck down the evil things that lurked there. But as the centuries passed, some of the Arys grew restless. Some tried to live as men, taking mortal husbands and wives, giving birth to the Vanha, neither Man nor God; something both more and less than either."

Triistan's mouth suddenly went dry. He knew he should stop there, turn the story back over to Mung or just claim his head hurt, but the riddle would not relent. He was overwhelmed by a sense that he *must* reveal his secret, that it was somehow *necessary*.

He ran his tongue across his teeth and gums and tried to work up enough spit to swallow before continuing.

"There was one among the restless, an Arys of great power and ambition, who went forth to live amongst Men, raising the tower of Talmoreth as the Dauthir had before him. His name was..."

Shocked that he had almost blurted it out, he coughed and cleared his throat awkwardly.

"I don't think we should speak his name, for names have power, but it is said that in his arrogance, he dared to share the language of the gods - the secret of Magic - with Man. But these teachings, and the... experiments that he conducted inside the obsidian tower angered Dauthir and Auruim alike. It was whispered that his thoughts were poisoned by Maughrin herself, and that he sought to release her from her bonds. Terrified that he might succeed, but unwilling to kill one of their own, the High Houses sent him away to... a place they had shaped to their will, where neither man nor god lived..."

He trailed off, his voice barely above a whisper as a powerful memory rose up in his mind. After making landfall on Aarden, he'd been asked to accompany Captain Vaelysia and the expeditionary group she was leading inland. At the time he had assumed it was because they wanted someone to scale the jungle canopy and scout ahead, but as they camped that first night, she and First Mate Tarq had approached him privately and asked that he begin mapping their route and documenting everything they saw and encountered on their journey. He had agreed, though at the time he had no idea what he would be agreeing to - the marvels they would see... or the horrors: horrors he had sworn an oath to keep secret.

He forced his mind in another direction, to a trip through an underground river with those who had survived, and the ensuing discussion about sending the *Peregrine* back to Stormgate. That was when Captain Vaelysia had made him swear not to show his journal to anyone other than the High Chancellor. The Captain and the Ship's Whip had been adamant, even threatening to have him flogged, scrubbed, or both if he failed. Even so, the compulsion to tell Scow and the others everything pushed him hard up against that oath. He could still stop: there had been no mention of what they actually found, so that secret was presumably still safe...

But what difference could it possibly make if he did tell them? It wasn't as if they could swim off and sell the information to someone else, and once - *if,* he reminded himself - they made port in Stormgate or Thunder Bay, they would all be required to testify before the Ministry of Commerce anyway. In that case, it might make his tale that much more plausible if his mates were part of its retelling, too.

"I've heard of Talmoreth, but I certainly don't know about any of that other business," Mung offered into the awkward silence. "You mean he was sent away like Maughrin was?"

Triistan was suddenly conscious again of the others watching him, waiting. His resolve hardened. Caught up in the story and a strange sense of fatalism, he had taken it too far, adding information he had come by on Aarden that was not part of the fable most people knew, but he hadn't broken his oath yet.

"Well... the rest of the story is a little confusing, at least what was told to me-" But Jode cut him off.

"I knew it," she said, eyes wide, all measure of comfort now lost. "Aarden is the Exile's Hold..."

Triistan's heart clenched. Of course she would know. Although she was not Khaliil, she had lived among them in Ghostvale for the first eighteen years of her life. There, knowledge of history was far more intimate.

"Exile's what?" Dreysha blurted out.

He fought for words to repair the damage he'd already done, but before he was pressed to confirm Jode's guess, they heard shouts from the mid-deck, where Voth and the others had been reorganizing their meager supplies. Biiko was on his feet instantly, even before Triistan could turn his head in the direction of the voices.

"I've got a bad feeling about this," said Mung. He hadn't moved from where he'd been standing, although he was at least craning his neck to see.

"You've got a bad feeling about everything," Triistan grumbled to his friend as he reached for a nearby line and pulled himself upright, relieved that he'd been spared from breaking his oath.

From where he stood, he could see the backs of some of his shipmates standing along the starboard bulwark. Beyond them, across the deep, black expanse of ocean, a red-orange orb was lifting itself from the ocean's edge.

"Blood Moon," someone whispered. Several of them turned in the opposite direction and spat.

A few times a year, inexplicably at least as far as he knew, the moon rose full and red. Sailors were an embarrassingly superstitious lot in Triistan's experience, eager to embrace every new phenomenon as a sign of impending doom, and they considered a Blood Moon to be the penultimate bad omen. Unless they were engaged in combat or exceptionally well-trained, most crews abandoned all of the normal routines and procedures, as well as their posts, and gathered below-decks until moonset. Most officers and captains joined them, some out of resigned practicality and some - those that had clawed their way up from the common ranks - out of practice. An extra ration or two of rum usually kept things orderly, but it typically took until the following normal moonrise before full discipline and operations were restored. He mimicked the gesture, though he felt foolish.

A furtive movement caught the corner of his eye. He turned to see Captain Fjord making his way forward, but something about the sight made him uncomfortable. The injured man's movements were wooden, his gaze fixed on something on the deck near the prow. He was clutching a small pack or purse of some kind to his chest. Everyone else seemed to be watching the moon rise, so no one took any notice of Fjord as he squatted next to one of the twin anchors and coils of line stowed neatly to either side of the prow. Triistan was about to point him out to the Mattock when Scow's deep rumble cut him off.

"Kraken-piss, somebody lend me a hand here!" Triistan spun around to find the master carpenter on all fours, trying to restrain Jode, whose body was convulsing violently. Her arms and legs were splayed out, fingers clawing at the deck planking. Two of her fingernails tore off as she dug at the wood.

"NOW GODS-DAMMIT!" Scow bellowed. Triistan dove across Jode's legs, forgetting Fjord's odd behavior for the moment. She arched her back with such ferocity that Triistan heard it crack. As he fought for

- 73 -

control of her legs, he glanced up, catching a glimpse of her jaw beneath Scow's chest and arms and was suddenly struck by her silence: she wasn't making any noise other than the sounds of her limbs and head hitting the planks, but the cords of her neck were as taught as main-stays in a gale and her mouth moved as if she were trying to scream. The sight chilled him.

Scow managed to pin both of her arms to either side, then swung one of his thick legs over her so that he straddled her chest, using his considerable weight to keep her lying flat. Her head thrashed back and forth and she gnashed her teeth, like an animal in full panic trying to free itself.

Then, just as suddenly as it had begun, her body went perfectly, eerily still. Her eyes opened and she lifted her head off the deck, fixing Triistan with a ghastly smile.

"He comes."

Her head snapped back again and her body tried to arch beneath Scow's bulk. They heard a horrible choking, wet sound as a fountain of blood erupted from her mouth, while her head smashed up and down on the deck, striking it in staccato harmony with the heels of her boots for several long seconds. He heard Mung retch from somewhere behind him, but he could not tear his eyes away.

Finally, the convulsions subsided and her head lolled to one side. Triistan could see she was gone, but even lifeless, her open eyes somehow fixed him with an accusatory stare until Scow muttered a curse and brushed his huge hand across her face, closing them and breaking the spell. Shaken, Triistan sat back on his heels and found himself staring across the launch at Captain Fjord.

"Oh, gods…"

Fjord was standing on the taffrail near the prow, one hand holding a nearby stay for balance, the other holding something bulky in front of him. There looked to be coils of line draped across his shoulder and around his torso. Triistan's guts twisted as he realized what Fjord was about to do.

"NO!" he shouted, struggling to rise, but it was too late. No one was anywhere near the man as he stepped off the railing into the hungry sea.

Biiko was the first to the rail, Triistan and Dreysha close behind him. The other end of the line he had seen the Captain loop around his body was playing out from what had been a large coil on the deck. The anchor it was typically attached to was conspicuously absent.

Biiko grabbed the line with both hands and braced himself against the taffrail, then began slowly pulling it back up. Triistan forgot his own weakness and grabbed onto the rope behind the Unbound, while his mind tried to calculate how far down the Captain must be by now. The launch carried two bowers, each with about eighteen fathom of rope. Based on how much was left on deck, Fjord must be over a hundred feet below the surface. They were pulling faster with his help, but not fast enough.

"Drey!" he said through gritted teeth, "help -"

The rope jerked unexpectedly in his hand for an instant, pulling him off balance and into Biiko's broad back. The warrior grunted and Triistan thought he must have let go of the line, until Biiko began hauling it in even more quickly. Triistan regained his balance and pulled on the rope as well, and for a few breaths it was all he could do to keep up with Biiko.

The line was coming up so easily now he decided Fjord must have changed his mind and was swimming back towards the surface. Maybe he had even managed to cut the anchor loose - but just as the thought occurred to him, the rope suddenly went taut with another powerful jerk, and then was ripped from their hands. Biiko hissed in pain and Triistan screamed, burying his palms under his arms in agony. With a sound like an angry swarm of bees, the loose coils they had hauled up on deck slid out over the taffrail so fast he would have become tangled in them and dragged overboard if Dreysha hadn't grabbed him by the arm and pulled him clear. Though the end of the anchor line was secured to a cleat at the base of the rail, Biiko tried to catch the last few coils and tie them off around a second cleat, nearly losing his fingers when the rope ran out and the boat lurched sideways from the force of whatever had the other end. The spikes fastening both cleats screamed as they tore loose, the line cracked like a whip, and hemp and steel disappeared beneath the bloody sea.

Stunned, Triistan collapsed against the rail, his burning hands held out before him, Jode's final words ringing in his ears.

He comes...

- 6 -

New Blood

"Are you ready for this?"

Casselle Milner looked up into the kind eyes of the older man that had asked the question. She nodded, but upon recognizing the man's rank from the marks on his torc, she added a quick and proper response.

"Captain, yes, sir," she said. Long drilled reactions compelled her to stand up and come to attention, though doing so in the full bulk of her new armor felt both clumsy and awkward.

"Hrm," came the reply, a bit of the kindness draining from his eyes as he cast a critical eye over her. "You're bigger than I expected." By "bigger," she knew he did not mean tall. That was fairly standard treatment from all of the instructors and captains she'd met thus far in the ranks of the Templars.

The Captain reached out and began to tug on various bits of her ensemble, making sure the buckles were properly fastened, the clasps properly locked, and that the armor was free from any distracting marks or blemishes. She stood resolute as he tugged here and there, being neither slight nor subtle with his adjustments.

"You have broad shoulders and big feet. Those will serve you well here," he said, finishing his inspection and moving to stand in front of her. "The faulds about your waist fit awkwardly, do they?"

"Yes, sir," Casselle replied. "They are small. My hips are... wide."

"I should suppose so," he said with another dismissive noise. Casselle did not flinch. She had trained such behavior out of herself years ago. Thankfully this officer did not belabor the point, nor did it seem like he was attempting to touch her for any lurid reason. "You are about to be inducted as a Templar. You should know how vital it is to have proper equipment ready. Look into fixing that."

"Yes, sir." Normally she would have said nothing, but regulations dictated all officers would be acknowledged verbally or with a formal salute. In the cramped quarters of the dressing chambers, a salute seemed out of place.

"It is a statement of the times that we live in such a world where we allow our women a place in line alongside our rightful defenders," he said, not wasting time to fit in another insult. Despite her bravery during the riot, these tiny jabs had increased. She assumed this was their last opportunity to shame her outright before she was bestowed her sword and became a Templar proper.

"Nevertheless," the old man continued, "you have finished your training and earned your blade, which gives you the right to stand amongst us. I will pray that you continue not to disappoint us."

Casselle took the insult calmly. He was not the first officer to express his displeasure, and he did so with a surprising lack of disgust in his voice. He dismissed her with a wave and moved on to check the harness of the next inductee.

She moved over to stand next to the rest of her squad, each wearing their newly forged Templar armor, a finer suit of mail and plate than the ill-fitting armor they had been forced into just before the riots. Each had a suit tailored to their measurements. More specifically, the suits had been tailored to be worn by men of their measurements. Casselle still looked a bit awkward, but other than the slight pinch at the hips, it fit her perfectly.

"He seemed nicer about it than most," Jaksen said in his thick rural accent. A sour expression from Casselle made him look away quickly.

"Gods, these things are awkward," grumbled Raabel, attempting to find a comfortable way to wear the empty scabbard they had each been given. The ceremony would end with each of them receiving a new sword, accepting their proper title and pledging a lifetime of service to the Laegis.

"The only thing awkward around here is you," said Temos, "stomping around like you're getting ready to invade the parade ground."

"Hush, Rabbit," Raabel grumbled in his favorite reply. Casselle and Jaksen shared a chuckle. It felt good. There had not been much of that in the wake of the riot, which seemed to have cast a brooding pall over the whole of the city. The graduation was not a solution, but at least it was a moment of bright enthusiasm for a hopeful future.

To Casselle, there was nothing better than the warm smiles and laughter of her squadmates. They had worked hard for this moment for years, and despite an ill fitting fauld, there was nothing that could dampen her enthusiasm.

"Hard to believe it'll be over," Temos said.

"Over, little one?" Raabel said, "You know that this is a pledge of service until *death*, right?" Raabel heavily emphasized the word "death", trying to make it sound ominous and imminent.

"Yes, but not always," Jaksen said. "There have been those that have been honorably discharged."

"Which will you trade for your release? A crippling injury or the loss of sanity?" Raabel scoffed.

"Must I choose now?" joked Jaksen.

"All I care about is that no one will be able to threaten to fail us or throw us out or send us packing ever again," Temos interjected. "We're past that now. No more of those indignant old bastards thumbing their noses at us being unworthy."

"I doubt they'll stop that," Jaksen said. "They will continue to think ill of us, but this time we'll be able to tell them to shove it up their cheeks without fear that we'll be out in front of the bunkhouse with our bags packed. They can think what they want. If I've learned anything - especially in light of recent events - it's that I'll be a better Templar because of my time on the farm. Unlike them, I'm not afraid of getting my hands dirty."

"Well said!" Raabel grinned, slapping Jaksen on the back.

"Alright, alright, it's not often it happens, but I'll admit Jaksen's right," Temos said with a grin.

"I might just get myself drunk tonight to celebrate," said Casselle, eliciting shocked looks from her squadmates.

"I feel sorry for the cask of ale that seeks to beat you in battle," Jaksen said first.

"I don't think I've ever seen you even take an extra portion of bread at mealtime. I'm not sure any of us are ready to see you deep in your cups," Temos confessed.

"Fear not, Rabbit," said Raabel, placing a protective hand on his shoulder. "I will make sure she leaves your virtue intact." Jaksen and Casselle couldn't hold in their laughter after that. Temos and Raabel joined in immediately afterwards. It was as they tried to keep themselves from bursting the buckles of their armor that Odegar Taumber found them.

"It is good to see the four of you in excellent spirits," the Templar Captain said with a wide smile. They cheered and pulled him into the circle, slapping him on the back and smiling all around. It was Casselle who first noticed that his grin was too quick to fade. He was also not wearing the ceremonial tabard and other trappings that they were expected to wear for the occasion.

"Are you not attending the ceremony, sir?" she asked. Some Templar still maintained regular duties during this time, but most (especially the instructors and captains) were expected to attend and show support for those receiving their sword.

"I am not. Unfortunately, duty compels me to come to you once again for assistance. Last time it was by luck, this time it is by design."

Casselle noticed the other graduates beginning to line up for the official procession out.

"I'm sure we will be happy to lend you our new blades for whatever work you have for them," Temos said, "but first we actually have to go out there and pick them up." The others smiled in response, but Odegar did not.

"The ceremony is long and burdened by its own excess. I have authority from the Templar High Marshall to give you your blades now if you will come with me. I have already made provisions for us to get horses and supplies at the stables so that we don't have to wait any longer than necessary." Their smiles evaporated. Nearby, the procession of graduates was slowly but steadily draining from the room as they marched for the parade ground.

Casselle spoke first.

"Ok," she said, her voice quiet, but firm. "We'll come with you." It took a moment - and a considerable amount of will - to take the first step towards the door that led away from the ceremony. She felt if she waited any longer to think about it, the disappointment might be too much to bear. It was best to get right to work. That was the right thing to do, after all.

She was surprised to find a firm grip on her arm, urging her to stay.

"No," said Raabel. Odegar looked over at him, shocked, but not angry.

"Respectfully no," Temos quickly added.

"Respectfully or not," said Jaksen, "still no."

Casselle shook off the hand and turned to face them. Jaksen rushed to explain.

"Before you say anything, we're not doing this for us. It's true that we deserve it, but it's not about that," said Jaksen. "It's not even for you, even though it is about you."

Casselle and Odegar exchanged a look.

"The three of us talked about this the other day," Temos said. "We expected it would happen sooner, but we thought that someone of rank might want to keep you away from the grounds for the ceremony, not necessarily to keep you from being a Templar, but just to keep you from being seen."

"Many people will watch this," Raabel said.

"It's a big show, like the Captain says" Temos continued. "There will be a lot of people here watching us swear by the blade. There are some who might prefer if the people didn't see you among those assembled. The high ranks already consider us... and you... a black eye on their face. If they can just keep you in the shadows, it will be almost like you aren't really there."

Casselle nodded, understanding his point. It was only in the last twenty years that the numbers of the Laegis had dwindled to a dangerous level. With the Gods dead, there was doubt the organization had a purpose other than reminding the people of a long lost past. The wealthy and influential sent fewer of their sons to be trained because there was less prestige in doing so. Rather than face the collapse of their own ranks, they began to allow initiates like Casselle's squad into the organization, people of more "humble" origins. When that wasn't enough, they even became desperate enough to let a woman attempt the training.

They hadn't expected her to succeed. It was mainly just to present the appearance of fairness. The fact that she passed the training with exceptional marks was almost scandalous. Regardless, it was clear that the Laegis didn't want the attention her promotion would bring. Undoubtedly she and her squad were to be used as little more than armored bodies to shield the more important ranks from harm. Her musing was interrupted as Odegar spoke.

"I am not here to take away the honor or title rightfully earned by any of you, but there is a real danger that..."

"With all due respect, sir," Temos said politely, "shut up." Casselle was no less surprised than Odegar by this, but Temos' mouth was already at work again before anything else could be said.

"I'm a loudmouth and a cad, Raabel is full of self-importance and Jaksen is honest to a fault. Frankly none of us would be standing here if we hadn't met Casselle. So the three of us took an oath to do anything necessary to make sure she was out there." Jaksen and Raabel nodded in agreement.

"Why?" Casselle asked.

"Because it's important that you be seen. People may not know you, but they know of you. Strossen is not so big that the news of a Lady Templar would get lost..."

"Just because I'm a woman..." Casselle began, but Temos kept ahead of her.

"I don't know if there were ever any before the Ehronfall, but there certainly haven't been any since then. I should know, I've checked. But, that's not the point... it's more than just that," he emphasized.

"Look. We're just three simple louts in metal jackets, but you represent everything that is best about what the Templars should be.

"But what the self-inflated bigots who want to take this pretentious, overstuffed ceremony away from you don't understand is that you've never been the type of person to rub their noses in it. You give of yourself because it's the right thing to do. Even now, you are willing to toss it all aside without hesitation just because people need your help," Temos said.

"Thank you for such kind words, but Captain Taumber wouldn't have..." Casselle began, before being cut off once again, this time not by Temos, but by the Captain himself.

"He's right," Odegar admitted. "It is important. I was so caught up in my own thoughts and hadn't really considered this as some sort of subterfuge. Though I think this is more of an ill timed coincidence than sabotage, I do agree with you that it speaks ill of all of us if we let them try to silence the best of us."

Casselle was taken aback by the honest change in his tone of voice. She met his eyes and saw, perhaps fully for the first time, the amount of admiration he held for her.

"Go. Be proud of what you've accomplished. Be proud of the Templar you've become," Odegar said sincerely. "I will make preparations for us to leave as soon as we can. I'm sure I have underestimated the amount of time required of me to prepare things before you must become involved. I'm sure there is just enough work to keep me occupied for roughly the length of a pretentious, overstuffed ceremony."

Temos turned away, slightly embarrassed at having his words repeated to him, even in good humor.

"Thank you," Casselle said in return, humbled by the support and confidence shown to her by her friends and mentor. There wasn't time to think on it further as the last of the procession was exiting the door. She moved to her place at the back of the line. Jaksen and Raabel followed her directly, but Odegar held Temos back for a moment.

"Did you really expect this?" the Captain asked.

"Maybe not this exactly, but something. The boys and I were prepared just in case."

"Prepared how?" Odegar asked.

Temos replied with a smile and pulled a bundle hidden in the small of his back, underneath his tabard, tucked into his belt. He pulled it on his head like a cap.

It was a wig, and a horrible one at that, but underneath the unbrushed locks, Temos might have been able to pass for a woman dressed in Templar armor, if but for a moment.

"Each of us was willing to be taken in on her behalf. Even if we stalled them just enough for her to get to the field, we figured they wouldn't embarrass themselves by hauling her off it with most of Strossen watching.

"You make a suitably hideous woman, Pelt," Odegar said with a smile.

"I bet you say that to all the girls, sir," Temos replied in a horribly fake high-pitched tone. Odegar pulled the wig from his head and shooed him off with a wave of his hand. The young man laughed as he jogged off to catch up with the others further down the tunnel.

***

Casselle was in a daze for most of the ceremony. Even though it was long and boring for the most part, she was buzzing with nervous energy, eager to wear the clasp signifying her new station and the blade awarded to her for her accomplishments. It was all she could do to concentrate on the front of the parade grounds, where someone talked endlessly about duty and honor and then introduced another speaker who lectured for another endless length of time about the same thing, with the words slightly rearranged. Casselle tried hard to keep herself in the proper parade stance and not look about at those standing alongside of her.

Out of the three hundred or so candidates that were originally admitted alongside Casselle, only thirty-seven of them remained. Nine squads of four with one remainder were assembled on the field. Casselle's group was the last group. Even the one squadless Templar stood ahead of them. That hadn't diminished Casselle's enthusiasm, however, nor had the lengthy, numbing speeches of the Templar's Captains, Commanders and Generals.

In fact, the number of "important people" on the stage threatened to outnumber those being sworn in. As yet another speech rumbled on about "honoring the legacy of the High Houses," Casselle tried to figure out some of the less familiar faces. Everyone in a Templar tabard was easy to spot, even if she couldn't put names with faces. She assumed a few without any armor at all must be members of the Elder Council or their representatives. Some of those in deep blue and silver would be constables or officers of the Strossen Watch, whose purpose for being there was clear. The Templar and the Watch often worked together, as they had in the riot.

There was a time when the Laegis Templar only took orders from the Gods, directed through whichever temple happened to be closest. But with things as they were, the High Marshall and his Generals worked closely with the Elder Circle, who had direct control of the Watch and the Outriders, the respective internal and external militias of Strossen. In fact, the Strossen Elder Circle had been so successful with their armed services that they stood as a standard of excellence for smaller cities across Gundlaan.

In the past, the Templars dwarfed these organizations, but since the Ehronfall, without the direct inspiration or guidance from the Gods, the organization was merely a shadow of its former self, save when it came to reputation and pagentry. Casselle recalled her conversation the other week with Odegar, wondering if the Laegis Templar were indeed the empty place setting, left alone only until it was decided that there was no longer a need for it.

Her attention was refocused as the formation began to move for the first time since they had marched onto the field and taken their parade positions. She watched as each squad moved to the side of the dais, each graduate marching up one at a time only when called by the High Marshall to receive the blade that would signify their induction into the organization.

Casselle couldn't be more excited. The act of standing still mustered a level of restraint she considered heroic, given the fact that she wanted to storm the stage and take it in hand herself. Instead she tried to quell her restless energy by occupying her mind with other tasks.

She focused on trying to suss out the strangers on the dais, like the distinctive pair that stood to the right of the High Marshall. One was a head taller than most of those on stage, with close cut hair almost the same shade as his darkened steel armor. He had the same sort of ageless face as Odegar, both old and young in equal measures. His companion was clearly younger, with no grey in his dusty brown hair, but still shared a strong resemblance to the first that was more than just the matching black and gold tabards they both wore.

If they were not Templar or Watch or Outriders, then who might they be? Perhaps they were commanders of a mercenary force? With the loss of the Young Gods and the stability they'd provided, there had been many that had attempted to seize the opportunity to establish their own authority. Large land owners with deep coffers provided many jobs for those with the talent to swing a sword and a lack of scruples when selecting targets. If these two were mercenaries, were they here at the behest of the Elder Circle or the Templars themselves? It seemed like they would have to be more important than simple sells words. She made note of the emblem on their tabards, a golden lion holding a sword with a blade of lightning. Perhaps one of the others would know.

She pushed these thoughts aside for the moment as her squad finally moved into position to be called up. Her squad mates went first, but not by her design; that was just the way they were arranged in formation. It was mostly quiet as she heard her name called, the last of the candidates to climb the steps.

She was not sure when she noticed it first, as her mind was still in too many places, trying to pay attention and process everything around her all at once. But at some point as she crossed over to the High Marshall with his finely embroidered cape, some noise in the background caught her attention.

The crowd outside the gates, a great assembly of the Strossen people from all walks of life, was cheering madly. Casselle paused, just shy of an arm's length from the highest ranking Templar in the world, holding out the blade that would make her forever bound in service. She looked at it, arms at her side, before looking up into the face of the High Marshall.

He looked older than Captain Taumber, with thick lines across his forehead and under his eyes. The weight of his armor caused him to slump slightly forward and it was obvious that he was sweating from the strain of a lengthy ceremony. She expected some sort of anger or resentment in his eyes, like those she'd seen from the Captains and Masters she'd met in the ranks. Instead, she saw a quiet reserve, perhaps even a little affection for the miller's daughter.

"With Ogund's blessing, I grant you this blade, to build and defend," he began. She replied in kind directly afterwards.

"The hearts and the homes I now swear to serve," she said, taking the pommel of the sword in her hand and gently lifting it clear of the arm he had presented it on. She kept the sword out as she walked towards the other end of the stage. She was going to leave quickly and quietly, but at the edge of the first step down, she heard one of the assembled old men clearly swear against her honest birth.

She should have let it slide, but she could not help but turn back to face the ranks of her people, the commoners of Gundlaan, watching her every move. She stabbed the sword in the air, holding it up over her head proudly. The crowd erupted in applause and cheers, thrice as loud as they had when she had first mounted the stage.

Temos was right. Even though she had been the one to endure, the victory belonged to all of them, every single man, woman and child that labored with the hope that their honest effort would be someday rewarded. There were no such guarantees in life, but Casselle stood tall, sword to the sky, proving that it was not impossible.

With a slight grin on her face, she left the dais, not even bothering to acknowledge the administrator who had mocked her. She preferred to imagine him now choking on his own bitter words. The cheers persisted until she crossed back over the field and took her rightful place with her squad. Jaksen, Raabel and Temos each had smiles that couldn't be hidden.

There was no time for congratulations or even sly whispers, however. One of the Commanders walked to the front of the dais to begin the recitation of the formal Laegis oath. In a loud voice, he challenged the assembled thirty-seven new Templars.

"To avenge the fallen..." he began.

"We guide the sword!" responded all of the graduates in steady measure.

"To defend the forsaken..."

"We steady the shield!"

"To hold the Dark at bay..."

"We lift high the torch!"

"To forge a better tomorrow..."

"We strike the hammer!"

"There are many tools..." the Commander began.

"But we are the hand that guides them," the graduates answered.

"And when the Gods themselves cannot reply," the Commander prompted them.

"We are the fist of righteous fury!" roared the graduating class.

"En'vaar et Laegis!" The voices of all of those assembled thundered, from those facing the dais, to those standing atop it, even the High Marshall himself.

As the city around her cheered, her heart swelled.

"En'vaar et Laegis," she repeated to herself. It meant more than "we are the Laegis." It was a declaration of permanence. We have been, we are, we shall ever be Laegis. Those who made it this far, by fate or by effort, recognized their duty was not a list of rules; it would forever be a part of them, as inevitable as the dawn of the next day.

The moment was fleeting, but pleasant. Casselle knew that their first mission already awaited them. She gripped the hilt of her sword, feeling confident of her training and hopeful for the future, whatever was yet to come.

***

They found Captain Taumber by the stables. He'd procured a half dozen horses, five saddled for riding, one loaded with heavy saddlebags full of supplies. He was going over tack and harness one last time with the stable groomsman. As they approached, the stablehand slipped away, leaving a satisfied looking Captain with the horses.

"I heard the cheers," Odegar said. "Hopefully for the right reasons."

"I doubt I could have paid for a better reaction," Temos said, grasping the hilt of his own sword. "For a moment I thought they were going to bust the gate down and crown her Queen of Everything, right then and there."

"Is Everything to the east or west of Strossen?" asked Raabel dryly.

"It was wonderful," said Jaksen. "It made us most proud."

Casselle blushed slightly and shifted the new weight of her sword off of her hip.

"Excellent," Odegar replied. "I wish I could keep the mood cheerful, but I'm afraid we ride towards an uncertain future. There is a danger growing in the west that threatens..." Odegar paused, grasping for the right words. With a slight sigh, he settled on saying "everything," with much less mirth than Temos and Jaksen had just referenced it.

"Go and change into travelling clothes," the Captain said. "Something comfortable. If we leave soon, we might be at Felbrank by the end of the long evening. Pack your armor as well, but not the ceremonial parts. We won't be needing those." With nods, the squad set into motion towards the barracks.

In her bunkroom, Casselle was a study in economy of motion. There was no wasted time or effort on her part as she removed her ceremonial tabard and adornments and stowed them in her footlocker. As Odegar had mentioned, there would be no use for these on the road. The major plates unbuckled quickly and she left her armorjack on as she changed her boots and pants. She pulled a shortcloak over her shoulders and fastened it with a hasp, then peeked out of her room.

Based on what she heard, it was clear the others were still struggling to get off their armored plates. Hers were already secured in the travel sack, which she set beside the door alongside her shoulder duffel full of clean underclothes and the small kit she always kept at the ready for grooming and minor wound care.

The only problem with her efficiency was having to wait while her squad finished their own preparations. She sat for a moment, looking around her room. Templars were supposed to live simply, which was not difficult for her. Unlike many of the recruits that were simply sons of rich merchants and bankers, Casselle did not come from money.

There were a few books on the table in her room, one borrowed from a former instructor, the other two bought after saving what she could from her small Templar stipend. They were luxury items to her, even though they were hardly noted classics; merely cheap, incomplete reprints of better books. The books themselves were more than her family could ever hope to own, not that they would have had any need for them. They were treasured because they were hers and because she had the skill to read them, something many millers' daughters thought to be just a fanciful dream.

Thinking of her family, she felt for the plain silver band she kept on a leather thong around her neck, just under her shirt.

The ring had been the wedding band her mother wore before her passing. Her father had remarried, but could not bear to use the same ring. He thought to sell it, but when Casselle asked him for it, he could not refuse her. She kept it as a reminder of them both, tucked under her shirt, kept warm against her skin.

Even though it was simply furnished, she counted herself lucky to have this room to herself, the place she'd ended most of her days during the years she'd spent training here with the Laegis. This room felt more like home now than the one she'd left. She took a deep breath and exhaled slowly. The open road was full of dangers, but she tried not to dwell on the thought of never returning here.

"Idle limbs give way to idle thoughts," she reminded herself, a favorite saying of many of the instructors in the Templar ranks. She banished those idle thoughts by putting her limbs into motion, taking up her bag and leaving her room behind her.

Casselle took her equipment down to the courtyard in front of the barracks and began the short walk over to the stables. This was the first time she'd made this walk with a Laegis blade at her hip. She always imagined that things would be different after receiving it, but the walk over felt like every other walk over. The only appreciable difference this time was that she'd be riding away on her own steed, rather than staying to service the horses for other Templars.

On her way to meet Odegar, she received a few lingering stares, leaving her with the impression that the ill will towards her might have actually gotten a bit worse after her graduation. Perhaps her grandstanding during the ceremony had only given them yet another example of why she was unfit to be a member of the Laegis.

She sighed slightly, wondering why her own accomplishments in any way diminished the organization that she had pledged her service to. Thankfully, Captain Taumber was in sight now, waiting for her patiently at the stables. His warm smile did much to dispel her worries.

It was not long after she secured her equipment to the dun colored mare that had been assigned to her when Temos, Jaksen and Raabel emerged from the bunkhouse. They were assigned mounts of their own and soon enough they were all trotting towards Strossen's west end.

***

The suns were winning the race to the horizon, descending slowly ahead of them. Despite Odegar's previous warning, spirits were high. Hearing her friends talk and laugh was reason enough for Casselle to enjoy the moment. She thought of the road ahead. She had only ever traveled such a distance once before, from her family's home to Strossen itself. She'd spent so much time in the big city that it had become comfortably familiar to her.

But this first assignment was a new adventure cut from a wholly different cloth. She managed to keep from smiling about it, knowing there would always be an element of danger, but that seemed comfortably distant for the moment.

The buildings leading up to the western gate were taller and closely crowded together. Outside the thick walls of the city, the architecture changed almost immediately. Much of it had started as development of convenience, a place to park outside the walls while conducting business inside. Over the years, it had become a second ring around Strossen, an unmanicured explosion of poorly constructed housing and utility. The road soon widened, though, eventually breaking free of the city outside the wall and leaving them mostly alone on the approach to Felbrank, one of the towns that marked the edge of what most townsfolk considered the reach of Strossen's direct influence.

People talked of Gundlaan, the greater area that was under the direct care of Ogund at one time, but it was still a very loose association of cities, Strossen being the largest. The smaller towns each had their own Elder Circle, but with trade agreements and contracts of arms for Outriders, it did feel as if Strossen's leadership had taken the place of the God that once lived there. With what she had seen inside the city of late, she wondered if that leadership had finally been stretched to the limit and how many smaller cities it could support before it broke altogether.

She tried not to ruminate on these things as her group traveled together upon the open road. There was lots of talking and jesting, with Temos mainly at the center of it all, but Jaksen and Raabel easily kept pace, sometimes even getting the upper hand every now and again. Casselle enjoyed hearing them banter and even caught sight of Captain Taumber doing the same, smiling more often than not. She considered herself lucky to be in their company.

The trail fell away beneath them, and leagues passed underneath the sure feet of their steeds. The long evening had settled in when they arrived at Felbrank, a small farming village known regionally for its delicious cheeses. They stabled next to a tavern called The Hairy Goat, with attached rooms for overnight stays. It was rustic, reminding Casselle of the village she had grown up near when she was younger. She knew it would be missing many of the refined features she was used to even in the less developed parts of Strossen.

The freshly minted Templars took care of their horses and made their way inside. They secured two rooms for the night, and Odegar apologized that Casselle would have to share one with him. It was not unexpected and she reassured him she was comfortable with it.

"Then stash your packs and wash off. We'll meet over in the tavern for dinner. There might even be enough coin in my pocket to cover a round or two of drinks to celebrate with my new Laegis brothers," Odegar said, adding as he nodded to Casselle, "and my first Templar sister." The boys hooted and moved to stow their gear for the evening.

Odegar followed Casselle into the room they would share and set his pack on the bed, rummaging around for a moment. Casselle thought to afford him a moment of peace, but he bade her to stay.

"I intend to tell the others in the morning, on our way out of town," he said. He freed a letter from his pack, a thick bundle of pages folded and secured with waxed red twine. He handed it across the bed to her. Warily, she took it, noticing that the seal of the Laegis had held the twine in place, but now it was broken, the letter already examined.

He didn't let go immediately. He made sure she met his eyes before he spoke again.

"You are the squad leader, Casselle. You should read this first, before I speak with the others. Familiarize yourself with the details. It is the bulk of what we know at this time."

She nodded briefly. Satisfied, Odegar let go of the letter.

The Captain set the rest of his pack aside and quickly folded his short cloak on top of it. He looked back once again just before he left, perhaps to add something more. Instead, he just motioned for her to read before he slipped out of the room, closing the door behind him.

She sat down on the bed and picked up the letter. Across the front, stained with dirt and dried blood, was a name she didn't recognize and the name of a town she knew was on the far western border of Gundlaan: Donnikaar. The paper was in good shape and the waxed thread showed minimal use. This hadn't passed through many hands.

Casselle untied the bundle and pulled the folded pages free. They were stiff in her fingers as she tried to flatten them out enough to read. The handwriting was plain but steady, and did not spare much space on the page, using as much of each sheet as possible. Conscious that the others were waiting downstairs, Casselle read as quickly as she could.

> I am a man not unfamiliar with letters, but I am not used to recounting such things by hand, so I will try to write plainly and true. Do not discount what is said here as I did once. I fear it may have doomed us all.

> I am Templar Captain of the Laegis, Renolf Crennel. I am stationed in Flinderlaas, a keep just past the border of Gundlaan in the Deckoraan Wilds, just beyond the Bay of Athoriss. Flinderlaas is the home of a small Gundlaan Outriders company as well as my double squad of Templars. We are the first response against the dangers of the Wilds. Normally this is occasional incursions by packs of hungry animals, bandits and the militant descendants of those states that perished during the Ehronfall.

> Gundlaan has been encouraging those in the Wilds to reorganize, to form new territories, but there has been little success. We have seen many new settlements spring up almost overnight, with many of them dying just as quickly. A few, however, have become welcome destinations while patrolling away from Flinderlaas.

> It was during one of these routine patrols that I first heard mention of the packs of wolves that came during the night to prey upon these outlying settlements. Initially, I discounted them altogether, but when the Outriders returned with increasingly wild tales, the last one being a story of a wolf as large as a small horse, I felt it was our duty to investigate. I took a squad of Templars with me and we set out into the Wilds towards a small settlement called Iselglen.

It took us close to a week to travel there through the Wilds. When we arrived, the town appeared almost empty. The people did not greet us, but watched us silently with suspicious stares. That afternoon, we met with the town Constable. He was nervous and new, having recently been promoted since the disappearance of the previous constable three nights back. He filled us in with as many details as he had, which sounded more like fiction than fact.

It was unsafe to wander far from town. It was unsafe to leave your house at night, or to stay inside and leave the doors and windows unbarred. Parents, those who hadn't left town altogether, kept children in sight at all time. This was the mildest of the news. There was talk from other outlying settlements that not only were the wolves attacking in broad daylight, but they were larger and more aggressive than normal wolves.

All of this I discounted as nervous superstition. I am not naive that the Gods once walked among us, and there are still devils in the shadows, but the only evil we have seen in daylight since the Ehronfall has been that perpetrated by man against other man. The constable invited us to stay in the safety of his office for the evening, but I told him we would keep an eye on the town from outside. Shortly I would come to understand for myself the look of horror I saw on his face.

I captained four fine Templar: Sten Vennel, Taric Steel, Falk Conner and Ran Bendbridge. I set Sten, Ran and Falk at the southern, eastern and northern cardinals of the town, taking the western for myself. Taric climbed the watching tower near the center of town in order to keep an eye on us all. I thought it a good plan and found a comfortable vantage on the west side, on the roof of the town sundries shop that had been abandoned in the last week.

It was a short evening that day and the darkness fell heavy over us. The moon was in seclusion, but the stars seemed to provide enough light for us to see the edge of the woods creep closer under the cover of night. I had my back to a chimney and my eyes on the worn footpath that led into the western woods. It was quiet there, the kind of unnatural quiet you hear before the first crack of thunder, when the animals have already hidden themselves away before the unrelenting storm. It was the kind of silence that should have warned me that something was amiss. The trip had been long, however, and my premonition did not overcome my fatigue.

I do not remember falling asleep, but I remember waking up. Since there was no moon, I could not tell what time it was, but my breath hung in the air and there was a layer of thick mist on top of the ground. I assumed this meant it might be close to sunrise, but I was mistaken. As I pulled myself up to my feet, I heard something below me, just over the edge of the roof. I looked to the watchtower, but saw no movement. I waved my hand for a moment, hoping to get a reply.

None came. Below me, there was another sound, one that chilled me to the bone. I crept quietly to the ledge and peered over.

Sten was on the ground, one hand wrapped around a bloodied throat, his voice a wet whisper gurgling through his fingers. The other weakly clawed at the side of the lodging. He was wounded in other places as well. Just as I looked for a way to drop down quickly, I saw something else that stayed my hand.

It was a wolf. A wolf larger than any I have ever seen, thrice as large as those that you have seen pelts for. It jogged casually out from the corner of another building and locked its jaws onto Sten's lower leg. As if he were no more than scrap left over from supper, it dragged him away effortlessly. Sten's free hand tried madly to grasp at the ground, to grab anything to keep from being dragged away. I moved reflexively to save him, but I stopped as another of the beasts rounded the corner, followed by a third. My blood chilled as they stopped in the middle of the path and began to tear him open, fighting for the opportunity to feast on his innards.

My blood was ice, freezing my limbs in place. I'd seen men fall to beasts before, but there was something else here, something deadly sinister that was as ever-present as the dark and equally oppressive. I stayed on the edge of the building, terrified and crying. I write these things only partially to confess my sins, but also to warn those that may come after me. As I was about to discover, there are things that inhabit the night that may strip a man of his courage, no matter how deep that well may run.

What brought me back to my senses was the cry of a child. When I heard it, something put purpose back into my heart. I found a way down on the opposite side of the building and hurried towards the sound of it. I felt my heart leap from my chest as I closed on the sound from around a merchant's store, hidden by the side alley. Ahead of me, from an open door, walked a woman with a screaming babe in her arms.

At first I thought she was in shock, because she had emerged from the home without any modesty, naked as the night sky. When I saw the wolves emerge from the house as well, I wanted to scream a warning to her, but was held in check by either fear or caution, I cannot say which. The wolves were not chasing her; they were following her instead, like faithful hounds.

I took a second look at her. She was not from the village. Her hair was long, wild and unkempt. It fell down to the small of her back in a dark, tangled cascade. Her legs also showed a light covering of short dark hairs and her feet were muddied and rough. Despite all of this, she had a natural beauty that I could not deny: a comely face with thick lips, a sensually curved figure and full, heavy breasts. She walked with such casual grace that I found myself aroused by her mere presence.

The babe cried again and brought me to my senses. He was cradled in one arm, his head pillowed on one of her ample tits, but he was not feeding, even though he looked to be the right age for it. She looked around lazily, the concerns of the child wholly ignored. Just when I thought the child would start to scream in earnest, she picked it up, holding it up to the night sky. Like a wild mother, she laughed and gently cooed at the baby as it's mood changed from annoyed to amused. She spun in a circle, listening to the child giggle as it orbited above her head. At that moment, she was intoxicatingly attractive, a beautiful untamed spirit that touched my heart and aroused my desires.

Then the woman tore the child in half as if it were made of parchment.

She was splashed with blood and viscera and the wolves immediately snatched up the remnants of the babe as she casually discarded them. I lost myself to vomiting for the next few moments, emptying the sparse contents of my stomach behind a crate in the alley.

When I heard a wolf howl, my legs moved of their own volition, straining for the closest path out of town.

I hazarded a look over my shoulder as I ran, catching one last sight of her, chest smeared in blood and sucking one of her own stained fingers, her eyes shining with every bit of savage lust as the animals that attended her.

I don't know how far I ran, or for how long, but eventually I collapsed, exhaustion winning out over caution.

The next morning, I began my long trek back to Flinderlaas, without mount or provisions. You read this letter as a testament to my success, the cost of which I cannot fully tally. I know Iselglen is lost, as well as the settlers that had lived there and the squad of Templars that had traveled with me. By the time I returned, there were already reports of attacks at settlements closer than Iselglen, and I know that Flinderlaas may well be consumed soon as well. The Commander of the Outriders has submitted his own report, asking for reinforcements or redeployment.

I fear this foe is more than just a plague of wolves. It is a vanguard of something more sinister. I feel it in my bones. I pen this to the Laegis Generals, in the hopes that my words will move them to mobilize a force to root out and cull this evil before it breaches our borders and threatens Gundlaan itself.

I submit this request for a cadre of Templars to face this threat to our lands and peoples. I send it with Iacob Ennis, a young man that has been a great help to me here at Flinderlaas, one that I would heartily recommend for an apprenticeship within the Templars.

En'vaar et Laegis,

Captain of the Laegis Templars, 3rd Expeditionaries

Renholf Crennel

Casselle folded the letter. It took her a moment to notice that Odegar had returned and was standing silently in the doorway, watching her with concern.

She held up the letter, hoping that there was something more he could tell her that would help lift the weight she felt on her heart at that moment.

"The letter was found two weeks ago on this side of the Bay. It was on the corpse of a young man, whom we assume to be Captain Crennel's messenger. He and his two companions had been killed. The Outriders who found them said that it looked to be the work of..."

"Wolves," Casselle interjected. Odegar, unfazed, merely nodded in agreement.

"Come," he said, "the others are waiting. Leave your worries here for the evening."

That was easier said than done. Though she wore a smile as she left with him, she disobeyed the order she'd been given. Her worries traveled with her, and weighed heavily on her heart.

7

Slivers

"A dedicated, efficient officer and member of the Seeker Corps, Captain Fjord carried out the duties of his noble office to the best of his abilities, and in a forthright manner consistent with the doctrines established..."

By all the gods, old, new and as yet unaccounted for, Lahnkam Voth's eulogy for the recently departed Captain Fjord was the worst Dreysha had ever heard in her twenty six years. And she'd heard a lot of them in her line of work.

She slipped a punch dagger from the top of her right boot, only half listening as Voth droned on about a man for whom the highest compliment he could come up with was "efficient". She loved the familiar feel of the knife's cross-grip in her hand. She'd had it custom-made by one of the best smiths in Mylesia so that the handle was set perpendicular to the blade, allowing her to hold it in a clenched fist with the business end protruding between her fingers. Although it had fit nearly perfectly the first time she'd held it, time and use had finished the job. Among her extensive collection of tools, this one might be her favorite; a small consolation since it was the only one to have survived the wreck.

The disaster wasn't a total loss, however: she was pleased by the comfort of her snug sealskin boots. Though Longeye's calves and ankles had been much thicker than Drey's, it seemed that their feet were the same size, and the sturdy laces that ran down the back, from just below her knees to the top of her heels, allowed her to draw the supple hide in tightly. The soft fur lining on the inside somehow kept her feet and legs cool, and the soles were remarkably tough despite being much lighter and thinner than the heavy Corps-issued clunkers the rest of the crew were forced to wear. Given the raw conditions they were struggling in, the boots were a singular luxury and well worth the price.

With the tip of the punch dagger, she set to work on a long sliver in her palm, the last of several nasty barbs she had acquired over the past two days as Voth and Scow pushed them hard to repair the damage done by the ridgeback's attack. Nobody complained, though; they were all in a hurry to get underway and as far away from that accursed spot as possible. The launch had taken a beating when the bitch crashed into them; they'd lost two oars and cracked three ribs on their starboard side, and sheared the rudder clean off when the vessel was shoved sideways. Worse still, they were taking on water; not enough to sink, but the threat was enough that they all forgot their empty stomachs and recent losses and worked with a collective focus. Dreysha knew how lucky they were to have Scow with them still; Lanky Lahnkam might be a heroic provisioner and crate-counter, but he couldn't lead the shit from his own arse, and for a career Seeker he knew remarkably little about the timber and tack of a vessel. Fortunately his life was at stake as well, and he was at least smart enough to get out of the way while the Mattock organized them into work parties. While he and Sherp worked at jury-rigging the rudder - something they could mount from topside as nobody was about to get in the water - Scow set Rantham to bailing duty, and Dreysha, Triistan and Biiko to gathering what they could from the floating debris around the launch.

Among the flotsam of Fjord's Folly (Mung had christened the makeshift raft while recounting their survival efforts leading up to their rescue), they had found two broken spars and several feet of deck planking they could use to shore up the hull. But the real treasure was the partially-full scuttlebutt Triistan had spied, still intact. Trying to gaff it and the other items and get them into the boat was not an experience she would ever wish to repeat, however. Dreysha had been in any number of tight spots, and gotten out of them again by keeping a cool, clear head no matter how bad things looked. In the process, she'd found fear to be a regular and sometimes useful companion for her. It forced you to take things seriously and helped push your body beyond its normal limits - as long as you were able to keep it under control. Terror was another matter altogether, though, and watching Biiko lean out over that black abyss, tap-tap-tapping on the barrel to coax it over to the ship... waiting for that fucking black bitch to appear again... *that* was terrifying. In a way it was worse than when she'd been in the water and it was chasing her. At least then she had known where it was, had even been pretty certain it couldn't catch her before Biiko could pull her from the water. But knowing it was somewhere below, unseen, waiting to strike... it was the very nightmare essence that made up what men called The Dark.

It took most of the next day to affect all of the repairs. While they worked, their nerves were rubbed raw, caught as they were between the strong breeze that sang mockingly in the damaged rigging above them and the vast, lurking Darkness below. By the time they finally got underway, everyone had retreated within themselves, backing into whatever felt to them like a safe corner, some sulking, others watching one another suspiciously.

As a result, Voth and Scow had decided to pass around the Morale Officer, allowing each of the survivors two pulls of the black rum. As she felt the spiced liquor spread warm fire through her gullet, she could see the collective mood on the boat begin to mellow, backing away from crisis, if only for the moment. They had all shared a glimpse of what was to come, however, and just like their food and water, the firkin of rum would only last so long.

"... and so we Seekers release his ashes to the wind," Voth's dry, whiny croak intruded on her thoughts, "that he may sail on, or return to the waiting Sea." He paused, allowing the rest of them to intone the Seeker's Oath:

"To sail beyond the Wind, to find that which has been Lost, and illuminate the Darkness with the torch of Discovery."

She said the words with the rest of the crew, but other than serving to maintain her cover, they were meaningless to her. She preferred the common sailor's version, said safely out of earshot of any officers: "To sail beyond our borders, take that which hasn't been given to us, and increase the cost of everything to fill the Sea King's coffers."

She was interested in what Voth would do next, however. At this point in the Releasing Ceremony, the speaker would typically add a few drops of his own blood to the remains - specifically onto arxhemical glyphs tattooed on the deceased's arms and face, triggering a phenomenon that most simply considered 'magic'. First the runes, and then the entire corpse, would burst into a heatless blue flame, which would completely consume the body in a few moments, leaving only ash and cinder. Most people called it "Veheg's Fire", alluding to Veheg the Traveler, God of Death. The fact that the gods had wiped themselves out a few centuries ago didn't seem to matter.

Dreysha's travels had given her a more practical understanding of it, though, and she knew the process had evolved from techniques mastered by the Ashen. She had been taught that everyone's body had a limited store of a fundamental material they called "xhemium", which could be ignited under the right circumstances. Ashen had learned to manipulate these stores and use the material as a sort of fuel or catalyst for their incantations. Somewhere along the way, they had taught the Seeker Corps and other mariners how to process their dead this way, providing an ideal method for cremating the bodies in dramatic fashion, but with very little heat where normal fire was a significant concern.

However today, since they did not have Fjord's corpse, there were no tattoos, no xhemium, and no inner fire to release. Seeker Protocol allowed for this too, of course. After all, it was fairly common to hold Releasing Ceremonies for naval personnel lost at sea. In those instances, they were supposed to use something symbolic to represent the deceased, such as any of their personal affects which could be spared. The items would be soaked in seal-oil and placed in a small sea chest, which would also be doused in oil, then set on the end of a wooden plank balanced on the taffrail and held in place by a member of the crew. At the completion of the Oath, the person giving the eulogy would set fire to the chest, wait until it had burned long enough for the contents inside to catch, and then give the command for the "planker" to tip his end up and deposit the symbolic remains into the sea. It was considered a successful ceremony and general good omen if the chest continued to float and burn until the ship was underway again.

In Drey's experience, it typically sank and went out after only a few moments, although she recalled one instance where the remains sank very slowly. They were sailing through Niht's Haven, so visibility was excellent and they could still see the chest several meters under water, when it had suddenly flared brilliantly. She had found out later from a clever young topman who'd helped prepare the chest that he had stashed a small flask of Shan's Fury inside - a homemade spirit banned on Seeker vessels because of its potency and, apparently, the fact that it was highly flammable. It had been one of her first glimpses of a side to Triistan that she didn't think most people knew existed, and she found his subtle resourcefulness and mischievous alter-ego intriguing.

Voth had been in quite a state initially, since Fjord had appeared to only come to them with nothing but his Captain's Sash, which he was still wearing when he had wrapped himself in the anchor rope and dove into the Dark. Seeker Protocol was very specific about how the Releasing Ceremony should be carried out, and Voth was very specific about maintaining Protocol. Fortunately for all of them, Mung came to the rescue; Captain Fjord had been fully-clothed when they had pulled him from the sea. He had been unconscious, with an ugly wound along his left temple, but it was not until after he woke that he inexplicably stripped off his uniform and underclothes and donned just the sash. Not knowing what else to do, Braeghan had collected the uniform, crisply folded it, and tucked it into a chest they'd found and absorbed into their flotsam raft. They had been putting anything of interest or value into this chest as they found it floating among the *Peregrine's* wreckage. Braeghan had called it the "Memory Box" and talked about how happy everyone would be when they were rescued and found something they'd thought lost forever. Mung had gone along with the idea, thinking the items might make good trade currency were they to wash up on less than civilized shores.

The locker had survived and been brought onboard along with the other odds and ends they had been able to salvage, but forgotten until Voth had nearly come unhinged because he had no way of properly conducting the Ceremony with no remains. Dreysha had thought the man was going to actually embrace Mung when he produced the chest and the uniform.

Now, Voth went through the ritual steps with characteristic rigidity, exactly as specified by Seeker Protocol, with one glaring exception that he was oblivious to: the Releasing Ceremony was meant to be a symbolic tribute to the victim's life, as well as a way for his friends and associates to bid him good-bye. If Dreysha had really cared, she might have felt sad that Voth had managed to transform a ceremony meant to honor Captain Fjord's memory into an emotionless, regimented routine whose sole intent seemed to be disposing of some unused clothing and a battered sea locker. After the chest was set afire, he waited just long enough for its lid to crack in the heat and then nodded to Rantham who was serving as planker.

The Rogue cocked his head slightly. "Perhaps we might wait just a moment long-"

"Now, Mr. d'yBassi," Voth interrupted.

"Aye, Sir." Rantham tipped up his end of the plank and the chest at the other end slid off into the sea with a hissing plop. The flames went out immediately and it sank like a stone. Dreysha pressed harder on the dagger to stop herself from laughing at the irony.

"Try not to cut it off, girl," Scow rumbled under his breath as he moved past her to take his place beside Voth, where he would deliver the eulogy for First Apprentice Jode Cooper. Under other circumstances, she would have quipped about her last lover saying the same thing, but she bit her tongue and hid a smile behind a wince as she worked at the sliver. It was half the length of her pinky finger and buried deep in the meaty muscle of her thumb.

She supposed Voth wasn't entirely to blame: the Seeker Corps as a whole was steeped in tradition, bound together by habit and ritual. Sailors thrived on routine. Everything they did, from the moment they woke to the instant they fell asleep in their hammock, was scripted; set out step by step in a schedule that was adhered to with a passion most religious fanatics would envy. Even emergencies had carefully-planned response strategies, and you would be hard-pressed to find a set of circumstances for which the Seeker Corps had not crafted a response plan to address. Dreysha knew; she'd looked.

Funeral ceremonies were no exception, of course. In the event where more than one crewmember needed to be interred, they were handled in order of rank, from highest to lowest. As a First-ranked Skilled Apprentice, Jode outranked Pelor and the boy, Braeghan, so her body would be interred next, and Mordan Scow - her mentor - would honor her memory.

Dreysha watched as the big Master Carpenter traced the arcane shapes of the arxhemist formulas that had been tattooed on Jode's skin during the previous day - they were the only portion of her body not wrapped in the spiced linens intended to help mask the scent of decay. She was thankful that Veheg's Fire only required the bodies to sit for two days; in this heat they were breaking down quickly and she could already detect the sickly-sweet, cloying scent of death despite the heavy odor of the spices.

The Mattock paused for a long moment, looking at his understudy's body, as Dreysha felt Triistan move up beside her. She knew it was him even before she turned and looked, though she couldn't say how. His face twitched through several expressions as if he couldn't decide which one was appropriate, ultimately wincing in what she supposed was probably embarrassment before turning away to watch Scow. She chewed on the inside of her lip to stifle another smile and glanced down to the bulge in the back of his Topman's Sash where she knew he kept his precious journal. She would have to make another attempt to steal it soon; her brief look at it a few days before had confirmed it was the reason she was stuck on this godsforsaken floating coffin, and she needed to see everything it contained.

She put those thoughts aside as Scow began to speak. Job or not, she genuinely liked and respected him, and what little she'd known of Jode had impressed her. She was interested to hear what he would say.

"First Apprentice Jode came to me as rough and green as the Forever Sea itself - and, though I didn't know at the time, nigh as deep as it, too."

The Mattock stood behind the makeshift table where Jode's wrapped body lay, hands behind his back, thick legs set apart in a stance she had seen him adopt many times before - usually whenever he was reviewing a crewmember's work. He drew his arm across his forehead to wipe the sweat away. Though one of the Twins was hovering just above the horizon, they were entering the long evening and it would be nearly a full watch before the second sun set. The steady wind they'd been running on had fallen to a light and fickle breeze that did little to relieve the tropic heat. What was left of the stained and ragged material that used to be Dreysha's uniform clung uncomfortably to her sweat-soaked body.

"I owed a favor to a friend and they asked me to take her in and train her." He grunted and shook his broad head. "She weren't no bigger than Braeghan at the time, and I didn't figure she'd had the brains or the brawn for ship-work.... but I was wrong. She was smart, that one - smarter than me, and by the end of the first week, we both knew it."

He looked out at the small group without really seeing them, bald head glistening in the late afternoon sun. "I've been sailing in the Seeker Corps for more years than I can remember, and at sea for half again that time before joining the Corps. Never took a wife, though most of you mud-foots will say I might as well have married the *Peregrine*."

Beside her, Dreysha heard Triistan laugh quietly, and Rantham caught her eye with a wink. The Mattock's romantic exploits with his ship were well-documented among the crew. He was confident enough in his leadership and his mates to go along with the joke, though, and had even improvised a roaring ballad the night they'd held a feast to celebrate making landfall on Aarden. The rum had been his muse, and when he'd finished belting out the last line at the top of his considerable lungs, most of the crew were either on their backs or knees, gasping for breath and clutching their stomachs in uncontrollable laughter. The memory brought a sudden poignancy to his efforts to speak here, where she could clearly hear the raw grief in his voice.

"When she went-" his voice caught and he coughed, shaking his broad head. "When the *Peregrine* broke, I thought it was the worst thing I'd ever felt... maybe the worst thing I'd ever feel again. If Halliard hadn't needed help telling up from down, I might've gone down with her."

He glanced at Triistan who nodded silently in acknowledgment.

"But this feels worse." He shook his head slowly again. "Ships can be rebuilt. But a good Seeker... so much potential. So much to offer to those who knew her... so much to offer the world. Jode was the best gods-damned apprentice cooper I've ever laid eyes on. I'd planned to make her Master sometime this year. But she was more than that. Captain material, without a doubt. She was..." he paused, groping for words, his wide jaw moving soundlessly for a second, eyes searching her body as if he expected to find them written out in the arxhemic tattoos.

"... she was good timber. And the world is a Darker place for having lost her."

Scow bent and kissed Jode's forehead - a tender, vulnerable act so incongruent with the man's size and temperament that it almost touched Dreysha, almost brought a lump to her throat. She dropped her gaze and dug harder at the sliver in her palm, hard enough to draw blood.

Keep it clean, Drey, professional.

The Mattock cleared his throat and led them in the Seekers Oath, but where Voth had worked mechanically through procedure, Scow's participation was reverent and infinitely more meaningful. He held one hand out over her body, then drew the blade of a small whittling knife across his palm. His hands were so thick with calluses, though, there was no blood, so with a soft, self-conscious grunt, he drew the knife across his beefy forearm. A line of crimson followed the tip of the blade at once.

Scow held his arm over Jode's and clenched his fist, sending a bright, twisting rivulet of blood running down to his elbow, where it collected, a small drop swelling fatter until it dripped to strike the dead flesh below. There was a sharp hiss as the blood struck the glyph at Jode's wrist, and Veheg's Fire took.

Magic or not, the results were impressive. A bright blue luminescence flashed at the point of impact before racing up her left arm as Scow leaned over her right. He gave a slight shake of his fist to jar loose another couple of drops, and when they spattered onto the tattoos on her other arm, the Fire caught there as well. At first, the iridescence followed the path of the tattooed symbols, etching them in a blue, veined light that would have looked like the hot glow of burning embers had it been orange or red. As the last symbol on her right arm began to smolder, there was a soft whump and spectral blue flames rose like dancing wraiths from the tattooed glyphs.

Scow stepped back, wearing an expression of childish awe, picked out in the unearthly cerulean glow despite the brilliant afternoon sunlight. Dreysha found herself holding her breath; from experience, she knew that the flames along Jode's arms were a small glimpse of the real conflagration going on beneath her skin, as the xhemium throughout the corpse caught alight. The process was remarkably effective, and it was hard to comprehend how it could be so thoroughly destructive without producing any more heat than if she'd held her hand near a watch lantern. Any moment now...

There was a sudden, blinding flash that forced her and the others to close their eyes or look away. Dreysha tried to shield hers behind an outstretched hand so that she could see the final transition. She was partially successful; with a soft sigh, the linen wraps simply turned to ash and sloughed onto the deck, and for an instant Jode's naked form was visible beneath. It was more a web of bright blue veins in the shape of her body, before, a heartbeat later, it flashed and was gone. A cloud of ash and feather-light blue embers rose up slowly, like smoke, until a sudden stiffening of the breeze caught them and sent them spiraling up and around the mainmast. When the cloud reached the top-gallant, it blew sideways, stretching towards the setting suns, streaming for a moment from the top of the mast like a signal flag before tearing away across the sea.

Dreysha watched it go. Everything that Jode had done and been and would ever be was gone, while the suns continued to crawl toward the horizon, the water lapped at the sides of what was left of her world, and those still clinging to it struggled on, thinking for some reason that they were different, that they still mattered.

Finished, the Master Carpenter and Voth stepped back to make room for Sherp. The men of the rowing pit were the lowest-ranking members of a Seeker crew, with the exception of non-ranked apprentices, so his brother Pelor's ceremony would come before Braeghan's. In this case, Dreysha was grateful for the Corps' stodgy adherence to tradition. Sherp was not taking his brother's death well, and seemed intent on making the most of every perceived slight. Apparently he blamed the boy and Triistan for his brother's death, and a good chunk of the tension on board the launch seemed to be emanating from those two. Well, moreso from Sherp if she was honest about it. Triistan was doing his best to avoid the big Valheim, though quarters were tight and that wasn't always possible. Fortunately for the young topman, Biiko seemed to have taken an intense interest in his well-being, and the warrior was never far away. Until this morning, his presence had kept the sullen oarsman at bay, but it was also making it decidedly harder to get closer to Triistan and his journal.

As Sherp shouldered his way up to stand beside his brother's body, Dreysha saw him shoot a baleful glance in Biiko's direction. The Northman was a big man, with the broad back, powerful shoulders, and thick neck of his profession. He kept his long, black hair and beard in a series of braids, which were now sludge-gray and encrusted with the salt and grime of their ordeal, as well as matted blood from his mangled nose. Above that crooked, purple and red mess, eyes the color of stone brooded from beneath a prominent brow, across which the ruddy skin seemed stretched too tightly. The last joint of the second and third fingers on his right hand were missing, allegedly from a tussle with a fourteen-foot ridgeback. Judging from Sherp's size and temperament, she did not envy the ridgeback, but she thought him a thrice-damned fool for picking a fight with an Unbound. He was fortunate to still be alive.

No one could quite figure out why Biiko had appeared in Thunder Bay, or how he was able to join their crew. Captain Vaelysia and the Ship's Whip, Tarq, seemed to have worked something out between them and given permission to the dark-skinned warrior to sail aboard the *Peregrine*, but no one else had any inkling why. There had been plenty of speculation among the other crew members, but the stranger had steadfastly ignored all direct inquiries. Since he'd come aboard, she hadn't heard him utter a single word other than when he chanted his evening prayers. Until this morning, that is, when he had broken his precious vow by voicing an ugly idea that had been working its way through her own thoughts as surely as the sliver in her palm.

Voth - she refused to acknowledge him as Captain Voth unless addressing him in person - had finally found a way to be useful by making a full inventory of their remaining food and water supplies, only slightly bolstered from what they had recovered from Fjord's Folly. Then he worked out a rationing system for them to follow. It was the one thing he was good at, and knew it, so he had attacked the task with zeal. He was equally zealous, even gleeful, as he read off the report and portions that would be allowed. What made it even worse was the fact that everyone knew he had wasted a third of their water by kicking over the scuttlebutt when the seal-oil lantern had broken and spilled. If Voth had been truthful enough to reflect this fact in his inventory and subsequent report, he certainly hadn't bothered to share it with the crew.

"Following is a complete list of food and water stocks as inventoried by me, Captain Lankham Voth, *SKS Peregrine* Emergency Launch, on this date, which we approximate to be Twelveday of the Month of Estre, in the Year Two Hundred and Fifty Seven Since Ehronfall. First Mate Mordan Scow was present for the inventory and will affix his seal to this document as witness."

The news was bleak. Most of the food supplies had been washed overboard during the wreck of the *Peregrine*, and what remained - one sack of moldy hardtack, four jars of pickled herring, and half a dozen overly-ripe jenga melons - might be stretched to last the eight survivors two weeks. None of the salted pork or boar had been saved. Water was slightly better: with one and a half barrels, they had enough to last them about a month, longer depending upon rainfall.

Or shorter if Lanky Lankham wasted any more of it, Dreysha thought sourly.

Sherp delivered the eulogy for his brother Pelor in Old Valheim. Dreysha had been extensively trained in four different languages, but had only a rudimentary grasp of the Northman's language. His voice was badly distorted by the damage done to his nose, but she recognized enough of it to understand he was uttering some type of prayer for the dead, if for no other reason than the number of times he invoked the name of Fjorvin, the long dead god of the Northern Wastes. The others remained silent and respectful, but it was clear from the stolen glances and shuffling feet that they weren't sure how to react. All but Biiko: he stood quietly to one side, his dark face impassive. The scar on the side of his face had a way of tugging down one corner of his mouth so that he always looked unhappy, but she imagined she still saw the slightest frown of disapproval.

His eyes suddenly shifted from the ceremony to meet her own, and it was as if she could hear him speaking all over again. *The fallen still have something left to give.* Her thoughts shifted back to that morning again.

Voth's rationing schedule had not been received well, and the crew had erupted in protests and curses. Voth squeaked out a call for order, which everyone ignored until Scow bellowed at them to cease and desist or he'd see them all strung overboard as bait. As the clamor died down, Biiko had uttered that one phrase. His voice was deep, with a quiet power that under other circumstances she might have found soothing. They all lapsed into a stunned silence, shocked both by the fact that he had spoken, and by the import of his words.

It was Mung who had spoken first. He seemed to have a knack for situations like this, though as usual his initial reaction was just wide of the mark.

"Brilliant! We'll use them as bait, yes?"

Sherp took a step towards him, snarling, "I'll gut you myself and use your fucking balls as bait before you touch my brother's body, nagracht!"

Mung's pallor was visible even through the painful red color of his sunburned skin. He stumbled backwards, pointing a shaking finger at the Unbound warrior.

"It was his idea!"

Biiko didn't move, but Dreysha had noticed he seemed to lean forward ever so slightly, as if he'd shifted his weight to the balls of his feet. Scow stepped between them, and although he was half a head shorter, the Northman stopped in mid-stride.

"Stand down, Seeker."

Sherp was seething, his deep chest heaving, big meaty hands clenching and unclenching, and for an instant Dreysha had thought he was going to try and push his way past. Thankfully, duty and habit had won through, at least for that moment. He frowned contemptuously, averting his eyes from Scow but raking the rest of them and settling on Biiko.

"If you touch my brother's body for bait, you die", he muttered and took a step back. She had been about to breathe a sigh of relief when Biiko spoke again.

"Not bait. Food."

This time the Northman erupted in fury. Scow, neck and face turning red with wrath, had partially turned to look at Biiko as if he were mad and Sherp took advantage of the distraction, shoving past and lunging for the Unbound while screaming something in Old Valheim. It was over in an instant.

Dreysha still wasn't completely sure what had happened, but one moment Sherp was charging forward and the next he was lying in a heap on the floor of the boat, with what looked like a bloody piece of meat on his face. Biiko stood quietly again, looking down at the oarsman with one eyebrow raised and a slight frown, as if he were studying a bug he hadn't seen before. Scow had crouched next to Sherp's body and bent his ear to the man's chest.

"He's alive. Going to have to do something with that nose, though, or he'll never be able to breathe out of it again." The Mattock then stood up again, looking at Biiko appraisingly. They studied one another for a long moment.

"You could have killed him," Scow had finally said quietly.

The Unbound said nothing, just lifted the one eyebrow further as if to say "Only if I intended to," then turned and made his way to the prow of the boat. He returned a moment later with a small satchel which Dreysha knew served as a sort of field kit for him. It contained several different types of herbs, poultices, ointments, and bandages, all kept dry and preserved in a waterproof inner pouch made from an animal stomach. She recalled that he had been chewing on something as he brushed past her and crouched beside Sherp's inert form.

The others stood uncertainly and watched while he tended to the Northman's face, first doing what he could to blot up the blood, then applying the same foul-smelling green paste she'd seen him use on Triistan's head after the ridgeback's attack. They all winced at the sound of grinding bone as he tried his best to realign the man's nose, and she remembered wondering at the time if Sherp was truly still alive; he didn't so much as groan during the whole process. Biiko had done him a tremendous favor by knocking him senseless.

In typical fashion, now that the danger had passed, Voth had tried to restore some semblance of order.

"There will be no - I repeat, NO - more discussion of... of THAT abominable practice again aboard my ship, am I clear?" His shrill voice and craven manner burrowed under her skin worse than any sliver and even now, thinking back on it, she ground her teeth. Looking up, she saw that Sherp had apparently finished his prayer and was moving to stand at one end of his brother's wrapped corpse. He leaned down until his forehead touched Pelor's own, placing both hands alongside his face, then began singing quietly in Old Valheim. This, she knew, was the Song for the Dead, in which a relative would recite the names of all of the family members that had died before him, summoning them to come and guide the fallen to wherever the Dead go. Her stomach rumbled and she wondered if Biiko had been right. In the end they were just empty husks and ash anyway.

At first no one had responded to Voth's question. Even the Mattock had remained silent, averting his eyes and looking out at the vast expanse of water and sky around them. At the time she remembered wondering if the hard truth of their circumstances was overwhelming even his once unshakable sense of duty.

"I said AM I CLEAR?"

"Aye, Captain!" squeaked one voice. *Mung. Of course.*

The next person to speak, however, had surprised her.

"Sir," Triistan said hesitantly, "I think we should consider... all... options, in light of the fact that we're -" But Voth had cut him off.

"We'll consider nothing of the sort, Boy," he spat. "We aren't Kingsbane cutthroats or some savages from the grasslands - we are Seekers! I ought to have you disciplined before the mast for insubordination. Which part of no more disc-"

"What are you so afraid of, Captain?" Dreysha knew she should keep her mouth shut, but that had never been one of her strong points. She'd had enough of this fool. "Not like we'll be looking at your bony arse for the noon meal."

Scow had rounded on her, bringing his face close to her own. "Stow that right now, Seeker! I don't care how bad things get, by the Seven High Houses I will not suffer belligerence or I will flay every single one of you myself - understood?"

She'd held her ground, but averted her eyes and said tersely. "Aye sir. Understood."

Voth had stepped close then, looming over her. He was tall, and she knew from watching him he took advantage of that whenever he could.

"Thank you, Mister Scow. Your loyalty will be noted in my report to the High Chancellor. It is comforting to know we may rely on a man of your experience and character. As for the rest of you..."

He had trailed off as the Master Carpenter - First Mate, she corrected herself - turned to address him, muttering quietly in a voice the others probably couldn't overhear. "Captain, with all due respect, I think we should hear the lad out. He's got a solid head on his shoulders and we're in a bit of a tight spot here if I may say so, sir."

She couldn't help but smile at the memory of Voth's face at that moment. His contemptuous, smug satisfaction had melted into sour uncertainty; beady eyes narrowing, jaw hanging slack as his purser's mind hit the end of its ledger, unable to reconcile this subtle challenge to his authority. He had just complimented the First Mate on his experience and character, and he desperately needed Scow's support, so he could not dismiss him now without seriously eroding it. He blinked a few times and closed his mouth as he completed the calculation.

"Very well. Go ahead, Boy. Speak."

Triistan had looked from Scow to Voth and then stolen a glance at her before clearing his throat and standing straighter, as if he were lining up for an inspection. "Thank you, sir. If I may point out to the Captain, sir, we have made our reckoning at five hundred leagues north of Sigil's Wrath. Or I should say we *were* five hundred leagues north of it."

He glanced up at the trailing sun, called 'The Copper Crone' because her light had a faint reddish-orange tint to it and she was older and slower than her sister. "We're more likely some four hundred and fifty leagues northeast of there by now."

"That's preposterous! We've been sailing north by northwest for nearly a full day. How could we *possibly* have gone *backwards*?"

The Triistan she had met before reaching Aarden would have mumbled an apology and retreated into his shell. But to his credit that morning, he plowed forward to make his point.

"I believe we're caught in the Godsfall Drift, Captain, and we'll need to make at least seven knots to outpace it, Sir. We've barely -" Mung and Rantham started talking at the same time, so that Triistan had to raise his voice to be heard over them: "- we've barely been making four or five, and that only up until the mid-day watch."

"SILENCE!" Scow ordered the others, who complied immediately. She recalled with distaste seeing Voth rubbing his temples with skeletal, ink-stained fingers and muttering "Gods, why is this happening to me?"

"By your rationing schedule, Sir, we've enough food to last us two weeks, and water perhaps a month - more if we're lucky and it rains." Triistan paused to take a deep breath.

And rains without another squid-fucking storm along with it, Dreysha filled in as she recalled the conversation.

"If we sail northeast to compensate for the Drift, and if the wind holds," he finished by saying what everyone else - even Voth - had already concluded, "we might see Thunder Bay in six weeks. If we tack north first to break out of the Drift, maybe we'll shave a week off from that time, and again, that's if everything goes our way, sir.

"We need to plan for two to three more *months*..." He trailed off, leaving the rest unspoken.

Voth had jumped into the silence before anyone else could say it for him. "Then we'll learn to fish better, and I will review the rationing schedule again! We can go hungry without starving, at least for the first few weeks. As long as we have sufficient water supplies, we can survive on that. Anything else is madness! I'd sooner starve than... than..."

"So you think now, Captain." It was Rantham, but he had sounded different to Dreysha, much more subdued - haunted. "I've sailed that course before, and I have no wish to go there again."

Voth had thrown his hands up in the air in a futile gesture and looked to Scow for help. The Mattock stared hard at Rantham. "Make your point, Midshipman."

Rantham d'yBassi, who shipmates referred to as "The Rogue" due to his uncanny luck, had looked at each of them in turn, his characteristic smirk nowhere in evidence beneath his black goatee. Dreysha thought now that he had looked like someone who knew his luck was running out.

"Aye, sir. Before I joined the Corps, I crewed a smuggler's ship called *Shadowplay*, out of Vorthr. We plied the Golden Gap from The Tooth all the way to Valheim. Weapons, artifacts, slaves, criminals, currency - if someone wanted something, and wanted it kept off of the ledgers, we hauled it." He laughed sadly, shaking his head. "Those were the best days, amazing days. The blood and thunder of raids; a mistress in every port and whores on board for the runs between... we ate jade and rubies and shat gold, and made the Sea Kings tremble with envy."

"Your *point*, Mr. d'yBassi?" Voth had said acidly. "I believe we're still waiting to hear it."

Dreysha remembered the look Rantham had given him then; his dark eyes nearly black, calculating and cold, but he nodded and shrugged in that familiar, insolent way that he had. "Of course, Captain. As you wish."

"They finally caught us just north of The Tooth. The *Red Waters*... a war galley, bounty class, with two rowing decks and three masts. She'd been waiting for us in a blind bay and swung in half a league behind us with full shrouds and all one hundred and ninety-eight sweeps in the water, pulling as if the H'kaan manned her benches. Gods but she was *fast*.

"We threw everything we had into *Shadowplay's* sweeps, hung every scrap of canvas, trimmed every inch of her, but it wasn't enough. They caught us late that afternoon - didn't even slow, just ran us down and rammed us."

Voth sneered. "The Ministry's arm is long and its justice terrible and sure, Mister d'yBassi. How is it that you can stand here today and recount these events? You must really be as lucky as they say."

Rantham had smiled sadly.

"Do you mean, why wasn't I hung or scrubbed, sir? Would that I had been, that I could forget." He stared coolly at Voth as he continued.

"Their justice was indeed terrible, Captain. The ram took us astern, smashing the rudder as well, not that it would have made any difference. The wound was fatal, and when the Red Waters reversed sweeps and backed her way out, we heeled to starboard almost immediately. You could hear the water rushing in through the hole and the ship groaning like some wounded beast as she started to go down. Our captain shouted our surrender and requested help getting his exhausted men aboard the galley..." He paused, his lips curling bitterly.

"... and received a half-dozen crossbow bolts in his chest as answer. The rest of us did our best to abandon ship, and some even thought to cut loose some of the remaining supply crates and barrels to use as rafts. Most began swimming for the war galley despite what had happened to our captain, assuming we would be taken aboard as prisoners.

"A few were shot before the Kings' Justiciar ordered his men not to waste anymore ammunition. He gave the order to come about and set his course for home, leaving us to drown."

Dreysha remembered looking around at her companions and watching the looks on their faces, from Biiko's impassive stare to Triistan, who was grappling with this unflattering portrait of his homeland. When her gaze came to rest on Voth, the smugly-satisfied smirk he didn't bother to conceal had made her want to rescind her earlier statement and roast him slowly over burning coals. Her stomach rumbled again in agreement.

Sherp completed his lengthy Song for the Dead and took Scow's dagger from him - she made a mental note to watch if he returned it after the ceremony. Overhead she heard Snitch chattering away. Since being rescued and surviving the ridgeback's attack, it had, with no rats aboard the emergency launch, made good use of its time endearing itself to the crew. Mung seemed particularly attached to it, and spent quite a bit of time teaching it simple tricks, though sometimes she wondered if it weren't the other way around. Since this morning's disagreement, however, the titch monkey had refused to come down from the top of the mainmast, as if it understood that its status had changed once again: from rat catcher, to pet... to food. She wondered when her own status would change, as her mind returned to Rantham's tale.

"We never had a chance to take a head count, so we had no idea how many men went into the water. Forty, perhaps. Crossbows took six of us, and at least another dozen drowned within the first hour while we gathered what debris we could and lashed it together to form a raft." He glanced knowingly at Mung.

"Not unlike yours, Mung, but smaller, with only enough room for four men to ride on it. We put the sickest on the raft, and the rest of us clung to the sides... feeling like a piece of bait dangling at the end of a line.

"We lost six more that night... from the cold, I think, or maybe they knew what was to come and just let go in the dark. Up there, the waters of the Golden Gap and the Forever Sea are cold; the ice flows north of Valheim melt in mid-summer, and the Gap's current channels that right down and out into the Sea. I found out later that this was what kept the big predators away, that the ridgebacks and kraken-eels prefer these warmer southern waters. I only wish we had known it at the time.

"At first light of the next day, there were twenty-one survivors left. Four or five had taken a chill and were in a bad way. The skies opened up, drenching us mercilessly for the rest of that day and the next. We drank what rain we could, though none of us thought to try and capture it. In fact barely any words were spoken at all for those first two days; our circumstances were so bleak most of us were just doing our best to hang on, numb with cold and shock. I remember thinking that the *Red Waters* captain was only trying to teach us a lesson and that he was waiting just over the horizon. That he would appear any time now to collect his prisoners. The things we tell ourselves...

"By the eleventh day, there were nine of us left. Each time we lost another man and pushed his corpse off of the raft, you'd see the hungry stares, or somebody's mouth moving, making that quiet smacking noise with their lips and tongue, while the cold hollow ache in our guts grew worse. We were sick and weak and it was only a matter of time before someone addressed the thought on everyone's minds, the question we were all obsessing over privately... the same one we're all thinking of now..."

He shook his head and made a soft, bitter sound - part laugh, part snort. His voice was barely a whisper, as if he were speaking to himself.

"Starvation is a terrible thing, my friends. The body, robbed of nourishment, begins to feed on itself. There is pain... so much pain... not the stomach aches that you are thinking of now, but everywhere. Your bones, your insides, your eyes... even your teeth hurt - before they begin falling out... Your bowels turn to water, although you aren't eating anything. And the mind can only stand so much..."

Dreysha could still see the faraway stare in Rantham's eyes as he paused. The others had gone completely silent as they contemplated their own fates. All but Voth, who seemed unaffected, still wearing that contemptuous smirk.

"And yet you survived, Mister d'yBassi. How were you rescued?"

Rantham closed his eyes and bowed his head, and for a moment Dreysha had thought he wasn't going to respond. Then he ran a long-fingered hand through his black curls and sighed deeply.

"I don't know how long we drifted. We were found by a mapper, a Seeker vessel updating charts of an atoll and surrounding reefs south of The Tooth. I have absolutely no memory of the rescue - only what others have told me. After recovering I was told by the young captain that she had found three of us on the raft, and no other survivors. Two of us lived, I and a freed pit fighter from Uthengaard. The third..."

He paused again, his head moving up and down silently in a nodding motion, until, with that same soft, bitter laugh he raised his eyes to look at them. "The third man died from his wounds shortly after we were rescued. His wounds..." he laughed again, and she had found the slight maniacal edge to it unsettling. His voice dropped to a hoarse whisper.

"There were strips of cloth tied tightly around both legs... here -" he made a slashing motion with the edge of his hand along the inside of his upper thigh. He grimaced and spit his next words out as though he could still taste his sins.

"From there down, most... most of the flesh... the *meat*... had been gnawed off both his legs."

8

The Game's Afoot

Sherp threw back his head and let out a long, ululating cry that raised the hair on the back of Dreysha's neck and jolted her back to the present. Veheg's Fire flashed through his brother's body as the Valheim lifted his heavy arms skyward. Dreysha didn't think the Fire was anywhere near as bright as it had been with Jode - she was able to look directly at it this time - and rather than rise and depart elegantly, the cloud of ash boiled around the corpse like steam or smoke from a wet fire, eventually getting caught in a swirling crosswind that scattered it around the onlookers and the boat. She could smell and taste the ash, feel it settling on her skin. She spat and fought the urge to jump in the sea to get clean, ridgebacks and gods-knew-what-else be damned.

At least the ceremonies were almost finished. Triistan would be next, speaking for Braeghan, and there would be no Fire for the boy. Just his head had surfaced after the ridgeback's attack and with Triistan unconscious, no one else had volunteered to recover it with that black bitch prowling below them.

Fortunately, one of the items Mung and Braeghan had recovered and placed in the Memory Box was Braeghan's favorite book. It was mostly ruined now, but it had been a beautifully-illustrated collection of children's stories about the misadventures of a narcissistic former Templar knight who, despite practicing death magic in his attempts to bring Darkness into the world, could not seem to avoid doing good deeds - purely by happy accident and despite his best efforts to the contrary. It had actually been quite popular with many members of the crew.

Triistan came forward with it now, and as Sherp walked by, the oarsman deliberately kept his shoulders square and jostled Triis hard enough to knock the tome loose. Dreysha's eyes slid immediately to Biiko, but the Unbound only watched, his face expressionless. Triistan scooped up the book without a word and continued forward to stand in front of Scow and Voth, both of whom were also watching, though in their cases Dreysha saw quite clearly what each was thinking: the faction lines were beginning to show, particularly after this morning, and their contrasting expressions told the tale of the simmering power struggle developing on board the launch.

She gently dug the tip of the punch dagger into the hole in her skin where the sliver had entered her palm, trying to enlarge it enough to get at the thorn's end, while her thoughts drifted back to earlier that morning.

It was just after Rantham had finished admitting he and another survivor had resorted to cannibalism, when Dreysha and the rest of the crew had fallen into a stunned silence. Voth, who had been aggressively trying to discredit Rantham's story from the beginning, had been the first to collect himself. He scoffed.

"Pathetic, Mister d'yBassi. What - are we supposed to feed on each other like rats?" His gaunt face was mottled with red and purple splotches and whenever he spoke, spittle tended to collect in a small froth at one corner of his cracked lips, as it was doing now. Drey knew if anyone was the direct focus of his attention, it was difficult not to become distracted wondering at what point the spittle would be launched in their direction.

Voth then drew himself up to his full height and looked at each of them.

"May I remind all of you that this is the Sea Kings' Seeker Corps, not some craven band of cutthroats! We took an Oath, to serve the Corps with *honor* until the Sea takes us or our own Fires are lit. We will honor that Oath, as we will honor our dead according to the Corps traditions!" He rounded on Rantham, shoving a long, bony finger in the man's face.

"As for you, Mister d'yBassi, you're a self-confessed thief and murderer, if your story is to be believed - which personally I find preposterous! Rather, I think you're nothing more than a frightened liar who enjoys making more of himself than the pathetically disappointing truth!"

Rantham's expression had darkened. "My story is true, sir, and I have nothing to gain by its telling other than to try and warn you, to warn all of us, what we're facing. You heard what Triis said - how long it's going to t-"

But Voth had heard enough. "What I heard was a young topman, a *line spider*, making navigational and logistics guesses best left to trained officers, of which I happen to be, Mister d'yBassi! Now, enough of this madness. The Ministry will receive my full report of your dissension and insubordination when we return - and we WILL return, I promise you all - at which time I can assure you, Mister d'yBassi, you can look forward to a complete investigation into your ridiculous claims.

"Perhaps you can also look forward to a Reformative Scrubbing to rid you of such horrible memories," he'd added mockingly. "Mister Scow, return these men to their stations and prepare the bodies for the Releasing Ceremony."

At their feet, Sherp groaned and began to stir. Biiko had still been kneeling beside him and helped the dazed Valheim struggle to a sitting position. Voth wasn't a complete imbecile, Dreysha thought, remembering the gleam that had crept into his eyes as he made a show of inspecting Sherp's mangled nose.

"See that the oarsman comes to speak with me when he is capable of standing on his own." With that, the ex-purser had spun on his heel and stalked off to the other end of the launch. She had no doubt he would try to take advantage of this little incident and win the embittered crewmember over to his side.

The others had looked to Scow, ostensibly waiting for his orders, but in truth wondering what he would do. As Dreysha watched Mung prepare the plank and chest for Triistan to place Braeghan's book in, she reflected on that moment, feeling that they were balanced much as Mung's plank was now, but rather than some boy's remains hovering precipitously over the dark water, it was their lives - *her* life - hanging in the balance.

The Mattock had stood quietly for several moments. She could imagine the wheels of his mind turning and feel the tension of his inner turmoil radiating from the way he stood at the time, though the only visible sign had been the rhythmic bunching of his jaw muscle. Finally he had looked at each of them in turn, and when she met his eyes, she knew that duty had won, at least for that moment. Mutiny was just not in the man's nature.

Scow issued his orders, and as the crew took to their tasks, she told herself that it had been a close thing, all the same. There was still time, and for all she knew Voth might be right about Triistan's estimates, though she did not believe that anymore than she believed what he had said about Rantham's story. She'd been through enough interrogations - on both sides - to recognize a lie when she heard one, and at the very least, Rantham certainly believed what he'd told them. No, the good Captain Voth was the problem. He was going to get them all killed at some point unless something was done about it.

She smiled as she finally exposed enough of the sliver to catch it between her broken fingernails and draw it from her palm. As she held it up for inspection, Triistan cleared his throat nervously and began his eulogy.

"Braeghan was a good lad, a good mate, and a good friend. Where most ship's boys tend to never be around when you need them, and stuck to your boots when you don't, he seemed to have this... this uncanny knack for timing, always showing up precisely when you needed him." He shook his head, unable to hold back a smile. "Wish I could say the same about his jokes though..." That provoked a few chuckles. Braeghan's jokes were so notoriously innocent and simplistic that even the most seasoned, salt-encrusted sailors onboard the *Peregrine* found it hard not to grin. Triistan seemed to relax a little bit, though he still looked like he'd swallowed a bucket of bilge water.

"As a junior apprentice cooper, he wasn't much to most people, but I count myself fortunate to have known him. I know he was only a boy - he saw his twelfth year just before we left Aarden - but sometimes he'd surprise you with... with a wisdom that was beyond his age. Like the way he saw people - he didn't just look at them like most of us do. I think we tend to see people the way they've been drawn for us by someone else, or even the way they may have drawn themselves, but we don't really *see* them, see their whole picture the way Braegs did..."

Now isn't that interesting... is that what you were up to, Triis? Trying to see me for who I really am? Be careful where you go sniffing around, little mouse.

Dreysha remembered the first substantial glimpse she'd had of his journal, just a few days before the storm had swept in and capsized the *Peregrine*. She had seen him scribbling away in the book countless times, though typically he tried to be very discreet - usually retiring to a rig-tit or some other out-of-the-way corner where no one could steal a look over his shoulder. This time he'd found a similar spot atop a folded bolt of spare sailcloth, his back against a low stack of crates near the stern. Scow had sent her aloft to install some chaffing gear in a few spots where lines had begun to wear, and after working awhile she found herself perched on a spar that was directly over Triistan's head. Partially hidden in the sheets, she had a reasonably good view of the open book whenever he drew back to inspect what he was working on, and when she got her first clear look at his subject, she gasped quietly and nearly fell from her perch.

It was a rendering of her. He was working on a close-up of her face, dark hair pulled back over one ear and head turned slightly so that she seemed to be looking just past the viewer. On the opposite page he had written in large, bold letters, as if he'd gone over them several times: "Everything is possible. What you think of as impossible is only what you do not know."

The quality and detail of the portrait were stunning.

She remembered being captivated, filled with a sense of both flattery and suspicion, not to mention a healthy dose of genuine admiration for his talent. At that moment he seemed to be focused on her eyes, shading and highlighting with his graphite stick as if it were a paintbrush. His movements were deft and sure, much like the way he moved through the ship's rigging...and nothing like the awkward way he handled himself when dealing directly with her, she mused. His memory must be quite keen as well, since she was sure that she had never sat across from him for any length of time, holding a pose like he had captured so realistically here. He was creating it purely from memory and imagination - no wonder Captain Vaelysia had insisted he join them on the Aarden expedition. His talents made him an invaluable tool for relaying their discoveries back to the High Chancellor and the King's Council... or anyone else who might be interested in them.

Dreysha had watched him work for a long time, until her arms began to tingle and she thought herself in danger of losing her grip. She was loath to break the spell, but a more practical voice inside - her professional voice, she called it - had reminded her of who she was and why she was there.

She had a job to do.

The *Peregrine's* crew knew her only as Dreysha, but in the streets of Mylesia, she was called by many names: Cat's-paw, The Red Smile, Veheg's Daughter, and Widowmaker, among others. In the gilded halls of most governments, she was known as well, but under a different name, and believed to be something else entirely.

To her handler, and to the few people who truly knew her, she was Tresha l'Sonjaro; thief, assassin, spy, freelance merc - "Whatever the job required" - as she was fond of saying. So what if the boy was infatuated with her? She could play lover as well, and in the right circumstances, she might even enjoy it.

She put that thought aside as Triistan finished his eulogy and held out a small flask of seal-oil, slowly pouring the contents over the book and chest as he led the others in the Oath:

"To sail beyond the Wind, to find that which has been Lost, and illuminate the Darkness with the torch of Discovery."

As he spoke, he used a taper to transfer a small flame from a watchlamp they had lit for this purpose to the chest with Braeghan's book inside, where it caught immediately. The Crone was nearly touching the far horizon now, and two-thirds of the sky had faded to a luminescent cobalt blue, as if the heavens themselves were aglow with Veheg's Fire. The sea stretched away in all directions, empty and ominous in its vastness and its secrets, deadly but beautiful, brushed by pink and gold to the west, and blending into dark infinity to the east. Several early stars had appeared in that direction, beckoning them homeward.

Watching Triistan now, she supposed calling him a boy wasn't really accurate, though she couldn't help thinking of him that way. He had only seen nineteen years to her twenty-six, and his shyness sometimes made him seem even younger, or perhaps her own experiences left her feeling as if she'd lived half again as long. He certainly had a man's body: the physical demands of his life in the rigging had carved it with lean, taught muscles stretched over a rangy frame. He stood a full head taller than her, with long, reddish brown hair that sun and salt had streaked with platinum, and the telltale bronze skin and bright green eyes of an Islander that had her thinking these... circumstances... could certainly be worse.

The seal oil in the watchlamps tended to burn with a greenish tinge, and as the flames enveloped Braeghan's chest, the glow was much more visible in the fading light than it had been when Voth had dumped Captain Fjord's remains over the side. Additionally, in contrast to Voth's hasty, mechanical approach to the final steps of the Releasing Ceremony, Triistan seemed determined to ensure that both the chest and the book were burning well before he completed the ritual. Several long moments passed before he finally spoke in a rough whisper.

"Fair winds, Braegs. Burn brightly wherever you go."

Tears ran freely down his cheeks as he nodded to Mung. The echoman slid the plank out, then began tipping his end up slowly, perhaps hoping to lower Braeghan's remains gently into the water. But the launch's taffrail was a full eight feet above the sea, and as the far end of the plank dipped perhaps a hands-breadth past the level, the burning chest slid free. It hit the water with a soft hiss and splash, but with only the book inside, it did not completely submerge. Instead, it bobbed along, sputtering and hissing, but burning fiercely nonetheless.

The crew watched for a few moments, and she supposed some were thinking it a good sign that the chest had not yet sunk and the flames refused to be extinguished. She knew the ink and the thick pages of the book Triis had chosen were extremely flammable, but she did not begrudge them their maritime superstitions. They might even be useful to her at some point. From her perspective, though, omens and curses, fate and the will of the gods held little sway. She couldn't think of a single instance where she had benefitted from divine intervention, and generally assumed that had they still been around, she doubted that the Arys would have had any specific interest in her activities anyway. This was a fact she was thankful for when she thought about it; after all, they had managed to destroy themselves and a good portion of the world at the same time.

There were other entities she needed to be concerned with. They were mortal, yes, but dangerous, powerful mortals who'd hired her to do a job. A job that wasn't working out quite the way anyone had expected. She reflected back on the conversation with her handler, Marquesso d'Yano, when he'd offered her the work.

For nearly eight years, d'Yano had been a reliable, reasonably straightforward contact between Dreysha and the cartel currently calling itself (laughably, in her opinion) "The Mylesian Citizens Concern". She had done many, many jobs for him, and the scope and terms had always been clear, accurate, and generous. They also varied wildly; assassinations, kidnapping, smuggling, document theft or forgery, the occasional rescue operation, and actual spying - listening in on key conversations or meetings, observing and recording troop or trader movements, shipping schedules, and the like. She'd even been hired to follow individuals and note where they went and who they met with. The jobs could be anywhere, and with such a diverse repertoire, it kept a naturally curious and extremely resourceful girl busy and always on her toes.

d'Yano kept a private (and expensive) room on the fifth floor of the Den of Dark Delights, a brothel with a well-earned reputation for discretion in a city where stealing secrets was an addiction. The building was a massive, rambling stone structure with a sweeping tile-covered roof that overshot its walls by a full wagon's length. Fat timber braces supported the cavernous eaves, each of which bore the likeness of a nude woman, carved and painted in exquisite detail, writhing sensuously on each brace like the figureheads on many of the ships moored in the nearby harbor. The Den loomed over the dozens of other buildings of nearly every size and shape that leaned and staggered along the busy quay, like a petulant giant squatting down amidst a crowd of drunken revelers.

Whenever d'Yano had a job for Dreysha, he would light one or more of the colorful lanterns that hung in the large window of his apartment. Known throughout the city as "love lamps", they were made of all shades of colored glass and could be seen in many a bedroom window. It was customary to light them when the rooms' occupants were engaged in amorous activities, for in Mylesia, whose people were deeply passionate about most things, such activities were meant to be celebrated, not hidden.

Not surprisingly, dYano hated them, thinking that the whole practice was boastful and tacky, which told Dreysha that he was most likely not a native Mylesian. But who was? Mylesia was the world's stew-pot. The self-proclaimed Knaves' Haven drew its denizens from the furthest reaches of Ruine, from every walk of life. Dreysha herself had originally been born in Argonne and had been told once that she was a tribe-daughter of The First, the three nomadic tribes that ruled over the sweeping plains. That was just an old tale as far as she was concerned, though, something that had happened to someone else. Her only memories were of her life in Mylesia, which, in her mind, made her Mylesian.

Regardless, the lamps made for a useful tell if d'Yano had something of interest for her, and so one evening in late summer, like any of the myriad moths drawn to one of the lamps, she drifted in from the night, landing whisper-soft on the small balcony adjacent to his room. She could see him through the window, seated in a heavy leather and oak chair with his feet propped on a matching ottoman. A small fire burned in the hearth across from him, the only other source of light in the room. He had a thick book lying open, face down on his lap, and was in the process of rubbing his eyes when she slipped a flat metal pick into the keyhole of the terrace doors. The lock sprung with a soft, satisfying "click" and she slipped in on cat's paws.

"Good evening, my Little Diplomat," he said, still rubbing his eyes with long, gloved fingers. At least, she assumed he was rubbing his eyes. As always, he wore a heavy cowl that hid his face completely. She had never seen his face, nor he hers, thanks to the Rotter's Hood and beggar's robes she typically wore during these meetings. The Hood was a worm-eaten, filthy hemp sack with two holes cut out for eyes. It stunk and made her head itch, but it was a convenient disguise, since it completely concealed her identity while warning others to stay well away from her or risk contracting the disease. Few would approach a Rotter, except perhaps the godsdamned Dark Devout, the doomsaying gutter priests who could not resist such pitiful charity cases - or easy converts, Dreysha thought cynically.

She had swept her gaze around the room habitually, noting the shadow-shrouded corners, larger pieces of furniture, and door locations, of which there were two; one led to the bed chamber and one to the hallway outside. Both were closed. Satisfied, she sauntered across the room, trailing one hand lightly across d'Yano's shoulders as she slipped by him to settle on a rather stiff divan set perpendicular to his chair and closer to the fire.

"Hello, Grandfather," she purred. d'Yano had always called her his "Little Diplomat", and she called him "Grandfather"; in part to needle him for patronizing her and in part because there was something elegant and paternal about his speech and the way he carried himself. She knew she was letting her imagination fill in the gaps around what he allowed her to know, but the slight tremor in his hands and in the timbre of his voice seemed legitimate. In truth, though, she could not recall if she'd first noticed those traits before or after giving him the elderly moniker - an oversight she constantly berated herself over. Either way, she wasn't naive enough to believe they might not be deliberate - just like his derisive comments about the love lamps - intended to paint a portrait of himself that did not reveal the artist. Ultimately it made little real difference to her. So long as he treated her fairly and honestly, and continued to feed her well, she didn't care if he'd seen twenty or two hundred years, except perhaps that the younger he was, the longer he might be around to send her work.

He chuckled softly, and she thought the rheumy sound of that laugh was authentic and would have been hard to feign. "You're late. An old man needs his rest, and it has been two days since I lit those ridiculous lamps."

"I wanted to be certain you were finished with that lovely little Minethian I saw leaving earlier, Grandfather. Surely you must have slept at some point? She looked rather... energetic, for your refined tastes, anyway."

He laughed again and closed the book, setting it on a low table to his left, beside a curiously-shaped bottle and an empty wine goblet. He took up both and poured himself a glass of dark, purplish liquid. He knew better than to offer her any.

"Sophilia is as sweet as she is... energetic, but she is a poor conversationalist. And as for sleep," he nodded his cowled head in her direction and she caught the glint of firelight from his eyes, "I find it next to impossible with all of the cats prowling around this place."

She reached over to place another log on the fire, then picked up a bronze poker to stir the coals. The handle was made of brass and cast in the likeness of a woman's body, while the opposite end was a soot-covered, admirably straight and hard phallus. The warmth of the fire had felt good; it had been an unusually cool, damp night outside, and she vividly remembered stretching languorously before reclining on the divan, completely unaware of the hole she was about to fall into.

"You have work for me?"

"Indeed. How do you feel about a nice, relaxing cruise to the Shattered Isles?"

At the time, she had felt pretty damn good about it. Her last job had been a fairly high-profile target, and worse yet, an old acquaintance of hers. It would be good to disappear for awhile. She didn't say that, of course; d'Yano knew nothing of the job as far as she knew and she preferred to keep it that way. Instead, she yawned and pretended to be mildly curious.

He explained that someone had taken an interest in the Sea Kings' surveying efforts around the Isles, and was looking to place a resourceful, competent "observer" on board one of their mappers. Her job was to be fairly simple; keep track of where they sailed and if they made any significant discoveries, and if the opportunity presented itself, copy any charts she could get her hands on. Although she had never taken this kind of job before, she was aware that they were fairly commonplace, especially where the Sea Kings were concerned. As Ruine's foremost naval power, they were constantly pushing back the unknown edges of the world. Frankly, she tended to avoid these jobs because they sounded incredibly dull to her and typically didn't pay very well. Besides, the Shattered Isles were impenetrable, their jagged shores and volcanic islands as dangerous a place to sail as any she'd ever witnessed. Even the Kingsbane avoided them.

When she pointed this out to d'Yano, he became subdued, gazing at his wine goblet. He sat silently for several long moments, while Dreysha listened to the crackle of the fire and the faint cries of someone sampling the Den's dark delights.

The silence stretched long enough for her to wonder if he'd nodded off. "Grandfather? What is it? Surely you knew that already?"

"That did occur to me, Tresha." He spoke slowly, choosing his words carefully, as one might choose where to place their feet when creeping across a loosely-tiled roof. "While the work appears to be... routine - I have already checked with my contacts at both the Ministry and within the Seeker Corps and all of the information the client provided is accurate - it is the client that concerns me."

"How so?"

"They are unknown to me. Someone very influential, and very wealthy. And someone with sufficient resources and... diplomatic talent... to persuade the Citizens Concern to offer me three times my normal rate and to insist that we work with the Client through anonymous channels. I ignored that requirement, of course, but although I was able to verify everything concerning the mapping mission, I came up empty with respect to our benefactor. Somehow he has successfully eluded my own network of informants... and you know how difficult that should be." She saw the faint gleam of teeth inside his hood.

"There appears to be a new player in The Game, my Little Diplomat. And whoever it may be is being very, very careful."

Dreysha wondered now how d'Yano and the Client would feel about Aarden, and about some of her mates' belief that it was the fabled lost continent, where some god had supposedly been exiled. Could the Client have been searching for it?

If so, it was a remarkably happy coincidence, she thought. The storm that carried the *Peregrine* so far off course could not have been predicted, and she had seen all of the charts and even a copy of the captain's orders; their exclusive mission was to chart the Shattered Isles - there was no mention or mark on a map indicating the belief or suspicion of Aarden's existence. Besides, there were any number of legitimate reasons to keep track of the Sea Kings' exploration; since Ehronfall, they had risen first from the ashes and had become the largest, most powerful kingdom on Ruine. As such they had their fair share of sycophantic countries begging their favor, one or two staunch allies of their own choosing, and many, many enemies.

But why pay so much? d'Yano's network was famously expensive as it was; to offer him three times those rates and insist on remaining anonymous bespoke more than an interest in updating charts and coastal surveys.

With the Releasing Ceremony concluded, Voth gave the command to get underway. Under The Mattock's shrewd eye, Dreysha and Triis soon had their two sails trimmed and full. Braeghan's tiny pyre slid away behind them, still burning fitfully, though only the frame of the lid was still visible above the waterline. As Rantham played out the log-line to gauge their speed, she sought out a relatively comfortable niche she had discovered near the stern, hunkered down, and tried to get some sleep before her watch began at moonrise. Her mind was not ready for rest, however.

She had to get her hands on that journal again, but she would need to be extremely careful. Biiko was clearly keeping an eye on the boy, even back then before the storm, and he always seemed to be hovering about on those few opportunities she had to approach Triistan. For his part, Triis was being very cautious with it, and the only other opportunity she'd had thus far had come just a few days ago - the day of the ridgeback attack, actually. He had been napping across from her and had become agitated, rolling over and murmuring in his sleep. His journal had slipped free of his sash and lay on the bottom of the boat, not two meters away from her.

She had looked carefully around the launch at the rest of the crew, but they all appeared to be either occupied or sleeping. It was a chance she had to take, so, moving slowly, she reached out and carefully lifted it from the bottom of the boat, holding her breath as the long flap on its protective pouch rustled open. Triistan had muttered something sleepily and rolled over, but did not wake.

She did not know how much time she would have, so she thumbed through most of it right there, scanning several written passages but focusing primarily on the illustrations. The book was thick, and it appeared that he had been writing in it for years, so much of what she saw initially were drawings and descriptions of all manner of things, from random people to odd-looking tools. Some were done in intricate detail as her portrait had been, and others sketched and scribbled, though these were usually ten to twelve versions of the same object viewed from different angles, all on the same page, the vast majority of the space between them filled with arrows and tiny, precise notes. She read through one collection of sketches of a capstan and realized that he had disassembled it in his mind and was examining each part, noting how it fit and what its function was, whether or not it was necessary, and finally how it could be improved. She estimated that there were well over a hundred of these dissections, from weapons to ships to animals to common objects like a lantern. There were a few portraits of other crew members, and most were only moderately-detailed sketches, but the expressions were so realistic that each time she came across one, she paused for a moment to admire it. Scow, Vaelysia, Tarq, Braeghan and Longeye were there, the last making her think self-consciously about her boots.

And then she discovered The Hold.

At least that was the name Triis had initially given it, written in heavy, dark strokes along the margin of a two-page spread depicting a highly-detailed drawing of what looked to be ruins. As with most of the pictures she'd seen, he had worked primarily with small blocky sticks of graphite, but in this instance he had also somehow added color, albeit in limited fashion. Hulking, dark stonework, emblazoned with arcane symbols from a language she had never seen before, framed the picture to either side. They were overgrown with a haphazard maze of twisting brown and green vines, some of which had forced their way into mortar joints between the huge slabs and moved them laterally, toppling some and leaving others perched precariously.

The rendering's perspective was looking between these two structures at a courtyard of sorts, ringed by tall black statues that resembled the colossal one they had seen guarding the entrance to Aarden, though each was of a different figure. She gave them scant notice, however, as her eye had been immediately drawn to the center of the courtyard, the floor of which was a long oval of some type of mirror-smooth, black material that looked like water or highly-polished black steel. Massive chains were affixed to thick metal rings set in the gleaming floor and ran in contorted paths over its surface, towards the center. Whatever they had been affixed to at the other end was destroyed; great chunks of a strange, translucent crystal material lay around the center, and in a few occasions, the pieces actually seemed to be floating a few meters above the oval's surface. She could see where two of the heavy chains actually ran through the crystal pieces on the ground and ended in broken manacles. Triis had drawn someone standing inside one of the manacles - it looked like First Mate Tarq. He stood with feet together, and the dark metal collar completely encircled his legs, wide enough to reach his knees.

The rendering was so well done and its subject so intriguing, unlike anything she had ever seen before, that she had felt herself drawn into it. Feeling foolish, she had reached out and touched it with her fingertips, idly tracing the serpentine vines that appeared to be dragging down the alien ruins before her very eyes. The effect was mesmerizing.

When Triistan had suddenly cried aloud and kicked her, she had nearly shat herself, but recovered quickly enough to distract him and toss the journal, unnoticed, to the small pile of his belongings next to where he had been laying. That was the day they had found Mung, Braeghan and Captain Fjord, the day of the ridgeback attack. With all that had gone on since then, she had not had another chance to try for it again.

Patience, Drey. It's not like he has anywhere to run to, she told herself. For some reason, that made her think about Captain Vaelysia and Tarq and the rest of the crew who had remained in Aarden to establish a colony. When she had first seen the drawing of the ruins, it hadn't really meant anything to her. In fact, it was so fantastical looking she had initially assumed it to be merely the product of an overactive imagination. But after hearing Triistan's story, and the way some of the others had reacted - particularly Jode - she couldn't help but wonder what the expedition had really discovered, and what those who had stayed behind might be facing.

They didn't have anywhere to run to, either.

- 9 -

Factions

Dreysha wasted little time trying to steal Triistan's journal. She decided to try a direct approach first to find out just how far she could push him, as well as to lay the groundwork for more subtle, long-term efforts. She hadn't met a man yet whose cock didn't influence his counsel.

To help the survivors move past the Releasing Ceremony and tension of the previous day, Scow set up a regular work schedule. The launch may have only been fourteen yards from stem to stern with a six-yard beam, but as far as he was concerned, it might as well have been the five-decked man-of-war that served as the Seeker Flagship. Dreysha could not conceive how there could possibly be enough work to do around such a small vessel that it could fill up a two-day schedule, but apparently the Mattock had no trouble doing so. The day after the Ceremony found her teamed with Triis again to man the 'billy' - the nickname the crew had given to Triistan's bilge pumping apparatus.

This particular duty was as much about morale as it was maintenance, she thought. Despite their continued efforts to shore up the battered launch, they were still taking on enough water to require bailing twice a day. With no oakum or tar onboard, there were some joints that time would eventually take care of, as the wood swelled and the hull tightened of its own accord, but some would never cease to weep. And water in the boot wasn't just uncomfortable, it was a constant reminder that, little by little, they were sinking.

Scow had assigned the second pumping shift of each day to Triistan and Dreysha, so in the heat of the late afternoon suns, Triistan stripped off his shirt and set it and his journal aside while they worked. Dreysha watched him wrestle the pump out of its storage locker, not bothering to disguise either her gaze or the look of admiration on her face as she watched him. Though he tried to hide it, she had caught a furtive glance or two and knew he was aware of her attention. It was difficult to tell with his sunburned skin, but she thought his cheeks and the tips of his ears might have flushed a deeper shade.

"By the dancing Dark, can it get any hotter?" she groaned and removed her own stained and sweat-soaked blouse. Beneath it she wore only a taenia, a narrow, tight-fitting linen wrap that criss-crossed over her breasts, looped across the back of her neck, and wrapped once around her waist. The breeze brushed her damp skin with cool fingers, raising tiny bumps on her back and arms, and causing her nipples to stiffen beneath the soft cloth. She closed her eyes and tipped her face up toward the suns.

"Mmm, much better." When she opened her eyes again she found Triistan staring at her, mouth half-open. *Excellent.* She flashed him a glowing smile and glanced down.

"Are you ready for some help with that?"

"Help? Wha-" His eyes suddenly grew wide and he looked down as well, wondering perhaps if the lightweight fabric of his trousers had betrayed him. Her laughter in response was genuine.

"Your other pump, Titch - the billy."The look on his face made her laugh again. She knew at that moment that work or not, she was going to enjoy this; perhaps even enough to forget the impossible circumstances they were in, at least for a little while.

"Oh - yes... yes, of course. Here - you can take the discharge tubing again," he held out one of the lengths of criedewood and she bit off another suggestive remark; she had the opening she needed and it was time to go to work. As she stepped forward to take the tubes from him, she deliberately kicked his shirt, knocking the journal loose. It came to rest near the edge of the murky pool of bilge water and he lunged for it, but she was quicker.

"That was close - sorry, Titch," she said as she scooped it up and opened it in one smooth motion. "What is it about this book that's so-"

"Ho there, give it here!" he cried anxiously and tried to snatch it from her. She took a step back and held the journal behind her.

"Easy, mate. I just wanted to have a little look is all."

"Well you can't - it's private, alright? Give it back, now!" He stepped forward and tried to reach around her. She smiled coyly, keeping her feet in place but bending back some, drawing him closer. She tsked playfully.

"Where are your courtesies, Titch? Can't a girl show a little interest in your work without you goin' by the boards?"

He glowered in response. "I'm serious, Drey. Give it back-"

He reached around her again, quick as a snake, catching her by the wrist this time. His grip was strong, but she had him exactly where she wanted him. She stumbled backwards just a moment too late, pulling him into her, trying to pull them both down.

Unfortunately, all of the time he'd spent living aloft as a topman foiled her ruse - falling was not something he did easily. He shifted one foot forward and held her, preventing them both from tumbling in a heap on the deck, but it wasn't a total loss. Their bodies had come together and rather than pull away, she swung one arm up over his shoulders and clung to him as if trying not to fall, arching her back and pressing against him in the process for good measure.

She heard his breath catch and they both froze, suspended. His face was so close that loose strands of hair from his sailor's knot brushed her cheek. For an instant, two or three heartbeats at most, she saw the protective veil lift from behind his eyes, felt him actually seeing her for the first time... and then it was gone and he was pulling her upright and turning her so that he could snatch the journal. He looked around the boat self-consciously and stepped away, shoving the book into the back of his topman's sash before crouching beside the pump to assemble it.

"I'll thank you to leave my things alone," he said gruffly. "And stop calling me 'Titch'. I'm no monkey."

She swallowed the lump in her throat and tried to look chastised. "Sorry, Ti- Triis. Don't mean nothing by it. Anyway if I can't look at it, maybe you could read one of your poems to me...?" She let her voice trail up hopefully as she squatted across from him and began piecing the criedewood tubes together. Without looking up from his work, he muttered, "Maybe. I'll think about it."

Well, she thought, that was that. Her test was informative, if mildly disappointing - she wasn't used to being rejected so easily, especially when she knew a mark was interested in her. But at least now it was clear that her instincts about the journal's importance were correct; his reaction went beyond mere shyness and embarrassment - he was protecting something. Based on the discussion they'd had the night Jode died, it seemed obvious to her now that the Aarden Expedition thought they had discovered something called the Exile's Hold.

The implications were overwhelming: such a discovery would literally change the world. Triistan's drawing of the ruins and broken chains rose up in her mind like a prophecy. What had been imprisoned there? She only knew snatches of the story, but could it have really been an exiled god? It seemed ludicrous to think a god could be contained by chains, no matter how large the links and manacles, but if not a god, then... what? And what had happened to it?

The more she considered it, the deeper her need became to see what else Triistan's journal contained. But how to get her hands on it with sufficient time to read it? If they had still been aboard the *Peregrine* or in port somewhere, she could have continued pressing him physically, perhaps even romantically, but under these circumstances, she knew it was only going to get more difficult. The tension among the crew was palpable, they were weeks if not months from home, and they were slowly starving to death.

Her stomach twisted, growling ominously at the reminder. *The fallen still have something left to give.* She found that she was glad they had gone through with the Ceremony and destroyed the bodies. She was hungry and tired, but not that desperate. Not yet. She was obviously not looking forward to the slow, painful decay Rantham had described, but it wouldn't be the first time she had been tortured. What Dreysha truly dreaded was the moment when the journal's contents and her assignment would no longer have any meaning, when she was too sick to care anymore. At that point, she thought, the dead might indeed have something more to offer than a pair of good boots.

For the next nine days, the gods, or fate, or the ruthless chaos of simple chance, continued to stoke the hot coals of their crucible. Scow kept them as busy as he could to help pass the time, but their poor diet and the effects of constant exposure were beginning to wear them down. She could see the skin beginning to sag on the other crew members as they lost weight, and they had a haunted, shadowed look around their eyes that reminded her of a Rotter child she had once glimpsed without his hood. Any exposed skin blistered and peeled from the constant sun, despite their best efforts to stay beneath the makeshift awnings they had hung from spare sail-cloth, and Sherp had lost one of his front teeth to go with his mangled nose. She thought one of the larger ones in the back of her own mouth felt loose and was constantly worrying it with her tongue.

Despite their pathetic rations, their food was running out. The first jar of pickled herring they opened had a broken seal and salt water had mixed in with the pickling fluid: the fish reeked of corpse-flesh when they opened it, sending Mung to the rail for another round of dry retching. Their ongoing efforts at fishing continued to prove fruitless, and the gods-damned titch monkey never left his roost at the top of the mainmast, at least while they were awake. Mung was the only one it apparently trusted, but even he was unable to coax it into a snare they'd made for it (which Mung was altogether too obviously happy about in her opinion). Biiko tried a harpoon shot, but the angle was bad and the monkey too quick. Voth was forced to reduce their already meager food rations down yet further, and the tiny morsels they received twice a day seemed worse than nothing - just enough to twist their guts with unsatisfied cravings. Dreysha took what little comfort she could in the notion that the fucking titch would starve to death soon and fall from his bloody perch right into a buttered skillet... not that they had a skillet.

The water situation was a trifle better, but still tenuous at best. It had rained only once so far, allowing them to collect a modest amount from the sails and the handful of small containers they had collected for that purpose. Voth had taken to marking the level of water on the outside of the scuttle they had fished from the wreckage of Fjord's Folly, which had been two-thirds full when they found it. The mark he'd made the morning of the sixth day looked to be just below the metal band encircling the barrel's waist: less than half, plus the other full barrel. The amount of rain water they collected and poured back into it may have moved the mark two fingers higher, but it was difficult to tell.

As she had expected, there weren't any opportunities to push things physically with Triistan, but she did continue trying to build some kind of friendship with him through casual conversation and by carefully navigating the increasingly turbulent political waters. Sherp was clearly Voth's man, now - whatever Lanky Lankham had said to him or promised him in the aftermath of his scuffle with Biiko had finished the job his brother's death had started. He only spoke directly to Voth, and said nothing to the rest of the crew but for the occasional sullen "Aye, sir" in response to a direct order from Scow. He avoided Biiko, but his hatred for Triis only seemed to deepen. Sometimes she would catch the Valheim staring at him, eyes full of murder. If the Unbound wasn't on board, she had no doubt that Triis would be dead by now.

So Biiko and Triistan formed the core of a separate faction, directly opposed to Sherp and Voth. Dreysha still hadn't figured out why the mysterious warrior was protecting Triis, but that was irrelevant. Whether it had something to do with his Kattha, or because Captain Vaelysia had charged him with guarding the topman and his journal - or it was due to something else altogether - she had come to the conclusion that her best chance at both survival and completing the job lay with them. It wasn't a decision she had made lightly, though. In fact despite her distaste for Voth, she had to consider that there was a chance that with Sherp's help and a surprise attack, they could overpower Biiko and Triistan, giving her what she really wanted: his journal. But convincing Voth seemed an unfavorable gamble at best and there was no way to determine what would happen afterwards.

And what about Mung, Rantham and Scow? Mung and Triis seemed to have become friends, though she didn't expect the self-professed coward to fight on either side until it had already been decided. She had expected Rantham to align himself with Triis, but since being chastised and humiliated for his tale about cannibalism, he had grown increasingly quiet and remote; a shadow of the swaggering rake he had been. He followed orders, but his actions were listless, and whereas before he would be the first to call out for a game of bones or a song to pass their idle time, now he spent almost all of it sleeping or staring out at the sea. Still, she thought that if it came down to bare steel and blood, Dreysha could not imagine him standing up for Voth.

Scow was another matter entirely, however, and really the key to everyone's survival. Without his experience and leadership, she doubted very much that they would ever make landfall. Unfortunately, he was as stubborn as the tide, and she knew that his real mistress wasn't the *Peregrine* - it was duty.

The Mattock was a career Seeker from stem to stern, and while she could see the signs of his bridling beneath a clearly inferior officer, she had not seen any indication that he would betray that duty. She knew that he had a strong affection for Triis, but if there were an outright mutiny, she honestly could not say which side he would choose. Ultimately that is what decided her to take Triistan's side: they needed Scow if they were going to survive another six or seven weeks at sea, and without a legitimate reason to attack Triistan, she thought he would oppose them, and the bloodshed would not stop with Triis. While Voth pranced about like he was the High Chancellor himself, the crew on both sides still looked to Scow and followed his example. If things deteriorated further, his side - whichever side that was - would have the greatest chance of coming out on top.

She was surprised at the level of relief she felt reaching her decision to back Triistan, but told herself she was just being practical.

She also found it curious that as conditions grew worse, her desire to read his journal only grew stronger. Initially she had feared that the overwhelming distraction of their situation would render the journal and the job irrelevant. Instead, getting her hands on his book became an obsession. Every waking moment found her watching him and imagining some new set of circumstances that would allow her to steal it. She had to keep reminding herself that, as she had watched Sherp, Biiko was most likely watching her. She must remain discreet, but that was steadily becoming more difficult: the image of whatever they had found in Aarden was an itch lodged deep inside her head that desperately needed scratching.

On the ninth day following the Releasing Ceremony and their eighteenth since the *Peregrine* capsized, Dreysha finally got the opportunity to scratch it.

"Foul weather on the way, Captain!" Mung's voice broke in mid-sentence.

"Where away, Echoman?" Scow answered from their makeshift helm. Voth was slumped nearby, dozing, and awoke with a start.

"Port aft, sir! She's... she's scudding in hard sir and will likely overtake us by the Crone's Watch." The Crone's Watch was the four-hour period from mess to the setting of the second sun at the end of the long evening.

Scudding in hard...? Scow must have had the same reaction, given the withering look he shot at Mung, a look he had honed to perfection over the years. "By the Dark's blind bollocks those are clouds you're talking about, not a fleet of warships. Now step lively, Mr. Azimuth, and prepare the containers."

"Yes - I mean aye aye, Cap- uh... Sir!"

While Mung's grasp of the mariner's vocabulary might still need working on, his forecast proved to be accurate. A small but furious storm swept down on them from the northwest, lashing the boat and its crew with wind and rain and the merciless pitch and roll of angry seas, from dusk until dawn, when it finally rumbled off into the gathering day. Thanks to the echo-man's warning, they had been prepared for it, though. It was a long, grueling night, but little damage was ultimately done and, since they had lashed everything down including themselves, nothing was lost. In fact, another two fingers' worth of water was added to the water barrel.

But the best possible news came after the water was measured. Scow convinced Voth to stand the crew down for the rest of the day, maintaining a "one-eyed watch", which meant only one person on lookout duty per four-hour shift. Seeing her chance at last, Dreysha volunteered to take the first watch and the rest of the crew were too exhausted to protest. She knew Triis typically kept his journal tucked into his topman's sash at the small of his back, but she'd picked enough pockets in her day to feel confident he'd be too tired to notice if she wiggled all the way into his breeches to get it. *Now there's an idea - let's see him reject that offer...*

She shook her head to clear her thoughts and moved to a spot on the boat relatively close to him, being careful to look casual. She noted where Biiko bunked down and placed herself on Triistan's opposite side, making a show of checking the forestays and belaying pins where she eventually wanted to sit so that the Unbound and the others would choose different spots. Once everyone had settled in, she moved quietly about the ship for another hour, waiting to be sure everyone had fallen asleep. She thought it would also help her stay awake, though she soon discovered that, with her quarry so close at last, she was full of too much nervous energy for sleep now anyway.

When she could finally stand it no longer, she crept back beside Triistan, listening intently to the gentle breathing and soft snores coming from both he and Biiko. Triis was sleeping on his back, but that wasn't really an issue, especially on a boat, and a leaky one besides. She went to the center of the launch and crouched in the boot, then cupped her hands together and filled them with bilge water. On cats' paws, she stole back to his side, extended her hands past his shoulder, and slowly began to let the water seep from them so that it ran down the planking behind and beneath his prostate form. After only a moment his breathing changed and he grumbled something, then rolled over onto his side. A half-dozen heartbeats later, his breathing resumed the slow, steady rhythm of slumber.

Child's play, my little Titch.

She was about to reach for the book but paused, her outstretched hand nearly touching it. It was early morning, and only The Maiden had risen. The Copper Crone was still abed and the departing storm was retreating across the sea, dragging its sullen cloak of clouds behind it. The light was a soft, pale orange, just now rising above the taffrail and picking out the red-gold tangle of Triistan's hair, the line of his cheek and jaw, and the base of his neck where she could see the slow pulse of his lifeblood. She was suddenly conscious of her punch dagger in its resting place inside her boot, pressing against the side of her leg, and wondered how it would change the equation if she killed him now.

Her eyes flicked to Biiko, who lay nearby on his side, facing them, his features barely visible in the shadows. She remembered how he had suddenly looked at her during the Releasing Ceremony, as if he could hear her thoughts, and repressed a shudder. His eyes were closed - she thought she could see that much - and his shoulder and side rose and fell in long, slow breaths. It was entirely possible that he was only pretending to be asleep, but if so it seemed unusual that he would have let her approach this closely. She doubted that even one of the Unbound was quick enough to prevent her from opening Triis' throat if she wanted to.

That was the real question, wasn't it? And what then? The rest of the crew would not ignore the murder, and some - like Voth - would likely call for blood justice and execute her on the spot. There mustn't be any evidence, and since slitting his throat would leave a mess, throwing him over the side afterwards wasn't an option - even if she could muscle him up and over the rail. She could strangle him with one of the laces in her boots, but the mark on his neck would likely be obvious, and what's more he would awaken and struggle. She thought she could probably still kill him, but Biiko was too close to risk him kicking and thrashing about. What she really needed was poison, but she'd lost her supplies during the wreck.

Or someone to blame it on, she thought. She could kill Triistan and plant the blade on Sherp, but that wasn't without risk either. She would have to use her dagger, which by now everyone on board had seen in her possession, and making it look like Sherp did it wasn't nearly as simple as it sounded, or so she told herself.

She tipped her head slightly and studied Triistan's sleeping form. Her hand drifted slowly towards his head, almost as if it were moving of its own volition, until it brushed the thick snarl of hair that made up his sailor's knot. She took some between her thumb and first two fingers, feeling the strands without really knowing why. She wondered what it might feel like to-

Her instincts flared suddenly and she pulled her hand back, looking around the boat. No one had moved; they were all fast asleep where they had been just a moment ago. A sound, perhaps? Had Biiko's breathing changed? She glanced at him again, and the light had grown sufficiently to see his face clearly now. His eyes were shut and his breathing seemed normal. She shook her head and chastised herself. If he was awake, she'd be dead by now. *You're getting sloppy, Drey. Take what you came for and do the job.*

She fished the book from Triistan's sash in one deft, smooth motion, froze for twenty heartbeats to listen for any change in his breathing, and then stole away to a secluded corner near the bow to claim her prize. Had she turned to look back, she might have seen the glimmer of Biiko's half-open eyes as the leading edge of the Crone broke the horizon.

- 10 -

Land of Secrets

Gods, what have we done?

Dreysha stared hard at the words on the last page of Triistan's journal. A tiny shiver of anticipation crawled up her back and across her dry, sun-and-salt-scratched skin. The rest of the crew slept soundly, worn-out by the previous day's storm and taking full advantage of the one-eyed watch Voth and Scow had called. Based on their exhausted condition, she should have a few hours to look through the book - provided she could remain awake herself.

At the rate her heart was beating, she didn't think that would be a problem.

She flipped from the last page to the middle of the journal, stopping on a drawing of an exotic tree, its most prominent feature a writhing nest of thick, snake-like roots curling around the lower third of the trunk and spreading out in all directions at its base. A "Citadel Tree" they had named it. For scale, Triistan had drawn the figure of a man standing under an arch formed by one of the roots. Above them, the trunk in the sketch ran branchless to the top edge of the page, but she knew from experience that it ran that way for fifty yards or so, straight and smooth, before the first of several sprawling, flat limbs began. They grew straight out from the massive trunks like so many huge hands held out, palms facing up, branches splayed out like fingers, alternating from one side of the tree to the other. High above their heads, green-and-gold leaves would have shimmered in the suns above and beyond their sight.

She had seen two of these incredible trees guarding the mouth of the river valley on Aarden where they had made landfall, mighty pillars reaching through the dark canopy above, while below their intricate root systems swallowed up all other undergrowth for a twenty- to thirty-yard diameter around the base. In some cases, thick, woody vines dropped from the canopy and attached themselves to the citadel trees' roots to create a chaotic, many-layered web or fence around their bases. For the most part, though, the giants provided oases of clear space in the otherwise dense jungle undergrowth. She had heard from the survivors of the expedition that there were more of them further inland, particularly once you left the river valley and found higher ground.

She knew she must be in the right section of the journal, but needed to find the beginning of Triistan's entries on Aarden, so she turned back several more pages, past numerous scribblings and sketches of all manner of flowers, strange insects, plants, trees, and bizarre beasts. Some of them looked particularly horrific to her, and as she stopped to flip back to some kind of giant dark-skinned lizard, she landed on another detailed illustration that covered two pages and caught her breath in her throat.

Five dugouts were in the foreground, drawn up on a grassy shore and laden with supplies. Leading away towards the center of the rendering, the banks of the river were roughly sketched, thick with overhanging foliage that seemed to reach out over the water to either side, like outstretched hands waiting for the boats to dare their passage. The river itself ran fairly straight and calm until it met with the foot of a massive stone structure that instantly reminded her of the ruins she had seen him draw before, as well as the huge warrior guarding the lagoon. It was some type of barbican extending from one end of the narrow river canyon to the other, towering well above the canopy based on Triistan's rendering - the rolling indistinct mass of shadows and half-sketched trees depicting the jungle ran hard up against the wall, stretching random tendrils up its sides, but unable to reach the crenellated battlements above. The river ran through a huge arch in the wall's mid-point, where its surface bubbled and frothed over and around the wreckage of broken gates; their shattered, twisted remains thrust up from the water like the jagged bone fragments of the Young Gods. That portion of the illustration was drawn in considerable detail, so that it became the central focus of the picture.

She turned to the following page and read the entry that began there:

Tenday, Vehnya, 256, 7th Day of the Expedition, 30th Since Landfall:

This most magnificent sight greeted us at dawn this morning. Previously our horizon was so close you could reach out and touch it, what with the clutching undergrowth I have already described and the close banks along this meandering stretch of the river. Consequently we have known little of what lay ahead, though as I've already noted, the Captain and Mister Tarq warned us to expect things like this.

We made camp late last night on a sandy shoal that thrust out into the water, around which the river bent its bewildering path, but at least from here it appears to run true for awhile. The bar was relatively clear of undergrowth and covered by that tough, bluish grass that is so prevalent here - a much better alternative to the rocks and roots we've been sleeping on since leaving the main camp. By the way, jharrls or no, I've resigned myself to sleeping on the ground for the rest of this expedition - the night before last I slung my hammock in a tree on the edge of our campsite, and woke cocooned by what must have been some type of large spider, though we never saw it. Oddly (and fortunately), it had not bitten me. After a good laugh once everyone knew I wasn't harmed, we theorized that it must wrap its prey in this way to preserve it for later...

Dreysha shuddered and turned back several pages, until she found his first journal entry after making landfall on Aarden.

Ten and Five, Tendres, 256 - LANDFALL!

I am as bone weary as I have ever been, even during the tempest that nearly sent us all into the Dark, but yet I find I cannot sleep until I have given an outlet to my crowded thoughts. After finding the bay and the Sentinel yesterday (so the crew has named the magnificent statue illustrated previously), Captain Vaelysia found a decent berth not far to the north-northeast of the falls. Mister Scow organized a party of climbers from the topmen and named me as one of them! Several men from the pit had some lewd things to say about me running off with a titch monkey if they let me off of the boat, but I don't care. The fools completely missed the point that I would be one of the FIRST to set foot on an unknown, previously undiscovered island!

There were five of us: Scaab, Lestin, Myles, Donner, and I. By the time we had gathered our pitons, grapplers and ropes and were ready to begin, it was just after the mid-day meal (which we abstained from under the circumstances). The first hour or so was fairly routine; there was a slight slope running away from us and plenty of small handholds and ledges to get a toe onto. At one point we even had a shallow channel in the rock to follow for fifteen or twenty yards, right to the lip of the ledge just behind the statue's knees. From there, the going became very slow, and the slight incline reversed itself (although fortunately it stayed fairly shallow). Enough to feel the weight of the rope and equipment, though.

It took us four more hours to reach the top of the falls and the mouth of the river valley, all the while making our way laterally as well as vertically, and climbing alongside the most incredible thing I've ever seen. The Sentinel was impressive when viewed from the Peregrine's deck, but clinging to the cliffside only a few yards away from legs as big as bastions was overwhelming and almost killed us all. Donner's as good a line spider as any of us, and without a doubt the strongest, so we put him last to anchor the line. But he became distracted and missed a handhold and slipped, and if Myles hadn't just tied off to the next piton he might have dragged us all to our deaths. He didn't though, and the five of us finished the rest of the climb without further incident.

When we scrambled up into the mouth of the river valley, we were dumbstruck. I will try to describe it here, and perhaps later will have a chance to sketch it.

The floor of the valley is of equal height to the giant's waist, it is at most a league across here at the mouth, and its sides run fairly sheer up to the level of the statue's broad paldrons. The falls themselves are relatively narrow here at the edge, perhaps only five or six yards wide, but further up and back, the river is at least twelve yards across. Over time, the water seems to have cut a deeper notch into the lip of the valley floor and funnels into this channel, shooting out and over the cliff in a great flume before tumbling to the waters of the bay below. It does not quite reach the back of the Sentinel, but nevertheless the mist it creates constantly soaks him, so that the stone on this side is skinned with slick, green moss. Plants, vines and roots spill over the valley's edge in a kind of "greenfall" that copies the river. It was not so thick as it appears to be further inland, fortunately, so we were able to climb through and over it, finally reaching a wide clearing where the river has spread out to either side and formed a good-sized pond perhaps as wide as the Peregrine is long, and running away from us, narrowing as it goes, for five or six hundred yards. The vista of the river valley stretching out before us was inspiring, its nearest edges gleaming gold in the evening light and its heart lost in gathering darkness.

A note was scribbled into the margin alongside this particular paragraph, and Dreysha rotated the journal so that she could read it. "If only we had known the real Darkness that lay ahead, I should have turned back then." She glanced over towards where Triistan lay sleeping, but she did not have a clear line of sight to him. She turned the book back to an upright position and continued reading.

The jungle is a thick, tangled thing crouching to either side, but towards the end of this elongated pond there are two magnificent trees standing on opposite banks, like the pillars of a gate leading to the jungle beyond. We have never seen their like before, but they would do well as towers, lacking only a curtain wall between them. I will have to study them in daylight and draw one of them here as they are truly remarkable!

Indeed much of the plant life here seems quite foreign to what we have seen before along the coasts of Nyah, and I suspect the wildlife will be as well. It is certainly vibrant! While the clearing we found ourselves in was quiet, the canopy and watercourse beyond was (is! It is perhaps even noisier now at night!) alive with screams and cries both familiar and alien. We could see the flash and flicker of brightly-colored birds moving along the edges of the jungle, and a hearty few returned to the clearing after having left it upon our ascent. Some heavy, three-toed creature left its prints in the sandy shore, and Myles, one of the Peregrine's Scouts, told us it had been there within the hour. Somewhere off to our east and (we hoped) fairly far away we heard a heavy crash and roar, but nothing challenged us directly.

As wondrous and promising as the new world before us, the view behind us was equally strange and unsettling. Looking out at the bay, with the Peregrine gently rocking far below, the vista is dominated by the upper torso of the Sentinel. What civilization could have constructed such a thing? The stone is completely foreign to me, though Mister Tarq said it could be mined from the Burning Sea immediately surrounding Sigel's Wrath - something to do with the earthfire that boils from the ground there he claims. When I asked him about the strange armor and weapon, and the bone-like material they were carved from, he told me he had better things to do than teach history lessons.

Despite the uneasy feeling the Sentinel gives the crew, the view from our tiny foothold is still stunning, to be sure. The bay we crept through in the morning fog is actually a large, three-sided bowl, open to the north-west where we entered, and through which we can glimpse the two tall spires of rock we passed just beyond its entrance. Like this river valley, the bay's sides are sheer cliffs, almost as if both were carved out of Aarden's coast. The eastern edge is much higher - the land there seems to rise towards some low mountains north and east of us, but the bay's western edge is still quite high - several hundred yards above the water, anyway. The Peregrine looks like a toy when viewed from up here, and the Sentinel and his fearsome warcat appear ready to crush it.

It was difficult to remember our duty, but eventually we set to rigging block and pulley, creating a crude derrick (here his writing was interrupted by a detailed sketch of the derrick accompanied by tiny notes alongside), and got to work hauling up our mates and supplies. The captain and Whip worked us hard, but nobody complained - everyone was glad to get their boots muddy on solid ground again. It took until moonset, but eventually we were able to get all hands up with enough gear to establish a very rough camp. The clear weather and warm southern night air allowed us to sleep out in the open, or we would have been forced to remain on the ship until first light - by the time we finished hauling everyone and everything up, no one had the energy to erect a single tent. All in all it was an impressive effort, and considering the distance of the climb, our off-duty list is brief. Nyth and Lansten both broke their legs when one of the lines snapped and a weapons crate landed on them, but Hiigens, the ship's Master Physic, says that they were clean breaks and he should not have to amp- (illegible).

I just fell asleep while writing this, so I will close this passage with a final note: Captain Vaelysia chose the name I mentioned earlier - "Aarden" - which I'm told means "Land of Secrets" in the language of the Young Gods. Looking forward to discovering some of those secrets tomorrow, and incredibly grateful I did not pull watch duty.

As she reached the end of the passage, Dreysha paused for a moment, looking about and listening for sounds that the crew were stirring, but she might as well have been completely alone; the low, lazy creak and sigh of the ship's breath and the soft slap of the water along their hull were the only noises she heard. She suddenly longed to hear a bird's cry, remembering how they had all complained bitterly about the cacophony in those first few days in Aarden. Indeed, the clamor of war had seemed sweeter then than the incessant tweets, screams, hoots, howls, warbles and whistles that assailed them day and night from the surrounding jungle. Now, staring at the empty, endless ocean around her, the lonely silence took on a whole new meaning.

Turning her attention back to her prize, she quickly scanned the next several entries regarding the establishment of their base camp, which someone had named "Falcon's Roost" - a bit of vanity too clever by half in her mind. Triis had made a fairly detailed drawing of the camp, which they had established on the northern shore of the pond.

That first week was spent clearing away the strange vegetation, erecting tents, and digging latrine ditches and fire pits. It was a blur of blisters, sore muscles, cuts, scrapes, strange skin rashes, insect bites (three fatal) and deep, dreamless sleep. But by the tenth day from Landfall, Falcon's Roost was an orderly encampment complete with a huge cooking pit and commons at its center, around which their tents had been placed in concentric rings. Its borders were protected to the north by the valley wall; to the northwest by the sheer cliff dropping to where the *Peregrine* was moored below; to the west and south by water; and to the east by a broad earthen rampart they had constructed and fortified with a nasty skin of sharpened stakes set into its outer slope. The top of the rampart was wide enough for three men to walk abreast, and since it was set inside the ditch left by their excavations, it stood twice as high for an attacker as it did for the defenders: it was a full twenty feet from the bottom of the ditch to the top of the fortification.

They left a narrow causeway between the pond and the southernmost point of the ditch, but made a shallow cut across its top to allow the water to overflow into the ditch, thereby creating a moat. They built wooden ramps to cross over the moat by lashing tree trunks together and attaching long lines to the far ends so that these could be hauled back into the encampment if necessary; when they were drawn in, the only direct way in and out of the camp was across the causeway or by boat. Eventually, they had constructed a palisade as well, but only after they'd had a chance to scout the surrounding countryside and determined that this was the best location for a more permanent camp - almost a month after Triistan and the others had left on their expedition.

Dreysha studied the drawing of the encampment - more of a map really, as though she were seeing it from above. She had to concede that its organization was impressive, though that shouldn't have come as a surprise; as with everything else, Seeker Protocol had standard operating procedures for building encampments in remote, potentially hostile locations, and she had no doubt that "Falcon's Roost" had been built exactly to those specifications. Their final touch was to erect one of the spare masts near the central fire-pit, from which they flew two impressive-looking standards: the seven golden crowns on a field of blue that served as the Sea Kings' sigil, and below that, the new ship's standard Hobbs the sailmaker had sewn to replace their colors, which had been lost during the storm. It was a detailed depiction of a screaming falcon poised to strike, wings and talons outstretched, on a white triangular flag trimmed with a brocade border of interlaced blue and gold. The falcon's head was an excellent facsimile of the

Peregrine's figurehead, and Triistan had included a detailed drawing of the standard fluttering over the camp, a brave white flash against the ominous shadow of the Sentinel in the background.

This was all familiar to her, though, so she skimmed through the rest of these passages, just to be sure she hadn't missed anything unusual. She was looking for what the Captain had told Triistan and the other members of the expedition when they were assigned to it, since Vaelysia and Tarq seemed to know much more about what they had discovered than anyone else, and Dreysha wanted to know how and why.

The next few entries were fairly mundane, however. Once the work on the camp was done, they had turned their attention to hunting and foraging. Scow took control of the foraging efforts, with the main focus on obtaining sufficient timber to refit the *Peregrine*, and it wasn't long after that they had discovered thick stands of criedewood growing along the far shore. Dreysha came to a number of pages covered in sketches, arrows and scribbled notes and couldn't help but smile when she recognized the billy - this must have been when Triis had invented it, and from reading some of his notes, Longeye must have helped him. "Sha'ni" he called her; short for her full Khaliilic name, Lang'quokasha'ni. Dreysha stretched her legs out in front of her and crossed her ankles. She frowned as she looked down at her calves and feet, wondering how close the two of them had been and whether she had misjudged the true cost of her new boots.

There was a frenetic quality to these pages that she hadn't seen in some of the other illustrations, as if he were rushed... no, that wasn't right. Obsessed would be more accurate. Many of the drawings had been gone over repeatedly, their lines scratchy and dark, and every empty space had been filled with notes, many in the form of a question and written over and over the way some of the drawings had been. She realized with a small thrill that she was catching a glimpse of his mind - his thought process - and wished she had more time to study it.

She still had a job to do, though, so she turned more pages, until one entry caught her eye:

Why me??

Captain Vaelysia and Mister Tarq have just left my tent, after first asking Mung to leave (I've given up trying to use his true name, as he seems to prefer the crew's version) then demanding to see my journal (which they seem to have been quite impressed with), and finally informing me that I have been assigned to the expedition preparing to explore the island's interior. Apparently, we'll be traveling upriver, and she has already ordered Mister Scow to prepare six dugouts for the journey. I am to be prepared to depart in four days' time. When I asked (respectfully, of course) what my role would be, a strange look passed between them before Mister Tarq stated that there may be some portage required and they were bringing two topmen with them to assist in those cases.

It seems clear that this was only partially true, at best - but it matters not. The chance to see more of this incredible land puts all other worries in perspective- the next four days are going to take forever!

I wonder who else will be going? Braeghan? Biiko? Apparently not Mung.

Dreysha??

She smiled to herself - the slow, secret smile of someone who has discovered something they shouldn't know - a feeling with which she was intimately familiar, and the one aspect of her profession which she never tired of.

No, my little Titch, she thought. *They did not invite me to your party. Be a good boy and tell me all about it...*

The next few passages were just distracted ramblings; he was obviously excited about the pending expedition, and he was writing in the journal more as an outlet for that nervous energy. She forced herself to scan through them, though, looking for any additional conversations with the Captain or Tarq. Aside from a fairly in-depth account of their Landfall Feast, the only thing of interest was an entry discussing the billy - "bilge pumping apparatus" he called it - and presenting it to Scow, who was predictably stoic. Clearly he'd thought enough of the invention to have it stored onboard the launch, however, for which Dreysha was very thankful. But what caught her eye was the date of that entry, because she thought it was the day before the Expedition left camp, and the next page in Triistan's journal confirmed it.

Fourday, Vehnya, 256, 1st day of the Expedition, 24th since Landfall:

And so it begins. Supplies have been laid in and the 6 dug-outs await us on the shore of what we're now calling Long Pond. They look to be sturdy things, and knowing that the Mattock oversaw their construction gives me comfort. This is the first time I have seen the entire Expedition assembled, and I think we are a capable, versatile group. There are 20 of us, and I shall list everyone here for history's sake, for surely this is a historic moment we will all look back on one day for its significance.

Captain Vaelysia - Second Officer Fjord has been left in command of the camp. He is a very capable officer.

First Mate, Tarq'nilonqua-hi (Mister Tarq) - I am surprised they are both going; further confirming my suspicions that there is more to this expedition than simple exploration.

Reaver, Firstblade Tchicatta - Commander of the Peregrine's Reavers, I'm not surprised to see him here with the Captain and Whip going. A fierce, brooding warrior with the unquestioning loyalty of his men and long years of faithful service to the Captain.

Reaver, Jaspins - One of Tchicatta's more promising recruits and, more importantly, Hiigens' very capable Medical Assistant.

Reaver, Miikha - A dour soul, but highly proficient with his bow.

Reaver, Creugar - A huge warrior from the central Sea King Isle of Chatuuku, known for his skill with axes - throwing, hand, and the giant battleaxe he wears strapped to his back. I have to note here that he also has an impressive singing voice (revealed at the Landfall Feast to everyone's surprise).

Reaver, Taelyia - Minethian; sturdy and dependable.

Scout, Myles - An excellent climber and topman, he is also a highly skilled tracker and hunter.

Scout, Wrael - A hunter and carpenter's apprentice, but not one of Scow's best men - we could have done better.

Triistan went on to list all twenty members in a similar fashion, and Dreysha could find nothing extraordinary about the people who were named, except for his last two entries:

Specialist, Biiko - While I have yet to understand the mysterious warrior's interest in my well-being, it is hard to imagine a more worthy or useful addition to our party.

Specialist, Triistan - Although Mister Tarq said I was chosen to facilitate our portages, I believe my real purpose will be to record our findings (though Jaspins is a more-than-capable archivist - I have seen the illustrations and notes in her medical journals and greatly admire her talent).

The Captain has delivered her final orders to Commander Fjord; everyone is saying their good-byes and I must do the same, then off to Find That Which Has Been Lost...

Dreysha remembered that day very clearly. Triistan's last line captured the mood perfectly - it had been such an optimistic, exciting moment, the Seeker's Oath in its purest form. Unfortunately for her, she had not been included in the final list despite requesting the assignment directly from the Ship's Whip himself. The way he had studied her before asking, and his refusal, had made her wonder if her true intentions and identity had been discovered.

Nothing had ever come of it, though, and ultimately she considered herself fortunate that she had not gone. The survivors who eventually made it back to camp had been strangely mute about what they had discovered. In retrospect, haunted might have been a better word, though at the time she had assumed they were all suffering from shock and exhaustion. Their losses had been horrific; twenty men and women had left on the expedition, and only six had made it back. They faulted all manner of hazards, from poisonous insects and plants to ferocious beasts, and made absolutely no mention of the ruins she had seen in the journal. According to Triistan, most of their losses had come from a pack of jharrls that had stalked them for several days, primarily striking at night when they were nearly invisible. She wondered if he and the others had made all of that up to conceal the fact that whatever had built the Sentinel and the gate and gods-knew-what-else was still there.

But why the secrecy? Why not let the rest of the crew know? The answers were in here, so she kept reading. The next page was another entry made later on that same day:

Fourday, Vehnya, 256, 1st day of the Expedition, 24th since Landfall (Evening)

Aarden is a name well-suited to this incredible place! Every league that goes by is a marvel of new plants and creatures. The river itself seems to wander aimlessly through the valley, so that our field of view is severely limited. We float suspended between the bend ahead, the curve behind, and the impenetrable jungle to either side, as if the land has drawn a cloak about itself and is slowly, reluctantly revealing its mysteries, glimpse by fleeting glimpse. There are flowers of every conceivable color and shape and size; plants with pale-blue stalks and leaves as large as a man, others with variegated black and red bark and brilliant pink thorns; vines everywhere - suspended from the canopy above, interwoven along the ground, and strangling the trunks of some of the larger trees, covered in pale-green moss or colored it seems to compete with the flowers; criedewood stands whose slender stems knock hollowly against one another when disturbed, creating an odd music; and other trees, some of which (like the trusty stonewoods) we recognize, but most of which I at least have never seen before (though nothing as fantastic as what we've taken to calling "Citadel Trees" - those two giants we sailed between when we left Long Lake).

Even the river guards its secrets well; by day the water below us is so dark it is nearly black, and by night some type of luminescent algae sets it to glowing like liquid moonlight whenever it is disturbed. Some of the mates are trying their luck at fishing, but so far the only catch they've made is a giant slug of some kind, nearly as long as my forearm and exuding some pinkish ooze that left painful blisters on Chelson's palms. There are fish, though; we've seen several break the surface to seize some poor floating insect, and at night dark shadows move through the water - some disturbingly large - but as of yet Myles and Wrael have yet to find a bait that tempts them.

They did manage to snare a large turtle, however, and as I write this my stomach roils at the heady scent of a stew they are preparing. After today's hard paddling, I am so famished I suspect that boiled grass would have the same effect! The current is swifter than it looks - we cannot touch the river bottom with a fully-extended paddle - and each boat of four is forced to keep at least two paddlers active in order to maintain any headway.

We are organized thusly: Captain Vaelysia, Mister Tarq, the Firstblade, and Izenya (the bosun's mate) are in the lead dugout; Chelson, Pendal, Welms and Jaegus in the second; Anthon, Jaegus (the younger), Thinman (who's anything but), and Brehnl the next; our boat is the fourth; and Creugar, Jaspins, Miikha, and Taelyia guard our rear. The sixth boat is being used to hold our extra supplies and is being towed by Commander Tchicatta's Reavers. I do not envy them their task, though Creugar is worth at least two normal men.

I am sharing my dugout with Myles, Wrael, and, of course, Biiko. It has been rather comical watching the two scouts' attempts to get Biiko to speak. Though everyone on board the Peregrine now knows who and what he is, duty schedules have kept both of these men from spending any significant time with him. So, like every other member of the crew to suddenly find themselves sharing a watch or a task with him, they have seized upon the opportunity to try and crack the eggshell of his silence and get to the golden mystery inside. They've a better chance of hatching a matu egg by sitting on it.

I have found over time that he has a very sharp sense of humor - nearly as keen-edged as that of his legendary scowl: when he tires of their barbs and blatherings, he will freeze them with that stare he has, holding it for as long as needed, until their words dry up, their nervous jokes fade into silence, and they eventually look away and make a point of finding something else to do or discuss. While Myles seems to be a clever lad, Wrael is anything but, and it did not take long for Biiko to tire of him this morning. When Wrael looked away, Biiko saw me watching and winked at me, though his expression never changed. He is as much of an enigma as this Land of Secrets is, though whereas Aarden's mystery feels ominous, I find Biiko's presence strangely reassuring. I don't doubt that he is an extremely dangerous person, but I think that danger is carefully channeled, directed, and in some strange way I have come to think of him as a friend.

We estimate that we made three or four leagues today - slow going, to be sure, and the truncated days don't help: dusk comes early due to the encroaching jungle. When we glimpse any sky at all, it is but a narrow ribbon of blue or gray, and then only for a hundred yards at most, before the boughs and vines close over us once more, and the strange glow emanating from the water actually makes it harder to see, the way a campfire makes it harder to penetrate the shadows beyond its glare.

Since there are very few clearings along the river, we were forced to land even earlier in order to clear our own campsite. If there were still gods to thank, I should be letting them know how grateful we are for Creugar and his axes! The other men and women, especially the Firstblade and his Reavers, are strong, hearty mates, but Creugar is unmatched, and the jungle seems to fall away before his sweeping battleaxe like wheat before the farmer's scythe.

Besides the turtle we've also caught a fairly good-sized ape of some kind. It is about twice the size of a titch, and was living (or hiding) in the bole of an old tree with smooth gray bark, gray-green branches and blood-red leaves. As we cleared the undergrowth from around the tree, it shot out of the hole and clambered up the trunk to a position only a few meters above our heads, where it stopped and chattered angrily at us. Miikha and Myles both went for their bows, but Miikha was the quicker and felled it with a single shot through its neck. Myles and Wrael have dressed the kill and are preparing to roast it on a spit even as I write this, though from their bickering I think each would just assume roast the other instead. There is no love between them, and I assume it is because Wrael resents the constant and very specific instructions from Myles. It's too bad, really, as I've had a chance to discover Myles' extraordinary knack for field cooking, and Wrael might learn something. Certainly the rest of us would benefit greatly.

The light is failing quickly now. Commander Tchicatta has created a three-watch rotation throughout the night, with two Reavers and one regular crew member standing sentry in each watch. I have volunteered for the first rotation, since despite my physical exhaustion, I know my mind will not give me peace for several hours yet. I will use the time to observe what I can about this incredible place.

One thing I have already learned is to recognize dusk and dawn by sound; there is an odd quiet that descends at these times. Presumably it is as one "watch" of beasts and birds yields to the other, and some type of code or animal courtesy prevents them from talking over one another. It is a blissfully tranquil moment that lasts less than an hour, when the new watch begins to call out tentatively, first in individual voices, then in pairs or small groups, building one on the next, until they are all in full chorus again. We are entering that moment now - with each passing sentence I inscribe, the quiet descends, though there appears to be a troop of unhappy Gray-Bole Monkeys (so we have named them) intent on ruining this evening's peace. I can recognize the same chattering call as that made by our pending supper, and we have caught glimpses of several of them moving through the canopy above us. Their hair is rust-colored, with a vivid green crest running down the center of their neck and back, rendering them nearly invisible when they move through the gray-bole trees. Wrael tried his luck, but missed three straight shots, so the Firstblade ordered him to stand down and save his arrows.

I hope that they are not vengeful creatures.

Below this last line, Triistan had drawn one of the gray-bole monkeys with his typical skill. She could make out individual hairs, and the creature's narrow, down-turned eyes were so lifelike she expected them to blink. She was familiar with them: while they waited for the Expedition to return, the beasts always seemed to be lurking in the shadows of the jungle canopy surrounding their camp.

She turned the page, then sat up straight, eyes widening as she read the next entry.

Fourday, Vehnya - Later that same night

I have the truth of things at last - or at least that portion which Captain Vaelysia and First Mate Tarq have decided to share with us. It seems that we are on a bit of a treasure-hunting and archeological expedition, one that could lead to substantial rewards and advancement for all of us.

After we had finished our supper, the Captain gathered us round the fire. Incidentally, dinner was - and may yet be - a bit of an ordeal: apparently Wrael deliberately added his own spices and ingredients to the stew, and it was all most of us could do to choke it down. Fortunately, he left the monkey to Myles, and it was delicious, though I'm not sure my insides can tell the difference after the fact.

"Corpsmen, you are poised on the edge of what might be the single greatest discovery of our time," the Captain began. I saw the relaxed, contented expressions most were wearing suddenly become serious, and we all sat up a little straighter. She sat with Mister Tarq on her right, and the Firstblade on her left. Tchicatta's head was bowed as he stared into the battered tin cup I know he keeps in his field kit; it is as much a part of him as the axe and sword dangling from his belt, and some say he'd sooner ride to war without one of his blades than forget that cup. The light from the fire has a way of making stationary objects appear to be moving, but it looked as though he shook his head, ever so slightly.

The Captain then nodded to Mister Tarq, who drew forth a worn leather satchel I noticed slung over his shoulder earlier. It looked like an ordinary map case, but when he removed the cap from one end and upended it, something far from ordinary appeared. It was an ornate scroll-case that looked to be made of whalebone, ringed several places in copper and covered in meticulous carvings - arcane words and symbols that I could not read, though I recognized some of them as the same arxhemical symbols tattooed on our dead during their Releasing Ceremonies. I have never seen its like, nor what came next.

Mister Tarq unsheathed a dakra from his belt and drew the blade across his thumb, then squeezed several drops of blood onto the device, mumbling quietly as he did so. There was a faint hissing sound and a tiny puff of smoke. I may have seen the symbols flash blue for an instant, but in the uncertain firelight I cannot say for sure. Several of us flinched as Mister Tarq uncapped the case and turned it over, but only a rolled up piece of parchment slid out into his waiting hand.

Dreysha felt that chill of anticipation again as she recognized the "device" Triistan had just described. It was an Immolation Case: a specially prepared container designed to explode if the proper counter-formula wasn't used before opening it, incinerating its contents and most likely killing the person holding it. She wondered if it had been customized to Tarq's blood for an additional layer of security, but even if not, it was a clear indication that whatever was inside was extremely valuable. It also suggested that they were not free-lancing this: Immolation Cases were very rare and costly, and setting the trigger was not something your average Ashen could accomplish. If it had been specifically attenuated to Tarq's blood, it narrowed the field even further: only Arxhemists with years of specific mastery could create one as far as she knew. Outside of their damned tower, Drey only knew of one, and he was certainly no friend of the Sea Kings. Regardless, she smirked at Triis's assumption that it was carved from whalebone; if it was a true Immolation Case, the donor was most likely either human or Vanha.

He unrolled the scroll and set it flat on the ground, placing rocks at each corner to hold it in place, as the rest of us leaned in closer for a better look.

It was a chart, but like none I have seen before. A long belt of jagged islands spanned the top of the scroll like a necklace of rotting teeth, and across these the Captain drew her finger, reading the words inscribed there in a tongue I did not know.

"Biithenni-Sigel... Sigel's Bones... what we know as The Shattered Isles."

Of course. Now that she had named them, I recognized the formation, though I was used to seeing them at the bottom of all of the charts I had ever known - they were the southern edge of the world. Before we fell off of it, I suppose.

Across an empty space and far below the Shattered Isles was another land mass. It was difficult to know the scale used, but relative to the Isles, it appeared that this land was nearly as large as Niyah. There appeared to be some questions written in the space between the Shattered Isles and this land mass, but they had been written in the same language as above, so I could not read them, and the Captain did not seem interested in translating them.

"Seekers...this," she pointed to the strange land, "is Aarden."

Several of us gasped or muttered aloud and then began talking all at once. Up until that moment, I think most had assumed we had discovered a large island - one of the Shattered Isles that had been caught in the Godsfall Drift, yet here was our Captain telling us that we had discovered an entire continent! The world the gods had left us had always been a finite, defined space. Yes there were still many islands and large stretches of the coast that remained uncharted, and even entire portions of Niyah that have not yet been explored - or at least recorded... but all of the instruction I have ever received has shown the Shattered Isles at the southernmost tip of Ruine. To sail beyond was to fall off the bottom of the world...

Captain Vaelysia raised her hands to quiet us. Next to her, I saw the Firstblade drain his tin cup, then walk to the river's edge and crouch to wash it out. The Captain's eyes followed him briefly before she continued.

"All of your questions will be answered in time; some by us, and others will be revealed to us as Aarden decides.

"For now, know this: The Sea Kings and the Ministry of Commerce have been seeking this place for decades, and we will be claiming it in their name, as an extension of our kingdom. The purpose of this expedition is to explore as much as we can while the *Peregrine* is being refitted. We have been told to expect more ruins like that of the Sentinel statue, and we will be recording everything we can about these discoveries (here, she looked directly at me) so that we can report our findings to the Ministry upon our return."

"Since we do not have maps to follow, we will pursue this river to its source, or as far along as its course allows. As we do, the land will climb, and hopefully at some point the jungle will recede somewhat and we will be able to get a better look around. We have allowed two full months to reach the source, after which we will turn back whether we've found it or no, returning the way we came. We anticipate that our descent will most likely be at about twice the speed of our ascent, so we should be back here within three months' time.

"You have already seen numerous new species of plants and animals. Assume that there will be more, and that many of them may not be overly pleased to see us. Should we encounter any trouble, I have every confidence that Firstblade Tchicatta and his Reavers will handle it easily. In those situations, you will follow the Firstblade's orders as if they were mine or Mister Tarq's, is that clear?"

A quiet chorus of muttered "Aye, Captain's" followed, and I raised my hand to speak. When she acknowledged me, I had to swallow three times before I could say anything.

"What about the ruins, Captain?" I asked. I thought my implication was obvious, but she didn't seem to grasp my point when she answered.

"I'll speak to you privately in more detail, Topman, but you will be expected to use your talents and record them in detail. Anyone else?" Across the fire, I saw the Firstblade returning, staring at me with a raised eyebrow.

"Yes, ma'am. I would be happy to record everything we see, but what I meant was-" But she wouldn't let me finish.

"Privately, Topman." She said and stared at me the way Mister Scow does when he wants me to stop asking questions. They ended the meeting then and called the first watch, which I am now perhaps a quarter of the way through. The gray-boles have finally gone silent, and everyone else is asleep or talking quietly near the fire. The Captain has not approached me privately yet, so I am left to ponder my unspoken question on my own: who built these ruins?

And where are they now?

"And how the fuck did the Ministry know to expect them?" Dreysha whispered to herself as a rush of excitement raised gooseflesh along her spine. And who had drawn the map showing Aarden to the south of the Shattered Isles? How long had the Sea Kings had this in their possession? Had it truly been "decades" as the Captain had told them? What did the writing he mentioned say?

She drew a deep breath and let it out, slowly. This was often the path her work took: the closer she got to the truth, the more questions must be asked, and each answer only bred more questions. She must stay patient, which was normally not an issue for her, but in this case, she had to rely on someone else to ask the right questions.

All she could do was read on.

- 11 -

Into the Wilds

Casselle was glad to be off of her horse for the day. The riding had been especially hard, even after yesterday when she thought that she'd finally gotten acquainted with it. Today they stopped just short of the Deckoran Wilds, the untamed forest that had stood for hundreds of years as the unofficial border of Gundlaan on the west. Captain Taumber's carefully-planned route brought them to the very edge of the expansive wood, where a simple stone tower stood on a bluff. The Templars tied off their horses to a couple of hitching posts in front.

There was a quick, silent inspection of the building to confirm it was not occupied. Save a few small rats, the tower was clear and empty. A breeze blew a lonely tune through the crumbling mortar joints.

"The Outriders should be keeping these towers in better working order," the Captain said, "but things here have kept them busy, I'm sure. Let's do ourselves a favor and clean up as best we can before settling in."

"I'd barely even call it a tower," Temos declared, "One window on the bottom and a rickety ladder to a tiny roof. I doubt we could hold off a flock of angry sheep here."

"I'm glad you've seen the roof, Pelt, you'll be spending a good deal of time up there," Odegar said, implying that Temos would probably be getting the deep watch later that night. The young Templar groaned slightly while the others snickered in amusement. Odegar divided them into tasks and with a nod, the squad set about their work for the evening.

In the stillness of the long evening, while the dinner fire licked the tiny cooking pots and Temos caught a quick nap before his late watch, Casselle left the shelter of the tower to finish gathering the wood needed to sustain them through the night. Armed with her sword and a small hatchet, as well as a cloak pulled over her armorjack for warmth, she made towards the tree line just beyond them.

A hundred yards or so from the tower, she looked back and caught sight of Jaksen waving from the top of the tower. She waved back. Jaksen looked so small up there, not that the tower looked large, she thought. It certainly gave her perspective to view it like this, the only man-made structure as far as her eyes could see. That wouldn't be disconcerting in itself, but the sudden awareness of how utterly disconnected they were from everything else unsettled her in a way she didn't expect.

She turned and continued to the edge of the woods, her thoughts captured by the vast distance beyond them. Some ten days ride behind them, at a considerable distance from the tiny tower, was the edge of all that was civilized. Regardless, the Elder Circles of Naar Deran, Osterell and Strossen considered this part of Gundlaan now. Before the Ehronfall, before the Wasting consumed Cartishaan, it had simply been an unclaimed approach to Senhaal, the column of Obed the Guardian. But Senhaal was abandoned now, perhaps even ruined, and the land was growing more untamed by the year. The warnings to not travel this far west had died with the Young Gods. Casselle was well acquainted with the rumors that the Elder Circles of Gundlaan were not the only ones sponsoring expeditions to this side of the continent. If there was money to be made, the Tau'riin and the Sea Kings would not rest until they had their cut of it.

But the Fallen Sea was impossible to cross into from the larger Southern Ocean and the routes that would have been used to get to where Cartishaan used to be were no longer traversable. Not to say that it couldn't be done. Casselle knew the best route was either overland or through the Golden Gap, but the Bay of Athoriss was firmly held by the burgeoning Gundlaan Navy, under the direction of the Elder Circle of Osterell.

Gundlaan had a stranglehold on the northern routes to the Deckoran Wilds, but not an exclusive one, which is why expeditions had been sent out to try and claim as much land as far afield as possible, in order to prevent others from doing so.

Casselle knew that any legitimate authority from Gundlaan really stopped leagues back, at the small fishing towns that dared reside on the western side of the Bay. At least they had walls and some measure of security provided by the Templars, the noble-funded Outrider militias, and the merchant marines that had been conscripted into the Gundlaan Navy only just recently.

But those towns were days and leagues away by even the most favorable of measures. Out here, beyond their walls, in the deep of the

Deckoran Wilds, the law of nature ruled. Recalling Crennel's story, she thought it likely something worse was in play as well.

Casselle moved into the edge of the forest proper, taking great care in doing so, now that she and Jaksen had lost sight of one another. She moved cautiously, scanning for proper sized limbs or logs to use as fuel for the fire. There had not been a lot out in the open, certainly not enough to last the night, so she was forced to move deeper into an outlying thicket, looking for dead wood in the branches or near the base of the trees. It was slow going as the long evening started to close, the weak light of the second sun steeping the land around her in deep shadow. She listened to the rising sound of crickets, frogs and other nocturnal animals as they roused for the night.

She tucked her hatchet in her belt and collected the armload of wood she'd scavenged. She'd wandered a bit deeper into the thicket than she'd intended, but the trip would give them enough wood to last until morning if used conservatively. Casselle had her thoughts set on a warm meal and a good sleep, so when the dark form stepped out from around the tree, it caught her wholly off guard.

Her forward motion and his sudden appearance put them uncomfortably close to each other. But when another hand from behind clasped onto her shoulder Casselle emptied her arms, knowing she was already at a disadvantage.

The heavy firewood crashed down on to the feet of the man in front of her. The soft leather boots he'd used so effectively to sneak up on her offered thin protection from the tumbling wood. He tried to avoid it with some quick footwork, but couldn't, and ended up stumbling backwards in the attempt. Casselle was moving as well, lunging forward with her left foot while dropping lower at the same time. She anticipated the hand trying to keep a hold of her cloak, but with her center of balance closer to the ground and some momentum, she easily pulled free and finished toppling the man ahead of her, running over him in the process.

She spun, unsheathing her sword, putting the fallen man between her and the unseen one that had been behind her.

"Taisha's tits, girl! Calm down!" He was much shorter than the man she'd downed, similarly dressed, but not as menacing looking. He pulled back his hood and held up his hands. "Put that thing away before you hurt someone!"

Casselle did not put her sword away, observing that her two assailants were not alone; another hooded figure was a few steps off behind, with a longbow drawn and ready.

"Outriders from Flinderlaas," the talkative one continued, pointing at himself and the one that had scrambled out from underneath Casselle's heavy boots. "I'm Nikk and that's Shayn. I hope you're with the Templars or Aileah is likely to shoot you where you stand."

"I have walked far, but my soul is not tired," said Casselle, hoping the challenge they'd been given was accurate.

"Then you must have good boots or good news." replied Nikk confidently.

Casselle sized them up, noticing that each of them kept their hands close to their hilts, still on edge even after the challenge. Reaching her own conclusion, she slowly eased into a more neutral stance, nodding to Nikk as she did so. As she sheathed her sword, she watched the bow relax and the Outriders' hands stray away from easy reach of their weapons.

Wasting no time, she moved to gather the wood that she had spilled. Even so she was careful to keep an eye out and noted that the Outriders kept a similar watch on her. After an exchange of whispers one of them spoke up.

"So... you need a hand with that? It's a bit of a way over to the tower."

"No," Casselle replied, standing up, the load of wood now properly managed.

"Sorry the tower's a bit of a mess," the other man offered, the one Casselle had knocked down. He had a wild, disconcerting grin. "We was going to fix it up, but we were busy."

She didn't offer a reply, anxious to be back in the company of the other Laegis so that someone else could do the talking. She marched out of the woods much louder than she'd entered, trailing the three Outriders behind her like a string of ducklings.

Casselle already had her eyes on the tower, knowing that Jaksen would be able to see them all at a distance and would warn the others of their approach. By the time the four of them were in the building's shadow, Odegar, Jaksen and Raabel were at the door, hands on hilts. Temos would be above them on the roof, covering with his short bow.

Casselle met Captain Taumber's questioning look and acknowledged that they had met the challenge. He let her pass and stepped forward, while she darted inside to deposit the wood to one side.

"Odegar Taumber," he said, introducing himself. "You come from Flinderlaas?"

"Aye, Sir. Well met. Nikk Bellows," Nikk replied, stepping forward with his hand extended. Odegar returned the gesture and the two shook hands firmly before Nikk finished his introductions. "Behind me are Aileah Blue and Shayn Fletcher." As Cass returned she took the opportunity to get a better look at all three of them.

Shayn seemed less menacing than he had in the forest, the grin on his face more wide than wild, and a gangly looking thing underneath his thick cloak. Nikk was short like Temos, but wide and solid like Raabel. Aileah was the most fascinating to her, with her long braid, cocky smile and lengthy stares at Jaksen, like she was ready to eat him up. Casselle was not sure she liked this, but she knew the Outriders were important to the success of their journey and the mission ahead, so she resolved not to let this first impression ruin the rest of the operation.

Odegar introduced the other Templars before finishing with: "...and you've already met Casselle Milner."

"Not by name, sir, but yes," Nikk confirmed.

"Excellent. Then you should join us for dinner," Odegar offered.

"We certainly wouldn't turn down something warm and tasty to eat," Nikk replied.

"I can only promise dinner will be hot," Odegar said. "Tasty's typically only on the menu when Jaksen cooks."

"Can't be worse than trailbread and jerky," Shayn said.

"Let's assume you're correct, friend," Odegar said confidently.

Casselle let the others enter the tower first. She was still a bit on edge and hoped the night air would cool her off. Aileah also lingered. Before the Templar knew what to make of it, the Outrider drew uncomfortably close to her. She even dared to put an arm around Casselle's shoulder as if they were old friends.

"Between us, you don't look like you have any of those fish on the hook, but I wanted to make sure before I tested the waters out."

"I... no," Casselle confessed, stunned by the woman's aggressive honesty.

"That's great, because I'm fairly fed up with the ones I already have." Aileah chuckled easily, perhaps expecting Casselle to laugh along. "You don't mind, do you?"

"No," Casselle replied coldly.

"Thanks, friend," Aileah said, patting her on the shoulder and then sauntering off to join the others inside the tower. Through the doorway, she watched the Outrider make a point of sitting close to Jaksen by the fire. Nikk was making a broad gesture with his arms and judging from the laughter of those inside, it must have been the punch line to something humorous.

"They seem friendly enough," Temos commented from the roof, leaning over to see as much down below as he could.

Casselle harrumphed in reply and suddenly felt the need to fetch more firewood by herself.

***

"She's awfully grabby," Jaksen confessed. He and Casselle were at the end of the line, trailing a good distance back from the others. She was surprised that Jaksen had actually rebuffed Aileah's advances. "Not that it seems to have bothered Raabel any. But to be that way without invitation is just not proper. Nor am I in a position..."

Casselle looked over at her friend, cocking an eyebrow. Aileah had started slipping away with Raabel almost immediately after the two groups had started travelling together, to rut the time away between long days of travelling and short nights of rest. Casselle wasn't so much as mad at him as she was impressed by his resiliency, and Aileah didn't appear to have any issues in that regard either. She understood the angry stares Nikk and Shayn were giving Raabel, but his indiscretions shouldn't be a concern of Jaksen's.

Though not condoned, there were plenty of Laegis back in Strossen that would spend time in the Pleasure Houses. Raabel having a casual acquaintance with the Outrider shouldn't be that shocking to him.

"I... have someone special back in Strossen," the young man finally confessed. "I know we are Templar and foreswear home and family for the good of the cause, but... I... we..."

It made more sense to her now and Casselle could tell Jaksen was very conflicted. It showed on his face and in the way his hands tightly gripped the reins of his horse.

"I understand," she said, reaching out to touch him lightly on the shoulder. When he turned at her words, she saw his face break into relief and gratitude.

"I figured you might," he replied. He let out a deep sigh. "Thank you."

The group travelled along a path that was cut through the thick of the forest. It was not paved or even well tended, so it was slow going for the horses. Nikk sent his fellow Outriders ahead, the silent scouts occasionally reporting back that the way remained clear. Casselle was beginning to wonder why they even needed the escort. It hampered their progress and though the Outriders were quick at finding secured camping sites for the evening, it did not appear they offered any real sense of security or advantage beyond what the Templars themselves could provide... not that Raabel would agree with her.

Odegar also seemed to enjoy their presence, frequently chatting with Nikk about this bit of nature lore or that. Temos hovered nearby, doubly frustrated that Aileah had put him below Raabel in the pecking order and that Odegar had forgotten his background as a trapper's son.

"I know things, too," Temos had confessed the previous night at dinner. "Just because I took the sword oath it's not like I suddenly forgot what Maidenleaf is used for." Jaksen and Casselle had been greatly amused over the past couple of days by his ruffled grumblings. Ironically, Raabel had actually eased up on him some. Perhaps even he realized that his normal bragging seemed a bit too cruel in light of his recent good fortune.

But as the distance to Flinderlaas shortened, Casselle kept wondering why more wasn't said about the wolves. Certainly the Outriders had been dealing with it for some time and since Odegar had briefed the others before they'd left Felbrank, there was no need for secrecy. Surely, she reasoned, she couldn't be the only one curious. Every step deeper into the Wilds seemed like an excellent reason for one of them to start talking about it, but the topic was avoided altogether, almost as if by design. She couldn't understand that, since the thought of it was like a splinter under her skin that she couldn't pull free. She was continually annoyed that it wasn't the first and only topic of conversation all the time.

Even now she was thinking about it when Jaksen tapped her on the shoulder and pointed towards the front of the group. Ahead of them, Shayn had appeared and was gesturing wildly. Jaksen let Casselle take the lead, the two of them prodding their horses forward to join the others that had stopped in the middle of the road.

"Slow down," Nikk was saying. "You saw smoke?"

"Leah, did, yeah," Shayn replied, breathing heavily. "She went ahead to get a better look."

"Damn it!" Nikk cursed. He tightened his belt and looked over to Odegar, who had been leading his horse as they walked. "Shayn and I will catch up with Aileah and see what's going on. Give us a fair lead and then proceed at a normal pace forward. Hopefully it's just some foresting and we'll meet back up and have a good laugh about it."

The Templar Captain nodded in agreement and watched as the Outriders ran on soft leather soles down the road and into the thick of the Wilds.

"We should be close to Flinderlaas," Temos said, eyeing the deeply canopied road ahead.

"Aye," Raabel agreed. "I was looking forward to a big meal and a bed this evening."

"You mean..." Temos began, obviously ready to needle his fellow Templar.

"I think he means we are all worried about the safety of Flinderlaas and those stationed there," Odegar said sternly. Temos flinched at the rebuff and gave a weak reply.

"Yes, Captain."

"Templar Pelt, have your bow at the ready," Odegar began in a tone that made it clear he expected trouble. "Milner and Furrow will ride ahead of him, Shuute and I will close in behind. That should give our archer some opportunity before melee becomes necessary."

"Yes, Captain!" Temos replied, this time with conviction.

"Plates and caps, brothers and sister," Odegar said, instructing the Templar to don their heavier armor over the more supple armorjacks before they moved ahead.

There was something in his expression that Casselle had not seen before. He hid it well, but it looked to her like fear.

**

Flinderlaas was a well tended fort on a modest hill, surrounded by a small town on three sides and bounded by a lake on the fourth. On that day, under the twin suns' fading light, it actually looked quite beautiful, standing proudly above the tiny thatched roof cottages and the well-tended gardens.

Despite the alarm that had preceded their approach, there was no invading army, no organized force of raiders and no wolves. In fact, it looked surprisingly serene given the tense run they'd made through the woods up to here. Shayn and Aileah had stopped at the forest's edge, waiting for the Templars to catch up, while Nikk had gone ahead to speak with the Outrider commander.

"It looks pleasant," Raabel said with a slight smile to Aileah, who appeared lost in thought. "I guess there wasn't much to worry about after all."

Casselle cuffed him in the back of the head, then used the same hand to direct his attention towards the south side of town.

"They're burning bodies," Jaksen said, looking at the small crowd gathered there, halfway between the edge of Flinderlaas and the start of the forest. As two men threw another swaddled body onto the pyre, Temos shivered visibly.

"Something's very wrong," Aileah said.

Odegar spurred his horse down the hill without bothering to question or comment. Aileah exchanged a look with Niik and Shayne before she and the rest of the group jogged after him.

As they came to the edge of the town proper, Casselle noticed that it was unnaturally quiet, even for the cusp of the long evening. Solemn faced mothers ushered wide-eyed children inside. Weather worn faces sized up the Templars as they approached and spared no friendly exchanges for the Outriders with them.

"I trust it's usually a bit jollier than this?" Raabel asked innocently enough.

"Please shut up!" Aileah snapped, obviously very disturbed by this turn of events. Raabel played the part of the scolded dog while the rest of them continued to take in the view of the village. Casselle noted that it was not a quaint little town like the ones which dotted the countryside around Strossen. Flinderlaas was too well planned. The row of houses and the lay of the paths out and in suggested it was designed well in advance of the settlers' arrival and had been organized to optimize defense for the fort. A few well placed barricades in key places would prevent an easy approach up the hill.

She also noted that even though its design was very much utilitarian in purpose, it was not devoid of beauty. In fact the houses themselves had handcrafted flourishes and there were several places in town that showcased a tiny sculpture or simple shrine to the fallen but not forgotten High Houses.

They stayed a distance from the fire, which had been constructed downwind of the town, thankfully. They watched the last of the wrapped bodies go into the pyre and the handful of men that had attended the duty back away, wiping soot-stained hands and faces. Shayn walked over to one of them and spoke to him in low, somber tones that Casselle could not make out.

Odegar nudged her, drawing her attention to the mixed party of people descending the hill, including Nikk Bellows. Foremost among them was an older man in heavy leathers, with hard features and alert eyes tucked under a furrowed brow. Beside him, straining slightly to hear what Nikk was saying, was a middle-aged man in what must have been a fine looking coat by the standards of Gundlaan's larger cities. Out here in the wilds, the blue and purple panels fastened with gold buttons and the matching hat were merely out of place. A confident young man wearing the livery of a Templar followed behind the group.

"Looks awful young, doesn't he?" Temos said.

"We all did once," Jaksen replied.

"Raabel never did," Temos quipped. "He'd already grown a full beard by his first birthday." Casselle silenced them by crossing her lips with her finger. They nodded and waited for the group to arrive.

"Captain Odegar, this is Commander Stone," Nikk began as they closed to arm's length.

"Royan Stone," growled the leather clad Outrider Commander. "Outriders of the Third Expedition Company. I hope you're the new Templar Captain. The one we got is crazy as a barn cat."

"Perhaps we can talk in private, Commander...?" Odegar began before being quickly cut off.

"I am Hedrek von Darren, and I welcome you to Flinderlaas, Captain... Taumber is it?" Odegar nodded and the man in the blue and purple coat continued in a very loud yet practiced manner. "Welcome to our small community, proud and growing. I'm looking forward to our collaboration together. Perhaps once you..."

"Who are you again?" Odegar asked.

"Hedrek von Darren. I said that already," he remarked, clearly shocked that he had been interrupted.

"I understand, sir, but why are you here with the Commander?"

"Ah! You're new, so you are unaware that it is the von Darrens that funded this expedition and have been granted the land rights by the Elder Circle of Osterell. In a way, I am the Lord of these lands." Casselle couldn't help but notice that Hedrek was talking to Odegar as if he were a small child. She also noticed that the young Templar to his side was grinning smugly as the older man talked.

"Pardon me, brother, but I don't recognize you either," Odegar said, trying to wrest the conversation away from Hedrek.

"Vincen von Darren," the young man said confidently, "squired on the battlefield by Captain Crennel after the loss of his squad. I speak on his behalf for the Templars here."

"Do you now?" Odegar asked, somewhat surprised.

"I do," Vincen replied, quite sure of himself.

"This day has blessed me with many surprises," Odegar said. It was a term he used often when things were either on their way or had already turned to mung. Casselle noticed that Temos bit his lip to keep from laughing.

"Wolves?" she asked, pointing to the bright pyre just outside of town.

"Aye," Commander Stone nodded. "They were out cutting lumber. Only one of the eight made it back alive, and he'll never swing an axe again.

Royan looked at Casselle and her squadmates for a moment before speaking again.

"I'm disappointed not to see more of you. I don't know enough to respect your skills or not, but it doesn't seem like you're enough to turn the tide against them things if even half of what Crennel said was true. Last few weeks... sure seems real enough."

"I agree Commander," said Odegar, "but we are not here to help defend Flinderlaas. We are here to help you evacuate it."

- 12 -

Dreysha's Folly

Dreysha stood and stretched, wincing. It felt as though her entire body was one raw wound; scratched and dry from sea-salt where it wasn't burned, and burned by wind and sun where it hadn't blistered. The rough rasping of her clothes against her skin was a constant torture. Her lips were cracked so badly that whenever she yawned the corner of her mouth split open and bled. Her insides felt twisted, her joints ached, and her eyes constantly felt like they had sand in them. And things were only likely to get worse.

She swore softly and glanced around the boat, but all was still quiet. After reading Triistan's journal for close to an hour, she felt comfortable that she had at least that much longer before anyone was likely to stir. Given their condition, it would likely be even longer than that, but she still had to return the book to its place and did not want to risk discovery. Biiko was sleeping only a pace or two away from Triistan and, though he had been through the same crucible of gradual starvation, exposure, and recent rough weather, he did not seem to be suffering nearly as much for it. She knew enough about the Unbound to know that they were well-acquainted with fasting, and many of their training rituals regularly involved feats of spiritual, mental, and physical endurance. She thought it likely that he would be the first to recover, so half the watch was all she would allow herself.

Both suns were up now, and she could tell that it was going to be a brutally hot day. The sky was a cloudless, endless arch of lapis, with nothing to temper the fierce glare of the light reflecting off of the sea, forcing her to squint and making her head ache.

And not a breath of wind, she thought. What little breeze there had been at dawn had died with the suns' rise, but whether for good or ill she was undecided. *No wind meant no need for a crew to sail the launch, but if the doldrums are setting in, we are as good as dead.*

There was nothing she could do about it, though. Scow had ordered the sails be left unfurled to dry them out, so she found a spot in the shade cast by the mainsail and opened the journal again to where she left off, which she had marked by folding a corner of the page.

Fiveday, Vehnya, 256, The 2nd Day of the Expedition, 25th since Landfall (Mid-day)

It seems the gray-bole monkeys are indeed vengeful - and clever.

This morning we woke to find our supply boat missing. We backtracked downriver, initially thinking it hadn't been tied off properly and may have just drifted some before becoming snagged in all of the undergrowth along the bank. But around the last bend we had navigated the night before, we found partially submerged, broken food crates and other supplies scattered everywhere, either strewn along the bank or dangling from overhanging branches. The dugout was nowhere to be found, and whatever hadn't been smashed or thrown was missing - taken by our assailants or the river we'll never know. We were only able to salvage perhaps half of our supplies.

Along the muddy banks on both sides of the river, Wrael and Myles found tracks that they believe belong to our pesky friends, or at least to another type of ape of roughly the same size. Captain Vaelysia ordered them to conduct a more thorough search of the immediate area. She didn't say it, but I believe we were all thinking the same thing: it is difficult to imagine beasts having the intelligence to do such a thing, but the two scouts found no other trail signs.

The Firstblade questioned each person who had shared the watch, but of course none of us had seen or heard anything. He was clearly frustrated, though he kept his temper in check. While his interrogations were direct, even harsh, he seemed to accept the fact that something or someone had slipped away with the boat during the night, and dragged it out of earshot before ransacking the supplies. With the cacophony of nocturnal noise emitted by the surrounding jungle, they would not have had to go far. We assume that the boat was either overturned and sunk, or carried further downstream. With no other obvious culprits, the Firstblade ordered that no more of the apes should be killed unless he had given the command himself, then asked Wrael how long it would take to build a replacement boat.

As I suspected, we would have been better served with another apprentice - Brehmer or Piasii would have bent themselves to the task eagerly. But Wrael answered in that laconic manner that he has that it would take him a few days without the proper tools. When asked why he hadn't brought a full carpenter's kit with him, he grew sullen and said that he had understood he was there "as a Scout, not a bloody shipwright". Perhaps he thought he could get away with such insolence with the Captain and Mister Tarq both safely out of earshot, but the Firstblade would have none of it.

"I'm not sure why you're here at all, boy. But if you don't check your tone and find a way to make yourself useful, it will be as bait, am I clear?" Wrael was at least smart enough to be cowed. He straightened some from his impudent slouch and nodded.

"Aye, sir. I meant no disrespect." The look he gave the Firstblade after the man turned his back spoke otherwise, though.

It soon became clear that we would have to make do with one less dugout, at least for now. After an hour of searching in vain, Captain Vaelysia ordered us to divvy up the remaining supplies amongst the other boats and we were underway by late morning. There was no sign of the monkeys, and I was pleased to bid farewell to the stand of gray-bole trees when it disappeared around the bend behind us.

The rest of the morning passed swiftly. The rains have returned, though not the deluge we experienced last week in camp, thankfully. The thick canopy of the jungle has a strange delaying effect - it may start pouring on our boats if the section we are in is open to the sky, hammering the surface of the river and making of it an infinite host of watery spikes, but the banks to either side will remain sheltered for several moments before the rain eventually finds its way through the overlapping layers of leaf, branch, vine and bush. Things are never dry of course; the air is thick and cloying, and everything glistens with a perpetual sheen from the humidity. But even so, it is intriguing to listen to the rain coming; a huge sigh descending on us as it works its way down.

The river has narrowed considerably and the current is now much stronger, so we've had some tough pulling for the past hour or so. We're rotating three men in and resting one, and have managed to maintain reasonable progress, but it is hard work. Myles and Wrael have actually found something they can agree on: they both seem to think we may be approaching our first portage based on their read of the river's changing personality.

I am more concerned about the encroaching banks, however; our path ahead has shrunken from twenty yards across to perhaps four or five, and the overhanging growth reduces this unencumbered space even further. We are forced to travel in single-file now, through a dark green tunnel, and I have to confess it feels very vulnerable. The jungle is dense, and those creatures we have seen thus far are striped or spotted or otherwise camouflaged to take full advantage of it: often times we only see them once we've drawn close enough to scare them into flight. Fortunately they have also been shy and unthreatening so far, but none of us are foolish enough to believe there aren't larger predators here which have kept hidden. If any were that naive, the angry roar we have heard twice since we left the Long Lake should cure them of their ignorance. It is very similar to the one we heard upon first entering the valley, and both times came from the southern bank. Wrael thinks it is the same beast, following us.

My rest break is over - will write more later.

Below this last line Triistan had sketched a portrait of Biiko, arms outstretched, paddle in mid-stroke, with the blade of the oar poised just above the water. He had even included a line of tear-drops from the bottom corner of the blade to the river's surface. Legs crossed, back as straight as a spear, the Unbound had stripped off the upper portion of his jiisahn, and the diagonal cross-straps of his twin blades formed a darker "x" against his black skin. Triistan had sketched in the narrow, elegant hilts protruding behind each shoulder, but where he had spent considerable time detailing the area around Biiko, the warrior and his clothing were uncharacteristically vague. She thought back again to the exquisitely detailed drawing Triistan had made of her, and his comment at Braeghan's Releasing - about seeing people for who they really are. The only thing clearly depicted in this drawing of Biiko was the warrior's eyes. Triistan had captured his uniquely-colored irises and their intensity with lifelike precision. It gave her the uncanny sensation that he was looking right at her; that he was coming for her because he knew she had stolen the journal.

She glanced up in alarm, half expecting Biiko to be standing there, but she was still alone. She turned the page to the next entry, which was made the following day.

Sixday, Vehnya, 256, The 3rd Day of the Expedition, 26th since Landfall (Evening)

Myles and Wrael were right; not long after I made yesterday's entry, we began to hear the muffled roar of a waterfall. A short time later, we came to a series of low rock shelves, across which the river ascended (or descended from its point of view). The shelves weren't steep and under normal circumstances would not have been difficult to scale, however they were strewn with fat boulders obstructing the river's passage, creating snags for passing branches and, in a few cases, whole trees. As a result, the shelves were really a series of broken, tangled dams and boulder-strewn pools, effectively impassable for us. We scouted the banks to either side, eventually locating a game trail on the north bank that wound its way up alongside the falls. It looks as though Myles and I will not be required to do any climbing just yet.

The basin at the foot of the cascades was wide and only waist-deep; the last "shelf" in the series of falls, really, since it stays shallow for approximately fifteen yards from their base before the rocky bottom disappears abruptly. Like most of the others, I took the opportunity to bathe quickly in the shallows, keeping well away from the dark line of the deeper water. It is quite curious that such a small body of water can convey as much or more of the same sense of hidden menace as the sea - I would not have believed it if I hadn't experienced it personally. By contrast, the water in the basin is clear and inviting, and there are thousands of tiny minnows nibbling at the roots of plants along its edge. Our aspiring fishermen have been foiled once again, however, since anything bigger than my little finger appears to favor the darker depths downriver. No doubt the minnows have learned the same lesson.

We camped alongside the basin, or rather in it if truth be told. The vegetation was so thick, and the slope so steep to either side that we were unable to find a suitable spot to clear. After the previous night's misadventure with the supply boat, we were loath to leave the dugouts here and camp at the top of the falls, so we simply tied them together and then ran additional lines to some of the sturdier trees on the shoreline. We posted our watchmen at these trees and the rest of us slept in the dugouts. With no fire, we supped on strips of dried lamb and some honeyplant melons. I suppose we should thank the gray-bole monkeys for those; while searching for the boat, we came across a sprawling honeyplant shrub and have harvested fifteen of the fat, succulent fruit.

After an uneventful, rain-soaked night, we spent the entire next day making our portage. Captain Vaelysia sent four men up the trail to widen it as best they could, while the rest of us went to work stowing as much of our supplies as possible in each boat and lashing them down. While that was being done, Mister Tarq created a rope harness for each dugout, allowing a team of four men per boat to slip a loop about their waist or shoulders and drag their craft up the steep incline. It was hard, hot work, and I am not looking forward to more of these along the way. Wrael says that the higher we climb, the harder they will be to traverse as the terrain grows more rugged. At that point, he says, we'll have to carry the supplies up separately rather than in the boats, and make multiple trips. I've noticed he seems to take a perverse glee in delivering unfavorable news.

We were rewarded for our efforts with a veritable feast, though. Myles, Miikha and Wrael managed to bring down a monstrous boar-like animal. It had the same pig-like body, but was nearly three times the size, with a broad head badly misshapen by old wounds. It was missing its right eye and ear, and rather than tusks, it had four long, curved horns protruding from the sides of its head. One of these was cracked and broken and considerably shorter than the other three. Lastly, the beast's right flank was marred by the puckered skin and off-color flesh of scars where something had raked it with its claws. I wondered at the titanic struggle that must have transpired, and whether the boar's opponent had survived. I held my hand up to the scars and spread my fingers, attempting to gauge how large the claw that left them had been, but was unable to match their span.

The meat from our kill was tough, but delicious. Wrael did not attempt to prove himself a cook this time, and even managed a grudging compliment for Myles' skill - adding chunks of the honeyplant melons to the spit and drizzling their juice onto the roasting boar (for lack of a better word) was brilliant!

Indeed, the overall mood of the expedition was very good as we feasted. We were tired, but spirits were high from our accomplishments; the climb and the kill felt like small but important victories over this wild, untamed place. Even the jungle seems to have withdrawn slightly - at the top of the falls, the river widens again and the ground is very rocky, thinning the undergrowth in a large arc along the banks and even allowing in a bit of moonlight. There is a relatively small citadel tree just on the edge of our campsite that must be very young; it is only the size of a stonewood tree, with branches starting a couple of meters off the ground. The limbs grow out so wide and flat that they seemed ideal to hang a rig-tit from and I resolved on the spot to sleep in one tonight - perhaps the bugs won't be nearly as bad as they are on the jungle floor, and I would feel a good deal safer getting up off the ground.

Dreysha couldn't help grinning at the spider he had drawn in the margin alongside this paragraph. "You were almost a meal yourself, Triis," she whispered, though her words were drowned out by the painful contraction of her stomach. She would give anything for a honeyplant melon or a slice of roast pig.

She heard a quiet chattering noise from somewhere above her.

She wondered how roasted monkey would taste with honeyplant. Somehow that damned titch monkey was still alive, still strong and agile enough to keep to the tops where nobody could reach it. Not a day went by that a member of the crew didn't try to entice it down to the deck, or set a snare in case it snuck down on its own during the night. She felt confident that monkey stew would taste even better than roast boar, and wished Triis would stop detailing every meal they ate along the way.

Even the Captain and Mister Tarq shared in our fine humor, and both were more approachable than I have yet seen. Jaegus the Younger challenged Thinman to an eating contest. The challenge alone drew loud guffaws, given that Thinman looks as though he could swallow Jaegus whole. How someone on a Seeker's regiment could accumulate and carry such girth is beyond me, yet he does with apparent ease. His arms and back are among the strongest aboard the Peregrine, and even that blackhearted Valheim Sherp cannot best him in an arm wrestle. Jaegus is a reed by comparison, though he must be a hollow one - never have I seen one man put away so much food so quickly! In the end he won by forfeit, since Thinman attempted to belch but retched instead, filling Wrael's boots in the process (apparently the Scout was having some blister issues and had removed them to rest his sore feet). That of course set everyone to laughing (well, everyone but Wrael anyway), and Thinman the worst of all, to the point of retching all over again. He made good on it, though, rinsing the boots out in the river. I thought it was a fine gesture, but judging from the sour expression on Wrael's face, I don't think he agreed.

Some of the other lads began boasting of past adventures, goading each other on in good-natured competition to see who could spin the most outrageous yarn. As each tale grew taller, the voices and laughter grew louder, until the campsite rang with a din that all but drowned out the surrounding jungle's clamor.

Only the Reavers refused to share in our revelry; Commander Tchicatta placed three of his men at watch about the camp, and he and Jaspins brooded quietly next to a small watch fire they've built adjacent to our dugouts. He seemed restless, periodically getting up and visiting his sentries, prowling about the edge of the camp like a stalking jharrl. I wondered whether he was concerned about what unwanted visitors we might attract with our merrymaking, or if he was just intent on ensuring that whatever had stolen our dugout did not have another chance. I didn't have to wonder for long before I had my answer.

From the dark, tangled mass of jungle on the far bank came the roar we have heard thrice before, but much closer this time. The laughter and shouting broke off abruptly and a few of us stood to look across the river, holding our hands to either side of our eyes to try and shield them from the glare of the campfires. Oddly, Biiko quietly crossed the camp to the opposite side, where the Firstblade stood, looking off into the jungle in the other direction. He stood rigidly, head tilted, listening...

I noticed at that moment that the jungle had also gone eerily quiet. We waited for several long, tense moments, the low rush and murmur of the river passing over the falls below us the only sound. I found myself wishing it would cease, so that we might better listen for approaching footsteps, or the crash and thud of something large moving through the undergrowth.

Then suddenly a second roar came from the north - from our side of the river. This one sounded farther away, but also deeper and more ferocious.

We all jumped at it, and most snatched up their weapons. I saw Jaspins rise quietly and draw her kilij, the well-oiled steel of the Reaver's signature blade barely whispering as it left its curved sheath. Myles and Wrael had both grabbed their bows and knocked an arrow, but where Myles looked calm and alert, Wrael's head jerked here and there, birdlike, as he looked about for the source of the threat. He was licking his lips and muttering something to himself. I stayed where I was, not because I was any braver than he, but because I was watching Biiko and the Firstblade. They stood side by side on the edge of our campsite, looking into the jungle towards the direction of the second call, but they did not seem to me to be alarmed. Neither had drawn a weapon or made any other preparation for an attack.

Finally Mister Tarq murmured something to Captain Vaelysia that sounded to me like "Not yet." She nodded and called out softly to the Firstblade.

Just then Creugar materialized from the jungle where he'd been standing sentry, and the Commander said something to him I couldn't hear. The huge Reaver nodded and gave a response that made both men chuckle, drew the great double-bladed axe from its sheath on his back (an impressive, customized sling that secures it tightly to his back yet lets him draw it with ease), and slipped back into the waiting darkness. As the big man disappeared, Biiko moved to the base of the citadel tree, reached up to grasp the first branch, and smoothly pulled himself up in one motion. Like the shadow of a passing cloud, he slid up into the tree and disappeared from view. Commander Tchicatta ordered Jaspins to take Creugar's watch and strode back to address the Captain.

He frowned and shook his head. "They will wait for the apex. The second call was most likely an elder, but there are too many of us for now." I still feel the cold breath of fear as I write those words, now several hours later.

Captain Vaelysia turned then and gave the Ship's Whip a look I've seen many times before. He nodded.

"Aye, Captain. The Firstblade speaks true, I think. They prefer ambush anyway; if they were going to attack, they would not be calling to one another."

"Just what in the Endless Dark we talkin' about here, Cap?" It was Wrael. He was still facing the opposite shore of the river, looking back over his shoulder. Next to him, Myles muttered something under his breath that I couldn't hear, placed his arrow back in its black quiver and returned to his seat by the fire.

"Fuck you too, mate. Since when do jharrls hunt in packs?"

First Mate Tarq answered him. "Since Tarsus made them, Mister Wrael. Stow your weapon and your tongue and maybe you'll learn something. Everyone else, come, gather round."

He told us that there were presently two jharrls of unknown age and size stalking the expedition. We most likely picked up an outrider - a member of the pack responsible for patrolling the edge of the pack's territory - when we entered the river valley. I assume that must have been the source of the roar we heard then, as well as the ones since. Between Mister Tarq, the Firstblade, and later Myles, (who was more than willing to answer all of my questions after the Ship's Whip and Commander Tchicatta had finished) I learned a great deal about jharrls over the next hour that was incredibly fascinating, if extremely unsettling. I will put it down here for future reference.

Apparently, they do form packs, which I had never heard before - like Wrael and most others, I had always thought they were solitary creatures. According to Myles, though, that is a common misconception - since they keep well away from man, apparently most encounters are with these outriders, leading to the inaccurate assumption of lone cats.

In truth, though, the packs are highly structured and typically led by a dominant male (the "apex"). They are highly territorial, and when an outrider learns of trespassers, it will alert another member or members of the pack, then stalk the newcomer until sufficient help arrives to attack. When I asked Myles about the "elder" that Commander Tchicatta had referred to, he told me that he thought elders were typically lieutenants of a sort, acting almost as a personal 'guard' or inner pack for the apex. As such, he assumed that they were usually the largest, strongest members of the pack.

The Captain, Mister Tarq and the Firstblade said that they were confident we did not need to worry about an attack until the apex arrived, and when someone - Miikha I think? - asked them how we would know that, the Firstblade smiled crookedly and said, "Because he'll tell us."

Without thinking (obviously), I blurted out "They can speak?"

The rest of the crew had a good laugh at that, until the Whip took pity on me and waived them to silence. "When the apex male arrives, he will stalk us with his pack mates, assessing our strength. Once he is satisfied, he will call several times, with such ferocity and power that you will not mistake him, Halliard. It is both a challenge and a warning."

"Then what?" I managed to ask.

"Then it will depend on us. If we flee, they will pick out one or two of our slowest and take them down. Think of it as a blood tax for entering their territory."

Creugar returned from the jungle as Mister Tarq was talking. When the Firstblade looked at him, the big Reaver only shook his head, no. What was that about, I wonder? Did they not believe everything they were telling us and sent him out to be sure?

"And if we stay?" Brehnl asked. He was a good, solid seaman who did as he was told and never complained.

"If we stay or press on, they will attack us at a time and place of their choosing."

Commander Tchicatta informed us that his Reavers would take the watch tonight, though the Captain assured us it was just a precaution. They explained that jharrl territories could span hundreds of miles, so it might be days yet before the apex arrived, especially given the dense undergrowth we have observed. While they can scale individual trees with ease, they must move along the ground over long distances, and then, because of the thickness of the undergrowth, they are forced to use existing game trails. Myles told me that he had never seen a game trail that ran where you wanted it to go, but I think he was just trying to make me (or himself) feel better. Unfortunately, as Wrael pointed out so helpfully, we had just finished a fairly long portage following a path that led us exactly where we wanted to go. When I looked back to Myles for a rebuttal, he chewed on the inside of his lip for a moment, perhaps unsure of what else to say. Finally, after I had given up on a response and thought our conversation ended, he said that the Captain and Mister Tarq seemed to know what they were about.

I seized on those words, as I had been noticing that very thing since we landed on Aarden. I asked him how they seemed to know so much about this place and these creatures. He shrugged and pointed to Mister Tarq.

"He is Khaliil, and they remember."

He would say nothing more, though I understood his meaning. Sha'ni taught me that saying - "We are Khaliil, and we remember." She explained that it is a common mantra of the Sand Ghosts. Their lush valley was deep enough to withstand the

- 177 -

devastation of Ehronfall, and so they are one of the few civilizations to have come through the fire intact. Their long life spans and strong tradition of oral history have preserved their collective memory of the way the world was before the gods nearly destroyed it while they were busy destroying each other. I would like to visit there one day; the wonders she describes are unlike anything I have ever seen, and some of their engineering feats sound like the stuff of my dreams.

I wonder how much of this place - Aarden - she 'remembers'? I will have to ask her when we return. Now I must do my best to get what sleep I can, no easy task with the thought of hungry jharrls stalking out there in the dark. Even though they are swift climbers, I still feel safer up here than on the ground, and I take comfort from the relaxed, easy confidence of the Captain. She has never led us astray before.

Nor did she this time, Titch. She let you go astray all by yourself, while she stayed safe and sound in Aarden, Dreysha thought with a bitter twist of her mouth. She knew it wasn't a fair accusation, but she needed to blame someone for their predicament. It wasn't Captain Vaelysia's fault that the *Peregrine* had foundered, and "safe and sound" was a relative term at best - the Dark only knew what horrors they were facing back there. But with no gods around to blame, the fact that Vaelysia had given the orders that had placed them aboard a doomed ship was close enough. And the fact that she apparently knew so much more than what she had told the crew was another sliver for Dreysha to dig at.

The next entry was brief, barely filling two-thirds of the page.

Nineday, Vehnya, 256, The 6th day of the expedition, 29th since Landfall:

Nothing much to note for past three days. Bone tired - the current's been stiff, and the Captain's been setting a hard (illegible). Rain has stopped, but heat and humidity relentless - we seem to be traveling through perpetual clouds of steam and I now know what it feels like to be stewed! Last two nights we camped in the dugouts again, well after moonrise - trying to outpace the jharrls I assume. Found a nice clear shoal late this afternoon, where the southern bank thrusts out into the river and makes a tiny island. Strange - not much but grass growing on it. Probably for the best after my experience in the citadel tree the other night. More tomorrow; too tired to write any longer.

River sounds odd; Wrael says its more rapids further upstream. Hope he's wrong.

The next entry was the two-page spread showing the massive barbican with the broken gates. The first time she had turned to this page, she'd been struck by a strong similarity to the architecture in his rendering of the strange temple with the broken chains, as well as the Sentinel statue. As she looked at it now, she realized that she had seen that architecture before as well, a few years ago.

She had taken a job to accompany one of Marquesso d'Yano's lieutenants to Derenthaal, Column of the Suns. She normally avoided escort jobs - standing around as a bodyguard was not only far too conspicuous for her tastes, it was about as boring as a corpse's cock. But this job was different: it brought her into a new fold of the serpentine maze that made up d'Yano's organization, exposing her not just to the purpose of this particular mission, but more importantly it put her in contact with other agents he had working for him. d'Yano preferred to compartmentalize everything and everyone, so including her signified a new level of trust. She hadn't exactly been scraping the horseshit from the stalls - it had been a long time since she'd been asked to shake down a local merchant or have a "discussion" with an errant thief trying to set up his own operation within earshot of d'Yano - but she knew he reserved the really choice opportunities for others. She was getting good, solid jobs, but she wanted more; she wanted to be his best.

As an added bonus, it was a chance to see a piece of ancient history. Derenthaal was the first of the Dauthirian Columns completed. Dreysha learned during their trip that Derant the Builder had reshaped a mountain to create it, shearing its sides where they needed walls, and building sweeping, arched spans to provide the only approach to each of the citadel's three great gates. The foot of each bridge was guarded by its own tower and gatehouse, each four hundred and fifty feet high and yet still dwarfed by the innumerable spires of the main fortress above, thrusting at the heavens like a forest of spears. Ganar's Bones partially shielded the northeast of Nyah from Ehronfall, but the western foothills and slopes are filled with leagues and leagues of boulders and scree - the shattered bones of the earth. As a testament to Derant's skill, however, Deranthaal still stands unbroken.

Small good it did them, she thought. In the end the gods had still managed to wipe themselves out, and for all their magnificence and grandeur, they were but shadows and dust now.

Still, the mountain fortress' incredible architecture had been so distinctive that although she had missed the connection the first time

- 179 -

she had skimmed over the drawing, she saw it clearly now. The battlements atop the barbican Triistan had drawn in his journal looked very much like the ones bristling atop Derenthaal, and the massive scale and black, glassy rock the Sentinel and possibly these other structures were made of was the same material Derant's Column had been hewn from, she was sure of it.

Her thoughts were suddenly interrupted by a deep, familiar voice that drove a cold fist of dread into her belly.

"He wakes."

She looked up in a mixture of alarm and embarrassment to find Biiko standing only a few paces from her, his face expressionless.

He moves better than I do, she thought and started to rise. Whatever might come next, she would face it on her feet.

- 13 -

Storm Coming

As Dreysha rose to face her fate, she held Triistan's journal up before her with her left hand as if offering it to Biiko. She gave him her most winning smile, but it was cut short by a wince as the corner of her mouth split again.

"Was just having a little peek is all. Seems our little Titch is quite an artist." As she stood, her right hand brushed the back of her knee, slipping her punch dagger free and palming it in a move she had performed countless times. She knew she was unsteady, but she hoped the motion was still as fluid as it had always been.

It wasn't.

Her exhausted body betrayed her. Her bones and muscles ached badly in a hundred places as she tried to straighten, so that the best she could manage was a clumsy lurch, her grip of the dagger so weak that she nearly dropped it. As a final insult, her head swam from standing too quickly and she had to reach out and grab the rail to keep from toppling over. The blade and her intentions were right there in plain view.

"By the Stormfather's barnacled balls, I was just starting to like you, Bright Eyes." She squeezed her eyes shut and shook her head, trying to clear it, then shifted her footing so that her back was to the rail and the hand holding her dagger was free. She was embarrassed to have been caught red-handed, but she was also furious with how frail she had become. She doubted she could land a single blow before he gutted her or snapped her neck. *So be it*. She opened her eyes and steeled herself.

"Come on then, and have done with it. Not really the grand exit I'd always envisioned, but I wasn't looking forward to eating any of you squid-fuckers anyway."

But Biiko only gave her a bemused look and turned away. Flummoxed, she just stood there, unsure of what to do as he ducked under the mainsail's boom and returned to his makeshift bedding.

So apparently he's not protecting Triistan's Big Secret? *It doesn't matter right now*, her instincts warned her. She needed to seize the opportunity she'd been given and return Triistan's journal to him before he woke completely - assuming that hadn't happened already. She could figure out Biiko's strange behavior later.

She shoved the punch dagger back into its sheath inside her boot, tucked the journal into her waistband, and then made sure there was enough of her tattered tunic hanging down to conceal it. As quietly as she could, she sidestepped the boom and crept back to where Triistan lay.

He had changed positions and was lying on his back again, one knee raised and his right arm draped across his eyes as if to block out the daylight. She paused, watching the slow rise and fall of his chest, willing herself to be patient. She glanced at Biiko, who lay nearby on one side, his eyes glinting from beneath half-closed lids, and wondered if he was waiting for the right moment to wake Triistan as she was trying to return the journal. What purpose would that serve, though? If he had wanted her caught, he could have done so at any time, or better yet, not bothered to warn her that the boy was waking in the first place. The only plausible explanation she could come up with was that he'd wanted her to see it - but why? She dismissed the worry and refocused her attention on Triistan. She began to count.

After fifty of Triistan's slow, rhythmic breaths, Dreysha crouched beside him, intending to slide the book into the hollow beneath his lower back. His tunic had bunched up underneath him, however, and a corner of the journal caught on it, tugging at the fabric. He sighed and started to move, so she let go of the journal and stepped sideways, so that she was now directly between Biiko and Triistan.

She stood perfectly still for one breath, two, three...

"Drey...?" His voice was thick with sleepy confusion. Even in her exhausted state, old habits died hard.

She took another deep breath, wondering if it would be her last, and crouched beside Biiko, blocking Triistan's view of his face, and shook the warrior's shoulder as if she thought he was sleeping.

"Your watch, Bright Eyes." She pivoted some so that she could see Triistan and held her finger up to her lips. "Sorry Titch," she said quietly, "didn't mean to wake you."

He closed his eyes and nodded groggily, then rolled onto his side, facing away from her. His journal lay on the deck beside him, right where it would be if it had worked itself out while he was sleeping. She was sorely tempted to pick it up again, but decided not to push her luck.

She still half expected a blow from behind, but when she turned to face Biiko, he was just lying there staring at her with those striking golden eyes. She was close enough to see the thin blue ring of their original color around each iris, and it gave his gaze a penetrating depth that made her feel like an animal suddenly confronted by a large predator; trapped and helpless, waiting for her fate.

Then, without a sound, he rose and crossed the deck to take up the watch, releasing her. She watched him go, too tired and confused to decide what to do next, then finally shuffled back to her own little nest of meager belongings to lay down.

But it was pointless: though her body desperately needed rest, her mind had other ideas. Each time she closed her eyes, Biiko's gilded irises stared back at her from the darkness, drawing her into their incalculable depths.

What game was he playing? Why had he kept her secret and gone along with her lie to Triistan?

Since coming aboard the *Peregrine*, it had gradually become clear that he was interested in Triistan's welfare; he followed Titch like a second shadow, and he'd been keeping a close eye on Sherp since the Valheim started blaming the boy for his brother's death. But while she had occasionally caught Biiko watching her, she had always assumed he was either assessing her as a threat or as a woman (both of which she was used to), but never considered that he might be watching out for her. Assuming that was true, it made no sense to her.

She wondered how much Triistan knew about him and whether he had recorded anything in his journal about it. He seemed completely at ease around the enigmatic warrior, which was notable in and of itself given the Unbound's demeanor, and just short of shocking when you factored in Triistan's typical reticence. Maybe they had reached some sort of understanding during the expedition, or perhaps Biiko had been forced to reveal his purpose.

Too late to check now. She wished she'd had more time with the diary so that she knew what she was really dealing with. Based on what she had read thus far, she thought this was quite probably the most significant job she had ever undertaken, and if she could get a better understanding of the whole picture, it stood a good chance of being the most profitable one as well. She wasn't sure if she'd have another opportunity to look at it before they reached a safe harbor, but one thing was absolutely certain: if they did reach safety, Titch was going to have to swallow the fucking thing to keep it from her.

She massaged her temples and tried to focus. As their plight lengthened, it had become harder and harder to concentrate. Analysis like this used to come instinctively to her, but now she had to force her thoughts to march in a straight line. And that was going to make what she did next very dangerous.

Yes, this was probably the most significant job she'd ever undertaken, but she no longer had the luxury of waiting until she had a better overall understanding of it. She needed to contact d'Yano and report what she could now, before she lost the ability to do so. She hoped it wasn't already too late.

She sat back up and slipped a small roll of waxed leather from the hidden pocket in her taenia, where the fabric crisscrossed between her breasts. Glancing around to assure herself that no one was watching, she unrolled the tiny packet to reveal two small seeds. She swore softly.

Both seeds had mottled white and blue skin, but where one was whole and hard, the other was partially crushed. She could see where water had found its way through the tightly-rolled leather, and when she prodded the damaged seed, it felt rotten. Well that certainly narrowed her options.

After d'Yano had awarded this job, he had introduced her to a disheveled old man who called himself Amiel. For the next two months, Amiel had trained her in the use of Nightshade - a potent plant whose seeds could be consumed and used to transmit messages over great distances. When a seed is consumed by a "Sender", they enter a dream-like state. If trained properly, they can retain control over the dream in order to communicate information to an "Interpreter". She wasn't told how the Interpreter gathered the information, but apparently it had something to do with eating the blossoms on the Nightshade tree that had produced the seeds; they established some type of connection, but that was the limit of her understanding on the matter.

Dreysha wouldn't be the only one to have Nightshade. She knew the Seeker Corp had a few dedicated Interpreters of their own, ready to receive messages from ships on high risk voyages. Given the nature of the *Peregrine's* mission, she assumed Captain Vaelysia had been issued her own supply as well, which meant Fleet Command should have been alerted when the ship set out from Aarden on its return voyage.

So presumably they were expected, but Dreysha didn't know what the protocol was for overdue ships, or even how long they would have allowed for their return in the first place. So she had already used the first of her three seeds to alert d'Yano of the shipwreck, trusting him to get word to the Seeker commanders to begin searching for them. It had been surprisingly difficult to keep that hope a secret from her shipmates - especially Triistan - but she'd buried it for the sake of the job.

That first Send had gone smoothly, because by necessity it had been brief and direct: she gave the date, her best estimate of their position, and reported that the *Peregrine* had capsized. She was pleased with her success, but reminded herself that the process was not without risks. Both d'Yano and Amiel had warned her about something called "drifting", where the Sender could lose their way when trying to deliver the message. Amiel had hinted that there were other risks as well, but refused to elaborate; the risk of drifting was enough to worry about, he'd told her. It was greatest for the untrained, but it existed for all Senders, in particular those suffering from some other malady that might compromise their mental state. Hence her present concern: she had to assume that slowly starving to death while being cooked by Ruine's twin suns counted as a "malady". At least the damaged seed prevented her from having to send again sometime in the future, when presumably she would be even weaker.

To reduce the chance of drifting, Amiel had taught her to organize her thoughts as if she were rehearsing a conversation she planned to have with d'Yano. She should think of exactly what she wanted to say, then envision how d'Yano would respond, including as much detail as possible. The more detail, the better: hand gestures, sighs, laughs, shrugs - the more real and natural her projection of him seemed, the easier it would be to stay within the Send and avoid drifting. The Interpreter did not typically communicate directly with the Sender, but if they were sufficiently skilled at it, they could project basic thoughts and very strong emotions. According to the old man, it could be mildly unpleasant, but not painful. When she asked Amiel if d'Yano was "sufficiently skilled", he had only smiled crookedly and said, "Don't get too comfortable."

A tiny shiver twitched through her shoulders now at the thought of someone else putting thoughts and feelings into her head.

"Bah, stop dithering like an old crone," she muttered to herself. "No risk, no riches."

She popped the undamaged seed into her mouth and swallowed it, settling the matter. If she drifted and became a drooling idiot, at least she would be spared the agony of slowly starving to death, or the horror of eating her dead shipmates.

She dropped the leather scrap and the damaged seed over the side and then did what she could to get comfortable. She knew from experience that the first indication the Nightshade was working would be an unpleasant sharpening of her vision, to the point where she would be able to see the tiniest fibers of pulp within the wood decking, or the individual droplets of water kicked up as the launch shouldered through a wave. It had given her a splitting headache the first time, so she closed her eyes and bent her vision inward to replay the scene she had been constructing in her mind for some time.

She imagined herself back in her benefactor's apartment in the Den of Dark Delights. His back was to her as she made her customary entrance, slipping in through the balcony doors. This time, however, there was no click as she picked the lock, so he did not turn to see her come in; if she was calling the shots in this dream, she was damn sure going to be perfect at her craft.

The room was just as she remembered it the last time she was there: heavy leather chair, matching ottoman, the stiff divan she sat on, and the fire burning in d'Yano's fireplace. Even the bronze poker was there with its phallic-shaped business end. Of course it was. She and Amiel had constructed this mental model together during her training, and they had based it on d'Yano's room.

She stretched and yawned as the Nightshade went to work, sending tendrils of warm relaxation through her body. Without the distraction of her vision being amplified to painful levels, she was more aware of other sensations. It was pleasant initially, as if she were slowly being lowered into a warm bath.

The sensation deepened to a heavy drowsiness, and she started to think how nice it would feel to just let it wash over her and fall into a deeper sleep. She knew where that would lead though, so she bit down on the inside of her cheek and forced herself to concentrate. It was something Amiel had taught her - simple, but very effective - and critically important given her physical and mental state.

During her training and the initial Send aboard the emergency launch, this part had been relatively easy, but it was already a strain just to hold onto the image of d'Yano's room. The walls kept shimmering, as if their oiled wood panels were seen through the heat of a fire. There were two doors, as there were in his real room, but a soft blue light was slipping through the crack around the one she thought of as the apartment's entrance. The rippling effect had occurred early on in her training, but she'd never seen that blue light before. She bit down again and shifted her mental focus to the figure of d'Yano.

"I have something for you, Grandfather," she said, then realized he was already bent over Triistan's journal, flipping through the pages and mumbling incoherently to himself. He turned towards her, but as was typical, she could not see his face within the dark folds of his customary robes. She began reciting the information she had learned so far, imagining that it was written on the pages of the journal in d'Yano's hand, just as she'd seen it in the physical copy.

Her handler's shrouded head alternately swiveled from watching her to looking at pages in the book. He turned the pages whenever she called up a new mental image of one, but otherwise did not respond to her for several moments.

Until they reached the page where Triistan had drawn a picture of Biiko, when d'Yano looked up sharply.

Khagan's Son

She had no idea what that meant. The thought came unbidden, with an emotional force that jolted her. A breath later, another word formed in her mind:

Unbound

She had not envisioned this part of the conversation ahead of time, but somehow she knew now that d'Yano was looking for confirmation that Biiko was an Unbound warrior. She sensed he wanted much more than that, though; the thought had the weight of unasked questions behind it.

"Yes," she answered.

Who

"He calls himself Biiko, Grandfather." The room around d'Yano rippled.

Who

The response came with such force that she moaned aloud. She heard it, felt her body move where it lay on the deck of the emergency launch, but it seemed to belong to someone else.

She realized that this time d'Yano was asking who Biiko had attached himself to.

"Triistan Halliard, the author of the journal." Suddenly a host of other images rose up in her mind; memories of conversations they'd shared being drawn from her, as if Triistan's name were a kite and these thoughts and feelings were ribbons tied to its tail. The figure of d'Yano tore a page out of the journal and held it up to her accusatorily. It was Triistan's rendering of her, the one she had seen when spying on him from the tops.

Before she could think of a response, however, d'Yano threw the sheet into the fire and the images abruptly stopped.

No time

She felt disapproval and a hint of sadness, but only for an instant. He held up the open journal again, pointing to the sketch of Biiko. It was much rougher than the original had been, little more than a shadowy outline, except for his eyes; they were even more lifelike than they had been in the actual rendering, and they bored into her.

Find out why

Another ripple of distortion flowed across the room, and this time over d'Yano as well. She glanced at the entrance door and found that it was open. The room beyond was a shifting miasma of indistinct shadows, all tinged with the same blue luminescence that had been leaking out around the door. She took a step towards it, wanting to see what was out there. One of the shadows looked vaguely like Triistan lying on the floor - except there was no floor, just the shifting light -

Focus

She bit down harder, tasting blood. She imagined d'Yano stepping in front of her, his cowled head blocking her view of the door, but she found herself looking *up*: he suddenly seemed much taller and broader than she remembered. The robes still covered him, but they were different somehow, layered, with flashes of something metallic visible in several spots -

And then he spoke.

These were not unbidden thoughts summoned from her mind: d'Yano was *speaking* to her. His voice was not the rheumy old gentleman's she was used to, but deep and full of quiet power. Part of her dreaming mind - the rational, watchful portion that would reflect on it later - thought the voice familiar, but could not or would not put a name to it.

"What have you done, child?"

"What do you mean, Grandfather? I did the job and brought you an incredible discovery... a whole new world."

"You know not what you say, Tresha l'Sonjaro, or you would quake with fear at its full import." It was odd that he had used her real name.

She tried to laugh bravely, but it felt hollow.

"I am not afraid, Grandfather." But she realized as she spoke the words that this was not d'Yano, not anymore. She glanced again at the open door. Whoever – whatever – this was must have traded places with him somehow.

"Then you are a fool." The hooded figure studied the book again, shaking his head and muttering as he traced the text with a long, dark finger. "But, perhaps, a useful one. My brothers misjudged you - your chain is deceptively strong... and entwined with his, I think."

He slammed the book closed, though it made no sound, and held it out to her. She took it, and dread swelled in her breast as her outstretched hand touched the worn leather cover. She opened it to the page containing Triistan's drawing of Biiko.

"Who is he?" she whispered.

"Your time is limited, assassin. Choose your questions carefully." Somehow, she understood.

"What... *what* is he?"

"Better. But you know the answer, do you not?"

"He is one of the Unbound - but you called him something else. Someone's son?"

The tall figure nodded. "Khagan's Sons: he is one of many that some call The Unbound."

Khagan? she thought, but although she did not utter the question out loud, the figure that was and was not d'Yano answered, his deep bass something she felt more than heard, like distant thunder.

"Each life - mortal and immortal alike - is a great chain, its links forged from individual events that connect the Past to the Future, and each chain binds a life to this course, lending its strength to contain the Living Darkness. Some chains are more significant than others, like the great beams of a citadel. But all must fulfill their purpose. Even the gods - Old, Young, and those not yet come - must follow the Chain forged for them.

"But chains are bound as much as they bind, and what you call Fate is the true prison."

She shook her head. "I don't understand." The figure and the room around them began to fade. A sense of urgency made her shout it again.

"I don't understand!"

The tall figure in d'Yano's robes raised his hands to the sides of his cowl, and for the first time she noticed they were covered in gleaming ebony skin. They were strong hands webbed with old scars... familiar hands. He pushed the hood back, but though she knew who it was, all she saw was a dark silhouette and two hot points of light, like stars where his eyes should have been.

"You will, in time." Biiko's voice carried effortlessly across the ocean. "For now, hear me, and remember..."

The figure and his surroundings were lost in darkness, only the two burning eyes still visible.

"Khagan forged the chains, at the command of Tarsus," his voice was all around her, resonating in her very bones.

...but it was a mistake, and the Sons must break them...

The room disappeared completely and she was falling, falling...

...and then she jerked awake, the hard boards of the launch's deck pressing against her shoulder and hip; the scratchy sting of her burned and blistered skin reminding her who and where she was. A long, low rumble of thunder brought her up sharply, but the sky overhead was still clear. For a moment she thought it must have been some kind of queer after-image from her dream, until she saw the dark line of clouds far to the south.

"I don't think it will bother us. Pretty far away," a voice said quietly. It was Triistan, sitting nearby, knees drawn up and arms resting comfortably. Both hands were wrapped around the journal.

She lifted her head and glanced around, uncertain of how long she'd slept. Sometimes a Sending could take mere seconds, but this one appeared to have taken much longer. She wondered if she had left d'Yano in the Sending and fallen into a deep dream. Was that "drifting?" How would she know? Perhaps it was just one of the other risks that Amiel had mentioned but refused to elaborate on.

"Just a godsdamned dream..." she muttered, trying to convince herself that's all it was.

But inside she was thinking how grateful she was for the loss of the third seed. At least the risks here were real, not imagined, problems she could fight with blade and wits. She cast an eye around to see what had changed.

Biiko's bedroll was empty, and a quick glance under the mainsail showed him sitting in the position he typically assumed when praying - except now she harbored a strong suspicion that he wasn't praying. The watch hadn't rotated to anyone else though, so she reasoned she must have only been asleep for an hour or two. She wondered if Triistan had been awake all that time, and whether he had been watching her as she slept. The notion left her feeling conflicted, as her professional instincts ran squarely into an unexpected sense of comfort. She pushed a hand through the tangles in her dark hair and stretched, cat-like.

"We could use the water, though I do not wish to be tossed about in another sodding storm," she answered sleepily.

"Could use a bit of shade as well," he muttered. "We're burning up."

It was definitely hotter than it had been when she'd fallen asleep. Whatever fickle breeze had been blowing had died off, and the boat hung suspended like a child's toy cast in a great blue ball of crystal. Another rumble of thunder echoed in the distance.

Khagan forged the chains... She could almost hear the words from her dream rolling across the sea, but what the fuck did they mean? And why was she dreaming about it?

"You were dreaming," Triistan said, breaking into her reverie. She put her head in her hands and groaned. The Nightshade's effects were lingering, making it hard to look at anything for long.

"Aye, so I was. Hope I didn't wake you." He shook his head and looked away, towards Biiko, one eye shut and squinting against the glare.

"No, I can't seem to sleep for more than an hour or two at a time, no matter how -" he opened his mouth wide and finished talking through a yawn, "no matter how tired I am." He turned back to her. "What did you dream about?"

She cocked her head to the side, trying to meet his gaze. "Well not you, if that is what you're thinking, Titch. Sorry - Triistan." He laughed self-consciously and dropped his head, fidgeting with the journal.

"I didn't mean- I mean, I didn't think-"

"Yes, that is rather obvious now, isn't it?" she quipped, unable to stifle a grin, which of course aggravated the cut at the corner of her mouth. The pain sharpened her focus, however.

"Actually, I think I was dreaming about your bodyguard over there, though he was dressed a bit differently..." Though she hadn't intended it in the way he took it, she enjoyed the look of surprised jealousy that flashed across his face. *By the Dark but they could be so simple sometimes.*

She jabbed his arm with her elbow. "Not that kind of dream, Triis. He was *talking* to me."

He rubbed his arm. "Oh - Biiko was speaking? About what?"

She heard the thunder again, and thought it sounded closer, though it was difficult to tell for sure; Scow and Sherp seemed to be engaged in a pitched snoring battle. She stretched out her left leg and poked the Mattock with her foot a few times. He snorted and shifted positions, breathing quietly again.

Candor did not come easily for Dreysha, so she answered, "A little of this and some of that. I'm not even sure it was him, but it sounded like him. Something about the Unbound - no, that wasn't the word he used, he called them something else -"

"Khagan's Sons?" Triistan had lowered his voice to little more than a whisper. *Child's play.*

She nodded. "Yes, that was it. Or close to it. And something about chains and fate..."

His brows furrowed thoughtfully. "How could you know that from a dream?"

That's a good fucking question, isn't it? she thought. "What do you mean? Know what? Do you know what they are - what he's even doing here?" He was no longer listening to her, though. He was flipping through the pages of his journal and muttering rapidly to himself. It was suddenly as if she wasn't even there.

"What day had that been - early, before the attack I think..."

Dreysha could glimpse some of the pages as he rifled through them, and she recognized a few of the illustrations, especially the one he had made of the citadel tree. Suddenly he stopped, and a cold hand raked its fingers down her spine. It was one of the journal entries she had read, beginning with this phrase:

> It seems the gray-bole monkeys are indeed vengeful - and clever...

It covered the entire left page and half of the right, and below that was the sketch of Biiko she had seen in her dream.

Triistan was fingering the upper left corner of the first page, which had a slight crease and bend to it. How could she have been so stupid? Such a simple, basic rule of fieldcraft! She must be worse off than she thought to have made that kind of blunder. Well, there was one rule she wasn't going to break, an old adage which had served her well through the years: "Lie 'till you die." No matter how guilty you looked, people wanted to believe in innocence, honesty, integrity - as if the act of getting caught suddenly made a thief into an honorable man. "Coming clean" for Dreysha meant a clean escape, and she would say and do anything to achieve that.

She waited for the accusatory stare, the wounded expression; she knew how much he worked in that journal, how much he obsessed over its condition - every bit as much as its contents - and she presumed that with the incredibly detail-oriented mind that he had, he would spot any blemish, crease or other inconsistency and know instantly that someone else had been reading it.

It didn't come, however. Though he had paused and she thought he was examining the crease, his finger abruptly moved across the page, following the lines of text rapidly; he was reading the entry, browsing for something. Then he flipped through several more pages in the same manner. *You dodged that poisoned bolt, you lucky bitch*, she chided herself.

Triistan seemed to find what he was searching for in a lengthy passage that trailed across three pages, their margins filled with the kind of tiny notes she had seen where he had been designing the 'billy' pump. He read in silence for several minutes, but unfortunately she couldn't make out the words well enough to read them herself. While the Nightshade had left her feeling groggy and slightly hung over, her eyesight seemed to have returned to normal: between that and the way he hunched protectively over the book, it was hopeless. She decided to try a different tact and reached out to place a hand on his wrist.

He froze. His eyes locked on her hand and she felt a flicker of embarrassment at the cracked, blistered condition of her skin. The absurdity made her voice harsher than she intended.

"What in the Dark happened back there on Aarden? What did you find?"

He stared at her hand for a long moment. His cheek muscle bunched rhythmically, a tell she had learned meant he was struggling over some internal debate.

She sensed an opportunity. The suns burned down from above, Sherp went on snoring away, and Scow appeared to be giving chase again. Mung, Voth and Rantham hadn't moved from where they lay in some time, either, and Biiko was at his post. This was about as alone as they could ever hope to be.

She reached up with her other hand, feather-soft, touched his cheek, his chin. It was rough with stubble, the same fiery copper-and-chestnut as his hair. His jaw stopped twitching and he closed his eyes, but did not resist as she gently turned his head to face her. She could hear the subtle trembling in his breathing and leaned closer, licking her cracked lips.

"Triistan, please... tell me what terrible secret you're guarding..." she whispered. It was barely a breath really, but his eyes snapped open as if she'd struck him. He looked so sad.

"I'm sorry," he mumbled. Then he was standing, gently disengaging himself from her, and moving towards Biiko on the other side of the launch. He paused a moment at the mainmast and she hoped he might come back, but he only turned his head, speaking over his shoulder without looking at her. His voice was heavy with sorrow.

"Please don't take my journal again." He still held the book open. With exaggerated care, he straightened and smoothed the folded corner before shutting the book gently. He then slipped around the mainmast and left her alone.

Dreysha sat there brooding for a long time. She was angry with him for rejecting her, and with herself for mishandling both him and his Dark-damned journal. Most of all, though, she was angry with herself for what she had felt when he'd looked at her.

After awhile Scow snorted himself awake. He groaned and stretched, then grumbled a greeting at her, getting barely a grunt in reply for his trouble. The Mattock stood and stretched some more, his massive frame providing some welcome shade. She sensed him watching her, could imagine him glancing across the deck at Triistan. He knew his men almost as well as his ship, which is why he stood there silently for awhile.

Thunder rumbled again, great boulders of sound rolling across the sea, and this time there could be no doubt it was closer. She rose and leaned over the rail. The southern horizon was lost in a dark shadow beneath towering columns of bruised, sullen clouds. She could smell the rain, though the air was as still as death. Beside her, Scow hawked and spat over the side.

"Storm's comin' ".

"Aye," she answered softly. "Been coming for some time now."

- 14 -

Wings of Darkness

Triistan sat on the taffrail, long legs stretched out before him, back resting against two of the clew lines. He held his journal in one hand as he watched the storm to their south, his index finger inserted between the pages Dreysha had marked. It seemed to be holding its line, still many leagues away. A very fortunate thing, given the storm's ferocity: above the black wall of shadow that formed the storm's front and its skirt of torrential rain, huge columns of silver and charcoal clouds towered into the heavens, alive with the flicker and flash of lightning. It reminded him of another tempest he'd seen on Aarden, not long before...

He pushed the thoughts away; there was too much horror and pain in those memories. Instead, he focused on Dreysha. The way her hand had felt on his face, the soft brush of her whisper on his neck, the long dark hair and the face he could draw from memory now... he ached for her, and for that one moment this morning he had been so certain that she was drawn to him in kind.

Or so he had thought until he noticed the bent corner of the page and something clicked in his head. He had awakened earlier to find her standing over him awkwardly, as if she'd been watching him. When he said her name she made as if to wake Biiko for his turn at watch, but something had seemed wrong with how low the suns still were in the sky: he'd still been half asleep and had not realized it was too early for the watch change.

But when he had felt the creased corner of the page in his journal - the only one of its kind in the entire book because he always remembered where he left off - he immediately thought of that moment and he knew instinctively it must have been her.

It was just past midday and he'd been sitting there for nearly a full watch thinking about the situation, no closer now to deciding what to do about it than he had been when he walked away from her. He felt hurt, betrayed. The journal was an extension of him, a reflection of his mind, and she had picked the lock and stolen into his sanctuary like a thief. He was having difficulty separating the fear that this was causing him from a host of other emotions. Embarrassment came just behind the fear when someone glimpsed his private thoughts. Anger immediately followed because she had done so without his leave. He was also intensely curious about what she thought - of the journal's contents and now of him. Under it all, he felt a deep frustration and sadness at a lost opportunity: if it hadn't been for the gods-damned thing and his promise to keep it secret and safe, he might be with her right now.

In addition to his mixed emotions about Drey, he was also grappling with a new feeling: for the first time, he actually wanted to talk about his experiences with someone. The secrets he kept were living things, growing and squirming inside him, and they did not want to be contained. They were slowly eating away at his self-control and the pressure grew daily to let them out. He knew from past experience that without some kind of outlet, his mind would just continue cycling through them over and over, with painfully realistic detail, forcing him to relive each moment as if he were actually there again. It was becoming too intense - well beyond anything he had ever been through before - and for the first time in his life he wasn't sure he could cope with his thoughts alone.

Biiko was here, but although they had reached some kind of strange balance and he felt a genuine companionship with the Unbound, conversation was not an option. Since he had been a part of the expedition, Triistan could talk to him about it, but he would get nothing in return, which he assumed would be no different than writing in his journal.

The only other person on the boat he felt close to was Scow, but he was afraid that the Mattock's rigid sense of duty would compel him to reveal the journal's significance to Voth, and he knew instinctively that the "Captain" was the last person he wanted to share his thoughts with, let alone empower with knowledge of what the book contained. Besides, it was really Dreysha he wanted to talk with anyway. Her intrusion was unwelcome, but at least she knew part of what had happened - could telling her the rest matter so much?

He tried telling himself that his oath was no longer important, that their circumstances were so dire now that it might actually be considered prudent to tell someone else in case he didn't survive. But his promise was like a giant boulder in the narrow path his mind often followed, and he simply could not get around it. He had sworn he would not share the information with anyone until he had delivered it to the High Chancellor, and so, regardless of circumstances or how badly he wanted to let someone else in, he would not break that promise.

He considered the book in his hands, turning it over and running his fingertips across the familiar worn leather jacket. He remembered in perfect detail how it had looked when he had received it as a gift, right down to the rich, dark brown of its original color and the sweet smell of the oil that had been worked into it to protect the leather and to mask any leftover tanning stench. Now, so many years later, salt and sun had bleached it to a blotchy gray, like driftwood, and its texture was rough and dry to his touch.

The inside had changed as well; now that it held so many secrets, it was like a foreign thing to him. There were times when he wanted to throw it as far out to sea as he could, or drop something heavy into the waterproof pouch he'd made for it and let it sink into the Dark. He had even spent most of one afternoon wondering if he could eat the damned thing and gone as far as chewing off a small corner of the pouch - he had heard of besieged soldiers eating boot leather once - but in the end he came back to the same thing he always did: he needed it, not just because of the promise he had made and the responsibility he bore, and not because it had become an extension of his conscience. Over the past few days, he had been surprised to find a small measure of solace in rereading his notes. Though it still meant revisiting everything the Aarden Expedition went through, he did not feel completely immersed in the events the way he did when the memories just took over. Somehow, the physical act of reading gave him just enough distance and control that the emotions he felt were dulled. It gave him a chance to view things analytically, the way he might in a discussion with someone about it. As a result, it seemed to keep the runaway stallion of his mind from taking the bit in its mouth and leaving his sanity behind - at least for now.

What else did you see, Dreysha?

He opened the journal again and reread the passage Drey had marked, recalling their encounter with the gray-bole monkeys and reflecting on how that had really been their first warning of what was to come. He didn't think this entry had anything particularly valuable or interesting in it for an outsider, though, so she must have paused or ended there. Unless...

At the end of the entry, at the bottom of the right-hand page, was a sketch of Biiko. He remembered how difficult it had been trying to draw the Unbound - for some reason at that time he couldn't seem to capture details about the man, to see him in his mind in order to render him on the page, the way he could with everything else he drew.

Except for the man's eyes; they were the only feature he thought he had done a reasonably good job of depicting, outside of the scenery around him. Even the twin swords strapped to his back were only vague sketches, despite the fact that he had done a study of one of the blades back before they had discovered Aarden. They were extraordinary weapons, with jet-black, slightly curved blades so finely crafted they looked like glass, while the elongated hilts were notable for their simplicity; apart from the fine silver chain that wrapped around the handles from pommel to guard, they bore no other ornament or inscription, nothing to glamorize their deadly purpose. *Much like Biiko himself*, thought Triistan.

Was that why Drey had marked this page? Was it something to do with the Unbound? The journal contained a couple of specific entries regarding Biiko - things Triistan had learned from First Mate Tarq or his own observations during the Aarden Expedition - so his best guess was that she must have read those based on what she told him about her dream. Either that or she already knew something of the Unbound and was just fishing, trying to see how much Triistan would reveal if she dropped a few key terms. She certainly wouldn't be the first member of the crew to attempt to solve Biiko's riddle. Maybe that was why she had taken his journal in the first place, he told himself, and the thought went a long way towards dulling the pain of her personal betrayal... which of course was why he eventually discarded the idea. Things were rarely that simple.

He tortured himself in this way for the rest of the afternoon, finally dozing off when the shadow of the mainsail swung around to offer some relief from the afternoon heat. The rest of the crew slept and woke intermittently in awkward, disjointed shifts. Despite their physical exhaustion, none of them could actually sleep comfortably for longer than an hour or two - except for Mung, anyway. He slept so soundly it was often difficult to wake him, especially when it was his turn to take the watch, and today was no exception. Scow eventually gave up trying and relieved Biiko himself, and Rantham relieved the Mattock after that, while all (except for Mung) watched the storm during their wakeful fits. It had indeed stalled, and might even have begun moving westward. They would have liked to believe that the launch was making some headway in the opposite direction, but there could be little doubt now that they were caught in the doldrums, and there had not been any noticeable current in any direction since they left the pull of the Godsfall Drift a few days before. The irony was bitter: the storm would probably rip them to pieces, but it would also bring fresh water and, just as significantly, wind.

As the Mistress touched the edge of the western horizon, the air began to cool. It would still be several hours yet before the Crone limped after her, but the long evenings were much more comfortable with only one sun in the sky. The boat's inhabitants began to stir, and Voth called them together for their daily ritual in futility: what passed for dinner and, laughably, the Roll Call.

"Wiliamund Azimuth, Reserve Echoman" Voth intoned with all of the severity of a ship-launching ceremony.

Mung yawned. "Aye, Captain sir."

"Try to stay awake for the entire roll, if it's not too much trouble, Mister Azimuth."

"Aye, sir. Sorry, sir I don't kn-" but Voth had already scored his point and cut him off.

"Biiko, Special Ambassador." No one knew how to classify Biiko, but Seeker Protocol required it, so the "Captain" had made something up.

The Unbound nodded silently in response. That had been something of a hurdle for Lanky Lankham during the first week, Triistan recalled, since Protocol also required a verbal response from each crewmember to assure that they were all, in fact, present and accounted for. Biiko did not seem overly concerned about protocol, though, staring stonily back until Voth had finally thrown up his hands in exasperation and ordered Triistan to answer for him. It had been hard not to laugh or snicker the first few times, but their plight had worn away the thin veneer of amusement fairly quickly.

"Aye Captain," Triistan said.

"Dreysha, Able Seeker, Midshipman First Class..."

"Aye." Voth looked up from his "Captain's Log" - a stained, tattered ledger they had found in the bottom of the locker where the billy was stored. Triistan smiled, recalling Drey's wry remark about "Lanky's Log" as he was wiping off the filth that had leaked onto it from the bilge pump.

Voth stared hard at her, waiting.

Dreysha sighed. "Aye, Captain." He grunted and looked down to read the next name. She caught Triistan's eye and winked. He ducked his head, trying not to smile.

"Rantham d'yBassi, Able Seeker, Midshipman Second Class..."

Rantham nodded and mumbled, "Aye, Captain." He did not look well. None of them did, of course, but besides the deep-set eyes, hollow cheeks, and myriad skin afflictions they all had, Rantham's behavior had changed substantially over the past two days. His swagger was gone, replaced by a limping shuffle - when he moved at all, which was

- 199 -

rarely. And the bravado everyone loved him for was hidden away behind a sullen shiftiness. He largely kept to himself now, backed into some corner or other, watching everyone warily and muttering to himself.

"Triistan Halliard, Able Seeker, Topman First Class..."

"Aye, Captain" he answered quietly.

"What was that, boy?"

He felt his cheeks and the tips of his ears grow hot. "Aye, Captain!" he blurted, louder, trying not to duck his head again.

"Mister Mordan Scow, First Mate..."

"Aye, Captain," rumbled the Mattock. Scow had lost weight as well, but he had plenty to spare, more than any of them except perhaps Sherp. The great keg that passed for his belly had definitely shrunken, but there was still considerable strength in his chest, shoulders and arms.

Lankham Voth paused and looked up from the log book, thin lips hooked slightly in a smirk and the familiar glob of spittle gathering at the corner of his mouth.

"And last on the roll today, I am pleased to call the name of Mister Sherpel Icefist, who I am hereby promoting to Second Mate for his exemplary service and discipline in these difficult times."

Sherp's eyes shone brightly above his broken nose. Shocked, Triistan glanced at Scow, whose surprise was easily readable on his craggy face, though the Mattock tried his best to conceal it. The fact that Voth apparently hadn't consulted with him was almost as unsettling as the promotion itself.

"Aye, Captain!" the big Valheim answered, far too vigorously. Triistan and the others exchanged worried or angry glances, and in a few cases, both. Technically, Rantham's rank should have qualified him for the position first, followed by Triistan and then Dreysha before a member of the rowing pit should be considered. As far as a Seeker vessel's hierarchy went, "The Pit" was barely one short step above the non-ranked apprentices only - what most of the ship's company referred to as "bilge rats". While a Captain certainly had the authority to promote anyone he pleased to any position except his own, it was highly unusual for many reasons, most of them good ones.

Dreysha caught Triistan's eye again and he managed not to glance away this time. Their earlier impasse forgotten in the moment, she shared a look and a slight shake of her head that said "This will mean trouble" as plainly as if she'd whispered it in his ear. *If only she had*, he thought.

It might have given him the courage to object out loud, but if he did, he wasn't sure if anyone would back him up. Mung maybe - but he would be the first to tell you that his most reliable trait was his utter unreliability. Rantham was struggling with his own demons and unlikely to confront anyone. Mister Scow would never question a superior officer openly, though from the ruddy tone of the back of his neck it looked like he might be considering it. Dreysha...

Come to think of it, why wasn't she challenging this? She was outspoken to the point of insubordination on a good day, yet here she was swallowing her tongue as they all were passed over for a promotion that was as unfair as it was absurd under their present circumstances. There was something here he was missing, but he would have to think about it later. At the moment, someone needed to speak out against Voth's decision, or at least question it. He took a deep breath and half a step forward, then caught Biiko's eye. He'd forgotten about the Unbound - not that he would have expected him to break his Vow for this anyway. But as Triistan was learning, he rarely needed words to get his message across.

Biiko was staring at him now with those liquid gold eyes, one eyebrow raised and a disapproving scowl on his face. And if that wasn't clear enough for Triistan to understand, he shook his head slowly, emphatically, "no". Triistan froze - as much by his confusion at Biiko's sudden intervention as in response to the warrior's message - and then the moment was gone.

Voth closed the log book with a dull thump and clasped it with both hands behind his back.

"I expect you all to recognize the Second Mate's authority after my own and, of course, Mister Scow's."

Triistan was seething inside. The bubble of spittle at the corner of Voth's mouth struck him as even more offensive than usual; they were all barely getting enough water to take a piss once a day, swallowing food was a struggle - how was this man still able to drool?

"We will now convene for the Evening Meal, after which we will return to a normal watch schedule, though it will be reduced to three hours per shift. Also, Mister Scow, please dispense one glass from the Morale Officer, to be passed among the crew to toast Mister Icefist's career advancement."

For the first time Triistan could remember, Scow did not respond immediately to a direct order. His hesitation caught Dreysha's attention as well; Triistan could see her watching Scow with an expectant look on her face. It took a moment more, but eventually Voth seemed to realize people were staring at him in the awkward silence. He coughed nervously and wiped his mouth with the back of his hand.

"Is- is there a problem, Mister Scow?" Despite his sunburned, peeling face, Triistan thought he suddenly looked pale. Next to him, though, Sherp was scowling fiercely, ready to defend his new title.

The Mattock's eyes slid from one to the other and he shook his head. "No, sir, no problem. Twill be done, Sir."

Triistan let out his breath as Scow turned away. He had hoped the Mattock would protest, but now that the moment had passed he was relieved: anyone could see that Sherp was spoiling for a fight and it would not have gone well.

Scow obtained the key to the storage locker from Biiko and went to retrieve the firkin of rum while the rest of them formed up in front of the Unbound to receive their rations: one ship's biscuit and one strip of cured boar no bigger than Triistan's pinky finger, and two ladles of water. As he approached to receive his share, he noticed the line marking the first scuttle of water was only a hands-breadth above the bottom. It seemed lower to him than it should have been, but he had not been paying much attention to it the past few days. They had been allowed three ladles per day - morning, mid-afternoon and with the evening meal. Two days ago - or maybe it was longer, it was growing harder to keep track - they had decided to shift the mid-afternoon water ration to double up on the evening meal after Rantham had almost choked to death on his hardtack. The biscuits were so dry and the men so parched that it was difficult to get them down without a healthy dose of water. Biiko had managed to dislodge the hunk of food by striking him in the stomach, but the real damage came from Sherp's taunt: "Ah, that's a shame, now. Thought maybe the rest of us had finally got some luck ourselves and we was gonna have some fresh Rogue-chops."

That was when Rantham's behavior had begun to change and he had grown more reclusive and suspicious with each passing day. Triistan could see him now, wedged up against a bulkhead towards the rear of the ship, eyes darting from one to the other of his crewmates while he nibbled at the hardtack. Triistan thought he looked like an absurdly large rat and wondered what Snitch would think of him now. He looked up but the monkey was nowhere to be seen. It had managed to avoid capture despite their best efforts, keeping safely to the tops, and wisely out of sight during supper.

They ate their meal in silence, each member of the crew lost in the struggle to break down the tough meat and biscuit. Almost every evening at least one person lost a tooth in the ordeal, and tonight was Triistan's turn. He felt a dull pain in his right lower jaw as a molar caught awkwardly in the bread and snapped sideways. He swallowed it with the mouthful of food rather than risk spitting out any water or bread along with the tooth, then immediately regretted his decision. The sharp taste of his own blood made his stomach clench harder in hunger. That was one aspect of slowly starving to death he had not anticipated - the wracking pain of hunger pangs, far beyond the mild pinching and aching he had known in what he was increasingly thinking of as someone else's life: someone he used to know well enough to know their fears, thoughts and dreams, their philosophies and beliefs, even their favorite foods - but, still, someone else. He wasn't sure exactly when the sense of detachment had occurred - sometime after his recovery on Aarden, of that much he was sure. But since then, each day he felt a little more distant from the person he thought he had been.

The next few days went by in much the same fashion, suspended in the endlessly still blue of their crystal sphere prison. The storm to the south eventually retreated to a dark shadow on the horizon, leaving them to pray for another to gods that supposedly no longer existed.

Morale continued to deteriorate. Even those who had been friends avoided each other, retreating to the ever-shifting, perpetually insufficient pools of shade and whatever diversions they could create for themselves. Except for Voth and Sherp, that is. The new Second Mate didn't bother with any pretense of dignity or professionalism Triistan would have expected from someone recently promoted. He spent far too much time bending Voth's ear for his own purpose, as far removed from the rest of the crew members as the boat would allow. From time to time they would summon Scow, who would stand their listening for a few moments but rarely saying anything in return. Triistan could tell from The Mattock's body language that he was not happy with whatever he was being told, and probably even less so with the frequent collusion of the Captain and new Second Mate.

Rantham seemed to have finally run out of luck, in addition to most of his teeth. He no longer responded to any efforts to engage him in conversation, though he would take up his watch when ordered. What good it did them was anybody's guess, but for that matter Triistan didn't see the point in holding any watches anymore, at least not until they had some kind of wind to follow and sails to hoist. But Lanky Lankham had already gone as far out on a creative limb as he dared by reducing the standard four-hour watch shifts to three, and he would not abandon the daily regimen. Had it been anyone else making that call, Triistan would have lauded them for recognizing the value of routine, particularly to sailors. If nothing else, it helped them mark the passage of time. But he knew - they all knew - it wasn't about establishing some stable ground for the crew, to give them some kind of normalcy to cling to. It was about "Procedure" and "Doing Things According to Protocol", and most of all, it was about Captain Voth using them to exercise his command.

So Rantham sat his watches, which is to say that rather than huddle at the back of the boat peering at his fellow crew mates and muttering to himself, he instead took up the Watchman's Post - either of two small platforms protruding to starboard and port of the ship's waist - and huddled there, peering at his fellow crew mates and muttering to himself.

Dreysha also largely kept to herself, spending most of her waking hours watching Voth and Sherp and honing the blade of her push dagger with a whetstone - where she got the stone, he couldn't say. He could ask her, but he still felt trapped by the awkwardness that had developed between them since he discovered she had stolen his journal.

Triistan wanted very much to get back on more familiar footing with Dreysha. Despite what she had done, he found that he missed her company, especially her wry sense of humor and brash honesty. The pressure to speak with someone about the Expedition continued to grow, and he had even come up with several different, semi-plausible theories for how the page could have been creased that would exonerate her, but he still could not bring himself to approach her. So, hoping to reign in his thoughts and dull their intensity, he did the only thing he could think of, delving into the journal itself and, in a sense, returning to Aarden.

He started first by scanning through some of the sections he had written before they had first sighted land, not really reading them, but rather perusing the pages themselves, looking for... well, he really wasn't sure what he was looking for to be honest. Another folded page? A smudged fingerprint? He didn't find either, nor any other clue that Drey or anyone else had been through it, even though he scanned all the way to his last entry. So he flipped back to the page she had marked and read it again, then turned to the next page.

Sixday, Vehnya, 256, The 3rd Day of the Expedition, 26th since Landfall (Evening)

Myles and Wrael were right; not long after I made yesterday's entry, we began to hear the muffled roar of a waterfall. A short time later, we came to a series of low rock shelves, across which the river ascended (or descended from its point of view). The shelves weren't steep and under normal circumstances would not have been difficult to scale, however they were strewn with fat boulders obstructing the river's passage, creating snags for passing branches and, in a few cases, whole trees. As a result, the shelves were really a series of broken, tangled dams and boulder-strewn pools, effectively impassable for us. We spent the rest of the afternoon scouting the banks to either side, finally finding a game trail on the north bank that wound its way up alongside the falls. It looks as though Myles and I will not be required to do any climbing just yet...

He remembered those falls and the picturesque basin at their foot very clearly. What struck him most about these entries was his innocent curiosity and excitement; at the time he had had no idea of the dangers they would face, though he paused to consider one particular passage for its chilling prescience:

It is quite curious that such a small body of water can convey as much or more of the same sense of hidden menace as the sea - I would not have believed it if I hadn't experienced it personally.

Triistan had a sudden strange sense of being there again, but as an observer, and wished he could warn the young man he saw wading in the water to trust his instincts and turn back - tell them all to turn back and leave this place before it was too late. For some, that moment was only a few pages away.

The next entry was very brief - only a few sentences - and made on the sixth day of the expedition: the day before they discovered the ancient battlements First Mate Tarq had called Ahbaingeata, "Rivergate":

Nineday, Vehnya, 256, The 6th day of the expedition, 29th since Landfall:

Nothing much to note for past 3 days. Bone tired - the current's been stiff, and the Captain's been setting a hard (illegible). Rain has stopped, but heat and humidity relentless - we seem to be traveling through perpetual clouds of steam and I now know what it feels like to be stewed! Last night we camped in the dugouts again, well after moonrise - trying to outpace the jharrls we assume. Found a nice clear shoal late this afternoon, where the southern bank thrusts out into the river and makes a tiny island. Strange - not much but grass growing on it. Probably for the best after my experience in the citadel tree the other night. More tomorrow; too tired to write any longer.

River sounds odd; Wrael says its more rapids further upstream.
Hope he's wrong.

He wasn't wrong. Triistan turned to his drawing of the Rivergate and felt his pulse quicken. He remembered the moment vividly, sitting in the strange blue grass and purposely drawing the dugouts first - only five after the sixth had been stolen or scuttled - while the rest of the expedition ate breakfast and discussed what it was, who or what could have constructed it, and what might have happened to them. He looked at the drawing and now, as then, his eye was drawn to the arched tunnel at its center: a gaping maw where the river emerged through the broken teeth of what remained of its gates. Although at the time he wouldn't have admitted it, he knew now that he had deliberately drawn the boats first because of the sense of dread he was feeling, trying to delay the moment when he had to acknowledge what his eye and mind had already calculated. Later that day, as they clambered over the twisted, blackened and melted steel, the rest of the party concluded the same thing.

He'd had plenty of time to complete the drawing and make the next journal entry, since the Captain had ordered the Firstblade and three of his reavers to approach the gate for a closer look, leaving only Jaspins behind with the main party. They took one dugout and returned just after midday to report that the gate and wall appeared to be unmanned, and whatever had occurred there had happened years before, judging from the amount of jungle growth on and around the ruins.

The rest of the expedition had already broken camp while they awaited the reconnaissance party's return, so as soon as the Firstblade had finished his report, Captain Vaelysia ordered them into the dugouts. Commander Tchicatta pulled her aside briefly for a discreet conversation, and Triistan recalled wondering if it had anything to do with his suspicions about the gates. He considered approaching them, but Wrael and Myles were haranguing him to help launch their dugout, and then there was no more time to worry about it.

The current was very strong here, so soon they were all paddling hard, working their way upriver. The wall steadily grew taller, rising an additional hundred and fifty feet above the emergent layer of the surrounding forest, dominating the valley. Triistan remembered very clearly how his early impression of the gated tunnel as an open mouth had continued to grow stronger and more menacing as they drew closer.

It had only taken Commander Tchicatta and the other reavers about two hours to reach the gates and return, but it took them all much longer in fully-laden boats and without the luxury of a Creugar in every craft. It was early evening before they found a suitable clearing to put ashore, though both terms were highly relative, Triistan reflected. The "clearing" was actually a small cave created by the arching span of roots from an odd-looking tree, one of dozens that grew along the banks here. The roots were limbless and as thick as a man's leg, emanating from the base of a trunk that began about fifteen feet above the water line. They cascaded out and down, some anchoring themselves in the bank, but most plunging into the dark river water, creating large cave-like spaces within their span. Some of them were large enough to moor several boats, so it was in one of these strange shelters that they chose to make their camp for the evening. They had decided not to push on in the failing light, since beyond the broken gates and the rapids that tumbled over and around them, a mass of river detritus had clogged the mouth of the tunnel.

He flipped the page with his rendering and quickly scanned the journal entry after that, shivering as he remembered waking in the citadel tree cocooned in what they thought at the time had been spider webs. He flipped again to the next entry and started reading it in detail.

Tenday, Vehnya, 256, The 7th day of the Expedition, 30th since Landfall - Evening:

We all agree: the gates were destroyed from the inside, as though something forced its way out. The sheer scale of them, as well as the wall towering above us, is both awe-inspiring and terrifying. It seems clear that these structures were built by the gods, or at least constructed during their reign and with their assistance. Either that or some race of giants unknown to us once walked this land - a race I hope has long since departed. I wish I had studied more of the ancient histories. Perhaps I was wrong in assuming that the gods were dead, so looking backwards was a waste of time.

Despite my misgivings I feel I must comment on the design, though: the engineering is well beyond our own abilities, and even the Ship's Whip is impressed, though I remain convinced that he knows much more about this structure than he has yet revealed to us. At least he gave us a name to call it by: Ahbaingeata in the Old Speech - literally, 'The Rivergate'. I hope to speak with him later and learn more than just a name.

But, I am getting ahead of events. Let me try to put this down in its proper order for the sake of recordkeeping, or as Doyen

Rathmiin used to say, "If you tell me the end first, boy, there's no point in saying anything else."

It was a very difficult day of rowing from our tiny hillock-camp to where we have tied off the boats for the night. The current was swift and I have a newfound appreciation for the strength of our reavers: the same trip that took them only half a watch took us nearly two - just over six hours to bring our boats and supplies upriver from what we've come to call "Bluegrass Knoll". It surprised me, actually, since the river is so much wider and deeper here. When I said as much, Wrael grunted and spit over the side.

"Deeper don't mean slower, boy." He then looked down over the edge of our dugout, frowning suspiciously. "Deeper just means darker."

Although I understood his implication, I chose not to respond to it. This type of insinuation is nothing new from Wrael, but a black mood has descended on the rest of the party as well. All the way upriver, I felt its weight growing heavier, and I know that others feel it too. Even the jungle grows quiet, and the silence has a tense, expectant feel to it. I have to admit that I am dreading entering that tunnel, despite my great desire to inspect the machinery that must lie within - I cannot conceive how it is possible to operate such massive doors, to say nothing of the portcullis. But all of that really misses the point, doesn't it? The real riddle here isn't the how, it is the why.

By the time we reached the shattered gates, others were beginning to consider the same question. Myles kissed the talisman that hung around his neck - a curious trinket made from a small brass ring woven through with strands of the Captain's hair - and Wrael muttered and swore to himself, then spat over the side again. Thinman sat looking straight up, wide mouth hanging open.

"By the blood of Tarsus, what ye fellas think they was looking to keep out?"

Wrael snorted. "By your great, bloody arse, they weren't keeping nothin' *out*."

Several others in the neighboring boats were also clutching various charms, similar to Myles' talisman, wide eyes crawling over the wreckage and reading the signs for themselves. I was nodding, finding some relief in sharing the thought that had been tormenting me since we first saw the Rivergate this morning. I suddenly found myself talking.

"He's right. These have been forced out from the inside - see those large steel cylinders up there, those were parts of the hinges - gods I wouldn't even know where to begin trying to calculate the load at those bearing points - but see they are all bent and twisted outward, just as the gates themselves are. And there -" Once I had begun I couldn't seem to stop myself. I pointed at the massive grid work of wide, flattened steel that had been a portcullis about fifteen feet inside the mouth of the tunnel. The bars that made up the grid work were as wide as my hand and two fingers thick, though that was a bit difficult to judge based on their blackened, bent and melted condition.

"See there, too, how the portcullis has been bent backwards and up - outwards, towards us? Do you realize what kind of force you would need to apply to that amount of steel, not to mention, that warped area there was melted... and up there some of the archstones on this side have been forced out also? But this, this is truly incredible here..."

I guess I was 'lost in the moment', because I hardly recall leaving our boat, but I suddenly found myself standing on one of the wrecked gates and pointing out its structure, composition, and - most importantly - the fact that the steel was somehow melted in several places. There were great, long scores, tears in what had once been the beautifully-engraved surface of the thick plating. Unfortunately my illustration does not do proper justice to the scale and feel of the scene. The gates themselves are monstrous: great, twisted steel shapes that rise from the river draped in decades' worth of undergrowth. Vines as thick as my wrist, flowers, shrubs, ferns of every size and description - even some of what we've taken to calling Caveroot Trees - all climb and clutch at them, trying to drag them back into the river. Everything was covered with a greenish-black slime, very slippery to the touch, and I must have looked like I'd lost my sanity slipping and scrambling over them, but I had to look at the engravings up close. I was determined to take some rubbings of them until I suddenly realized that everyone was staring at me -

Wait - something is happening. I hear Welms and Jaegus shouting about... something moving in the tunnel?

The entry abruptly ended there, and Triistan did not need to turn the page to recall why. Welms and Jaegus (the older) had climbed to the top of the debris pile to attempt to see if the tunnel was clear behind it. The dam was a mass of dead tree limbs, roots, leaves, and gods-knew-what-else that had gradually lodged in the twisted grate of the portcullis, so it was relatively easy for them to scale. When they reached the top, Welms thrust a torch into the gap at the top of the dam, between the debris and the opening's arched pinnacle, while he crouched and tried to see into the darkness beyond. The jungle around them was indistinct in the gloom, as the Maiden had set some time before and the Crone was well beyond the encroaching jungle's looming horizon. In the bloody gloom of the long evening, the river's strange luminescence was just barely visible.

Jaegus called down that Welms had heard something. The Firstblade immediately ordered two of his reavers to scale the debris pile to investigate, but as they reached the halfway point, a terrible screaming noise began emanating from the tunnel. Jaegus stumbled backwards in alarm, catching his foot in amongst a tangle of branches and momentarily hanging from that leg while scrambling for purchase. As Welms stood, waving his torch, dozens of dark winged shapes exploded from the opening. The noise of their screams and the whisper and crack of their wings rose to a deafening pitch as dozens became hundreds. They were little more than dark silhouettes against the fading sky, just broad wings, tails and teeth. They tore past Welms, striking him so that he spun sideways, first one way and then the other, sending his torch spinning into the air, and then he began to fall, disappearing for a moment as the black shapes swirled around him...

It was one of the images indelibly etched in Triistan's mind, one of the worst memories from an expedition steeped in blood and horror. An instant after Welms disappeared, he reappeared again, flying in the midst of the swarm of creatures, tumbling and jerking through space, first one way and then the other as dozens sank their claws and teeth into his clothes, hair and flesh, fighting over him as crows might fight over a scrap of meat. And then his body just came apart in pieces, blood and gore showering down upon the rest of the party as the swarm rose into the evening sky above them, a huge living shadow that sped up and over the trees. Hundreds more continued rushing from the tunnel for several moments, until finally the last of them disappeared into the gathering night, and darkness and silence descended on the expedition.

Jaegus was nowhere to be seen either, and when they called out for him there was no answer. Commander Tchicatta tossed torches up to the reavers that had been climbing the pile and ordered them to search, starting where he had fallen and working their way down. It hadn't taken long.

All that remained was the lower half of his leg, still stuck in the boot where his foot had caught in the debris.

- 15 -

The Wolves of Flinderlaas

Casselle lifted a small girl up to the waiting arms of her mother. The family's wagon was filled with everything too important to leave behind, including a couple of angry chickens. The mother offered her thanks to Casselle, who smiled and nodded politely in reply. The young girl nearly fell out of the cart trying to hold Casselle's attention with her infectious smile and flailing waves goodbye, but was restrained by her patient parent. The Templar managed a smile in response, comforted slightly by the unbound optimism that only being young could provide.

This was the second caravan leaving Flinderlaas in as many weeks. Once away, only the direct retainers of Hedrek von Darren would remain with Casselle's group and the handful of left over Outriders and Templars that had been stationed here. In the weeks since her arrival, she had gained an appreciation for Outrider Commander Royan Stone and those in his command. They were not as highly trained or heavily armored as the Laegis, but they had a dogged determination to do right for the people of Flinderlaas, and Casselle respected that greatly. Even Aileah, who had originally set her on edge, had become less abrasive as they worked together to get the townsfolk packed for relocation. Most of her initial irritation was due to the relationship Aileah had struck up with Raabel. Since then, it had blossomed into a more genuine affection during the time they'd been there, and it was good to see Raabel happy.

The edict to move the settlers had been handed down by the Gundlaan Elder Circle. The settlement was to be abandoned until a sufficient force could be recruited, trained and supplied to provide a "compelling deterrent against those seeking to oppose Gundlaan's development of Flinderlaas and the surrounding areas of the Deckoran Wilds." Temos was particularly fond of repeating that specific part of their instructions to anyone who asked. He did so in a comically deep tone, so as to properly portray his complete lack of respect for the language of the document. His irreverence had been a big hit with the Outriders, who consequently offered him full access to their own private ale reserves in return for more of his comically exaggerated tales of big city life.

Jaksen remained the least changed by their new surroundings and often found excuse to work closely with Casselle while they performed their duties. She assumed it was because he missed the girl he'd left waiting for him in Strossen, but he had not mentioned it again since that day they had first arrived here. He seemed to feel the most satisfied when he was helping, so she let him lend a hand wherever necessary.

To be honest, her thoughts were preoccupied with other things. She had seen Captain Taumber infrequently since he'd been introduced to Renholf Crennel, the Captain that had been assigned to lead the two squads of Templars here. Crennel had been the reason they'd come. The account she'd read about in his letter seemed horrible enough, but after seeing the man for the first time, she could tell that his experience had profoundly changed him more than she'd imagined. He was terrified of being in the dark and the keep's physician said he had refused to sleep since returning. He was haggard and lean, more skeleton than man by the look of it.

Captain Taumber had begun to work with him almost immediately, calling for the stash of medicinal herbs he kept in his saddlebags. He was no Arxhemist, but he had a way of finding the right formula for burns, cuts and upset stomachs to make them vanish almost immediately. Casselle wondered what mix of plants would be necessary to restore Renholf Crennel's sanity. She never did find out, because Odegar set them to work immediately, doing what they could to coordinate with the Outriders and the town leadership to pack the settlers up for relocation back beyond the Bay of Athoriss.

The Outriders and most of the inhabitants of Flinderlaas were very appreciative and eager to get themselves and their families to safety. The only real resistance was from Hedrek von Darren, or more specifically, his son Vincen, who had assumed command of the remaining squad of local Templars after Captain Crennel's unfortunate excursion. Casselle was reminded of this as she watched Vincen von Darren stroll down through the center of town, having come at his leisure, well after the wagons were finished loading.

The caravan hoped to be underway shortly, before the morning suns climbed any higher in the sky. The Outrider escort that would accompany these families also wanted nothing more than to be well on their way long before nightfall. Although no more people had died after their arrival, the nights seemed full of strange noises and unseen terrors, leading to disturbing reports each morning. Casselle had pulled a watch duty just the other night, and was convinced half a dozen times that the wolves had amassed at the edge of the forest only to have the silvery light of the rising moon chase the shadows away. Her nerves had been honed to a brittle edge since then, and she had little time for Vincen von Darren's preening "inspection walks".

Both von Darren's had mentioned that Captain Crennel had squired Vincen on the battlefield. His rise to glory was slightly less noteworthy when heard through the lips of the Outriders, however. Shayn Fletcher, one of the three scouts that had led them through the woods, told them that Vincen and his father had been buying the affections of the newest squad of Templars, a group who had graduated just a year before Casselle, Temos, Raabel and Jaksen. They'd been green when they had arrived and they had not tried hard to prove themselves to anyone, preferring safe positions inside the keep rather than duties that would expose them to the dangers of frontier life. Shayn told them that the veteran Templars, the ones who'd been out with Renholf, had not bothered to hide their disapproval.

Vincen had been riding around the perimeter of the von Darren lands in the company of his entourage the day that Renholf Crennel had returned from Isenglen. The Templar Captain had used the last of his strength to pen the letter that would eventually arrive in the care of Captain Taumber. Shayn couldn't say when Crennel had made the proclamation, but the morning after, the younger von Darren showed up in full, fitted armor.

"With an attitude like one of the Young Gods themselves had come back to life just to anoint him King of the Wilds," Shayn had concluded with as much derision as he could wring from his voice.

Casselle wasn't entirely surprised. Vincen's new squad was just like many others she had seen in Strossen; the sons of rich fathers, who still felt having a family member in the Templars was a status symbol. The Templars allowed such things because they needed the bodies and the money that accompanied such recruits. She didn't need any help to fill in the rest of the details herself. Out in the Wilds, these four became quick friends with Vincen and the luxuries he could afford them. Backing him and his dubious claim was only a natural extension of the honor they'd already traded for easy amenities.

The thought of working alongside all of them made her teeth clench, but that was before she realized they wouldn't be doing much work at all. With Renholf incapacitated, they'd been busying themselves with pushing others around. While there was no official relationship between the Outriders and the Templars, the former had always deferred to the long standing expertise of the latter. Casselle couldn't help but think that a responsible Templar wouldn't abuse that relationship, but Vincen von Darren did not bother to bear the weight of being responsible. While this chafed her to no end, Captain Taumber had made it clear that she and her squad needed to focus on the townspeople. That was why they were here, after all.

She reminded herself of the Captain's words whenever Vincen poked his face around, criticizing the way her team was helping organize the evacuation, shoring up defenses, or securing resources. She'd stopped Raabel several times from busting his gloating smile into pieces, no matter how much she wanted to see that happen... or to do it herself.

"That's the last of it," Temos said, appearing from behind the final wagon just off to Casselle's side.

"Signal them to ride out," she said. "They're already late in leaving." Temos nodded and waved at the Outrider horsemen at the front of the short column. A young ginger-haired woman waved back and whistled loudly at her team. The others returned the signal and she gave the final call to get things underway. A middle aged man at the head of the caravan looked around to confirm they were starting before urging the team hitched to his wagon to begin. In short order, the motley train of carts began to roll out of the village.

Jaksen and Raabel moved to stand by Casselle and Temos as they watched the wagons go. The travelers were protected by a thin force of Outriders. Their total number had been small to begin with, before being crippled further by being cut in thirds, with two groups assigned to escort the first two caravans and one skeletal crew to accompany von Darren and the remaining Templars back. Casselle thought it was foolish to waste Outriders on von Darren, who would be flanked by the far better armed and trained forces. Even if Vincen and his cronies were worthless in a fight, their iron-clad corpses would make better barricades than a living leather-clad Outrider. She tried again to purge the venom she felt for the younger von Darren as he approached Casselle's squad.

"Sent them along, did you?" Vincen said loudly. "Just as well. They were always underperforming anyways."

"And you would know this," Temos said, "because you have firsthand knowledge of what constitutes a lack of performance?"

"A properly educated man knows lazy when he sees it," Vincen replied. There were a few snickers in agreement from Vincen's squad.

"So you have consulted with a properly educated man, then?" Temos asked. Vincen's face soured, but he did not take the bait.

"Now that your squad has sent the peasants away, I expect you to help catalog everything that remains. That way we can properly account for it on our books," Vincen began. "Since those settlers have abandoned this property, by default, it and anything left behind is now rightfully an asset of the landholder, which happens to be the von Darren family."

"You're taking everything that was left behind?" Jaksen asked, shocked at the audacity of the request.

"I don't have to 'take' anything, *boy*," Vincen said, making sure to add emphasis to his dismissive address of Jaksen. "It became ours when those scruffy dirthuggers turned tail and ran."

"They left on orders of the Elder Circle," Raabel growled. Casselle could hear his thick leather gloves squeak slightly as he clenched his fists.

"That same Elder Circle wrote the property laws that I'm looking to fairly enforce," Vincen replied mockingly. "You may not like the laws, but we are here to make sure they are applied equally. Are we not?" The last question was not open ended. The hastily promoted son of Hedrick von Darren was looking squarely at Casselle when he said it, waiting for the squad leader to acknowledge him.

Her jaw was clenched tightly as she nodded once in agreement.

"You see, even the little princess..." Vincen couldn't even finish the insult. Casselle was not surprised one of her team struck the arrogant bastard in the face, she was just surprised that Jaksen beat Raabel to the punch. She was also not surprised that every one of Vincen's squad recoiled, stepping back at the sudden assault.

Vincen spiraled in a tight circle before tipping over on his way to the ground, the one punch being sufficient to throw the young man off balance. As he clattered to the ground, hands finally started to clasp hilts, but before the first blade could be drawn, Casselle stepped forward, cleanly calling for attention in her most authoritative tone. Like trained hounds, both squads immediately stopped and snapped into position.

"Templar Furrow! You have been witnessed striking a fellow Templar," Casselle spoke swiftly, but clearly. "Do you deny this?"

"No, sir!" Jaksen replied, though somewhat confused. Casselle could see on the ground that Vincen was very angry, but equally confused.

"Templar Pelt, what is the recommended punishment for unauthorized combat against a fellow Templar?" Casselle asked sharply.

"Depending on the severity of the crime, a review from the Masters that could lead to expulsion from the Laegis or loss of off-duty time for additional work assignments," Temos replied before quickly adding, "sir!"

Casselle did not bother to look at Jaksen, though she knew he must be sweating slightly. During training, Casselle would always be the one to assume the worst punishment possible. Whatever fault her instructors found with her - and they looked hard to find many - she would always take the full measure of punishment for any infraction. She did it without argument or complaint and served each to a full measure and then some. One night when Temos asked her why she willingly took on all the extra work, she answered succinctly:

"Because the world outside these walls does not hand out easy punishments."

After that, the rest of her squad willingly accepted as she did, regularly assuming the worst duties and punishments without question and often accomplishing more than asked. It was something the other cadets didn't understand. They never brought up with each other why they had all chosen to follow Casselle's lead without question, but Temos noticed something different after that day. Many of the instructors who had retired after a life in the field acted differently around them. They didn't treat them with favor, in fact many times they often gave them the hardest tasks, but they never did so dismissively. Often times they would accompany the squad, giving them extra tips or training as they worked. When Temos mentioned it to the rest of them, he didn't dare call it respect, but they agreed it often felt like it.

Casselle could tell that Jaksen was ready to hear the worst. All in all, it was not as bad as he expected. The rest of the week he had extra kitchen duty, enough to keep most of his "free" hours busy.

"Yes, sir!" Jaksen said promptly in return. Vincen von Darren scrambled to his feet, shrugging off a helpful hand from his own squad mates.

"You arrogant peasants! Don't think for a minute that I won't have you drawn up on charges the minute I..." Vincen began to froth. He cowered back as Raabel broke line and took a step forward.

"I wouldn't mind an extra week of kitchen duties myself," Raabel growled in his deep baritone, fists already clenched. Before another incident could occur, Casselle shoved her way between them.

"One week cleaning stables," Casselle growled, and as Temos started to make a face, she added with an authoritative finger, "one week supply services." They quickly snapped to attention and accepted their punishment. As they stood there, thinking on how they'd each like to throttle Vincen von Darren, Casselle turned to face him.

"My squad is now occupied with other duties," she said calmly. With a slight nod of her head, she turned and began marching back to the castle. Jaksen, Raabel and Temos watched as she passed them and then took one last good look at Vincen's rapidly reddening face and the dumbfounded looks of his men. The three of them couldn't help but smile as they moved to catch up to their squad leader.

"Did you plan that?" Temos asked, looking at Jaksen, "the two of you?"

"No... I... no," Jaksen replied somewhat dumbfounded in discovering he had unwittingly gotten them all out of fattening the von Darren treasury.

"How did it feel?" Raabel asked.

"I've never felt quite so satisfied pulling extra duty," Jaksen said.

"I meant punching him," Raabel grumbled, sounding somewhat upset he'd been cheated out of taking a shot as well.

"Oh... that," Jaksen said with joy in his voice. "That felt very good indeed."

Casselle fought hard to keep from smiling.

***

After a quick lunch, she made sure her squad was working off their extra duties before retiring to the small room they shared inside the Keep. Casselle had plenty of work to do as well. She had to fill out a report for each of the extra duties she'd assigned. She wanted to make sure the incident and subsequent actions were well documented in case Vincen tried to carry through with his hollow threat of attempting to press charges against any or all of them. She didn't honestly expect that his commission would stand up when they returned to Strossen, but she wasn't going to let a lack of proper paperwork be the rope they would all hang by.

Casselle didn't even realize she'd missed dinner until a bowl of savory smelling stew and a thick roll were set down on the tiny table next to her papers.

"Jaksen told me he'd never been so proud to peel potatoes than he had for this stew," Odegar Taumber said as he set the food down. "It seems a shame to let such a thing go to waste."

Casselle chuckled and cracked open the roll, dipping the knot she'd pulled off into the stew before biting into it.

"Temos and Raabel also seemed equally elated. Strange behavior for Templars that have been given extra work shifts for a full week," Odegar added, taking a seat of his own on one of the simple framed beds. He leaned back against the wall, not even pretending to hide a grin. "You also may not be at all surprised to hear that Vincen von Darren happens to be sporting a rather ugly black bruise on his face, just under his left eye."

"That is... a tragedy," Casselle said calmly before returning to her meal. Odegar allowed himself a small laugh. Casselle couldn't help but notice how weary her old teacher looked, especially as the mirth faded from his face. The two sat quietly, leaving her slightly self conscious about how loudly she had started eating her stew. She took a moment to clean her mouth with a nearby rag, trying to brush some silence over her embarrassment.

Her teacher was clearly not paying attention, though. She could tell by the look in his eyes he was far away, somewhere between exhaustion and a richly deserved nap. Hunger goaded her to finish the meal, which she did as quickly and quietly as possible, her preferred way of doing most things.

Captain Taumber fought off sleep with a snort, pulling himself forward on the bed, away from the wall.

"I feel it's important to tell you that Captain Crennel is lost to us," Odegar confessed as he rubbed one of his palms against his eyes. "His body is barely surviving. Whatever remained of his spirit will drag his health along with it as it inevitably leaves."

"He wasn't just hurt, was he?" Casselle asked.

"No. Whatever this thing was that he saw, it was more than a simple pack of wolves. It's clear the experience did more than just injure his body," the Templar Captain confirmed.

"And the woman?"

"I think you're being overly kind calling her that. I wouldn't," Odegar said.

"Why?"

"You've yet to fight the H'kaan, and by all the fleeting memories of the High Houses, I hope you never have to," the Captain said, wringing his hands together at the thought of it. "There are a few of us who know that there were... things... Well, just imagine all the bad tales you've heard of the H'kaan and their bloody hunger. Now imagine there was a way to hollow out a person and put all of that inside them."

"You mean that as a clever description, don't you?" Casselle asked, her throat tightening slightly, "Like a wolf in sheep's clothing?"

"I certainly hope so," Odegar said. "Let us hope that we are never in the position to find out. Now, let us put that aside"

He was trying to bury the conversation. Though Casselle yearned to speak about it further, she did not press him for more. Instead, she scooped her reports into a neat pile and folded them in half, tucking them into a small leather satchel that she handed off to her superior officer. He acknowledged it with a nod and turned to leave. He paused for a moment at her door.

"We are scheduled to leave in a week, after the von Darren's have finished their packing and looting, and the keep itself is sealed and shuttered. That being said, we may not have a week left to us. If that is the case, I want you to do everything you can to get back to Gundlaan proper," he emphasized. He took a step away, but added one last thing, speaking over his shoulder without looking at her directly.

"The Templars already have too many like that black-eyed idiot, Vincen. They will need you and your squad ten times over if this is as I fear it."

She was humbled by the compliment, but surely he exaggerated again. She wanted to ask him to explain further, but Odegar was gone, striding quickly out of the doorway.

***

Casselle had assigned herself to the second shift watch, which would carry her up to the peak of the night. But second shift only afforded her a short nap after dinner. By the time that nap was over, the long evening had ended and she walked outside to a pale crescent moon hanging overhead in a starry, cloudless sky. She worked her way to the top of the ramparts, checking in with the Outrider Watch Captain as she did. At the top of the wall, she relieved one of the older Outriders, a bald man with a long gray beard. Smiling, he left his post, confessing he was eager to close his evening with a mug and a pipe before heading to bed.

Casselle checked the walk, seeing who else she would be sharing it with. There were two Outriders she recognized by their faces, but couldn't place names to them as she'd never been properly introduced. Rounding out the quartet was Aileah Blue, who was walking towards her.

"It's a nice night. Nice and quiet," Leah said. Casselle nodded in agreement. She was wondering if the Outrider was planning to talk to her all night. More importantly, she was worried about what the topics of discussion would cover. She didn't have to wonder or worry for long.

"Vincen and his boys didn't even bother to show up for supper," Leah said with a snicker. "They're likely hiding back in Daddy's house, applying expensive unguents to their damaged egos." Casselle smiled.

"I must say that I sure would like to have been the one to cuff him," she continued. "I've been waiting to see someone rub dirt on that one's face ever since I got here."

"We should..." Casselle made a slight motion with her hand. Being on watch actually required them to walk the walls, so they could survey the castle grounds and the wild just beyond.

"Right, right," Leah replied with a smile, patting Casselle on the shoulder as she passed by, as if in acknowledgement and approval that she had been the one to directly engineer Vincen's humiliation. The Templar smiled as she began her rounds, keeping an eye on things below and beyond.

The other two Outriders were Carshill and Ela, Casselle discovered, greeting them both as she met them while her shift progressed. She ran into Leah several more times as well and was glad to discover that not all of her talk was about bunkhouse conquests. Indeed, Casselle felt as if she might have to reconsider her opinion of the Outrider after several short but pleasant exchanges.

The moon peaked in the sky and Casselle was looking forward to spending the rest of the night in her bunk. Carshill and Ela had finished their shifts roughly halfway through her own and had been replaced a short while back with Varr and Wilkers. Unlike the Templars that shadowed Vincen, the Outriders had been nothing but pleasant and professional.

As her shift approached its end, Casselle looked for Temos, who would be arriving shortly to replace her. Currently he was nowhere in sight. As she approached Leah for the last time that evening, she could tell she was not the only one eager to be relieved.

"I hate these long shifts," Leah said with a yawn. "Keeps me worn out when I could be doing more important things, you know?" There was a subtle prod accompanied by a wink and a smile. Casselle knew exactly what she meant and was pleasantly surprised that this was the first time she'd brought it up. Leah was intently scanning the courtyard for her replacement while Casselle took another long look around at the edge of the town, towards the forest.

She felt her paranoia creeping up on her again as the shadows at the edge of the tree line flickered and shifted. It looked like something was out there moving.

She convinced herself it was just her imagination. If there was something there... the thought hung, like a snowflake held aloft by a sudden updraft. Casselle had no idea what the tactics of these beasts would be like. Up to this point she'd trained against opponents with two arms and two legs, opponents that could be unbalanced and disarmed, opponents she'd trained herself where best to strike and how much force was required in order to disable or kill. This would be a whole different breed of danger.

She tried to shove her troubling thoughts aside as Leah nudged her again.

"Do you think he should be up and about?" she asked, pointing to the figure staggering across the open courtyard towards the front gate. It took a moment for her to place the man, since the only time she'd met him before now was when they'd arrived and she'd witnessed him huddled up in the corner of a room, thin limbs lashing out at anyone who dared get close to him.

"Renholf Crennel," Casselle replied with a whisper.

"He don't look any better, but he's on his feet," Leah observed, before asking the more obvious question. "What's he doing out here?"

Casselle was already moving with purpose as the gaunt Templar Captain approached the front gates. Aileah picked up on the Templar's unspoken urgency and followed after. By the time they arrived on the ground, Crennel was already trying to force his way past the gate guards.

"Let me out! By the ghosts of the High Houses, let me out!!" he screamed. Casselle knew he posed no real threat or challenge to the able Outriders at the gate, but the wild desperation in his eyes was profoundly disconcerting.

"Calm down, sir," one of the guards said, "we'll get you back to the infirmary."

"No time!" Crennel yelled. "They are nearly here! They are upon us! We must flee!"

"Sir, I'm sure whatever it is..." one of the Outriders began in a calm voice before the wild-eyed Templar Captain lashed out with a strike that his frail arms would have seemed incapable of. It was enough to club down the Outrider, giving Crennel an unobstructed moment of freedom to run to the gate. Cursing, the Outriders were but a step behind, followed by Casselle and Aileah.

Though it was impossible to open the full gate by himself, he had managed to unbolt the smaller sally port off to the side and had actually cracked open the entrance before the Outriders fell upon him, wrestling him to the ground.

"Oi there!" one of the guards struggling with the crazed Templar Captain grunted at Casselle, "get that door closed!"

Casselle stepped around them, giving her clear access to the door. As she approached it, the cry came from above them.

"Sighting!" barked one of the remaining sentries on the wall. "From the North!" The other sentry confirmed it with a similar call. As Casselle took hold of the door handle she looked out at the town, turning her gaze northward.

At first it merely looked like boulders tumbling down a long slope, but very quickly she was able to discern the leading edge of the slide and it was most certainly not a cascade of rocks. It was a wave of hunched hairy beasts, charging madly, like a stampede of Harox, kicking up dirt all around them as they stormed forwards.

The wolves were upon them. Casselle's heart began to race, but she fought to keep her calm.

She could tell that they moved with purpose, not some random happenstance. The wolves were quiet, focused and quick. It was chilling to watch them peel away from the forest and run full tilt towards the edges of town, splitting into smaller groups with almost military precision.

She slammed the door shut and slid the bolt back into place, only slightly reassured when it locked into position. Any confidence she had managed to retain, threatened to melt when Crennel surprised them all with another blood curdling scream.

"She is here! It is too late! The Wolfmother has come!" The Templar Captain was raving mad at this point, with flecks of foam flying from his lips, his eyes unfocused and distant.

"Shut him up!" Leah cried, half panicked herself. Casselle left the madman to the gate guards and climbed the stairs to the ramparts. She had to see what was happening. Upon reaching the top, the scene appeared even worse than it had from the ground.

The wolves were everywhere, already tearing up the village. Casselle had only ever seen wolves at a distance, and not often, but she could tell these were abnormally large. They rooted through anything outside the abandoned homes with savage ferocity. Others beat against barred doors with reckless disregard until the portals were forced open or destroyed altogether.

"Watch the doors!" cried one of the other sentries, though Casselle was too fixated on assessing the situation to tell which one it was. But on hearing the cry, she looked down at the outside of the door that she had barred herself. Certainly it was too thick and well-fortified to break down. But as her eyes fixed on the scene below, she saw the real danger. Two powerfully muscled wolves were fiercely scrabbling at the dirt underneath the door, trying to find a way under without the need to break it down. Someone else cried out before she could put words to flight.

"We need archers up here!"

Casselle gripped the hilt of her sword in frustration. It was useless from this height, and the last thing she wanted right now was to feel useless. Even though she had little practice with a bow, she yearned for one at this moment. Her heart was pumping with excitement and for a fleeting moment she contemplated what would happen if she simply jumped from this height, knowing full well that if the fall did not kill her, certainly the overwhelming number of wolves against a sole Templar would. The presence of someone pulling up next to her was reassuring, especially when that someone drew her bow and leaned forward for a clear shot over the wall.

The first arrow flew wide, but the lean-faced Outrider was quick to adjust, sending the next one deep into the flank of the beast. The single missile did not seem to be enough of a deterrent, however, and the wolf continued pawing at the packed ground.

"Rutting bastards!" hissed the Outrider as she nocked another arrow. Her next shot was joined by a few more from other archers that had also mounted the wall. Casselle heard more cries of alarm behind her, as the sentries tried to rouse every able bodied person remaining in the keep to assist.

A feeling of dread crawled down her neck, sliding down her spine. There, just past the center of town, walking from the shadow of one building across the open space to another was a woman...

...the witch from Renholf Crennel's letter had arrived.

She was just as he had described her, dirty feet and a thick cascade of hair affording little modesty for her otherwise naked body. Casselle was going to point her out to an archer, but she was already gone, only visible for that moment before another home blocked her from view. Trailing behind her, now also slipping from sight, was something equally hard to believe: two beasts bearing the general appearance of wolves, but which were even larger than the ones currently attacking the fort. Far more disturbing than their size, however, was the way they moved; less like wolves and more like large men hunched forward, with overlong arms to help them lope along.

"Yes!" cried the archer next to Casselle in triumph. She looked back just in time to see one of the large wolves at the gate finally stagger to the side and fall over. More arrows flew and more wolves fell, but for each one downed, others replaced them, swarming the sally port. In a short time, they doubled the progress the first couple had made at digging underneath the front wall.

Behind the gate, Outriders moved thick burlap sacks of sand and rock to throw against the bottom of the doors, or any other breach under the wall, in an effort to further bar any attempts to break through or tunnel under. *That would most certainly work*, she thought. It had to work.

She wanted to feel helpful, like she was doing something. Every muscle in her body was tense, waiting for some opportunity to contribute to the fight, no matter how small.

Then Casselle heard something over the shouts of the defenders at the wall. The sound was faint at first, easily disregarded. Then it grew, spreading from the town, doubling over and over again as each member of the pack lifted its head skyward to howl. It was a loud and sinister chorus that made the young Templar's blood run cold.

And just as quickly as it had crescendoed, the howling stopped altogether. The keep's defenders were as stunned as Casselle, watching as the wolves suddenly turned and retreated. The pack slipped silently and quickly behind or into the ruined houses in the village below.

The keep was quiet after that, as was the night that surrounded them, until one brave Outrider raised his voice in victory. Like the wolves before them, other voices soon joined in, until everyone was cheering. Casselle did not join in.

"Aren't you happy, ma'am?" the Outrider archer next to her asked, wearing a wide grin herself. "We beat them back!"

"No," Casselle replied simply, finally relaxing the grip on her sword hilt. She left the parapet to retrieve Renholf Crennel and take him to Captain Taumber.

They were already understaffed, threatened by an enemy they did not understand, and now they were out of time. No, she wasn't happy.

She was afraid.

- 16 -

Dark Passage

A single round eye fixed Triistan with its stare, the crescent-shaped pupil like a dark claw slicing the yellow-orange cornea around it. Its head was turned in profile and cocked a bit sideways, showing the spiked ridge of cartilage that ran from between its bony brows, back along the center of its broad skull and down its long, serpentine neck and back. Leathery wings tipped with small, razor sharp talons - four on each "hand" - were spread wide, displaying its corded chest and shoulder muscles, as well as the elongated, segmented body, much like the belly of a big snake. It was supported by two powerful legs and a narrow, tapering tail nearly half again as long as the rest of the creature. The ridge crest and wings were a deep jet, the rest of the body a stormy gray, but Triistan knew he had only lightened the tone in those areas so that he could clearly depict the lean muscle and sinew and convey the texture of these brutal predators. Next to the drawing he had made in his journal, he had written the name that the expedition had given the creature: Kongamatu, "Killer Matu", the terrible cousin to the reptilian birds that nested along the sea-cliffs of his homeland.

He traced the illustration with his forefinger, remembering the Aarden Expedition's first encounter with them. They didn't realize it at the time, but it was the moment their primary mission began to change from exploration to survival.

After the reavers Miikha and Taelyia reported finding only Jaegus' lower leg, Captain Vaelysia ordered everyone to begin a thorough search of the area. They all assumed he had been carried off and devoured in the same manner as Welms, but there was a chance he had been dropped or knocked somewhere nearby. Commander Tchicatta placed three of his men atop the dam as lookouts while the rest of them scoured the river, the banks and the debris pile itself. Triistan remembered the sour feeling in his stomach as he saw several of his mates looking up, searching the trees, and realized they weren't just keeping an eye out for the returning swarm; Jaegus' remains might have been anywhere.

After an hour or so it became too dark to continue the search, and by then they all knew it was fruitless. In addition, they were terribly exposed and vulnerable, spread out as they were and surrounded by a wilderness they did not understand. Triistan recalled the relief that had washed over him when the Captain ordered them back to the boats. Most of the party rushed to comply, seeking even the limited protection of the trees' overarching root systems until they could get the boats back out into the river and escape downstream. Consequently there was some pushing and shoving as men tried to get to their dugouts too quickly, until First Mate Tarq reminded them why he was called the Ship's Whip. He climbed up on the knobby knee of one of the roots and his voice cracked sharply over their heads.

"Ease down you mud-footed whoresons! I'll not have a panicked rout over a flock of fucking matu is that understood?" He immediately had their attention. "You there, Anthon, give Halliard a hand with the crate you've knocked overboard! Thinman, stow that galley of an ass you're carrying before you swamp your mates. The rest of you, to your benches and shut your scuppers or you'll have more than baby wyverns to worry about!"

The water under the roots had been waist deep and was glowing relatively brightly thanks to all of the splashing about they had done, causing the underside of the Caveroot Tree above them to ripple with reflected light and shadow. Everything had a blue-green, ghoulish under glow, allowing them to see each other and their immediate surroundings, which calmed them somewhat and helped to reinforce the Whip's discipline. For Triistan, though, it had only served to increase the feeling of approaching peril, since all that could be seen outside of their shelter by then was gloom. He remembered how his heart had jumped into his throat when he saw a bulky shadow move across one of the openings between the roots, before he recognized the massive double-bladed axe that Creugar carried on his back. Commander Tchicatta had picketed his men in a ring about the base of the tree, while he leaned on one of the roots just beyond and to the left of the Captain.

Triistan remembered how calm Captain Vaelysia had been, standing with her arms crossed and her long, booted legs knee-deep in the water at what passed for the "front" of their shelter: a sort of hollow in the bank where the boats' mooring lines had been tied to a broken root.

"Thank you, Mister Tarq. Well said, as usual." She looked at each of them in turn. As she did, backs straightened and shoulders squared, and the nervous whispers faded to silence. When her eyes had locked on Triistan's, he too had felt her strength and confidence shoring up his own resolve.

"We need to know what it is we're dealing with. Now, did any of you get a good look at them?"

Several shook their heads, but someone said it had looked to them like a giant matu, and a few others, including Triistan, agreed enthusiastically. Some heated discussion followed, since everyone was familiar with their much smaller and more colorful cousins, but no one had ever heard of them attacking anything larger than rodents and fish. It was true that they nested in large numbers - some communities along the southern coasts of Niyah and the Sea King Isles hosted thousands of matu - but they were solitary hunters, preferring fish over anything else (though they were not above picking off the occasional rat or other small mammal). At worst they were a nuisance, when several of them might descend on a fisherman's nets in hopes of a free and easy meal, but like most birds they could easily be shooed away. Some of Triistan's earliest climbing experiences had been scaling the sea-cliffs along the coast of Siitsii, stealing eggs from their nests. The more aggressive matu would batter him with their wings, but most would simply fly erratically around him, wheeling and screeching. Clearly the kongamatu were very different beasts, despite the strong resemblance to their distant island relatives.

Triistan had sketched the one in his journal while listening to the rest of the expedition arguing amongst themselves, and now, as he studied the picture, the conversation came back to him quite clearly. He could almost hear their voices, as if they were there on the launch's deck with him.

"Well whatever they was, they done for poor Jaegus an' Welms an' we'd better haul wind back downriver." A chorus of "ayes" greeted this from Chelson, but the Captain shook her head.

"I'm afraid not, gentlemen - not yet. This expedition will continue upriver. There is far too much at stake here, and I'll not have it said that the crew of the *SKS Peregrine* couldn't stomach a bit of danger for the sake of making history. Make no mistake: we *will* go through that tunnel, lads..." she paused, sweeping her gaze over them again.

"But we won't do it blindly or foolishly. First we are going to get to know our enemy a little better. At the moment we believe they have gone out to hunt - more than likely they do so at night, and nest in the day."

"Or maybe we spooked'em and drew them out, then fed'em a little snack is what I think," Wrael interjected.

"No one asked what you think, Corpsman, so stow it. We're going to find out one way or the other, because for now, we're staying right here." She waited a moment for the murmuring to die down, but before she could continue, Jaegus the Younger spoke up.

"Your pardon, Captain, but what if they come back? We're just rats in a barrel here..."

"Aye," she answered. "That's why we'll be shoring up this barrel and doing our best to hide it." She shouldered her way through another wave of murmuring.

"What about the jharrls?" several people called out. She nodded.

"We've discussed that possibility. Unless the apex arrives, we don't expect them to attack, making this our most defensible position until we've got a better idea of what's inside that tunnel."

"And if it does?" asked Wrael.

She fixed him with eyes the color of storm clouds. "By then we should know what's beyond those gates, and we'll respond accordingly." She held Wrael's gaze while she raised her voice to address the entire crew. "This discussion is over. I suggest the rest of you reach into your breaches and make sure you didn't leave your balls aboard the ship as well. Mister Tarq, I want two details - one gathering every vine and pliable bough within fifty paces of this camp, and another weaving that material into blinds, using this tree's roots as support posts. It needs to be a screen, not a solid wall - we need to be able to see out on all sides - and leave an opening large enough for one boat to pass - and by that I mean width and height, Whip. We're going to wait these things out, while the Firstblade sends two reavers inside to find a way through. I want the scouts to go with them - Myles, Wrael, grab torches and your weapons and report to Commander Tchicatta.

"Questions? Then get moving, people. We may not have much time."

They set to their tasks with a limited amount of grumbling; they were afraid, but they had been in tight spots before, and they still had faith that their Captain would see them safely through this one. The Firstblade advised the clearing detail to leave a good sized buffer of vegetation around their hide-out to augment their camouflage, and they all bent enthusiastically to the task: it was a welcome distraction, the way it always felt better for men awaiting an attack to sound general quarters and prepare their ship for war.

Their efforts were wasted, however. Myles and Wrael were just reporting to the reaver commander with their gear when suddenly a deep, guttural roar erupted from somewhere in the night, much louder and longer than anything they had yet heard. It spoke of terror and death, and not a man among them had to ask what it was. The apex jharrl had arrived.

Everyone froze as the call died away and silence poured into the terrified vacuum in its wake. Not an insect, bird or beast dared challenge that call for several long moments, until his three pack mates answered from different points around them - not as loud, but nearly as savage, and much closer. The Firstblade barked commands at his reavers. Several of the crew cursed, others cowered. Even now, so far removed, Triistan felt his pulse quicken and imagined he could again smell the sour odor of urine as more than one of his comrades lost control of their bladders in fear. He was sliding back into the moment, and it was even more terrible the second time because he knew what was coming.

The first roar had touched some primal instinct in most of them, reducing them to rats scurrying for a place to hide. The answering calls, so close and all around them, had those same crewmen thinking only of escape. They began stumbling back into the dugouts and scrambling for their paddles.

"NO! Leave the boats and pack up only what you can carry!" Captain Vaelysia's voice cut through the tumult, clear and strong. "Mister Tarq, distribute torches, a pair to every third man, but don't light them yet..."

"HAVE YOU LOST YOUR BLOODY MINDS?!" Wrael shouted. "We've got to get in the boats and get back downriver..."

Wrael's voice cut off abruptly as he found himself staring cross-eyed at the tip of the Captain's rapier. Her voice might have been harder and colder than the steel blade.

"If I hear you so much as breathe again, Corpsman, I will have you flayed and hung from a tree as jharrl bait. At least that way you would be of some use to me. Do we understand one another?"

The scout opened his mouth to answer, then promptly snapped it shut in the face of her icy promise, nodding silently instead. She sheathed her blade and said quietly, "Smart lad". She turned to face the rest of the party and spoke in measured, calm tones.

"That call came from downriver - no further than Bluegrass Knoll or my ears have been stopped up with more than a craven's crying. You all know what the river is like past there - so narrow that we had to row in single-file. A perfect spot for an ambush, and apex or no, we'd be torn to shreds with no room to maneuver and no solid footing. That leaves two options. Follow the wall into the jungle in the hopes of finding a suitable place to make a stand before they're on us, or go through the wall and use the tunnel as a choke point. I prefer the tunnel.

If they pursue us, we will choose the ground and hold the advantage. You have five minutes to pack your gear and form up outside. MOVE!"

They were ready in three. She led them up the side of the giant dam of tree limbs, twisted steel and shattered stone, casting fearful glances behind them, to their sides, and to the sky above. Triistan remembered trying to decide which would be worse - an ambush by the jharrls or the swarm of kongamatu returning as they were cresting the dam. Both seemed unavoidable as they reached the top to find the way blocked by what remained of the portcullis. It had been bent and twisted up and out, but it was still intact where it disappeared above into the channel that housed it when raised. At first glance it appeared there was no escape that way.

However, Jaspins had been one of the reavers to first climb the dam and wasted no time leading the Firstblade to the left, where a few of the vertical steel bars had snapped. The rest of the party followed them through an opening there and plunged down into the wet, waiting darkness.

To their relief, it was not completely black. The strange incandescence of the river brushed the tunnel's stone flanks to either side, as well as any other obstruction the water had to find its way through and around. It was not enough light to reach the ceiling, but at least they could see the base of the pile they were descending and something of a path ahead. It would not be an easy passage: everywhere they looked, the eerie bluish glow outlined broken stone and timber. Whatever had destroyed the gates had first fought like the damned to get there.

Captain Vaelysia called for a halt after they had descended for several minutes and ordered the torches to be lit. There were several exclamations of surprise and wonder as the light revealed more of their surroundings.

They had come a little more than halfway down the huge mound of tangled branches, vines, plants and other debris that had been trapped against the bent portcullis over the years. Triistan had estimated that the mouth of the tunnel was some hundred or more feet tall, and the dam came nearly to the top, so they were still relatively high up when they stopped, giving them a decent view of what lay ahead.

The water was like a glowing underground lake in some yawning cavern, but choked with debris. The sheer size of the timbers and stones that had been pulled down was awe-inspiring, whispering of gods and giants and heroes long forgotten. The telltale black streaks and partially-melted stone and metal spoke of powerful arxhemistry as well, and for a moment he had forgotten the danger that pursued them as he took in the incredible scene. Closest to them, the ceiling was still intact, but not far from where they had entered, a huge section had collapsed and the largest of these fallen remains thrust from the river like a finger, pointing.

Triistan remembered letting his eyes trail up from the broken, blackened beam to the ceiling far above. He could tell from where the roof met the gate opening that it was vaulted and riddled with murder holes - he had counted six dark squares immediately above where they had stopped to light their torches, and he saw several more just within range of their light. Arrow loops were also visible at three levels along the nearest wall, with the lowest being about fifteen yards above the river's waterline. He assumed the opposite wall contained them as well. But out away from where they stood, just above the first pile of rubble, the ceiling and part of the wall had been torn open, revealing the honeycombed chambers that gave defenders internal access to the defenses. It gave Triistan a unique view of the barbican's construction and he recalled wishing hard that he had time to study it further. He held his torch up higher, catching a flicker of reflected light and wondering what the defenders had left behind - weapons or armor, or some kind of artifact, perhaps?

The jungle had found its way into the tunnel as well; thick dark vines snaked out from the broken ceiling, or slipped in through the twisted portcullis like long, black fingers festooned in heavy webs of grey-green moss. In hindsight, Triistan now wondered how much of the destruction they saw had been caused by those searching vines, slowly prying even the strongest mortar joints apart, or dragging down weakened sections of the walls and ceiling. In Aarden, all manner of life seemed to favor savagery and malice.

Captain Vaelysia had them form up in the same order as their boat assignments, except for the reavers, who had split their group. Miikha and Commander Tchicatta were in the front, while Jaspins, Taelyia and Creugar held the rear. Triistan's dugout crew was just in front of them, and he had been comforted knowing that Biiko and three reavers had his back. It helped him to ignore the obvious fact that if the jharrls followed them in, the van would take the brunt of their initial attack.

The Captain and Mister Tarq followed the Firstblade, and after one last check of their line, gave the order to set off again. Triistan remembered Myles casting a wistful glance at the opening above and behind them just then. There was still just enough bloody daylight left in the sky that it was clearly visible.

"Seems to me we ought to be making a stand right there in that chokepoint."

Safely out of the Captain's earshot for the moment, Wrael had embraced the chance to peck at someone else. He snorted in derision. "And what happens if those man-eating matus come back while we're waiting for - or worse - engaging the pack? What then, oh Mighty Strategist? Those poor sods were eaten alive, and I've no intention of joining them. And the Cap's leading us right into their fucking nest..."

"And she'll be leading us right through and out of their fucking nest as well, Wrael the Rotten," chuckled a deep voice. Creugar loomed over them, a wide, bright smile on his dark face. "If you are quiet, maybe the matus don't stop their fucking long enough to even know we are there."

Triistan smiled sadly, remembering. So many good men and women. He missed the big reaver. Despite his fearsome size and appearance, he had a relaxed, untroubled way about him that put most of them at ease. His sharp wit and ever-present grin (even his teeth were big) made him one of Triistan's favorites, while his ruthlessness in battle endeared him to the entire expedition. He certainly proved his worth that day, and in the days that followed.

Once the expedition had made it down to the waterline, they were surprised to discover that the river was both deep and swift there. Most had assumed that the dam ran all the way to the bottom, but as they probed with a long branch to find out the river's depth, they discovered that it was largely unobstructed four or five feet below the surface. They reasoned that floods upstream must wash large amounts of debris downstream, where it would jamb up against the portcullis. Significant floods must raise the waterline in the tunnel and deposit new debris higher up, eventually leading to the massive logjam they were standing on. As to why it wasn't also collecting below the waterline, their best guess was that it was deep enough that the river's current was gradually clearing out anything that wasn't caught by the portcullis above.

A narrow ledge ran along each wall just above the surface of the water, barely wide enough for one man to walk on. They followed the left side in single file, weapons or torches in their right hands, away from the wall. Sounds echoed in a strange staccato pattern, caught between the surface of the water and the hard stone of the tunnel, while the river murmured wetly, sliding around and under the wreckage like a great dark serpent slowly slithering away from Aarden's mysterious heart. There was no way of knowing how far the tunnel ran; between the rubble, the uncertain lighting, and the fact that it was now dark outside, the opening at the other end could have been two or twenty thousand paces away and they would not have known. Triistan found that to be intensely frustrating - even if it had been two *hundred* thousand paces, he could have calculated how long it would have taken them and monitored their progress and how much further they had to go. Instead the darkness seemed to stretch infinitely beyond the reach of their flickering brands, and every step only brought them closer to nowhere. In addition, after days growing accustomed to the steady background roar of the jungle, the hushed gurgle of the river felt ominous. From time to time they heard other noises, too: the rattle and splash of falling rocks, the hiss of occasional loose dirt or gravel raining down, or the swish and plop of something moving in the water. They made as little noise as possible themselves, very much aware of the crouching quiet and straining to hear any sounds of pursuit.

Although the damage around the area they had entered was the most severe, the rest of the tunnel was nearly as bad. Huge timbers and haphazard piles of massive, broken stones barred their way, forcing them at times to either climb over or swim around them, slowing their progress to a crawl. On a few occasions where they had to swim under the water, the torches had to be extinguished, wrapped tightly in their waterproof covers, and then re-lit on the other side, slowing them even further. Climbing wasn't much better, as some of the debris was unstable - one misstep could cause an avalanche that would bury anyone further down. The treacherous footing soon became the least of their worries, though, for it was near the top of such a climb that they discovered the nests.

They were scaling a large pile of rubble that took them high enough so that their torchlight reached into the chambers above the ceiling, when a sour smell of decay and something fouler assaulted their nostrils, growing stronger as they climbed. Something long and serpentine, with dozens of spidery legs, skittered across Triistan's hand and he pulled it back, shaking it in revulsion. Glancing down he nearly lost his footing as he saw dozens more like it crawling through the wreckage. A fat purple beetle as big as his thumb scurried out of a hole near his foot and flew off into the darkness.

"The place is crawling with bugs..."

"Softly now, little Titch," Creugar said quietly. Their line snaked back and forth as they made their way up the rubble pile, so that the reaver was just below him even though Biiko, Jaspins and Taelyia were in line between them.

"They are more afraid of you than you of them I am telling myself, though myself is having a hard time listening. He seems to think if they were larger we could use our axes to squish them." For emphasis, he stepped on another beetle with his boot, then scanned the ceiling warily. "I tell him he should be careful what he wishes for."

Triistan shuddered and kept climbing. Creugar was right: better these than what was hunting them. He risked a glance up, saw more of the reflective flashes he had noticed earlier and tried distracting himself by imagining what else may have been left behind by the defenders. There might even be a library...

Suddenly Tchicatta stopped and raised his gauntleted fist, holding it there. They all froze, and he motioned for them to lower their torches before signaling to Miikha to raise his. As he did so, there were several sharp gasps as they realized what was shining back at them.

Eyes.

Miikha took an involuntary step back, stumbling, but the Firstblade was there to support him.

"Give me the torch," he growled quietly.

He climbed a few steps closer, moving very slowly, lifting the torch higher, until they could all see into the chamber just above the tunnel. Its walls and ceilings were covered in creeping vines of all sizes, and nestled in amongst them, like pale, bulbous lilac flowers, were hundreds of egg clusters. Dozens of the creatures that had swarmed from the tunnel were hanging upside-down from the surrounding vegetation, wings folded about their bodies like cloaks, bright round eyes watching them.

"Carefully, Commander," whispered the Captain. In response, he climbed the last bit to the top of the debris pile. He was a big man and had he stood to his full height and extended the torch, he could have brushed what was left of the ceiling with it. Instead, he kept in a crouch so as not to startle the nest, then slowly and quietly drew his kilij from its curved sheath. An axe hung from a short strap on his left hip, but he left it there in favor of the torch, which he lifted into the air and waved in a slow, wide arc. The kongamatus did not move, though their eyes still shone brightly as the torchlight swept over them.

Encouraged by their apparent docility, Tchicatta rose from his crouch, still moving the torch back and forth. He froze when a few of the creatures stirred, and one even extended its wings briefly before folding them again, but that was the extent of their agitation. He stood straighter still and lifted the brand higher, examining them as best as he could from his vantage point. After a long, tense moment of this, he waved the torch a few more times, a bit more rapidly, then nodded to himself and climbed carefully back to where the rest of the party had stopped.

"These seem smaller to my eye than the ones that killed Welms and Jaegus," he rasped. "They are either asleep or blind... or perhaps both. Hard to get a clean look, but what I first took to be their eyes are more likely protective lids that reflect the light - probably to give predators and egg-thieves second thoughts. They did not track my torch at all. Many of them appear swollen - pregnant, I assume."

First Mate Tarq spoke up. "The sand wyverns in Ghostvale enter a deep trance when nesting - like the summer beasts do when the snows come in the north."

"That may be," answered the Firstblade. "Either way, they don't seem to know or don't care that we're here, and I think we can pass beneath them as long as we're careful."

"How many?" the Captain asked.

He frowned and shook his head. "At first I thought less than a hundred, but that is only in the one chamber directly above us." He raised his eyes to the ceiling, scanning it. "But this is just one of many in a network of access tunnels and rooms - part of the defenses. I would guess there could easily be ten times that in the adjoining spaces."

A few within earshot cursed and groaned at this news, and the rest wanted to know what in the Endless Dark was going on.

Mister Tarq hissed for silence.

The Captain studied the opening in the ceiling above them, then turned to look back the way they had come. "Caught between storm and shoal..." she muttered in exasperation, but a captain didn't have the luxury of indecisiveness.

"Alright, let's move quickly. Take us through, Commander."

"Aye, Captain. Miikha, take the lead and light another torch. Keep it near the ground until you're past the nest and begin your descent, then hold it up as high as you can - the other side has a pretty steep drop-off and I don't want anyone stumbling over it in the dark. Jaspins and Taelyia, keep yours, but anyone else with a torch, put it out. Tael, I want you near the top with your brand held low - enough light for our people to pick their way past but not enough to disturb the nests. Jas will bring up the rear with her torch, so once you see her, move on through with the rest of the party. Everyone else, sheath your weapons and use both hands for climbing. Do not speak and make as little noise as possible. Let's move."

The Firstblade crouched next to Taelyia at the top of the pile, torch in one hand and kilij in the other. The rest of the expedition followed Miikha with painstaking care and at a maddeningly slow pace, while the smell grew worse, until it soon became obvious where it was coming from.

"Shit," grumbled Wrael, so quietly that Triistan barely heard him. "Shit, shit, shit. Never going to get my hands clean and everything I eat is going to taste like the inside of a matu's ass for the rest of my life..."

Triistan wondered if the swarm brought food back to the nest, then quickly realized that they were probably climbing over worse things than dung. He had to swallow several times to keep from retching.

By the time he reached the top of the pile he was soaked with sweat and their collective panting sounded to his ears like waves crashing on the shore. Any moment he expected the kongamatu in the nest to swarm and attack. He looked up nervously, but Taelyia had done as commanded and her torch was too low to reach beyond the ragged hole in the ceiling. Commander Tchicatta had kept his near the ground as well, though Triistan could still see the eyes flickering above, like overlarge stars. Although he now knew it was just a trick of the light reflecting off their eyelids, it still made his skin crawl.

Biiko was behind him, Jaspins, and Creugar bringing up the rear. The Firstblade motioned for Taelyia to cross to the other side and descend with her torch, and Myles and Wrael crept after her. As Triistan moved to follow, he heard a noise from somewhere above - a hard, scraping sound, like claws on stone, followed by a long, soft hiss. He froze, holding his breath, and locked eyes with Commander Tchicatta, crouched only an arm's length away. Something wet and viscous dribbled down onto the surface of the stone, not far from his right hand.

The Firstblade remained perfectly still, except for his eyes, which slid up and over Triistan's head. When they widened ever so slightly, Triistan knew there was something moving above him, coming out of the nest.

Tchicatta's eyes flicked back to meet his own, narrowing with deadly intent.

"Move!" he whispered fiercely and then erupted in a blur of motion.

Triistan dove forward. Something hot grazed his right calf and smashed into the large slab of stone he had just left, but his attention was on the empty air in front of him; he had lunged over the lip of a cliff of sorts and there was a steep drop to a wide, heavy beam about twelve feet below. He crashed headlong into Myles and Wrael, who were still on the beam, and somehow the three of them managed not to go tumbling over. While Wrael cursed him for a clumsy mud-footed whoreson, Triistan struggled to his feet and looked up.

Above them, the Firstblade was fighting a nightmare come to life. At first glance it looked to be a much larger version of the kongamatu they had seen thus far, though it was tough to distinguish any details during those initial moments. Most of its body was suspended up inside the chamber above them, and it was striking at Tchicatta with a thick, barbed tail that moved like a whip, fast and deadly. For the moment the Firstblade was faster, alternately dodging and parrying the strikes while he tried to get at the head - a broad, reptilian horror of long sharp teeth and glistening black skin. As Triistan watched, he aimed a cut at the tail, but the curved blade of his kilij only glanced off one of a multitude of sharp chitinous spikes that covered it. Tchicatta swore viciously and dodged sideways, dropping to one knee as his foot slipped off of the edge of the slab Triistan had been on only a moment before.

Sensing an opening, the creature opened its jaws impossibly wide, slaver running freely from curved fangs, and lunged at the Commander. Just as it stretched forward, a long black blade erupted from its snout, just in front of its eyes, and the jaws snapped closed for the last time. The beast shuddered and went limp, most of its body still hanging lifelessly from the hole in the ceiling above Biiko's head.

Commander Tchicatta regained his footing and thrust the torch at the opening. From Triistan's vantage point, he could only see part of the hole and the chamber behind, where the kongamatu were making a terrible din, screeching and flapping their wings in agitation.

"Go!" the Commander whispered hoarsely. "Get down to the water, quickly!" Wrael and Myles immediately began scrambling down after the others, but Triistan scurried up, gaining the lip of the slab and swinging himself over just as Biiko was removing his blade from the creature's gullet. Above their heads, the kongamatu were still screaming and fluttering their wings, but they did not appear to be leaving their perches. He had an instant to really look at the creature that had attacked him before the Firstblade rounded on him.

"May the reefs rake the flesh from your bones, boy, what don't you understand about 'go'?!"

Triistan flinched, but stood his ground, suddenly conscious of a throbbing pain in his lower leg. He wasn't entirely sure himself why he had climbed back up; he just knew that he had to see the thing for himself.

"I - I just wanted to... to thank you, sir. For saving my life."

The Commander's scowl froze, then lengthened incredulously. He opened his mouth to speak, closed it again, then managed a strangled, "Now?"

A deep chuckle saved him. "Come on now, little monkey man, the Commander has better things to do than listen to polite courtesies. And methinks that leg needs tending to, but not here."

Creugar scooped him up effortlessly and threw him over his shoulder like a sack of grain, then nimbly followed Jaspins and Taelyia over the edge. Biiko fell in immediately behind them, followed by the

Firstblade bringing up the rear. Triistan saw the grizzled warrior give him an odd look as Creugar lowered himself over the side, and he glanced away, embarrassed.

The kongamatus continued their screeching, but it soon became clear that they did not intend to leave their nests. He wondered whether another one of the bigger ones might come in response to the noise, and how many of those might be lurking in other chambers, but he remembered feeling strangely untroubled by the notion, distracted, as if things were happening to someone else. He had started feeling cold and a bit dazed, and by the time they reached the bottom, the pain in his leg had grown from a dull, throbbing ache to a sharp burning sensation that made him wince at every jostle. Creugar set him down gently on another large, flat slab like the one they had crossed at the top of the pile. It lay at a slight angle, with the bottom third disappearing into the river, but still leaving plenty of space for the entire expedition to gather. It occurred to him just then that these were the stone blocks that made up the walls of the tunnel and he was struck again by the huge scale of everything. He would have loved to have seen this incredible structure as it was being built.

Biiko crouched beside him, blocking his view while he removed some contents from the field kit he carried. Triistan struggled to a sitting position, propping himself up with his hands, so that he could see over the Unbound's shoulders.

He immediately wished he hadn't. His pant leg had been ripped away to expose his lower leg. There was a long, deep gash from just below his knee, running down and across his calf to his ankle. His bronze skin seemed pale and waxy in contrast with the bright blood running from the wound, and for a moment Triistan thought he would be sick. He lay back down, shivering, while Biiko began shoving leaves into his mouth and chewing rapidly. Jaspins appeared just then and knelt beside him, taking his hand in hers. It felt remarkably warm and he smiled weakly at her in thanks.

"Here, use this to stop the bleeding." She handed a roll of bandages and a wooden stake to Biiko. Still chewing, the Pathfinder tore off a length of the cloth, wrapped it twice around Triistan's upper leg, then broke off half the stake and handed the other half back to Jaspins. He used the piece he had kept to twist the bandage tighter and then tied it deftly in place. Triistan gasped as a moment later he felt a sudden cold sensation along the wound, but the pain receded almost immediately, and a few moments later it had gone relatively numb.

Jaspins was frank. "The good news is that we don't see any sign of poisoning. The cold you're feeling is an herbal paste that will ease the pain and - normally - keep the wound from festering. But we've got to get out of this tunnel, and that means more swimming -"

"And that's the bad news..." he managed with a weak smile. She nodded.

"Aye, that's the bad news. At best the river will wash out the paste, and at worst it will infect the wound and you'll lose the leg. We need to cauterize it, seal the wound by searing the flesh."

Triistan's guts twisted and he began shivering more violently. He could only nod and look away, hoping she wouldn't see his fear. Then, through clenched teeth, "Do it."

They moved quickly. Biiko signaled the three torch-bearers to lay their brands on a small circle of rubble, heads together. Jaspins handed him her steel knife, which he set so the blade was laying on top of the torches, then extracted a small pouch from his field kit. He undid the drawstrings and removed a pinch of a black powder, which he sprinkled over the blade. The flames from the torches flared hotly, and tiny sparks hissed and crackled along the knife. In seconds the fire around the steel edge took on a bluish hue, and the blade began to glow brightly. He met Triistan's eyes and nodded, his expression not unkind and somehow softer than Triistan had seen it before. He took a deep breath and nodded back.

"I'm ready."

"Here, bite down on this." Jaspins placed the broken stake in his mouth and then hastily removed her cloak and folded it into a rough pillow. "I'm going to place this over your mouth to help you keep quiet. Okay?"

He bit down harder on the stick and nodded, waiting for the pain...

Triistan winced now, remembering, and looked down at the ugly scar that coiled around his calf muscle. In the end it hadn't been necessary to use her cloak, as he had passed out after only a few seconds. He was told later that Biiko had to reheat and apply the knife half a dozen times in order to cauterize the entire length of the wound. The few moments he could remember were bad enough to make him squirm uncomfortably even now.

"What's done is done," he whispered to himself. Jaspins had been wrong about an infection, but none of them had ever had any experience with creatures like this, so he couldn't fault her for not anticipating what happened to him after.

He shuddered and opened the journal again to the rendering on the next page. It was a drawing of the creature that had wounded him - a much bigger, heavier mutation of the kongamatu. Wingless, it was close to fifteen feet long from nose to tail, with six legs - four sturdy, tightly-clustered front legs and two long, powerful rear legs - all ending in four-fingered "hands" of a sort. The "fingers" were set in opposing pairs with thick webbing between them, and while the front feet housed sharp, curved talons like the kongamatu's, the rear feet were covered in small, hooked suction cups similar to a squid's. Its skin color was blended; a random, swirling pattern of smoke and midnight, and its entire body was covered in some kind of foul-smelling slime. A larger version of the kongamatu's broad reptilian head was set on the end of a strong neck, and the same bony crest ran from its flat forehead, down the center of its back, until it merged with the hooked spikes that emanated in all directions from the last meter of the thing's deadly tail. Nearly half the monster's entire length, the tail ended in a curved and barbed stinger that made Triistan shudder to look at again. If he had been half a breath slower, he would have been impaled.

They had brought him back by waving a tiny snuffbox of smelling salts beneath his nose. As he regained consciousness, his first thought was that he could not feel his leg and they must have removed it after all. He panicked and struggled to sit up, gasping in relief when he saw that it was intact and wrapped tightly in a clean bandage. A pair of strong hands aided him, and when he looked up, he saw that they belonged to Biiko, kneeling beside him. The hint of a smile turned the corner of the warrior's mouth and he nodded his approval.

Triistan reached down to poke at his leg, but although his fingers had felt the pressure of the contact, his shin and calf were completely numb. He glanced at Biiko and shook his head. "I can't feel anything."

The warrior raised his eyebrows and nodded, then touched his hand to his own chest and held it out towards Triistan, palm up, in a gesture he had learned meant "You are welcome".

He felt foolish as he realized that the Unbound must have applied something to dull the pain, but he was surprised that he felt nothing at all in the leg and wondered if it was just from the medicine. He wanted to ask, but not wishing to appear ungrateful, he merely nodded and smiled. "Thank you. And thank you for killing that creature and saving the Firstblade."

Biiko seemed partially amused at that, as if they had shared a private joke, then stood up and helped the boy to his feet. He found that there was some sensation in his right foot, but with no feeling at all from his ankle to his knee, it was difficult to put any weight on it. He tried taking a step and Biiko had to catch him as his knee gave out, but when he tried again, he was at least able to manage an awkward limp. As he was wondering how he would keep up with everyone, Jaspins arrived with a grin and a long stick. He liked Commander Tchicatta's protégé. She was tall and strong, with long strawberry-blonde hair that she wore in a flat, braided plate that reached to the bottom edge of her shoulder blades. Intelligent, pale blue eyes glinted mischievously from a pleasant face. It was somewhat flat, but her pug nose, smattering of freckles, and a pair of big dimples came alive when she smiled, and you couldn't help but smile back. She was the polar opposite of the dark, dour Firstblade.

"Good to see you on your feet, Triistan. Here, brought you something." She handed him the stick, which he saw actually branched at the one end and was long enough to tuck under his arm as a crutch. Too long, actually - they had to cut about six inches off of the other end for it to fit correctly.

"Guess she thought you were taller," Taelyia teased and he realized that he was actually looking up at both of them as they stood facing one another. Feeling suddenly self-conscious, he straightened as best he could. He was tall in his own right - a good hand span more than most Seekers he knew - but both women still had an inch or two on him. There were several different theories of why this was so amongst the crew, but at that moment he blamed it on the slope of the slab they were standing on.

Captain Vaelysia had them form up again, impatient to get underway and put as much distance between themselves and the nest as possible. Although the screams of the kongamatu had subsided to an occasional angry croak, there was no telling how many of what they had started calling "guardians" might be around, or when the hunting swarm might return. For all they knew, the creatures had some way of alerting their brethren and summoning them back.

The right ledge was clear as far as their torchlight reached, so Miikha and Tchicatta led them across the base of the rubble pile and clambered up onto it. The others followed: Izenya, Pendal, Anthon, Thinman, Brehnl, Jaegus the Younger, Chelson, Wrael, and Myles. Triistan had an awkward time with his crutch, particularly over the broken, jumbled debris field, but eventually he reached the ledge and Myles held out one end of his bow, helping him make the short hop onto the walkway. Biiko crossed effortlessly, and as the Unbound landed on the ledge next to him, Triistan glanced back at the three reavers in the rear. Creugar was next, with Jaspins and Taelyia to either side and a little bit behind him. Taelyia's torch must have either gotten wet or the seal oil it had been soaked in was burning low, because the flame was sputtering fitfully and making the shadows around her jump and twitch. The odd effect of the lighting made it look like the rubble pile was moving.

With a chilling certainty that still made his chest ache as he recalled it all of these months later, he realized it was.

"BEHIND YOU!" He had screamed, too late. Taelyia was jumping from a large block of stone to a nearby fallen beam when something sprouted from the center of her leather cuirass and her body shot into the air. Blood fountained from her open mouth, her back arched and her arms flew wide, sending her torch tumbling to the ground. In the sudden pool of light below her Triistan could see another creature like the one that had attacked him. All six legs were braced firmly on the ground, while its tail arced up over its back like some giant scorpion, Taelyia's skewered body dangling from the other end. With unbelievable strength, it waived her body above itself before smashing it to the ground.

Creugar and Jaspins had reacted instantly to Triistan's warning, both dodging to the side and turning to face the threat. There were three more of the beasts; one that was close enough to strike at Jaspins, and the other two scrambling sideways across the pile, moving towards Creugar and the rest of the expedition. Their odd coloration blended in almost perfectly with the chaotic mass of shadows and debris, making them difficult to see whenever they stopped.

The one near Jaspins struck out with its tail, lightning quick. It barely missed her, burying its tail-spike in the same broad beam Taelyia had been jumping towards. It stuck there, and as the creature tried to free itself, Jaspins brought her curved kilij down in a two handed overhead swing, striking the tail just above the barbed section. The blade bit deep and the creature hissed at her, still struggling to free itself. She wrenched her sword loose and lifted it for another blow, but before she could land it, the monster gave a tremendous heave and literally tore its own tail off, leaving the barbed stinger in the beam and using the remaining stump to knock her sideways with astounding speed.

The creatures moved incredibly fast, their tails alternately rising and striking or whipping out at their opponents almost too quickly to see. As Jaspins was knocked sprawling, Creugar flung one of the three hand-axes he carried in his belt at the guardian attacking her. It flew end over end, striking home in the side of the thing's skull, just below and behind its eye. It hissed in rage and spun on him, while the other two closed in from his left flank. He hefted his huge battle axe and grinned fiercely.

"Come then, No-Tail. This axe is much bigger, and I would rename you Split-Skull!" All three charged him at once. For half a heartbeat, Triistan thought him doomed, but he underestimated the reaver squad and how well they fought together. Suddenly Creugar was no longer alone. Jaspins had recovered her balance and attacked her original assailant from behind. She leapt and rolled beneath its thrashing tail, coming up to a crouch next to its left rear leg and swinging with all her might at the back of its knee. She severed both thick tendons, causing the leg to give out and the guardian to lurch sideways, rearing its head back in agony. Creugar roared and brought his axe around and over his head in a one-handed arc that ended with a sickening crunch in the middle of the thing's skull. It collapsed to the ground, dead and renamed as promised.

The attack had left the big reaver's flank exposed, but as Triistan watched, it was covered an instant before the other two guardians could strike. Biiko appeared from nowhere in front of the closest one, a wraith brandishing twin black blades before him in a cross-guard stance. Triistan hadn't even noticed him leave his side when the battle began, and the guardians seemed just as surprised. The first beast reared up and lashed out with its tail-spike. Without changing his stance, Biiko simply rotated his arms, swinging the twin blades in one sharp motion, and the last two meters of the creature's deadly tail dropped to the ground. The fluidity and control of his fighting style made him seem unhurried, though he moved much more quickly than anyone or anything else in the battle. There was no discernible difference between his guard and his attack; each flowed into the next as if it had all been planned out ahead of time, choreographed like an elaborate dance. As he finished his first cut and the severed tail began to fall, he spun the blades in his hands to reverse his grip, rotated a half-step and drove them to the hilt in each of its eye sockets. He held them there for a heartbeat, perhaps two, while the guardian's body shuddered and its severed tail thrashed back and forth. Then he yanked both blades free and looked for another opponent, leaving the last one still twitching on its feet for a moment longer before it crashed to the ground.

At the same time the Unbound appeared before his guardian, Commander Tchicatta leapt from the ledge, his kilij in one hand, axe in the other. He landed on the broad back of the third surviving beast as it was side-stepping Biiko, its focus still on Creugar. Using the momentum of his jump, Tchicatta struck hard with both weapons at the back of its neck. His axe bit deeply, but his kilij glanced off the spiked crest in the center. He braced a knee against the crest and held onto his axe for leverage as the guardian kongamatu bucked and writhed, all the while lashing its tail at him. Ducking under the blows, he swung the kilij around and drove the blade point-first into its flank, just behind and below its right shoulder, seeking the thing's heart for a kill-shot. He failed to kill it, but it was badly wounded: the guardian slowed noticeably, and it began making a strange coughing noise. Tchicatta's sword would not come free, however, so he swung off its back, using his weight to pull the axe out with his other hand as he half-fell and half-slid to the ground. He easily side-stepped another strike from the tail, which was much slower and poorly aimed, as if the guardian were having trouble controlling it. An arrow suddenly appeared in its neck, causing it to shake its head back and forth violently, then stagger sideways. It opened its wide mouth, exposing fangs as long as Tchicatta's forearms, and hissed at him, but before it could strike again, two more feathered shafts sprouted from its right eye, killing it instantly. Triistan glanced to his right and saw Miikha, another arrow knocked and drawn, searching for his next target.

While the Firstblade was placing a booted foot on his dead opponent and attempting to free his kilij, Creugar and Jaspins converged on the guardian that had attacked first. Taelyia's torso was still stuck on the thing's tail-spike. It had become enraged trying to dislodge it, repeatedly smashing her body on the rubble, oblivious to the rest of the battle until Creugar parted its head from its neck with a great two-handed blow. Triistan couldn't imagine the force of the impact as Creugar's axe sheared through flesh, bone and cartilage, bouncing off the stone slab beneath them and sending shards of the blackstone in all directions. His teeth hurt just thinking about it.

Just as suddenly as it had begun, the battle was over, the tunnel quiet but for their labored breathing and the whispering river.

Commander Tchicatta did not allow them the chance to rest - or mourn. "Creugar, Jaspins, grab her gear. Miikha, you'll take her place in the rearguard. Let's go."

Without bothering to see if his orders were being carried out, the Firstblade waded to the ledge and pulled himself back onto it, taking the lead. Behind him, Creugar and Jaspins removed Taelyia's pack and weapons from her battered torso, then severed the tail above the spike and tossed her grisly remains into the river. Miikha retrieved his arrows and took up his new position between Jaspins and Creugar. Triistan remembered the pain in their faces, and the admiration he felt at their stoicism. Others were relying on them and they had a job to do. He wondered how many Reavers had fallen thusly, far from home, their comrades forced to abandon them. For most, their fellow warriors were the only 'home' and family they had. He knew many had once been criminals, scrubbed of any memories of who they were and then "reclaimed" by the Reavers, trained to become a part of one of the most feared fighting forces in the world. Many men wiser than he had argued both sides of the Reformative Memory Cleansing practice. Without knowing what they had done, however, Triistan could only judge them by who they were now.

Without fully understanding why at the time, he asked Jaspins if he could have Taelyia's kilij.

"Why?" she had asked him. "What do you know of the sword?" Like most sailors, he was fairly proficient with his dakra. Most of them carried one or two in their sashes, and knife-fighting was a popular diversion for them when not on duty (using wooden training knives of course - unless someone had gotten into the rum, had a score to settle, or both). As a matter of protocol, all Seekers were trained in swordplay as well, but most did little to practice or expand those skills while at sea. That's what the Reavers were there for, after all.

"Some - but I would learn more. Can you teach me?" She gave him a curious look, but before she could answer, Creugar interjected.

"Bah! Don't waste your time on those sticking-pins, little monkey man. Let Creugar teach you how to use a real weapon!" He held up his double-bladed axe and kissed the blade for emphasis. Triistan grimaced; there was still gore on it from the battle.

"Might as well try fighting with a ship's anchor," she fired back. Then, to Triistan: "I suppose I could, though I am unsure why Taelyia's..."

"To honor her," he said, stopping abruptly and turning to face her. He needed her to agree, to understand - before he lost his courage. "To honor all of you and... and do my part." Thus far, he had been a bystander, a passenger on the expedition, relying on the others to tell him what to do, where to go, how to get there; relying on them to hunt for him, to protect him... to die for him. All while he just observed, treating this entire expedition like some kind of naturalist's adventure. Yes, he had been ordered to record everything in his journal, and he knew that the Captain considered that task to be vital, but Taelyia's death and his own close call had badly shaken him. He was looking right at the godsforsaken things - why hadn't he seen them earlier? If he could have warned them an instant sooner, she might still be alive. By the Deep Dark, if he hadn't needed his wounds tended to, they would have been away much sooner. Commander Tchicatta had reacted quickly enough, warning him to move in time, then was nearly killed himself when he attacked the guardian. He was tired of feeling like an outsider or a burden... like a child. He wanted to take up the fallen warrior's sword, and with it, her purpose, so that in some sense she would go on, that all she had been and done would not be reduced to a slab of torn meat left to rot in the Darkness.

"She shouldn't just be forgotten," he muttered, cognizant of the looks he was receiving from all three reavers. Biiko was watching him as well, his face unreadable as always.

Jaspins searched his eyes. He returned her gaze without flinching away, thinking that perhaps she was not so different from the Firstblade after all. There was a hardness in her eyes that he hadn't noticed before. After a moment she pursed her lips and nodded, sounding much like her mentor and commander when she said: "We shall see. First honor her memory by staying alive and helping us all get out of this godsforsaken, overgrown sewer."

They pushed hard. Tchicatta and Captain Vaelysia set a brisk pace, but no one complained or lagged. Biiko and Creugar worked together to help Triistan keep up. All could feel the mounting urgency; they had spent too much time climbing, swimming, and crawling over and under obstacles. Too much time healing him and then fighting the nest guardians. In truth, that entire engagement - from the first attack that had wounded Triistan to the instant they set off again - had taken less than an hour. But every delay brought their hunters closer, and the threat of another ambush seemed unavoidable. The guardian kongamatu were wonderfully adapted to this environment: they were nearly invisible with their gray and black markings, and their strength and speed made them deadly under the best of circumstances. While there had been no sign or sound that the jharrls had pursued them into the tunnel yet - most assumed that the nest of kongamatus and the water kept them out - no one felt confident enough in that assessment to dismiss them. Besides, even if they hadn't, and even if there weren't any more guardians following them, the returning swarm of kongamatu hunters - creatures that had stripped the flesh from two corpsmen in mid-air - was more than enough threat. Strung out in single file along a narrow ledge or picking their way through piles of fallen rubble left them exposed and vulnerable, while the erratic play of light and shadow thrown by their torches made it difficult even to see what they were climbing over at times. It was the longest journey of Triistan's nineteen years.

Suddenly, Wrael came to an abrupt halt, and Myles cursed as he ran into him. Triistan and the others behind him stopped as well, grumbling their own invectives and asking what the problem was.

"Shhhh! I thought I heard something..."

"I hear lots of things," Myles muttered, "like the sound of everybody else's footsteps fading as they run away and leave us..."

Wrael hissed and made a chopping motion with his hand. They all paused, listening. For a moment, what Myles had said was true: all Triistan could hear was the patter and shuffle of the men in front of them, gradually receding as they pulled ahead. But just as he was about to suggest they had better hurry and catch up to the rest of the party, he heard something else - a flapping noise, coming from behind them. They all turned to look back the way they had come.

The tunnel was a gaping black abyss. Beyond their meager torch, the only light came from the phosphorescent traces wherever the river brushed past something in its path or along its blackstone flanks. It was like looking down a well you knew you were about to be dropped into - or in which you knew something was lurking, waiting to leap out and snatch you.

The sound abruptly stopped, but then started again from somewhere off to the side. A strange hollow piping noise echoed down the hall - softly, but so unique that it was easy to discern above the wet whisper of the river. The flapping began again, and this time Triistan thought it was clearly coming from the left side of the tunnel and growing louder. When it stopped, he heard the rattle of small stones.

After a few moments of tense silence, Jaspins caught Wrael's attention and pointed in the direction they had been going while mouthing the words "Tell the others". He nodded and began jogging up the passage. Myles remained with them, and Jaspins motioned to him and Biiko to start moving before turning back towards the noise. She pointed to Creugar and Miikha, then to her eyes, then back down the tunnel. They nodded, and when she followed Biiko, the two reavers dropped back a few paces before trailing after them, keeping their backs to the wall and watching behind them. Creugar had moved to the rear, holding a torch up with his left hand and his huge axe in his right, while Miikha still had his bow, arrow knocked and ready.

As soon as they started forward, they heard the alternating flapping sounds again; first from one side of the passage and then from the other. Now that they were all paying attention, it was easy to hear, especially when whatever was following them repeated the piping call. It also became clear that there were actually two sources of the noise, as sometimes they would alternate to either side, and several times they could hear both simultaneously.

They proceeded this way for several long moments before they caught up to Wrael and the rest of the expedition, who had stopped to wait for them. The Captain and Commander Tchicatta had moved to the rear of their group, beside Wrael, and when they were close enough, Jaspins held up two fingers and brought her hand down in a chopping motion across her other forearm. Triistan had learned that was the hand signal the Reavers used to indicate the presence of possible enemies, with the number of fingers held out indicating how many. The Firstblade nodded and then tilted his head, listening. After a moment of silence, he sighed impatiently and flung the torch he had been carrying in a long, high arc, back the way they had come. His aim wasn't bad, considering; the torch struck the wall just above the walkway they were following, then careened off both and disappeared into the river with a distant hiss. Before the light was snuffed out, however, it illuminated the unmistakable figure of a kongamatu perched atop a broken column, watching them with bright orange-yellow eyes.

As if it were accepting a challenge, it flew out of the darkness to land on a pile of rubble barely thirty feet from them. There was an unmistakable brazenness to it as it lifted its head and made the hollow piping noise they had heard earlier. A few seconds later they heard more flapping, and a second beast appeared and landed not far from the first. It piped back, and the two studied them with unnerving interest.

"Amazing," breathed Jaspins, to no one in particular. "Communication, coordination..."

"What is so sodding amazing about that?" Wrael hissed.

"It means that unlike you, squid, they appear to be somewhat..."

"Intelligent," Triistan finished for her. Jaspins glanced at him, nodding, and he recognized the familiar blaze of excited curiosity in her eyes. "Which means..."

The first kongamatu opened its curved jaws and screamed loudly, extending its wings and puffing up its chest, but its cry was cut short when a long black arrow suddenly sprouted from its throat. The other kongamatu screamed and flew off into the dark before Miikha could get off another shot.

The Firstblade finished Triistan's thought. "Which means we're being scouted. Captain, we've got to get out of here, now." He looked at Triistan, then at Biiko. "Carry him if you have to; we're out of time."

With that, he and Captain Vaelysia pushed their way back up to the front of the line and led them off in a loping jog. Although he still could not depend on his lower leg, Triistan had gradually become aware of a dull ache below his knee. As he sat here reading his journal and looking at the scar, he remembered how foolish he had been, thinking that was a good sign, hoping the feeling would return so that he could walk and run on his own. At the time, he'd had no concept of the agony still to come.

He leaned on Biiko, limping and hopping along as best he could, determined not to be carried, either literally or figuratively. His left leg burned fiercely from having to compensate for the injured right, but he kept up, distracting himself by trying to calculate how far they had traveled. He remembered wondering how thick the wall above could possibly be, unaware that they had passed out from under it several hundred feet earlier, not far past the point where they had fought the guardian kongamatus.

They came to another sudden halt, and a swell of excited murmuring rippled down the line. The first word that came back was "The gates! We've reached the gates!", followed almost immediately by word of a cave-in blocking them. Wrael laughed bitterly.

"Of course there is. Now we're trapped down here, waiting for someone to sound the bell for the evening meal. We'll make a fine bowl of brown when we see that fucking swarm coming down that tunnel, and half you mud-foots foul your breeches..."

"Shut your scupper, Wrael, and listen," urged Myles.

As he did, the party began moving forward again. Triistan was listening as well, and thought he heard the sound of water falling.

"Boil my bullocks, you're right - and look how the water glows here," Wrael answered. "You can see its bein' stirred up somewhere not far ahead. 'Sides that, where the fuck's it all coming from if it's blocked?"

"Aye, has to be a sizable breach through somewhere or we'd be a lot darker'n drier on this side..." Myles trailed off as the tunnel spit them out into a cavernous chamber.

"By the High Houses," he breathed incredulously.

Triistan had indeed heard the rush of falling water. It had been muffled by the strange acoustics within the tunnel, but now, as he stepped into the chamber, it was loud enough you would have to shout to be heard over it - were anyone speaking. At the moment, most of them were just staring, awestruck. The walls at either end glowed with the greenish-blue luminescence they had seen in the river, and it took Triistan a moment to realize that it was from water, cascading down from massive grills set at the juncture between the walls and the ceiling, some two hundred feet above. Below these, huge scuppers also poured great gouts of glittering liquid into the room, like waterfalls of moonlight. They looked to be made of the same ivory or bone material that they had seen on parts of the giant Sentinel statue. There were seven in all, each carved in the likeness of one of the High Houses' sigils, and they were spaced evenly across the two end walls and the wall through which they had just passed.

Wide channels at the base of the walls caught the falling water and directed it around the perimeter of the room, eventually intersecting with the river, just in front of the tunnel entrance. The room itself was much wider than the tunnel - perhaps four hundred feet on a side - through which the river cut a glowing swath down the center. Triistan was glad to see two wide plazas to either side of the channel. They were covered in elaborate mosaic tiles that may have once depicted some kind of scene or landscape, but so many were broken, missing, or covered in grime it was impossible to tell.

No one was paying much heed to the floor mosaic, though.

In the center of the huge chamber, four towering statues rose from the plazas, a pair on either side, very similar to the one in the bay they had named The Sentinel. They were formed from the same semi-translucent black stone, accented with bone or ivory to form similar arms and armor. Each pair stood back to back, giant bladestaffs in one hand and crossed with their twin on the opposite side of the river. The glassy texture of the stone they were hewn from absorbed some of the eerie light, so that the statues almost appeared to be glowing of their own accord. They were magnificent, imposing, even terrifying. And yet they were still not the focal point of the room.

Every pair of eyes in the expedition was drawn past the enormous statues to the far side of the chamber, where the true spectacle loomed.

The entire opposite wall wasn't really a wall at all; it was a mountain of rubble and ruined, twisted metal that might once have been another set of gates. At the base of the cave-in, a giant carcass unlike anything they had ever seen before was partially buried in the debris, with only its mammoth head, a foreleg the size of an ironwood trunk, and the heavily-spiked leading edge of a giant shell showing. Water trickled through the collapse in a thousand places, coating everything in the soft, blue-green glow and making it difficult to distinguish details from where they were. But they could make out the creature's gigantic head, with its broad, triangular cap of thick bone or cartilage, prominent brow, and the four curved horns emanating from either side, each twice as long as their tallest man. Its neck was twisted somewhat, so that the head lay partially on its side, propped up on a large broken slab as if it had fallen asleep there. The lowest side was partially submerged, and the water glowed brightly around it, as if the beast were the source of the luminescence. A hollow eye socket big enough for one of them to stand in upright stared vacantly from the side closest to them, phosphorescent water bleeding from it like glowing tears.

The ledge they had followed widened out as they entered the room, giving them a platform about ten feet across between the wall and the channel that funneled the water from scuppers and end walls. From where Triistan stood, it looked like the platform ran along the closest wall all the way to the corner, and possibly turned there to follow the end wall. The channel itself was only about ten feet wide, though he could not tell how deep.

"Look!" Chelson shouted above the din of the falls. "There must be a way through - look at my torch!" He was standing next to the river, holding it high, grinning broadly, his ruddy face almost childlike. The flame danced and sputtered ever so slightly, and the greasy black trail of smoke was drifting lazily back towards the mouth of the tunnel. It wasn't much, but perhaps it meant an opening, some breath of air finding its way through somewhere near the top of the cave-in, above where the water was seeping through. Not much, but something for them to cling to...

"Oh, that can't be good." Wrael's sardonic tone made Triistan turn back towards Chelson and his torch. As he watched, an opposing breeze scattered the smoke and sent the flames wavering in the other direction. The flame resisted, straightening bravely for an instant, but then an even stronger gust nearly blew it out. Chelson's grin faded, and he looked at the others, eyebrows knitting with worry.

Jaspins had remained at the mouth of the tunnel, while Creugar and Miikha were a little ways back, keeping an eye out for pursuers. Triistan had a clear line of sight to both of them, though, so when Creugar turned to face Jaspins and made a fist, then brought it down on his other forearm, he read the sign aloud:

"Enemy approaching, too many to count."

They began to run.

Softer on the Inside

As Triistan continued reading from his journal, his memory of the events it detailed was so strong that even here, months later and hundreds of leagues away, he still imagined he could feel the pain flaring in his injured lower leg as he scrambled to keep up with the rest of the Aarden expedition. He remembered how determined he was not to slow them down, but when they started leaping over the wide channel in the floor, he faltered. He could probably have run on the leg if he had to, but there was no way he could jump off of it just yet.

"Swim." It was Biiko, standing next to him, then grabbing a fistful of his tunic and half-pushing, half-dragging him into the water. The channel was only about four feet deep, so with the warrior's aid, he managed to wade across before being helped out on the other side. The Expedition sprinted across the plaza, following the main channel of the river towards the cave-in with the blind hope they would find an opening to escape through. Tchicatta and his Reavers naturally took up positions to the rear of the party, and Biiko fell in with them. The sound of steel being drawn shivered through the chamber behind him as Triistan hobbled along with help from Myles, desperately trying to keep pace. At least with the pain came more responsiveness and control over the limb, and he was able to manage a limping run.

They had just reached the base of the towering statues near the center of the chamber when they heard the shrieking wail of the kongamatu echoing up the tunnel, faintly at first, but growing louder by the instant. The breeze grew stronger, pushed ahead by the huge mass of creatures moving together, beating their wings and driving the air down the long passage. He tried clinging to the small hope that they were just returning to their nest, but the primeval rage in those cries and the speed with which they grew were unmistakable; they were on the hunt again, and he and his friends were their prey. They were coming.

"Into the water!" the Captain shouted.

She and the Whip fanned out to either side as the first few men jumped into the river. Izenya and Pendal dove in first, followed by

Anthon and then Thinman - who couldn't swim, so was forced to lower his huge bulk over the edge carefully, holding onto the edge with desperate fingers. The first two were caught immediately in a strong current and began drifting downstream, back towards the mouth of the tunnel. They came up sputtering, eyes wide with panic, and swam hard for the bank while their comrades dove over their heads, oblivious in their rush to escape. Brehnl, Jaegus the Younger, and Chelson followed, then Wrael and finally Myles. Triistan balked, though. He had noticed the current and something about its strength was nagging at him. Something Myles or Wrael had said just before they had first entered the chamber...

"Move it, Corpsman!" the Captain ordered and someone shoved him from behind. The screams of the kongamatu were growing louder; any second they would come pouring into the room.

He resisted, rolling away from whoever had pushed him. *The current... why is the current so strong?* His leg was throbbing badly, but he ground his teeth against the pain and tried to concentrate. He glanced up at the pile of rubble; there were hundreds of places where the water trickled through, tumbling down in a myriad of ghostly waterfalls from boulder to beam to slab, and eventually into the river. It did not seem like *enough* water, though. As wide as the main channel was here it was also deep - none of the sailors in the water were touching the bottom, that was clear...

But before he could finish thinking it through, they ran out of time.

The kongamatu exploded into the chamber, a great boiling cloud of teeth and claws, leathery wings, and piercing screams. The roiling mass poured from the mouth of the tunnel, swirling up into the lofty room, filling the space with their fury. They did not immediately attack the party, however, giving Triistan the impression they were searching for them. Perhaps the statues hid them momentarily, or the strange light of the falling water affected them some way...

"By the gods..." he breathed.

"The light!" he shouted. "Follow the light!" He lurched along the riverbank, towards the cave-in, pointing at the water around the massive head of the carcass buried in the rubble. Like the water falling along the walls or cascading in great flumes from the scuppers above, it glowed brightest where the water churned around the strange beast. Captain Vaelysia understood at once.

"You heard him - get moving! Swim for the carcass!"

Triistan did not wait to see if they complied. He ran as fast as his injured leg would let him, hoping he could reach the thing's head in time. He heard the kongamatu swarm overhead and was vaguely aware that their screams had changed pitch, but he ignored them, fixing most of his attention on the huge creature in front of him. Now that he was closer, he had a better sense of its enormous size: the head was easily thirty feet across, the horns another fifteen feet beyond that and as thick as the *Peregrine's* mainmast. There were two on each side, sweeping out sideways from a wide, bony plate that seemed to be part of the creature's skull. One of the horns was snapped off where it disappeared into the water. The skin that covered the armored plate, the broad forehead below it, and the wide, blunt snout looked to be made of thick, overlapping scales. The corpse was desiccated, its hide clinging tightly to the skull beneath, but it seemed to be intact - at least where he could see it along the head and jaw, and back along its giant neck up to the point it vanished in the rubble pile. Overhead loomed the leading edge of a massive shell, like the back of some gigantic, armored turtle. It was lined with huge horned spikes that jutted out at varying lengths, and several of those were also splintered and shorn.

All of that Triistan remembered afterwards, though. At the time, he was focused solely on its eye - or lack thereof. The empty eye socket was the key to everything. From his approach, he would somehow have to jump across to the broken slab that propped the thing's head up, then scramble up the broken horn and...

He was suddenly struck from behind and lifted into the air. His heart stopped beating and the breath rushed from his lungs from the force of the impact. Something clawed his shoulder and buffeted his head. Wings and teeth and claws swirled around him, and then suddenly he was falling and plunging into cold water. He panicked. He couldn't breathe. Something had a hold of him, constricting his chest and stomach, tight and unbreakable like thick iron bands, holding him under, squeezing... then he was pulled to the surface again, gasping for air; sweet, cool life pouring in to quench the fire in his chest. Two breaths, three, while around him he heard shouts and screams, terrible screams. He opened his mouth, inhaling deeply to call for help, and then whatever had hold of him pulled him down again.

Fortunately this time he had air in his lungs, and with it the sense to fight back. He kicked and struggled, pain shooting up his right leg when he connected with something solid behind him. He tried desperately to get his hands on whatever had a hold of him, until he realized it was someone's arm around his chest. He opened his eyes and looked down, going limp when he saw Biiko's familiar dark skin.

The Unbound spun him around so that they were facing each other, keeping one hand bunched in Triistan's tunic. He could feel the current trying to pull him away and saw that the warrior was holding onto the submerged end of a broken beam with his other hand, anchoring them both. Triistan grabbed the lip of a twisted piece of metal that might once have been part of a portcullis so he could resist the current on his own... Biiko released him and held up a finger, waving it in front of Triistan's eyes to make sure he had his attention, then gestured towards the surface, followed by an open-palmed motion he understood meant "cautiously". The young man nodded in response, and they both rose a few feet, emerging into a world of chaos.

They were floating alongside the huge rock slab at the foot of the cave-in. Above, the great head of the carcass looked down on them with its empty eye socket, and Triistan realized that Biiko had not actually been holding onto a beam, but the end of the broken horn he had noticed earlier. The air was filled with the deafening shrieks of the kongamatu. They were everywhere: swirling, banking, and swooping down on the surface of the river. Triistan had just enough time to notice several of the other party members floating nearby before he was forced to take another breath and duck under to avoid being raked by a pair of dark claws. He held it as long as he could before resurfacing, and for the moment it was clear, giving him time to discover that they were somewhat protected by the dead beast's horns and the edge of its armored skull-plate. The carcass provided enough overhead cover to prevent more than one or two kongamatu at a time from attacking them, and those that did try had a difficult time of it given their wingspans. It created a strange bubble of calm - the eye at the center of the ravenous storm.

Other members of the expedition had found similar shelter in amongst the tangled wreckage of the cave-in, but five or six of their comrades were still struggling out in the open. The main body of the swarm had shifted their attention to these easier victims and was alternately hovering, swooping, wheeling and banking, trying to get at them. Unlike the matu of his homeland, though, which would dive-bomb for fish from great heights, plunging deep into the ocean before reappearing with their catch, these appeared to have an aversion to the water. Rather than plunging from the air, they were circling, trying to glide along the surface and attack with their claws. Nevertheless, a few ended up in the water despite their efforts. At first it was just those that struck at the swimmers and misjudged their angle of attack, but as he watched, others began dropping from the air much less gracefully, dark feathered shafts protruding from their bodies.

Triistan craned his neck back and found Miikha perched in a pocket in the rubble pile above him, drawing and releasing arrows with astonishing speed. Myles and Wrael were just clambering up from the water to join him, black shafts held crosswise in their teeth, phosphorescent water streaming off of them so that they looked like drowned spirits climbing from the sea. Above them, Miikha targeted any of the creatures that dared approach their little pocket of shelter first, but there were relatively few of those, so most of his deadly rain fell upon the swarm. The Reaver's quiver was already a quarter empty, though, so Triistan turned his attention back to the swimmers, wondering how he could help.

There were six that he could see still in harm's way: Captain Vaelysia, Jaspins, Pendal, Chelson, Izenya and Brehnl. They were surviving by swimming under water as long as they could while making their way slowly towards the shelter provided by the carcass, then surfacing for a quick breath. The Captain and Jaspins were doing their best to urge the others on while fending off any kongamatu that came too close, but there were simply too many of them. Each time someone surfaced, they were struck. Sometimes they managed to grab hold of one of the creatures and pull it under with them, but then they would lose ground, struggling with their opponent rather than swimming upstream. He did not see Thinman, Creugar, Jaegus, Anthon, the First Mate, or Commander Tchicatta and hoped that they were somewhere in the rubble pile out of his line of sight.

Two of the kongamatu struck at Pendal just as he surfaced, one latching onto his left arm and the other tangling its claws in his hair. He screamed as they beat their wings furiously and, incredibly, began to rise, lifting him bodily from the water. He kicked and squirmed, clawing wildly at them with his free arm as his torso lifted free of the water. A third swept in, talons extended, aiming for his exposed belly, but there were too many of the beasts in the way now and Triistan lost sight of the beleaguered Seeker. He caught a glimpse of Jaspins rising up from the water, curved kilij carving through the swirling throng, and then he lost sight of her as well.

"There's too fucking many of them!" Wrael screamed in rage from over his shoulder. "Where the fuck did Penny go..."

Suddenly, Jaegus the Younger burst from the water next to Triistan, gasping for breath, followed shortly after by Anthon and then the Firstblade. Strong swimmers, they had come the entire way safely underwater. A fourth body surfaced; Commander Tchicatta was dragging the First Mate, who had a nasty wound to his face and was either dead or unconscious.

"We're not stopping here. This was your idea, boy - get him up into whatever that sodding thing is!" He shoved Tarq's body towards Triistan and the others, took a deep breath, and dove under, heading back towards the struggling swimmers. Jaegus and Anthon climbed onto the slab, dragging Tarq's limp form out by his shirt collar as Triistan pushed on him from the water. Two kongamatu broke off from the swarm and tried to attack them, but Wrael brought one down with an arrow and Anthon managed to fend the other one off, wounding it with his dakra. Smelling blood, a dozen other beasts attacked the injured creature as it clawed and lurched its way past the horns, tearing it to shreds.

Triistan looked for Biiko, but the Unbound had already left to assist the others. Hoping to gain some leverage to help drag Tarq's body to safety, he started to climb out onto the slab when something hard bumped his legs, startling him so that he all but leaped from the water.

Creugar surfaced where Triistan had just been, one massive arm wrapped around Thinman's chest. The big Reaver had a hand clamped over the sailor's nose and mouth, and Triistan remembered that he couldn't swim. While they caught their breath, he pointed up towards the huge eye socket above them.

"We need your help getting the First Mate up there. It's our only way out."

Creugar looked up at the eye socket dubiously; it was close to fifteen feet above their heads.

"Up there? I do not see a way out, little Titch. All I see is a very big creature I am very glad is very dead." Despite the chaos around them, Triistan couldn't help but smile. In a sudden wave of giddiness at the audacity of his idea, his smile widened to a grin.

"Exactly."

Creugar looked at him curiously, then up to the eye socket and back again. Triistan watched realization dawn on the big Reaver, until he flashed his own fierce smile in response and nodded vigorously.

"Yes! Creugar likes this plan, little Titch! When a beast so terrible as this - or his friends, in our case - tries to eat you, jump down his throat, for he is surely softer on the inside!"

Despite his wound, Triistan remained as nimble as his nickname as he climbed the side of the giant head, bracing himself between the horns and the thing's jaw line. He could see the water pouring from its mouth now, confirming at least part of his wild plan. A kongamatu crashed into him, nearly knocking him from his perch. It tried to dig its sharp claws into his shoulder, but one of the archers must have hit it, because it fell away almost immediately. He set his good foot on the closest horn and lunged upward, catching hold of a great fold of rough skin he assumed had been the creature's eyelid when it was alive, then pulled himself up into the hole. Since the giant beast's head was tilted, it was like climbing up into the look-out's perch atop the mainmast, with the eye socket playing the role of the hatch. Once he was inside the thing's skull, it was exactly what he had hoped to find.

He was in a large cavern made of bone. The walls dripped and glimmered in the reflected glow of the water, while before and a little below him the river churned and frothed on its way out from the dead beast's throat, through its jaw and out past broken teeth the size of tree trunks, all of it glowing brightly and contributing to the increased phosphorescence he had noticed in the water outside. Though the random patches of dark, hanging moss looked like scraps of flesh, there was no soft tissue left. It was all bone, cartilage and rough, scaly hide. The creature had likely been dead for some time and the kongamatu or other scavengers had been feeding on its insides, while the thick hide and shell kept the carcass largely intact - or so he hoped.

On the opposite side of the giant skull, somewhat above him because of the angle of its head, the other eye socket was partially staved in. The splintered end of a broad wooden beam jutted through the jumble of wreckage above it, and Triistan wondered if that had been the killing blow. To his left, the thing's throat was a yawning cave mouth leading off into the ghostly gloom, and his heart leaped when he saw that it wasn't completely submerged. He had half expected it to be, since the water seeping through from so many places, so high up the rock fall, was a clear indication that the water level on the other side was much higher. If he was correct, the cave-in had created a dam, but the husk of this huge creature had made a bizarre tunnel through it. The main flow of the river was getting through from somewhere, hopefully beyond the cave-in, and he meant for them to follow it to daylight and freedom.

But first they needed to get everyone else inside.

He stuck his head out of the hole again to find that Captain Vaelysia and the other stragglers had gained the relative security below. With their strength consolidated and the protection provided by the surrounding rubble and the dead thing's skull and horns, they were managing to hold off the kongamatu, but it was a costly battle. Everywhere he looked he saw bloody wounds. The first mate still lay unmoving on the slab below, and he didn't see Pendal anywhere.

"I think we can get through! Throw me a line!" he shouted down.

"Here!"

Triistan was relieved to see that Myles still had his climbing gear, including his grappling bow, which he tossed up to Triistan. It was one of his favorite tools, a crossbow that fired a collapsible grappling hook.

It was surprisingly powerful, capable of punching a hole through heavy canvas at fifty feet. The line they used was unusually light and strong, woven from Minethian silk, and he was confidant it could easily bear the weight of their heaviest man, so he secured the grappling hook on the edge of a boney ridge, disengaged the release mechanism on the crossbow's line spooler, and dropped it through the hole.

Jaspins had made it to the slab and was waiting next to Tarq's body. She caught the crossbow and deftly unfastened the line before tying it under the first mate's arms and around his torso. Then she leaped and grabbed the line a good ten feet off the ground and pulled herself up hand over hand into the skull. Triistan was impressed with how rapidly she made the climb; he was considered one of the best line-spiders aboard the *Peregrine*, but the Reaver's skill clearly matched his own. When she came through the eye socket, though, he was shocked at what he saw; the right side of her face was a mask of blood; her shoulder pauldron on the same side was missing and the flesh beneath it was torn and bleeding, and there were several rents and corresponding wounds across the back of her black chain-and-leather hauberk. He couldn't believe she could stand let alone move and climb as she was doing.

"Are - are you alright?" he stammered. He wasn't sure quite how to address any of them, save the Commander, since although Reaver contingents were standard additions to any sea-going Seeker vessel, they tended to keep themselves separate from the crew. Technically they fell under the Captain's command, but other than the Firstblade, the regulars remained aloof and somewhat enigmatic. As a result, there was typically little love lost between most Reaver squads and the nonmilitary sailors they were supposed to protect, a rather odd arrangement Triistan had always thought. With the possible exception of Creugar, Jaspins was the most approachable Reaver he'd met, and he was grateful for the way she had helped to treat his wound. But right now she looked furious.

"I'll live. Make way."

Creugar pulled himself up the same way she had, and the two of them were able to haul the Whip up and manhandle him through the hole while the others continued to fend off the kongamatu attacks.

As Jaspins and Creugar pulled the next man through, Triistan retreated to fashion a crude harness for carrying First Mate Tarq. He could see the Whip's wound now: a deep gash along the left side of his face, from high on his forehead to his cheekbone, bisecting his left eye. Bone was visible on his forehead and Triistan couldn't tell if his eye was still there, but he was relieved to find the first mate's skin was warm and he was still breathing. They hauled Thinman up next, freeing Jaspins to work on the First Mate.

"I am thinking you need a new... image, my friend," Creugar groaned and rubbed the small of his back.

Thinman grunted as he took over for Jaspins. "Don't know what my image 'as to do with it. Mebbe if you bloody crab-backs would haul a line once in awhile, instead of spendin' all day fondlin' your steel, you might be in better shape."

"I am thinking my steel would not agree with you, not-so-thin-man!" Creugar laughed as he pulled Izenya through.

By the time Triistan was finished with the harness, Jaspins had cleaned and bandaged the First Mate's wound as best as she could, and all but Biiko, Commander Tchicatta, and the Captain had made the climb.

Without the covering fire provided by Myles, Wrael and Miikha, though, Captain Vaelysia and the others were hard-pressed. The kongamatu, frustrated by their inability to get at their prey, had grown even more frenzied, throwing themselves at the obstacles in their way, some hard enough to injure themselves. Anytime one of the creatures faltered, several of the others fell upon it and tore it to shreds.

More were landing on the carcass, then crawling towards the eye socket, but since they were only able to do so in small numbers, they were easy to fend off for the moment. The bulk of the swarm flew against the rubble and the skull itself, making dull thuds as they beat against the outside, dislodging some of the smaller debris and sending it rattling and thumping off of the husk. There was a louder booming noise, followed by a low rumble like distant thunder, and Triistan locked eyes with Jaspins.

"We should go," he said. She nodded, and there was another low rumble. Something heavy smashed into the top of the beast's skull, sending a cascade of dust and rocks raining down from the rubble clogging the other eye socket.

"Soon," he urged. She was already kneeling beside the rope and calling down to the Firstblade on the huge slab below.

"Commander, this rock fall isn't stable..."

"Understood, Lieutenant. I'm not sure these things care very much, though. Captain, go! Biiko and I will hold them off until you get clear..." he lopped off the head of one of the kongamatu with his axe, then spun to cut another one out of the air with his kilij, cleaving the thing from neck to tail.

There was another ominous rumble, and more bits of rubble and dust drifted down from the other eye socket. The kongamatu continued throwing themselves at the outside of the husk, smashing into it or crawling across it, looking for a way in. The survivors could hear the rake of talons as well, though it appeared the thing's tough scales were more than a match for their claws. More were attacking the socket itself too, forcing the Captain to hack her way through as she held onto the line and they simply hauled her up. As she climbed into the skull, there was another loud impact on the outside, directly overhead. They all flinched as a large slab of blackrock was jarred loose from where it had been suspended in the other eye socket to smash into the opposite side, drenching them as it landed partially in the water passing through the thing's jaws. Several smaller pieces followed amid a shower of dust and luminescent water, and Triistan realized there were a handful of thin streams falling from the blockage now. The beam was still there, although he swore it was penetrating farther into the skull. If they could just coax it the rest of the way...

"Everyone but the scouts, Creugar and Thinman into that tunnel. We'll have to hope Mister Halliard's hunch is correct. Jaspins, you have the lead while we get the Firstblade and Biiko up here." The Captain turned to Myles and Wrael. "You two, provide what cover fire you can; they'll be bait on a line until we get them up. Then we'll do our best to buy ourselves some time."

"Captain, may I -" Triistan began, gesturing towards the other eye socket.

"I see it, Corpsman. Now get out of here!"

Two kongamatu suddenly burst through the hole, screaming, stretching their wings and pumping hard to get up into the open space. Wrael and Myles both drew and fired on the same target, dropping it, but the other one slipped past and into the space above them. Before the scouts could draw and shoot again, three more came through the hole.

Jaspins grabbed Triistan by the collar and pulled him close, so that all he could see was her face.

"You heard the Captain, WE ARE LEAVING!" With that she shoved him in the direction of the tunnel made by the dead creature's throat. The last glimpse he had of the others as he turned away was a desperate fight at the entrance, while above them several more kongamatu now flew in erratic patterns. He still had not seen the Firstblade or Biiko come through.

Jaspins put Miikha in the rear to guard against any pursuit and told Jaegus and Chelson to carry Tarq, using the harness that Triistan had fashioned for him. She pushed her way to the front and led them down the monster's throat.

They had to duck beneath a low section where its neck joined the huge skull, pulling themselves along against the current in water that was up to their chests. Once they were through, they entered a strange passageway formed from bone arches that made up the beast's skeletal structure. Like the inside of its skull, there was no flesh left - just dark scraps of moss hanging here and there, clinging to the pale bone. The walls were made of its scaly hide, largely still intact, although they glowed and glistened in places where water seeped in. Triistan hoped they never met a living, breathing version: he guessed that it would be impossible to bring down based on the strength and resiliency of its hide alone.

The river filled most of the animal's neck and throat, and while it was over their heads in the center, it was only waist-deep along either side. Overhead, the bone arches formed a ribbed roof for the passageway that reminded Triistan of an ancient temple he had once visited when picking up a package for Doyen Rathmiin. Fifty or sixty paces later, these archways began to grow larger, the tunnel widening as the neck thickened near its base, until it ended abruptly and the walls and ceiling opened up into another huge, bizarrely beautiful cavern.

They must have passed into the shell-like structure Triistan had glimpsed in the mountain of rubble, but its size was hard to comprehend. The gigantic shell's walls and ceiling stretched beyond their sight, although they had a good estimate of how high it was by the glimmering threads of luminescent water streaming down in multiple places. Far above their heads, they could just pick out the source of each delicate, liquid stalactite, and wherever they fell into the river - which in this wide area was more like a large underground lake - the glowing ripple and splash of impact created ghostly sprites that seemed to dance upon the mysterious surface. It was difficult to reconcile the horror of the setting with the transcendent alien beauty around them.

Jaspins led them to the right, staying close to the outer wall of the shell. It was still only waist-deep there, and the current wasn't as swift once they moved away from the neck. Triistan glanced back as he left the mouth of the tunnel, hoping to see Biiko and the others following, but beyond Miikha the tunnel was empty. He paused, trying to listen for them as well, but all he could hear was the rush of water passing through the neck, and then Miikha pushed him ahead.

They had not travelled far when they heard a loud crack and boom, followed by another rumble, this one much longer and louder than the others. It went on for fifteen or twenty seconds, and they could even feel the floor and wall vibrating. When it stopped, some of the streams falling from the ceiling trickled and died out, though one off to their left grew much larger. The group waited, looking back the way they'd come. Some of the regular Seekers also looked warily at each other, while Triistan saw Jaspins and Miikha exchange a knowing glance.

"Do you know what that was?" Triistan asked Miikha. The archer glanced at Jaspins and she nodded tacitly.

"Likely something called Sigel's Fury. The Unbound make it. You saw some of it when your friend used it to heat his dakra before cleansing your wound. Used in sufficient quantity, it can create a small explosion."

"They must have tried dislodging the debris in the other eye to block off the entrance," added Jaspins.

"Sounds like they brought the whole rutting mountain down," said Chelson as he looked around nervously.

Triistan shook his head, "No, I don't think so. You would hear the water, and a lot more than that I think."

"The water?" asked Izenya. His pale skin and shock of red hair looked ghoulish in the eerie glow of the shell-cave.

Triistan nodded. "Aye, that whole landslide we saw has created a dam, and the carcass of this creature seems to be a part of it, but fortunately for us it remained intact, and a portion of it must be above the water lev-"

"Wait, *above* the water level? By the moldy old gods, Titch, are you saying we're actually *under* water right now?!" Izenya's voice had an edge of hysteria to it.

"That is exactly what he's saying, mate," Brehnl said in a hushed, almost reverent tone. A stocky man with a nasty crook in his nose and close-cropped black hair, he was one of their best helmsman, having worked for years as a harbor pilot in King's Crossing. "Ain't you noticed all the water comin' in from up high? Feels like bein' down in the *Peregrine's* bilgeway after a blow, don't it? The way her sides would weep until Ol' Scow had us patch her up again. By my bonnie, though, can you believe the size of this thing lads?"

"I known a docksie used to tell me that every time I dropped my breeches!" snickered Chelson.

"No doubt she meant the pox-boil she gave you on the end of it," quipped Wrael and several of the others chuckled in response. The laughter sounded forced, though, and Jaspins put an abrupt end to it.

"Alright, stow it and hold your positions. Miikha, double back and find out what happened to the Commander and the others." She turned her attention to Tarq's wounds while they waited, ignoring her own, as well as the rest of the party's, though none were as serious as the First Mate's. He could see the suppressed rage in her awkward, jerky movements and the stiffness in her back and shoulders. He wondered why she was so upset and whether he should offer to help her.

Instead, he told himself to mind his own business, turning his thoughts to Biiko and the others. Triistan had thought collapsing the other eye socket offered their best chance of sealing the swarm out, but he could not think of a way to do it without being buried in the process. He had never heard of Sigel's Fury before, and wondered how it would have been applied or triggered, anxiously picturing Biiko having to climb up and somehow affix it to the rubble. Could it be made into a paste, perhaps? Or maybe thrown in some kind of flask? And then how could it be set alight? He didn't see how it would be possible without someone putting themselves in jeopardy. And that was assuming that Biiko even made it inside and they set it off intentionally. His heart sank as he pictured the far more likely scenario that the Unbound was overwhelmed, and somehow the kongamatu set the material off when they tore him apart the way they had Jaegus and Welms.

Brehnl gave a sudden glad shout as the trailing members of the expedition entered the cavern, looking weary and bloodied, but alive. Captain Vaelysia and Commander Tchicatta came through first, with Miikha just behind, talking animatedly with Thinman, Myles and Wrael. Triistan held his breath, then felt warm relief wash over him as Biiko and Creugar emerged from the tunnel a moment later, bringing up the rear. The big Reaver was bleeding from his left ear and a ragged gash in his upper arm, but otherwise appeared hale; Biiko seemed uninjured and implacable as always, though some of the fabric portions of his jiisahn were badly torn. Unlike the rest of the party, who paused to gaze in awe as they entered the huge shell-chamber, the Unbound made his way directly to Triistan and the others as if he had been here before.

Triistan couldn't suppress a wide grin as Biiko approached, and he clasped the warrior's shoulders. "It is good to see you. I'm glad you made it back."

The warrior nodded formally but said nothing. He gestured towards Triistan's leg, lifting his eyebrow questioningly.

"Painful, but at least I can walk on my own now. Feels like it's on fire, though the water helps some. It is much worse when I leave the water."

Biiko nodded sagely, chewing on the inside of his lip, then pointed in the general direction of what they all assumed was out, then at Triistan, then at himself and finally the pouch on his belt that Triistan knew contained his healing supplies. *When we get out of here, I will treat it again.*

Triistan nodded and thanked him as the Captain, Firstblade and the others joined the rest of the expedition.

"Our thanks indeed, Biiko," said Captain Vaelysia as she passed them. "Without that Fury powder, we would still have those squid-humping things all over us. Now if I could prevail upon your skills once more..." She went directly to the First Mate, who was propped against the carapace wall, held up between Jaegus and Chelson. Jaspins was still examining his wound, dabbing at it with a folded strip of cloth.

"How is he?" the Captain asked quietly.

"Still unconscious, sir. But that is a mercy; he's lost the eye and is going to be in considerable pain when he wakes. He'll live, but we need to get the wound cleaned and dressed-"

But the Captain had already heard all she had needed to hear: *he would live*. There was another matter that needed settling.

"What happened to Pendal?" she asked, her voice sharp with command. Only then did most of them realize they were missing someone.

Jaspins' hand froze and she bowed her head, then dropped both arms to her sides and turned to face the Captain. Triistan was surprised at the hard defiance he saw in her expression when she squared her shoulders and lifted her chin. The blood had dried on the one side of her face, giving her a dark, savage look.

"Gone, Captain."

"I see that, Reaver. I asked what happened to him."

Jaspins' jaw muscle bunched and she turned her head to address Commander Tchicatta, speaking through clenched teeth. "Sir, Seeker Pendal was... overwhelmed. I tried to reach him, but one of those things had opened up his belly and his..."

"I asked you the question, Reaver," Captain Vaelysia said coldly. "I want to know what happened to my man."

The Reaver lieutenant glanced at the Captain, then back at the Firstblade, hesitating. He nodded, and Jaspins faced the Captain again. Triistan felt sympathy for her as he realized she was struggling to keep her composure. She bit off her words as if she didn't like the way they tasted in her mouth.

"Yes, Captain. The last I saw of him, his guts had been pulled out and were tangled around his legs. I tried to reach him anyway, at least to end his suf-" she stopped and shook her head. "But there was no way - too many of them. I made a tactical dec-"

"A tactical decision?"

Jaspins swallowed, but her voice strengthened. "I made a tactical decision. He was already dead - he just didn't know it yet, and they - they seemed distracted by the kill or I would have been next. Our resources are limited, our orders clear. One Reaver to four sailors, Captain."

A chill crawled up Triistan's spine as he realized what the Reaver was saying. Several of the others who had watched the exchange stared in numb horror. He waited for the Captain's outraged response, but she was silent, studying Jaspins' eyes for a long moment. When she finally spoke, the sharpness was gone, replaced by a weary sadness.

"You did the right thing, Lieutenant. You did your duty." She asked Biiko to dress Jaspins' wounds and then to double-check Tarq's dressings.

As she turned to address the rest of her anxious crew, she spotted Commander Tchicatta, who had been standing quietly nearby, observing. She spoke softly, but Triistan was close enough to overhear.

"She's a good pick, Commander, but four to one is a little high. My people are worth more than that."

She bent over and splashed water on her face, rinsing some of the blood and grime from it. Triistan could see claw-marks on her left temple, still bleeding freely. She typically kept her thick, blonde hair bound back with a corded leather braid, but it was gone and her hair was matted and bloody. He saw that the black bracer she usually wore on her sword arm was also missing, and her arm was wrapped in a makeshift bandage from elbow to wrist.

"So what happened, Cap?" Brehnl asked, unable to contain his curiosity any longer. "Are those... things... still after us?" She dipped her whole head under the water, then stood, swinging her long hair up and over her back. She produced a short length of cord from somewhere and used it to tie her hair back as she spoke.

"We collapsed the other side of the skull." Here she met Triistan's eyes for a moment and gave him a slight nod, acknowledging that she knew he had thought of it as well. "Nothing will follow us through there now. We can cover the details as we go, but right now we need to find a way out of here."

"We are passing through some kind of carapace..." Triistan offered, but she cut him short.

"Speak plainly, please, Mr. Halliard," asked the Captain brusquely. He felt his cheeks and the tips of his ears growing hot but mustered his courage and pressed on.

"Sorry, Captain. The shell - I believe we're inside a massive shell-like part of this creature's body, much like a tortoise or a shield-crab. If we follow the wall here, we should pass its legs and then eventually find its... back end, or perhaps a tail if it is like the crabs we know. The river has to be entering from somewhere. I believe the tail end of this creature is sticking out the far end of the dam, allowing both water and air in - like a spillway."

"Or the whole rutting thing is under water and we are as good as drowned," muttered Wrael sullenly. But Triistan shook his head.

"No, I don't think so. If that were the case, this entire husk would have filled by now."

Brehnl grunted in disagreement. "Not so sure, Titch. Ever turned a skiff or even one of our dugouts over? Air gets trapped underneath."

Triistan saw some of them nodding, but he also saw others looking out at the great pond and its ghostly waterfalls. He smiled.

"Not if you knock holes in her, Brehnl. She'll sink and take you down with her. This boat has holes in her hull, but she's still full of air. So we just need to find the one that leads to daylight." They all looked out at the strange site of the luminescent streams of water falling from somewhere in the darkness above. Somewhere out there was their path to freedom.

When Jaspins pronounced that they had done as much as they could for Tarq, the Captain reorganized their line, taking the lead with the Reaver commander. They were followed by Jaegus and Chelson carrying the unconscious First Mate, then the remaining Seekers, with Triistan and Biiko at their rear. Impressed by their archery skills, Captain Vaelysia placed Myles and Wrael under Tchicatta's command until they were safely out of their current predicament. The Firstblade had them keep pace in a parallel line alongside the group's left flank with Miikha and Jaspins to their fore and rear. The Reaver lieutenant was brooding quietly, still carrying Taelyia's sword on her back, and a much heavier burden besides. Behind them all, Creugar took the rear guard by himself. He had lost half of his left ear in the fight and now had a lopsided bandage wrapped around his head, but otherwise seemed none the worse for wear, alternately whistling and humming quietly to himself as if he were strolling along one of the beaches of Chatuuku.

As they set off again, Wrael fell in beside Triistan.

"Never thought I'd be looking forward to being shat out the bunghole of a giant tortoise-monster," the scout drawled.

Then, more quietly: "Better hope you're right about this, Titch. Because as certain as nothin' can follow us in here, the Cap's made damned sure we can't go back out that way, neither."

They followed the outer wall, climbing over ribs and leg-joints as big as stonewood trees. They were surprised to find that there were four joints on the one side, since they had all been essentially envisioning the creature as a giant turtle. Each one was like the mouth of a cave partially concealed by the trunks of huge trees whose bark had all been stripped off to leave the bleached wood beneath. In most cases the hide was pressed in against the bones near the top and sides, with some folds creating gaps, particularly along the underside of the leg bones. The gaps were tall enough that they could have walked into them without stooping, but they did not. As with the main body, there was water in the legs as well, but with almost no current and no falling water to disturb it, the tunnels were dark and full of hidden menace. As they passed by each one, Triistan was grateful that they had to work their way around the joint, putting some distance between them and whatever might be lurking further back, hiding in the shadows.

When they passed the last opening, the torso narrowed sufficiently for them to see the other side and the opposing joint. The current of the river had grown stronger, and it pushed at them, so that each footstep became a struggle. Captain Vaelysia called a halt and ordered them to tie a line from person to person, making sure that they also slipped the rope through the First Mate's harness. When the group was sufficiently tethered and each man had given a firm tug on his section of rope to satisfy himself he would not be drowned if he lost his footing, they started forward again.

It seemed to grow brighter as they progressed - not the ghoulish glow from the river, but real daylight filtering in from somewhere ahead of them. The 'cavern' they had passed through shrunk to a broad tunnel that sloped up as it ran away from them, and when he felt the ground rising, he knew his theory had been correct.

Something moved through his hair and he put his hand up to ward it off, then realized what it was.

"Do you feel that?" someone asked from up ahead. He inhaled sharply and tears stung his eyes as he caught the scent of flowers. There was a fresh breeze entering the tunnel from somewhere up ahead.

The light continued to grow, until the walls shimmered from both the glow of the rushing water as well as the rippling play of an external light source reflecting off of the river's surface. As they advanced, it grew brighter still, and the left-hand wall began bulging inward. The dried, armored skin of the carcass was soon lost behind a tangled mass of roots, interlaced with the same searching vines they had seen when they had first entered the western gate: the jungle was slowly reclaiming the giant creature's remains. More importantly, they knew they must be getting close to the surface.

The slope in the floor grew steeper, until they were forced to climb, using the roots and vines to assist them, as well as the gigantic rings of bone that formed the skeletal structure of the monster's tail. With each new hand- and foothold, the glow from the river slowly receded, despite the fact that it was falling everywhere around them now, noisily cascading down over the bone rings and running down the walls; pouring down upon their heads from the irregular patch of blue far above them in a glistening, joyful rain. It was the blue of the early morning sky, and the eerie glow from the river water was giving ground to the light of Ruine's newly risen twin suns.

It became almost a vertical climb at that point, with the bulk of the river roaring down to one side, tumbling into the darkness below. They kept the main falls to their left, scaling the mesh of plant life while water ran into their eyes and down their beards, necks and backs. It made the roots and bone ledges slippery, but by then the tangle of vines and interlacing roots was so thick it didn't matter. Once the climb became that steep, they ran four lead lines from the harness Triistan had made for Mister Tarq, tying them around the waists of their four best climbers. The shared burden and the taste of open air were such that Triistan and the others barely slowed, and then only when Creugar, who followed alongside Tarq's unconscious form, was forced to free the First Mate from a snagging root or vine.

When they finally gained the summit and burst into the open air, their first impression was that they were climbing out of a tear in the surface of a wide, calm lake surrounded by stone ruins. The remains of the beast's tail had created something of an atoll, reinforced by the thick, leafy vines that climbed from the water, along its scaly sides and down into the tunnel they had just emerged from. The end of the tail itself had been ravaged by something, leaving only a ragged, elongated opening where the water of the lake poured through like some giant drain. Over time - decades, probably - silt and other debris drifting on the surface of the water had become snagged in the vines and on the remains of the tail, gradually building up the island they now stood upon. Triistan looked up at the open sky, reveling in the warm caress of the suns and the sweet scent of fresh air.

They were overcome with elation. Some wept openly; others shouted and slapped each other on the back. A few of the regular sailors frolicked and splashed in the calf-deep water as if they were children. Creugar erupted in a rousing song about some 'merry maiden's monstrous moon'. Triistan thought he was making it up as he went along, but that didn't stop the others from trying to sing along with him.

Wrael stood at the edge of the thing's severed tail, looking back down the hole they had just emerged from, and favored Triistan with a rare grin.

"Well, Titch, looks like you were right. But I still feel like shit."

- 18 -

Fickle Winds

Someone was shaking him roughly by the shoulder.

"Ho, there, Halliard, wake up now! Triis! Wake up, lad, you're yammerin' loud enough to..!"

Startled and disoriented, Triistan bolted upright and smacked his head on Scow's square jaw. The Mattock swore and rubbed his chin.

"Damn me, boy! I'm losing teeth fast enough without you knockin'em out for me!"

Groaning, Triistan lay back down and massaged his forehead. The pain helped him reorient, however, and he felt the wings of panic recede as he realized he was aboard the *Peregrine's* emergency launch. He must have dozed off while reading his journal and started dreaming, though at the moment he felt like he had just simply shifted, from here back to Aarden, slipping from present to past. It was difficult for him to tell where his conscious thoughts had ended and the dream began. It had felt so lifelike, as if he were there again, with none of the strange alterations or illogical sequences of other dreams. It was all exactly as it had happened during the expedition. He shuddered, remembering the hot kiss of Biiko's knife and the terrified flight that had followed as he and his comrades tried to elude the swarm of kongamatu.

The scar on his leg itched terribly, so he sat up again to scratch it, then ran his fingers through his tangled, matted hair. It itched as badly as his scar, and he had half a mind to shave it off with his knife. From the look of the suns, it was early in the long evening, still hot with not a breath of air to be found. His journal lay open, face-down in his lap.

"How long-" he began.

"Don't know, lad. Not sure when you drifted off." Scow worked his jaw from side to side. "By Shan's storm-blown shaft I always figured you for a hard-head." He settled his bulk down beside Triistan with a groan.

"You missed your watch. No, no don't get your bullocks in a bunch - Drey took it for you. Besides, it was my call. None of us but Mung are sleeping well enough to pass up a good hard nod, and you were out for at least a couple of hours before your watch even came up."

Remembering Dreysha's earlier theft of his journal, Triistan looked down at it in alarm, but Scow chuckled.

"Not to worry, lad. Blackblades never strayed far from ya, an'I kept an eye out as well. Nobody but you's laid so much as a finger on that book." Triistan breathed a sigh of relief and mumbled a thank you, though it was hard to accept that he'd been asleep for that long. He felt nauseous and stretched out inside, not at all like he had been resting for several hours. More like someone who had been running and climbing for his life.

"Care to talk about it, lad?" Scow was looking at him with quiet concern.

"Talk about what?"

The Mattock gave him his "Do you think I learned to sail yesterday?" look, narrowing his bright blue eyes and lifting his white bushy eyebrows. It was a look that had dragged many a hard truth out of Triistan in the past.

He wanted badly to confide in Scow. The vivid reality of his dream, or flashback, whatever the Dark it was, made him long to unload at least some of what he carried inside, and the Mattock was certainly someone worthy of his confidence.

And the discoveries they had made! By all the gods, Old and Young, when they had finally come through the long dark tunnel beneath Ahbaingeata and learned the full scope of its construction and purpose - to say nothing of the incredible creature they had passed through to get there, or the heroic sacrifices made by the fallen... it was overwhelming and astounding and terrifying all at the same time. It was too much for a boy of only nineteen years to be asked to contain and keep secret. With each passing day he felt his resolve weakening.

Even though he shouldered all that weight, he knew he couldn't break his promise. The way his mind worked, the oath he had made to the Captain and First Mate would have been difficult for him to ignore under normal circumstances, but after what they had gone through together, it had taken on an even greater significance: just the act of thinking about telling it to Scow or Drey - or even to Biiko, who had been with them - felt as though he was betraying them. Though by refusing to share his experiences with his fellow survivors now, he couldn't help wondering if he was betraying them at least in equal measure, if not more.

Caught between storm and shoal, he told himself. *They weren't part of the Expedition, so until we reach home and turn this over to the Ministry, you can't include them.*

Once again he felt a strong compunction to hurl the book over the rail; there was such a long shadow of misery that trailed from its pages all the way back to Aarden's heart of darkness. But the journal was a part of him: the more he read from it, the more he realized how much of himself he had placed in those pages.

He searched the Mattock's eyes, trying to find a way to tell him all of these conflicting thoughts and emotions, but he was unable to withstand Scow's shrewd gaze for more than a moment. The Mattock sighed as Triistan looked away, and he thought he'd never heard the man sound so tired, or so sad.

"I'm sorry, sir," Triistan said. "I just- I can't. I took an oath."

Scow snorted.

"We'll all be riding our precious oaths and honor into the Deep Dark, make no mistake." The bitterness in his tone took Triistan by surprise.

"Sorry, sir?"

The Mattock waived a big, calloused hand and changed the topic.

"I remember the first time I saw you in Siitsii, perched up on those crates like a damned gull, that blazing torch you call your hair all knotted and tangled, stickin' out in all directions like it is now. Your face was an even bigger mess than your hair - looked like someone had beaten you pretty badly. I figured you for just another wharf rat - 'till I saw you scribbling in that Dark-damned book of yours. Not many rats can read and write, and not a one of'em will sit that long in the open; always somebody after them for something."

Triistan smiled. He also remembered that day in North Harbor, and the week before as well. He had spent several days watching the *Last Horizon*, mesmerized by the complexity and organization of her rigging, gradually realizing that he needed to get aboard one of these marvelous ships. The *Horizon* was a ship of war though, well-guarded, so he had set off to find a civilian ship and eventually wandered out onto the *Peregrine's* quay. She was even larger than the monstrous *Horizon*, but much sleeker looking. There was an elegance to her lines - a *grace* he remembered thinking at the time. More importantly, she was taking on supplies and looked to be making preparations to sail.

"Was I that obvious?"

Scow chuckled. "As obvious as a boil on my bunghole, lad. But mind you, I keep nearly as close an eye on my lady's berth as I do on her. Or did, I suppose I should be sayin' now," he ended wistfully. "I don't expect I'll ever sail the likes of her again..."

Triistan knew how painful the topic was to Scow. He would never forget the look on the Mattock's face when the sea had finally broken her. To distract them both, he tried steering the conversation back to the day he had stolen aboard the doomed ship, several years before. "Did you really know where I was hiding the whole time?"

"Eh? Oh, aye, lad. Not a hole aboard that ship that I didn't know about, be it spider, rat, rot or weevil."

"Then why did you leave me there so long?"

"Oh come on, lad," he chuckled. "Four days is none too long aboard a Seeker ship, as you well know now."

Triistan did his best to sound indignant. "I could have starved though, or died of thirst!"

"Not at the rate you was thieving bread and fruit, boy! At first I blamed it on our titch - he was a fat, lazy monkey and never had been much of a ratter, not like Snitch and Snatch, who came later. I figured he just wasn't keeping up with his duties. It was our Fore Echoman, Mhorokai, who actually found you, only a few hours out of port. He was checking on the emergency stores in the launch when he found you sound asleep, tucked up under a thwart. Now Protocol required he drag you before the Captain immediately, where on most ships you would have been tossed by the boards and told to swim home."

Triistan swallowed, knowing that probably would have meant his death. Back then he was not a strong swimmer, and besides, every one of the harbor entrances for the Sea King Isles was teeming with jibfins - smaller cousins of the ridgeback but still deadly. They ate anything that moved.

"Why did he tell you first?" he asked.

Scow smiled. "Old Mhorokai had a soft spot for fellow Islanders. Not that Captain Vael would likely have thrown you overboard, but as it happened 'Kai knew I was short an apprentice and figured if I was the one to bring you to the Cap, she'd give me first dibs on putting you to work."

Triistan picked at one of the ragged corners of his journal. "That didn't exactly turn out very well, did it?" he said sheepishly.

Scow grunted, smirking. Like many of Triistan's doyens before him, he was perpetually frustrated and overwhelmed by the boy's questions. As the *Peregrine's* Master Carpenter, he was always busy with multiple tasks and had very little patience for - or experience with - constant queries from his men. Most apprentices were terrified of him. Triistan was intimidated as well, but that had never seemed to get in the way of his appetite for learning. One day, Scow finally decided he'd had enough and assigned Triistan to one of the line crews to get the boy out of his hair (he'd still had some silver stubble back then). Triistan had turned out to be a natural at it - climbing, sliding, balancing and leaping through the rigging better than half the crew on his first day. He never looked back. His new duties gave them enough separation from one another that Scow eventually missed the boy and his ideas, and started seeking him out for his views on one topic or another. Their respect and admiration grew for each other over time, until he saw Scow more like a father than an officer.

He slapped Triistan on the back. "I'd say it's worked out pretty well, actually." Then he grew quiet and looked out to sea, staring silently for so long that Triistan began wondering if the older man had fallen asleep with his eyes open. When Scow finally spoke, there was a note of weary resignation in his voice.

"I took an oath too, lad. The Officer's Oath. 'To obey, promote and protect the person and will of my commanding officers, until death or the Corps release me.'" He shifted his bulk and studied his hands.

"I've been a sailor all my life, Triis. A Seeker for the better part of that. I've never disobeyed a commanding officer, or questioned them or their orders in public. Oh part of that is I've been lucky to serve under Captain Vael for a good many years, and Mister Tarq was as fine a First Mate as you're likely to find anywhere. But I've had a few... greener sashes to answer to over the years, if you take my meaning, so I've heard my fair share of bad ideas from the top.

"When I went through cadet school, that was the credo they drilled into us: 'Gods' will, Captain's will.' You take that Oath, you place your fate in your Captain's hands. Do your duty, fulfill your Oath, and the Gods and your Captain will work out the rest." He made a wry face. "Now that the gods are all but bedtime stories, you can see where the Corps places the Captain in the grand scheme of things."

Scow paused and looked around the ship to see if anyone was within earshot. Biiko was the only one close enough to overhear them, but he and Scow seemed to have some kind of understanding between them that Triistan hadn't quite figured out yet. The Mattock leaned closer all the same, and lowered his voice to the nearest thing his rough growl could come to a whisper.

"But I've always known - *always*, lad - that the ship and the crew were better served if I did my duty and stuck to my Oath, and so long as anything I took a dislike to I dealt with privately, man to man, everything would work itself out and the right thing would eventually be done. I've always believed that oaths were about my honor... honor's important, make no mistake. Honor makes you dependable, believable - trustworthy. Something to take pride in.

"But that's a ship without sweeps or sheets, Triis. Honor must be about sacrifice, too, for it to be worth more than a bucket of bilge; putting your ship and crew above yourself, always. Because honor without sacrifice is something else altogether. It's nothin' more than self-righteousness... and that can be a very dangerous thing."

Scow glanced down at the book in Triistan's hands, then patted the young Seeker on his forearm.

"That's the funny thing about oaths, lad: sometimes you worry s'much about keeping them, you forget why you took'em in the first place." He heaved himself to his feet. Triistan looked up at the broad silhouette of the man he'd almost come to think of as his father. He couldn't see them, but he imagined he could feel those bright blue eyes burning with a new purpose.

"You're a good lad, Triistan Halliard - a good man I'm proud to call mate... and an honorable one too, I think. Trust yourself, and you'll do the right thing..."

"What about you, sir?"

Scow paused before answering.

"Me?" He gazed out to sea, sounding distracted.

"I've got some hard thinking to do, lad. About oaths and gods and captains..."

He stopped and turned to the west. Triistan had felt it as well and stood so quickly his head swam. He dropped his journal, scooped it back up, and absentmindedly slid it into its customary spot between his sash and the small of his back.

It was just a soft brush, the barest whisper across his cheek and neck, but he knew as every man of the sea knows, deep within his bones, when he's been without it for so long.

The wind was coming up.

***

As it turned out, the breeze was a shy, delicate thing for the rest of the night and well into the next morning, teasing the shrouds and the desperate survivors with each brief gust, torturing ship and crew alike. Scow and Voth could not know this, of course, nor were they willing to wait for it to strengthen; as soon as they had felt its first hesitant touch, they ordered the rest of the crew to their stations. For the remainder of that afternoon, they all forgot about their demons and even their empty stomachs. Hope lent strength to their limbs and purpose to their actions; even Rantham regained a touch of his old swagger, exchanging a few barbs with Dreysha and Scow as they trimmed the sails. Snitch made a brief appearance during the evening meal as well, perhaps encouraged by the comparatively buoyant mood of the crew, but a near miss from Sherp's throwing knife sent it scurrying for cover in the tops again.

Voth decided on the spot that they had tolerated the titch monkey's presence long enough. When Mung protested with peculiar vehemence, Voth accused him of insubordination and ordered him to climb up the main mast and flush the thing out himself. Although Sherp laughed overloud and added a choice comment about Mung having a chance to make it up to the monkey first in the privacy of the new crow's nest, the rest of the crew grew quiet.

"May I have a word, sir?" Scow asked, and they stepped to the stern, speaking in hushed voices. It wasn't hard to guess the nature of the conversation, especially since they were all thinking the same thing. Renewed morale or not, their strength and coordination were severely diminished, and whatever confidence and vigor they felt now were just phantoms. Mung was the worst climber among them, as clumsy and uncoordinated a sailor as Triistan had ever laid eyes on. Sending him up to the tops after the titch monkey was risky and potentially deadly.

Triistan's thoughts inadvertently drifted back to his earlier conversation with Scow. Although he knew that at least in part he had been referring to Triistan and his journal, he also felt sure that the Mattock had serious misgivings about Voth. If ever there was an example of someone who had risen above their station, it was the *Peregrine's* former Master Provisioner. He had been abrasive and arrogant to begin with; as acting Captain, he was nearly intolerable. New to command and wholly unsuited for it, he was overcompensating for his lack of confidence, in some cases issuing orders just for the sake of exercising his authority. Worse, he had somehow managed to coax Sherp to his cause. The newly-minted second mate was a cruel, brutal man. Years of manning an oar in The Pit had strengthened him physically, and the fact that he'd never been able to rise above that station had left him hard and bitter. He was not burdened by thoughts of honor or sacrifice, and he and Voth together created a dangerous faction. Triistan wondered just how far Scow was prepared to go with his concerns if things continued to deteriorate. At the moment, he looked to be making every effort to contain his frustrations as he implored Voth to reconsider.

"Captain" Voth would not relent, however, though he did grudgingly acquiesce to Scow's final demand that a safety line and harness be used. If Mung fell, the Mattock and another member of the crew should be able to support him easily until he regained his footing.

From the look on his friend's face, that made little difference to Mung. He was visibly trembling as Scow began fashioning a makeshift harness around his torso.

"I suggest you all s-stay clear of the mainmast. My bowels were already as loose as a drunken doxy's not-so-private petals... well, at least as loose as I imagine them to be. My mother forbade me from whoring-"

"Stow that, Corpsman!" A bubble of spit shot from the corner of Voth's mouth as he spoke. "That mouth of yours is what put you in this place to begin with. Another word out of it other than 'Yes Captain' will see you before the mast, am I understood?"

Mung dropped his head and managed to stammer a "Yes Captain", but Triistan had seen enough. He was halfway up the mainmast before anyone else noticed. In fact, he'd climbed it so quickly his own body hadn't had time to register its fatigue; his limbs, hands and feet moved instinctively, with the fluidity of long practice and superior skill despite his deteriorating physical condition.

"Halliard!" Voth shouted hoarsely, and Triistan could imagine the spray of saliva shooting up in his direction. "What is the meaning of this? Come down here this instant!"

But a strange recklessness had come over him and Triistan kept climbing, even as he began wondering how he had come this far. Healthy, he could have made the climb with just his hands while singing at the top of his voice, but now his limbs shook and his left hand felt weak where he gripped one of the ratlines. He brought his right leg up and used it to push himself higher, while reaching with his right hand for the next rung. He was panting heavily, as if he'd been sprinting or swimming. He doubted he could even recall the words to a song just then, let alone have breath to sing it. *I wonder if Biiko could catch me if I just let go...*

"Say the word, Cap'n. I'll bring him down." It was Sherp's voice, and Triistan shot a quick look down between his legs. The Second Mate held a harpoon in one hand, arm cocked and ready to throw. Triistan closed his eyes and thought about swinging around to the other side of the mast, a move he normally could have made as easy and cat-quick as taking a step, but the trembling in his arms and shoulders made him hesitate.

"I don't think you want to do that, *sir*." It was Dreysha's voice, hard and deadly. He opened his eyes again and looked down. She was standing behind Sherp with the tip of her punch-dagger poised just behind his right ear, her left hand gripping the collar of his tunic. Triistan also noticed that Biiko was now standing within arm's reach of

Voth, though at the moment he held no weapon that Triistan could see. The Valheim slowly lowered the harpoon while Voth's head twitched back and forth between Biiko and Dreysha, mouth opening and closing like a fish stranded on the ship's deck.

"Everyone, STAND DOWN!" Scow thundered.

"Mr. Icefist, stow that squid-pricker! Dreysha, you too, and step back! Have you all taken leave of your senses? The boy's the best climber on board. Who better to go after that rat-humping monkey?! Azimuth isn't even a rated seaman! Is your intent to humiliate a member of the crew or secure a food source, sir?"

On this last point Scow looked squarely at the Captain and everyone, including Triistan, held their breath. His arms were trembling, so he ran a leg through the webbing of the ratline, squeezed his eyes shut again, and concentrated on the cool, hesitant stroke of the breeze on his cheek. Below him, Voth found his voice, though it was low and rambling at first, almost as though he were talking to himself.

"I'll report every single one of you when I get back, that's what I'll do. Belligerence, insubordination, dereliction of duty, disobeying a direct order... mutiny, yes, that's what this is. You dare to question my-"

"Sir!" Scow interjected, trying desperately to keep the situation from fraying further. "This is no mutiny, sir. You are the Captain and the ship and its command are yours. I am... *respectfully* suggesting that Seeker Halliard is better equipped than Mr. Azimuth for this task, and provides us with a much better opportunity to procure the food source, sir."

The pause that followed was enough for Triistan to steal another look down. For once, Voth actually stopped and thought before he spoke. Dreysha had stepped away from Sherp, but Biiko still stood close enough to reach both him and the captain. Voth's eyes darted around the boat, flinching from one crewman to the next while he worried his lower lip. Scow had stepped across a line Triistan felt sure he had never crossed before - at least not publicly - but he had realized it and tried to give Voth a way out where he would not lose face. But would the captain take it?

Voth's gaze settled on Sherp last, and Triistan thought he saw the captain nod to himself, though it was difficult to be sure from this angle. Finally, he spoke, and once again his pettiness showed through.

"Very well, Mister Scow. We will do this your way; a good captain considers the input of his officers," he craned his neck back to look up at Triistan, raising his voice pointedly. "Since Mister Halliard has shown such initiative, he may continue. In fact, given the gravity of the task, he may continue until it is completed. See that he does not come down again until the monkey has been caught. Given your confidence in the young man, Mister Scow, that shouldn't prove to be too difficult. Besides, we've gone too long without a set of eyes aloft and he can spend the next watch up there regardless."

"Aye, sir," rumbled Scow. To his credit, he did not reach out and strangle the man. Oblivious and apparently satisfied that he had regained the upper hand, Voth dismissed them all and ordered them to return to their duties.

At least the delay had given Triistan a chance to rest, so he was able to climb the last fifteen feet up to the new crow's nest. Even so, he was trembling badly again by the time he reached it. Fortunately, one of the tasks Scow had come up with to pass the time was to fashion a slightly more comfortable and somewhat sheltered lookout's perch than the loop of line and wooden crosspiece they had rigged in the first few days. At least now there was a proper basket and a solid floor to stand on. As Triistan stuck his head through the rough hatch in the floor, Snitch screamed at him and scampered up and over the side, then out onto the topgallant's yardarm. He heard mocking laughter from below and assumed it was Sherp's, but did his best to ignore it as he hauled himself into the nest, panting heavily again from the effort.

There wasn't enough room to lie down, but he could sit once he'd closed the hatch, and the curved walls of the basket made a decent backrest. As for Snitch, Triistan could hear it chattering away angrily a few yards away.

Stay out there for awhile, Snitch, he thought. He was in no hurry to climb back down anyway, and Voth had unknowingly done him a favor by ordering him to stay aloft for the next watch. Besides the fact that he lacked the strength to climb back down now, there were far less pleasant places to spend the night than up here. And the longer he spent aloft, the more time the rest of the crew would have to cool off. He knew tensions were high - you couldn't help but hear it in the tone of people's voices, or the ugly, stolen glances - but he hadn't realized that they were so close to boiling over.

We're a thin fin away from murder.

He had been very surprised - and pleased - that Dreysha had come to his aid. They had spoken little since he had accused her of stealing his journal, and he wondered why she would intervene on his behalf now. She had pulled a knife on an officer, risking severe discipline and placing her future in the Corps, not to mention her personal freedom, in jeopardy. He couldn't fathom why she had done it, but he had to admit it made him feel good.

When he had regained his breath, he stood carefully. Mindful of the last time he had been up in the lookout's perch and had seen the ominous shadow of the ridgeback, he fixed his eyes on the horizon.

The Maiden had already disappeared beyond the edge of the sea, but the Crone still trailed a few hours behind her. To the north and east the skies were clear but for a few high, thin streamers. To the south, a faint, hazy layer of clouds was advancing, brushed with the dusty red color of the long evening. Triistan knew at a glance that they would not bring rain, however. The best hope for that lay to the west, where he could faintly see a few large, billowing clouds that often piled on top of each other to form a storm. At the moment, though, they were very distant and altogether innocuous looking. No matter which direction he looked, the sea stretched to the horizon, blue-gray and empty.

The breeze stiffened and he closed his eyes, lifting his face to it, steeling himself to look down at the water immediately surrounding the ship. After everything he had experienced already, he felt utterly ridiculous, but he could not shake the memory of that long, sinuous shadow gliding beneath the prow, and he was convinced it would be there again if he dared look. Finally, he took a deep breath, held it, and opened his eyes.

There was nothing there but the deep, dark ocean. *Idiot.* He let out his breath, laughed at himself, and settled in as comfortably as he could. He would wait for Snitch all night if necessary, determined to enjoy the privacy and seclusion as best as his aching body would allow. The next watch wouldn't start for another two hours, so he had some time to himself.

He listened to the sounds of the boat, the creak and groan as familiar to him by now as the sound and feel of his own heart and breath. Whenever the uncertain breeze blew, the hushed whisper of sailcloth intruded on his thoughts and he would wait for the distinctive rustle and snap that would mean they were underway again. The occasional order and response of the other crew members drifted up to him, but they were few and brief. The launch was ready if - *when*, he corrected himself - the wind steadied, so there was not much for the crew to do right now but wait. If Voth were smart, he would initiate some kind of routine chore to help re-establish the familiar rhythm that most Seekers lived by, to move them away from the recent morale crisis rather than leave them all to their dark thoughts.

But Voth's not smart, is he? Scow was, though, and Triistan wondered why he hadn't stepped into the void as he always had in the past. He leaned out to see what everyone was up to down on deck and, not surprisingly, found the Captain and Second Mate huddled near the fore, talking to each other. Sherp seemed to be doing most of the talking, waiving his huge, hairy arms around for emphasis. It was said in the Isles that the Valheim were direct descendants of the great bears, which explained their people's tendency towards size, strength and ferocity. Triistan thought it had more to do with how hairy they all seemed to be, and Sherp was no exception.

Rantham was nowhere to be seen. Probably hiding in a corner somewhere, he thought. Scow was talking to Dreysha, not far from the base of the mainmast. Mung had joined them, and Biiko was kneeling a few yards away, hands on his knees, meditating.

The breeze tugged at his hair briefly, carrying a snatch of Drey's voice along with it, making him smile. He pictured her the way she had looked in those first few days after being rescued, when Scow had ordered them to man the billy together: eyes flashing from under her dark, lustrous hair; the way her hips swayed when he had followed her up to the prow; the ample curve of her breasts beneath her taenia; the smell and feel of her as he brushed by her... he groaned and stretched to relieve the growing pressure in his groin, nearly toppling from the nest when Snitch, who had apparently stolen back up to the edge of Triistan's perch, screamed and scampered away again.

This time he took a closer look at the titch monkey, who was out on the yardarm again, perhaps fifteen feet from where Triistan stood. There was something strange about its appearance, but it took him a few minutes to figure out what.

"Dark be damned, you look... healthy." He would have expected to find the animal emaciated, its coat of sand-colored fur matted and thinning, even missing in patches. The monkey was thin, but it did not look to be starving, and its fur actually looked as if it had been groomed recently. Nor did it act like it was malnourished; it had scampered out of harm's way with the same quickness and agility that made the nimble titch monkeys such effective ratters.

So where had it been getting food? Though it was unlikely, there might have been a couple of rats on board when they first boarded the launch, but an animal Snitch's size - they weighed close to forty pounds when healthy - would have gone through them in the first few days. And what about water? He suddenly remembered noticing that the level of the scuttle had seemed lower than it should have been. Snitch must have been sneaking down to the deck in the middle of the night and stealing water. But the food was kept crated, locked, and under constant guard - he could not imagine how the titch monkey could be stealing that on a regular basis. Someone was either secretly feeding it their rations, or the monkey had figured out how to conjure food out of the air.

Wiliamund. It made sense. He had shown a certain fondness for both Snitch and Snatch when they were aboard the *Peregrine*, even feeding them the odd piece of fruit or biscuit now and again. It would explain why the echoman had protested the monkey's slaughter, and perhaps why his friend was always sleeping; not only was he taking in less food, he was also most likely having to stay awake in the middle of the night to feed the thing. Triistan didn't know whether to feel sorry for him, or be outraged that he was wasting his own rations while squandering an opportunity to provide additional food to the entire crew. *Probably a bit of both*, he decided.

But what should he do about it? They needed the food, so there was little question that Mung's new pet would have to be sacrificed. But Triistan didn't relish the idea of being the one to do it, and wished that he could have at least talked with his friend beforehand to clear the air between them. He glanced down again to find Mung staring back up at the crow's nest, shielding his eyes against the glare of the sinking suns.

Well I'm not going to kill myself to get to him, he thought. He was fairly certain that wasn't the kind of sacrifice Scow had in mind; the monkey might provide a day or two's rations for all of them, certainly some much-needed meat, but not worth a man's life.

He shivered, though not because it had grown cold. With only the trailing sun, it was relatively cooler, but the Crone still burned high and hot. He was thinking again of Rantham's tale of starvation, wondering what the others might do with his broken body if he did fall.

Unwilling to pursue that line of thinking any further, he tried forcing his thoughts back to Dreysha, trying to remember that moment when they had almost kissed, but instead he found himself studying the scar on his leg and wondering how much meat his calf would yield and how many people it would keep alive for how long. His stomach growled.

Get a hold of yourself, Triis. Your mind is wandering, that's all. Left to its own devices, there was no telling what his imagination might conjure up. He needed a distraction.

He pulled his dakra and raised his head up slowly to look for Snitch. The monkey was still sitting out on the yardarm, grooming itself. It had something small and dark in its right hand, but he couldn't make out what it was. "Here, Snitch. C'mere little monkey stew. No? Don't like stew? How about a nice, succulent roast titch, then..."

Snitch barely glanced at him, intent on the thing in its hand - an elongated, flat, sharp-looking object. At first he thought it was chewing on it, but then realized it was using it to pick at its teeth, the way a man might with a knife or fork. Could it have just eaten something? He looked around the floor of the nest again, but saw no evidence that it had been eating up there - not a bone or crumb or discarded melon peel anywhere.

He gave up trying to coax it over to him, resolving instead to remain as inconspicuous as possible, hoping to catch it whenever it left its perch in search of food. He considered asking for one of the harpoons to be sent up, but they were slow, ungainly things and he knew he'd never be able to hit his mark with it. In the meantime, there was nothing to do but wait. He scanned the horizons and the water around the boat (the latter with his breath held again), then looked once more towards the setting sun.

He sat up quickly, his heart skipping.

He thought he had glimpsed a flash of white far out to the north and west, but when he shielded his eyes and leaned out of the nest to try and confirm it, there was nothing. He watched the spot for long moments, waiting - sometimes a smaller vessel with jib-cut sails could disappear if she tacked at just the right angle. If her course was towards you, eventually she would reappear, but if she was hull-down and running away, her line could easily take her all the way over the horizon before she tacked again.

"More likely a coxsil," he muttered to himself. The huge birds were known to travel thousands of leagues and their great white wings sometimes caught the sun. Light was a tricky thing at sea, especially during the Crone's Watch, when weary eyes and the single sun conspired against the good intentions of many a lookout. Triistan had learned the hard way how captain and crew alike loathed an errant sighting of land or sail, and under their present circumstances, it was hard to think of a crueler jape to play on them. He told himself it had been nothing and settled in once more to wait out the titch monkey. They were alone and most likely thousands of leagues away from any shipping lanes.

His thoughts returned to his conversation with Scow, about sacrifice and honor. It was not a new concept to him; he had witnessed plenty of it during the Aarden Expedition, though Scow would have no way of knowing that.

But he should. He needs to know, he told himself. *He needs to know how critical this information is, how important it is that we reach home safely and deliver it to the Ministry.* The truth was terrifying, but the rest of the world needed to prepare.

He fished his journal from the back of his sash, unwrapped its oiled, waterproof cover, and flipped it open. As if the journal itself wanted him to return to the events in his past, it opened to the long entry he had made after they had finally exited the Rivergate. It was a detailed account of their flight beneath the wall, nearly everything he had dreamed so vividly, so he had no desire to go through that again right now. However, in the pages before and after the entry, as well as in some of the margins, he had made numerous sketches and notes, and a handful of very detailed renderings. They were like artifacts he had collected along the way, relics of things they had discovered and which most of the world had forgotten; things that they must remember again to prepare for what was coming. And it was his responsibility - his alone - to ensure they were delivered into the hands of those who would know what to do with them.

But I can't do this alone. He and his secrets were lost at sea, yet he understood that the greater, more immediate danger lay in the fact that they were adrift internally as well. They desperately needed a strong, capable captain, and Triistan had no doubt the most qualified man aboard was Mordan Scow. Unfortunately, he was also the least likely to take the role by force. Triistan briefly toyed with the idea of trying to recruit Dreysha, Biiko, Wil and Rantham, hoping that if all of them acted to depose Voth, Scow would have no choice but to assume command. He could show them the journal's contents - that should convince them to join his cause, give them a reason to fight for their survival rather than leave it to the uncertain winds of Voth's ineptitude. But, if he told them, why wouldn't he show it to Scow? He owed it to the Mattock, didn't he? And what of his oath to Captain Vaelysia and First Mate Tarq? He knew that Scow had been partially right: he was fixating on the oath itself rather than its purpose. But he also knew that wasn't by accident. If he was honest with himself - if he "trusted himself" as Scow had urged - he had to admit that he was hiding behind the oath because he didn't believe in its purpose. Captain Vaelysia's primary concern was her duty as a Seeker officer to protect their discovery, to give the Sea Kings every opportunity to exploit it before the rest of Niyah was even aware of Aarden's existence. The Sea King Isles were his homeland, and he was a sworn member of the Seeker Corps. He'd been entrusted with a vital mission by one of the Corps' most highly-regarded officers, and he was duty and honor-bound to fulfill it.

But, gods help him, he knew it was wrong.

He ran his hand through his tangled hair in frustration. *By the High Houses, why does everything have to be so... complicated?* He had never asked for this role. He longed for the innocent excitement, the simple thrill of discovery that had been there even after having faced the horrors beneath the Rivergate. He remembered the sense of exhilaration he had felt when they had climbed out from the carcass of the creature they had eventually named Armaduura - "Armored Giant" in the ancient language of the Ghostvale. Besides the relief and joy at having survived, it was also an incredible moment of exploration - a true Seeker moment - as they emerged into a world that had been forgotten centuries before. Captain Vaelysia had pulled him aside and commanded him to record everything he could, and to get to it as quickly as possible.

"I want it all, Mister Halliard," she had said. "Maps, pictures, everything we saw, everything we did, down to the color and markings of those things' skin, understood?"

He had thrown himself into it with the ferocity the Reavers gave to combat. He had written and sketched almost non-stop during that first day, until his fingers and hand were so badly cramped he could no longer hold his stylus, then switched hands and wrote with his left. He could not draw with his off hand, but he had learned under Doyen Rathmiin to write with either one, so the script from his left was passable. Though his stamina on that side was severely limited, it allowed him to periodically rest his right hand. Once he began switching methodically back and forth, he was able to continue all through the first night as well. He was as exhausted as the rest of the expedition, but he didn't stop even when Biiko came to change the dressing on his injured leg and inspect the wound. He couldn't; there had been too much to record, too much to process and too much more to explore.

And too many sacrifices, he thought, remembering Taelyia and the others. He turned a few pages until he found the first passage he had written almost as soon as they crossed from the atoll around the Armaduura's tail over to the southern shoreline.

Ten and One, Vehnya, 256, The 8th day of the expedition, 31st since Landfall - Mid-Morning

The suns have never looked so sweet, nor the open sky so blue and endless. We have survived the dark passage of Ahbaingeata and its guardians, both wondrous and deadly, and won our freedom through the most unlikely means I could heretofore have imagined. The Captain has commanded me to record the terrible events of our passage, as well as the amazing discoveries we have made on the other side.

There is so much to tell, I scarce know where to begin, so I will first take note of our losses, so that their names are not forgotten.

The Fallen of Aarden:

Welms - Died on Sevenday, Vehnya, 256. Killed by native wildlife in the act of exploration.

Jaegus - Died on Sevenday, Vehnya, 256. Killed by native wildlife in the act of exploration.

Taelyia, Reaver - Died on Eightday, Vehnya, 256. Killed by native wildlife defending her companions.

Pendal - Died on Eightday, Vehnya, 256. Killed by native wildlife defending his companions.

'And so do we Seekers release their ashes to the wind, that they may sail on, or return to the waiting Sea.'

I should write something else here to honor their memory, but am presently unable to do so. The Captain calls us to council.

They were the first to give their lives to this cause, but certainly not the last. Triistan turned the page and instantly thought of the Captain's meeting, since the primary topic of discussion was sprawled across two pages right here on his lap. It was a drawing he had begun during the council, attempting to illustrate what he had been having difficulty explaining to the rest of the Aarden Expedition: where they were and how they had gotten there. The Captain and one or two others had understood intuitively the same thing he had realized when he had urged them into the armaduura's skull: they had needed to go up to get out.

Originally they had all assumed that the barbican had been named 'The Rivergate' simply because the Glowater passed through it in a tunnel capped by fortified gates at either end. That was only half the story, though: the river and its approach were actually part of the fortifications. He studied his drawing closely - he was proud of the finished product now, although it had begun crudely enough. Most of his companions had not understood what he had been trying to describe to them, so there had been plenty of shouted questions and more than a handful of insults as he rushed to illustrate it more clearly, all the while burning with embarrassment... at first. But then an odd thing happened. As his picture took shape, the questions grew quieter, more respectful. Focused on their increasing understanding, he forgot about his embarrassment, gradually taking command of the conversation and earning their rapt attention as he drew and explained each element of Ahbaingeata's complex design.

He had used a 'cutaway view', something he had learned from a master builder once. The method showed a structure in profile, with most of the outer wall removed, allowing the artist to depict what was inside. Triistan had done the same thing here, showing the huge wall, the valley floor on both sides, the great hall with its magnificent waterfalls and statues, the mountain of rubble, and a long, sloping ravine on the far side of the collapse, where the armaduura lay, and through which the Glowater passed. The rendering also showed the significant elevation change from the floor of the river valley they had followed in from the coast, up to the highlands on the south-east side of the wall. A cliff separated the two, close to two hundred and fifty feet high, and the wall, built to rest on the valley floor, covered its face and rose another three hundred feet beyond that, obscuring the dramatic change from the lowland side.

His drawing also showed why the tunnel had been so long. Barely a tenth of its length was actually beneath the wall; from there, it sloped gradually upwards until it joined the great chamber just inside the eastern gate, where they had battled the kongamatu swarm and eventually escaped into the armaduura's skull. Up to that point, the incline was so sleight that with all of the debris and the constant threat of attack, they hadn't even noticed it. Beyond the great chamber and the cave-in, the slope was much more severe, so the river made most of its elevation change through this sloping canyon cut into the land above, using the empty remains of the armaduura as a conduit through the rubble. Triistan had surmised that the beast must have tried to work its way through the eastern gate, either during or long after whatever great battle had occurred inside and demolished the western doors. Its efforts had caused the outer chamber and part of the reservoir above it to collapse, trapping it there, but providing the Aarden Expedition a most opportune path to freedom. Above everything, from the damaged tail end of the armaduura to the wall, he had drawn a series of vague shapes, rectangles and columns, arches, stairs, trees, pyramids and spires: Ostenvaard, Stronghold of the Forgotten. At the time he had intended to survey the city and flesh out those crude shapes, but he never had the opportunity.

Based on what they found in the city, Triistan theorized - and later confirmed - that the lake was part of Ahbaingeata's natural defenses as well: it was an intentional consequence of closing the eastern gates. Although the dam caused by the cave-in had triggered the same effect, the gates that led from the great hall to the ravine had been crafted with such exquisite precision that when barred, they created a watertight seal, so unlike the western gate with its truncated design, they did not allow the river to pass beneath them. Consequently, the narrow canyon through which the river descended as it approached the eastern gate would flood, filling the canyon and then spreading into a sprawling plaza that had been built to act as a reservoir above the ravine. The armaduura's tail lay near the eastern shore of this "lake", not far from where the Glowater dumped into it. The top twenty feet or so of the great chamber where the thing's head lay rose from the center of the lake to their west, the grates they had observed from inside it allowing the water of the reservoir to pass through into the chamber, preventing the main city from flooding and allowing the Glowater to continue on its journey to the sea - all by design. The north, south, and western shores of the reservoir were actually marble steps leading up to broad stone streets, along which the ruins of Ostenvaard rose in ancient splendor. Beyond those, to the west and north, the top portion of the wall loomed like an advancing storm front. To the east, the Glowater exited the city and was visible for perhaps half a league before it was engulfed by the waiting jungle, rank after rolling rank of soaring trees, layer after layer of leaf, plant and vine, like an army preparing to storm the gates.

Considering the virulence of the surrounding wilderness, the city-fortress of Ostenvaard was remarkably intact. Most of the buildings and bridges were festooned with grasping vegetation, like giant green cobwebs, but the majority of them still stood, a testament to their initial construction. *And to their monstrous scale,* Triistan reflected. Everything they explored in Ostenvaard had been built for a much larger race. A land of gods and giants...

He considered his drawing of the armaduura. This particular rendering was less about creating an accurate portrait of the creature than it had been about diagramming how its remains had provided the critical tunnel through the wreckage. Consequently, it was very crude, and other than its relative shape and proportions, it bore little resemblance to the actual living creatures they encountered later in the expedition. He wished he had one of his charcoal pencils with him now so that he could amend his picture some. They were magnificent creatures, and the tiny, simplistic rendering he had made did not do them justice.

He held the book at arm's length, looking at the whole illustration with a critical eye. He had gone over it many times, adding details that he hadn't had time to put in at first, but which were indelibly etched in his mind. Once an image embedded itself there, he could recall it to his mind's eye as if he were seeing the subject firsthand. For things like this, it was a gift. But as he had grown older, and learned that there were some things better off forgotten, it was also a curse.

On the following page was a very detailed drawing of a kilij, the traditional Reaver sword. It was meant to be Taelyia's weapon, which Triistan remembered asking for after she had been slain by one of the kongamatu guardians. He had drawn it after the meeting had come to a close. Once they all had a solid understanding of their position, the Captain and Commander Tchicatta had moved on to a discussion of their options. They decided to make a temporary camp on the near shore to tend to the wounded and inventory their supplies, while the Firstblade, Miikha, Myles and a grumbling Wrael set out to scout their immediate surroundings. From all appearances, the city was abandoned, but that didn't mean it was empty.

Below the drawing was another entry:

Ten and One, Vehnya, 256, The 8th day of the expedition, 31st since Landfall - Late Morning, Entry #2

The council was interesting, to say the least. Captain V. ordered me to explain our situation - that is, where we are and how we got here - to the rest of the Expedition. At first it was very difficult, as no one was willing to listen to me. I think they were frightened by their lack of understanding. Notsomuch the reavers - they took up positions around the council, keeping watch - but Seekers are accustomed to the fixed and defined area of their ship, for the most part. They find large expanses of land disconcerting under the best circumstances, and the fact that we have been traveling beneath and through strange ruins on a foreign shore while grappling with fell beasts has made them edgy and impatient, to say the least. I admit I was rather intimidated at first, but eventually they grew calmer as I did a better job of explaining things. Illustrations seemed to help immensely, and the diagram you see on the preceding pages is the poor sketch that seems to have won the day. We were finally able to move on to the Captain and Firstblade's important agendas.

Our temporary camp will be made in a large guard house at the base of what must once have been a watch tower. The door into the tower is buried beneath heavy undergrowth, which we will have to cut our way through, but I look forward to gaining the top and an elevated view of our surroundings. I would like to refine my diagram to capture the ingenious layout of the wall and its defenses. As noted, I suspect that we are actually hundreds of feet above the floor of the river valley we followed in, but I need to gather more information to confirm my assumptions. I am reasonably confident in them, however, since our journey through the ARMADUURA - what an amazing creature! - was exactly as I envisioned it would be. We were clearly climbing the entire time, and the roof of the Great Hall with its grates and waterfalls is visible above this man-made lake's waterline, exactly where it should be.

Commander Tchicatta has taken Miikha and the two scouts, Myles and Wrael, to explore the city, which I have learned from the Captain is named 'Ostenvaard' (her knowledge of this place continues to both impress and baffle me). Their plan is to return before nightfall, while the balance of our party establishes a defensible camp. After our ordeal in the tunnel, the nature of our adventure has changed considerably, and now has the feel of a military campaign moreso than an expedition.

Speaking of which, I must explain the sword I have sketched above. Jaspins, the young Reaver Lieutenant and protégé to the Firstblade, has done me a great honor. After the Captain's council, she approached me and handed me Taelyia's blade. Her manner was solemn, and when I thanked her quietly, she said that I had earned it.

I will provide a full accounting of the Reaver's death once I have an opportunity to record our passage through Ahbaingeata. For now, I will only say that in the moments immediately following her death, I was moved by her and her fellow Reavers' courage and sense of duty, and asked if I might take up her sword, so that she and her courage should not be forgotten, and that I might do my part for this battered - but far from beaten - company.

More later. First I must assist making our temporary camp and have my leg tended to. Then I will give an account of our incredible journey through Ahbaingeata.

He thought of Taelyia, of what she and so many of the others had given, and about Scow's comments about honor and sacrifice, while his finger absently traced the outline of her sword. And he thought about something else: what this entry did not say.

Possibly for the first time ever, he had deliberately omitted something from his journal. In part it was because it was difficult to explain – he wasn't entirely sure what had happened when he had accepted the sword and wrapped his fingers around the hilt for the first time.

"I know now the choices made are mine alone to make."

The words had come to him like a sudden memory, and he had simply whispered them aloud. But he had no idea where they had come from, or why he had felt such a strong compulsion to say them out loud.

"What was that?"

He looked up suddenly and realized he was standing before Jaspins, holding the partially-drawn kilij out before him.

Confused, he just shook his head and mumbled something about being honored. She told him he'd earned it, felt his forehead and the side of his face to see if he was feverish, and then moved on to check on Tarq's injury.

He drew the weapon several more times, but nothing else happened. Feeling self-conscious, he found an area out of sight of the others, so that he could study the sword more closely. It was a finely wrought blade, well-balanced and meticulously maintained. Taelyia had carried the scabbard on her back, and given her height, it had only needed some minor adjustments to properly fit him. The curve made an over-the-shoulder draw somewhat awkward for him, but he told himself he would practice with it until he could not only draw it smoothly, but actually wield it skillfully enough to help defend his comrades.

He began slowly moving through the few sword strokes and guard positions he had learned as a Corpsman. Although his motions were awkward, there was nevertheless something right about the feel of the hilt in his hand and the weight of the kilij, as if it were an extension of his arm. When he noticed Biiko standing there watching him, though, he blushed and started to lower the blade, feeling like a child playing with a wooden stick. But with a step, Biiko was suddenly inside his guard, strong fingers locked around Triistan's wrist. Wordlessly, he moved his sword arm back into a ready position, adjusting his elbow and the angle of his wrist. Then he moved behind Triistan and tilted his head just so, moving his hands along the young man's shoulders and upper arms, repositioning them slightly and showing him how the different parts of his upper body now lined up. Lastly, he kicked at

Triistan's feet until one was a step forward of the other rather than placed squarely under his shoulders, forcing him to rotate his hips and place more of his weight on the back foot. His injured leg was beginning to ache, but he didn't dare protest.

Biiko made a few more adjustments before taking a step back to inspect his work, hands clasped behind his back. Triistan remembered smiling awkwardly then, still feeling like a child performing for his teacher and waiting to be shown what to do next.

The teacher was not pleased.

Moving so quickly Triistan saw nothing but a shadowy blur, the Unbound drew one of his twin blades, spun, and knocked the kilij from Triistan's stinging fingers with a backhanded blow. With the grace of a ribbon in the wind, he finished his motion by sheathing his sword and coming to rest in the same position he had started.

Then he fixed Triistan with his golden irises and did something that truly startled the boy: he spoke.

"The weapon does not wield itself. Nor a life. Without will, they are meaningless."

Biiko stalked off, leaving him to retrieve his sword and ponder this new mystery.

On the surface Triistan thought the warrior's metaphor was pretty obvious. After all, his need to contribute to their mission, to be more than just another burden for the rest of the Expedition to shoulder, had driven him to ask for Taelyia's weapon in the first place. He thought Biiko had recognized this compulsion and decided for whatever reason to acknowledge it. But there had been something else about their exchange, a strange familiarity to the Unbound warrior's words, just like the phrase Triistan had uttered when he had grasped the pommel of the kilij the first time: it was a sense that he'd been there before, that it was what he was *meant* to be doing.

He looked up from his journal, wishing he still had the kilij. Like most of their possessions, it was lost when the *Peregrine* foundered. He pictured the cold steel glimmering faintly as the blade sank into the depths, now a meaningless artifact buried at the bottom of the sea.

The weapon does not wield itself.

"Nor a life," he whispered, echoing Biiko's words.

If he did not do what needed to be done, they would all share the same fate.

- 19 -

The Well

For a moment, just one hopeful moment, it looked as if the rider would make it beyond the edge of Flinderlaas. That hope was crushed as Casselle watched a large wolf leap from behind one of the buildings, crash into the rider and knock her clean from the saddle.

More wolves were already there, savagely ripping the bodies of horse and rider apart until the remains were small enough to drag away, carried back to wherever it was the beasts remained hidden during the daytime. Jaksen clenched a fist and slammed it angrily against the fortress' high wooden walls. Cries of anger and disappointment rose up in unison from those assembled on the ramparts looking out over the town.

"That was our last good horse," remarked Vincen von Darren off-handedly. Vincen was yanked off-balance, the front of his armorjack used to pull him close to the face of Royan Stone, which was red with rage.

"We lost an excellent Outrider with that horse, you damn fool!" the Commander barked fiercely. He had a look that suggested Vincen would be lucky to merely end up with a second black bruise to match the one already under his left eye.

"Yes, Commander, I just meant..." Vincen began before Royan pushed him away. No further words were exchanged as Vincen quickly evacuated the scene.

Casselle knew what Vincen meant, despite the tactless way that he offered it. There were a few horses left, but they were either too old, unfit or untrained for the type of punishing run it would take to break through the wolf-infested ruins of Flinderlaas. This rider and her mount had been their last chance to get a message out.

It had been days since the wolves had taken the town, an eternity of long, weary double work shifts since the last caravan had left for the Bay of Athoriss and the edge of Gundlaan proper. Even if those returning reached their destination quickly, by the time they could tell the authorities, it would still be far too late for them to send sufficient help to those trapped here at the private fort of the von Darren family.

Before attempting this last run, there had been some discussion about sending the Templars out as a vanguard, backed by Outriders, in order to clear the town or at least secure an escape route for the von Darren family, but that had been scrapped the same evening by the overwhelming number of wolves threatening the gates.

"Even if we had heavy armor, they'd crush us by sheer bloody numbers," the Outrider Commander had commented. So for the last couple of days since then, they'd tried to send individual riders to break through, hoping to outrun the wolves. Since the wolves prowled at night, there were hopes that letting the riders out during the day would provide the best chances. But no matter the time of day, the results had always been the same: the wolves took down every single one.

Terri, the last rider, had the idea to build up momentum in the courtyard before charging the gates. When they were opened, her horse was already running at full tilt, sprinting out into the town. She had hoped that it would give her just enough of an edge to get past them before they had the chance to react.

She was wrong, and when she fell, the collective hopes of the keep fell with her. Atop the wall, outrage settled into a sorrowful silence as Templars and Outriders mourned the loss of the brave rider and her mount.

"Let's get our people back to regular duties," Templar Captain Odegar Taumber said to Commander Stone in a quiet aside. The Outrider leader, his fists still clenched and shaking, nodded politely. As mad as he was, it was clear he knew what needed to be done, and instructed his remaining soldiers to return to their schedules.

The duties were largely ceremonial at this point, though. Weapons were sharpened, arrows fletched, materials for fill and repair were stacked at the ready, and provisions had been recounted any number of times. The work was there to distract them all from the unnaturally organized pack of wolves at their door… and its leader.

Casselle thought once again of the wild-haired woman she'd seen that first night, annoyed and disturbed that no one else had caught sight of her since then.

At the foot of the stairs leading from the wall's ramparts, Casselle watched a couple of Outriders return to their inspection of the walls, adding fresh dirt and stone to shore up any areas that appeared vulnerable. As with the first night's attack, the wolves had continued their attempts to dig under the walls on each subsequent night. It was only through constant vigilance that the defenders had kept them out.

Casselle knew that they were fighting more against time at this point. This fort was not built to withstand a prolonged siege. Truthfully, there were barely enough provisions to last them through the rest of the week.

She watched Jaksen, Temos and Raabel file down after the others, trailing behind the remaining Outriders and family servants. Her squad would also resume their assigned responsibilities. Today that involved a lot of physical labor, moving rocks from the inner courtyard to the edge of the wall. She could tell that the death of the rider added to the fatigue they already admirably bore.

Casselle did not go with them, though. She followed Odegar, who was walking next to Commander Stone. They were headed for the center grounds, where a good deal of dirt was being dug up, cleared and leveled to make changes to the keep's well. Those with woodworking skills were putting the finishing touches on modifications to the pulley system used to haul water up from below. It had been reinforced to bear more weight and allow for a draft horse to help work the winch.

"I still think this is a bit of a fool's errand," Royan commented to Odegar.

"It may be, but the theory is sound enough," Odegar replied. "There is a natural cistern under the hill suggested by the architect's plans I found. If you look off the back side of the keep, you can see the flow of water from the hill into the lake. If there is a passage from the cistern to the lake, we might be able to sneak out the back. I think we can both agree that leaving through the front door is no longer an option."

"Better on two legs with a sword in hand than out like a turd through the cesspipe, I'd say," the Commander retorted.

"Elegantly put, though inaccurate," Odegar chuckled.

"And then getting down boats and supplies..." Royan began.

"One challenge at a time," Odegar interjected with a smile. "Let's see if we can put wheels on the wagon before we attempt to ride off on it. Before we plan too heavily, we need to confirm that it's even a viable alternative." The Outrider Commander gave a rough grunt of agreement. Casselle moved up to Odegar's other side.

"I'd like to be the one to go down," Casselle said. The older Templar turned to face her. Their ordeal was weighing heavily upon him, despite his attempts to remain positive for the others. She could see it etched across his face in lines of worry and in the sunken look in his eyes. She had figured out several days ago that he didn't expect them to survive, but he'd been putting all of his energy into finding any plausible means of escape in order to prevent utter despair from breaking out.

"I know you are not the sort to volunteer foolishly for the sake of pride. Why then, might I ask, would you wish to do such a thing?" Odegar asked, genuinely curious.

"Temos and I are the smallest capable warriors. It will be easier for us to maneuver up and down the well and the space below," Casselle answered. It was true. For the last day or so, she had evaluated all of the Templars, even von Darren's otherwise useless squad, and the much more useful Outriders that remained. All of the warriors were considered, some more easily discounted than others. Aileah Blue was a close call, as she was the same height as Temos. Casselle eventually deferred to her history of trust and experience with her squadmate instead.

Odegar scrutinized Casselle for a moment, chewing on her words and most likely running through several scenarios in his own head. She waited patiently.

"You sure this is the most tactically sound choice?" He asked. Casselle shrugged.

"Too much we don't know," she said. Odegar took a deep breath and then exhaled, nodding his head in agreement.

"I'm too tired to argue with you about it," he replied, "not that it would do much good anyway." Casselle cracked a slight grin despite it all. For the first time since the wolves had penned them in, so did he. The moment of levity was short lived.

"Finish up your afternoon tasks and then you and Temos take your meal. If you had evening duties, assign them elsewhere. I want you both fully rested for the morning. We'll get started early," Odegar instructed. "I have a few things to check and prepare myself." He paused for a moment, looking at his own clenched fist before unfolding it and placing it briefly on Casselle's shoulder.

Casselle was surprised, but warmed by this sudden display. She smiled and patted the old Captain's hand with her own. He nodded in return and left, heading back to the space he'd been assigned near the former Templar Captain, Renholf Crennel.

Since the assault, Renholf had been completely withdrawn, slowly wasting away as he accepted neither sustenance nor medicine. It was disconcerting news, and something they had tried to conceal from the others to keep it from having a further impact on morale.

Casselle mused that there were certainly plenty of other things to worry about. She had certainly taken on an extra measure of it for herself and her squad. Unbidden, her thoughts turned to home. Her father was at the mill, worn and dusty from a day's work at the stone. It was as clear as if it had happened just yesterday.

If she died here... if they all died here, it was likely he would never hear of it, but would be left to assume the worst. He would not be the only one. Raabel's father, Temos' family and even Jaksen's special girl, the one he dared to love despite the Templar code...

There was a proper time for such thoughts, which was most certainly not now. She packed them away and moved with purpose to fulfill her duty for the afternoon.

***

Jaksen checked to make sure the straps on Casselle's armor were secured on the side. The Outriders had loaned them leatherjacks for protection. Like the Templar armorjacks, they were coats that fit snugly to protect their chests, upper legs and upper arms, but these were reinforced with leather, not metal, making them lighter and easier to maneuver in. Casselle had not expected to need weapons or armor, but Odegar insisted on basic protection and close combat weapons.

"That should do it," Jaksen said, a bit of concern on his face. He leaned in closer. "Are you sure we can't just shove that von Darren brat down the hole and see if he comes back alive? If not, at least we're no worse off than we are at the moment."

Casselle smiled, alleviating some of Jaksen's visible worry.

"There you are, rabbit," Raabel said, finishing a similar check of Temos' armor nearby. "Now you're all ready to go into the warren."

"Hilarious," Temos dryly responded. "Can we go now before this well meaning fool tries to shove carrots down my throat?"

Nearby, Nikk Bellows clumsily suppressed a laugh as he inspected the rigging that would allow the old draft horse to work the winch. The improvised additions to the mechanism allowed them to lower and raise much more weight than the original well equipment had been designed for. Casselle had seen them test it on loads of heavy rocks earlier this morning and felt confident that it would pose no problem for her and Temos.

She moved closer to the edge, where several other people were gathered.

"Old Honey and I will make sure you two have a smooth ride," Shayn Fletcher said. He was holding the reins of the horse working the mechanism, slowly stroking the animal's neck.

"I trust you will. I don't have to remind you I'm a bit more delicate than a bunch of rocks," Temos quipped. Raabel teased Temos again, but Casselle paid no mind to the exchange. Odegar had set up a small table a few feet from all of this and was busy with an odd collection of bowls and jars. She stood off to one side, so as not to disturb his last minute preparations. On the table were three small leather lanterns. She watched as he finished adding a measure of powder to two vials of milky liquid. The reaction was almost immediate as the vials began to glow with a bright blue light. Odegar stoppered the two vials tightly and gave each a vigorous shake to make sure they stayed sealed.

"This is an Arxhemic light. It should last you quite a while, hopefully long enough to get down and back. They're waterproof, too, so if you drop your lanterns, they shouldn't go out," he said as he affixed the vials in the slots normally reserved for candles. Then he secured the simple leather catch across the front, closing each lantern in kind. Casselle smiled and nodded, taking both lanterns in hand.

"I won't go on about being cautious and not taking risks. I trust the both of you." He walked alongside Casselle to the well, where she handed off one of the lanterns to Temos. A simple strap was sufficient to secure them to their respective belts. Odegar tied the final lantern to a loop in the thick rope that would lower them down. This one he had strapped open, to provide a visual marker for the rope in the darkness below. Then he held the rope steady for Casselle.

She stepped up to it, beside him. There was a small, round wooden disk they had threaded the rope through, to give them a secure place to set their feet. They had also tied a few more loops in for Casselle and Temos to affix a climber's hook to. Should they lose their footing and grip, it should keep them from falling outright. Not that she had any intention of letting herself fall, but she was still grateful for the extra precaution.

"I know how loud you can whistle, so if you get in any trouble on your way down, just whistle up. The well should make it easy for us to hear," Odegar said. Casselle nodded and secured the climbing hook to the rope before stepping on the platform. She steadied herself and then signaled to Shayn and the others that she was ready.

Odegar and Temos helped steady her as Old Honey followed Shayn's instructions to turn the mechanism, allowing the winch to lower the rope. There was a bump and a jerk initially, but as Casselle's head slipped past the edge of the well, the ride smoothed out, continuing down at a slow but steady pace. At first, she was merely attentive to the sensation of her controlled descent, but after a few minutes of watching the daylight above slowly contract out of sight, she felt a tiny bit of fear creep in.

She gripped the rope with one hand, while she held the other out to the side of the well to steady herself. She felt the mortar between the stones become rougher, even through the leather of her gloves, as she descended further. She closed her eyes and began silently counting to herself, trying to distract herself from her fear. She focused on her breathing, trying to keep it as normal as possible.

Just as she was getting into a comfortable rhythm, she felt nothing but empty air around her and the shock of it sent her into a slight panic. She flailed outward with her free hand and sent herself into a lazy spin, watching as the light from the lantern above her spun as well, throwing an incandescent glow onto the ceiling and the walls around her. Most of the panic faded, replaced by silent fascination. The light was faint further out, but the walls were not as rough hewn as she expected them to be. They almost looked carved, constructed to be a proper dome.

She moved her own lantern from her belt to a strap around her wrist, just in time to see and feel the water on her feet.

It was cold, almost numbingly so. She inhaled sharply, as tiny cold needles pierced her outer garments and prickled her skin. She fumbled clumsily for her climbing hook, unhooking it from the rope and tucking it into her belt, not wanting the weight of the rope to impede her. She kicked and paddled in the frigid water, hoping the exertion would warm her up, even if only a little.

She needed to find someplace drier, somewhere more stable. Determined to accomplish her task and get out of this place as quickly as possible, she clawed at the latch that opened the flap of her lantern with numb fingers. The light seemed brighter, fiercer down here in the dark than it did on the surface. Grateful for it, Casselle searched to find the edge of the cavern. She knew for certain the cistern couldn't be larger than the hill. Directing the light ahead of her, she found where the curve of the ceiling met with the water.

By the look of it, she was not so far away. She tried to swim with her free arm and both legs, but was confounded by the light armor she'd been pressed into wearing. In the water it felt restrictive and heavy, threatening to drag her down at any moment, and she struggled to rein in her fear that she would not reach the wall at all.

She caught a mouthful of water and coughed it back up, but it focused her concentration and she worked twice as hard to make progress. After what felt like a small eternity, her fingers finally brushed against the smooth stone and she groped around for a moment trying to find anything to grip on to. At first, any sort of handhold eluded her, but she forced herself to remain calm, knowing there must be something for her to latch onto, somewhere within reach.

She finally found a break in the wall. It was just a crack, but it was deep enough that she could stuff her fingers into it, giving her a point of contact. Now she had more than just her aching legs to keep her head above water. Steadied for the moment, she saw the rope vanish altogether, leaving her light as the only one remaining.

She knew it was just being pulled up so that Temos could come down to join her, but watching the attached blue light disappear up the well shaft was terribly frightening. Teeth chattering from the cold, she whispered a quick thanks to Odegar, and in the same breath, wished for Temos' quick arrival.

With the other light gone, she extended her arm and swung her own lantern around, starting on one side and then rotating as far as she could, hoping to survey the whole of the cistern.

Unfortunately, the light did not reach the other side, so all she could see was more of the same dark water she was already immersed in. With her grip on the wall, she braced her legs against it, giving them a momentary reprieve from work. While she tried to keep her teeth from chattering, she swept the lantern light along the curve of the wall on either side of her.

Something around her legs shifted.

Fighting the fear crawling in her guts, she tried to hold herself still. After a long minute or two, she was able to pinpoint the sensation. There was a current moving below her.

She swung her lantern in that direction and noticed for the first time several eddies in the surface of the water. It was subtle, but telling. Though she could not see the far side where the current flowed towards, she used the wall to kick off in that direction. Her motions disturbed the telltale marks on the surface, but she could feel the water pulling against her legs now, so she swam along with it, confident it was flowing towards the outlet that emptied into the lake outside.

Casselle heard Temos descending into the cavern as the far wall came into range of her lantern's light. She kicked her legs a bit harder as the twin lamps of Temos and the rope made a controlled descent from the well shaft.

"Over here!" Casselle called out, her voice echoing between the water and the rounded dome of the cistern. Out of her peripheral vision, she saw his light swing and search for her as she reached for the far the wall. Almost immediately to her left, there was a breach in the dome, a black hole in the perfect smoothness.

"I see you!" Temos replied. "I'm almost to the water. Is it cold?" Casselle maneuvered closer to the hole without answering. She could tell now it was not accidental: like the ceiling, it appeared to be carefully crafted, a large arch that looked more like a window than an accidental crack or fissure.

"You're not saying anything. Are you giving me that 'of course it's cold, you idiot' look? I can't see your face well, so I kind of assume that's what you're doing," Temos chattered. A moment later, he let out a cry of shock and alarm.

"Rutting Balls that's cold!" he yelled, filling the dome with smaller echoes. Casselle pulled herself up to the bottom edge of the window, a good couple of feet from the surface. It was more difficult than she had expected. Even though she was in excellent shape, it felt like she was trying to lift half of the well water along with her.

"I'm coming, I'm coming!" Temos called out through chattering teeth, while noisily splashing closer by the moment. Hanging from her arms at the bottom ledge of the opening, she used her light to inspect the space just beyond it. Inside was a well-constructed room with finished walls, floor and ceiling, and three passageways leading out in different directions. It was clear that the cistern was not a naturally occurring cave, regardless of what Casselle had heard Odegar tell Commander Stone. Clearly someone had been mistaken.

"Is it the way through?" Temos asked, now close enough to see the hole for himself. Casselle turned enough to shoot him a frustrated expression before devoting her energy to pulling herself up through the window. It was not pretty or graceful, but the Templar managed to get herself up and over the sill and into the room beyond. She wanted to rest for a moment, but she forced herself up, lantern in one hand and the other hand ready to draw steel at the slightest sign of trouble.

But there didn't appear to be anything to worry about. Another quick look verified that the room was virtually barren save for some cobwebs and dust. S

"Hsst!" Temos grunted, trying to haul himself up as Casselle had, but with considerably less luck. She let her lantern dangle from her wrist and helped him through, where he landed in a wet heap on the ground at her feet.

"Since you haven't told me to shut up you stupid bastard, I'm assuming we're the only ones here?"

Casselle nodded.

"Perfect," he complained, "now all I have to worry about is being sopping wet and likely to freeze to death."

She rolled her eyes and helped him to his feet. One corridor was directly ahead of them, opposite the window, but two of them were spaced an equal distance apart on either side of that one. Casselle nodded towards one of the side portals as she moved to the other. With the light in hand again, she saw stairs leading downward, curving around a corner. Though she couldn't see anything, she heard the rush of water from below.

"Wherever the water flows out from the cistern back there," Temos said, looking through the door on the opposite side of the room, "these stairs connect to it. If we follow them down, we might be able to see the way out."

"Not yet," Casselle said, motioning for Temos to look down the center corridor between them. Drawing his short sword as he moved along the wall, Temos flashed a quick look around the corner as Casselle took up a position on the other side of the entrance. It led to a short hall that split three ways, with two new passages branching out at slight angles away from the main corridor. Each ended in a door, or one's broken remains, as was revealed when they inched down the main corridor.

She motioned to the far left and he nodded in return, the two of them drawing their swords with trained precision. It was difficult to actually tell if they were sneaking up on anyone or anything, since the light must have been an obvious warning, but they did their best to remain silent at the very least. They reached the end of that first hall, which turned out to be half collapsed by age and decay. As Temos directed his light through the open half of a rotting door, his hand brushed against what was left. It splintered easily, the pieces of it clattering to the ground. Casselle shot him a sharp look.

"Rut it all!" he cursed, only half under his breath as he broke through the rest of the door, abandoning caution altogether. Casselle glanced behind them to the empty darkness before following.

The room inside was larger than the one they'd climbed into, but round and capped by a domed ceiling, much like the cistern, but on a smaller scale. Whatever had been in the room at some point before had fared even worse than the door. Perhaps a bed and a table, some fragments of clay pots for certain, and a few metal bits that were half rusted. Temos pointed out what might have been a bookshelf, but was little more now than a pile of pulped and mossy remnants.

"How long do you think this has been down here?" he whispered. Casselle shrugged as she ran her lantern around the room, searching the smooth stone walls. Unfortunately, anything that could have been painted or hung there was now lost to time.

"Let's check the other two then," Temos said, moving back to check the hallway past the broken door. It remained empty and silent. He moved first, leading the two of them back to the junction. Casselle joined him and then moved up the middle corridor until she reached the next door, which looked remarkably intact. She stopped short and signaled Temos to do the same. There was something... wrong.

After a few tense moments of observation, Casselle carefully closed the shutter on her arxhemical light. Temos looked confused in the blue glow of his own lantern, but finally did as she had done, closing the leather flap over the opening. As his eyes adjusted to the darkness, Casselle heard him gasp, announcing his surprise to see a flickering light from the slight gap where the door met the floor.

Casselle edged forward, her breath coming shallow and quick, her heart racing as she reached the door. She paused at the entrance, ears straining for any trace of activity, but it remained as quiet as a graveyard. She tightened her grip on her sword and put her other hand against the door, pushing on it slightly.

That gentle touch was enough. The door swung inward easily, revealing the room beyond.

The light was soft, but it fully suffused the room with a golden glow. It came from a single flame, an ornate oil lamp suspended from the ceiling, just above head high, centered over a massive stone table in the middle of the room. There were many stems on the lamp, but only one was currently lit. This room was also circular with a domed ceiling, but there was nothing in ruin here, though age was evident. Around the stone table there were bookshelves, one after another, emanating from the table like spokes on a wagon wheel, their far ends touching the wall but leaving aisles between them where someone could walk. On a nearby shelf, the two Templars could see stacks of scrolls, piled so high in some places that the weight of them bowed the shelves.

The shelves and the massive table were the only fixtures in the large room, and Casselle noticed the table was just above waist height for her as she and Temos quietly approached it. Draped across its length, from one end to the other, was another scroll, two to three feet wide. Vials and bowls of pigmented paints were spread haphazardly across the edge of the table closest to them, just above the top of the scroll. Some were dry and cracked, but others were fresh.

Casselle could make out something on the parchment, a drawing of some sort, and as she stepped closer to examine it, she was startled by the sound of footsteps. From her left, behind one of the shelving units, came a man in armor.

Casselle drew back, holding her blade out in front of her. Temos moved up beside her, his weapon also at the ready.

But the armored figure simply ignored them.

"What the..." Temos let slip as they both noticed his metal helmet. It was fashioned like a crude face, rusted over on the left side, with several large holes where corrosion had eaten completely through. But where they expected to see a head through the gaps, they saw nothing. Metal hands moved with purpose as the figure set jars up near the top of the open scroll, where the bowls had been sitting. It did not set the last jar down, but opened it instead and poured a portion of its contents into an unused bowl.

After setting the last jar down, it picked up two brushes, one in each hand. The figure paused, then began painting with almost mechanical precision, tiny clicks and clacks rhythmically punctuating its movements.

Temos and Casselle shared a look. She signaled for him to go around the left side of the table, while she moved around the right. Certainly he... it, she corrected after looking once again at the rusted holes in its head - certainly it had seen them. It must be able to see, after all, or else it wouldn't be able to paint. But as the two of them circled around to stand behind it on either side, they confirmed it either did not see them or did not care about their presence.

The figure swapped out the brushes for two others as it continued to paint, a stylized, deft, but depthless representation of a castle on a hill, flanked by water to one side and a town to the other.

"That's us!" Temos exclaimed, perhaps a bit too excitedly. There were drawings of tiny wolves in the town, flanking a woman with a wolf's head. She also saw what Temos was pointing to, a couple of small figures in a room under the hill below the castle. The space on the scroll on Temos' side was blank, but there was more on Casselle's side, to the left of the artist. The scene continued on to the edge of the table, where the rest of the scroll remained rolled up. She could not make out the markings, but there was another painting of the wolf-headed woman, leading a group of wolves through a town towards a hill in the distance. The markings of skeletons around the town left her little doubt this was the former town of Iselglen.

"What's before that?" Temos asked, looking over the artist to the side of the scroll Casselle was scrutinizing. She rolled open the scroll as far as it would go on the table, revealing another picture of the wolf headed woman rising from... darkness? Had she come from the Dark? Her curiosity unsatisfied, she tried to unroll the scroll even further. It slipped away from her fingers and fell off the table with a clatter, unrolling until it was stopped by the edge of a bookshelf.

It revealed more blackness, until that blackness became a dragon; a massive beast of wings and claws and slavering jaws consuming the wolf headed woman. Gooseflesh rose along Casselle's forearms.

"That's terrifying..." Temos confessed, now squatting with Casselle in front of the scroll on the floor.

"Look at the others," she said, pointing to other figures roughly the same size as the wolf-headed woman. There were several of them: a plump woman with a broad smile, a skull headed snake with wings, a raven headed man holding hands with another woman who was carrying a child. There was a three faced man holding a lightning bolt, next to a wild cat that appeared to be on fire, just ahead of a squat, hooded man. All around them were tiny figures, fat impish things of varied appearance: some with wings, some tails and a hundred other variations. All of these things were falling into the jaws of the dragon, being consumed by the darkness.

"Is that who I think it is?" Temos asked.

"You know of any other dragons?" Casselle replied with a question of her own, already knowing the answer. It was Maughrin, she was certain of it, the very same dragon that was beaten and imprisoned in the Dark forever by the last of the Old Gods. That's how the story went... but it was only a story wasn't it?

"Are these the Old Gods?" Temos asked. "Did she eat them before...?"

"I... don't know," Casselle replied, her mind trying to grasp the scope of this. Some part of her wanted to say no, because it felt wrong, but she was unsure what would make her leap to that conclusion. Her thoughts were interrupted by the movement of the metal artist. Temos stood up quickly, weapon at the ready again. The artist took steps in their direction, but stopped abruptly, blocked by the Templar.

"What's he doing?" Temos asked, confused. Casselle was trying to protect the unrolled portion of the scroll, which had more of her attention than her teammate. She looked up to see the artist attempting to get around him, but not in a forceful or aggressive way. Before she could say anything more, the young Templar pushed out with his hands.

She knew he was only trying to keep it away from her while she could put things back in order, but it flew back at his touch, as if it were made of paper rather than metal. It staggered backwards, flailing its arms and striking the oil lamp suspended above the table.

The next few moments were filled with fire and panic. The lamp shattered on contact with the metal limb, the force of it spraying oil behind it. But there wasn't just oil. The one tiny spark in the lamp turned the splash of fuel into an arc of bright flames that sprayed against the bookshelves and the scrolls stacked up inside of them.

"No!" Casselle yelled as the fire immediately caught hold. The metal thing with the rusted face crashed backwards against another shelf, its arm still alight with flaming oil. There was nothing that could be done. The ancient bookshelves may have resisted the flame by themselves, but the scrolls and the paints on the shelves spread the blaze with reckless abandon.

"Come on!" Temos yelled, tugging at Casselle to move. The heat in the room was building up at an astonishing rate. Casselle tried to take the scroll with her, but it was too heavy and awkward to lift easily.

"Leave it!" Temos yelled. She relented, knowing that they didn't have the time to save any of it. They fled the room, pursued by the roar of hungry flames.

***

"You did what you had to do," Odegar said. Casselle's head hung low. She wasn't exactly sure what she had destroyed, but her heart sank with the thought that it felt irreplaceable.

"The third room was empty, but we did confirm the stairs led to a lower passage," Temos added. "Looks like a hall that leads to the big flooded room. The doorway is partially blocked, but from the part that's busted open, there's a steady stream of water leading away and out. It's for sure what's feeding the lake."

"Is there enough room for us to navigate it?" Odegar asked.

"Us? Yes," Temos replied, his voice heavy. "No horses, though, or supplies past what we could carry - certainly no boats."

"Could we build them at the top of the stairs and take them down?" Jaksen asked. "In that room beyond the window?"

"You'd never get them down. The stairs are too narrow," Temos replied, "and there isn't any real space at the bottom, either."

"What else?" Odegar asked.

"We'll need some climbing gear to get down the side of the hill to the lake. It's pretty much a straight drop, and it'll be dangerous," Temos said. Casselle recalled the sight of it: slick rock near the edge of the opening, falling straight down into a jagged pile of boulders that marked the edge of the lake against the cliff. Dangerous was a generously polite description.

"And there was nothing else on the scroll?" Odegar asked. Both of them shook their heads no.

"But I think I can redraw most of what I saw," Temos said. "Maybe not perfect, but close enough. I'm not so bad at that sort of thing." Odegar looked somewhat surprised, almost pleasantly so.

"Yes, Templar Pelt, I would like that," said the Captain. Casselle was not as shocked. She'd seen some of Temos' work back at Strossen. He'd drawn animals and plants that had been common around his home and shared them with his friends. He'd also drawn his fair share of caricatures of other Templars, much to the squad's amusement.

Still, Casselle was distracted by the thought of all they had lost. The fire burned itself out, spectacularly quick and brutal, but thorough. The room was a toxic miasma of smoke and caustic fumes that stung at her face when she had opened the door.

There was nothing left worth salvaging. Even the metal artist was but a pile of steaming debris, as if whatever had been holding him together had burned up as well, leaving only a jumble of half-melted pieces behind. Most depressing was the loss of whatever information had been recorded on those scrolls. Who knows what they could have told her about the lady outside their gates... who she was... what she wanted... how she might be stopped or reasoned with... or...

She felt Odegar's hand on her shoulder, interrupting her worries.

"You've done good work," he said. Casselle heard the sincerity in his voice. She looked up at him and he nodded in affirmation. "We need to secure waterproof sacks and prepare what we'll need to travel."

"You expect we're going to get across the lake and outrun all those wolves?" Raabel asked.

"I do," Captain Taumber said.

"I'm as optimistic as the next fellow," Temos replied, "maybe even a measure more, but how do you expect we're going to do that?"

"I thought we'd start by throwing our guests a farewell party," Odegar replied calmly.

- 20 -

Monkey Business

Given their condition and their plight, the last thing Triistan Halliard would have expected was to be aroused, yet that is exactly how he found himself as the Crone touched the steel-blue line of the western horizon. His bones ached, his teeth ached, his lips were cracked and blistered, and where he didn't have active blisters, he had scabs and cracks from ones come and gone. But at that moment, all he could feel was the press of her body against his, the cool touch of her hands on his neck, and the warmth and hunger of her mouth on his.

He had been scanning the pages of his journal, his mind restlessly seeking some form of distraction while he waited for Snitch to reveal its secret larder, when a shadow fell across the pages and he looked up, startled. She was between him and the setting sun, an indistinct silhouette framed in red-gold fire, but he knew who it was the instant he lifted his gaze.

Dreysha.

She had foregone the hatch in the base of the crow's nest, instead climbing the jack ladder that ran from the lower port shrouds to the futtocks above him. He stared dumbly at her, feeling both annoyed and excited at the same time. And perhaps even just a little bit terrified.

"Aren't you going to invite me inside?" She didn't wait for an answer, but swung a leg over the edge of the basket and started to move into the nest beside him.

"Inside?" was all he could muster for an answer anyway.

She had removed the supple boots she had stolen from Longeye's corpse, revealing strong, brown calves and bare feet that were suddenly straddling his own. The crow's nest was only built for one person, and although two people could fit in it, they could not do so without making contact. At the moment she was half-sitting on the edge, with a hand on one of the shrouds to keep her balance and her knees to either side of his right leg. If she slid all the way in, it would be more than her bare feet straddling him.

She tilted her head and smiled, while he blinked and tried to breath. It was a good thing the basket came up above his sash or he would have fallen out.

"Mmm, cozy," she purred. "How's dinner coming?"

Their plight was taking its toll on her as well - dry, cracked lips, the lines of her cheekbones and jaw too sharp beneath her sunburned skin - but her eyes looked like liquid sapphire to him, and she was so close...

"D-dinner?" he stammered. "Oh, Snitch?" He looked away towards the titch monkey, grateful for the opportunity to break eye contact with her. "Did you see him?"

"Do you always ask so many questions?" Dreysha teased, and he realized he was behaving like a complete fool - next to her, he always seemed to feel like a child. What's more, she was deliberately making him feel that way, enjoying every second of it. He felt his ears growing hot, though the heat in his groin was worse.

"What do you want?" he managed.

At least it hadn't been a squeak. Her black hair was pulled back in a loose pony tail that hung below her shoulder blades. It was dull and hopelessly snarled, yet his fingers itched to run through it all the same.

She favored him with a sultry half-smile. "There's another one, and this'n more loaded than most, Triis. I want to take care of some... unfinished business." She glanced down and back and raised a suggestive eyebrow. "Well...?"

He glanced down as well, feeling somewhat panicked; could she see his...

"Aren't you going to move over and make room before I fall out?"

"Oh, sorry, yes - yes, of course." He edged sideways, allowing her to let go of the line and move completely into the crow's nest. She was then able to turn and lean her back against the basket, but she was still pressed against his side.

"That was a near thing down there, wasn't it?" she asked. "Why did you do it?"

"Do what?" he asked and immediately wanted to kick himself. But it was difficult to think clearly; the pressure of her thigh and hip against his own was distracting him. Was she leaning into him now?

"Spared Mung the indignity of shitting himself while we hauled his mud-footed ass into the tops, that's what. And ignoring Lanky in the process. You'd best be careful or someone might think you're trying to lead a mutiny."

He hissed and looked around in alarm. "Don't say that! Sherp is just looking for an excuse to flay me for what happened to his brother.

Besides, I... I don't know why I did it. I guess that I couldn't see the point of Mung being needlessly humiliated."

"Oh, you're welcome by the way. Maybe he'll have us both before the mast ere sunset tomorrow."

He knew she was referring to the fact that she had drawn her blade on Sherp to prevent him from skewering Triistan with a harpoon. He wanted to ask her why she had done it, but all he was able to mumble was, "Thank you for - for that. For saving my life."

She smirked. "A debt I'm glad to be owed. I'll have to think of some way for you to pay me back."

He was suddenly conscious of his journal, clutched in his left hand. He closed the protective flap and began winding the leather cord sewn to one corner around it. Dreysha placed her hand on his, and he looked up at her, eyes narrowing. She had already stolen it once - did she truly think he would just forget it and forgive her?

"I'm not here for that, Triis." Her expression confused him - there was an unguarded sincerity to it that he hadn't seen before. "Except to apologize, anyway. I should not have taken it. I thought it was just some silly book of sketches and notes from your experiences on Aarden and aboard the *Peregrine*. I didn't realize it was... that you had put so much of yourself in..."

"It's ok," he mumbled. *No it's not - it's not ok.* Why in the Deep Dark did he say that? He knew she was manipulating him. "I don't care."

"I mean, I do care - just not about that... the part about me, that I..." He sighed. This was hopeless. He certainly did care. The more he read it, the more he realized how personally revealing it really was. If she had realized that as well, in the limited time she had access to it, it must be even worse than he thought. But he couldn't tell her that, so he seized on the only other legitimate reason he could think of that he felt he could share with her: his oath.

His knees were trembling and he hoped that she couldn't feel them, though he wasn't sure how she could possibly miss it. Struggling for some kind of control over his rebellious body, he awkwardly disengaged his hand from hers and finished wrapping the book up. Staring hard at the journal, he was aware that she was watching him, that their bodies were still touching, and that she was dangerous. Something in that combination gave him courage.

"I'm under orders and I gave my word - took an oath. There are things in here - important things - that need to reach the High Chancellor and the rest of the Trade Ministers... the Kings' Council as well. They need to know - the world needs to know what we found. Not just the fact that Aarden exists, but..." He heard her laughing softly and looked up, frowning.

"I'm glad you find me so amusing." He tried moving away but there was nowhere to go; the crow's nest was affixed to one side of the mainmast and partially cut around it, so that the mast itself blocked his way. All he could do was turn slightly to try and minimize their contact, but that only brought him around to face her more directly.

She shook her head, green eyes glinting. "No, no not at all. It is just that, after all of my efforts to find out more about your precious diary -"

"Journal. It's a journal."

"Journal, then... after all of my previous efforts, you've told me more in the past ten breaths than throughout this entire bloody misadventure. That is what I find amusing." She stood nearly a foot shorter than him, so her head was tilted back, exposing her neck. He was momentarily distracted by its smooth, strong curve and tried to work up enough saliva to speak.

"Then... then what did you mean by 'unfinished business'..?" He lifted his gaze and trailed off, lost in her eyes.

She reached up and slid both hands around his neck, pulling herself against him, stretching up, lips parted. He felt her breasts push against his chest, where his own heart thundered as he bent to kiss her. Just before their lips met, she breathed "This..."

He dropped the journal and wrapped his arms around her, crushing her to him. She winced and he started to pull back, apologizing, but she wouldn't let him, holding onto him with surprising strength, kissing him harder. Her lips were rough, dry, but they yielded to him all the same. He tasted blood and thought he'd bitten his tongue, but there was no pain - no pain anywhere in fact. Just her; her tongue, her teeth, her hair in his hands, her body pushing against his... and the voice of his conscience warning him, telling him that she was playing him for a fool. But as he bent to kiss her neck and bury his face in her hair, all he heard was her moaning softly in his ear.

She slid her hand inside the front of his breeches as she pushed her body hard against him. He gasped and opened his eyes briefly - and met Rantham's unabashed leer from across the boat. The Rogue was standing at the starboard Watchman's Post with a clear, unimpeded view of them.

Startled, Triistan swore. He felt the blood leaving his manhood even before Dreysha released him.

"What is it? What's wrong?" They were both panting and he saw the hot flush in her cheeks - that at least couldn't be an act. He bent down to scoop up his journal from the floor of the crow's nest, waving his other hand in Rantham's direction.

"Seems we've an audience." His loins ached fiercely, but there was some kind of relief inside him as well. Dreysha wasn't ready to give up, though. She reached for him again.

"Then let's give him a show he won't soon forget - he can flog 'imself and we'll have given his morale a good fuck as well. The Dark knows he needs it."

His conscience said no, but his heart and body wanted her so fiercely now that he was almost able to forget Rantham and lose himself to her touch. He tried. He closed his eyes and concentrated on the feel of her hand stroking him. For a moment he began to respond in spite of everything, but as he moved his own hand down to return the caress he became aware of his journal again. Suddenly mindful of its weight and significance, the moment was lost.

With his free hand he brushed back her hair, touched his forehead to hers. "No. Not like this. I'm sorry, Drey," he whispered, feeling her body tense. She pulled back as much as she could in the confined space and looked up at him.

Once more she surprised him. He had expected some kind of mockery or frustration, even anger. But what he found instead looked like sadness as she turned away, though not before he noticed that the corner of her mouth was bleeding. When he reached out a hand to touch her, she blocked it and faced him again, her gaze defiant. The sadness was gone, hidden, and it seemed to him that her eyes had lost some of their luster.

"Your loss, Titch. I've got blisters on my ass anyway and the last thing they need is to be pounded against the side of the nest."

"Drey, I -"

She placed her hand on his lips. "Enough. Save your regrets for someone who cares to hear them. Maybe Snitch can lend a hand, though I'll wager it won't feel as good as mine." She reached for one of the shrouds and pulled herself up onto the edge of the crow's nest. He had to stop her from leaving, so he blurted out the next thing that came to his mind.

"Wait - did you see the monkey?"

She turned back with a sour look. "No - I was looking for the serpent, remember?"

He dropped his head, embarrassed, but couldn't suppress a grin in response. "No - I mean yes, I remember. But Snitch - have you seen him? His condition, I mean?"

She shook her head, then swung around some to look for the titch monkey. "Why, what are you getting on about?"

"Over there, out on the yardarm. Look at him." Triistan leaned in and pointed past her to where Snitch was still perched on the end of the spar, grooming itself. "Look closely."

The flat object it had been playing with before was nowhere to be seen. Not that Triistan noticed just then; the breeze had caught Dreysha's hair so that some of it was lightly brushing his face and neck. He closed his eyes for a moment, savoring it.

"I see a titch monkey licking his bullocks - is that why they call you 'Titch' by the way? Can you do that? Because then I might be able to understand why you wouldn't need a woman."

He couldn't help but laugh, and it was all he could do to keep from seizing her in his arms and pulling her back against him. He wasn't sure she would let him, so he kept talking to distract himself. "Look at his coat, his weight - does he look like a starving animal to you?"

Although the Crone had almost set completely, there was still sufficient light to see Snitch. Indeed, in the ruddy glow of dusk, his coat looked even healthier, richer somehow. There was also no doubt that the monkey had some meat on its bones. But Dreysha seemed nonplussed.

"I think Mung's been feeding it some of his rations," Triistan pointed out. If he was feeling overly clever, she soon put an end to it.

"Of course he is," she said. "Been giving it half his hardtack since we rescued both of them."

That caught him by surprise. "You knew? How?"

She elbowed him in the ribs. "What exactly do *you* do on watch, anyway? You do know why they call it that, right? You're supposed to be *watching* things? I noticed he never ate his rations with the rest of us, so I got curious. Damn thing comes down almost every night to pay him a visit. Gets its biscuit and then runs off somewhere aft."

"And you never told anyone?"

"Why should I? I figure he's been fattening the thing up for the rest of us. Well, keeping it alive and edible, anyway."

"But we need the f- " he had started to say 'food', but realized the significance of what Dreysha had just said. "Keeping it alive and edible." *Fresh meat.* As if she had read his thoughts, Dreysha nodded.

"Aye, now you're using that over-ripe melon of yours, Titch. How long do you think that skinny ratter would last us - all of us?" He caught her additional emphasis on the word 'all', but answered as if he hadn't noticed it.

"I don't know, a few days, a week maybe."

"With eight of us, at best a few days. I'd give it four, but then I'm no purser. Let's just say a week for argument's sake, but it doesn't matter, because we're nowhere near anywhere and a week isn't going to do it. Anything short of a month's worth of meat might as well be none at all."

She paused and glanced down towards the deck. She was still balanced on the edge of the crow's nest, with one hand on the shrouds. After sweeping her gaze along the length of the ship, she turned back to face him, lowering her voice even though they were well out of earshot of anyone.

"But I don't expect there to be eight of us for much longer." She fixed him with a penetrating stare, waiting to see what his reaction would be. He could not disguise his dislike for the idea.

"What are you suggesting, Drey? That we murder someone, or were you serious about a... a mutiny?" He dropped his voice to a whisper on the last word. She gave him an odd look, but then shook her head.

"I wouldn't dare suggest anything of the kind, Titch. But you saw what happened earlier, and that stew's been bubbling for a long time now - it's likely to boil over soon. Ranth is convinced he's on the menu soon as the rations run out. I'm not sure when the last time he closed his eyes was, but he can't go on that way for much longer afore his hull splits. And if Mung keeps feeding half his rations to the monkey, he won't be around much longer, either.

"*And* let us not forget the good Captain and his Second Mate. If they don't kill us all by their sheer ineptitude, they're certain to provoke another incident like we had today." She smiled crookedly and arched one dark eyebrow. "Don't expect me to be such a lady the next time. Hear me, Triis: the decks will be bloodied."

"Scow won't stand by while -"

"Are you sure about that?"

That took Triistan by surprise. "What do you mean - did he say something to you?"

"It isn't what he said, so much as what he didn't say that caught my attention."

Triistan thought he knew what she was inferring; he'd been speculating about it only a little while ago.

"Because he didn't reprimand you for drawing on Sherp." That was completely out of character for the First Mate, for whom discipline and Seeker Protocol were a religion. *Gods will, Captain's will.* The Scow he knew was equally demanding of everyone, even Triistan. Dreysha's actions should have been punished, and normally it would have been

Scow meting out that punishment. There was also the conversation Triistan had with the Mattock earlier. It was hard to imagine he would contemplate a mutiny, but the signs were certainly there if you looked closely enough.

He also thought it strange that Voth had not pursued the matter. Maybe he was waiting for things to cool down. Or perhaps he recognized that he and Sherp were outnumbered and feared to challenge them openly. Triistan would have preferred it if he had; Voth and Sherp were not the type of men to let something like that go. If they thought they were outnumbered, they would be working discreetly to better their odds.

Dreysha was nodding in response. "Exactly. You're not so dumb after all, though many a man who's fancied these might argue differently." She gave her left breast a squeeze and he groaned inwardly, cursing himself. Then he cursed Rantham and would have started down a long list of other targets worthy of damnation if she hadn't swung a leg over the side and started to pull herself onto the ladder. He caught her by the wrist.

"Wait. Stay... please."

She studied him, the hint of a smile returning to one corner of her lips. The dark smudge of blood was there as well; her blood, which he had tasted only moments ago. He held her stare, heart racing, somehow managing not to melt or duck his head. The Crone disappeared beyond the sea, and the western sky turned a soft blend of orange and pink in her wake. Overhead, he knew stars would be visible in the pale blue, but he could not look away to see them.

"And do what? You've made it clear that you do not want me," she paused and looked down meaningfully, "well, *most* of you doesn't want me. I'm no tavern wench for you to summon whenever your jack needs filling..."

"But we still haven't solved the monkey problem."

"The monkey problem?"

"Aye, the monkey problem. You said that Mung has been feeding it his hardtack. Have you ever seen him give it anything else?"

She shook her head. "No. Just the biscuit." She tilted her head. "Why?"

The smile came easily to his lips. "Stay with me and I'll show you."

When she gave him a calculating look rather than a sharp retort, he knew he had her.

"You do have some skill at this game, Titch," was all she said, and climbed back into the basket.

They talked for a time, periodically checking to make sure Snitch hadn't left his perch yet. Dreysha told him that it typically visited Mung after moonset, so they probably still had some time to kill. When she pressed him to tell her what he planned to show her, he had to confess that he didn't quite know himself yet, adding quickly that there was no way the animal could be as fit and healthy as it was if it was only eating half of a ship's biscuit every night, so while he had no idea how or where, he was certain it was getting food from somewhere else. That seemed to be enough to keep her there, though: he had piqued her curiosity, which he was learning was as difficult to resist for her as she was for him.

Overhead the stars blazed to life, here and there hiding behind drifting clouds - pink and indigo sails catching the day's last light. They gave the sky a certain depth that made the stars seem impossibly far away, and the clouds close enough to catch. He fancied himself plucking one from where it hung and offering it to Dreysha, but the notion made him feel suddenly embarrassed. *Fool*, he told himself. She would laugh in his face if she knew what he was thinking. Maybe - that kiss had certainly felt real enough, and once again he was all too aware of the press of her body against his.

He had to create some space between them, so he hoisted himself up onto the rim of the crow's nest, leaning his back against the mainmast and hooking an arm through one of the shrouds. He typically sat his watch like this anyway, as it allowed him to stretch his long legs out before him. Since at this height any roll of the ship was greatly exaggerated, he had to keep one leg in the nest for stability if there was any kind of weather. Right now, the breeze was still weak, the sea calm and flat, but he left his right leg inside all the same. He didn't want to create *too* much space.

Dreysha took advantage of the additional room and hunkered down in the bottom of the nest, arms wrapped around her knees. He was glad when she leaned her head back against his thigh and had to resist the temptation to touch her hair. Instead, he reached back and fished his journal from its customary place, tucked into the back of his sash. Seated as he was, it was digging into his lower back, so he held it on his lap instead. Dreysha's eyes were closed, but somehow she sensed what he had done.

"You shouldn't play with that thing so much," she grinned.

He grunted noncommittally. He should have kept it out of sight and dealt with the discomfort, but a part of him was enjoying their little game. He knew she wanted to read it, though he was wrong about why.

"Hmm," she mimicked, but when he didn't respond, she tried a different tack. "What do you think they will do with it, these Sea Kings of yours?"

Triistan shrugged. "I don't know. My orders are actually to deliver it directly to the High Chancellor, but without the Captain, I'm not sure how I will even gain an audience with him." By 'Captain' he meant Captain Vaelysia, of course - the Dark only knew what would happen if he had to rely on Lankham Voth to sponsor him. But as for being seen by the Chancellor, he wasn't being completely honest with Dreysha: Captain Vaelysia had also given him a sealed letter that she said would guarantee him an audience. She'd warned him to keep it a secret as well lest it fall into the wrong hands and be misused, so he had tucked it into a hidden flap on the inside of the journal's waterproof cover.

"I wonder why," she said.

"Why what? Why I wouldn't be able to gain an audience with High Chancellor Tiigan?"

He felt her head shake from side to side against his leg. "No. Why the Cap told you to deliver it directly to Tiigan, instead of using a fleetfoot. That way you wouldn't need a sponsor." Fleetfoots were what the regular sailors called the members of Fleet Courier Service, a network of carefully-screened runners who were responsible for transferring important documents between the vessels of the Seeker fleet and the Ministry's offices. Ships' manifests, captain's logs, even sealed orders were all entrusted to the Service, so on the surface it made sense to seal the journal in a courier pouch and send it on its way. But Captain Vaelysia had ordered him specifically to deliver it personally, using her letter to authenticate her sponsorship.

"She didn't say," he answered as casually as he could. "But given the magnitude and... sensitivity of our discovery, I think she was worried about word getting out to our rivals before our claim could be legalized and bound by treaty."

He left out the fact that she and First Mate Tarq were certain that the Corps had been infiltrated by foreign spies. He had overheard them arguing about it once during the Aarden Expedition, though they had never directly addressed the issue with the rest of the crew. It had first caught his attention because disagreements between the Captain and the Ship's Whip were rare; there was a great deal of mutual respect and admiration between them and although they debated often, it was usually a friendly competition: almost always cordial, sometimes spirited, but never openly antagonistic. On the topic of who could be trusted, however, both argued bitterly for their cause; the Captain for following the Ministry's orders, which were apparently to only inform the crew if and when it was absolutely necessary; and Mister Tarq, for sharing the information that they had with those being asked to put their life on the line without fully understanding why.

Dreysha had said something but he'd missed it.

"I'm sorry, what was that?"

"I said, how are you going to gain an audience? Especially if Lanky files his report and has us all in the brig for sedition?"

He shook his head, wondering if she had found the letter when she took his journal and was just playing games with him again. "I'm worried about the same thing. I guess I can go before the Kings' Council first, and trust that they will work it out with the Ministry. It isn't what the Captain wanted, but it may be my only alternative." And given the nature of the information, it might be the better alternative, anyway.

She snorted. "You'll need all of the Rogue's bloody luck for that. This is a Seeker ship, a Seeker mission. It falls completely within the Ministry's jurisdiction and they'll have splinters in their fat, self-important asses if they think the Council is interfering with Trade."

Not exactly, thought Triistan.

The Sea King Isles was a confederacy of seven large islands in an archipelago originally known as Shanthaal - The Columns of Sea and Storm. One of the famed Dauthirian Columns, it had been raised from the sea floor by Shan the Stormfather thousands of years ago. As with many of the wonders built by the Young Gods, people came to live in its shadow, and Shan encouraged them to form their own Elder Circles, bodies that helped settle matters without the need for his direct intervention. Over time, the Elder Circles governed all matter of affairs, and so it remained, until the Godswar.

Thankfully, the island citadel was well removed from the site of Ehronfall and thus it and its people were spared the devastation many of those living on the mainland had experienced. Whole cities were laid waste, and in some regions entire generations who had fought or otherwise worked in support of the war were lost. The citizens of Shanthaal had sacrificed a good share of their ships and warriors as well, but the citadel and the majority of its people endured.

Left to find their own way in the wake of Shan's passing, the seven islands chose to eventually consolidate their power by creating a collective governing body, formed from representatives from each of the islands' separate Elder Circles. Recalling the legends that Shan promised the islanders that they would be hailed as "kings of the sea", the Council members adopted the moniker, declaring themselves formally as the Council of the Seven Kings' Isles, or more simply, the Kings' Council. "Seven Kings, One Kingdom", as the saying went.

The Sea Kings, as they soon became known by the rest of the world, had not only been spared annihilation, but their most valuable resources - shipbuilding, fishing, and, most importantly, trade - were now the driving forces for rebuilding the world in the aftermath of the Godswar. The Kings' Council created the Trade Commission to lead the reconstruction efforts, and with missionary zeal, they spread the religion of commerce all along the coasts of Niyah. Over time, the Commission's power grew, until it rivaled the Council's, prompting a power struggle and botched assassination attempt on two Council members.

A bloody inquisition followed, as the Council and its supporters sought to root out those behind the assassination attempt, and a series of reprisal killings of lower officials on both sides led the Isles to the brink of civil war. But the Trade Commission had done an excellent job of making Coin the real King amongst the islanders, so when an independent group of cunning merchants circulated their estimates of the cost of a civil war, cooler heads prevailed. A last-minute peace was brokered and a new, two-headed government was born. At one head, the Kings' Council would continue to rule over the daily lives of its citizens, as well as be responsible for overseeing the confederacy's political and military concerns. At the other, the newly-minted and empowered Ministry of Commerce would oversee exploration, trade, and the rising kingdom's burgeoning economy. As a result, the Seeker Corps was birthed, providing the Ministry with a substantial naval force to fulfill its duties, as well as offset the marine and citadel watch forces commanded by the Kings' Council. All in all, it was an elegant solution, inspired by the balancing scales used by those very same merchants, assuring that power would be shared in equal measure.

Therefore, although Dreysha's statement that this was a Seeker mission and thus fell within the purview of the Ministry was technically correct, the nature of their discovery and all that it entailed had dramatically changed the game. He knew Captain Vaelysia didn't see it that way; she was a Corps Captain, through and through, which was why she had directed him to return his journal to the High Chancellor. But there was little question that it would have a monumental impact on far more than just commerce, and Triistan knew that the Kings' Council should be consulted immediately. Something this significant required the attention of both governing bodies: not just for the safety and welfare of all the Isles, but the rest of Niyah needed to be warned as well. The thought was overwhelming.

One thing at a time, Triis, he told himself. *You can only do so much.*

The problem was, that isn't what he'd sworn to do, and what's more, he'd be disobeying a direct order. This was dangerous ground for him, not just in terms of sharing too much information with Dreysha, but also within his own mind. He felt the weight of his own words as if they were physical chains, so he tried setting the conversation on a different tack.

"Do you think we'll even make it that far? Make it home, I mean?"

"Depends on what you call home," she said, so softly he wasn't sure he heard her correctly.

"What was that?"

"I said I really don't know, Triis. I've seen worse odds, but I've seen better ones, too. With Lanky at the helm..." she shook her head slowly.

They lapsed into silence. He thought about Scow. If they could overpower Voth and Sherp - preferably without killing them - the Mattock would become captain and their chances of survival would go up considerably. But even after their discussion that morning, he just could not envision Mordan Scow starting a mutiny. It was going to take some kind of spark to push him over that final edge, and with circumstances as they were, they might as well be packed to the beams with pitch: one spark and the whole launch was likely to go up. Unless...

He looked at the worn cover of the journal in his lap. *Unless the spark was something only Scow could see.*

Voth was dangerous; Sherp even more so. It was wrong to entrust the fate of so many to them simply because Protocol demanded it. Triistan's duty - and Scow's - went beyond their oaths, beyond the Corps. He had to show the journal to Scow, or at least tell him what was in it, so that he would understand that it was more than just their lives and their loyalty in the balance, and that they needed to do everything in their power to see that the journal and its terrible secrets made it back.

And what about Dreysha? What stake did she have in all of this? He was loath to admit it, but he had to consider the fact that she might be one of the spies that Captain Vaelysia and Tarq had been so concerned about. Her interest in him felt genuine - he desperately wanted it to be genuine - but he could not ignore the possibility that her relentless curiosity about his journal had more to do with Aarden's secrets than his own. He had deliberately avoided discussing Captain Vaelysia's letter for that very reason.

So what if she was? It's not like she could steal the information, then swim home and warn anyone. Nations and politics be damned, *this* was their kingdom now. This launch and the ocean around them, and as long as their mutual goal was survival, what happened after would be someone else's problem, wouldn't it?

It is going to be everyone's problem soon enough anyway, a voice in the back of his mind whispered.

Voth and Sherp might as well be foreign agents; they were the ones posing a threat and making it difficult to fulfill his mission, not Dreysha. She had already made it clear that she was on his side, even going so far as to imply they should kill Voth and Sherp. And, she had a point as far as food and water were concerned. Scow's leadership would not change the equation that two fewer mouths to feed meant an increase in their supplies of one quarter.

But murder wasn't mathematics; he could not bring himself to reduce human lives to simple arithmetic. He thought Scow would agree, but Drey would take some convincing.

He looked down at her. Her head was leaning slightly to the side, as if she were dozing. He couldn't see her eyes from this angle, but the slow rise and fall of her shoulders and chest made him wonder if she had fallen asleep.

"I don't want to kill them," he whispered to the night.

"They're not likely to give you a choice, Triis," Dreysha answered and rolled her head back to look at him. From where he sat above her, the taenia did not cover much, making it difficult to maintain eye contact with her. "What do you plan to do, ask them nicely?"

"No. But aren't there enough of us to just... I don't know... surround them? Surely they wouldn't fight back if they had to face all of us."

"All of us being you and I, the Mattock - who might just as easily side with the captain for duty's sake; Rantham, who is convinced we're all going to eat him; Biiko - the dead gods only know what Blackblades will do; and our beloved monkey-master, Mung? Lanky will likely shit his breeches on the spot, but Sherp will never strike his sails. He'll come straight at us - straight at *you*, Triis."

She was right. Sherp blamed Triis for his brother Pelor's death, even though everyone else seemed to recognize the incident for what it had been, a tragic accident. Triistan thought the oarsman probably blamed Braeghan more, but the young cabin boy was dead and gone, so Sherp had chosen the next best target for his anger.

He was tempted to say that Biiko would protect him, but he hated the thought as soon as it formed. Had he not resolved during the

Expedition to stop sitting back while other people risked themselves for him?

"The weapon does not wield itself," he muttered, echoing Biiko's own words.

"You know it's not very polite to keep talking to yourself when I'm sitting right here," Drey said.

"Sorry. What about capturing them at night, when they're sleeping?" he offered weakly.

Dreysha turned more so that she could look directly at him. "Aye, we might be able to pull that off, though you know how poorly we've all been sleeping, and catching them both in a good nod won't be easy. So you're planning to feed them, then? Waste our rations on them, so that if we manage to make it back, they can sing a pretty song about mutiny? You do know that they're scrubbing for that now?"

He knew.

He looked out over the ocean, now darkened to a blue-black, nearly the same color as the night sky, except where the partial moon reflected off of it. He shook his head. "We can't do it, Drey. We can't murder them because it's convenient or we're no better than they are."

"Maybe you can't, but I can, and in my world, the living are always better than the dead." The hard cold steel in her voice unnerved him, reminding him again how little he knew about her, and how dangerous that could be.

They fell back into silence, each retreating to their own thoughts while they waited. The pale dagger of a moon arced across the night sky, accompanied by a host of stars, while occasional clouds drifted by. The irregular breeze had grown a bit steadier, and he thought the dawn would see them moving again. He did not know if it would last, but he liked the way it was strengthening slowly, and told himself they would be sighting land or sail within the week, and all of this talk of murder and mutiny would be for naught.

He dozed lightly, peeking through half-closed lids every now and again to see if Snitch moved, while his mind replayed their kiss. He must have drifted off more deeply, though, because he was kissing her again and it felt so real, but when he tasted blood and tried to pull away, Dreysha wouldn't let him go. This time it was his blood and she was sucking at it eagerly. It was exquisite and excruciating at the same time. He began to moan, but out of pain or pleasure he could not say... and then he woke with a start.

"Triis!" It was Dreysha. "Wake up, the monkey's gone." She was standing beside him, pushing at his shoulder. He reached a hand up to his lips but there was no blood, no injury.

"Only a dream," he mumbled aloud.

"Judging from that harpoon in your breeches it must have been about me. I'm afraid you'll have to settle for Mung and his monkey, though. Snitch is gone."

That brought him awake completely; if they didn't catch it in the act, there would be no way of knowing how it was getting extra food.

They slipped over the side of the crow's nest and climbed quietly down the port-side shroud, keeping the mainmast between them and Rantham, who was still in the starboard watchman's post, though he was slumped over and turned away from them. The moon had nearly set, but the skies had cleared completely and the stars were so bright the masts and rigging cast shadows on the deck. Everything had an enchanted, pale glow to it that reminded him suddenly of the Glowater River. He shivered involuntarily.

Dreysha led him aft. He was surprised by the quiet fluidity with which she moved; a wraith drifting across the deck from shadow to shadow. The rest had done him good, as he was able to keep up, though to his ears he was making a great deal more noise. Apparently not enough to wake anyone, though: they weren't challenged, and when they found Mung he nearly jumped out of his skin as they appeared beside him. Dreysha had anticipated his reaction and was there to clamp a hand over his mouth before he could scream. Unfortunately that meant she was close enough for the warm puddle of urine to reach her bare feet, and when she opened her mouth to curse, Triistan clamped his hand over hers. She glared at him furiously while sidestepping the puddle and wiping her foot on Mung's pants.

Mung was whimpering and Triistan was worried Dreysha might snap his neck, so he removed his hand and silently appealed to both of them for calm. She grudgingly agreed and eased her grip some on Mung, but did not release him for another few moments while he continued making plaintive noises. She finally drew her blade with her free hand, held it in front of his nose and said in a barely audible whisper: "Silence." His eyes went white and wide, but at least the echoman finally stopped mewling and grew still.

Dreysha made a soft, disgusted noise and released him, stepping around the puddle to stand beside Triistan, but keeping her knife directly in front of Mung's face. Triistan felt sorry for him; he was shaking so badly he imagined he could hear the man's teeth rattling in his head. He smiled to show him they meant no harm.

"Softly now, Wil - we're not going to hurt you. We only wanted to talk to you... about Snitch." From the look on Mung's face, he would have pissed himself again had they not all been dehydrated. He looked around quickly - Triistan assumed for the monkey, who was nowhere to be seen - and then would have fallen to his knees had Triistan not caught him up under the arms.

"P-please don't tell anyone, Triis. Please, especially not C-Captain Voth or Mister Sherp. I only gave it my own rations and didn't think it would harm anyone and was taking care of it ever since we found him and Captain Fjord and built our raft I was so happy when it wasn't eaten by the ridgeback he is so smart so much smarter than Snatch ever was-"

Dreysha clamped her hand over his mouth again, and Triistan set him on his own two feet. He was surprisingly light, and he could feel Mung's ribs beneath his tunic.

"Slow down, Wil. Where is he now? And how much are you feeding him?" Mung nodded, wide eyes sliding from Triistan's to Dreysha's and back again. She removed her hand and he took a deep, shaky breath.

"Okay, I'm sorry. I don't know where he goes; he always d-disappears after I feed him my biscuit. Well, half a biscuit usually. He takes it and runs off somewhere. I always thought it was because he was worried I might take it back or maybe he's just shy about eating you should see how fastidious he is he always bathes right after-" he stopped abruptly when Dreysha made as if to muzzle him again, then squeaked, "Sorry," and went quiet. His eyes were still big and white, and they darted back and forth between Triistan and Dreysha.

Dreysha started to say something, but Triistan held his hand up. "Did you hear that?"

"No," she hissed in annoyance. "I couldn't hear my own thoughts over his chattering teeth and a tongue that somehow runs more than his piss."

"I thought I heard something - a splash, maybe."

Dreysha rolled her eyes and pointed at the puddle at Mung's feet, but that wasn't what Triistan had heard. The noise had come from the stern. He always bathes right after, Mung had said.

After what? On a sudden hunch, he sidestepped Mung's liquefied fear and made his way to the rear of the ship as quietly as he could. The breeze was stronger, but when he glanced over the rail, the sea was as still and flat as black ice. Overhead the sails rippled and sighed softly, but did not fill.

As he approached the stern, he heard the sound again - plunk, splash. He was very close to it, and could now hear water dripping as well. There was something long and sinuous curled around the tiller, one end of it weaving slowly from side to side: Snitch's tail.

He slid quietly to port as he drew closer, until he could see over the rail, where he found the titch monkey hanging nearly upside down next to the rudder, using his tail as an anchor and freeing both hands for something the rest of the survivors had been unable to master and all but given up on: fishing.

The monkey's left foot was resting on the side of the rudder and its right was on the back of the boat. Directly below it, tiny burps and splashes disturbed the surface of the water, which Snitch was watching intently. Something glinted in the monkey's left hand just before it struck, and Triistan heard the noise that had first captured his attention as its hand and the object hit the water. The speed of the monkey's strike was surprising, quicker than Triistan's eyes could track in fact, and quicker than its quarry could avoid. When Snitch drew its hand from the water, a slick, silvery prize writhed on the end of the elongated object Triistan had seen in the monkey's hand earlier that day. He was close enough now to see that it was a harpoon blade, and all he could think to do was smile and shake his head.

He felt Dreysha move up beside him and heard her sharp intake of breath. "By Theckan's lucky stones... is he doing what I think he's doing?"

Triistan's grin widened. "Well he's not licking his bullocks."

He grunted in pain and surprise when she drove her elbow into his ribs. Snitch squealed, snatched the fish from his harpoon, scampered along the taffrail and then up a backstay, and disappeared into the tops. Rubbing his side and trying not to chuckle lest he be hit again, Triistan leaned out over the stern to look at the water. It was calm at the moment, but there were still a few pieces of biscuit crumbs left. Even as he watched, one disappeared with a soft swish and plop, just as Mung appeared beside him.

"You - you didn't hurt him, did you?"

"Did we hurt him?" Dreysha hissed through clenched teeth. "We're supposed to catch him and eat him, remember? Nice of you to fatten'em up for us!"

Mung winced and Triistan hastened to intervene. "No, Wil, we didn't hurt him, but... did you have any idea what he was doing with your hardtack?"

Mung shook his head. "No, none. Why? Was it something bad? Did he break something?"

Triistan grinned. "No, actually he-"

Now it was Dreysha's turn. She slipped in between them and placed her hand over Triistan's mouth. "We need to talk." She looked pointedly over her shoulder at Mung. "Alone."

The echoman gulped. "Ok I - I'll just go check on Snitch. Sometimes he doesn't finish it and gives it back. It can be a little soggy for some reason but given how stale they are I don't mind..." Dreysha was staring at him through narrowed eyes. She still had a hand clamped over Triistan's mouth.

"Sorry," Mung squeaked before turning and tripping over a stay, then collecting himself as best he could and heading off in the direction the monkey had scampered a few moments before. Dreysha sighed and shook her head in disgust. She turned back to face Triistan, who was still standing there waiting for her to explain herself.

"We need to think carefully about what we saw, and what we're going to do about it," she began. He was taken aback. His overactive mind had already thought of three or four ways they could take advantage of Snitch's unexpected fishing prowess.

"I don't understand. This is fantastic - we knew they were good ratters, but *fishing*... we can teach him to fish for us, or rig a net of some kind and bait them as well..."

She was nodding as he spoke, but the look in her eyes told him she didn't necessarily agree, at least not with everything he had said.

"Yes, but until we know just how well that will work and how much fish we can catch, we need to keep it our little secret."

Triistan shook his head, confused. "No, why would we do that? This could save us - *all* of us, Drey. You said yourself the monkey wouldn't go very far feeding all eight of us, but now we can actually use him to produce food." His voice was rising in excitement as he talked, so she hissed at him to keep quiet, looking around in alarm to see if anyone had heard. Except for the soft noises of the night and the low creak of the rigging, the launch remained quiet.

"The Dark be damned, I thought you were the smart one, Triis. Do I have to write it all down for you?"

"No," he bristled. "I doubt you would even know which end of the stylus to use anyway!"

She actually grinned. "The pointy end, Triis. It's always the pointy end."

He wasn't amused. "We have to bring this to the captain's attention and figure out a way to take advantage of it for everyone's benefit-"

"The captain? What captain?" she hissed. "Lanky? Do you have anything behind those pretty blue eyes of yours? If you say a word of this to Voth the only thing you can be sure of is that he will find a way to fuck us with it!"

"Well we can't just keep it to ourselves. I cannot let the others slowly starve while we have the means to prevent it." Could she really be that cold-hearted?

"That's very noble of you, Titch. So much for your oath I guess. It seems very convenient for you."

"What is that supposed to mean?"

"It means," she shot back in an angry whisper, "that at every turn you seem to be making decisions that compromise that oath. You need to start thinking about survival, Triis. About doing whatever gives you and that damned journal the best chance at making it home!" She paused and took a deep breath, trying to calm herself, then reached out and touched his forearm. Even now, while part of him recoiled from her ruthlessness, the contact felt like bees buzzing beneath his skin.

"Look. I'm not saying we should let'em all starve. I'm only saying we should think about this before we run off and give it over to Voth. He and Sherp already hold too much power for my taste."

Triistan didn't like it, but she had struck close to home with her comment about his oath. He had to at least consider his options. "What about Wil? He already knows."

Dreysha shook her head. "No, I don't think he does. He's so wrapped up in his own fear he can't see what's on the deck in front of him 'till he's pissing on it. He still thinks the bloody monkey is only eating the 'tack, then washing up after. He's not likely to say a word to anybody as long as he still thinks we're looking to eat it."

The whole conversation gave him a sour feeling in his stomach and he took a half-step back, withdrawing his arm from her fingertips in the process. He needed to think it through on his own.

"I'm going aloft, back to my post. I'll think about it." He was glad he couldn't read her expression; he was afraid of what he might find there.

He passed Mung on the way back to the shrouds. The echoman looked up at him questioningly, but Triistan merely put a friendly hand on his shoulder and slipped past, then clambered up the ratline, thinking hard the whole time. By the time he reached the relative safety of the crow's nest, he knew what he needed to do. He supposed he had always known.

The night passed slowly. He dozed off and on, but the comfort of true sleep eluded him while he thought about what he would say and when he might have the opportunity. He thought several times about seeking Scow out now, but he knew Dreysha was waiting somewhere below and he did not think his resolve would hold if he had to speak with her again beforehand. She was right about one thing: Voth was a catastrophe waiting to happen and they - *he* - needed to stop entrusting his fate to the jumped-up purser. He had known from the first few hours that Scow was best suited for command, and judging from comments the Mattock had made the other day, Scow knew it as well. It was time to trust his old mentor with all of his secrets, not just Snitch's potential but the journal and his mission as well. It meant breaking his oath, and he felt queasy and nervous inside thinking about it, anxious that some calamity would occur because he broke faith. Logic told him that there were far greater calamities coming if he did not take steps to ensure his survival, but there were certain situations for him where logic struggled with compulsion. If asked, he could not have explained what might happen if he broke a promise or why; he only knew that it made him terribly afraid to do so.

In fact, he was pretty certain he had never broken a promise before - ever. It had definitely made moments in his life more difficult, but he knew those situations would have been worse if he had not kept his word. He also knew that in this case, his oath to the Captain had kept him alive. In those final, desperate days, when what was left of the Aarden Expedition were fleeing for their lives, scattered and hunted like beasts, it was that oath that gave him the strength for one more step, one more breath. It had been in the steel of his borrowed sword when they were finally brought to bay, and it had given him the resolve to go on when so many of the others had fallen. It had been a lifeline that he'd clung to, climbing hand over bloody hand from the darkness of Aarden's interior to safety.

And now he meant to sever it.

Sometime in the quiet hours before dawn, he heard a soft noise and looked up to find Snitch perched on the opposite edge of the crow's nest. It was grooming itself nonchalantly, the fur on its arms and chest gleaming wetly in the starlight. The harpoon tip was nowhere to be seen, and Triistan assumed it must have some hiding place for it.

He watched the titch monkey for awhile, studying its lines and textures with an artist's eye, noting the movement of muscles beneath its fur, and the methodical way it proceeded from hand to wrist, from wrist to elbow and from there to its shoulder before starting on the other arm. From time to time it would glance up at him with wide, chestnut-colored eyes. He was intrigued by its sudden trust in him, as if he were no longer a threat now that he had discovered its and Mung's little secret. Or perhaps it was only taunting him; when he moved to relieve a cramped muscle in his calf, it hissed at him like a startled cat and fled to the safety of its perch out on the yardarm.

He stood and stretched, yawning. The ocean around them was a vast black shadow, the sky above a deep, twinkling blue; but for the stars, it was impossible to discern where the sea ended and the sky began, as if they were suspended in an empty void of darkness. He wondered if this were a premonition, a vision of what it might look like if Aarden's evils were unleashed upon the rest of the unsuspecting world.

Triistan pushed the thought aside and looked to the east, waiting for the dawn. When the line of the horizon slowly appeared beneath the pale glow of its approach, he checked that his journal was still tucked into its place beneath his topman's sash and opened up the hatch in the bottom of the crow's nest.

It was time to find First Mate Scow. It was time to light the spark.

- 21 -

Boiling Point

Triistan found Scow at the watchman's post as the Maiden sent tentative fingers over the horizon, reaching out for a new day. The post was a narrow gangplank with a crude but sturdy railing protruding about four feet from amidships. There were actually two; one on the starboard side and a matching one to port. Scow had just replaced Rantham, who had withdrawn so far into himself that he shuffled past Triistan without so much as a glance. Triistan had been bracing himself for some kind of stinging remark about his time with Dreysha, but he found the man's silence even more disconcerting.

"Captain" Voth and Sherp were still abed where they had set up their hammocks near the fore of the launch. Triistan knew they would be up soon, so he would have to work quickly to convince Scow. If he was quick enough, perhaps they would be able to avoid any bloodshed and take the two in their sleep.

He cleared his throat and spoke quietly. "Good morning, sir."

Scow turned from where he had been scanning the sea and Triistan felt his heart sink. The former Master Carpenter had always been a powerful man, broad-shouldered and deep-chested, with a bull's neck and tree trunks for legs. If a ship were to be somehow transformed into a living man, that man would be Mordan Scow.

...or would have been. The man that turned to face him now was a derelict. His arms hung loose and heavy from sloped shoulders and he moved gingerly, wincing and grunting quietly with every breath, like an old man. Beneath the cracked, blistered skin of his face, there was a definite yellowish hue, which was also obvious in the whites of his eyes. When he saw Triistan, he smiled, which only made the boy feel worse. Scow normally had a large gap between his two front teeth, but it was now accompanied by three more from others that had fallen out. Despite all of this, though, the Mattock's voice still rumbled with the deep power of the sea.

"A fair mornin' to you too, Triis. About as fair as we've seen in some time I think. The wind's woke up and I'd bet my last biscuit that before the day is done, she'll blow like a doxy on our first night of shore leave."

Triistan glanced around quickly again to confirm that they were alone.

"We... that is I - I mean - ". He paused and took a deep breath, while Scow chewed on the side of his lip and stared at him as if he were trying to steal that last biscuit.

"We discovered something yesterday - well, last night actually. Dreysha and I. And Mung. Well not so much Mung, he was there and he already sort of knew that Snitch was eating something, but -"

The Mattock was shaking his head. "What in the Deep Dark are you trying to tell me, lad? Take a breath and spit the whole wad out instead of dribblin' bits and pieces at me."

Reflexively, Triistan came to attention. "Aye, sir. Sorry sir." He tried to gulp down his nervousness, only partially succeeding. "Snitch is catching and eating fish, sir. He's using Wil's hardtack as bait, and then snatching them out of the water. I'm not sure how many, but I saw him catch one off the bow and I think we can either train him to fish for us or set up a net of some kind to catch them."

Scow whistled and rubbed the side of his jaw. Triistan could hear the rasp of the Mattock's calloused fingers over thick stubble. *Now comes the hard part.* He looked around once more and then squared his shoulders.

"I don't think we should say anything to Captain Voth, sir." The rasping sound stopped, and Scow's sharp blue eyes locked on his.

"Why is that, Topman?"

Triistan reached back and drew his journal out. He had expected to have a difficult time turning it over, but now that he had begun, he was intensely relieved to finally have someone he could share his burden with. Oath or not, he knew beyond any doubt that he was doing the right thing, remembering their talk from the previous day. Honor without sacrifice is nothing more than self-righteousness - they were Scow's own words.

"Because of this, sir." As he handed it to the First Mate, Scow's bushy eyebrows shot up in recognition and surprise. He accepted the battered book gingerly, barely holding onto it, leaving his hands out before him, palms up, as if Triistan had just filled them with water. Triistan looked around again, suddenly fearful that Dreysha would see them, but the deck was still clear. Even Biiko was conspicuously absent from his line of sight. He lightly placed the fingertips of both hands on the edge of the journal and pushed it towards Scow.

"Please, sir," he whispered. "I would prefer that no one saw you reading this. And you must swear that you will not show it to anyone else. I am already disobeying a direct order from Captain Vaelysia by giving it to you, though I think now she would call me a fool for not having done so sooner."

Scow gave him an appraising look, and for a moment Triistan thought that he was going to give the journal back. Instead, his mentor nodded slowly and slipped the book inside his tunic.

"Very well, lad. But I don't like this business about Captain Voth, and I can't keep that information from him even if I did. It's my duty, and yours. It might be our only hope to avoid starving. The way rations are dwindling, we'll be chewin' on the canvas soon."

Triistan had expected this, but he still wasn't sure how to broach the whole subject. "I understand, sir. That's just it, though - we're starving, but we're dying in other ways too, sir. Everything the man touches..."

He trailed off, hoping Scow would finish the thought, but the big man just stared at him, waiting. From past experience, Triistan knew that he could do that for as long as he needed to.

"I gave her my word, sir. Captain Vael. She - she knew how important it was that this journal make it back home. What we found... something terrible is going to happen, sir, and the Ministry and the Kings' Council need to know about it. If she were here, with us, I know we'd be much better off than we are now and we'd stand a chance, but..."

"But she ain't, lad. And we need to make do with what we've got."

Triistan nodded and took another deep breath. "Aye sir. And we have you, sir."

One of the things Triistan loved most about Scow was his shrewdness. Most of the seekers who worked under him believed he could read your mind if he looked at you the way he was looking at Triistan right now. It made it very difficult to keep anything from him, but if you didn't have much to hide, it made him a very effective leader, mentor, and friend. He knew exactly what Triistan was hinting at, which spared him from having to say the words aloud.

"Tell me about this bloody monkey," he growled.

So Triistan did. He spoke rapidly, in a hushed whisper, fearful that any moment Voth or Sherp would wake. Even though he was careful to leave out the intimate parts about he and Drey, as usual he had the sense that Scow deduced more than Triistan was telling him. The Mattock's questions seemed more pointed around the holes in Triistan's narrative, though thankfully he said nothing specific to indicate that he suspected anything until Triistan had finished.

"And here you are alone," Scow finally said.

"Sir?"

"Where are Drey and Mung? Why did you come forward on your own?"

If his body had the water to spare, Triistan knew he would have started sweating. This was one question he hadn't anticipated. "Well... um... they - that is, Wil, he... he doesn't know, sir."

There went the eyebrows again. "Doesn't know? Mung ain't the brightest star in the sky I'll give you that but didn't you say he was giving the titch his 'tack?"

Triistan nodded his head vigorously. "Aye, sir, that he was. But the monkey would leave and go somewhere Wil couldn't see him. He just assumed Snitch was eating in private somewhere and never saw him fishing."

"And why didn't you tell him when you found out?" Triistan knew he was treading dangerous waters now. And Scow knew it, too.

"I thought it best to come forward to you on my own, sir." That much at least was true. Dreysha didn't want him to come forward at all; she wanted to keep it just between the two of them.

Scow nodded, chewing on the inside of his cheek and squinting through one eye at Triistan. He did that for a long, awkward moment while the young Seeker did his best not to squirm or fidget.

"You did the right thing, lad," he finally said. "Though you're not tellin' all of it. Still, the holes are clear enough, and none large enough to sink your story." He patted his side and Triistan heard the soft thud of the book tucked under his shirt. "I'm going to want to have a look at this diary I suppose."

"Journal, sir."

"What was that, son?"

"It's a journal, sir. Not a diary."

Scow grunted. "Ok, lad. A journal it is, then. Now, I'd suggest you take over for me here and I'll go aloft. About the only place on this ship a man can be alone." If his expression left any doubt he had surmised at least some of what Triistan and Dreysha had been doing earlier, his next words made it perfectly clear.

"You're a good friend to Drey, but I'm not sure the benefits go both ways, so you'd best watch the weather on that horizon."

The young man ducked his head.

"Thank you, sir," Triis said to the Mattock's feet.

As Scow clambered down from the watchman's post to make room for Triistan, they heard Sherp groaning as he stretched and climbed out of his hammock. They watched quietly while the big Valheim scratched various parts of his body on his way to the taffrail to relieve himself. Triistan was grateful that Scow hadn't left yet; Voth had told him to stay in the crow's nest until he caught Snitch, so he expected trouble once the second mate noticed he was on the deck.

The Mattock expected it too and stood next to him, waiting. Sherp was preoccupied with digging something out of his left ear, which he held up for inspection before wiping his fingers on his breeches. When he pulled the long, tangled mass of his black hair back from where it hung over his face, he noticed them for the first time. His features hardened from the vacant, dim-witted expression he'd been wearing to an angry, equally dim-witted scowl.

"'Fuck are you looking at Titch? Ain't you s'posed to be aloft buggerin' that bloody monkey?" As an insolent afterthought, he turned to Scow and nodded. "Sir." Triistan's shoulders clenched in anticipation of what he knew was coming. Sherp might as well have shoved a hot ember up a bear's arse.

"I don't give the Storm Father's right bullock if you're newly-minted by the captain, Mister Icefist - you will address a superior officer properly or by the dead gods I'll flay you and serve you to the crew. I've half a mind to promote the monkey to Head Cook now that the precedent's been set!"

Sherp straightened, blinking stupidly. Triistan wondered if he was trying to puzzle out Scow's insult or just come up with the proper address, but Voth spared him any further effort.

"Is there a problem, Mister Scow?" Whatever his personal misgivings were, the Mattock showed Sherp exactly how it should be done: eyes fixed on the middle distance straight ahead, chin up, shoulders square, back stiff and straight as a mast, hands clasped behind his back high enough so that his elbows jutted out, and feet spread at shoulder width. A lesser man might have shot a contemptuous sidelong glance at Sherp to be sure he was watching, but the Mattock didn't so much as blink.

"No sir, Captain."

Voth's beady black eyes found Triistan and he frowned under his hooked beak of a nose. He made a show of looking around. "And where is the monkey, Halliard? I trust you have managed to catch it before leaving your post? Have you left him lying on a butcher's block we have stashed away somewhere I wasn't aware of?"

Triistan followed Scow's example and came to attention as well. "No sir, Captain. The monkey is still aloft somewhere sir." Nervous, he felt compelled to say more, but he clamped his mouth shut and told himself to wait. One of Scow's favorite admonishments came back to him: "If you're talking, you're not listening. If you're not listening, then you really don't know what you're talking about."

Voth's beady eyes seemed to shrink even further. "Then why are you not aloft looking for it?" A fleck of spittle hit Triistan square in the cheek, but he didn't flinch. "I gave you an explicit order not to -"

"I relieved him, sir," Scow interjected. Voth's head twitched sideways like a gull's.

"For what purpose?!" he sprayed at the First Mate. Triistan was just as surprised.

"We've a fine westerly beating up, sir, and I mean to get every ounce of speed out of this launch while it blows. I've a mind to rake her masts and wanted a look at her lines from the nest. I ordered Topman Halliard to take my position here since there's only room up there for one, sir."

Clearly Voth was stumped. He was a purser, not a sailor. Despite his long years in the Corps, they were primarily spent with his nose in the ship's ledger, down in the hold, or, as many a crewman had quipped before, up everyone's arse making sure they weren't hoarding kernels of corn. Furthermore, Scow's longevity and reputation, not to mention his bulk, had always given him an air of authority that surpassed his actual rank. As a Master Carpenter, there might be one or two men in the entire Seeker fleet who could be considered his equal. Captains and other commissioned officers routinely deferred to his knowledge and experience, so his answer sounded perfectly plausible to Voth, no matter how much he disliked it, or how ridiculous the concept of raking the masts on this particular vessel was. Triistan struggled to keep a straight face while he watched Voth's little black eyes flitting from the masts to Scow, no doubt trying to come up with something reasonably captain-like to say.

"Very well, Mister Scow," he finally muttered. "But be quick about it; I would like to address the crew after we break our fast this morning. There are... issues to be addressed and your presence will be required."

Scow lifted one bushy eyebrow. "Issues, sir?"

"Yes, Mister Scow. Issues." But clearly he wasn't going to provide any more detail than that. He dismissed them both, and Scow made for the foot of the mainmast while Triistan retreated to the relative safety of the watchman's post. They were only wide enough for one person to walk and stand, so at least he could gain some separation from Sherp and Voth.

The next hour passed slowly. Day crept shyly into the sky while the launch and its tiny crew came to life. Triistan watched Scow make a show of inspecting the masts and the ship from the very same spot that Rantham had watched him and Dreysha. From time to time, the Mattock would stand in such a way that Triistan assumed he was reading the journal, being careful to keep it out of sight by shielding it with his body. He wondered how well the First Mate could read and if he would glean enough information to convince him. He wished he had planned this more carefully and somehow walked Scow through the journal personally. If the Mattock didn't turn the whole thing over to Voth, perhaps he would still have that opportunity.

Biiko appeared in a small clearing on the deck, not far from the watchman's post. It was an area he often chose to meditate from, though Triistan could not have said why; it seemed no different than several other locations on the boat. Dreysha appeared next, ignoring Biiko as she casually leaned on the taffrail nearby. She pretended to be merely admiring the sunrise, but Triistan knew better. He saw the way she swept her gaze over the rest of the ship, pausing for one extra heartbeat where he knew Voth and Sherp were standing near the fore. When her eyes met his, he lost that extra beat, though he quickly recovered it and many more as she approached him.

"Mornin', Titch," she said. Despite her apparent nonchalance, he thought he could hear a slight note of tension in her voice.

"Drey," he said with some effort, thinking his voice sounded admirably steady this time.

She leaned on the rail where it turned to run out around the watchman's post, her back to him, shielding her eyes against the rising sun and pointedly looking up at the crow's nest.

"I thought the First Mate had the dawn watch and you were supposed to stay aloft 'till you caught our hairy little fisherman?"

"He - Mister Scow that is - asked me to swap with him so he could inspect the masts. Thinks he's figured out a way to rake them." He tried to sound casual, failing miserably. Unlike Voth, Dreysha would know better. The look she gave him over one shoulder said as much.

"That so? Rake the masts you say? Well if anyone can figure that magic trick out, it'd be the Mattock." Dreysha let her gaze drift up and down the boat again and turned to face him, still leaning on the rail, and dropped her voice.

"Tell me you didn't talk to Voth?" she whispered harshly. Triistan glanced at the acting captain, who was discussing something quietly with Sherp. Neither one of them were paying attention to he or Dreysha.

"No, I didn't say anything about Snitch to Voth." Something in the way he added "to Voth" at the end roused her suspicions and she looked at him sharply. She was worse than Scow when it came to reading minds - at least his own. She looked up at the crow's nest again, then back at him where he squirmed uncomfortably, like a fish caught on the end of a harpoon.

"Oh, Triis... tell me you didn't. Tell me you did not tell the most single-minded, stubborn, stone-headed sailor in all the fleet, who's suckled at the Corps' tit since he was a babe and views 'duty' the way most of us view the air we breathe?"

He winced and thought about going for a swim. "I don't know... maybe?"

"*Maybe*?" she said incredulously. "Maybe?! By the Dark and all its secrets why would you think that would be any better? You know him better than any-" when she stopped in mid sentence, he knew he was really in trouble. He could see her putting the pieces together in her head. Even in the face of her wrath, he had to admire her for it. Bit by bit, he was discovering that her mind was every bit as agile and beautiful as she was.

"You showed him your bloody diary, didn't you?"

"Journal, it's a j-"

"I don't care what you call it!" she hissed. "You said no one could see it but the Ministry, - that you'd given your word - and then you broke your oath and you gave *him* your bloody journal!" She turned away from him and stalked aft.

He wanted to call out to her, go after her, but he was suddenly conscious of Captain Voth and the Second Mate staring at him curiously. They must have heard Dreysha's outburst, but how much did they understand? He shrugged and smirked back at them as if to say he didn't understand her either, then turned to look out to sea. He waited for several long minutes while he scanned the horizon in all directions, expecting to be hailed or hear footsteps on the planks behind him. But when the call finally did come, it was from Scow, summoning them all to the morning meal. The First Mate met him at the end of the gangplank, putting an arm around Triistan's shoulders and gesturing out to sea as if he were showing Triistan something. When both their backs were turned to the others, Scow shoved the book into Triistan's tunic. He didn't say a word, but gave Triistan's shoulder a hard squeeze.

They broke their fast as they had every morning for the past several weeks; one strip of dried boar, one ship's biscuit, and one swallow of water. Dreysha avoided him, sitting by herself and eating silently. Biiko sat on one side of him, Scow on the other. When Rantham accepted his rations and made to move away from the group to eat in his customary solitude, Sherp stopped him and told him that the Captain would be addressing the crew shortly. Rantham's eyes - yellow and bloodshot - darted around the group as he searched for a safe spot to sit down. He finally selected one with his back against the hull, as far removed from the rest of them as possible.

Triistan chewed on the tough strip of dried meat resolutely, while his mind worked on Dreysha's reaction and what to do about it, if anything; the more rational side of him knew his task would be far easier if they left each other alone. He tried catching her eye, but she sat facing in another direction and stubbornly kept her gaze out to sea. The breeze had grown steadily, maturing from its fitful gusts to a steady caress, enough to move her hair, making it ripple and flutter slowly, like a black silken flag. The rise of the wind should have lifted their spirits in kind, but the silence was oppressive, each of the survivors weighed down by their own thoughts.

When they had finished eating, Voth stood and cleared his throat.

"Mister Scow, call the roll if you please."

"Aye sir," the Mattock rumbled and went through the charade. Triistan watched him carefully, hoping to find some indication that Scow might be nearing the end of his patience, but his face might as well have been carved from stone as he read through the short and painfully obvious roster.

"Excellent," Voth began in a slow, deliberate manner that was as over-officious as it was ludicrous under the circumstances. *We should be manning the sails and rigging*, thought Triistan. *Trimming the vessel to squeeze as much speed out of her as we can possibly manage, heading for home*. Instead, the Captain gave every appearance of starting a speech for a cadet graduation ceremony.

"Officers and able crewman, proud members of the Seeker Corps and my fellow survivors of the *SKS Peregrine*, I have called this assembly to address some growing concerns that have troubled me of late. Discipline is flagging, and with it our morale. This is not acceptable, and I will not allow it to continue. Our hope of survival will follow in kind if we do not take steps to restore these things. I have given the matter much thought, and called upon my officers to do the same."

Triistan saw Scow's eyebrow twitch upward, though the rest of his expression remained still.

"As a result, the Second Mate, Mister Icefist, has made some very interesting observations and suggestions to improve discipline and security on board this vessel. After much consideration, I have agreed to implement some of these suggestions for the benefit of us all.

"As you all know, Seeker Protocol has very specific provisions for non-officers carrying weapons when the ship has not adopted a military stance. Therefore, any and all weapons not belonging to an officer will be confiscated immediately. As Second Mate, I have charged Mister Icefist with securing these weapons, to be distributed if and when the need arises, which will be determined at my sole discretion. You will turn over all personal weapons to the Second Mate immediately."

Drey swore viciously and spat, but managed to keep her tone in check, thanks in large part to the restraining hand Scow laid on her forearm. "Begging the Captain's pardon, sir, but what in the Dark's going on?" Triis thought he knew. Voth wasn't as dumb as he appeared. He knew he had morale and respect issues and must be worried about open rebellion, so he was shoring up his position. No doubt Drey knew that as well, but she wasn't going to make it easy for him.

Voth turned to face her, smiling in self-satisfaction beneath the curved beak of his nose. "We'll start with you, Seeker. I'll have that dagger you keep tucked in your boot."

A slow grin spread across her face, but her eyes were cold and flat. "You should be careful what you wish for, sir..."

Despite himself, Voth blanched and took a step backwards.

Sherp stepped between them and reached for Dreysha, but Scow was already there. "I'll take care of it, Second."

For a moment, everyone froze. Sherp glanced from Scow to Voth and back again, as if considering whether to challenge the First Mate's authority. Old habits died the hardest, though, and he reluctantly took a step back, mumbling a barely audible "Aye, sir." Triistan realized he had been holding his breath, but wasn't ready to release it just yet. *Now, sir - do it now. Please... we'll never get a better opportunity...*

But if Scow had read anything, it had not been enough to persuade him. "Midshipman, you will relinquish your weapon as instructed. Now." Triistan let out his breath and it was all he could do not to drop his head in disappointment. Scow held out his hand and for a moment it looked like she was going to spit on it, or worse. Without taking her eyes off of Voth, though, she reached down and slipped the punch dagger from its sheath and handed it to Scow.

"Take good care of that please, sir" she said to him.

"As if it were my own," Scow answered. Dreysha's eyes found Triistan's then, fixing him with cold accusation.

- 341 -

Scow approached Biiko next. The Unbound had taken to carrying one of the harpoons with him since the ridgeback's attack, and had it now. Of his twin blades, he had only one when they rescued him, and that he kept out of sight under his bedroll, wrapped up in a bolt of rough spun cloth. The mattock slipped Dreysha's knife into his belt and held out a hand for the harpoon.

Surprisingly, Biiko complied without so much as a raised eyebrow.

Voth might make a lousy captain, but he rarely forgot an inventoried item. "When we're through here," he sneered, "you will also turn over your sword." Biiko stood impassively, not deigning to even look at the captain. Triistan supposed that he didn't really need any weapon for his own protection, and wondered how Sherp and Voth would address that fact: even unarmed he was a threat to them if he chose to be. He had already demonstrated that to Sherp with painful clarity, so Triistan doubted that part had been overlooked.

He gave up his own dakra without protest. Sherp ran his thumb along the eight inch curved blade before slipping it into his sash, giving him a sick, sinking feeling; his plans for a mutiny had just become a great deal more complicated.

Mung had no weapon. "Just my deadly wit, sirs, of which I give freely and often."

Rantham, however, kept a finely-wrought silver stiletto in a leather bracer on his wrist. When Scow and Sherp approached him, he drew it and backed away, brandishing the weapon, eyes wild. He started shouting at them to get back, that he wouldn't be the first. Scow held out both hands, palms out, and tried to calm him down.

"Easy, Mate. No one's going to hurt you. The Cap is just trying to make things safe in case it gets worse out here, that's all." Triistan caught a glimpse of Voth muttering something to Sherp, but then Rantham gave a short, shrill laugh that pulled his attention away from them.

"I've heard that before! Not this time, though!" He gestured towards Voth with the stiletto. "He's got it all figured out, now, doesn't he, sir? Don't you, Lanky? One at a time, when... when we give him any little excuse-"

"STAND DOWN, SEEKER!" Scow bellowed. Rantham was brought up short, years of working on the *Peregrine* under the whip of the Mattock's authority cutting through his confusion and paranoia. He literally came to attention, placing his hands behind his back, though he did not release the blade. His mouth opened and closed several times, but he seemed to have been momentarily struck mute, caught between trying to formulate an apology and blind fear of Scow's wrath. Whether or not he agreed with Voth's decisions, Mordan Scow did not tolerate insubordination, ever.

"Hand me the blade, Midshipman. *Now.*"

Rantham shook his head, slowly. There were tears in his eyes. "I'm s- I'm sorry, sir... I can't do that..." Scow extended his hand, palm up, and took a slow step toward Rantham. The panicked Seeker brandished the knife, yellow eyes bulging in fear.

"Stay back, sir! Please!" The sharp boney lines of his shoulders heaved in a sob.

Triistan's heart sank as he watched the already flickering hope of forcing Voth out of command snuffed out. Biiko might be a living weapon, but unarmed, there was no way the others would dare attack Sherp and Voth. They were doomed.

"Alright, lad, just breathe easy now. We're all in a bad spot - *NO!*" Sherp emerged from behind the mainmast and drove Triistan's dakra into Rantham's back with such force that it lifted the man bodily off the ground. Scow roared and charged in a blind rage. Sherp used Rantham's body as a shield, while the dying man made a keening, gasping noise. Triistan realized he was trying to scream, just as a dark blur brushed past him: Biiko.

Scow had managed to grab Sherp by the throat, with Rantham's body still between them. The dakra was lodged in the man's spine, forcing Sherp to release it to free himself of the dead weight. He grappled with Scow, who was now driving him back towards the taffrail. Rantham's body slumped to the ground, completely limp, though his eyes were still open and he continued making that horrible gasping noise. Triistan saw the silver stiletto fall from his limp hand, but just as the blade touched the deck, Biiko was suddenly there. He rolled over the dagger, snatched it up, rose and lunged, all in one incredibly smooth motion like some kind of exotic dance, the flash of the stiletto darting out from the end of his extended fingers like a bolt of silver fire.

It flew straight and true, lodging itself in Sherp's neck, but not before the big Valheim had his revenge. As Biiko was lunging for Rantham's blade, Sherp had found the handle of Drey's punch dagger in the Mattock's belt while they struggled. He tore it loose and drove the knife deep into Scow's side just as Rantham's stiletto hit home, and together, both men crashed to the deck.

- 22 -

Best Laid Plans

Casselle watched Hedrik von Darren nervously descend down the well. At one point he had actually argued that being eaten by wolves was preferable to drowning. Drowning in the cistern below, however, was now quite unlikely, as they had secured several guide ropes in the days after Casselle and Temos had returned from it. Now it was much easier to navigate through the chilling water to the window. There was even a short hanging ladder to help with climbing up and into the chamber beyond.

"Does this have any chance of working whatsoever?" Temos asked.

"I thought you'd like the idea of retreating back down your hole again, Rabbit," Raabel jested.

"I'm talking about the other bits, you enormous lunkhead," Temos replied.

"It'll work," Jaksen interjected forcefully, trying to quell the bickering. Casselle turned to look at him, but noticed they were all focused on her instead, waiting for her reassurance.

"It will work," she said confidently. It was Odegar's plan and she had faith in him. It would work. Her assuredness seemed enough for the three of them and they went back to their tasks. Casselle left the side of the well now that Hedrik von Darren had disappeared into the dark below.

They had constructed a palisade around the well out of materials scavenged from the buildings inside the walls of the fort. Although it was not a solid wall, it was a strong barrier nonetheless; a fort within the larger fort. The barricade bristled with spears, spikes and sharpened sticks, anything they could affix to it to make it decidedly unfriendly. There was only one way in, a door sized portal that had a simple gate that could be pushed into place and buttressed from the inside.

A couple of platforms had been nailed into place, allowing archers access to the top of the inner wall and providing them with an excellent vantage of the open ground between the barrier and the front gate.

Casselle saw Captain Taumber speaking with the Outrider Commander near the gate and walked past the large pits where the remaining livestock sat roasting over open flames. The air was thick with smoke and the smell of cooked meat. Rations had been tight the last few days, and like others she'd noticed, her own eyes lingered on the food as she walked by. She banished the thought of stealing a bite for herself and continued on to the gate.

"This is a horrible plan," she heard Commander Stone say under his breath as she approached.

"It will work," Odegar Taumber reassured him with a thin smile. "Just remember your part in it all." He caught sight of Casselle and motioned her to join them.

"Hedrick's down then? Everyone is in position below?" the Templar Captain asked. Casselle nodded in affirmation. "Well then. Not much left to do except open the gates and invite our friends in for a bite."

"I may not agree with the rest of it, but you don't have to worry that me and mine won't give them a mouthful of trouble," Stone growled.

"That is the plan," Odegar said, sounding relatively confident. That alone was enough to bolster Casselle's courage. "There's still a few things left to fix, so let's get them done before the sun climbs any higher in the sky."

"Wouldn't want to be late, for our heroic defense of the cesspipe," Stone quipped.

"Just think of the ballads they'll sing," Odegar replied cheerfully.

The normally stoic Commander of the Outriders actually cracked a smile at that one.

***

"I'm sorry, Old Honey," Shayn Fletcher said as he rubbed the nose of the horse that had been previously working the winch mechanism. "It's time now."

He carefully removed her bridle and gave her another friendly pat on the flanks. The three other remaining horses waited next to her, each of them at the end of their days and only used for light draft work.

"Needs to be done," was the only thing that Nikk said, a short distance away at the front gate. He and a couple of the other Outriders were poised to open those gates, which had been sealed tight since the wolves had begun this bizarre siege.

Ever since the initial rush, they had not attacked the keep in force, but had constantly scouted around the smaller guard portals on the sides of the keep, once or twice attempting to dig under the wall during the cover of darkness. Their attempts had failed, though not without a cost to the defender's strength and security. They were slowly being worn away, gnawed on like an old bone.

"Do it then," Shayn said. Nikk signaled the Outriders at the gate, who threw back the locking bolts and kicked free the buttresses. With effort, they pushed the doors outward, opening them wide to the village below.

"YAH! GO!" Shayn yelled, slapping Old Honey on the flank. Startled, the mare snorted and lurched forward. The other horses followed, the beasts running out of the keep as fast as they were able. They galloped past the wall and down the slope toward the town below.

"Move!" Nikk Bellows yelled, urging his fellow Outriders to make their way back to the inner palisade, without a glance back at the beasts they'd sent to their deaths.

And death did come for them, bearing down on the horses from the shadows with gnashing fangs as soon as the animals reached the town. In the daylight the difference was obvious: these wolves weren't hunters. They hungered for the kill, not the meat. Most of them did not even wait to see the horses torn apart before they began their quick dash up the slope, towards the open doors.

Aleah Blue loosed her arrows as quickly as she could nock them, firing from one of the platforms that gave her view over the top of the palisade. She was trying to deter the fastest wolves from closing on Nikk, Shayn and the others before they could reach the safety of the barricade.

One of the other Outriders that had opened the gate turned to look behind him. Leah recognized his face, but couldn't remember his name. It wouldn't matter shortly, though. Already lagging behind, he tripped over a stone, tumbling to the dirt. She put two arrows in the back of the lead wolf, but it wasn't enough to stop it from reaching the young man and grabbing him by the leg. He thrashed for a moment before others were there, swiftly finishing what the first one had started.

"Close the rutting door!" Nikk yelled as he ran through the opening in the inner wall. The palisade's gate slammed shut so quickly that it almost hit the last of the Outriders passing through.

"Brace it!" ordered Commander Stone, his thick hands already at work around the haft of a spear ready to stab out through the gaps. He watched two heavy timbers fall into place, locking them inside the ring.

"Outriders! Make 'em bleed!"

Leah was already putting as many arrows as she could into any wolf that presented a target, of which there were plenty. It looked like they had all entered the fort through the outer gates.

A small group of them were knocking over the roasted meats that had been left cooking on spits, snarling and snapping at each other for a taste. Leah was sighting one of these down when one of the larger pack leaders came up to bark at them. She was chilled by the sight of the wolves deserting the easy meal in response, as if the alpha had reminded them that the real prey was still up and about on two legs.

It was not natural. It was the kind of thing that would haunt her dreams, assuming she survived. She didn't want to think of that right now, so she tied that fear to an arrow and sent it into the flank of the next wolf she saw.

The wolves were spreading out everywhere, filling the courtyard and surrounding the palisade. Some were attempting to break into the buildings inside the courtyard, scratching or battering at closed doors in an effort to gain entry at whatever might remain inside.

"Carshill! The signal!" commanded Royan Stone, who was putting his weight behind the spear sticking through the wall and into the back of a snarling wolf. One of the Outriders behind him put a horn to his lips and sounded a long, clear note.

* * *

"This is the worst plan ever," groaned Temos as he took the rope in his hands and looked over the edge of the fort's outer wall.

The Outrider signal had not even finished sounding, but next to him Casselle was already climbing over, beginning her quick descent.

"Over the wall, Rabbit," said Raabel, getting a good grip on his own rope.

"En'vaar et Laegis, my large friend," Temos replied.

"We are indeed," replied Raabel, smiling fiercely.

Inside the keep, the stairs leading up to the battlements at the top of the wall had been collapsed in advance. Even if the wolves had detected the five of them, which was unlikely given all the other scents they'd been putting in the air over the course of the long morning, they'd have no way to reach them. But being undetected was an essential part of the plan as Captain Taumber had laid it out.

Temos concentrated on lowering himself down as quickly as possible, controlling the speed of his descent by working the rope wound around his body. Thankfully, his leather gloves and the thick padding of his armorjack saved him from uncomfortable burns as he descended, but he was still afraid that he would make a mistake and lose his grip. Then there was nothing between him and the hard ground at the base of the wall.

He devoted so much energy to worrying that he was surprised when his feet bumped onto solid ground. In a surge of joyful relief he turned to check on the others, only to notice Raabel limping off behind Casselle.

"What'd you do, you big oaf?" Temos asked as he caught up with his squad mate, moving as quickly as his legs would carry him.

"I came down too hard on my leg. I think I twisted my ankle. Nothing serious." Raabel smiled with a wince as he lumbered forward awkwardly. Temos considered calling out to Casselle, but he dismissed it, knowing that the Captain's plan left no time for incidental injuries.

As they approached the main gate, they heard the calamity inside - horns and howls, barks and war cries. The doors were open wide and across the open space, behind the far door, Temos knew Captain Taumber and Jaksen were there, ready to swing it shut. They would have to be quick: once the gates were closed, they'd have to brace them using beams they'd dropped over the wall the night before.

Fortunately the doors were easier to close than open, thanks to counterweights installed on the inside. Regardless, the five of them faced a serious challenge. Temos moved next to Casselle, who was peeking out around the side of the door, looking for a familiar face on the other side. She must have seen one because she nodded and then held up three fingers.

"Count of three, then," Temos whispered to Raabel, who already had his hands on the door. The big man nodded and Casselle brought down her fingers in succession. When the last one folded over, she immediately opened her fist and pushed her palm against the door.

Raabel and Temos pushed with all of their might as well, but nothing happened. Their half of the massive wooden gate did not budge.

"It's not going to work!" Temos hissed, feeling the desperation leeching the strength from his limbs.

"It will work!" Raabel grunted, his face red from the effort.

"C'mon you rutting..." Temos began, half pleading, half cursing at the stubborn thing until he felt it start to move.

"Harder!" Casselle encouraged, her arms out and head down, legs slowly pushing forward.

The momentum built as the doors began to swing together. Temos felt his heart leap as his footsteps quickened and his effort grew less strenuous. By the time they reached the halfway point, the doors practically moved themselves into place, slamming together with a thunderous crash.

"Braces!" yelled the Captain, already grabbing one of the thick timbers on the ground around them. Jaksen helped him, and the two Templars quickly moved to the gate and wedged it into place just behind where the doors met. Temos and Casselle were working on another while Raabel struggled valiantly to set a third one all by himself. Temos could tell it hurt his ankle further, but the big warrior did not complain.

"Will that hold?" Temos asked, raising his voice over a series of heavy thuds from the other side as the wolves attempted to force the doors back open.

"Two more," Captain Taumber ordered, pointing to the other beams still lying beside the gate. "We have to make them hold."

"That may not be our only problem," Jaksen replied between heavy breaths, his hand straying to the hilt of his sword.

Temos turned away from the door, looking back towards the town.

Too short of a distance away, beside the closest building, stood a woman, naked as a newborn babe, a wild tangle of dark hair cascading down her back. Each one of her slender hands rested on the back of some hunched over, monstrous creature with the head of a wolf. She stood there, head cocked slightly to one side, looking almost innocently confused.

"Oh, fuck me," Temos cursed as his hand moved quickly to the hilt of his own sword.

***

"The doors are closed!" Leah shouted down, nearly falling over as a wolf attempted to climb over the back of another to get up to the top of the palisade. Thankfully, Royan Stone was there to intercept the beast with his heavy spear and pushed it back. As the wolf tumbled away, it took the spear with it, ripping it from the Commander's fingers.

"Time to move, people!" Royan barked. "Outriders, we are leaving!"

"You heard the man," Nikk said to Leah, holding up a burning brand for her. Pulling one of the prepared arrows at her feet, she lit the end and then looked out to the barracks, only a short distance away. Set next to the closest corner was an open barrel of pitch, some of its contents already freshly applied to the wooden walls all around the container.

"Remember when I couldn't hit the broad side of a barn?" Leah asked of no one in particular, just before loosing the arrow. She watched as it arced over the heads and backs of the beasts, missing the barrel, but hitting nearby, in one of the freshly painted side timbers.

"Thankfully that's all you have to hit," Nikk replied with a smile as Leah lit up a second arrow, aiming for the small stable house.

On the other side of the ringed palisade, one of the other Outrider archers was also sending out flaming missiles of his own, catching the main fort proper, the place Hedrick and his freshly minted Templar son had called home up until recently. Leah's only regret was that she hadn't been the one to light the fire herself.

Not every building had a barrel next to it. There hadn't been enough to go around. But there were enough to help start fires on the largest of the buildings. From there, the fire was certain to spread.

The Outrider archers came down from their perches as their targets began burning in earnest. Shayn Fletcher was already helping one of them down the well; a simple loop in the rope and a couple of pulleys was all that was needed for Shayn to control their descent.

"Be quick about it," Stone ordered, having found another spear to jab out at the attacking horde.

Leah noticed that the wolves had turned wilder now, not just angry, but frenzied by fear as well, slamming themselves at the barricade, oblivious to the damage they were inflicting upon themselves.

More chilling, however, was the sound rising up behind the vicious barking and growling: a chorus of howls soared into the sky, climbing up and over the walls of the burning keep.

***

"I know she wants to kill us, but I'm very conflicted here," Temos said. "She is very attractive..."

"Stop," Casselle said flatly, her fingers gripping, but not drawing her sword.

"You're right," Temos confessed quickly, "she's probably not my type."

"Why do you think she hasn't..." Jaksen began, leaving the question unfinished, but clear.

The woman that Renholf Crennel had called the Wolfmother was gazing skyward, up over the tops of the walls of the keep where her pack had raised its sorrowful cry. That was not the only noise, though. The buttressed main gate behind them was being assailed by constant banging and scratching, and over that they could hear the growing roar of a town on fire.

She was still. Her eyes squinted and searched, her nose lifted slightly and sniffed at the air, and her mouth was set in a tight line. On either side of her, the wolves with the limbs of men stood hunched over and yet still shoulder height with her, snarling and growling. She was their tether, Casselle was sure, the only thing keeping them from charging the small squad of Templars.

Her squad was not in full armor. The plan hadn't allowed for that. Armorjacks only, they had decided, the thick thigh-length coats of mail locked between layers of cloth and leather. They were heavy, but not as restrictive as the plate they wore in full battle. No shields, only swords and long knives, things that they could reasonably have rappelled with.

Now they stood at the ready, between the blocked door to a burning Flinderlaas and a woman who controlled an army of wolves, flanked by two things that could only be described as monsters.

"Is she H'kaan?" Temos asked.

"I do not believe so," Taumber said. The Captain of the Templars had not yet drawn his blade, but stood ready to do so while he tried intently to read her face. "If what the two of you discovered is any indication, I think she's something else."

"Well, I think it's safe to rule out that she's friendly," Jaksen offered, his sword in his right hand, his left drawing the long knife at his belt.

"Without being able to talk to her, we'll never know," Captain Taumber replied, sounding almost disappointed.

"Not the best time to attempt a parley," Temos said.

"Agreed," the Captain replied, his voice more determined. "The only thing we must make certain of is that the doors remain closed."

Casselle knew that if the wolves escaped the fire, they would be able to track down the group assembling on the far side of the lake. Without horses, there would be no way for the survivors to escape on foot. Their only hope was to kill all of the wolves here, or kill enough of them to give the fleeing townsfolk a fighting chance.

A low growl began, deep in the throat of the Wolfmother. Her features darkened and her gaze fell to the Templars standing between her and the gates. Her mouth jerked open and a series of short barks erupted from it. The wolves to her sides sprang into motion, bearing down upon the squad, all gnashing teeth and raking claws.

No command had to be issued. They paired up to tackle the charging beasts while Odegar rushed the Wolfmother, nimbly slipping up the middle before drawing his blade. Casselle split away from Raabel, the two of them moving to support Jaksen and Temos, respectively.

Jaksen met the first one head on, a gray-maned thing that went directly for his throat. He brought his knife up with his left hand and gave the beast a taste of steel instead. Neither scored a telling blow, but both drew blood. Casselle was there as they broke apart and slashed at the wolf's side, but it had already moved, circling to the left.

Temos jumped back to avoid the brown wolf as it lunged in his direction. The monster charged blindly and did not see Raabel closing in until the Guundlander crashed into it, knocking them both off their feet. Temos tried to take advantage of his teammate's maneuver to score a definitive hit, but the wolf was already rolling away to regain its feet. Raabel could not regain his as quickly, so Temos stood between the two of them, sword gripped before him with both hands.

Several yards away, Captain Taumber had closed to a few feet from the Wolfmother, one hand held out in a gesture to keep her at bay, sword ready in the other.

"I don't know who you are, but I will not allow you to pass unchallenged," he said in a commanding voice. Casselle could only glance at the two of them, as she did not dare divert her attention from the gray wolf. It was now moving purposefully to flank them. Even so, she was still distracted as the Wolfmother charged Odegar with astonishing speed, arms outstretched to grab him.

The Templar Captain moved just enough to evade her, instantly slashing out against her exposed back with the skill and reflexes honed by decades of combat. Casselle was shocked as his blade rebounded, unable to break the naked flesh.

"Watch out!" Jaksen said, pushing Casselle off balance to the right. As she tried clumsily to regain her footing, she was aware he had saved her from a vicious overhand attack from the gray wolf. Its thick talons caught on Jaksen's arm instead, opening up a bloody gash below the elbow where the armorjack could not protect him.

Angry at herself more than the beast, she put her strength into a sideways slash, cutting deeply into its powerful, hairy arm. Blood flew in an arc away from the two of them, propelled by the force of her stroke.

The beast roared and turned on her, slashing at her with its other hand and catching her in the side. The armorjack prevented its claws from reaching her flesh, but it still struck her with astounding strength, batting her aside and forcing the air from her lungs.

Jaksen used the moment that it had overextended itself to drive his own sword into the thing's ribs. But his hand was weak and slick with blood, so he lost his weapon as the thing thrashed in pain and pulled away. He was already bringing his knife back up to bear as Casselle drew deep, painful breaths, trying to shake the spots from her eyes.

Her vision cleared just as the gray wolf clamped its jaws around Jaksen's wounded arm, even as he was driving his knife deep into its neck. She leapt forward, stabbing into its side, ramming her blade in all the way to the crossguard.

As the wolf bit deeper into his arm, Jaksen stabbed it over and over again in the neck with desperate strength. There was a sudden loud snap and he fell back screaming, his forearm torn off just below the elbow. He tumbled back down to the dirt.

Tears blurred Casselle's vision, but she refused to quit. She twisted her blade and pulled it free, blood jetting from the wound. The wolf yelped, letting Jaksen's savaged limb fall from its mouth. It backed up and lunged at Casselle, bloody fangs wide.

She used her size to her advantage, dropping down into a wide stance as she stepped towards it, ducking under the lunge. She stabbed forward and up, pushing with all of her strength.

She opened its exposed belly up to the point where her sword was stopped by its ribcage, before sliding free as the wolf thrashed away to the side. It crashed to the ground, lifeblood and innards spilling out into the dirt. She wasted no time in bringing her sword down on the thing's neck, making sure the job was finished.

Her lungs heaved with exertion as she took a moment to quickly survey the field.

Jaksen was curled up around the shattered end of his arm, desperately trying to stem the flow of blood.

A short distance away, Raabel was wrestling the other beast, both of them reared to full height and bleeding profusely. Temos lay in the dirt at their feet, a nasty cut across his forehead.

Beyond them, Odegar clutched at his left leg, shuffling as if he couldn't put any weight on it, blade extended towards the Wolfmother.

"Not like this," Casselle whispered to herself.

***

"Here!" yelled Leah, stabbing a spear through a hole in the palisade. The fire had started to spread to the wooden barricade, brought by wind and maddened wolves attempting to break through. The Outriders had pulled a few buckets of water for just such an occasion, but it did not seem like there would be enough here to be effective.

Someone threw one haphazardly on the spot closest to her. There was a slight hiss as the fire briefly sputtered, but she could tell that it was already too little, too late.

"How many left?!" Royan barked, wiping the back of his hand against a cut on his head; a gift from a wolf's claw that had managed to get past the lattice. He was bleeding from his leg as well, the blood falling on the dead beast that had managed to climb over the backs of those crushed up against the wall.

"Once Varr gets to the bottom, just the four of us," Shayn shouted. He was exhausted and hot, as were the rest of them. Getting them down the well by hand was taking far too long.

"Blue and Bellows and then we'll figure it out," the Commander yelled, trying his best to be heard over the tumult of battle and flames.

"We're not going to have that kind of time!" Nikk said, listening to the wood groan in protest from the pressure exerted against it. It had already given in where he was standing, but the stack of bodies prevented it from collapsing any further.

"Varr is down!" Shayn replied excitedly.

"Tie it off!" Royan ordered. "We'll go down by hand. Bastards won't be able to climb down after us."

"Sir!" Shayn answered, acknowledging the command. Thankfully that would be simple enough. A couple of thick knots should suffice to secure it to the frame over the well. Invigorated, he coaxed energy into his sore fingers and worked quickly to fix the rope in place. After a minute or so of tense work, he indicated it was ready.

"Go!" the Outrider Commander yelled.

Leah went first, pulling on her riding gloves for protection before kicking her legs over the edge of the well. Taking a deep breath, she wrapped herself around the rope like it were a pole, letting herself slide down naturally, using her hands and crossed legs to provide a measure of control.

It was not a smooth ride. She banged into the sides of the well on the way down, bruising herself and almost losing her grip more than once. But she held firm, glad when the sides of the well ended and the cistern began.

Nikk was coming down behind her, even less gracefully than she had managed. She lost sight of him when the light from the lanterns out shown the faint light reaching from above. She felt awkward hanging in the air without the walls of the well around her, so she slid just a few more feet before letting go completely, allowing herself to fall freely into the water.

She broke the surface and caught sight of the window, lit up in the darkness below. Varr was there, waving her on. She paddled forward a bit awkwardly, trying not to swallow water before she grabbed the guide rope that would take her to the side.

Nikk's cry startled her. He came plummeting out of the shaft, not even having cleared the sides of it before letting go of the rope. *What was he thinking?*

He hit the water hard and awkwardly. It took a moment to register that he wasn't the only thing falling. As she swam towards him, thinking he may need help to reach the guideline, she noticed the rope was still in motion, whipping around like a dancing snake.

No, it wasn't moving, it was *falling*, twisting as it fell down the shaft and into the water. Nikk broke the surface, coughing and gasping for air. Leah called for him, reaching out with one hand, the other tightly gripping the guide rope.

"What happened?" she screamed, panicked that the Commander and Shayn were still above.

"I dunno. I was just... and then the rope..." Nikk struggled, obviously still disoriented. "There was a crash... like something fell..."

Leah looked up at the well, one hand helping Nikk to the guide rope, the other holding on herself. Varr was calling to them from the window nearby, but Leah just stared up at the black hole in the ceiling above them.

***

Odegar's leg was broken. It was all he could do to remain standing. *This Wolfmother is strong, like an elder Vanha,* he thought. Strong like the Young Gods had been. His sword had been casually deflected by her bare arms, like he'd been a child attacking a tree with a willow reed. He was surprised to even see scratches there, the only evidence that he'd even made contact.

She had broken his leg with one hit.

Jaksen was down and most likely bleeding to death. Temos was struggling just to get up. Raabel was barely holding the remaining wolf at bay. Casselle was moving to help him, having managed to dispatch the first one.

He had gravely miscalculated her strength. He thought if she had been like the H'kaan, she could be wounded, even killed, if enough force were brought to bear. But his worst assessment had been well short of the mark, and now it looked as if they might all die here.

A glance behind him confirmed that Flinderlaas was burning freely. Soon there would be nothing left alive in there, either. At least he found some comfort in that.

Odegar noticed that the Wolfmother kept looking back as well, glancing past them at the barricaded front gate, which was splintered and buckled in some places, but remained unbroken. The calm demeanor she had displayed up to this point had evaporated, and now her eyes were full of hurt and rage.

She walked forward towards him and he shuffled into a position that allowed him to balance on his good leg. He reached deep inside, awakening that part of himself that was born of something older, something powerful. He felt the strength pulse through his body and he lurched forward, surprising her with his unexpected aggression.

His sword was a blur, slashing out quickly. She threw up her arms again to ward off the blow. In that moment, he saw his opportunity. With the last bit of strength he had, the last bit afforded him by his Vanha heritage, he thrust past her defenses, driving the point of his sword into the middle of her neck.

His arm broke from the impact.

His sword shattered at the tip, as if it were made from glass rather than steel. The pain came at once, making him scream. He would have fallen backwards if she hadn't hit him instead, batting at him with one of her naked arms and knocking him into the dirt where Jaksen lay several yards away.

His vision was spotty and breathing brought sharp pain and uncomfortable pressure. Noises around him seemed hollow and distant.

He knew what was coming next. Nothing could stop it.

So he prayed.

And then, most unexpectedly, Death answered.

- 23 -

Turning Point

Triistan saw the blade punch into Scow's lower back. He heard the impact and the heavy grunt. An eternity later, both bodies crashed to the deck. He had to physically choke back a scream, just like the one that had been torn from him only an hour ago when he had watched it happen for the first time - when it was real and not just his mind forcing him to relive it. He wrapped his arms around his knees and rocked back and forth, trying to regain control of his thoughts.

"I think we should make a slight heading correction," someone said tentatively. He shook his head: *that wasn't how it went*, he thought. No one had said that after Sherp and the Mattock went down.

It was all just screams and shouts, chaos. Dreysha had knocked Voth to the ground, then wrapped her legs around his throat. He remembered Lanky's face turning purple as she strangled him and told him that she could break his neck but didn't want him to die so easily. A moment later, Biiko had crouched beside her and said something that Triistan couldn't hear, but whatever it was, it had convinced her to release Voth. She didn't let him go completely, however, and shifted like a snake to slip her arm around his throat. Triistan had been kneeling next to Scow, trying to shove Sherp's inert body aside and wondering why Biiko was trying to save Voth when Mister Scow was so badly injured.

There had been so much blood. Biiko's throw had sent Rantham's silver stiletto all the way through Sherp's throat, burying itself up to the hilt on one side of his neck and sticking out the other. The oarsman's blood had spurted out the side, splattering the deck and taffrail as well as Scow's face and chest. In the few moments it had taken Triistan to reach and push Sherp's body off of Scow, the big Valheim had nearly bled out all over his superior officer. Triistan could still smell the copper tang.

But it wasn't Sherp's blood that concerned him; it was the growing pool beneath Scow. Triistan was no healer, but he knew something vital had been hit for there to be that much blood so soon.

"Triis? Begging your pardon, but we're beating too far to the east; I think we need to swing at least ten points to the north-northeast... sir." It was Mung's voice. *Wil*, he corrected himself. *Since when did Wil know anything about navigation?*

Triistan rubbed his eyes. They were red and raw, though there were no tears, no matter how hard he drove his knuckles into them. Scow lay before him in a makeshift litter, unconscious but clinging tenaciously to whatever life remained to him. He lay partially on his side, and Triistan was watching his chest move erratically. His breathing was strange - short, shallow gasps separated by long pauses, with a ragged, ever-changing rhythm. It was maddening to listen to, but he found he couldn't stop; he kept waiting for that next breath, hoping it would be deep and steady, fearing that there wouldn't be one at all.

The man lying before him had been a father, teacher, and friend to him for over a third of his entire life. Triistan was only fourteen years old when he had stowed away aboard the *Peregrine* and had eventually been caught and assigned to the ship's Master Carpenter. He had grown to manhood under Scow's watchful eye. Without him, the future seemed bleak and desolate; an infinitesimal, unknown sea upon which he would drift without sail or sweep. His body felt as though it were trying to come apart, like he had been the one released by Veheg's Fire to scatter to the winds as so much smoke. He hugged himself tighter.

A soft voice sounded from nearby and he looked up to find Dreysha and Wil staring at him expectantly. *Why are you asking me?* he wanted to scream at them.

"Whatever you think is best," he croaked. It felt as if someone else had answered with his voice. He hadn't even heard the question, but his response must have sufficed. Thankfully, they left; he couldn't stand the way they were looking at him.

Why ask him? What was it that they saw in him? He was just a boy who had stowed away on a doomed Mapper, and because he could draw and write, he'd been pressed into service and caught up in events that were far too big for him. He was adrift in a raging river, being hurled from one calamity to the next, always in danger of being dragged under or smashed against the rocks of his own futility. He was so tired; tired of his thoughts constantly spiraling with memories he did not want and fears of a future he could not grasp. Most of all, he was tired of watching people die.

He glanced over to where Rantham lay nearby. After intervening between Drey and Voth, Biiko had moved quickly to the injured midshipman and immediately wrenched the blade free. At first Rantham wouldn't stop screaming - anguished cries of pain mixed with desperate pleading for someone to help him. "I can't feel my legs!" he kept crying over and over, until Biiko finally forced some kind of medicine into his mouth and clamped his hands over his jaw and nose to make him swallow it. The Unbound then gave Wil a bandage and commanded him to keep it pressed against Rantham's wound; by the time he reached Scow's side, the midshipman's cries had faded into sleepy murmurs and then to silence.

Whatever Biiko had given him was still working, keeping him mercifully unconscious. *It would be more of a mercy if he died though,* he thought grimly. The knife had struck dead center in the middle of Rantham's back. Triistan had witnessed his fair share of back injuries from topmen losing their grip or mistiming a jump and falling to the deck below. Based on the location of Rantham's wound and his panicked complaints that he could not feel or move his legs, Triistan feared the worst.

Unlike Scow, Rantham had not bled much, so as long as they kept the wound clean, he would probably survive. But Triistan knew that was only half the battle; the mental and emotional toll would be far more difficult to deal with for both Rantham and the other survivors. He had already been convinced that the rest of the crew was going to resort to cannibalism once the food ran out. Now, Triistan thought how terrifyingly possible Rantham's worst fears would appear to him, when he could not walk or even sit up without assistance. He knew what Dreysha would have him do, and on some practical level he could not fault her for it.

Don't leave me here like this, sir, he thought as he looked at Scow again. *We need you. I need you. I can't do this alone... I'm just a boy. I'm not supposed to be here!*

"Better a boy at the helm of this floating coffin than this fucking old fool," he heard Dreysha's voice saying again. And just like that, everyone else had started looking at him for answers.

As Biiko treated Rantham, Drey had dragged Voth over to the mainmast, where she then secured him with a length of rope. Although the acting captain was much taller than her, she handled him easily. Even if Voth had decided to put up a fight, Triistan had no doubt that Dreysha could have subdued him quickly and probably thanked him for giving her the opportunity. As it was, though, the up jumped purser appeared to be in shock, offering no resistance, just pleading not to be killed over and over again. Somehow that made things even worse. The sight of the sniveling, conniving old man, whose ineptitude and pettiness had brought them all to the brink of death, filled Triistan with bitter disgust. It had taken every ounce of his self control not to kick

Voth and scream at him to shut up. *None of this matters!* his mind had raged. Roll call, Protocol, Chain of Command... it was all just noise, a ripple on the surface of the sea while the real storm gathered just beyond the horizon.

He had been so focused on Scow that he'd only half heard Drey when she suggested he would make a better captain than Voth. He couldn't even be sure what had prompted her to make the comment - whether she was just thinking aloud or had someone else suggested they mutiny? Maybe it had just been on everyone's mind already, so that when things unfolded as they had, it just happened naturally, as if they had planned it.

Whatever had occurred with the rest of the crew, he had missed it. All he could remember was rolling the Mattock onto his side and pulling his blood-soaked tunic up to reveal a puncture wound half the length of Triistan's forefinger and nearly as wide. Thick red blood was pulsing out of it - darker and thicker than any blood he had seen before. It terrified him, but the look Biiko had given him had scared him even worse.

"You can save him, can't you?" he had pleaded. "You must save him - just... just stop the bleeding. You can do that, right?" For the first time since Triistan had known the mysterious warrior, he looked uncertain and strangely sad.

"The chain is forged regardless. His path is to lend his strength to yours," he said. He hesitated a moment, then nodded as though he had decided something. "Still, I will try. Get a piece of rope and put it between his teeth. There will be much pain." It was the most Triistan had heard the Unbound ever say, and yet it told him almost nothing; he did not understand what Biiko meant and thought he was contradicting himself. Triistan wanted to think it sounded hopeful - how could Scow possibly help him by dying - but he could not shake Biiko's odd behavior.

Please. I cannot lose another like this. He felt so alone and small. "I'm sorry, sir," he whispered to the Mattock's prostate form. "This is all my fault. Perhaps if I'd told everyone, people would have understood and none of this would have happened. But she ordered me and made me swear, sir. I gave my word..." he trailed off feebly.

Even as he spoke the words though, he knew they were hollow. If he had entrusted the journal's contents to Scow, it might have changed the entire dynamic on board the launch. With Drey, Wil and Biiko behind him, he could have convinced Scow to take command much sooner, sacrificing his own honor and duty for the greater good.

- 360 -

But instead he'd let himself drift along once again, hiding behind his oath the way a child hides behind a lie, and now the one person they needed most lay before him, unlikely to rise again. Captain Vaelysia should have entrusted it to someone else.

"I don't belong here," he whispered bitterly.

"You cannot hide behind that sentiment any longer, Mister Halliard." It was another voice remembered: the Captain's. She sounded as clear as if she were standing on the deck of the launch behind him. He ducked his head and ran shaking fingers through his tangled hair.

He remembered when she had said it to him, the day after they had fought their way clear of Ahbaingeata. On the southern edge of the lake they had emerged from, they had found a sturdy guardhouse squatting at the foot of a tall, slender watch tower. They made their camp in the tiled plaza outside. The guardhouse was covered with heavy undergrowth, but most of the tower's base had been clear. Like Ahbaingeata, the look and feel of the architecture reminded him of some of the old fortifications at home, remnants of the Stormfather's Column, Shanthaal. They were similar, using many of the same materials and built at roughly the same oversized scale as the ancient structures on the Sea King Isles. But there were subtle differences as well; strange ruins carved into the stone, and ornate decorative detailing made from the same bone-like material they had seen on the Sentinel statue.

There was no visible way into the tower - arrow slits penetrated the curved stone exterior, but the first of those was at least thirty feet off the ground - so they reasoned that it must be accessed through the adjoining wall of the guardhouse. Serpentine vines, like long, searching fingers as thick as a man's waist, had penetrated the barrack's clay tile roof in several places. Once inside, the vines had branched out in dozens of tendrils, creating a tangled web throughout the structure. They spent the remainder of their first day recuperating and treating the wounded, while those of the expedition who could swing an axe or a sword had set to cutting their way through it.

It was hot, hard work, and slow going. The mesh of woody vines was thickest towards the back of the building, so that the wall adjoining the tower and the door in its center were completely hidden on the inside. It had taken them all day to locate it, so they were well into the long evening before they finally gained access to the tower, where they were once again reminded of the scale of things on Aarden. The door's lintel was some twelve feet high, the iron-banded wood so thick and heavy it took three of them to push it open. Captain Vaelysia threw her own shoulder into the effort, impatient "to get topside for a look around", as she had put it then. Commander Tchicatta and his scouts had not yet returned.

Broad marble steps had followed the inner curve of the wall, spiraling slowly up to the landing at the top. A thick layer of dirt and debris covered the floor and steps, but other than a few thin creeper vines that had managed to worm their way around and under the door, the tower itself had been empty. Because of his leg, Triistan had to take the steps slowly, even with Biiko there to assist him. It had given him time to study the steps and walls more closely, though, and he began to notice signs of damage similar to what they had seen beneath Ahbaingeata. There were patches of broken stone visible where whole chunks had been torn off, and in other places they were pitted and somehow warped, as if from a tremendous heat source, though at the time he had known of no fire that could reshape stone. Similar marks marred the leading edges of some of the steps, growing more severe the higher they climbed, and Triistan remembered wondering at the titanic struggle that must have occurred there.

Eventually he had limped up through a ragged hole in the floor of the circular room at the top, which must have once served as a trap door. Now, however, the edges of the opening were badly warped and scorched and there was no door in sight. The room itself was huge, its outer wall an arcade of arches separated by columns of the same glassy black rock that the colossal statue in the lagoon had been carved from. The floor was covered in more of the mosaic tiling they had seen in the massive chamber with the dead armaduura, though much of it was blackened and battered, mimicking the ceiling above. The strange black pillars around the room's perimeter seemed virtually untouched, however. Beyond them there were no railings or battlements to obstruct the view, so from where Triistan had emerged on the staircase all he could see beyond the arches at first was sky. As he had limped his way awkwardly across the tile floor, the spectacular vista that lurched into view was stunning.

Even now the memory was so vivid he felt a hint of vertigo. After gaining the summit of the watch tower, he had pulled out the rough map he had sketched during the Captain's meeting earlier that day, looking to compare it to the actual landscape. He remembered feeling very proud of how accurate his assumptions about the layout of Ahbaingeata had been, particularly how far the underground river and causeway penetrated past the monstrous wall they had seen from downriver. Across that distance sprawled a ruined city the world had forgotten, though how something so magnificent had simply faded from history was beyond him.

After having a good look herself and sharing a few words with some of the others who had made the climb, Captain Vaelysia had come over to stand beside Biiko and Triistan. At that moment he had been looking eastward; something about the view in that direction was bothering him, but he hadn't been able to put his finger on it just yet.

"Do you know what you are looking at, Mister Halliard?" Her tone was hushed, almost reverent. He had strained to hear her.

"No, Captain," he answered softly, nervously licking his lips. He was always struck by how formidable a figure she presented up close. As a topman, Triistan's duties rarely brought him into her immediate presence, so on those rare occasions when they did, he found himself cowed by the aura of strength and confidence she portrayed. He was considered tall, but she looked down on him all the same with grey eyes the color of mist. Her shoulders were broad and powerful, her legs long and strong, with a seafarer's thick calves and ankles. Bronze skin and golden hair shot with streaks of red betrayed her Island heritage, but there could be little doubt that the blood of the Vanha ran through her veins as well. She wore her hair pulled back in a tight pony tail from a fair, seemingly ageless face. She was actually quite striking, though the intensity of her gaze and the quiet power she radiated made it feel dangerous to think of her that way. Triistan tried to meet her eyes and failed.

"This," she'd said, "is Ostenvaard, City of the Faithful and home to the Laegis Centuriis... The Thousand."

He had never heard of Ostenvaard until that moment, although he was aware of some half-forgotten myths concerning The Thousand from a book he had stumbled across while serving as a scribe for Doyen Rathmiin. Well, more like a librarian and custodian, if he were honest about it. Most of his time had been spent either fetching or returning books for the Doyen, or cleaning up the seemingly endless supply of clutter around the old man's desk. On one such trip he was returning a stack of books nearly half as tall as he was when his foot caught the hem of his ill-fitting apprentice robe and he went down in a tumble of dust, leather and parchment. One of the books had landed open before him, displaying a fantastic two-page illumination of a fleet of strange-looking ships, their sails full and hulls heeling hard as they raced away from the viewer. Several indistinct figures in elaborate costumes stood in the foreground, and they reminded him of other drawings he had seen of some of the Young Gods. There was an air of sadness and farewell to the portrait that had captured his imagination, and he had immediately begun scanning through several pages of the book without even bothering to get up and dust himself off. It wasn't long before Doyen Rathmiin came looking for the source of the crash he had heard, but it was long enough for Triistan to learn that the book was about some kind of ancient host that had been assembled and sent off to a war far from home. At the time, he had thought it was just some old fable, though his master rarely wasted his time on fireside tales. He knew better now, and a chill slid down his back as he recalled the words written on the old tome's final page:

"Where this wind ends, our Oath begins. Remember us. En'vaar et Laegis."

He had repeated the phrase aloud, and the Captain looked at him appraisingly.

"Impressive. Where did you learn that?"

He told her of the book. "What does it mean? What is all of this for?" He gestured out at the city.

The Captain turned to face him, arching one eyebrow and studying him for a moment. She pursed her lips, but instead of answering his question, she held out her hand. "May I see the diary?"

Triistan frowned and muttered something about "journal" under his breath as he held it out to her.

"What was that?"

"N-nothing, Captain," he had answered, thinking twice about correcting her.

She studied his drawing of Ahbaingeata, then flipped back through several pages. Her eyes scanned rapidly, and every now and then she nodded, while he waited and tried not to fidget. The sweat trickling down the center of his back had not made it easy. Finally, she handed it back to him.

"Excellent work, Topman. Your journal is exactly what I had hoped for."

"Th-thank you, sir," he stammered. He could feel the tips of his ears growing warm. "But anyone could have done this for you," he demurred. "Jaspins is more than capable, and a student of the healing sciences besides... why me, Captain? I mean... I just don't feel like I belong here..."

She arched an eyebrow. "No? And why not?"

He had opened his mouth to answer, but a long list of self-doubts seemed to crowd together, trying to come out all at once, and he hadn't been able to decide where to begin. Instead he just blinked, rather stupidly he thought in retrospect.

The Captain hadn't been interested in hearing his feeble protests anyway. "You cannot hide behind that sentiment much longer, Mister Halliard," she began. "Soon or late, you must accept what you are." Her words made him uneasy, but she continued before he had a chance to interject.

"You have as much right to be here as any other member of this expedition, perhaps more than most... and you proved that to us beneath Rivergate."

"But I was almost killed, and others were killed. Taelyia - Taelyia died because of me..." The thought made his voice break. Captain Vaelysia's eyes flashed.

"No. Do not flatter yourself. She died doing her duty, for all of us. That is the way of it with the Reavers; ask any of them and they would gladly have died in her place." She drew a deep breath and her voice softened somewhat. "It was you who found our escape route, Mister Halliard. If not for you, her valor might have been for naught." Her gaze shifted from him to Biiko, then back. She placed a hand on his shoulder and forced him to meet her gaze.

"But that isn't the whole of it, lad. What do you know of the Unbound?"

Triistan shook his head again. "Little. Only that they are an ancient order of seers - oracles with a penchant for martial training." He lowered his voice, feeling awkward with Biiko standing nearby. "Wil told me they were the best single-combat fighters in all of Ruine. They do not speak unless the need is urgent, and they are devoted to their faith, though no one seems to know what that faith is as they do not preach. Why? And what do you mean by 'my guardian'?"

"Only that he seldom leaves your side. And the Sons of Khagan are much more than oracles."

Triistan glanced at Biiko. The warrior stood as he always had; hands behind his back, feet set at shoulder width and flexed slightly, so that he was balanced on the balls. If one looked closely enough, you could slip a sheet of parchment between his heels and the floor. His face was impassive, though his eyes were locked on the Captain.

"So what is he, then? And what does he want with me?"

She withdrew her hand from his shoulder and smiled crookedly. "You will have to ask him, topman. But if the Sons have taken an interest in you coming here, then you, Mister Halliard, *are exactly where you should be*."

Scow coughed weakly, startling Triistan out of his reverie and bringing him back to the present. The Mattock said something in a hoarse whisper, but Triistan missed it, so he leaned in closer. "I'm sorry, sir, what was that? Sir?" Scow's lips parted and he breathed out one word, so faintly that even though Triistan's ear was only a few inches from the Mattock's lips, he still barely heard it.

"Water."

"Aye sir! Right away!" He leaped up and sprinted to the scuttle, filled the ladle and then had to force himself to move slowly so as not to spill it on the way back. He helped Scow turn his head by partially lifting it, dribbling the water onto his lips. Most of it ran down his cheeks and jaw, but his mentor was able to take a couple of tiny sips just as Biiko appeared beside him with a clean bandage. He took hold of Triistan's wrist with one hand to hold the ladle steady, then dipped the bandage into the remaining water. Once it had absorbed the liquid, the Unbound carefully set one end in Scow's mouth and the other end in Triistan's hand, gesturing for him to hold it up. The Mattock sucked at it like a giant babe being fed goat's milk, with all of the water going into his mouth rather than down his chin. His eyes came open but he couldn't seem to focus them on anything, and after a moment they rolled back and he fell unconscious again. Still, Triistan felt his spirits lift at even this tiny rally. He looked at Biiko hopefully.

"That's a good sign, isn't it?"

The warrior shrugged his broad shoulders and frowned noncommittally. *Perhaps*, the motion said.

***

Scow woke twice more during the afternoon, though he did not speak either time. Triistan used the bandage as Biiko had shown him, and although the Unbound examined the Mattock's wound periodically, Triistan could not get him to answer any more questions. It should have driven him mad with frustration, but after having been up all night chasing Snitch, and then the morning's explosion of violence, he was exhausted. He drifted in and out of sleep, stuck mostly in a sort of numb trance, unable to tell the difference between the two states. Someone - Wil, he remembered later - shook him awake and handed him his rations for the evening meal. He took them, listening to the ragged catch and rasp of Scow's breathing. He wondered if anyone would bother taking a roll call, and then wondered more seriously if anyone would bother to feed Voth. That led to other thoughts he did not want to contend with just then, so he pushed them away and drifted off again.

Day slipped into dusk, dusk into nightfall. The stars and moon wheeled overhead, and when dawn broke, thin clouds drifted in, like bandages stretched across the raw red wound of the rising suns.

The wind held steady, and the rhythm of sailing pulled them along despite their battered state. Rantham seemed to be weakening. He had yet to awaken from the sleeping draught that Biiko had given him the day before, though by now its effects should have worn off. Scow woke from time to time and asked for more water, and each time Triistan thought he seemed a little stronger. If the Mattock was anything, he was stubborn, and they all agreed he was probably too stubborn even for death.

They argued over what to do with Voth, with Drey pushing hard to slit his throat and dump him overboard - to conserve food, she said, but Triistan knew it was more than that. She blamed him entirely for their predicament. She was not wrong, but Triistan could not bring himself to murder the man, no matter how much he despised him. If they were rescued, Lankham Voth would be forced to answer for his crimes. Triis had to fight her alone, though, since Wil refused to take a side and Biiko held to his customary silence. He thought it odd that Drey didn't just kill Voth anyway - with so few of them on board, and in the state they were in, she could have easily done it when no one was looking. He supposed it might have been Biiko's presence - by now it was clear to everyone that he had assumed the role of Triistan's protector, for lack of a better word - though part of him wanted to believe she had other reasons. He had not forgotten their intimate moment in the crow's nest, and wanted to believe she had real feelings for him.

She did relent on the idea of keeping Snitch's fishing skills a secret, however. Not that he had given her a choice. He was done keeping secrets, done with factions. If the rest of them were going to survive, they were going to have to do it together. He made his decision as they were breaking their fast in sullen silence, each of them cocooned in their own thoughts, an arm's reach from one another yet leagues away inside. He simply blurted it out without preamble.

"Snitch is catching fish."

Wil stared at him uncomprehendingly. Biiko was examining Scow's wound, but Triistan thought he detected a trace of a smile on the warrior's dark lips. Drey's jaw muscle twitched, but she said nothing.

He had expected her to give him a hard time about this, and took courage from her silence. "We saw him the other night, the night before -" he glanced at Scow and Rantham, shook his head and gestured with his hand, "... this."

"I don't understand, Triis. How..?"

Triistan looked at his friend. "We have you to thank, actually, Wil. He was using the hardtack you shared with him as bait, then he spears them with a harpoon blade when they come up to feed on the crumbs. He hangs off the tiller so he can get close to the water, and he's quick. Very quick and very clever, actually."

He knew he had made the right decision when a slow smile stole across Wil's haggard face. He looked aloft, shielding his eyes with a trembling hand, but the titch monkey was nowhere to be seen.

"That's the best bloody news we've had since this whole wretched business began. Who knew being oblivious could be so bloody brilliant?"

Dreysha snorted in disgust and Triistan laughed, surprising himself. It felt good, though, and once he started, he found he couldn't stop. Wil caught the infectious giggle and joined in, and after a moment Drey's derision gave way to a head-shaking, lip-biting and eventually useless attempt to resist it. They laughed until their sides were fit for bursting and each was gasping for air, while all the while Voth stared at them as if they'd gone mad. *Perhaps we have,* Triistan thought. It certainly looked that way as they all handed the monkey their hardtack later that evening.

First they had needed to overcome Snitch's well-earned fear of the crew, however. Wil surprised them by confidently telling them to leave the task to him, and spent the rest of the day coaxing the monkey down to the deck and getting it used to the idea that it was no longer being hunted. By early evening, as the suns retreated before the gray line of cloud marching westward, the survivors were gathered at the stern, watching Snitch ply his fishing skills in the launch's wake and trying to count the silver flashes roiling just beneath the surface. There weren't many - perhaps a dozen - but even one or two would seem a feast after eating the same thing, and precious little of it, for so long. Besides, large schools attracted predators, and there were worse things than ridgebacks in the dark depths of the open sea.

They began to wager on the number of fish that Snitch could catch, betting shares of their anticipated meal. Wil won with five, though in truth they all won with that kind of a catch. There were four vesher and one of the bony skrell, which they threw back; the fish was not well-tolerated by most healthy sailors, and even as hungry as they were, that type of illness could easily kill them. On the other hand, the vesher were a staple for most coastal towns. Known as Stripefish by the locals, they were fat and succulent. Even one of the smaller fish would be enough for one man to eat as a daily ration: in that evening's catch, two of the vesher were as long as Triistan's foot, and the other two measured about half that. They feasted like kings.

Although Islanders ate raw fish routinely, most sailors had a strong preference for cooked, so they decided to risk a small fire on the aft deck. There was a wide, cast-iron bowl in amongst the rations for that purpose, with four curved legs to keep the bowl's hot metal base off the deck. Triistan suddenly remembered the Morale Officer and fished the firth of rum out of the storage locker. They passed it around as they ate, each pulling tentatively at first, but by the third pass any thoughts of rationing were washed away in a flood of food and fiery liquid. By the time the long evening relented and the early stars were swallowed by the advancing clouds, they were stretched out, trying to relieve the pressure of their full stomachs and vying to see who could belch the loudest. Biiko stood quietly at the helm, watching them with a bemused expression, as Drey put the others to shame with a deep, guttural roar that would have made the Mattock blush.

Among their provisions, there was also an iron pot with a long handle, which they had salvaged from the raft of flotsam that Mung, Captain Fjord and Braeghan had been rescued from. Wil used it to make a fish broth, even adding some bits of cured boar to it to give it some more flavor and substance. They tried spoon-feeding it to Scow and Rantham, but while Rantham surprised them by swallowing three or four spoonfuls, Scow murmured it tasted like bilge-broth and asked for more water. They tried to encourage him to eat, to help regain his strength, but he waived them off and went back to sleep. Triistan looked at Biiko with concern, but the Unbound only frowned and shrugged noncommittally.

"What about him?" Wil asked, nodding towards Voth. The ex-purser-made-captain-made-prisoner was still bound to the base of the mast, although they had changed his bonds to a short tether around his ankle. When it was time to sleep, they would tie his wrists behind his back so that he could not free himself, but otherwise at least he was able to change positions, stand up or stretch out on the deck. Drey had objected, of course, but Triistan had insisted on it.

"Lanky? Why, I'll give'im my meal when I'm all through with it - in a few hours, I'd wager. It'll be nice and softened up for'im." She grinned and slapped her backside, in case he missed her point. From the look on his face, he hadn't.

Wil gave a wan laugh and looked at Triistan, who smiled crookedly but shook his head. "Give him his standard rations, Wil. We'll test our luck again tomorrow; if it holds, we can share some with him."

Drey snorted derisively and made a show of stretching out, using a roll of sail as a pillow. The firelight bathed her dusky skin in amber, and as she lay back, the ragged edge of her shirt pulled up to reveal her flat belly. She stared into the fire, one hand tracing idle circles around the dark hollow of her naval. It suddenly felt like someone was sitting on his chest, so Triistan shifted positions and made a show of stirring the coals with his dakra.

As she stirs mine, he couldn't help thinking. He set the knife on the deck and found a spot where he could lay down comfortably, thinking of his journal and the secrets it contained. Tomorrow he would share it with them all, and tell them everything. Keeping it hidden from a fully-crewed mapper made sense, especially if they were concerned about it falling into the wrong hands. The only thing that mattered now was that it and the warning it contained made it back to Niyah, and the best chance of that occurring lay with all of them working together. Besides, they deserved to know. They'd earned that right and he wasn't going to deny it to them any longer.

A thick fog of weariness stole over him, and he closed his eyes. He felt almost happy as he drifted off to the soft snores of his comrades, the sigh of the wind in the launch's sails, and the gentle song of creak, hiss and gurgle sung by a ship underway.

He dreamed.

He was standing atop a massive, sloped wall in Ostenvaard again, looking out over a sprawling plaza tiled with slabs of stone. Two crumbling towers flanked the wall, with rivers of glowing blue water bleeding from their bases, curving out in a graceful arch across the plaza. A third river with hard edges of cut stone ran from their confluence off towards a dark line of buildings only barely visible through a haze of smoke.

The air was thick, heavy with anticipation. His head throbbed. He was aware of others around him, tall shapes in strange armor. Several held bladestaffs, twins to the one held by the sentinel statue in the bay. They were all facing north, toward the roiling smoke. A storm had gathered just beyond their sight, and this was the last breath before the thunder.

A horrific scream rose up from somewhere, so high and loud it was excruciating, driving long spikes of sound into his skull. Seconds later, a tide of darkness emerged from the smoke, flowing across the plaza toward him, a living, seething shadow of mottled black and gray flesh, teeth, and claws. The H'kaan had come, but they weren't alone: *He* was with them -

Triistan jolted awake, panting. Biiko knelt beside him, and Triistan knew instantly that something was wrong.

- 24 -

Broken Links

Preparing a body for a Releasing Ceremony was painstaking work.

Out of respect for the fallen, they were washed and clothed in their best garments, their hair combed and arranged. Wounds were cleaned and dressed, to the extent that it was possible, but the real task was preparing the corpse for immolation through Veheg's Fire. This required that the skin of the deceased's arms, legs and face be tattooed with arcane triggering formulas, from shoulder to wrist, groin to ankle, and neck to hairline. Those charged with tending the body spent close to two days bent over it, dipping a needle in an iridescent blue ink and using it to puncture the corpse's skin, one dot at a time, one symbol at a time. It was a lengthy process by design. Even if you could mark the body faster, the ceremony would not work immediately afterwards; certain changes occurred within it over those two days that were required before you could light the arxhemic fire.

Because the process took so long, the body must also be wrapped in strips of linen soaked in heavily-scented spices to help preserve it and mask the smell of death. Fortunately, the Corps insisted that all sea-going vessels, right down to the simplest of skiffs, be fitted with an Embalmer's Kit - what most regulars referred to as the "Body Bag" - and the emergency launch was no exception. Their kit was a multi-pocketed leather pack, about the size of a set of folded saddle bags, stuffed full of the linens, spices dyes and quills required for properly interring a dead sailor. It even contained instructions and detailed diagrams of the required trigger symbols.

An outsider might interpret this regulation as the Seeker Corps' commitment to honoring its fallen, but ask any bow-legged deckhand and he could recite the proper steps for taking a piss. The Corps had procedures and plans for *every* eventuality.

The preparation was tedious, mind-numbing work, but Triistan was grateful for it, because it gave him something to do, something to help distract him from his own pain. Thanks to Snitch's knack for baiting and catching fish, the specter of starvation had receded somewhat, though it still haunted the periphery of their existence. They were keeping a close eye on their water supply as well, but given that there were fewer thirsts to quench, they could reasonably expect to ration what they had long enough to last until the next rainfall. The wind had held strong and steady, and no one had touched an oar since the last ridgeback attack. All things considered, after the doldrums that had plagued them immediately following the wreck of the *Peregrine*, they could not have asked for better weather. Since the launch was designed for handling by a small crew, there was plenty of idle time - too much for the overactive mind of a young man struggling to come to grips with still another loss.

He dipped the quill into the luminescent dye, counted slowly and deliberately to five to allow sufficient time for the dye to be absorbed, then bent to his task. He placed the sharpened tip against the corpse's skin and pushed, applying enough force to puncture it, before plucking it out and moving to the next dot. If the tip didn't break off, the quill held enough dye for eight to ten punctures before it had to be dipped again. This body's skin was tough, though, especially along the arms, and they had already broken two quills. They had five left, which he hoped would be enough.

Triistan tried hard to focus on the deliberate, steady rhythm of the process. Dip, count to five, place the tip of the quill on the spot where he'd left off, move it to where the next dot must be tattooed, see the symbol in his mind to make sure he had placed it correctly, and then finally push down, puncture the skin and withdraw, the light tug as the quill pulled free a tactile counter that kept the rhythm in time. It was simple, methodical, and it helped hold back the overwhelming tide of his grief, instead allowing him to explore it carefully, the way one might probe a sore tooth with his tongue. What's more, it gave him the chance to honor a man who had come to mean more to him than his own family, while he tried to prepare himself to say goodbye forever to Mordan Scow.

He was working on The Mattock's right forearm, while Dreysha sat opposite him, working on the left. They had finished his legs at moonset the night before, taking advantage of the ghostly blue-green glow of the ink in order to finish and wrap as much of the body in the preservative linens as possible.

We should be able to finish his face tonight, he thought. One more day to ensure the dye was sufficiently absorbed, and then they could hold the ceremony the morning after. *In less than two days' time, he will be gone completely.*

The image of Scow's body being consumed by flame intensified the ache in his chest. Though the man he knew was gone, there was still something vaguely comforting about tending to his body. He could almost pretend that his mentor was only sleeping.

Almost. Perhaps the boy he had been just a few short months ago might have been able to imagine that for a little while, but not now.

That boy doesn't belong here anymore, he thought. *Not since the moment Biiko woke me and I knew... I knew...*

The Unbound had not said a word, only shook him awake and stood, waiting. As Triistan had looked around the boat in alarm he saw Dreysha and Will crouched next to the Mattock. Triistan lurched to his feet and stumbled over to Scow's side, a low moan forcing its way out from the back of his constricted throat.

"I'm sorry, Triis," Wil had whispered as tears streamed down his blistered cheeks. Triistan fell to his knees beside the Master Carpenter's still form. "He must have... d-died sometime during the night - I came to see if he wanted water or might have a bite to eat... but I couldn't wake him. He's gone."

Gone. How could such a man, such a force in his life, be gone? And why him, while Rantham still lived despite having nothing to live for but fear and horror?

He had been consumed by bitterness and despair for the next several hours, at one point even wishing they still had Sherp's body so that he could rip it apart with his bare hands. But they had all agreed previously that the Valheim oarsman did not deserve a releasing ceremony because of his actions, and had dumped him overboard instead, giving him to The Dark the same as any other common criminal would have been. He considered doing the same to Voth, but knew, deep down beneath the rage and pain, the man he grieved for would not approve, nor would it bring him back to life.

As he dipped the quill in the dye once more, he heard Dreysha humming faintly. The tune was a familiar one, but it took him a few moments to place it. When he did, a sad smile slipped out from beneath his mask of grief: it was an old sailor's cant that Scow and several other members of the crew had gotten very creative with at the celebratory feast they had held after making landfall on Aarden.

The memory drew him back there again. The night was warm and humid, the foreign smells of plant and animal intoxicating. He closed his eyes and inhaled slowly, still able to recall the scent with surprising clarity, and with it the soaring emotions that had intoxicated the *Peregrine's* crew. Perhaps the fact that they were on solid ground again had given them the sense that they had eluded their fate, that rather than being smashed to pieces at sea and swallowed by the deep and endless Dark, they had instead discovered a new world that was theirs for the taking. Whatever the reason, they had felt drunk long before the first tankard of rum was hoisted.

At the center of their encampment, they had dug a great pit and piled it high with cut logs and deadwood. It was too large a fire for cooking, so they had dug five smaller pits around it for their roasting fires, fitting each with spits large enough to hold a harox. Since there were no more livestock left by the time they had reached Aarden, they had been forced to hunt for their meat. Fortunately, there proved to be no shortage of game, and over each cookfire, some curious new creature crackled and sizzled and popped, filling the air with a heady aroma. Most appeared to be distant cousins of familiar beasts, but a few were even more exotic, particularly some of the larger birds they had managed to bring down. Some were extremely dangerous as well, like the twenty-foot-long, green and yellow lizard that had taken Mynder's arm off at the elbow. He should have survived, but the beast's maw was foul and the wound had festered; fleshrot consumed the rest of his arm before the infection spread to his insides. He died screaming several nights later.

Nobody had known this at the time of the feast, however. It was a night of wild celebration, where they ate and drank, sang, danced, then drank and ate some more. That was the night they had discovered that Creugar had such a beautifully sweet singing voice it moved several of them to tears. Later on had come the tune Dreysha was humming now, led by the Mattock himself: Scow's bawdy, self-deprecating rendition of "The Captain's Mistress", wherein he changed most of the familiar words in order to poke fun at himself and his notorious "love affair" with his ship. Several mates joined in to offer their help - some a bit too zealously, Triistan had thought at the time - but the Mattock took it all in stride, roaring out each new line louder than the would-be bard who'd first penned it. Scow's favorite had been one that Longeye, the lookout, had come up with:

The Mattock's Mistress be lean,
As swift on the seas as any vessel I've seen;
But her secret lies not in her rigging,
nor her sheets be they square-cut or jibbing,
For on her heavy-beamed aft,
There's no rudder, there's a shaft
And ole Scow driving hard at her ribbing!

Triistan's smile grew as he recalled both of them staggering around the huge fire, leading the rest of the crew as they repeated the lines several times, until it became hard to tell the difference between the singing and the raucous laughter that accompanied it. The memory was bittersweet.

Now, both are gone forever. The backs of his eyes burned as he began tracing the last glyph on Scow's wrist.

They had been so full of life and joy, he recalled vividly, when Longeye had thrown her supple arm over his shoulders and yelled overloud in his ear.

"Come now, Triis! Let's have a song from ye! There mus'be all sorts of fine 'arpoons ye'can drive in'a Mattock's arse - now's your chance!"

He remembered how painfully self-conscious he'd felt as he smiled and shook his head. "Some other time, maybe. I don't know what I would say, or who'd want to listen to it anyway."

"Suit yourself," she hiccuped into his face, then staggered away as someone began a whirling reel with a pipe. She grabbed hold of Scow's arm and tried pulling him into the gathering body of dancers, but he held his ground for a moment longer.

"Someday that'll change, boy. Someday you're going to have plenty to say, and many and more will want to listen."

The Mattock had always been telling him things like that, trying to build up his confidence and ease some of his shyness, but looking back now, his mentor's words took on a prophetic quality he found unsettling. He suppressed a small shiver and returned to his work.

Tattooing the glyphs on Scow's face proved to be much more difficult than what they had done thus far, both physically and emotionally. Triistan had to stop several times, whenever the tears welled up and spilled over. Thankfully, there was only room for one person to work, so Dreysha left him to do it alone. Other than her quiet humming, she had kept unusually quiet during the entire time they had spent on Scow's legs and arms, only answering if he spoke to her, and when it became obvious they could not work on such a small area together, she had wordlessly clasped his hand before moving away.

He was touched by her sudden sensitivity, though he was also surprised, having grown accustomed to her irreverence. He wondered if it was a ruse for his benefit, or if she felt genuine affection for the Master Carpenter. Probably both, he decided. When this was done, he would find out if any feelings she might have for him were legitimate, or simply a ploy to get a hold of his journal. After the Releasing Ceremony, he planned to begin his accounting of what had happened during the Aarden Expedition. It was time to tell them all, everything. Once her curiosity was satisfied, he was afraid she would have no more interest in him

It took hours, but eventually the work was done. In place of Scow's broad face, the body now wore a faintly luminescent mask of strange markings that matched his bulky arms and legs. Triistan felt his friend slip further away. The pain was still intense, but strangely, the empty hole in its wake seemed less so. Instead, a feeling of calm was growing within him, helping to sooth the wound. Whether it was exhaustion, or the knowledge that he was finally going to be free of the burden of his secrets, or something else altogether, he did not know. But he had a sense of strength and balance inside that he wasn't used to.

He straightened and stretched, groaning at the tightness in his lower back. The moon had long since set from a cloudless sky, leaving a glittering wake of stars. The night was warm, but pleasant. The wind that had filled their sails earlier that day had slackened to an intermittent breeze, so in between gusts, the surface of the ocean was calm and flat enough to mirror the sky, and but for the soft slap of the water against their hull, all was silent, still. For just a moment it felt as if the boat were floating in some unknown place with no horizon, where sea and sky had become one; an endless field of blue and white fires, glittering in the distance like the hopes and dreams of other people.

He wondered if this is what it had been like to be a god, when the Arys had lived among the stars. Then the wind dragged across the sea, and he was mortal once more.

He grunted quietly. "Gods help us." The bitter irony of the words tasted like dried blood.

"There are none left, remember?" said a soft, throaty voice. Dreysha appeared beside him, materializing from the night as if she had been standing there all along, reflecting the stars as the sea had done. "And even if there were, they'd give more thought to their own shit than to the likes of us."

"Maybe," he answered quietly, "but the stories tell us differently."

She grabbed a line and swung a lithe leg over the taffrail, straddling it. "Finished then?" she asked, nodding her head in the direction of Scow's wrapped and tattooed body.

He stared at it and sighed wearily, then slumped onto a nearby crate. "Yes... I think so. Though I've only ever helped before - I've never been responsible for the whole preparation."

"You did well, Triis. I'm sure it will be fine."

"Thanks." He tipped his head back and gazed up at the night sky.

They sat together in companionable silence for several moments before Dreysha said softly, "Surprised to hear that comin' from you though."

"Surprised? At what?"

"Would you really look to the gods to solve your problems? Seems odd."

More than you know, Drey, he thought to himself. He reached back and touched the hard edge of his journal, verifying that it was tucked securely in his sash.

"I didn't really mean it like that - I was being ironic. But what do you mean by odd? The histories are clear. The Young Gods asked for something more than simple beasts, something they could relate to. That's why Tarsus created us, so they could nurture and guide us... I think they did actually care for us..."

Dreysha scoffed. "That's all books and stories now, Triis. Even if they were here I don't think you - we - would want them meddling in every little thing we did. I mean... maybe it's because I know how clever you are, how... self-reliant. You're the last person I would expect to be looking to them for answers."

He snorted. "We could use a few now, don't you think? Just look at us..." he made a helpless gesture towards Scow's body.

"I am, which is more than they would've done if you ask me. They killed each other, Triis, and tried to take us along with'em. Good riddance, I say - let's fend for ourselves, stop waiting around for someone else to do it for us. I think most folks have had it all backwards for a long time."

"And I suppose you've talked at length with 'most folks' to figure that out?" he shot back. She gave him a crooked smile.

"Don't give a monkey's bunghole about the rest of you, though I'd wager my last coin that same monkey's arse has got much better sense when it comes to this."

Triistan couldn't suppress a smile. "And I suppose you've talked at length with a monkey's arse to figure that out as well?"

She grinned back and sketched a mock bow. "Haven't had the time, Captain Titch, Sir. What with you keeping your head up there most of the time." They both laughed quietly.

Dreysha continued. "My point is, little Snitch over there has a problem, he faces it on his own. He does something about it. He doesn't waste his breath singing hymns or building temples to Mung the Mighty or some other godhead. He and his kind have lived just fine without gods getting in their way, and I say we would, too. But people - most people, anyway - they're always looking to blame their luck on something or somebody else, instead of looking to themselves. And what better crutch than a group of all-powerful, all-knowing and conveniently absent beings?" She turned her head and spat over the side.

"Piss on'em. We're better off without their meddling - better off making our own decisions, determining our own course. It's like the Cap's tattoo: 'Fate is the Wind - you can trust it to take you home, or you can seize the helm and make it.' Words to live and die by, Triis. I've never had the pleasure of divine intervention one way or the other, and I like it that way. Not like they got it right the first time 'round anyway, or even the second for that matter."

I know now the choices made are mine alone to make...

The phrase came back to him again, a whisper from an old memory he couldn't quite grasp, which had originally surfaced back on Aarden, when he had drawn Taelyia's kilij for the first time. He had tried drawing the weapon several more times with no effect, and hours of practicing with it since hadn't produced anything other than sweat and aching muscles. He'd eventually dismissed it as a product of his leg injury and the horrible experience that followed, but now...

Dreysha gave him a playful kick in the shin. "Well, nothin' to say? No sage musings on the secret metaphysical lives of monkeys, or maybe a history lesson on the esoteric qualities of life as a puppet dancing on deific strings?"

He smiled and shook his head. "With what comes out of your mouth sometimes, I think you've more in common with that monkey's arse than - ow!" She kicked him in the shin again, but much harder this time.

"Dammit, Drey that hurt!"

"Just lettin' you know I'm real, unlike your bloody gods, or whatever it is you think you've found back on that Dark-damned pile of rocks. You'd be much smarter saving your fear and supplication for me," she grinned mischievously.

Her reference to Aarden chilled him. He thought about everything that had transpired there, what they'd found, what they'd seen.

"If you knew what I knew, you might think differently."

"Maybe you should tell me then," she replied, her voice softening.

He wanted to tell her - that and much more - but there was a manipulative note to her response that rang false to him. He heard Scow's growly warning again in his head: "You're a good friend to Drey, but I'm not sure the benefits go both ways, so you'd best watch the weather on that horizon."

It wasn't so much that he didn't feel right sharing the information with her; he'd already decided that it was time to let them all know everything that he knew - her most of all. He ached to let her inside, someplace he never let anyone. But as much as he wanted her, that sense of being manipulated made him wary. He still thought there was something genuine in her affection towards him, but right now the gleam in her eye had more predation than passion to it.

He shifted his leg to break contact. "After the Releasing Ceremony," he answered, more coldly than he'd intended.

He saw the playful smile stiffen on her lips. One of her eyebrows twitched up as well, and he groped for some way to soften his response. Perhaps he didn't have to let her inside, but he didn't want to push her away, either.

"I think Biiko would agree with you about not relying on the gods," he offered, hoping to keep the conversation going. "He said a weapon didn't wield itself, and neither did a life. You had to exert your will or it was meaningless. Something like that."

"For a mysterious warrior sworn to silence, he seems to have a lot to say," she muttered. Triistan smirked.

"He does have a way with words."

"I wonder if that's what he meant about the chains..." she trailed off, pursing her lips thoughtfully.

Triistan remained silent, waiting for her to finish her thought.

She glanced up at him and shrugged, trying to appear casual. "Do you remember that dream I had... of Biiko? It was just before Voth and Sherp started to lose what little sense they had..."

He clenched his jaw. He remembered. He remembered every detail of every conversation he had with her, but even if he hadn't, he would not have forgotten that particular conversation: in the middle of it he had discovered she had stolen and read part of his journal. He nodded, still without saying anything.

She winced, searching his eyes for a moment. "About your journal, Triis. I'm sorry I took it, it's just..."

"It's done, Drey," he said awkwardly. As always, his feelings about her confused him; he wanted to be angry with her, but at the same time he was afraid of pushing her away. "I'd rather not talk about it anymore. What were you going to say, about the chains?"

"Well, he told me something about the world being made up of chains - no, that's not right. He said that each life was a... a great chain, connecting events in the past to other events in the future, something like that. 'Each chain binds a life to this course,' he said. Some strands are more important than others, and somehow all these chains together help 'contain the Living Darkness'."

He stared at her incredulously. "Biiko told you that?"

She nodded. "Well, at first I was talking to... someone else. Then it was like he just, I don't know, took it over. It was his voice - at least, that's what I thought in the dream. Has he ever said anything else to you about this?"

Triistan glanced over his shoulder, looking for the Unbound. Biiko stood at the helm, a faceless wraith wrapped in shadow and mystery. Triistan shook his head. "No - aside from that one instance, he's only ever said a handful of words to me, and never anything else about chains or fate." He snorted. "And certainly never anything in my dreams."

Drey laughed quietly, shaking her head.

"What? What's so funny?"

"Only the fact that one of the deadliest warriors to walk the face of Ruine has been following you around like your personal bodyguard for how long and you don't even know what his favorite color is, let alone why he selected you as his master! You must know something, Triis - you knew about Khagan's Sons-"

"And so did you," he cut her off.

She shrugged. "So I did, but I told you how. Seems I'm doing most of the talking here. You still haven't told me how you knew what your guard dog is or why this idea of yours is so close to my dream, to say nothing of whatever it is that has you all twisted up inside."

"Everything!" He lurched to his feet, but then caught himself and looked around. The rest of the launch's skeleton crew did not stir. He stood there for another moment, mouth working in soundless frustration, until Dreysha giggled at him.

"Oh sit down, you look like some maniacal fish with flaming hair for Dark's sake."

He sighed in exasperation and sat back down heavily. When he spoke again, his voice was quiet, resigned. "Okay, fine. I suppose I owe you that much. The Captain told me some things, though she had a knack for taking much more information from me than she gave."

Dreysha sat forward, wrapping her arms around one bent knee, still perched on the taffrail. "What did she tell you?"

Triistan glanced over his shoulder again, but Biiko had not moved. "Not much, really. I already knew most of what she told me of the Unbound - what most people seem to know anyway. Their Vow of Silence, their legendary discipline and martial abilities - all you have to do is watch him move and you can figure that part out. I've never seen anyone move that fast, that... gracefully... he's like a ghost..." He trailed off, recalling some of their encounters on Aarden.

"Triis..." Dreysha prompted.

"Sorry. Anyway, as I said, she didn't tell me much I didn't already know, except when I asked her why Biiko had shown so much interest in me. She told me that I should be honored that he had chosen me, that I must have some great role to play." He laughed self-consciously. "I know, it sounds ridiculous, doesn't it? I'm a stowaway nicknamed for a bloody monkey. I'm nobody, no different than anyone else in our crew. That's what I told the Captain."

"And what did she say?" she asked quietly.

He shrugged. "She didn't, not really. She told me I had to ask Biiko that question."

"So did you?"

Triistan laughed. "Of course, and of course you know that he just stared at me in that... that Dark-damned bemused way he has, like he's privy to some incredibly rich joke he's playing on you."

Dreysha smiled knowingly but didn't say anything.

"So I asked the Whip," his laughter died off and he stared out at the sea, remembering. "He told me quite a bit, actually. The Khaliil 'remember', right? Their tradition of passing along oral histories from one generation to the next makes for great storytelling. He told me about Khagan's Sons, the original name of The Unbound. Khagan was some type of... construct I think he called it. Tarsus actually made him for a specific purpose, as a smith would forge a tool."

"What purpose?"

"Ironically, he was a blacksmith. After Tarsus defeated Maughrin but realized he couldn't kill her, he created Khagan to forge and maintain the chains that bound Her in captivity."

Drey shook her head in disgust. "So the old bastard couldn't kill her, and the best plan he could come up with was indefinite imprisonment by this 'construct'? Like I said, piss on the gods."

"I don't think it was that simple, but we were focusing on the part about Biiko and The Unbound. Whatever he was, Khagan was formidable. Different than the Arys, but just as powerful, if not more so." He frowned, remembering something else First Mate Tarq had tried to explain to him. He did his best to convey it to Dreysha.

"He wasn't just one person - or tool, I guess. There were actually five of them. 'Five physical embodiments with separate functions but one voice' was how the Whip described it." He shrugged. "In any event, these five 'constructs' are referred to simply as 'Khagan' in all the old stories."

Triistan remembered how formal Tarq had become as he relayed the tale.

"And Khagan did gather unto him ten disciples, so that each of his embodiments might have two acolytes, to learn the art of the Forge and the secrets of the Great Binding. But he did not choose from the ranks of either Auruim or Dauthir for this task. Instead, he chose the Children of Tarsus.

"There are some who think Tarsus had commanded it, because he trusted these new creatures more than the Young Gods he'd created. But others believe that it was Khagan's decision alone; that his cold logic could not be swayed by pride or vanity, and thus he was not blinded to the rift that might come to pass. He thought then that Maughrin's Binding must survive the breaking of the world.

"Whatever his reasons, it is agreed that Khagan chose five women and five men from amongst the Children. He trained them in earnest, for the body of Maughrin still lay near the Forge, and the slow drumbeat of her heart yet pulsed. The Binding Chains must be learned and maintained, and the sooner the better, lest some flaw escape his notice now, that she might exploit when she awoke in years hence.

"Just as she was bound in chains, He demanded of them a binding oath, the Vow of Silence, that they might not speak of their knowledge to those untrained, for to do so would be catastrophic. For each chain in the Great Binding was forged of a life, and its power lay in the ability of that life to follow its true course, to fulfill its true purpose. This Khagan did call The Path, and charged his disciples to defend it.

"Unto them he gave the gifts of Longevity, Wisdom, and Discipline, that they may be strengthened in their cause. He then beseeched the Young Gods to adopt his charges and teach them the ways of the High Houses. This was done, save for the House of Pleasures, for these things did Khagan see as a weakness and potential threat to their Duty.

"His acolytes labored for decades, learning from the Young Gods even as the Arys learned the ways of this new world Tarsus had left to them, until Khagan deemed them ready.

"He called them to the Forge of Stars, and made them listen to the doom-filled beat of Maughrin's heart. There they saw what Tarsus had known would come to pass, that it had grown stronger, the beat faster. And Khagan said unto them:

"I am an instrument of something greater, forged for a Purpose that must endure, though my creators could not. And though I am not of flesh and blood, I have labored to reshape you in mine own image. As I am made of stone, your bodies have been strengthened. As I am forged of steel, your minds have been sharpened. You have been taught to see the Binding Chains, and now you must go forth among your fellow man to protect them.

"But you are few, and for every life, there is a Chain. Therefore, you will find and teach others our Purpose, as I have taught you. But even this will not be enough. Seek the Great Chains: they are as the great limbs of the tree, rather than the myriad small branches. They are the Paths that must be followed, lest all our work be undone, and the sacrifice of those who came before rendered meaningless. Go now, and be true."

"And thus through knowledge and labor and purpose were Khagan's Sons forged."

Of course Triistan had to paraphrase most of it, but Dreysha listened intently the whole time and did not interrupt him. He enjoyed having her undivided attention so much that he'd forgotten his concerns about being manipulated.

"Was that all? Was there anything else?"

Triistan shook his head, "No. I kept asking him, but he refused to say any more on the subject, until he finally threatened to stake me out in the latrine pits if I didn't stop pestering him about it." He glanced over at Dreysha with a self-conscious grimace.

She drew up her other knee and hugged them both. She was chewing thoughtfully on her lower lip.

"So Khagan's Sons were sent out to train other fighters to see and protect these 'chains' - which we are to believe are actual people's lives...? And somehow these people-chains were somehow keeping Maughrin imprisoned?"

"Yes...?"

"And Biiko is one of them... and he's attached himself to you..."

Triistan blushed. He knew where she was going, and had considered it as well, but the prospect that his life was one of these 'Great Chains' was preposterous. He thought it far more likely that somewhere along the way, the legend of Khagan's Sons had been greatly exaggerated, assuming it hadn't been a complete fabrication to begin with.

He said as much to Dreysha, adding, "Besides, that story makes it sound like the Sons believed that a life had a specific, pre-ordained path to follow - fate, if you will."

"So?"

"So what about 'the weapon doesn't wield itself'? Biiko told me I had to exert my own willpower for my life to have meaning. Doesn't that strike you as the opposite of this whole chains idea?"

Dreysha hugged herself like she was warding off a sudden chill.

"Fate is the real prison, and 'chains that bind are bound themselves'," she said, her voice barely above a whisper.

"What?"

"It's from my dream - almost the last thing Biiko said to me before I woke up."

"That sounds more like him. What else did he say?"

"He said that it was all a mistake, and that 'the Sons must break them'." She fixed him with those deep, dark eyes, and his heart stopped.

"Triis... what did you find on Aarden?"

He stared back.

Images of tall alien spires hewn from black rock rose up in his mind, surrounding him, fencing him in. It was a vivid memory and it threatened to swallow him - one of those he had obsessed over in his journal in fact, going over the lines of his illustration over and over again. "The Hold" - that was the name they had initially given it. He remembered scrawling the words above the picture, writing it countless times until he was in danger of wearing through the paper. He didn't need to pull out his journal to see it again in every detail.

Arcane symbols from a language he did not know were inscribed on hulking, dark stonework. The stones were overgrown with twisting vines, some of which had forced their way into mortar joints between the huge slabs, shifting some and toppling others completely. There was a courtyard ringed by tall black statues that resembled the Sentinel they had seen guarding the entrance to Aarden, though each depicted a different figure. Most of the ground was covered by a long oval with a dark surface that shown like water or highly-polished, black steel. A structure of some kind had once occupied the center of the oval, but now all that remained of it were great chunks of a strange, translucent crystal that lay on the ground or, in a few occasions, actually floated a few meters above the floor's surface.

And among these, there was something else. Large bands of black metal as thick as a man's waist were set in the floor at the foot of each statue. Heavy rings of the same material ran haphazardly across the floor, from the bands, through the shattered crystal pieces in the center...

"Chains," he whispered.

"We found broken chains."

- 25 -

The Wake

"How long do we wait?" Leah asked.

The question caught Nikk off-guard. If not so much the question itself, the implications that went along with it.

"I... I don't think we should," he said. "I mean, the Commander and Captain Taumber said we should just go. If everything went according to plan, we should meet up with them at the tower."

"But it didn't go according to plan," Leah replied solemnly. The Commander was dead. Shayn was, too. They had waited hopefully at the window overlooking the cistern until the embers came down the shaft, the flickering remains of the framework that had been constructed on top of it.

By then it was clear nothing else could have survived. Hearts heavy with regret, they joined the others below, in the long cavern where the water from the cistern exited the hill, cascading over a steep drop to the lake below, just as Temos and Casselle had described it. Carshill managed to break his arm on the climb down and one of Vincen von Darren's fool Templars had managed to drown himself on their way across the lake, but the rest of the refugees had made it safely.

Even Renholf Crennel had survived, despite his state of delirium, at least until an unguarded moment when he ran off into the woods on his own, slipping away when attentions were elsewhere.

Much to everyone's displeasure, Hedrik von Darren's mouth had also survived their harrowing escape fully intact. He loved hearing himself talk and he did so constantly, most recently complaining to anyone who cared to listen (as well as those that didn't) about his family's property and loss. That much was not in dispute: Flinderlaas was in flames, even now a bright burning spot on the hilltop across the lake from them.

"No," Nikk Bellows finally replied to Leah. "Not at all according to plan." He hung his head for a moment, chewing on the risks and possibilities.

"You're the closest thing to a Commander now," Leah said. Nikk looked around. The remaining Outriders nodded in agreement. Carshill, Ela, Varr, Wickers, Blane and Runders all looked to him now. The von Darren's seemed content to keep their own company, and the other two remaining Templars stood guard near them. Hedrik had a couple of nervous stewards, young men that couldn't sit still, constantly trying their best to keep the old man comfortable.

Nikk was responsible for all of them.

"We shouldn't wait, then," he said. "We need to get going."

Provisions and equipment were spread amongst the survivors. Each had a waterproofed sack with food and a blanket. Hedrick had an additional bag of "important documents" that he would probably take to the Strossen Elder Council to seek redress for his losses, as well as a lumpy sack of "irreplaceable valuables." Nikk could not care less. As long as he wasn't required to carry it, von Darren could drag a gold plated carriage behind him.

Unfortunately for the young stewards, they were charged with both bags and Hedrick's provision bag, leaving the old man only a head full of complaints to carry around. Nikk was not pleased to discover he was more than happy to share those at his own discretion, which was often and at length.

"You know, there might still be wolves around," Leah finally snapped at the foppishly dressed dandy as they made their way through the forest, heading slightly North and East towards the tower at the edge of the Deckoran Wilds. That seemed to work for a short while, perhaps not silencing Hedrick altogether, but at least quieting him to a more tolerable level.

When the long evening began and the night began to fall, they looked for a place to set up a sparse camp.

"No fires," Nikk instructed. "Carshill, I'm going to need you to still pull a watch, but you can have one of the first. Vincen, I'm going to need you or one of your Templars for a watch as well."

"You have no authority over me," he scoffed. "You're not even the Commander."

"You arrogant little piece of..." Leah snapped, before one of the other Outriders pulled her aside.

"That's true," Nikk replied calmly. "If we don't have any Commander, I suppose we're just undisciplined layabouts."

"Everything I've seen points to that," agreed Vincen smugly.

"Which means there's nothing to keep us from wandering off in the dark while you sleep," Nikk said calmly.

Vincen's eyes narrowed for a moment while he studied Nikk's face.

"Is that a threat?"

"Just an observation," Nikk replied. For the first time, he noticed how much smaller the younger von Darren looked without his fancy Templar armor, which had to be left behind when crossing the water.

"I could have you stripped of your position... or worse," Vincen threatened coldly.

"You'd have to take that up with the Outrider leadership. Assuming you can navigate the Wilds back to the Bay. Bit of a hike though," he said, looking off to the distance. After a moment, he gave Vincen a second look and then shook his head slightly, like he'd finished calculating the odds of them making it that far. It wasn't that tough of an equation to solve. He'd seen Vincen's previous attempts at woodcraft firsthand. It'd take a miracle larger than they could muster to make it even half the way back.

"Now, now, let's not fight amongst ourselves," Hedrik von Darren chimed in eagerly. "I'm sure all of us know that we stand the best chance of me surviving if we work together."

"It's true," Nikk agreed confidently. Vincen rolled his eyes and groaned.

"Fine. Take whichever one of them you need and don't bother me with the details," he said. Nikk nodded and quietly exhaled. He had anticipated conflict, but was glad that the exchange went better than expected.

"I say we leave them anyway," Leah commented as the Outriders assembled around Nikk some distance away from the von Darren's.

"Don't think I'm not tempted," Nikk said. "Because I am. Very tempted."

The other Outriders chuckled. Nikk relaxed slightly, the burden of leadership settling on his shoulders, still somewhat uncomfortable, but at least bearable. He assigned everyone evening tasks, making sure none of them went off alone. It was still too dangerous for that.

During the first watch, after a cold dinner, Leah found Nikk leaning against a tree, staring into the dark forest that surrounded them.

"What if they don't come?" Leah asked. Nikk had heard that tone in her voice before. She wasn't just curious. She was worried. "What do we do then?"

"We return to Gundlaan. We notify the Outriders and the Militias and the Laegis. That's the only thing we can do," Nikk said.

"We could look for them. Some of us... One of us could look for them..." Leah said.

"You really care for that tall one, Raabel?" Nikk asked. He was curious because it wasn't like Leah to form attachments for long.

"Yes... I mean, not like that. I do care, about all of them," she said, her gaze wandering.

"What's this about?" Nikk asked.

"I just want to do something," she said, her voice more resolute.

"Look," Nikk said, "we did our best. That's all that Commander Stone ever asked of us. He knew what he was doing when he ordered us down first. He knew it would be risky to stay longer, but he did it so that we could walk out of there. So *you* could walk out of there.

"Raabel and the Templars knew the same. They knew there would be risks, but they took them, so we all would have a chance to survive. The only other option was that none of us would," Nikk said. "I know you want to go find them and help them, but the truth is, we can't. We just can't."

Nikk watched his words sink in, hoping Leah would let go of any thoughts of fanciful heroics. After a long pause, she drifted away, moving to another spot to rest before her watch shift began.

He shrugged to himself and stared off into the woods, thankful not to hear the howls of nearby wolves for once.

***

"There's a light on in the tower," Leah reported with excitement.

"It would make sense," Nikk replied. "We actually had a farther distance to travel." They had actually made good time, but provisions and tempers were running thin. Even so, he had ordered the rest of the group to hold back: a mistake here could cost them everything.

Nikk and Leah watched the tower from the woods, cautiously inspecting it from a distance. The light inside the rundown building flickered and steady wisps of smoke rose from the roof. But they had still not seen any people, and with everything that had happened of late and with his new responsibility, he was being extra careful.

"Go with Ela and Varr. Take a peak," Nikk told her. With a wide grin she started to move, but he put out a hand to restrain her.

Leah met his gaze and acknowledged his concern, her face going blank the way it did when she was ready to work. She motioned to Ela and Varr. The three of them spread out and moved towards the tower from different angles, sticking to scrub for cover whenever possible.

Nikk tried to keep track of them, but lost Leah about halfway there. Varr was a bit more obvious, though, and he was able to track him almost up to the tower, until he ducked behind a low, crumbling wall that may have been a more legitimate defense many years ago.

Nikk counted upwards in his head, unclear what number he would need to reach to convince him to charge in after them. His counting was interrupted as he heard voices rise up in joy and the clear peal of Leah's whistle across the intervening space. With a lighter heart, Nikk signaled the rest of them to move forward.

As he approached, he could tell things were not as well as they hoped. Leah was off to the side, by herself, most likely trying to keep others from seeing her cry. Temos was at the door, waving them forward, a stained bandage across his forehead. Inside the tower, Nikk saw Casselle rising up from someone's prostrate form, but from this angle, he couldn't tell who. He assumed by Leah's tears that it wasn't good.

"Thank goodness! An actual roof!" Hedrick shoved his way past the Outriders, making his way to the relative comfort of the interior of the tiny tower. The stewards followed and Vincen and his Templar cohorts were not far behind. Nikk was fine with leaving him to the building. Over the past few days, he'd been wishing for some sort of barrier to block him from the whole von Darren family experience.

Casselle and Temos left the suddenly crowded interior to come outside. Casselle was glad to see Nikk, who was talking quietly with the remaining Outriders he'd brought with him. They glanced inside, but apparently decided against joining the von Darren entourage.

"Commander Stone? Shayn Fletcher? Captain Crennel?" Casselle asked.

"Shayn and Royan are gone. Dead, we assume," Nikk answered solemnly. "Crennel actually escaped with us, but when we were regrouping after crossing the lake, we found that he'd run off. I made the call not to look for him."

Casselle nodded in agreement. Beyond her he was able to see that it was Jaksen laying on the ground, his face pale and his body swaddled in blankets

"I don't see..." Nikk began.

"The Wolfmother was outside," Temos answered. "She wasn't alone either." The Templar gave a sidelong look at Leah, still off to one side by herself. He lowered his voice slightly.

"Raabel died protecting me," he said solemnly, "and Captain Taumber ... he might have made it, but he gave his life to save Jaksen's."

"I'm so sorry," Nikk said. He wanted there to be silence... some measure of reverence. He was tempted to yell inside the tower at Hedrick von Darren for chattering on about his minor inconveniences when clearly there were more important things that had been lost. Instead he bit his tongue.

"To you and yours as well," Temos replied sincerely. Nikk fumbled in his vest for a moment before retrieving a small metal flask.

"A proper drink is in order for later, but for now..." He unscrewed the cap and took a swig before handing it over to Temos.

Quietly, the Templar accepted the flask and took a swig of his own, wiping the lip with his tunic sleeve before offering it to Casselle. Nikk watched her consider the offer before finally taking the flask and taking a quick slug herself. She coughed and handed it back to him.

The temporary Commander of the Outriders took a final sip himself and tucked it back into his vest.

"We can leave at first light tomorrow. Best to make for the Bay as quickly as possible," he said. Both the Templars nodded in agreement. "If you two can supplement the watch schedule, I won't have to rely on Vincen's folks. They did more complaining than watching anyway."

"Absolutely," Temos said. "We just need to keep an eye on Jaksen. He seems stable now, but tired."

"I'll have my folks help out."

"Thank you," Casselle said. Nikk nodded and moved to each of his Outriders in turn, handing out assignments until he got to Aleah Blue.

"Just tell me when," she said, refusing to turn and look at him.

"Whenever you're ready," he said. He turned to walk away, but he reconsidered, retrieving his flask once again and offering it to her.

She took it from him gingerly and gave it a quick shake.

"There's not enough in here," she said.

"No, there's not," he said. "But it's all yours." He saw her nod, though she still would not turn to face him. He considered saying something more, but he hesitated and then felt like the right moment had passed him altogether.

He moved to join Blane on the roof of the tower, giving them a better view of the surrounding area.

As he approached, he saw Temos inside, weathering the company of the van Darren's to check on Jaksen. Casselle brushed by him, moving over to where Leah had secluded herself. He hoped the two women might be able to offer some solace to each other.

***

"He wanted me to tell you..." Leah heard someone say.

Surprised that the voice wasn't Nikk's, she glanced over her shoulder and saw it was Casselle looking quite pained. She was standing just a few feet away, her armorjack still stained with blood, her face dirty and unwashed. Like the rest of them, she looked exhausted from the hasty retreat from Flinderlaas. Leah pulled the flask from her lips and used the heel of her hand to clear the tears from her cheeks.

"...He asked me to tell his father what he had done, to tell him that he had died bravely," Casselle said. Leah was shocked. This was probably the most she'd heard from her since they'd met. Even after the evening when they shared a watch on the wall, it was certainly the only time she'd honestly opened up about anything.

"He also wanted me to tell you that he was sorry," Casselle added. It was obvious that her throat was tight. This wasn't easy for her, something Leah understood more than she wanted to admit.

"Sorry for what?" Leah asked.

"I don't know. He died after he said that," answered the Templar. "I don't know if he meant to say more or not."

"Oh," Leah said, "I see." Casselle was looking off in the distance, across the grassy fields on the edge of the Deckoran Wilds, to the starry horizon and perhaps beyond. Leah put the cap back on Nikk's flask before putting it inside her shirt. She stared off with Casselle, listening to an occasional gust of wind rustle the weeds around them and whisper in the untamed shrubs and thin limbs of scrub trees.

The sounds of night were joined by the voices of those in the tower, a smattering of laughter and light conversation, the sound of people no longer in fear for their life, eager to put these experiences behind them.

"Thank you," Leah said, continuing to look out towards the horizon.

"You're welcome," Casselle said, her voice heavy with grief.

They shared that moment in each other's company just a bit longer before Casselle turned and walked away, leaving Leah alone once again.

***

"Can I ask what happened?" asked Nikk.

"Sure," Temos replied. It was the next evening and the Templar was clearly pleased that von Darren's stewards had taken over cooking responsibilities for the survivors. The result had been filling, which was pretty much the only quality most soldiers looked for in a meal. The fact that it had been quite tasty was an added bonus they both appreciated. "I'm afraid I can't tell you the whole story, though."

"Why's that?"

"I was out for most of it, I'm afraid to say," said Temos, tapping the bandage on his head. "I'm lucky to still have this intact."

"But you got the doors sealed," Nikk said, scraping the last bit of the stew out of his bowl.

"We got down the walls with far less trouble than I expected. Then we got the doors sealed, just like we had planned," Temos explained. "After that she showed up."

"The Wolfmother," Nikk confirmed.

"Aye," Temos confirmed, "It was her. Naked but for a smile and flanked by two..."

"Wolves?" Nikk asked, curious why Temos had paused.

"By the look of them, sure, but big, and by that I mean tall, because they loped along like they should be walking on two legs, but were all hunched over. More like wolf-men? I suppose that's a more accurate description."

"Wolf-men?"

"Unless you want to think of a better name. They were ugly... strong, too," Temos added, "really strong. Raabel and I attacked one of them while Cass and Jaksen tackled the other. Though I should say we tackled ours, because that's just what Raabel did. He tackled the thing after it tried to charge me. I went in to see if I could finish it off, but it caught me across the head, almost knocked it clean off. Things went blurry and I hit the ground.

"I heard a bunch of things, but I can't say that they make any sense to me, it was all just loud noises and screams at that point," Temos continued. "When I finally could understand what was going on around me, Raabel was dead. Jaksen looked dead, but I found out he was just passed out from Odegar sealing his wounds up. Casselle was next to the Captain, listening to something he had to say before he stopped talking altogether."

"And the Wolfmother?" Nikk asked.

"Gone. Just gone," Temos said. "Like one of the stories about monsters you heard as a child. But they were real... the bodies were real enough."

"And you didn't ask her..?" Nikk tilted his head towards Casselle, who was standing off on her own now, lost in thought.

"No," Temos replied, his head dropping slightly, his tone more somber. "I didn't ask her because I felt like she'd tell me when she was ready. If she's ever ready to tell me, that is.

"The only other bit I got was from Jaksen, but he's half fevered and lost a lot of blood," the Templar added. "He told me that the Captain had saved his life, had closed up his severed arm, to keep him from bleeding out altogether. But he heard some of what Odegar told Casselle. He said 'Death led her away.' By her, I assume Odegar meant the Wolfmother. But Death... well, I don't know what to assume about that."

"At least you know something," Nikk said. "We just have to assume the worst about Commander Stone and Shayn."

"Wilkers told me they just didn't make it down," Temos said. "Do you think they cut the rope themselves?"

"Dunno why they would. Wolves can't climb ropes, up or down."

"Oh yeah," Temos said, "I guess they can't."

"Well, we should reach the Bay soon," Nikk said. "Hopefully this whole thing will be behind us."

"But will it?" Temos asked. "I mean, we didn't stop her. It's not like there are a shortage of wolves out there in the Wilds. What if more of those wolf-men show up? And, by all the High Houses, what if she's not the last one? What if one of those others shows up? The ones we saw on the scroll?"

Temos fumbled for a small book from the inside of his armorjack. After flipping open a couple of pages, he showed Nikk one of the sketches he'd been working on.

"So this is the Wolfmother, but what if one of these comes trotting up to the gates of Strossen? Like this fellow," Temos said, pointing at a picture of a black cloaked man with a raven's head. "Do we have to fight an army of angry birds, too? Who knows what these others do."

"This was from under the hill?" Nikk asked, taking the book offered to him and flipping through the pictures.

"Yeah. Before it went up in flames, this is what we saw, at least as best I remember it," Temos answered.

"You think all of these are still out there somewhere?" Nikk studied the pictures, not quite sure what to make of what he saw.

"Who knows? Until the other day, I thought most of this was the concoction of a half mad old Templar. I don't know if I'm a good judge of such things."

"Does that mean this is real, too?" Nikk asked, holding open a couple of pages in the journal. Temos' face blanched when he saw the gaping black maw.

"I always thought it was a story... you know, like a metaphor or something. Tarsus was all things good and virtuous while the dragon was all things bad and the story was just about morality and ethics, the eternal struggle between good and evil and all that. I never really considered it might still actually be real, much less alive. I mean... how old would it be?"

"Do you need a drink?" Nikk asked, handing Temos his journal back and fishing for something out of his own pockets. He produced a second small metal flask, the one he normally didn't share with others. Given the circumstances, he was just glad he was alive and able to make the offer.

"To be honest, I'm not much of a drinking man," Temos answered, "but right now I might be able to put a pub out of service."

Nikk grinned before taking a long pull, then passed the flask over to Temos.

The two of them drank as the long evening came to a close.

***

Casselle hadn't shown anyone the mark on her shoulder. It had been easy to hide under her armorjack. She wasn't sure who to talk to now that Odegar was dead, and although she felt bad withholding the truth from Jaksen and Temos, she wasn't even sure what the truth was at the moment.

They would be at the Bay soon enough and into Gundlaan after that. She would certainly have to talk to the Elder Circle in Strossen, but if she couldn't collect her thoughts to speak to her own squadmates, how in the world was she going to talk to them? They would ask about the deaths of Odegar and Raabel, the loss of Captain Crennel and the destruction of Flinderlaas. What was she going to tell them?

"You tell them the truth," she whispered to herself, knowing that the truth was...

The thought stalled, tripped up before she could even complete it. What was the truth? She admitted to herself that she wasn't sure anymore.

She worked her hand inside her armorjack, under the padded shirt to touch the mark. It was still cool under her fingertips, a chilling reminder of where that thing had touched her. At first she thought it to be some sort of bruise, but it hadn't gone away, and last night, she swore there were white spots, like flickering lights, just below the skin. She wondered if it was some sort of infection; was this how it had begun with Renholf Crennel?

She stared over her shoulder at the campfire, watching the survivors keep company with each other. But instead of longing for their companionship, she only saw the fire, thinking of the city left in flames behind them.

Casselle turned away from the light. It was already far too easy to remember sights and sounds from that day.

The second wolf-man had torn out part of Raabel's shoulder. He was bleeding uncontrollably as Casselle ran her sword through the thing's side, through its heart. When it fell, it took Raabel to the ground with it. She was on her knees in an instant, trying to pry them apart.

By the time she was able to muscle the bulk of the wolf-man off of him, she thought it was too late. His face was ashen and his body still. She was reaching out to brush his eyes closed when he suddenly grabbed at her arm, using the last of his strength to speak to her; a few desperate words that would have to provide a lifetime of consolation to his family and to Aileah Blue. Casselle wanted to tell him to save his strength, but he was already gone.

She had to keep moving. Temos was alive as far as she could tell, but Jaksen and Odegar were in bad shape, and the Wolfmother was closing on them.

If Captain Taumber could not stand against her with his years of experience, backed by all of his Vanha strength and stamina, she knew she had little chance. But it was not in her character to stand to the side while her friends died. Summoning her courage, she yelled at the Wolfmother, some sort of wordless, visceral challenge. The creature did not acknowledge Casselle at all, like she was not even there. The Templar let her rage drive her actions and ran between her friends and the Wolfmother, arms outstretched.

"No!" Casselle screamed. Suddenly confronted, the woman's face twisted in a confused expression.

The Wolfmother made her own quick assessment of the battlefield, and noticed that the second wolf-man now lay dead beside Raabel's corpse. When she looked back at Casselle, her face was full of rage, her lips drawn into a hateful scowl.

"You cannot have them," Casselle yelled. "I will not let you!"

The Wolfmother tensed, preparing to rush forward. At that moment, Casselle thought she heard Odegar muttering something that sounded like a prayer. She didn't believe in prayer - the Gods were dead - but she was willing to take any help she could get.

She held her sword out before her, gripping it with both hands, preparing herself for the worst.

An attack never came. The tension left the Wolfmother's body and she suddenly straightened. She was no longer looking at Casselle, but past her.

The Templar felt something on her arm, a light touch, as if someone were bidding her to stay her hand. Her instincts told her it was Odegar. Her heart assured her it was Odegar. Who else could it have been?

An instant later, her arm ached fiercely, as if it had been kissed by a hot iron. As she recoiled in pain from the touch, a figure stepped out from behind her.

It was not Odegar. It was taller than her Captain and draped in layered black robes with torn and frayed edges. A hood was drawn low over its head, and a tattered scarf was wrapped around its nose and mouth. The fingers that withdrew slowly from her arm were thin and pale, almost skeletal, and certainly stronger than they looked.

"How did I not know?" came a voice from inside the hood. The words sounded like they were scraped off of wet stone. "How did I not know you had returned?"

Casselle stepped back. She could not see the face of the hooded figure, but the Wolfmother's anger had faded altogether. In its place, her expression was full of joy, her face streaked with tears. The Templar watched the two close on one another, arms outstretched, as if they would embrace.

Why had she turned away at that point? She couldn't remember, and that was bothersome. All she remembered was moving to Odegar's side.

"Move me closer to Jaksen," he instructed her. She helped him up, supporting him on the side of his broken leg. It seemed to take forever to reach their fallen friend, who was already unconscious from loss of blood.

"Quickly," Odegar said, "set me beside him."

She moved Odegar into a position to help, where he could lay his good hand on the ruins of Jaksen's mauled arm. She remembered hearing Odegar speak, his words measured and foreign. His skin grew warm underneath her hands as she held him in place.

She watched as Jaksen's flesh sealed, closing up neatly on its own, leaving a stump where his arm should be, but a stump that was no longer leaking blood. It was a clean seal that seemed to be at no risk for rot or infection. Jaksen was pale and unconscious, but his breathing steadied. He was still alive.

Casselle remembered saying something aloud about finding a way to make a litter for each of them.

"It's too late for me," Odegar confessed. "I'm overextended. I was never disciplined enough to be an Arxhemist." His breath was hot and he was sweating.

"I'm proud of you, Casselle Milner," he said, his face calm and relaxed. "We have done good work. But now Veheg is here to take me someplace you cannot follow."

Casselle looked back to where the cloaked figure had met the Wolfmother. Is that who he meant? Even if he did, wherever they had gone, they were no longer in sight.

"They're gone," she told Odegar.

"It doesn't matter," he replied with a weak smile. "This isn't over, and you will need to be ready for what comes next. The Templars must be ready. Train hard. Prepare..."

Odegar was burning up with fever. Sweat beaded on his face. His breath was incredibly hot. She almost thought she smelled smoke when he spoke, but with Flinderlaas burning a short distance away, everything smelled like smoke.

"We will," Casselle assured him. "I'll make certain of it."

"One last thing," Odegar said with a forced smile, "When you return, visit my sister and tell her of this. Tell her I thought of her at this time. Tell... her.... there are... flowers... here... beautiful... fl-" He convulsed slightly, as if he was trying to cough, but didn't have the strength.

"I will," Casselle said quickly, hoping he could still hear her. "I will tell her!" Odegar's good hand gripped her arm tightly.

His body convulsed again, and his face was pained, but only for a moment. A small wisp of azure flame escaped from his open mouth and dissipated into the air. His eyes grew distant, his chest stilled and his body went limp.

There, in the shadow of the burning keep, there had been no time to mourn. But here, away from the tower, removed from the Outriders, the remains of her squad, and the survivors of Flinderlaas, Casselle finally allowed herself to cry.

Her mother had died when she was young and Casselle had sobbed for days. She couldn't understand why her mother could not come home anymore. Her hand strayed to the ring hanging around her neck. But this was different. The process of death was not a mystery to her anymore. This was just release, as if her eyes could not hold in the painful images anymore, so they tried to wash them away.

When Odegar passed, she had done what was needed to get Temos and Jaksen to safety. Her mind had been focused on leading them away. There had been neither time for grief nor even time to dig so much as a shallow grave for Raabel and Odegar. It was all she could do to get Temos to help her move Jaksen into the woods and away from the town.

The three of them had survived, though not without scars, and it was clear none of them would ever be the same. At least for now she was in good company, and safe for the time being.

The tears ran freely, though she did not sob. There was a lump in her throat, but she did not wail. There was no pain in this, merely emptiness, like a part of her that had been hollowed out.

She cried until her tears were exhausted. Then she tucked the ring back under her shirt and watched the stars glint in the night sky above them.

The way they twinkled reminded her of the flicker under her skin, and she found herself absently rubbing the mark on her shoulder, hoping to warm the spot with her fingertips. Her thoughts strayed to Odegar's final remarks, about being prepared for what was to come next. There was more going on than the troubles of this small group.

Something was changing in the world, something that would not stay isolated on the far side of the Deckoran Wilds.

"Prepare," Odegar had told her.

Behind her, the camp had settled down for the evening. Soon Temos would come by to check on her and tell her to get some rest.

The tears were well and gone by now. She used her thumb to brush away any lingering evidence. The time for mourning had passed. There was work to be done.

They had to be prepared for what was to come next. Shouldering the legacy of those who had passed, the burden of the dead must now be borne by those who remained.

- 26 -

We Who Remain

"We Who Remain have come to bear witness to the Release of Captain Mordan Scow," Triistan began, his voice hoarse with grief.

In one hand he held a scrap of paper he had written notes on, which crackled and snapped as if trying to wriggle out of his grasp. It was only an hour past dawn, and with the rising of Ruine's twin suns, the wind had returned with renewed vigor. It pulled at his hair as well, sending it streaming out behind him in a banner of red and gold.

Scow's body lay on a crude dais they had cobbled together by shoving three of the food crates into a line and covering them with a sheet of canvas soaked in sea-water. Unlike actual flames, Veheg's Fire only consumed its host, but they were all sailors, and no matter how many times they had seen the Ceremony, fire was still fire and they would take no chances.

"Formerly the Master Carpenter of the *SKS Peregrine*," Triistan continued, "Class One Blue-water Surveyor and the pride of the Second Fleet, and First Mate of this vessel..."

He paused and drew a deep breath, steadying himself.

"More than anything else - her captain, her crew, her record of discovery - The *Peregrine* was what she was because of Mister Scow. He was not her commander, but he was her keel: solid, deep and true... the essence of what the Seeker Corps imagines itself to be, and the finest person I've ever known."

"We who remain..." The traditional opening words of the Releasing Ceremony had rarely been more meaningful. Dreysha stole a glance at her fellow survivors: Mung stood immediately to her left, with Snitch perched on his left shoulder.

Rantham was to Mung's left, propped up in a sitting position between the two remaining water barrels, his uncanny luck finally having deserted him. *So much for your namesake, Rogue.* Though Rantham grew stronger each day, he still could not move anything below his waist. She considered that to be the worst kind of luck. *Biiko should have let you die*, she thought.

The Unbound stood a little behind and to Triistan's right side, one hand on the helm. Lankham Voth completed the crude circle to Triistan's left, still hobbled to the base of the mainmast.

She did her best to stifle a yawn, thankful that Triis wasn't looking at her just then. She hadn't been sleeping well to begin with, but she was completely exhausted from helping him prepare Scow's body over the past two days. After their conversation about gods and gods-knew-what-else the night before, she had slept fitfully for what little was left of it, haunted by unsettling dreams she was grateful she could not recall when she awoke this morning.

"We found broken chains," Triis had said, and when she pressed him, he had finally drawn forth his journal and showed her the drawing he had labeled "The Hold". She had seen it before, of course, as it was one of the first pages she had examined after pilfering the book what seemed like years ago.

She could feel one hard corner of it now, digging into her belly where she had shoved it inside her sash as they gathered for Scow's Releasing Ceremony. Though he had refused to let her keep it last night, this morning, just after waking, Triistan had simply walked up and handed it to her.

"Why the sudden change of heart?" she had asked. He shrugged and seemed to be searching for his answer.

"I don't know. Maybe I just thought you should see it before everyone else... or maybe it's to make sure I go through with this - telling everybody, I mean."

Whatever Triistan's reason, it was strange to have it again, and this time with his full knowledge. She was eager to steal away on her own and read it.

"Mister Scow taught me everything he could about seamanship: navigation, carpentry, knots... anything and everything he could think of, whenever he had the opportunity and thought I was listening. It didn't take me long to learn not to let him know when I wasn't." They all chuckled quietly.

"But he was more than a Master Carpenter to his charges, and more than a mentor to me. He was - he was like a father to me..." He looked down for a moment, clearing his throat. She could see his lips quivering as he gazed at Scow's body, fighting to keep his composure. Finally, he took another deep breath, lifted his gaze, and looked at each of them in turn.

"Besides the skills and knowledge to be a better seaman, Mordan Scow also taught me how to be a better man. He showed me every single day in the way that he lived. He taught me about kindness and compassion... strength and perserverence... honesty and loyalty. He taught me how to admit when I was wrong - which was often - and how to act when I was right."

"And he taught me about honor and humility. He was tough, demanding, but always fair and always truthful - sometimes, brutally so." Dreysha couldn't help but smile; Scow's temper and the vocabulary that came along with it were legendary, though she had never seen him lose it without good reason.

"He once told me, not so long ago, that honor without sacrifice is merely self-righteousness..."

His grief was palpable, but as he spoke, Dreysha gradually realized that something had changed in him. At first, she couldn't put her finger on it. Beneath his raw emotions, she glimpsed a new strength and solidity that he had not shown outwardly before. She knew him well enough to know it had always been there, but he typically kept it hidden, carefully locked away inside.

She studied him more closely. The hollows beneath his cheek bones and his eyes were still there, like everyone else, and his lanky frame was leaner than ever - she could clearly see his collar bone, and the largest part of his arm was his elbow joint. Still, he seemed taller somehow, larger. Then she noticed his familiar boyish slouch was gone; replaced by square shoulders, a straight back, and feet planted firmly on the deck. He stood the way the Mattock and many other officers stood: with confidence and authority.

Best way to find out if a man can swim is to throw him in the sea, she thought. It was an old Seeker proverb - one of Scow's favorites, actually. Clearly, Triistan was finding out that he could swim just fine. In fact, the more he spoke of Scow, the more he revealed about himself.

Command suits him, she thought. *The strengths and qualities he lauds the Master Carpenter for are the same ones we all see and respect in him.* Apart from Voth, anyway. The ex-purser's long, thin face was stretched even further by a scowl of bitter disdain. In Triistan's first official duties, he was already twice the captain Voth would ever be, and Lanky knew it.

She fidgeted with the journal, trying to move it into a more comfortable position. After Triis had handed it to her and walked away, she had not had any time to read it before the Ceremony started, so she was anxious to find a corner out of the way and delve into it. Having it in her possession, without being able to look at it just now, was maddening. She tried to distract herself by picturing Marquesso's reaction when she returned with it.

d'Yano will shit himself when he sees what I brought him, she thought. From even what little she had seen and heard from Triistan last night, Marquesso d'Yano was going to get far more than he had bargained for when he had made arrangements for her to join the *Peregrine's* crew. Of course she had no way of knowing exactly what he had been expecting them to find, but she was reasonably confident that the discovery of a new continent, and thus the chance to enter the race to exploit it, was probably at the top of his list. She still hadn't learned what the terrible 'secret' was that Triistan kept hinting at - he was surprisingly mum on that point last night, saying only that she would learn it when he addressed the rest of the crew - but ancient artifacts and archeological sites like the ones she had glimpsed would only add to the value. Whatever Triis was worried about, she was sure d'Yano and his supporters could handle it, and make her a very rich woman in the process. Perhaps rich enough to disappear to some hidden bay along the Minethian Coast. She could take Triistan with her - if she could convince him to forgive her for -

Her thoughts were interrupted when Triistan suddenly snapped his boots together in rigid attention and called out, his voice ringing crisply in the morning air.

"Wiliamund Azimuth, Echoman!"

"Um... aye, Sir?" came Mung's reply.

"Biiko, Special Ambassador and Master-at-Arms!"

"Aye, Sir," Biiko answered. The Unbound's verbal response spoke volumes about the respect Scow commanded.

"Dreysha, First Mate." She caught the slightest stammer when he said her name. *Still such a boy in some ways*, she thought, suppressing a smile.

"Aye, Sir!" she replied.

"Rantham d'yBassi, Able Seeker, Midshipman Second Class!"

"Aye, Sir." Rantham's voice was thready, but clear.

"Lankham Voth, prisoner!"

Voth jerked up his balding, age-spotted head and sneered at Triistan. "I won't be party to these theatrics,'" he spat, quite literally. "You're all guilty of sedition and mutiny and -"

Dreysha gave him a sharp kick in the back of the leg, dropping him to his knees. "He says he's present, sir."

Triistan nodded and paused, chewing on his lower lip.

"Mor-" his voice broke and he had to clear his throat to try again, forcing the words out through clenched teeth.

"Mordan Scow..."

The launch creaked quietly and the sails rustled, but The Mattock did not respond.

"Captain Mordan Scow!" he repeated in a stronger voice, but still no one answered. There was only the sound of wind and water. The moment stretched out, and Dreysha found herself holding her breath, wishing that Scow would respond, however irrational that seemed.

Triistan called out one last time. "*Captain Mordan Scow, SKS Peregrine, report!*" There were tears in his eyes as he struggled to maintain his composure.

But the only reply was the creak of timber, the whisper of the wind, and the endless song of the sea.

Several painful moments later, Dreysha tried to answer, according to the Ceremony. For just an instant, her throat constricted and she had to swallow hard to get the words out.

"The Sea answers for him, Sir."

Those who remained repeated the same phrase: "The Sea answers for him."

Dreysha's eyes stung and she was surprised at the strength and suddenness of her grief. *Damn you, Scow,* she thought.

Triistan held his arm out over the Mattock's body. In his other hand he held his dakra, its curved blade flashing in the early morning sun. He drew the dagger across his left forearm, a line of blood following in its wake. Tears flowed freely down his cheeks as he spoke the final words of the Ceremony:

"And so do we Seekers release his ashes to the wind, that he may sail on, or return to the waiting Sea." Triistan clenched his fist and bent his arm at the elbow, sending fat red drops spattering down onto the tattooed glyphs on Scow's forehead.

With a sudden *whump*, blue flames ignited, writhing across the glyphs on Scow's exposed skin like spectral dancers. In seconds, his body was completely engulfed, the fire swirling, stretching upwards, reaching for the matching cobalt sky above. There was no heat to Veheg's Fire, but there was sound; a low, hissing roar like a strong downpour, or a gale wind moving through the trees. It was mercifully free of the crackle and pop of normal fire, though it consumed its host just as voraciously. It was not long before the Mattock's bones were visible, glowing a blue so brilliant it was nearly white. The light was so intense that most of the onlookers had to shield their eyes, but she could not look away. An instant later, something happened she had never seen before, despite having witnessed well over a hundred Releasing Ceremonies.

The flames suddenly vanished, as if they'd been drawn back into his remains, leaving only the hotly-glowing bones for one heartbeat... two... three... and then with a final, brilliant flash, they burst into blue fire again. There was a sharp crack like thunder and a rush of air, and Scow's bones disappeared, consumed in a swirling pillar of cerulean flame and ash. The flames went out, and the wind carried the ash into the sky, where it flirted briefly with the top-gallant as though it were making one last adjustment to the launch's trim.

And then her eyes betrayed her, the world blurred, and Mordan Scow was gone.

***

When they had finished cleaning up after the Ceremony, Triistan addressed them.

"There are... things we need to discuss. Things that I need to share with you that... that I should have shared a long time ago. But I'm not ready yet - I need more time to gather my thoughts." He drew a deep breath and squared his shoulders.

"In the meantime, Wil, take the helm so that Biiko can change the dressing on Rantham's wound. Maintain our current heading, and when Biiko's done, let's trim her up to get as much out of this wind as we can."

"Aye, sir," Mung answered crisply.

"Dreysha, get up in The Nest. From now on I want eyes topside on all watches, or as close to that schedule as we can come."

"Expecting company?"

"Aye, maybe."

That caught her attention. "Oh? Mind telling us who, Captain?"

He gave her a strange smile and said, "No one in particular, but a friend once told me we should fend for ourselves, and stop waiting around for someone to do it for us."

With that, Triistan left them and went to stand by himself at the prow, staring out at the sea. Mung took the helm, and Biiko went to fetch his field kit. Voth sat in his customary spot, back resting against the mast, boney arms resting on his boney knees, and Rantham sat quietly, propped up against the scuttles while he waited for Biiko to change his dressing.

Finally, Dreysha thought.

She pulled herself up one of the ratlines, heading aloft. She was grateful for her orders. She needed to be alone, and the crow's nest would offer the closest thing to privacy that the launch could offer. The intensity of her emotions during Scow's funeral had caught her off guard - she was not used to... whatever that feeling was. And the way the Mattock's Fire had behaved at the end, she wanted to talk with Triistan about it to see what he thought, whether he had ever seen anything like it. That would probably have to wait, though, as she sensed he was in no mood for conversation right now. She knew the rest of the crew probably took it for some kind of *sign*, and she grunted dismissively as she pulled herself through the trap door in the bottom of the crow's nest.

Sailors, by nature, were a superstitious lot. They saw signs in the simplest of coincidences, and most had a personal arsenal of wards and charms to help influence the outcome of events in their favor. Dreysha had always taken a cruel pleasure in mocking them - she had less use for signs than she did for long-dead gods, which was to say little to none. She kept her focus on things she could control. She had learned that there was quite a bit about her life she could influence through her own actions, without relying on a lucky lock of hair or spitting in the proper direction at precisely the right moment. *Signs* - and for that matter, gods - were for the weak-minded.

Or so she had always thought.

She settled into The Nest and brought out Triistan's journal, but held it closed on her lap for several moments, staring at the cover. The leather was cracked, the edges worn rough, the color a sickly mottled green and grey, like a Rotter's face. Now that she had it in her grasp again, she was suddenly reluctant to open it. Instead of the rush of excitement she felt when she "borrowed" it the previous times, she now felt a strange sense of unease. She tried telling herself that it was just a simple letdown, that without the thrill of having lifted it, it had lost some of its mysterious allure. But the feeling persisted, like a dark line of clouds appearing on the horizon.

Steeling herself without understanding why, she flipped the journal open and began searching for the passages she had read before. She planned to skim through those to refresh her memory and help establish the Expedition's timeline. She did not know how much time she had before Triistan planned to begin telling them his tale, nor did she know how long he intended to let her keep the journal, so she wanted to pull as much information out of it as she could, while she could. She used his elaborate sketches as a crude guide, thumbing through several pages at a time before focusing more intently on any particular passage that might interest her. She was looking for significant events - landmarks in the journey - to help her plot the whole expedition out.

She found his entry on the thirty-fifth day of Tendres, which he had labeled "LANDFALL!". Scanning it quickly, she smiled at the youthful enthusiasm and pride he had displayed at having been selected to join the climbing team and be one of the first to set foot on Aarden. Off in the margin was his contrasting note, referring to the "real Darkness" they had discovered later in the expedition.

"Fuck this superstitious nonsense," she grumbled and rifled through the pages until she found the drawing he had shown her last night.

Triistan's skill was impressive. Some of his illustrations were so detailed, it felt like she was looking directly at his memories, or looking back through time, seeing the events or scenery through his eyes. It lent an intimacy to the experience that she found both mesmerizing and unsettling at the same time.

She ran her fingers lightly over his picture of The Hold, taking care not to smudge his work as she studied the strange architecture of the surrounding ruins. She looked more closely at the statues ringing the courtyard with the shiny black floor and counted seven of them before inhaling sharply. Dreysha had never been a student of religion, but she had enough worldly experience to recognize the dress and features of the towering figures depicted here: they were unmistakably Arys, the Young Gods.

She did not recognize all of them, but Thunor's great wings and curved tulwar were familiar to most. She also knew Shan - called 'Stormfather' by Triistan's Islanders - by his twin daggers and thick mane of hair. His image, in one form or another, was tattooed somewhere on the flesh of most sailors. She also recognized Derant, the Builder. But she could not name the other four. Based on the status of the three she did know, she supposed them to be the other leaders of the High Houses. A tiny shiver slid down her spine.

She turned to the previous page and began reading the entry there.

Twenty and Three, Vehnya, 256, 23rd Day of the Expedition, 46th Since Landfall

[There were a few sentence fragments that had been crossed out to begin this passage.]

It is difficult to comprehend what we have been through, let alone capture it in words. After several failed attempts, I have decided instead to use the next two pages following this one to record Aarden's greatest - and darkest - secret, while it is still fresh in my mind. Perhaps after illustrating it, I shall find the words I need to describe not just this incredible discovery, but all that we have gone through - and lost - to get here.

Since I have space on this page, I suppose I should begin by describing our approach and first glimpse of what Danor calls "Exile's Tears" - a name that will foreshadow this place's significance to those who know their history.

Dreysha frowned. She did not recognize the name "Danor". Was Triistan referring to some obscure historical scribe? She made a mental note to ask him and returned to the passage.

We climbed from the ravine out into a valley dominated by a narrow, winding lake, which ran away from us until it disappeared in the foothills of a tall, sharp range of mountains that march off to our south and west. We are trying to decide what to name them, having pared our list of suggestions down to two: "The Stonefangs" and "Aarden's Teeth", by which you can discern their menacing appearance. Danor's people have apparently named the range -

"Danor's *people*"? That did not sound like a reference to a historian. That sounded like someone they had met, who might even be traveling with them. But if so, then why hadn't any of the Expedition's survivors ever mentioned discovering other people on Aarden? *That's what you get for skipping around, Drey*, she told herself. After finishing this passage, she would have to backtrack and find out who in the Dark this Danor was.

Danor's people have apparently named the range, "Te'Sanginele", which The Whip tells me is "Ice-that-cuts-the-eyes" in their language. Indeed, they are blindingly bright and difficult to look at it in the full light of day.

Aarden is not only a land of secrets, but a land of strange places and breath-taking views as well. The valley was no different. While we were below the snowline, it was still much cooler than while traveling up the Glowater, and on one morning the tips of the grass were white with frost when we awoke...

Dreysha forced herself to stop reading line for line. She needed to skim the journal systematically, objectively, to gather as much information as she could before she had to return it. But she had not expected her work to be so difficult; she actually found some of Triistan's written descriptions more captivating than his illustrations. There was something about hearing his voice in her mind, the direct exposure to his thoughts and how he viewed the world, that drew her closer to him... closer than she wanted to be.

So she placed her index finger on the page and began reading through the rest of this particular passage as quickly as she could. There were definitely other names mentioned she didn't recognize, so she was going to have to backtrack and read it more thoroughly when she had more time. She flipped to the pages immediately following his drawing of "The Hold". Although by now she had a pretty good idea of what they thought it was intended for, she needed to read the words; to hear the thoughts of a mind she had great respect for, hoping it would help her come to terms with a fundamental shift in everything she thought she had ever known. Triistan may have learned the trick from Scow, but Tresha l'Sonjaro could not easily admit when she was wrong.

For the rest of the afternoon, she poured through the journal's contents. Resisting the pull of Triistan's prose was no longer an issue; she could not read fast enough to stay ahead of the questions each new page and illustration raised. Just after the second sun had set behind a low, thick bank of clouds, turning them the color of a bloody bruise, Rantham gave a shout of surprise from where he was lying in his makeshift bed.

"Did anyone feel that?!"

Dreysha jerked her head up; she had become so engrossed in the journal she was surprised to find it was dusk.

"What?" she heard Triistan's voice from below.

"Something struck the sodding boat! Didn't anybody feel it??"

The journal lay in her lap, so she gathered it up carefully and tucked it into her sash, then leaned over the edge of the Nest to get a look at Rantham. She could see him lying directly below her. Triistan sat nearby, and Mung looked to be pissing over the side of the boat. Well, he was pissing *onto* the side of the boat now, as he backed away from the edge. She looked down at Rantham again. His eyes were wide with fear and he was trying to prop himself up using only his arms, looking around wildly. Had he finally lost it? She was surprised he had held on as long as he had, actually. Unless...

She looked out at the infinite water around them. It was the color of red wine - the color of blood. A cold fist clenched in her gut. *Shit, not again.*

Biiko made his way over and crouched beside Rantham, laying the back of his hand on the man's cheeks and forehead. He shook his head, then hefted his harpoon and went to the side of the launch, peering cautiously over the taffrail at the dark water. Triistan did the same on the opposite side of the boat, but there was still too much glare from the sunset to see anything below the surface.

"M-maybe it was just s-someone's footfall, or a dream...?" Wil stammered hopefully.

"No, it weren't no fucking dream. It was right underneath me! I'm telling you something str-"

Thump.

They all heard it that time, and the icy fist in Dreysha's stomach squeezed harder.

"Ohshit ohshit ohshit ohshit..." Wil moaned aloud.

"Smells more like piss to me" Dreysha muttered as she slipped an arm through the lanyard they had rigged for use during rough seas.

Biiko retrieved a second harpoon from a rack amidships, then drifted out onto the starboard Watchman's Post, one weapon raised and ready to strike, the other held loosely at his hip.

They waited in tense silence for several more heartbeats, and then they heard it again. This time it seemed to be right under Triistan's feet, and it was followed by two more in short succession; *thump... thump, thump!*

What in the Deep Dark...?

"LOOK!" Triistan cried, pointing down at the water.

She spun around, her back to the setting suns, and gripped the edge of The Nest. The water immediately adjacent to the launch was now in shadow, and something triangular and nearly as wide as Triis was tall darted into view. By some trick of the light, it shimmered under the water as it raced toward the boat. Three more appeared in the launch's shadow just as the first slid out of sight beneath them. They heard a soft scraping noise, but this time there was no impact, and when the next three disappeared, there was another thump, but only one, and again it did not strike the hull with much force.

She lifted her gaze, looking out to the southwest, and her breath caught in her throat. "By my balls, if I had'em...." she whispered.

A broad, low wave was rushing at them from starboard aft, shimmering as it reflected the last light of the sunset. No, that wasn't quite right - as it drew closer, she could see that it wasn't reflecting the light at all; it was *glowing*, lit from underneath. As the swell raced towards them, its leading edge became more defined: a wide, sinuous line of those same triangular shapes, undulating as they swam around one another, some diving, some rising, but all speeding directly towards the launch as if they meant to overwhelm it. She knew what they were now, though she had never seen them in such numbers before. They were spinners - sailor's cant for "spinnaker fish": large, flat creatures shaped like a spinnaker sail. They were considered to be docile, though some carried long, whip-like tails tipped with a poisonous barb.

Dreysha had seen several in her lifetime, but never in groups, and never at night. Until now, she'd had no idea that they glowed.

"Triis, you should be up here! You have to see this!"

"What? Would somebody please tell me what is happening?!" Rantham screamed, his voice raw with panic.

"It's ok, Ranth!" Triistan reassured him. "It's going to be ok. They're just spinners - a whole school of them headed towards the boat." Rantham was looking at him as if he didn't understand, but Triistan didn't stay to explain. He scrambled up a ratline, gaining the crow's nest in the span of a few heartbeats, just as the swell struck the side of the boat. As he slid in beside Dreysha, the impact jolted them, and although it wasn't forceful enough to damage the boat, being up as high as they were meant that every movement was greatly exaggerated. Drey let go of the safety line and was nearly knocked out of the nest, but he steadied her with an arm around her waist and gasped at the stunning sight below them.

The water churned around the ship as dozens upon dozens of the spinnakers parted around them or dove beneath. Many struck the side of the boat as the first ones had, but it seemed to be incidental, as if they were being carried along by the current of their fellows, somewhat unable to control their course. Behind them, a long, golden swath of ocean glittered, as if the sun had just set beneath the waves barely half a league from their position. There must have been thousands of them in the school, all chasing the last remnants of the day. It was breathtaking.

As they watched the display, Dreysha felt Triistan's arms tighten around her waist, so she pressed back against him.

"It's the most beautiful thing I've ever seen," he breathed into her hair. She said nothing, but reached up without turning to clasp his neck. He held her tighter, and they watched the spectacle together, until the rest of the school passed them by and faded from view, nearly an hour later. As the last of the daylight drained from the world, the sea, as it always did at night, became an ominous black void again.

When she finally felt him begin to relax his grip, she turned quickly to face him, expecting him to retreat from her as he always did. She had so many questions she wanted to ask him, things that could not wait until he shared his story with all of them. But he did not retreat, and when he bent to kiss her, she found herself rising eagerly to meet him.

His kiss was tentative at first, but she responded hungrily, despite the painfully cracked and blistered skin of her lips. His tongue found hers and she moaned softly in the back of her throat, pressing herself harder against him. After a moment he drew back, searching her eyes.

He touched her face, tracing his finger along the line of her jaw, then pulled her head to his chest, holding her tightly. She lost herself in the moment, in the surprising strength of his arms around her, in the gentle touch of his hand as he slowly ran his fingers through her hair.

Let the gods rot in the Dark, she thought. She wanted to live in that moment forever.

As if he had sensed her thoughts, he suddenly stiffened.

"Tarsus..." she heard him breath.

She smiled, her face still pressed against his chest. "It was good, but it was still just a kiss. Stay with me up here and I'll have you singing the names of every member of the High Houses -"

He suddenly took her by the shoulders and turned her around, pointing over her shoulder at the horizon.

"No, it's the constellation, Tarsus! Do you see?"

She did. He laughed and kissed her again, grinning the whole time.

"I think I know where we are now..."

He vaulted over the side and slid down one of the ratlines, calling for the sextant and charts.

Dreysha stood alone in the crow's nest, not knowing whether to laugh or cry. Above them, the star-filled sky glittered with the possibility of reaching home. Below, the Sea kept its secrets close; a vast world of shadows and unknown menace, but a world she had long ago come to terms with.

She looked to the south, back the way they'd come, thinking of what she had seen in Triistan's journal. She hugged herself against a sudden chill.

Somewhere out there in that infinite darkness was a world she no longer understood.

"Gods, what have we done?"

- 27 -

Leavings

Casselle understood that she had not been away from Strossen for long, but things felt different in a way that neither the count of days or leagues could adequately measure. Upon her return, she found that the city was still tense as the Elder Council found ways to dance around the requests of Jonn Harrell, a merchant and supposed champion of the hard working men and women of the largest of Gundlaan's cities.

She recalled defending the Elder Council against an angry mob, most of whom were legitimate supporters of Harrell. She was convinced the rest were simply amused by lighting fires and breaking things. It was depressing to think how many people fell into the latter category.

Harrell's imprisonment and the riot it sparked felt like a lifetime ago. It was jarring for her to come back to a place that had changed so little when she felt like everything else in the world had changed so much. She tried not to linger on the thought while she made her way towards the address she'd been given.

At least she was in motion. The alternative would be to wait while the Templar Officers discussed the news that had been delivered to them, starting with the wildly exaggerated claims of the von Darren family, which she attempted to "correct" in her detailed reports while accurately recounting the grim events that lead to the burning of Flinderlaas and the survivors' return to civilization.

She walked on, turning south at the Cel'Dama, the massive amphitheater considered by most to be the center of Strossen. As she traveled further, she noticed a marked change in the appearance of the buildings around her. They simply looked cleaner. It wasn't just the buildings that looked different. The roads were wider and walkways in front of people's homes were, more often than not, blocked by locked gates. Power lived on the south end of the city, made up of coin, influence, and a combination of the two.

Casselle was not used to such affluence, though she was more than familiar with the looks she was getting. Disapproval had a consistent look even as far away as her small home town. She was not wearing her armor, but rather a casual garment that lacked the sophistication of the surrounding crowd. It might not have been the wisest choice to leave her official uniform behind.

Such regrets were too late now, as the large square building just beside the Temple of Ogund that served as the simple Headquarters of the Laegis in Strossen was quite a distance away. She straightened her cloak, trying to seat the Templar clasp so that it was more visible on her shoulder, and hoped it might deflect some of the stares.

Her immediate observation was that it did not. Thankfully, the constables of the Watch saw it for what it was and let her pass without question. It was hard not to notice how many more of them were here in clean uniforms, walking in pairs down the streets in plain sight of the city's most wealthy. On the north side of town, home of the city's industry and the working families that supplied the raw labor, constables of the Watch were much less present.

She looked down at the slip of paper she'd been given by Brother Maynard, the Librarian. The old man hadn't recognized her at all, at least not as the "fat young boy" he assumed her to be the last time they'd met. Not that she was surprised. Her journey to Flinderlaas had transformed her in several ways, including the start of her transition to the harder, more weathered physique of a soldier.

Maynard had been quite distressed to learn of Odegar's passing. Her discomfort with his previous offhanded slight seemed trivial by comparison, so she had kept her mouth shut.

She looked for the name of the street the librarian had marked on the slip of paper. Brother Maynard had said it would be "quite clear," and that was confirmed when she easily spied the sign at a distance, further down the row. Questioning a helpful constable at that corner ensured she turned properly left and continued on.

She couldn't help noticing how much extra space there was here. The further she travelled, the more greenery she noticed; trees and beds of bright flowers and even sprawling lawns that seemed intended just to emphasize the luxury of having so much space that the residents need not use it for any purpose at all. It was a far cry from the buildings everywhere else in the city that were huddled so close together they seemed to fight each other for every inch of ground.

Not that she was unfamiliar with space. The small farm that was her childhood home did not have any immediate neighbors in any direction, but any passing similarity ended there. These homes were far larger, stern and unyielding instead of quaint and comforting. Her father, stepmother, two little stepbrothers and she would have thought such homes were designed for a dozen families. She harbored no such delusions, but then, she was no longer the same simple farm girl that had arrived in Strossen all those years ago.

The address on the paper matched the house at the end of this street, which had even more space around it than any of the others. It was also cleaner than the other homes, slightly more polished, and noticeably more organized, especially if you took the time to scrutinize it. She wondered if this was the way people with means insulted each other, by very discretely attempting to outdo those around them.

The gate was closed, but not locked. There did not appear any way to signal up to the front door from the end of the walkway, so Casselle let herself in and made her way up. The stones under her feet looked as white as bleached bone. It was discomforting.

Captain Odegar Taumber had died in Flinderlaas, sacrificing himself so that her friend and squad mate Jaksen Furrow might live. Until that moment, the fleeting talk of the Captain's family had always seemed remote, as if they lived in a land far away and long ago. The thought of meeting one of them now to deliver something so personal weighed heavily on her.

She paused in front, feeling unexpectedly embarrassed to knock. Thankfully, that pause gave her time to spot the small chain that would ring the bell to signal her arrival. She pulled it gently, hearing it jingle on the other side of the polished wooden door. She took a step back, feeling self-conscious about her appearance. It took a moment before the door finally opened.

A respectable gentleman with a receding hairline and dressed in a clean black coat opened the door. He cocked an eyebrow when he saw Casselle. The gentleman looked past her, as if he was expecting someone else to be following behind her, someone more important, she surmised. Still nervous, she knew she'd have to speak up to explain herself.

"Laegis Templar Casselle Milner to see Elleane Taumber. I bring news of her brother," she said.

After another look, his eyes fell upon the clasp holding her cloak in place.

"He is not with you?" the gentleman asked with a curious eyebrow lifted.

"He isn't... I mean, he can't..." Casselle wrestled with the words, not having expected to explain herself to the doorman.

"I understand," he said, his stern face softening slightly. He opened the door fully to allow her entrance.

"You may wait here while I inform Lady Taumber," the man said. He paused for a moment to make sure that Casselle understood, before nodding slightly, turning on his heel and vanishing into the room just behind the entryway and out of sight.

The inside of the house was no less spectacular than the outside. Everything was clean and bright. Several large windows pulled light in from outside, filling this room and those beyond with a soft radiance. The way everything was neatly ordered and arranged leant the home a certain amount of unreality, as if she had stepped into a museum. For a time, she lost herself in the details of a nearby painting, a scene of mountains just beyond green meadows.

The gentleman in the black coat returned and signaled her to follow him. He was already walking away again, forcing her to take a hurried step or two to catch up as they passed under the balcony of the floor above them. They entered an open room with several wide couches and a large dulcimer as the predominate feature of one corner.

Eventually he led her to a more somber colored room, lined with bookshelves from floor to ceiling. Behind the handful of chairs it contained, a set of double doors led out to a wide balcony running along the back side of the house. The gentleman in the black coat stepped through the doors, holding one open for Casselle, but did not move further. Once she was outside under the early afternoon sun, he adjourned from the balcony, closing the door softly behind him.

Casselle was immediately captivated by the view of the colorful garden just behind the house, below the balcony. The lush, deep greenery contrasted sharply with the bright white of the house's stonework. The open tops of stone planters burst with brightly colored flowers, and wooden trellises nearby added softer, accented contrasts. A stone-lined path wound like a serpent through the garden, meticulously designed to appear like a natural path, though there was not a pebble out of place. In fact, there were no wilted leaves left on the ground and no unmanicured plants anywhere her gaze happened to fall. It was impeccable, even more pristine than the approach from the front.

A woman sat on a bench next to the balustrade, her face serene, her gaze distant, and her hands resting in her lap. She had silver hair pulled behind her head in a braid that lay halfway down her back. Her face was soft and her eyes sharp when she finally looked over at the Templar. The tiny wrinkles at the corners of her eyes betrayed the only real signs of age that Casselle could see.

"It is not like my brother to send anyone in his stead," she said, her voice calm and strong. From the side it hadn't been quite as apparent, but looking at her head on, the family resemblance was clear. So much so that it caught Casselle by surprise. She saw Odegar in his sister and it hurt her heart.

"I am so sorry," Casselle began, her tongue already stumbling over itself. "He... I..."

Elleane Taumber held up two fingers, signaling the young woman to stop. She let her head dip for a moment and smoothed out a wrinkle in her dress. Once she was done, she lifted it to look back out over the garden. Casselle bit her lip and remained silent. Odegar's sister sat quietly for a moment before clearing an offending bit of moisture out from underneath her eyes with a slight brush of her hand.

"Your name, Templar, I would know it," she said calmly, still not making eye contact.

"Casselle," she answered, pausing unintentionally for a moment before quickly adding, "Milner."

"Ah," came the response, as if she expected to hear it. "He's spoken of you. Highly, if it pleases you to know." It did not exactly please Casselle to hear this, as it made her only miss him more acutely, but she did not say anything of the sort aloud.

"On our many walks around the grounds," she said, motioning to the garden beyond the balcony, "he would talk proudly of you and your fellows. Ever the patient sister, I indulged his little meanderings."

"Was it a heroic death?" she asked, changing the subject suddenly. She attempted to sound merely inquisitive, but a note of bitterness betrayed her emotions. "He always hoped that if he had to die, it would be so. He was afraid of late that he would soon be old enough that it would be considered more foolish than meaningful... if death was ever meaningful. I, for one, have no desire to make a pageant of my passing."

"He thought of you," Casselle blurted out. She was not used to expressing pent up emotion like this, so it tumbled out of her roughly. She took a breath before speaking more calmly. "This is no exaggeration. His lasts words to me were of you. 'Tell her there are flowers here,' he said, 'beautiful flowers.'"

"I see," she responded, her gaze never wandering from her immaculate garden. They stood there this way for some time. Casselle was used to standing still in formations, and found herself settling into a formal stance quite naturally, one she could maintain for some time.

Elleane eventually stood and turned toward Casselle, then stepped closer to get a better look at the Templar. She was put together almost as flawlessly as her own garden, immaculately dressed and groomed.

"Do you know what his words mean?" she asked, seeming neither hurt nor angry by the message that had been delivered.

"No, Miss, I do not," Casselle replied honestly.

"Tell me what you know of my Brother," she said.

"I... I know him from my first days of training with the Laegis. He has been a Captain of that Order for longer than I have been alive. He has met and killed twenty five confirmed and many more unconfirmed H'kaan in single combat. He has received..."

"No, no," Elleane interrupted, slightly irritated. "Tell me what you know of Odegar, not the rank and accomplishments of some Templar officer."

Casselle stopped, taking stock of her thoughts and feelings. It took a while to speak again, unsure of how she should begin.

"Odegar cared," she finally said. "He cared for us, for all of us, not just my team and I. He felt life was a gift that should not be squandered or thrown away casually.

"He cared for your mother and longed to know about his father. He mentioned once that his father was a soldier of Derant's during the Godswar, but he never knew him personally. I feel like he was always trying to honor that memory through his service." Casselle paused for a moment to look over at Elleane. She acknowledged it and motioned her to continue.

"I did not know he had other family until he told me of you," Casselle confessed. "It always felt like he was kin to me... supportive, understanding... at least these are the things that I associate with family. I know they are not always that way."

"They are not," Elleane gently confirmed. "Please continue."

"He was slow to anger, and approached duty with respect and focus. But it was not about simple service for him. I think he felt it was a way to pay back, in some measure, the gift of his own life.

"That seems a very kind picture you paint of my brother with your words," the lady said.

"I do not think him without faults, all of us have them," Casselle said. "Nor do I think his life was without worry.

"I think he was lonely," the Templar continued. "Because he did not speak much of others with us, nor did I know him to fraternize with many other Templar. I think his duty was both a source of pride for him and a way to shield himself from the pain in his heart."

"He feared for you all," the lady said, "and he cursed the High Houses for failing those they were sworn to protect. I think he tried to shoulder too much of that burden himself."

"For all the right reasons," the Templar replied.

"That is where we disagree," Elleane replied. "I did not see you as worthy of that level of sacrifice, nor am I the only Vanha that feels that way."

Casselle felt like she'd had the wind knocked out of her. To her, Odegar always seemed so understanding and generous. She did not know any other Vanha, certainly not in the familiar way she knew him, but she realized now her assumption that they were all equally kind and caring was wide of the mark. They were children of the Gods, weren't they? She assumed Odegar's sense of duty was born of that, that on some level, it was an innate part of what made them Vanha.

"I see that comes as a shock to you," Odegar's sister observed dispassionately. "Those of us that feel that way are not always vocal, but we remember our parents or grandparents back from a time when Ehronhaal still rested amongst the clouds. There are many of us that feel our family members were sacrificed for an unworthy and ungrateful mistake."

"Mistake?" Casselle asked, clenching her fists. "Is that how you see us?"

"The Children were crafted as a delusional flight of fancy by Tarsus. We cannot confirm this, mind you, but it's not a theory without some merit. Your short lives, your fleeting memories, your entitled sense of self. Like all other common animals, it seems the one thing you were designed to do was to spread without thought or concern and without surcease. Unlike other animals, though, you are not content to merely inhabit, you feel it is your responsibility to despoil everything you touch.

"In this garden of ruin, you are the weeds," Elleane said dispassionately. Casselle had been in plenty of fights, but she'd never struck out of pure anger before. She didn't think she had that in her, but the way Odegar's sister spoke to her, the way she wanted to discount his sacrifice, made her more than willing to consider it.

"Your brother gave his life trying to save one of ours," Casselle retorted sharply, "and had I the talent, I would have gladly done the same to save his!"

"I believe you just might have," Elleane replied, seemingly surprised by the Templar's outburst. She gave Casselle a cold, dispassionate look that quelled some of the younger woman's anger.

"We're not your garden," the Templar said, a bit more in control of herself. "You think we're the weeds in your garden, but we're not. We're not the flowers either.

"Outside your walls, there are thorns, vines, mushrooms, trees... a whole world that doesn't fit into your manicured, insulated view of things. I don't think your brother was ever suggesting we deserve to be in here. I think he was inviting you to take a walk out there... with him," Casselle said. She paused for a moment, her head still full of busy thoughts and hot emotions. She fought the urge to say anymore, fearful she'd already said too much.

Convinced she'd overstayed her welcome, she turned to leave, not waiting to give Elleane Taumber the satisfaction of dismissing her. She made it all the way to the door before the lady spoke again.

"Wait." The word was gentle, the way she spoke it, almost pleading.

Casselle paused, her hand outstretched, just shy of the door handle. She did not turn back, but she did not move forward either.

"That was the last thing he said to me..." Elleane confessed, "before he left. 'When next I come, let us take a walk outside the garden.'"

Casselle let her hand fall.

"I can see what he saw in you," she continued. "In a way you remind me of him, when he was younger. Those are the kindest words I can find, and it pains me to say them.

"But I cannot forgive you. I hate you all for taking him from me," she finished coldly.

Casselle strained for something to say. Temos would surely have come up with a clever reply, some stinging barb, but she could think of nothing. So she opened the door and left.

***

The wide, bright streets narrowed and darkened as Casselle moved north, back towards the center of town. She felt strangely vulnerable thinking of her friends, especially the ones that had been taken from her. It was not a good feeling, and she wished to be rid of it, like she was now rid of the responsibility of speaking with Odegar's sister. The encounter had left a bitter taste in her mouth. In the shadow of the Cel'Dama, she stopped at a food cart to get a fresh bite of fruit to eat along her way back to Laegis Headquarters.

She discarded the core in a public waste bin and wiped a bit of juicy pulp from the corner of her mouth as the spires of Gundhaal began to rise up behind the buildings ahead of her. Eventually, the street fed into the open space in front of the temple, a great square where people assembled under the proud bronze statue of The Crafter himself.

Ogund stood an impressive figure, with broad shoulders and thick arms; one hand held a heavy forging hammer, the other was resting on an overlarge water pump that continually poured into the basin around the statue. Many of his other inventions were arrayed around him: a spoked wheel leaning against the pump, a pulley with rope draped across it, tools and measures resting next to an anvil. His face seemed stern, but his eyes always struck Casselle as kind and insightful. She had been told one of his greatest students had crafted the statue as a present to the Young God and he displayed it proudly for all to enjoy.

When she first came to Strossen, years ago, she found these gatherings disrespectful, but later she grew in appreciation of them. She felt it was good that people were here, living and eating, talking and laughing in his presence. The more she learned of him, the more convinced she became that he would have liked it.

Histories wrote that people moved from the wild to settle around the great Columns the Dauthir had created and in the shadow of these towers, the Young Gods nurtured them. The name Strossen was coined by Ogund, who claimed it was an old word for "safe ground," where the Children of Tarsus could live under his protection. It seemed only fitting that these people felt comfort here, whether they were reminded of these things or not. Casselle much preferred to think of the Gods that way.

Elleane Taumber called all of these people a mistake, a great mistake on the part of the Gods, both Young and Old. She couldn't help but think of her father.

"Regardless of how hard we try, we'll always leave mistakes for our children to sort out. Best we can do is try to give them better tools than we had to fix 'em."

If they were indeed a mistake, how would they sort themselves out? Was that even possible? Is that why the Young Gods ended up killing themselves? Would the same happen to them?

Worse yet, if they were indeed the Children of Tarsus, what other mistakes had been left for them to fix?

She pondered these things as she approached Gundhaal, the home Ogund had crafted for himself, where the ancestors of Strossen had come to live and know him.

She was told it was not as ostentatious as the other Gods' homes. On its own, it was a structure taller than the other buildings surrounding it, but not as boisterously large as the Cel'Dama or the business cluster known as the Korristraad. For a hundred years after the Ehronfall it sat untouched, waiting on the western edge of town beyond the Temple of Passages and the attached Elder Circle building. The Lord High Marshall finally convinced the Elder Circle to put it to use because that's what Ogund would have wanted for it. It had since been renovated as a hospital, and it was there that Casselle was headed.

The magnificently crafted doors Ogund had originally carved for the building were left in place, though smaller, more sensible entrances had been cut into the base of the great portals, allowing access for normal sized folk. A few young Templar stood guard out front, more ceremonial than anything else, but it gave them good practice being patient. She smiled to herself as she passed them, remembering her own experience from years back.

The white-robed acolyte at the central desk just inside the doors pulled out a list and directed Casselle to the large stairwell on the left. She began her climb, noting the slow but steady flow of traffic in this central lobby. Fewer people were on the stairs. Most of the attention was focused below, so that those requiring the most immediate help were afforded the quickest care. A small staff of Arxhemists specialized in healing the body of injury and ailments was typically stationed there. They were few in number, but were supplemented by more conventional healers, as well as clergy of several faiths who had been trained to ease the pain of both mind and spirit.

The second floor was for recovery, for those that needed rest and care, but were not in immediate danger. She stopped on that floor, heading down the rightmost corridor. She glanced at the stairway that continued upward, knowing that the third floor was a place that she'd heard Templars often spent their last days, under the best of care until they ceased having mortal concerns.

Jaksen was not on the third floor, however. He was recuperating on the second and doing well if Temos wasn't exaggerating. Casselle passed several doors as well as groups of acolytes speaking in hushed tones so as not to disturb those resting. As she approached the room that Jaksen was convalescing in she heard laughter, bright and quick, before it was shushed by a heavier voice.

"There are other people worse off than I," Casselle heard Jaksen say.

"And I cannot be happy because of them?" a delicate voice asked in return.

"I wish to respect them during their recovery. It is the least I can do for them."

Casselle paused at the doorway. She was glad to hear strength in Jaksen's voice, but she did not want to disturb this moment for him. She considered turning around and leaving altogether as the two people inside the room whispered and laughed quietly. Thinking that it might indeed be for the best, Casselle turned to leave.

- 421 -

"I have to get back to the shop. I will come back after it closes and I will bring you something sweet," the young lady's voice said, bringing Casselle to a stop. Jaksen said something that made the girl giggle uncontrollably and Casselle blushed, assuming it had been something private. She shoved the thought out of her mind and stepped around the corner and into the room.

The girl was easily a year or so younger than them, but taller than Casselle by a good amount. Just the right size for Jaksen, she thought. She had soft golden hair bound in a loose bun and expressive blue eyes that displayed a bit of shock at the sudden arrival of a new visitor.

"Casselle!" Jaksen said with pleasure and surprise.

"I did not mean..."

"You're not interrupting anything," the young lady said, saving the Templar any further words. The shock had left her face and was replaced with something brighter. "It is good fortune for me that you are here. If it were not for you then Jaksen..."

Rather suddenly, she dashed forward to throw her arms around Casselle.

"Thank you," the young lady said tenderly. Casselle did not know how to reply, but the embrace did not last long.

"Visit with your friend! I will be back." With a lightness in her step, she threw a glance back at Jaksen before exiting the room, leaving only the pleasant smell of freshly baked bread in her wake. It took Casselle a moment to regain her bearings.

"That was her?" she asked.

"Jessamine is her name," Jaksen said with a wide grin. "I can't tell you how happy that makes me to be able to say out loud. We're going to be married."

Casselle was shocked.

"But you're..."

"Not anymore," Jaksen said, lifting up the bandaged stump that was all that remained of his right arm. Casselle moved in closer to speak, but he waved her off with his good hand. "I know what you are going to say and although the Laegis would keep me on as a steward or some such, I'd rather not.

"I joined to protect those that I loved," Jaksen said calmly. "Since I can't very well do that anymore, I'd rather just spend my time with them. I already had Temos help me write up a letter."

Casselle nodded. It made sense. It was selfish of her to expect him to stay on.

"Oh don't be that way," Jaksen said with a smile. "Maybe this is the way it was meant to be. Jessamine's father is a baker. He says that

I'd still make a decent one myself, even with just the one arm. I plan to have a good life, with no regrets.

"And don't you go taking on any more of your own on my account," he finished. Casselle took a deep breath. He knew her well enough, and he was right. This would be good for him. Seeing him so cheerful lifted her spirits. It was the first time since returning back that she felt something akin to happiness.

Regardless of what had happened, it was as Odegar had said. They had done good work. Jaksen would survive and have a family. The villagers of Flinderlaas had been sent away safely before the Wolfmother had arrived in force. There was loss and heartbreak, but life continued on because they had been there to fight for it.

There was a solace in that. There was also great comfort in the friends that remained.

"Confess, Jaksen, what do you know about baking bread, anyway?" she asked, drawing close enough to sit down on the end of his bed.

"Well, it involves flour and water and fire. Not all at the same time, mind you," Jaksen said with mock seriousness.

"Sounds dangerous," Casselle replied trying to suppress her own smile. "Please tell me more."

"Actually, I suppose that's about all I know at the moment," he laughed, "but I expect you to come by the store to see how well I'm sorting it out."

"I most certainly will," she said.

"Good. Now, although I am no baker yet, I do know a great deal about eating baked goods!" Jaksen said proudly. "Did you know there is more than one type of bread? And I'm not talking about cake, mind you."

"Fascinating!" Casselle replied, almost sounding sincere. "Please go on!"

"Pies and rolls, buns and breadsticks, there is virtually nothing I have not sampled," Jaksen began.

Casselle listened to him go on with enthusiasm for a good while about sweetbreads, nut breads, shortbreads and cakes, chuckling to herself the entire time. At the end of his animated descriptions, the two of them shared a laugh and it felt quite good.

***

"I think part of him doesn't want to face what he's given up," Temos said. "He's clearly in denial."

Casselle shrugged and hung her cloak up on the wooden pegs beside her door. During her travels they had assigned her and her squad rooms in the part of the barracks reserved for pledged Templars. It was only a few hundred feet away from the rooms they'd occupied as initiates, but it was nice to find her few possessions neatly packed and waiting for her in a clean room, one unburdened by shared memories of a group forced apart by circumstance.

"Did you meet the girl? Did you know he's been seeing her all this time?" Temos asked, following her into her room. "I knew he was fond of getting fresh bread, but I always thought it was because he liked doing things for us. I had no idea it was so he could go visit his secret sweetheart."

"I think it was a bit of both," Casselle said, pulling an armorjack from her wardrobe and setting it on her bed. She pulled out her tabard next and laid it beside the heavy leather jacket.

"Oh right," Temos said, turning away from Casselle, towards the door. He reached out to touch it, making sure it was fully closed. Behind his back, she removed her overshirt and chemise. The binding cloth around her chest was restrictive and uncomfortable, so she took it off as well. The armorjack had enough weight to keep things flattened and out of the way, though she did put back on her more comfortable undergarment before sliding on the thicker doublet that would keep her warm and padded underneath the armorjack.

"I just worry that he's rushing off into something that he's not prepared for," Temos continued on while Casselle finished dressing. "I mean, marriage? Baking? Do we know if he's well suited for either?

"And what do we know about this Jessamine? I mean, she seems nice and all, but how do we know she has his best interests at heart?" Temos pondered aloud as Casselle tied her tabard into place.

"Truly," Casselle said solemnly. "Perhaps she'll throw him in the oven the first chance she gets."

"You're joking," Temos replied sharply before doubt crept in. "I mean are you joking? I can't tell. I can never tell when you are joking." He turned around to see Casselle smiling at him.

"You're horrible," he grinned.

They were interrupted by a knock at her door. Checking for her approval first, Temos opened it when she nodded.

Standing outside, almost filling the doorframe, was a sturdy man in standard Templar uniform. A patch covered one eye, barely hiding most of the accompanying scars. The hair on his head was black, as was his close cropped beard, but gray had begun to brush his temples and whiskers. Casselle recognized him almost instantly, since he had been one of their first trainers when they had started as initiates of the Laegis.

"Captain Ardell!" Temos said, snapping to attention.

"Never mind that, Pelt," Greffin Ardell said, "I'm here mainly for Milner, but this probably will affect you, too, I wager."

Casselle met the Captain's gaze.

"You're wanted in the Rounder," he said, using the most common nickname for the Officer's war room, the circular conference hall with the large round meeting table.

"What for?" Temos asked.

"I don't know, I was just asked to fetch her," he said irritably. Casselle noticed that there were others in the hall, two Lancers, Templar spearmen who were common on the grounds as guards, often times to escort prisoners.

"Am I under arrest?" Casselle asked bluntly.

"You're under review," replied Greffin, which is something that had already been made clear to her almost as soon as she had returned, missing her Captain and squadmate.

"I don't know any more than that," he added with a touch of sincerity that was somewhat uncharacteristic for him. That frightened her more than anything else.

"Why just her? She wasn't the only one there. She..." Temos was arguing as if Captain Ardell had the power to do something. Her friend was obviously just as frustrated as she was, but was taking it out on the wrong person. Casselle reached over to grip him on the shoulder. As he turned to look at her, she shook her head slightly: this wasn't the time to argue.

Temos sighed in resignation and remained quiet as Casselle took a deep breath.

"Let's go," she said. "I'm ready."

The trip to the Rounder was short, though it seemed as if it took a thousand more steps than necessary to traverse to the double door exterior, which was flanked by a Templar on either side. Captain Ardell announced them both and the guards opened one of the doors to let them pass.

The room was sparsely decorated, an unwritten Templar tradition, with only a picture of the Laegis crest on one wall and some stained glass windows high up on the opposing side, casting filtered light down onto the table below. Casselle was surprised to see the black and gold standard in one corner of the room next to the Templar banner: on it was the familiar design of a lion holding a sword with a blade of lightning.

"Templar," someone said, drawing her attention back to the table. She saw some high ranking members of the Laegis, including General Raandol Vaughn, the right hand of the Lord High Marshal. Next to him were two men, one far older than the other, both in darkened steel armor with matching black and gold tabards. She remembered them from her graduation, how she had been surprised to see a banner so wholly unfamiliar and guests that had been given such a position of prominence. Why were they here?

"General Vaughn," Captain Ardell spoke. "Templar Casselle Milner delivered at your request."

"Thank you, Captain," the General said in a steady tone. He was not wearing full armor, or even an armorjack, but was decked in a formal coat under a Templar tabard as well as a respectable longcloak. He took his seat, along with the others on the side of the table opposite Casselle. There were six in all, she noted, one of them clearly there to take notes, seated at the far left end. Casselle stood at attention until the rest of them were seated and motioned for her to join them. Captain Ardell remained standing at rest just behind her chair.

"This is an informal review of the report filed on the siege and evacuation of Flinderlaas, by Templar of the Shield, Casselle Milner, following the death of Captain Odegar Taumber," the general began. The tone of these comments already struck Casselle as being all wrong. She'd filed the formal report only a day after she'd arrived back, but for the review to have involved this level of attention and scrutiny so quickly... she had already assumed the worst.

Did the von Darren's really have that much influence? Had she dismissed that too quickly? How likely was it that she could be drummed out of the Templars so soon after being inducted?

"General Raandol Vaughn presiding, with Commanders Hrain and Curt as well as Captains Ardell and Everliin. Also present is Sergeant Meercer as scribe, and guests of the Laegis, Lords Richard and Arren Lockewood," the General said.

Guests of the Laegis? Since when did strangers outside of the Templars sit in on field reviews, regardless of how important they might be? Furthermore, what would prompt a General to conduct an informal review of a lowly Shield Templar?

She had assumed the account of the Wolfmother would bring her under scrutiny, but this seemed like a disproportionate response, like when one of her first drill instructors had attempted to scare her out of the Initiate ranks by making her fight three other trainees simultaneously.

She suppressed a grin.

She'd won the respect of her future squadmates by limping off that field the victor. She wasn't about to let these old men scare her either.

"Let it be noted that we have all read the review by Templar Milner and are here to ascertain further information in order to get answers that may not have been made clear in the body of the report," the General continued. He paused.

"Now then," he said. "Templar Milner, is there anything in the document you've presented to us that might be interpreted incorrectly?"

"The facts are exactly as I represented them in my report," she recounted. "Our arrival at Flinderlaas, the meeting with the von Darren's to inform them of the Elder Circle's decision to retrieve the settlers, the subsequent assault on the keep by a hostile force, the discovery in the cistern under the keep and the plan that was executed for the best chance of our survival are accounted for *exactly* as they happened. I've even detailed the return to Strossen and provided a list of references among the Outriders that should be able to corroborate this account. Temos... Templar Pelt is currently working on reconstructing the paintings that we discovered. Hopefully they should be ready soon. I also indicated that in the report in the appropriate section."

"Your report is very thorough, Templar, but it's also very sterile," the General replied. "We need more than simple descriptions."

"These creatures you describe," one of the Commanders said, "some look like wolves, but others don't. Are you sure they were wolves at all?"

"I'm sure they were more than they appeared, Commander" Casselle answered.

"H'kaan?" the other Commander quickly interjected.

"Captain Taumber said they were not, sir," Casselle replied.

"But what else could they be?"

"I don't know if I have an answer for you, sir," Casselle said. "I have not heard of anything like this before."

"Have you ever seen the H'kaan, Templar?"

"No, sir."

"Then how do you know that they were not?"

"I trust the assessment of my Captain," Casselle replied, perhaps too sharply before adding, "Sir."

"The man in the hood," Captain Everliin questioned, stepping on the heels of Casselle's last reply, "you claim he appeared out of nowhere. If he was not H'kaan, do you think he was Arys?"

"The Gods are dead, Captain," Casselle replied as calmly and certainly as she'd heard it repeated to her so many times before.

- 427 -

"That's not what I asked," the Captain retorted.

"I don't have anything to compare him to, sir. The Gods were long dead when I was born," Casselle replied. "If he was, I would not know." She absently wrapped her left hand around her right arm where he had touched her, where her skin still felt cold, even now.

"What would you do if you saw this Wolfmother again?" General Vaughn asked.

"If she posed a threat, General, I would oppose her," Casselle replied.

"Why do you say, 'if'? Do you not understand that she poses a clear danger to all of Gundlaan?" one of the Commanders questioned.

"She posed a clear danger to Flinderlaas, sir, that I do not dispute," Casselle said. "But she did not pursue us, when she easily could have. I am unaware of her motives beyond that."

"You intentionally kept a squad of Templars out of the fight," the other Commander declared. "Who deemed Vincen von Darren unfit for combat? You did not approve of the battlefield commission Captain Crennel made, did you?"

"My Captain did not require my approval," Casselle replied, "He was more than able to make that assessment on his own."

"So you didn't consider that Templar von Darren's squad might have made a difference in your battle with this Wolfmother? That having them there might have saved the lives of two others?" the Commander shot back. Casselle's jaw clenched at the mention of Raabel and Odegar's death. She bit down on her first reaction.

"If I may be blunt, sir?"

"Please."

"Vincen von Darren is beneath my consideration in most things," she replied icily. "But Captain Taumber tried to limit our exposure to loss by only deploying one squad over the wall."

It was at this moment that she thought she caught a smirk on the face of the elder of the two strangers, the one she assumed to be Lord Richard Lockewood. It was the closest thing to an emotion that she'd seen on his face since arriving. It quickly faded though as the next verbal barrage began.

"Are you telling me, Templar, that your squad was willing to face an army of wolves by themselves?"

"At most it was two Fists of wolves, sir. While certainly a lot, it was not an army, and Captain Taumber's plan, though unorthodox, seemed likely to succeed. It did, in fact, work as planned."

"At the cost of Captain Taumber and Templar Schute," General Vaughan stated. "Not completely successful, I should say."

"Only the Wolfmother herself seemed immune to our direct assault. The other monsters, while dangerous, did fall to our blades. It was clear that she was a threat, but we were unsure of her physical abilities. There was a risk she could ruin the plan, but we still felt it was our best option given the time and resources available to us."

"Knowing what you do now, would you still have followed your Captain's orders?" General Vaughn asked.

"Sir, yes, sir," Casselle answered confidently. "I put my faith in Captain Taumber and the strength and skill of my squad.

"We are the hand that steadies the Shield. To defend those in need," she added with emphasis, quoting her vows. She had planned to stop there, but Captain Ardell's muttered "En'vaar et Laegis" from behind emboldened her.

"Two of us paid with our lives, but we were all ready to do so in order to safeguard those that escaped Flinderlaas before us. With respect, General, even you will not make me dishonor the memory of those that sacrificed themselves by trying to get me to admit it was a mistake!"

The assembled old men exchanged glances with one another. Most of them appeared to be in a state of shock, except for the General, who was studying her intently instead. It suddenly made her feel incredibly self conscious for reasons she couldn't understand. She was grateful when he turned his head away, but was equally shocked when she followed his gaze to meet that of Lord Lockewood at the end of the table.

"Well?" asked General Vaughan.

"Give her to me," Lockewood replied.

"Very well," the General said. "I'll have the orders processed."

Casselle didn't understand. Was this some new form of punishment?

"You cannot strip my title from me!" exclaimed Casselle. "I am a Laegis Templar. I will not be traded like a horse."

"You speak out of turn!" one of the Commanders barked back. Casselle began to stand, but felt Captain Ardell's hand on her shoulder.

"Calm down," the General told them both. "You're not losing your title, Templar Milner, and you're not being bartered away. You're joining a Fist of Templars, a special detachment working on behalf of the Laegis with Lord Lockewood."

"For what purpose?" Casselle asked.

"A direct question deserves a direct answer," Richard Lockewood responded, stepping forward. "The Gods may be dead, young Templar, but their problems did not get buried along with them. Those problems are our inheritance, and unless we are prepared for them, they will bury us just as surely as they did those before us.

"Simply put," Lockewood said, "you're going to help me save the world."

Epilogue

The Gardener

Keri Lugger set both bare feet on the warm stone floor and stifled a groan. He bent over double, reaching his arms out as far as he could, trying to alleviate the tightness in the small of his back. Long dark hair fell forward around his face and helped to dim the insufferable morning light. He tried to hold the position but could not as the nausea that had first awakened him threatened to turn violent, so he straightened slowly, stood up, and shuffled over to the sideboard. A silver pitcher waited there patiently on a plate made from polished flatshell.

He touched the platter briefly with a well-manicured finger, in the absent way one does a thing that used to have meaning, but which has long since lost its significance. It was a fine piece that had been harvested from somewhere along Khatiita's northern coast, where the shells grew as large as dining tables in the azure waters of Niht's Haven. There was a time when he would have gazed at it for several seconds, tracing one of the jade-colored veins that made these pieces so distinctive, while remembering fondly the adventures of a childhood spent along that same coast. But now they were just the memories of a child he no longer recognized.

He seized the handle of the pitcher a bit too quickly, sloshing the liquid inside and sending a few drops leaping out onto the flatshell, their red color obscene against the clean white. He cast about for his cup and found it resting on its side near the foot of the bed, just below the shapely ankle, delicate arch and dainty toes of... well, he could not quite tell from here whose it was. Somewhere beneath the rumpled satin sheets above were three more just as shapely.

Damn the Dark, what were their names again? That would cost him extra if he didn't want to see them pout. He put long, bronze-skinned fingers to his temple and squeezed his eyes shut. Melva, Maedra, Meln- Maesa, that was it! Maesa, the dark, sultry bitch from Khiigongo. This was not Maesa's foot though, he could see as he drew closer; the skin was too light, the calf too slender. And, at present, he had not the slightest notion of what this one's name was or where she hailed from. He needed something to chase the heavy cloud cover from his mind and settle his unruly stomach, so he bent to pick up the cup, bringing his face very close to that supple curve. He breathed in deeply, taking in the heady scent of the pleasure oils they had used, and stifled another groan, but this time for very different reasons. He *must* remember her name, so that he could request her again.

Cup in hand, Keri returned to the sideboard, filled it deftly, and padded towards the balcony, where the early afternoon suns burned like melted gold through the sheer drapes billowing slowly there. As he passed the end of the sideboard, he swept his left hand out and palmed a small leather pouch. He drank a mouthful of wine, swallowing just as he stepped into the hot wash of sunlight, deliberately timing the two sensations for maximum effect. Shuddering with pleasure he drained the cup, then refilled it with a deft, practiced motion before setting the silver pitcher on the edge of the parapet wall that formed the outer edge of his veranda. Beyond the sand-colored wall with its painstaking mosaic of inlaid shells, the world hung; a fat, succulent fruit waiting for him to pick.

He regarded the pouch, fingering it slowly, then decided to wait a little and set it on the wall adjacent to the pitcher. One of the seeds in the twineroot garden had flowered - "The Garden of Secrets" some called it, though he just called it 'The Garden' or 'The Plot' (which he thought surpassingly clever) - so he would have to keep his head relatively clear, at least through the preparation. It was the young Azimuth's seed, and would require extra care, not only in the preparation and interpretation (*especially the interpretation*, he thought with a wince), but ultimately also in discreetly delivering the information to Abet Quesso. An image from one of those messages rose unbidden in his mind - more of a feeling, really, an overwhelming sense of confused terror and horror and then excruciating pain as teeth closed around his torso and thighs...

Keri shook his head and pushed the memory away. Whoever the poor bastard was who'd sent that particularly nasty vision wasn't Azimuth, and Keri doubted very much he would be hearing from this new Sender again.

The Isles keep me, I hope not, he thought with a shiver. Still, perhaps just a bit of sap to "sharpen the edges", as he liked to call it; to accentuate the infinitely fine line that separates one object from another, one color from the next, one sensation from the myriad others that, unless you concentrated very hard, all just blended together in a bland paste that was excruciatingly dull. Sapping did wonders for the concentration part, as long as you were careful with it, and Keri could be very careful when he needed to be.

He drained his cup again, refilled it, and looked out across The Gap at Chatuuku's western coast line, squinting against the suns' glare. Tier after tier of streets, houses, buildings, markets, walls, towers and delicate foot bridges marched up the island's steep flanks, a jumble of structures that overlapped and overshadowed one another, like jungle plants struggling to reach the sun. It was a friendly competition, though - at least, when viewed from a safe distance - a merry riot of rich colors, from the tan and rose-colored walls to the deep browns and reds of the curved clay tile roofs, all of which were draped and dotted with every other color imaginable: the Gap was less than a thousand feet across at both banks, so Keri could easily pick out drapes, plants, trees, laundry, awnings and even - if he was sapping just right - individual articles of clothing. At water level, that was no great feat of course, but up here where the Wise and Powerful lived, it was god-like.

Keri's quarters were in the South Tower of Khatiita's sprawling Palace of the Suns. It dominated the northeastern end of this island, commanding spectacular views of Stormgate, Shelter Bay, the island kingdoms Juuma and Juu to either side, and across Shelter Bay on the central isle of Chatuuku, the capitol city itself: Kortaga, City of the Seven. At its feet, the Great Harbor lay like so much scattered treasure. Ships bobbed in their berths or plied the waters of the Bay like thousands of misshapen pearls, all encircled by the long, bejeweled arms of the harbor and its countless quays, docks, dry-docks, granaries, merchant stalls, warehouses, whorehouses, inns, taverns, stables... the list was endless, and Keri did not wish to waste the day ticking them all off in his overactive mind. He just wanted to absorb it, to *be*, here, in the Cradle of Ruine.

Natives of the Isles did not call it that as an idle boast. Sheltered by the main continent and distance, it was one of the few areas of civilization that had not been devastated by the destruction of Ehronfall and the Passing of the Gods. As the rest of the world crawled and clawed its way out of the wreckage, the Sea Kings' small confederacy had seized the opportunity by the throat, transforming the archipelago-fortress into a bright signal beacon calling those cast adrift by the great storm of the Godswar to safe harbor.

And how they had come, in their hundreds and their thousands! He raked long locks of hair back with his free hand, watching the matus wheeling below him while imagining what it must have been like. On horseback or on foot, sway-backed mules or even harox, the great shaggy beasts of Argonne, they were ferried shoulder to shoulder across Niht's Haven on huge barges. Some pushed or pulled carts or wagons full of their sole remaining possessions; others, their loved ones, who in many cases had coughed out their last breath as the barges drew within sight of Shanthaal's towering sea-walls. Some came with nothing but the ragged clothing on their bent and weary backs.

But all came with a powerful combination of knowledge and gratitude. The culture and teachings of dozens of different races from all across Niyah were given willingly - joyfully - in exchange for shelter and a place to begin again. The Sea Kings, newly risen to power in the wake of the Young Gods' passing, accepted it all, eagerly intent on building an empire that, Keri was certain, those same gods would now envy.

"Seven Kings, One Kingdom," he whispered the familiar mantra to the wind. "One bloody magnificent kingdom above all, if I have anything to say about it."

True, there were other areas of growth and prosperity. There was Atau, of course - if anything their closest rival, but burdened by too much tradition and mistrust to ever achieve real success. The combined Gundlaan cities of Strossen, Naar Deran (in the shadow of Deranthaal) and Ostrell made up perhaps the greatest industrial and agricultural giant on the mainland, but those cities were landlocked and ill suited for trade. It was also no secret that they were rife with civil unrest and very near to boiling over. The scrap of Cartishaan that remained attempted to give itself relevancy again by lending its legacy to Minethia. Fortunately, they only cared about wine and lazy afternoons, so that confederacy was of no particular concern. And finally, Talmoreth, with its arcane secrets and earnest scholars, busily working away at... whatever it was they did, for which Keri had neither the time nor the inclination to care.

All could make a claim, but none of them could match the combination of beauty, power, resources and reach of the Sea King Isles. Keranos Lugger - "Keri" to his friends, of which he had many - was *here*, a person of influence in the most influential place in the wide, wide world. For a man who had not yet found the limits of his appetite for stimulation, he could not conceive of a better place to be in all of Ruine.

Just then, he heard soft voices from the bedchamber behind him. He glanced at the pouch on the parapet wall and reasoned that waiting would be easier if he found something else to occupy himself with. His thoughts skipped to the flowered twineroot seed and the responsibilities it entailed - *his* responsibilities - then skipped again at the sound of a woman's husky laughter.

Vya. Her name is Vya.

Grinning broadly, he decided that there was probably one place that was, strictly speaking, better than where he was standing at the moment. The wine had cleared his head and settled his stomach, but he refilled his glass all the same; no sense leaving an almost-empty pitcher. Then he drained the goblet and threw it over the parapet wall, watching as it spun end over end, glinting in the golden suns, until it disappeared from view long before it landed somewhere far below.

The twineroot seed and Quesso's Cause could wait just a bit longer. He returned to bed and the soft, warm flowers that waited for him there.

***

Sometime later, as the Crone slid behind Juuma's verdant bulk to the west, Keri stepped through the heavy iron door into the Ministry's Twineroot Garden. He felt *fine*, like a blade that has just been cleaned and sharpened. His body hummed with energy. His mind felt agile, his thoughts clear, uncluttered. All of his senses were alive, extended; reaching out from his mind like the tentacles of some fantastic sea-creature.

After his tumble with Maesa and Vya - The "Ah! Sisters", he had called them and oh, how they had squirmed and giggled at that! - he had bathed and put on a clean white shirt and trousers. Over these, he donned a ruby-colored surcoat made from heavy Minethian silk, but eschewed its silver buttons, preferring the way the coat billowed as he made his way about. He thought it made him look rather roguish.

Keri held up the small leather pouch he had been carrying around earlier and lightly shook it. He had intended to save the sap for when he arrived at the Garden (the first few moments of its effects were always the most powerful), but he was feeling as *fine* as the soft hair on Vya's mound, and he did not want that feeling tempered in the slightest. Catching sight of himself in the mirror, and in particular the annoying blond roots beginning to show along the crown of his head, had sealed his decision.

He loosened the drawstring on the pouch and upended it over a small silver tray. Two misshapen, amber-colored granules tumbled onto the platter, which was perched over a tiny brazier about the size of his fist that he kept on the counter next to his wash basin. Rather than a bed of firestones, this brazier held only a fat round candle, which he lit with another slender taper that burned among a dozen or so nearby. These were nearly spent now, having burned and danced all night long even as he and the "Ah Sisters" had done the same.

In a few moments, the granules melted into a thin, orange-gold syrup, into which Keri dipped a slender wand made of brass, with a small, pea-sized ball at its end. The wand was curved, as though it were bending beneath the weight of something affixed to its end, but this was its permanent shape, which made the task it was designed for somewhat easier.

He moved the end of the wand in a circular motion, collecting as much of the syrup as he could, then quickly raised it high, tipping his head back as he did so. He positioned the wand so that the end with the syrup-covered ball hovered just over his left eye, then tapped it lightly against the bridge of his nose. A single drop of twineroot sap dislodged and fell into the inside corner of his eye, causing a hot flash of pain that was erased and forgotten almost before it had time to register.

What followed was a rushing wind of ecstasy; warm pleasure and brilliant lights exploding through his head, then radiating out through the rest of his body. He stood perfectly still, unaware that he had stopped breathing, his entire body one single nerve vibrating in pleasure. He knew that if he opened his eyes he could become lost in the finest details of what he saw around him as the visible world became so sharply focused as to be almost transparent... and that if he administered one or two more drops, he would be able to move *through* that layer into what lay beyond and between. But he didn't, because as exhilarating as that experience would be, he knew he would be lost for the rest of the day, and there were Things to Do. Important Things. *But oh, it was so tempting...*

... and then the first rush was past. He gasped and shuddered, then whooped in delight. He sucked the last of the syrup from the end of the wand and wiped out the small amount of residue left in the silver tray using his index finger. He was about to lick that off as well, then grinned broadly. He had a better idea. He spread it on his lips, strode into the bedchamber, and kissed each of the "Ah Sisters" goodbye. As he left his apartment, they were grinning too, and he could hear the soft smacking noises they were making with their tongues.

So now here he was in The Garden, feeling *fine* and doing his Duty, which as it so happened was a Duty to two completely different masters. His official master was the Trade Ministry, or more specifically, the Regent of Information, one of four very powerful men who served in the High Chancellor's inner circle. In addition to Keri's master were two other Trade loyalists, the Regents of Finance and Diplomacy. The fourth advisor to the High Chancellor was Regent-Commander Fenn, who had the rather envious and eminently dangerous position of commanding the Seeker Corps. The High

Chancellor and his Regents thus formed one head of the Isles' two-headed government, and the Kings' Council the other. Complicated, but it had served its purpose and ensured relative peace and growing prosperity since the Treaties were signed nearly two decades ago.

Prosperity, he thought and would have grimaced or scoffed had he not been feeling quite so *fine*. Some might call it that, but he and many he knew considered it folly to think of these past eighteen years as "prosperous", when there was so much more that could be accomplished. So much more that *would* be accomplished... perhaps starting right now.

He scanned the long trestle table set in the middle of the Garden, his eyes immediately drawn to the vivid orange and black blossom that burst from the plant at the far end of the table like a tiny frozen flame.

Shan be praised, there is only one this time, he thought. It was no bigger than his thumbnail and shaped like a star, with seven vivid orange petals surrounding a jet-black cluster of stamen. None of the other twineroot plants had blossomed, but even if they had, he would have tended this one first. This plant - a stunted tree, in truth - had birthed the seeds given to Minister Azimuth's son, and there were many among the Powerful who craved news of him and the ship he sailed upon, The *Peregrine*. It was standard practice for Seeker captains on "special" voyages to be given the seeds as well, but Captain Vaelysia's tree had been strangely silent. Judging from the disturbing, fragmented messages sent through Azimuth's seeds, everyone feared the worst.

He glided over to a workbench squatting in one sunlit corner of the room. It was set against the right-hand wall, and just beyond it was a cozy, curving portico. Beyond the ornate stone and marble balustrade that formed the outer wall of the porch was empty blue sky touched with the faintest blush of evening's purple. Keri knew that unless he walked out onto the balcony and all the way to the railing, the sky was all that he would see. Although the Ministry of Trade's main palace anchored one corner of the capital city Kortaga, the High Chancellor had also established campuses on each one of the Isles, relatively small but well-appointed compounds built adjacent to each of the Sea Kings' royal households. The Garden was hidden in the Ministry's Khatiita campus, on the topmost floor of a tower even higher than the one Keri resided in, safely beyond the reach of prying eyes or ambitious thieves.

Well, beyond their reach if they weren't ambitious enough, he thought to himself with a wry smile.

In addition to security concerns, its location had also been chosen to cater to the notoriously difficult and demanding needs of its principal occupants. The list of Twineroot's needs was as long as Keri's leg (which he could of course recite from memory) but chief among these requirements was indirect sunlight. The waxy, succulent leaves would yellow and shrivel after only a few minutes in direct sunlight, while repeated exposure brought on a blight of gray scales that would eventually kill off the plant entirely, root and stem. As a result, great care had gone into The Garden's location and design. Besides the balcony on the northwestern wall, filtered sunlight also found its way in through a series of layered wooden lattices set in a wide shaft that pierced the ceiling. Other than these two openings, there were no other windows; even shuttered ones posed too great a risk should they be left open unexpectedly.

As a result, the porch and the workbench he now stood before were the only places in the large circular room where the suns' rays managed to find their way in for a few moments each evening. Keri enjoyed watching the struggle between light and shadow as the suns sank and the beams moved. Whether by clever design or sheer coincidence, the last rays would slide across the floor until they just brushed the legs of the table upon which the Twineroot trees grew, before finally surrendering to the onrushing night. It was fitting, for Twineroot's true essence and power made it a child of darkness, where dreams and secrets thrived.

Dreamweed, Whisperwillow, Nightshade, Farspeak, Dreamchaser... it had many names, and many uses if you knew the plant's ways. Keri was intimately familiar with all of them, although he favored sapping. For one, the preparation was simple and straightforward, unlike the task at hand. Also unlike the task at hand, the effects of sapping were usually much more pleasant, if not quite as useful. When he first began to learn the forbidden art of Sending, he had been excited at the prospect of reading someone else's dreams. And early on, during the rigidly controlled lessons, it had been just as thrilling as he'd imagined it would be. There was something about stepping through the door of another person's mind that had touched a powerful chord within him. Of course in his youth, he had understood far less than he thought he had, and so seen all of the potential power of such a skill and none of the risks. Oh, he had learned the practical concerns well enough, like not preparing the blossoms properly and corrupting the send, or even losing the message completely. There was also the prospect of incorrectly interpreting the Sender's intent by reading the dream too literally, but these were all simple details, steps to the process that his agile mind had easily mastered.

But no matter how many times he had heard a lecture about drifting, or even just the effects of a poorly-organized message sent by an ill-prepared Sender, he saw opportunity where others perceived danger. Some instinct told him that this was the cutting edge of the Art, where its real power could be tapped. Drifting - the concept of becoming lost out there on the other side of that door, trapped in a Sender's nightmare or someplace his instructors hinted was worse - did not frighten him. On the contrary, it excited him, and if his instructors were too timid to recognize the opportunity it presented, then there would be that much more glory for him once he graduated and became an Interpreter in his own right. Back then, he was absolutely convinced he would become a Master, discover the secret power these old fools were too meek to grasp, and live out the rest of his days basking in the wealth and glory of his achievements.

If he wasn't feeling so *fine*, he might have acknowledged how wrongheaded his thinking had been back then; how a bit more humility and trust in his elders might have helped him realize those youthful dreams of success. He had been a promising Adept before learning what drifting really meant; when he had lost his way in The Between, and Night astride his dark horse had ridden him down...

Keri suppressed a shudder and stepped out onto the sun-washed porch. But he *was* feeling *fine*, the warm rays reminded him. Anyway he'd survived all of that unpleasantness, hadn't he? He was wealthy, and glory was... well, glory might be just around the next bend if he and Abet Quesso had anything to say about it. Their faction - Quesso's Cause, some were calling it now - was growing stronger day by day, despite the best efforts of the Kings' Council to suppress it. You could hear their positions being argued in nearly every tavern, barracks, outfitter, outrigger, outhouse and whorehouse; wherever people gathered and wagged their tongues, among other things.

A matu glided past, several feet below him, leathery wings the color of jade spread wide and glistening in the suns' light. He could see every scale; count every long, blood-red whisker that trailed from its lower jaw and neck like a beard. It banked to one side and rolled a cold black eye in his direction, emitting a piercing scream before suddenly folding its wings and diving from view. Rather than the familiar plaintive cry, though, this one seemed to chastise him. "Enough dithering, Keranos", it seemed to say, "you have your role to play, so go and play it!"

The sooner it's done, the sooner he could get back to Maesa and Vya, and another drop of sap. *A big drop. Maybe big enough to fly*, he thought with a dreamy smile, and returned to the work bench to begin preparing to receive young Azimuth's message.

He cast a nervous glance over his shoulder to confirm that there was still only one blossom on the Twineroot tree, as if it might have sprouted several more while his back was turned. One of the last messages he had received still troubled him deeply, and he was loath to experience something like that again. He wasn't in any danger - at least, he didn't think so - but that did not make it any less horrific. Whomever had consumed that particular twineroot seed - *seeds*, he reminded himself, as three flowers had blossomed simultaneously - had apparently met with a most unfortunate and painful end. He could not be entirely sure, but he suspected that the supply of seeds Azimuth had given to his son had somehow fallen into someone else's hands, who for whatever reason did not understand their use. The poor stupid bastard had apparently eaten three of them, gone mad, and then flung himself overboard.

But that wasn't the worst of it. Poor Stupid Bastard had then gotten himself eaten by something very large, most likely a ridgeback, if the monstrous shadow Keri had glimpsed wasn't a hallucination or a 'ghost' - the term he used to refer to someone else's lost memory that had somehow gotten caught up in a send. Certainly the pain and terror were the most visceral, real things Keri had ever experienced during an Interpretation, and the abruptness with which the message had ended led him to conclude that the Sender had died. At least, he hoped so - for their sake and his.

So now there was yet another send, and Keri was understandably hesitant to harvest it. He knew that consuming two seeds could trigger a sort of temporary madness that could last several hours; if three seeds had been consumed, he had no idea how severe the effect might have been, or whether it could cause some kind of... fragmentation, delaying some of the Sender's message so that it was now coming in pieces.

"By the cold dead gods, I hope not," he muttered to himself. Still stalling, he began clearing some space among the clutter atop the workbench. There were several clay pots, one with a recently-deceased twineroot tree still in it, which he set aside for later. It needed to be stripped of its valuable bark before tossing its remains in a brazier squatting against the wall an arm's length away. In addition to the pots were a haphazard pile of blank scrolls, a smaller stack of papyrus sheets, an inkwell and pen, a large silver mug, three different sets of pruning shears, a whetstone, mortar and pestle, a hand shovel, half a dozen candles, a lantern, and several delicate instruments for harvesting the sap. The workbench had a raised shelf along the back where it rested against the wall, and he began stacking and organizing these items along it, grumbling as he did so.

"Amiel, you old blind fool. Just once it would be nice if you would return things to their proper place!" Although they rarely saw one another, Keri shared his duties with another Interpreter, a man thirty years his senior. He was also a member of Quesso's faction, and had in fact recruited Keri on behalf of Abet Quesso himself, while training the brash young man to be an Interpreter. Amiel's internal clock kept its own time, so he tended The Garden from the very early, pre-dawn hours until late morning. "The old need less sleep than the young," he liked to remind Keri whenever they did see each other, "because they are far less apt to waste their energy doing foolish things the rest of the day." Keri had no complaints, as he did have plenty of other things to do - *countless* things when you came right down to it - and he did not consider a single one of them to be wasteful or foolish. Since most of those things seemed to need doing all night long, he was grateful for the schedule the old man kept.

In truth, he was actually quite fond of old Amiel, and he was smiling as he groused, deliberately mimicking the old gardener's favorite phrase: "How can you expect to find a dream when you can't find your own head without shoving your hands up your arse?"

When he had finished straightening and stacking, he took a small straw brush and swept the bits of potting soil and dead leaves off of the workbench and into a wooden pail. As he did so, his thoughts returned to the Azimuth tree's previous sendings, and what this new one might entail.

Wiliamund Azimuth's very first message had come through nearly nine months ago. Although he had undergone some training prior to the *Peregrine's* departure, his message had been fragmented and difficult to interpret - which, to be fair, was normal for someone's first sending. What's more, some of the important information had come through. For instance, it was clear that the *Peregrine* had set sail on its return voyage, and that they had discovered something the boy considered extremely important. He had even managed to include the date they had sailed, which was a vital piece of information for those trying to predict their return. Then the send had begun to break down. There might have been another passenger carrying some kind of powerful artifact, or possibly some terrible secret, but after that the message had become too blurred by Azimuth's own fear and excitement. The only solid impression that Keri took away after that point was the image of a colossal warrior towering over the *Peregrine*. He dismissed this impression as youthful fantasy, especially after the send devolved into an embarrassing moment with him exposing himself to a woman who was laughing at him. He was loath to consider who the woman might actually represent.

Keri grimaced and picked up a shallow bowl made of copper, his smallest clippers, and a pair of tweezers. He crossed the room to where the flowering twineroot tree stood waiting. It was perhaps the height of a young child, coming to nearly mid-thigh if he had set it on the ground and stood beside it. Its trunk and limbs were covered in smooth, gray-green bark, the delicate branches spreading broadly in alternating directions, giving the tree a very balanced appearance. Keri knew that they could grow in any direction, but this particular one had been meticulously pruned to give it this shape. He had no idea why Amiel had chosen that particular form, or any of the others for that matter. The old man did most of the pruning work - "training", he called it, which was more accurate, Keri had to admit - and each tree bore a different design. When Keri had asked him once where he drew his inspirations from, Amiel had told him he had seen each tree at one point or another in the Between, and would say no more.

The old gardener had done something Kari hadn't seen before with this one as well. He had spent countless hours working on the tree's roots, inserting small rocks in different places to 'train' the roots to grow up and over the stones. After several weeks, he removed the rocks, leaving the roots arching away from the base of the tree for a few inches before returning to the soil, reminding Keri of the arched buttresses that supported some citadel walls.

He sat down on a wooden bench and carefully set his tools on the table beside the plant. Several weeks ago - over eight months after that initial message - the three blossoms had appeared at once, and Keri had known right away that this one had not been sent by Azimuth's son. Messages sent through this process were very personal and carried a distinct feeling, or quality, enabling an Interpreter to distinguish between different Senders, much like the sound of a person's voice was unique to that person. Only a very experienced Sender could disguise this, and then only with limited success. Young Wiliamund Azimuth was anything but experienced, and presumably he would have no reason to hide his identity, so as soon as Keri slipped into the Interpreter's Trance, he knew this send had originated from someone else.

The message began with promise: the Sender was a Seeker Officer, formerly of the *SKS Peregrine* - *"formerly", now that seems strange*, Keri had thought at the time, and then the send had unraveled from there. The person could not recall their name or rank, and seemed to become fixated on this point for several minutes, before any semblance of coherent thought dissolved into a series of disjointed images that assaulted Keri's mind. They were raw bits of memory as far as he could determine - just images, sensations and emotions, with no structure or overriding consciousness to explain them. Keri's best guess was that the Sender had been caught in a terrible storm and might have been washed overboard.

One very strange detail emerged in the middle of this chaos: a book of some kind.

The Journal! The Sender's consciousness had suddenly found its voice. *Save the boy's Journal!*

Then the chaotic images had returned, with even less order and relevance than before: scenes of someone's childhood, of a military graduation ceremony, of a Corps uniform that had become unbearably itchy and had to come off, and when he took it off it was full of tiny pearl-colored crabs or spiders, Keri couldn't tell which. The flurry of images had eventually subsided, and then crystallized to the scene that had caused Keri to dread this next Interpreting: the Sender tying himself to an anchor line, cradling the anchor in his arms, and jumping overboard.

Keri picked up the pair of clippers and delicately grasped the branch from which the flower had blossomed with his free hand. Pushing down slightly to expose the point where the slender limb joined the main trunk, he clipped the branch as close to its base as he could, and extracted it and its precious blossom from the surrounding foliage. His movements were careful and precise; dropping the flower at this point would be disastrous.

As the blossom and stem came free, he realized he had been holding his breath and let it out slowly. He lowered the flower over the shallow bowl, then, using the tweezers, gently pinched it at its base to remove it from the stem. It settled into the copper bowl with the soft rustle of a sigh.

Keri followed suit, sighing with relief that he hadn't dropped the flower or upset the stamen. In order to capture the entire message, it was critical that all components of the blossom were collected; a lost stamen or petal would corrupt it to the point of illegibility.

He glanced over at the workbench and saw that it was still in the sun, so he pushed the bowl a bit further onto the table, away from the edge, then rose and went to retrieve the rest of his tools; he would prepare it right there on the growing table.

He was pleased to find that Amiel had left a full kettle of water on the brazier, and began humming tunelessly as he stoked the coals beneath it, still musing on the previous sendings.

Perhaps, he told himself, young Wiliamund has only lost some of his seeds, and has worked up the nerve to send again. It would be nice to deliver some good news to the boy's father.

But as soon as the thought formed, Keri knew it was hollow. Because there had actually been a third Sender, whose message had come a few days after Poor Stupid Bastard's. Keri had nicknamed him (or her, he wasn't quite sure) "The Counter", and while most of his message was useless (not to mention disturbing), the one informative detail that had emerged was definitely *not* good news.

That send had come as a surprise on several levels. For starters, Keri hadn't expected there to be any more messages - which was absolutely fine with him after the last experience, by the by. But not three days after Poor Stupid Bastard's Send, another of the orange blossoms had sparked to life on young master Azimuth's tree.

Keri had gone through the same ritual then as he did now, though then it had taken him twice as long due to his trembling hands. It had taken him nearly *three* times as long to achieve an Interpreter's Trance, but as soon as the link began, he knew it was someone new yet again.

The Counter did not identify themselves, and for the first time since he had been Interpreting, Keri was not able to determine if the Sender was male or female. The random, somewhat violent nature of the link did not allow him any time to consider this unusual fact, however, as Keri had then been assaulted by a series of random images - some of them extremely disturbing, like the woman who appeared to be chewing on someone's genitals. After that, the Sender ran through a rapid series of vague images of people, along with the names of each. Presumably a roll call of the crew, but none of the faces were very clear. There were other disturbing visions as well, and it was clear that this Sender was not only untrained, but unstable as well.

The send finally attained some semblance of normalcy as the Sender began to concentrate on what appeared to be an inventory of the stores on board some kind of ship. Judging from the meager quantities, Keri had thought it to be a small vessel. This began to devolve into a series of calculations on how long it would take to burn through each item, until the link to the Sender began to fade. The individual must have realized this, for suddenly the Sender's thoughts crystallized; enough for them to indicate they were aboard the *Peregrine's* emergency launch and drifting somewhere near the Burning Sea. And then the link was broken and the message ended abruptly.

Keri shuddered and shoved the coals around some more. Steam was rising from the water in the pot. Very soon it would start to boil, and all too soon after that he would enter the Interpreter's Trance and harvest... what? Only the dead gods know.

Quite often - too often, in Keri's opinion - messages from unskilled or troubled Senders also contained a reflection - the term most Interpreter's used to describe an overlapping and often confusing impression formed from the Sender's emotions and subconscious. Keri thought of the phenomenon more as a 'shadow', because it rarely "reflected" the message the way a pool of still water or a mirror might. Instead, it tended to be a dark undercurrent; traces of the fears, hopes and inferences the Sender attached to their intended message. Just like their 'voice', an experienced Sender could mask this shadow, but for the novice, they often provided the Interpreter an unintended glimpse into their secret thoughts and feelings.

To Keri's disgust, The Counter's message had contained not one but *two* reflections. The first was fairly routine: a jumbled mixture of false pride, self-doubt and bitter resentment that Keri had experienced in many Interpretations. But beneath the principal, conscious message and that reflection was something much darker, much more worthy of Keri's 'shadow' moniker. Even as The Counter ran through their actual inventory of hardtack and herring, they were ticking through the names on the roll call, evaluating each one's chances of survival, and doing so with relish. There was a degree of hungry vengeance to it that had sickened him.

Recalling that last message, he was no longer feeling quite so *fine*. He went through the remaining preparations mechanically, heart heavy with dread. Normally he enjoyed the vivid display of color from the petals as he crushed them in the pestle, particularly as some of the xhemium contained in the stamen was released, setting the mixture alight in blue flame for a few seconds. But not today. Today the orange looked red in the light of the long evening, like blood.

But still he persisted in his Duty. As the matu had said, he had a role to play. The Powerful were awaiting him, Keranos Lugger, and he would not disappoint them.

He scraped the pasty mixture from the pestle into the kettle of hot water, then carefully set the mortar and pestle in the pot as well, before crossing to the brazier and setting the kettle back on the bed of coals. As he stirred the mixture with a long wooden spoon, he began chanting under his breath, a slow cant that rose and fell. By the time he was finished, both suns had set, and the Garden was cloaked in a deep gloom. Had there been any other open twineroot blossoms, they would have yielded a soft blue light, but now the only light in the room came from the brazier. Its baleful glow picked out the high points of Keri's sharp nose, cheeks and chin, but left the hollows of his eyes in darkness.

Still chanting, he lit a taper from the coals and set it to one of the candles on the workbench, then held the brand over the pot to look inside. All of the paste had dissolved, giving the water a ruddy hue, like summer ale. He could see that both mortar and pestle were clean, and deemed his brew ready.

He wrapped the sleeve of his surcoat around his hand and grasped the pot's handle - momentarily annoyed that the expensive silk did a much poorer job insulating his palm than the rough spun wool rag he normally used - and poured the mixture into a large silver mug, being careful not to let the mortar and pestle tumble out in the process. One edge of the pot had been hammered into a short spout of sorts, but still he had to be careful not to spill anything, which was doubly difficult thanks to the burning pain in his palm. He tipped the last dregs into the mug and set the pot down with a curse, waiving his hand in the air to cool it. He tried inspecting it in the light of the candle, but could not see well enough to know if he had actually burned the skin. Still waiving it and muttering curses - he was definitely no longer *fine*, even in the slightest sense of the word - he stepped out onto the balcony.

The view there always picked up his spirits though, especially on a clear night, and tonight was no exception. The sky had taken on a magical, luminescent color over distant Minethia, somewhere between cerulean and deep jade. It was reflected in the still waters of Niht's Haven, and without the faintest breath of breeze, the water of the bay had captured every detail of the islands and coast along its edges. Had the sap not already worn off, he fancied he might have been able to see his own reflection peering back up from the impossible depths of an inverted, underwater tower.

The tea needed to cool, so he set it carefully on a low table by the balustrade. There was a divan next to the table, and he bent to arrange the pillows before settling onto it. Plucking the mug from its resting place on the balustrade, he took a sip to test its temperature. It was perfect.

Having run out of ways to stall, Keri took a deep breath, let it out slowly, and drank the mixture down. It was still hot, but not enough to scald him, and he savored the sensation as the heat poured down his throat into his belly. The warmth began to radiate outward, at first not unlike the feeling after a good pull of black rum - Shan's Rage, not the cheap piss they fed to Seekers - and soon after its power began to thrum in his veins like the heat of desire.

He picked up the low, singsong chanting again, but now it grew louder, deeper, reaching a register he only found possible after drinking the tea. The deliberate cadence of the chanting was meant to sooth, the vibrations from his chest and throat becoming hypnotic, slowing his breathing and heart rate, helping him to first clear his mind, and then to open it; or rather to open the door between his mind and the Sender's.

As the stars flared to life overhead, Keri did not see them. Instead he saw another's twilight, many leagues to the south and east, while his body lay sprawled on the divan, eyes staring vacantly into the night sky. A thin glitter of saliva seeped from the corner of his mouth. He would lie that way for a full two hours before slipping into a deep sleep. During those first hours, however, he would learn the identity of the Sender he called the Counter, and hear of the incredible discovery of Aarden, its detailed recording in the journal of a boy named Triistan Halliard, and the subsequent mutiny and betrayal of that same boy.

The Counter had learned how to speak through the Twineroot, and it was clear he had much to tell.

~ The End ~

###

Appendix A

Of Gods and Other Monsters

The Arys and Their High Houses:

The Young Gods were given life by Tarsus. They were divided into two factions, the Auruim and the Dauthir.

The Auruim - "The Winged Ones", "The Sky Gods", who lived in Ehronhaal, the city in the clouds:

The House of Knowledge: For those who seek to master intricate skills or lore. Learning and experience are the foundations here.
Heraldic Symbol: Burning torch
Ekoh the Archivist, God of History and scribe of the High Houses
Flynn the Bard, God of Music and Stories
Lyrin the Judicator, Goddess of Law and Philosophy
Minet the Creator, Goddess of the Arts

The House of War: The frontline against the Endless Spawn of Maughrin, led by Thunor.
Heraldic Symbol: Gauntleted fist
Thunor the Conqueror, God of War
Wicka the Herald, Goddess of Competition, Sport and Glory
Obed the Guardian, God of Vigilance and Ancestry
Heketh the Ravager, God of Vengeance, Famine, Pestilence and wanton Destruction

The House of Pleasure: Celebrates passion, desire, and fulfillment.
Heraldic Symbol: Two cupped hands held together; sometimes holding wine or flower petals
Eris the Maiden, Goddess of Love, Chastity and Romance
Taisha the Whore, Goddess of Pleasures
Paola the Matron, Goddess of Hospitality, Food and Comfort
Theckan the Rogue, God of Luck and Fortune

The House of Secrets: Dreamers, schemers, visionaries - all those who covet The Unknown.
Heraldic Symbol: Eyes peering above a veil
X
Veda the Scholar, Goddess of Math, Magic and Arxhemistry
Estra the Dreamer, Goddess of Insight and Intuition
Sylveth the Silent, Goddess of Cunning, Riddles and Deceit

The Dauthir - "The Shepherds", "Ruinebound", who lived on the ground amongst the huunan, the Children of Tarsus.

The House of Storms: Where the raw power of Ruine itself is both harnessed and worshipped
Heraldic Symbol: Lightning bolt
Shan the Stormfather, leader of the Dauthir and master of both Storm and Sea
Iemene the Gentle, Goddess of Rain, Nourishing Waters, Mist and Rainbows
Ganar the Unbroken, God of the Undergreen, Patron over Rocks and Metals
Niht, wife of Shan, Goddess of the Night, Lady of the Gentle Breeze and the Trade Winds. It is said her anger (though infrequent) is also the cause of heavy winds and tornadoes.
Sigel the Untamed, lord of Fire and Rage. Unlike any of the other Arys, Sigel has been depicted as both male and female.

The House of Passages: Often directly associated with the construction of things, but also relates to the passage of time, distance, and journeys.
Heraldic Symbol: An astrolabe
Derant the Builder, God of Design, Architecture and Carpentry
Ogund the Crafter, God of Invention, Tinkering and Smithing
Cartis the Navigator, Goddess of Exploration and Mapmaking
Vell the Eternal, Lady of Spring and Summer, Birth and Youth
Fjorvin the Reaper, Lord of Fall and Winter, Maturity and Death

The House of the Wilds: The true caretakers of Ruine, devoted to all manner of wildlife and the wilderness, as well as agriculture and domesticated beasts.
Heraldic Symbol: Jharrl's head, roaring
Arcolen the Verdant, Goddess of the Green, Plants and Wild Places

Udgard the Planter, God of the Harvest, Farming and Animal Husbandry

Feness the Wild, Goddess of Wild Animals and The Hunt

Tauger the Scavenger, God of Vermin and Resourcefulness

Beyond the High Houses

Maughrin - *The Living Darkness, the Demon Dragon, Mother of the Endless Swarm and Destroyer of the First World.* To some, she is vanquished. To others, imprisoned forever. To most, she is a fairy tale, a terrifying adversary that was ultimately defeated by Tarsus, never to be forgotten, but never again to plague the Huunan. Only the H'kaan carry on her legacy, and even they have been seen infrequently since the Ehronfall.

Khagan - Known by most only as a patron of the Sons of Khagan ("The Unbound"), he is generally regarded as the Forger of Fate.

Veheg - Viewed by the Young Gods and the Children of Tarsus as Death incarnate, it is said he existed before the Old Gods and is believed to harvest the final spark of life from the dying. To what purpose is no longer known.

About the Authors:

You made it! Thank you for reading our book. We hope you enjoyed it, and if so, we would be most grateful if you took a moment to leave us a review at your favorite retailer.
Yours Very Truly, TBS and RWH

T.B. Schmid lives in upstate New York with his wife, two children, and two Norwegian Elk Hounds. When not haranguing R. Wade Hodges about their joint venture, Lions of the Empire, he enjoys football, movies, music, motorcycles, gaming, rum, and cheering on his kids.

R. Wade Hodges feels like author summaries sound too much like obituaries. He enjoys giant robot anime, good whisky, gaming and anything involving bacon. He is grateful to be part of Lions of the Empire and the world of Ruine. He has survived by spite and the efforts of his wonderful daughter and his fantastic wife.

Discover other titles by Lions of the Empire:
Feral by T.B. Schmid
Tales of Yhore: The Chronicles of Monch by D.F. Monk

Connect with us:
Official Website: www.lionsoftheempire.com
On Twitter: @lionsofthempire
On Facebook: search for "lionsoftheempire"
On Smashwords and Goodreads, look us up under Beyond the Burning Sea, T.B. Schmid, or R. Wade Hodges

Excerpt from the Chapter <u>There Again</u>

It was close to moonrise later that same night, and Triistan was scrawling feverishly in his journal, intent on carrying out the Captain's orders and recording every scrap of detail surrounding their journey through Ahbaingeata. After swimming the short distance to shore, the Aarden Expedition had set up a temporary camp adjacent to what they assumed had probably once been some kind of guard barracks. A tall, stone drum tower rose up from the tangled vegetation that grew around, over and into the barracks. After searching the base of the tower, they discovered that the only access into it was through a large door in the rear wall of the barracks. It took them most of the day to clear out the dense undergrowth and force the door open, but at least they had been able to get topside for a good look at the alien landscape around them. The vantage point had helped Triistan confirm his assumptions of Ahbaingeata's design, in particular the use of the river passage and reservoir as a form of defense, and he had felt intensely proud of how accurate his diagram was.

He was sitting outside on the ground now, leaning against the barracks wall, in order to take advantage of the light from the watch fire burning just a few paces away. Taelyia's kilij lay nearby in its scabbard. Biiko had just finished changing the dressing on his wounded leg and had gone back inside. The unmistakable sounds of slumber drifted from the doorway leading into the guardhouse, where most of the crew was housed and presently trying to recuperate from their ordeal. Other than the sentry posted at the top of the tower, only Captain Vaelysia and Jaspins remained on watch here on the ground with him. They had been pacing impatiently around the perimeter of the camp since dusk, waiting for Commander Tchicatta, who had left shortly after mid-day with Miikha, Myles and Wrael, intending to scout the ruined city. They were supposed to return by nightfall, but as of yet there had been no sign of them.

Occasionally, either the Captain or the Reaver lieutenant would stop and listen, as if they'd heard something, but with the jungle's infiltration into the city, its nocturnal denizens had moved in as well. Given the cacophony of cries, hoots, whistles, screams, grunts and snarls coming from the ruins, Triistan wondered whether they would have heard the Commander coming if he'd ridden up on horseback.

Just before midnight, a drenching rain began quite suddenly, as it often did in the jungle. Triistan welcomed it at first, seeking relief from the oppressive humidity, even though he knew now from experience that unless it were a major storm moving through, it would probably only grow muggier. Still, the first light shower felt cool on his skin. Even better, the din seemed to be subsiding as well, suppressed by the soft hiss of the rain. He closed his journal and lifted his face to it, enjoying the peaceful hush as it descended around them. But the reprieve was short-lived, as before long, the hiss grew to a roar and drove the three of them back into the barracks for cover. Their fire sputtered out soon after, and the night closed in.

Biiko joined them as they stood huddled together in the doorway, listening to the drumming downpour as it hammered away across the uneven floor of the plaza. There were channels cut through the flagstones, bisecting the area in a wide grid pattern, which Triistan knew acted as gutters to help carry the water away. Earlier in the day he had noticed a square depression with a twisted tangle of vines as thick as his waist growing from it. What looked to have been a heavy iron grate was barely visible at its center, and he reasoned that it must be a drain leading to a sewer system, now choked with vegetation. The rain soon overwhelmed the gutters on the surface, and the plaza began to flood. He was thankful for the shelter the guardhouse provided, briefly wondering if the scouting party was tucked away in some similar place.

"Should I fetch a tor-" he began, but Jaspins placed her hand over his mouth, silencing him. She pointed back out into the darkness.

"Storm and sea..." the Captain whispered beside him.

The impact of the heavy rain had caused the surface of the reservoir to glow with the same ghostly luminescence they had observed in the tunnel, wherever the water was disturbed by a swift current or as it brushed past some obstacle. The light rose a short distance above the lake, creating a faint, blue-green fog as it lit the falling rain, but it was not strong enough to illuminate the surrounding ruins.

It was eerily beautiful, but it was not what Jaspins was pointing at. Triistan inhaled sharply.

Much closer to them, perhaps twenty or thirty paces off to their left, a pair of large, almond-shaped eyes shown from the darkness. They glowed a deeper, richer blue than the water, and were at least as large as Triistan's hand, widely spaced, and floating two or three feet off the ground. They disappeared for a moment, then reappeared again, narrowing to a pair of inverted crescents. Triistan heard - or felt, perhaps, it was hard to be sure - a low rumbling noise which he first took to be distant thunder. It made the hairs on his neck and arms stand up, and he took an inadvertent step back.

The eyes rose higher into the air. When they reached a height of seven or eight feet, the rumbling noise ended abruptly in a low huff, the eyes winked out, and the rain and the night returned...

Continued in Book Two of Fate's Crucible

55457400R10274

Made in the USA
Lexington, KY
24 September 2016